MW01505919

MIRROR KINGDOMS:
THE BEST OF PETER S. BEAGLE

PETER S. BEAGLE

Edited by Jonathan Strahan

SUBTERRANEAN PRESS 2010

First Edition

ISBN
978-1-59606-291-7

Subterranean Press
PO Box 190106
Burton, MI 48519

www.subterraneanpress.com

DEDICATION

For Victoria and Jack Knox,

Kalisa Beagle and Farhad Torkamani,

Dan and Robyn Beagle,

my family.

TABLE OF CONTENTS

Introduction

What strikes me most immediately, looking over the table of contents of this book, is the obvious and remarkable gap between the two earliest and everything else. "Come Lady Death" first saw print in the Atlantic Monthly in 1963, though it had been written a couple of years before, while "Lila the Werewolf" was originally published in Terry Carr's *New Worlds Of Fantasy #3* in 1971, then reprinted as a chapbook by Capra Press in 1974. And except for a couple of non-fantasy stories I'd written for college classes and published in my teens, that was absolutely it for me and short fiction until 1994.

I have excuses. I worked on one novel, *The Folk of the Air*, through eighteen years and four separate versions; and I was constantly diverted during that stretch by movie and TV gigs, which paid me far more money than I'd ever seen, even though precious little of what I wrote ever made it to the screen. And then I wrote another novel, *The Innkeeper's Song*, which was published in 1993. But in looking back, the real reason for the complete lapse in my short-story production strikes me as the fact that I was simply afraid of the form. There's probably a Latin term for the phobia; I'll have to look into it.

To me, short stories have always ranked with poetry as the most difficult of literary forms, primarily because the writer can't afford to make a single mistake. One broken rhythm—one missed moment of revelation, one wrong word or line of dialogue—and it's all over: the trick revealed, the illusion of magic gone. Novelists have it easy, by comparison, unless you're someone like Vladimir Nabokov, who *is* writing poetry. The rest of us can make every stylistic and technical error in the book and still get away with beating the reader into submission with detail, character, or plain action. (I offer Theodore Dreiser as the ultimate poster boy in this regard.) As the film director Michael Curtiz said when it was pointed out to him that a particular Errol Flynn movie lacked any logic in its development, "Don' worry—I make the sonabitch move so fast, nobody notice." He did, too, and so do we. Often.

Also, I'm a comparatively slow writer, with a distressful tendency to make things up as I go along. I felt that as much time and effort as a story cost me, I might just as well be working on a novel. So this sudden explosion of short fiction between 1994 and the present is hard to explain, even to myself. Both "Professor Gottesman and the Indian Rhinoceros" and "Julie's Unicorn" (the former remains my personal favorite still) were written specifically for a two-volume anthology of unicorn stories called *Peter S. Beagle's Immortal Unicorn* (largely edited, in all candor, by Janet Berliner; I mainly committed my stories and some introductions to the enterprise, and let my name be added to the title to satisfy the publisher's marketing imperative). Then my old friend Annie Scarborough cozened me into writing "The Last Song of Sirit Byar" for *Space Opera*, a collection of fantasy stories based around vocal music, which she co-edited with Anne McCaffrey. "Sirit Byar" was a return to the world I invented for *The Innkeeper's Song*, and it set me off on writing a series of five related stories, which became the collection *Giant Bones* (a.k.a. *The Magician of Karakosk* in every foreign edition, and in the upcoming American reprint.) All of these were written in the mid-1990s, and I'm still very proud of them.

But the real flood starts in 2004, with "Two Hearts," the tailpiece or coda to *The Last Unicorn*. Connor Cochran, my business manager, *de facto* agent, accountant, chauffeur, first reader and editor, and all-purpose accomplice, persuaded me to write it, just as he is responsible, in one way and another, for the existence of all the stories that followed. *Two Hearts* itself exists because Connor noodged me into creating a bonus gift of a new story for the first 3000 people to order the CD of the audiobook of *The Last Unicorn*. "You don't even have to use any of the same characters—that world must have plenty of other stories in it," he said in response to my initial refusal. So, naturally, I wound up writing the quasi-epilogue I did, which inevitably became a bridge to a true sequel novel that I am now working on. This happens a lot.

My tales tend to run long, often falling into the more or less arbitrary novelette or novella category: ironic for someone whose short-story idols include Chekhov, John Collier, Saki, Avram Davidson, Jessamyn West and Eudora Welty. I attribute this to my pattern of taking forever to find out what the hell I'm doing, and what the story's *really* about. (Connor calls me the King of the Second Drafts; but "The Tale of Junko and Sayuri" went through seven passes, and both "What Tune The Enchantress Plays" and "Vanishing" hit twelve. I can think of one that took me a good sixteen, but it's not in this collection, and I'll never tell which one it is when it does appear.) The novelette length suits me in many ways: it leaves me room for digression—for what someone called "incidental felicities"—to move around and make discoveries, to take my time letting the tale unroll, and above all to surprise myself, which is crucial, whether you've got it all plotted and charted from the beginning or, like me, you're fumbling around trying to trick the story into telling itself. All of that time and effort invested so that someone can later tell you, meaning to praise, that the story seemed to have flown out of you in one smooth burst of inspiration. If I hate one word in this world...

I don't think of my fiction as notably autobiographical, except as all writers cannibalize our lives—just as we do other people's—for the odd episode, memory or insight. (*I See By My Outfit*, my nonfiction book about a cross-country journey on motorscooters, is still occasionally taken as a novel to this day.) We use what comes in useful, however we may dress it up after the fact. "Giant Bones," while an Innkeeper's World fantasy, unquestionably draws its—okay, *okay!*—inspiration from affectionate recollection of a small boy named James, who wanted desperately to grow up to be six feet, seven inches tall, weigh two hundred and forty pounds, and play football. Damn kid used to drive me crazy, swinging from the lintel of every door in my house, trying to stretch himself. (He's six-three now, and surfs.) Then there's "Uncle Chaim and Aunt Rifke and the Angel," which draws consciously and heavily on my New York childhood as the nephew of three Russian Jewish painters; while "The Rock in the Park," one of five stories I wrote and recorded as podcasts for The Green Man Review website, goes back even more specifically to my old Bronx neighborhood, and employs my oldest friend as a character. In that sense, at least, I have been able to go home again, and I'm increasingly grateful for it as the years pass.

From my earliest childhood, I have spent a great deal—perhaps a majority—of my time in this world in the company of imaginary friends. A lady once tapped my head and said, rather sadly, "All those people partying up in there, and I'm not invited." I explained, as best I could, that I'm not always invited either, and that I often end up crashing the party, or eavesdropping through doors, walls, windows. They rarely confide in me, my characters, but they do leave trails of breadcrumbs for me to follow.

In short stories, you don't get much time to hang out with your imagined cast of characters: to have a beer and talk, to let them divulge, confide, let slip—and lie as well, for characters who lie will lie to their author, as they would to anyone else. I can be more confident in a novel, more assured that I'm in control, as I feel I really should be. But if these stories hold your interest, maybe it's because with them I'm *not* assured, that I no more control what's going on here than you do—and maybe less, because you can always close the book. On this side of the page it's a bloody mosh pit, and I'm just doing my best to keep surfacing: writing for my life, and the lives and lies of my imaginary old friends.

Professor Gottesman
and the Indian Rhinoceros

Professor Gustave Gottesman went to a zoo for the first time when he was thirty-four years old. There is an excellent zoo in Zurich, which was Professor Gottesman's birthplace, and where his sister still lived, but Professor Gottesman had never been there. From an early age he had determined on the study of philosophy as his life's work; and for any true philosopher this world is zoo enough, complete with cages, feeding times, breeding programs, and earnest docents, of which he was wise enough to know that he was one. Thus, the first zoo he ever saw was the one in the middle-sized Midwestern American city where he worked at a middle-sized university, teaching Comparative Philosophy in comparative contentment. He was tall and rather thin, with a round, undistinguished face, a snub nose, a random assortment of sandy-ish hair, and a pair of very intense and very distinguished brown eyes that always seemed to be looking a little deeper than they meant to, embarrassing the face around them no end. His students and colleagues were quite fond of him, in an indulgent sort of way.

And how did the good Professor Gottesman happen at last to visit a zoo? It came about in this way: his older sister Edith came from Zurich to stay with him for several weeks, and she brought her daughter, his niece Nathalie, along with her. Nathalie was seven, both in years, and in the number of her there sometimes seemed to be, for the Professor had never been used to children even when he was one. She was a generally pleasant little girl, though, as far as he could tell; so when his sister besought him to spend one of his free afternoons with Nathalie while she went to lunch and a gallery opening with an old friend, the Professor graciously consented. And Nathalie wanted very much to go to the zoo and see tigers.

"So you shall," her uncle announced gallantly. "Just as soon as I find out exactly where the zoo is." He consulted with his best friend, a fat, cheerful, harmonica-playing professor of medieval Italian poetry named

Sally Lowry, who had known him long and well enough (she was the only person in the world who called him Gus) to draw an elaborate two-colored map of the route, write out very precise directions beneath it, and make several copies of this document, in case of accidents. Thus equipped, and accompanied by Charles, Nathalie's stuffed bedtime tiger, whom she desired to introduce to his grand cousins, they set off together for the zoo on a gray, cool spring afternoon. Professor Gottesman quoted Thomas Hardy to Nathalie, improvising a German translation for her benefit as he went along.

> *This is the weather the cuckoo likes,*
> *And so do I;*
> *When showers betumble the chestnut spikes,*
> *And nestlings fly.*

"Charles likes it too," Nathalie said. "It makes his fur feel all sweet."

They reached the zoo without incident, thanks to Professor Lowry's excellent map, and Professor Gottesman bought Nathalie a bag of something sticky, unhealthy, and forbidden, and took her straight off to see the tigers. Their hot, meaty smell and their lightning-colored eyes were a bit too much for him, and so he sat on a bench nearby and watched Nathalie perform the introductions for Charles. When she came back to Professor Gottesman, she told him that Charles had been very well-behaved, as had all the tigers but one, who was rudely indifferent. "He was probably just visiting," she said. "A tourist or something." The Professor was still marveling at the amount of contempt one small girl could infuse into the word tourist, when he heard a voice, sounding almost at his shoulder, say, "Why, Professor Gottesman—how nice to see you at last." It was a low voice, a bit hoarse, with excellent diction, speaking good Zurich German with a very slight, unplaceable accent.

Professor Gottesman turned quickly, half-expecting to see some old acquaintance from home, whose name he would inevitably have forgotten. Such embarrassments were altogether too common in his gently preoccupied life. His friend Sally Lowry once observed, "We see each other just about every day, Gus, and I'm still not sure you really recognize me. If I wanted to hide from you, I'd just change my hairstyle."

There was no one at all behind him. The only thing he saw was the rutted, muddy rhinoceros yard, for some reason placed directly across from the big cats' cages. The one rhinoceros in residence was standing by the fence, torpidly mumbling a mouthful of moldy-looking hay. It was an Indian rhinoceros, according to the placard on the gate: as big as the Professor's compact car, and the approximate color of old cement. The creaking slabs of its skin smelled of stale urine, and it had only one horn, caked with sticky mud. Flies buzzed around its small, heavy-lidded eyes, which regarded Professor Gottesman with immense, ancient unconcern. But there was no other person in the vicinity who might have addressed him.

Professor Gottesman shook his head, scratched it, shook it again, and turned back to the tigers. But the voice came again. "Professor, it was indeed I who spoke. Come and talk to me, if you please."

No need, surely, to go into Professor Gottesman's reaction: to describe in detail how he gasped, turned pale, and looked wildly around for any corroborative witness. It is worth mentioning, however, that at no time did he bother to splutter the requisite splutter in such cases: "My God, I'm either dreaming, drunk, or crazy." If he was indeed just as classically absent-minded and impractical as everyone who knew him agreed, he was also more of a realist than many of them. This is generally true of philosophers, who tend, as a group, to be on terms of mutual respect with the impossible. Therefore, Professor Gottesman did the only proper thing under the circumstances. He introduced his niece Nathalie to the rhinoceros.

Nathalie, for all her virtues, was not a philosopher, and could not hear the rhinoceros's gracious greeting. She was, however, seven years old, and a well-brought-up seven-year-old has no difficulty with the notion that a rhinoceros—or a goldfish, or a coffee table—might be able to talk; nor in accepting that some people can hear coffee-table speech and some people cannot. She said a polite hello to the rhinoceros, and then became involved in her own conversation with stuffed Charles, who apparently had a good deal to say about tigers.

"A mannerly child," the rhinoceros commented. "One sees so few here. Most of them throw things."

His mouth was dry, and his voice shaky but contained, Professor Gottesman asked carefully, "Tell me, if you will—can all rhinoceri speak, or only the Indian species?" He wished furiously that he had thought to bring along his notebook.

"I have no idea," the rhinoceros answered him candidly. "I myself, as it happens, am a unicorn."

Professor Gottesman wiped his balding forehead. "Please," he said earnestly. "Please. A rhinoceros, even a rhinoceros that speaks, is as real a creature as I. A unicorn, on the other hand, is a being of pure fantasy, like mermaids, or dragons, or the chimera. I consider very little in this universe as absolutely, indisputably certain, but I would feel so much better if you could see your way to being merely a talking rhinoceros. For my sake, if not your own."

It seemed to the Professor that the rhinoceros chuckled slightly, but it might only have been a ruminant's rumbling stomach. "My Latin designation is *Rhinoceros unicornis*," the great animal remarked. "You may have noticed it on the sign."

Professor Gottesman dismissed the statement as brusquely as he would have if the rhinoceros had delivered it in class. "Yes, yes, yes, and the manatee, which suckles its young erect in the water and so gave rise to the myth of the mermaid, is assigned to the order *sirenia*. Classification is not proof."

"And proof," came the musing response, "is not necessarily truth. You look at me and see a rhinoceros, because I am not white, not graceful, far from beautiful, and my horn is no elegant spiral but a bludgeon of matted hair. But suppose that you had grown up expecting a unicorn to look and behave and smell exactly as I do—would not the rhinoceros then be the legend? Suppose that everything you believed about unicorns—everything except the way they look—were true of me? Consider the possibilities, Professor, while you push the remains of that bun under the gate."

Professor Gottesman found a stick and poked the grimy bit of pastry—about the same shade as the rhinoceros, it was—where the creature could wrap a prehensile upper lip around it. He said, somewhat tentatively, "Very well. The unicorn's horn was supposed to be an infallible guide to detecting poisons."

"The most popular poisons of the Middle Ages and Renaissance," replied the rhinoceros, "were alkaloids. Pour one of those into a goblet made of compressed hair, and see what happens." It belched resoundingly, and Nathalie giggled.

Professor Gottesman, who was always invigorated by a good argument with anyone, whether colleague, student, or rhinoceros, announced, "Isidore of Seville wrote in the seventh century that the unicorn was a cruel beast, that it would seek out elephants and lions to fight with them. Rhinoceri are equally known for their fierce, aggressive nature, which often leads them to attack anything that moves in their shortsighted vision. What have you to say to that?"

"Isidore of Seville," said the rhinoceros thoughtfully, "was a most learned man, much like your estimable self, who never saw a rhinoceros in his life, or an elephant either, being mainly preoccupied with church history and canon law. I believe he did see a lion at some point. If your charming niece is quite done with her snack?"

"She is not, " Professor Gottesman answered, "and do not change the subject. If you are indeed a unicorn, what are you doing scavenging dirty buns and candy in this public establishment? It is an article of faith that a unicorn can only be taken by a virgin, in whose innocent embrace the ferocious creature becomes meek and docile. Are you prepared to tell me that you were captured under such circumstances?"

The rhinoceros was silent for some little while before it spoke again. "I cannot," it said judiciously, "vouch for the sexual history of the gentleman in the baseball cap who fired a tranquilizer dart into my left shoulder. I would, however, like to point out that the young of our species on occasion become trapped in vines and slender branches which entangle their horns—and the Latin for such branches is *virge*. What Isidore of Seville made of all this..." It shrugged, which is difficult for a rhinoceros, and a remarkable thing to see.

"Sophistry," said the Professor, sounding unpleasantly beleaguered even in his own ears. "Casuistry. Semantics. Chop-logic. The fact remains, a rhinoceros is and a unicorn isn't." This last sounds much more impressive in German. "You will excuse me," he went on, "but we have other specimens to visit, do we not, Nathalie?"

"No," Nathalie said. "Charles and I just wanted to see the tigers."

"Well, we have seen the tigers," Professor Gottesman said through his teeth. "And I believe it's beginning to rain, so we will go home now." He took Nathalie's hand firmly and stood up, as that obliging child snuggled Charles firmly under her arm and bobbed a demure European curtsy to the rhinoceros. It bent its head to her, the mud-thick horn almost brushing the ground. Professor Gottesman, mildest of men, snatched her away.

"Good-bye, Professor," came the hoarse, placid voice behind him. "I look forward to our next meeting." The words were somewhat muffled, because Nathalie had tossed the remainder of her sticky snack into the yard as her uncle hustled her off. Professor Gottesman did not turn his head. Driving home through the rain—which had indeed begun to fall, though very lightly—the Professor began to have an indefinably uneasy feeling that caused him to spend more time peering at the rear-view mirror than in looking properly ahead. Finally, he asked Nathalie, "Please, would you and—ah—you and Charles climb into the backseat and see whether we are being followed?"

Nathalie was thrilled. "Like in the spy movies?" She jumped to obey, but reported after a few minutes of crouching on the seat that she could detect nothing out of the ordinary. "I saw a helicopiter," she told him, attempting the English word. "Charles thinks they might be following us that way, but I don't know. Who is spying on us, Uncle Gustave?"

"No one, no one," Professor Gottesman answered. "Never mind, child, I am getting silly in America. It happens, never mind." But a few moments later the curious apprehension was with him again, and Nathalie was happily occupied for the rest of the trip home in scanning the traffic behind them through an imaginary periscope, yipping "It's that one!" from time to time, and being invariably disappointed when another prime suspect turned off down a side street. When they reached Professor Gottesman's house, she sprang out of the car immediately, ignoring her mother's welcome until she had checked under all four fenders for possible homing devices. "Bugs," she explained importantly to the two adults. "That was Charles's idea. Charles would make a good spy, I think."

She ran inside, leaving Edith to raise her fine eyebrows at her brother. Professor Gottesman said heavily, "We had a nice time. Don't ask." And Edith, being a wise older sister, left it at that.

The rest of the visit was enjoyably uneventful. The Professor went to work according to his regular routine, while his sister and his niece explored the city, practiced their English together, and cooked Swiss-German specialties to surprise him when he came home. Nathalie never asked to go to the zoo again—stuffed Charles having lately shown an interest in international intrigue—nor did she ever mention that her uncle had formally introduced her to a rhinoceros and spent part of an afternoon sitting on a bench arguing with it. Professor Gottesman was genuinely sorry when she and Edith left for Zurich, which rather surprised him. He hardly ever missed people, or thought much about anyone who was not actually present.

It rained again on the evening that they went to the airport. Returning alone, the Professor was startled, and a bit disquieted, to see large muddy footprints on his walkway and his front steps. They were, as nearly as he could make out, the marks of a three-toed foot, having a distinct resemblance to the ace of clubs in a deck of cards. The door was locked and bolted, as he had left it, and there was no indication of any attempt to force an entry. Professor Gottesman hesitated, looked quickly around him, and went inside.

The rhinoceros was in the living room, lying peacefully on its side before the artificial fireplace—which was lit—like a very large dog. It opened one eye as he entered and greeted him politely. "Welcome home, Professor. You will excuse me, I hope, if I do not rise?"

Professor Gottesman's legs grew weak under him. He groped blindly for a chair, found it, fell into it, his face white and freezing cold. He managed to ask, "How—how did you get in here?" in a small, faraway voice.

"The same way I got out of the zoo," the rhinoceros answered him. "I would have come sooner, but with your sister and your niece already here, I thought my presence might make things perhaps a little too crowded for you. I do hope their departure went well." It yawned widely and contentedly, showing blunt, fist-sized teeth and a gray-pink tongue like a fish fillet.

"I must telephone the zoo," Professor Gottesman whispered. "Yes, of course, I will call the zoo." But he did not move from the chair.

The rhinoceros shook its head as well as it could in a prone position. "Oh, I wouldn't bother with that, truly. It will only distress them if anyone learns that they have mislaid a creature as large as I am. And they will never believe that I am in your house. Take my word for it, there will be no mention of my having left their custody. I have some experience in these matters." It yawned again and closed its eyes. "Excellent fireplace you have," it murmured drowsily. "I think I shall lie exactly here every night. Yes, I do think so."

And it was asleep, snoring with the rhythmic roar and fading whistle of a fast freight crossing a railroad bridge. Professor Gottesman sat staring in his chair for a long time before he managed to stagger to the telephone in the kitchen.

Sally Lowry came over early the next morning, as she had promised several times before the Professor would let her off the phone. She took one quick look at him as she entered and said briskly, "Well, whatever came to dinner, you look as though it got the bed and you slept on the living room floor."

"I did not sleep at all," Professor Gottesman informed her grimly. "Come with me, please, Sally, and you shall see why."

But the rhinoceros was not in front of the fireplace, where it had still been lying when the Professor came downstairs. He looked around for it increasingly frantic, saying over and over, "It was just here, it has been here all night. Wait, wait, Sally, I will show you. Wait only a moment."

For he had suddenly heard the unmistakable gurgle of water in the pipes overhead. He rushed up the narrow hairpin stairs (his house was, as the real-estate agent had put it, "an old charmer") and burst into his bathroom, blinking through the clouds of steam to find the rhinoceros lolling blissfully in the tub, its nose barely above water and its hind legs awkwardly sticking straight up in the air. There were puddles all over the floor.

"Good morning," the rhinoceros greeted Professor Gottesman. "I could wish your facilities a bit larger, but the hot water is splendid, pure luxury. We never had hot baths at the zoo."

"Get out of my tub!" the Professor gabbled, coughing and wiping his face. "You will get out of my tub this instant!"

The rhinoceros remained unruffled. "I am not sure I can. Not just like that. It's rather a complicated affair."

"Get out exactly the way you got in!" shouted Professor Gottesman. "How did you get up here at all? I never heard you on the stairs."

"I tried not to disturb you," the rhinoceros said meekly. "Unicorns can move very quietly when we need to."

"*Out!*" the Professor thundered. He had never thundered before, and it made his throat hurt. "Out of my bathtub, out of my house! And clean up that floor before you go!"

He stormed back down the stairs to meet a slightly anxious Sally Lowry waiting at the bottom. "What was all that yelling about?" she wanted to know. "You're absolutely pink—it's sort of sweet, actually. Are you all right?"

"Come up with me," Professor Gottesman demanded. "Come right now." He seized his friend by the wrist and practically dragged her into his bathroom, where there was no sign of the rhinoceros. The tub was empty and dry, the floor was spotlessly clean; the air smelled faintly of tile cleaner. Professor Gottesman stood gaping in the doorway, muttering over and over, "But it was here. It was in the tub."

"What was in the tub?" Sally asked. The Professor took a long, deep breath and turned to face her.

"A rhinoceros," he said. "It says it's a unicorn, but it is nothing but an Indian rhinoceros." Sally's mouth opened, but no sound came out. Professor Gottesman said, "It followed me home."

Fortunately, Sally Lowry was not more concerned with the usual splutters of denial and disbelief than was the Professor himself. She closed her mouth, caught her own breath, and said, "Well, any rhinoceros that could handle those stairs, wedge itself into that skinny tub of yours, and tidy up afterwards would have to be a unicorn. Obvious. Gus, I don't care what time it is, I think you need a drink."

Professor Gottesman recounted his visit to the zoo with Nathalie, and all that had happened thereafter, while Sally rummaged through his minimally stocked liquor cabinet and mixed what she called a "Lowry Land Mine." It calmed the Professor only somewhat, but it did at least restore his coherency. He said earnestly, "Sally, I don't know how it talks. I don't know how it escaped from the zoo, or found its way here, or how it got into my house and my bathtub, and I am afraid to imagine where it is now. But the creature is an Indian rhinoceros, the sign said so. It is simply not possible—not possible—that it could be a unicorn."

"Sounds like *Harvey*," Sally mused. Professor Gottesman stared at her. "You know, the play about the guy who's buddies with an invisible white rabbit. A big white rabbit."

"But this one is not invisible!" the Professor cried. "People at the zoo, they saw it—Nathalie saw it. It bowed to her, quite courteously."

"Um," Sally said. "Well, I haven't seen it yet, but I live in hope. Meanwhile, you've got a class, and I've got office hours. Want me to make you another Land Mine?"

Professor Gottesman shuddered slightly. "I think not. We are discussing today how Fichte and von Schelling's work leads us to Hegel, and I need my wits about me. Thank you for coming to my house, Sally. You are a good friend. Perhaps I really am suffering from delusions, after all. I think I would almost prefer it so."

"Not me," Sally said. "I'm getting a unicorn out of this, if it's the last thing I do." She patted his arm. "You're more fun than a barrel of MFA candidates, Gus, and you're also the only gentleman I've ever met. I don't know what I'd do for company around here without you."

Professor Gottesman arrived early for his seminar on "The Heirs of Kant." There was no one in the classroom when he entered, except for the rhinoceros. It had plainly already attempted to sit on one of the chairs, which lay in splinters on the floor. Now it was warily eyeing a ragged hassock near the coffee machine.

"What are you doing here?" Professor Gottesman fairly screamed at it.

"Only auditing," the rhinoceros answered. "I thought it might be rewarding to see you at work. I promise not to say a word."

Professor Gottesman pointed to the door. He had opened his mouth to order the rhinoceros, once and for all, out of his life, when two of his students walked into the room. The Professor closed his mouth, gulped, greeted his students, and ostentatiously began to examine his lecture notes, mumbling professorial mumbles to himself, while the rhinoceros, unnoticed, negotiated a kind of armed truce with the hassock. True to its word, it listened in attentive silence all through the seminar, though Professor Gottesman had an uneasy moment when it seemed about to be drawn into a heated debate over the precise nature of von Schelling's intellectual debt to the von Schlegel brothers. He was so desperately careful not to let the rhinoceros catch his eye that he never noticed until the last student had left that the beast was gone, too. None of the class had even once commented on its presence; except for the shattered chair, there was no indication that it had ever been there.

Professor Gottesman drove slowly home in a disorderly state of mind. On the one hand, he wished devoutly never to see the rhinoceros again; on the other, he could not help wondering exactly when it had left the classroom. "Was it displeased with my summation of the *Ideas for a Philosophy of Nature*?" he said aloud in the car. "Or perhaps it was something I said during the argument about *Die Weltalter*. Granted, I have never been entirely comfortable with that book, but I do not recall saying anything exceptionable." Hearing himself justifying his interpretations to a rhinoceros, he slapped his own cheek very hard and drove the rest of the way with the car radio tuned to the loudest, ugliest music he could find.

The rhinoceros was dozing before the fireplace as before, but lumbered clumsily to a sitting position as soon as he entered the living room. "Bravo Professor!" it cried in plainly genuine enthusiasm. "You were absolutely splendid. It was an honor to be present at your seminar."

The Professor was furious to realize that he was blushing; yet it was impossible to respond to such praise with an eviction notice. There was nothing for him to do but reply, a trifle stiffly, "Thank you, most gratifying." But the rhinoceros was clearly waiting for something more, and Professor Gottesman was, as his friend Sally had said, a gentleman. He went on, "You are welcome to audit the class again, if you like. We will be considering Rousseau next week, and then proceed through the romantic philosophers to Nietzsche and Schopenhauer."

"With a little time to spare for the American Transcendentalists, I should hope," suggested the rhinoceros. Professor Gottesman, being some distance past surprise, nodded. The rhinoceros said reflectively, "I think I should prefer to hear you on Comte and John Stuart Mill. The romantics always struck me as fundamentally unsound."

This position agreed so much with the Professor's own opinion that he found himself, despite himself, gradually warming toward the rhinoceros. Still formal, he asked, "May I perhaps offer you a drink? Some coffee or tea?"

"Tea would be very nice," the rhinoceros answered, "if you should happen to have a bucket." Professor Gottesman did not, and the rhinoceros told him not to worry about it. It settled back down before the fire, and the Professor drew up a rocking chair. The rhinoceros said, "I must admit, I do wish I could hear you speak on the scholastic philosophers. That's really my period, after all."

"I will be giving such a course next year," the Professor said, a little shyly. "It is to be a series of lectures on medieval Christian thought, beginning with St. Augustine and the Neoplatonists and ending with William of Occam. Possibly you could attend some of those talks."

The rhinoceros's obvious pleasure at the invitation touched Professor Gottesman surprisingly deeply. Even Sally Lowry, who often dropped in on his classes unannounced, did so, as he knew, out of affection for him, and not from any serious interest in epistemology or the Milesian School. He was beginning to wonder whether there might be a way to permit the rhinoceros to sample the cream sherry he kept aside for company, when the creature added, with a wheezy chuckle, "Of course, Augustine and the rest never did quite come to terms with such pagan survivals as unicorns. The best they could do was associate us with the Virgin Mary, and to suggest that our horns somehow represented the unity of Christ and his church. Bernard of Trèves even went so far as to identify Christ directly with the unicorn, but it was never a comfortable union. Spiral peg in square hole, so to speak."

Professor Gottesman was no more at ease with the issue than St. Augustine had been. But he was an honest person—only among philosophers is this considered part of the job description—and so he felt it his duty to say, "While I respect your intelligence and your obvious intellectual curiosity, none of this yet persuades me that you are in fact a unicorn. I still must regard you as an exceedingly learned and well-mannered Indian rhinoceros."

The rhinoceros took this in good part, saying, "Well, well, we will agree to disagree on that point for the time being. Although I certainly hope that you will let me know if you should need your drinking water purified." As before, and so often thereafter, Professor Gottesman could not be completely sure that the rhinoceros was joking. Dismissing the subject, it went on to ask, "But about the Scholastics—do you plan to discuss the later Thomist reformers at all? Saint Cajetan rather dominates the movement, to my mind; if he had any real equals, I'm afraid I can't recall them."

"Ah," said the Professor. They were up until five in the morning, and it was the rhinoceros who dozed off first. The question of the rhinoceros's leaving Professor Gottesman's house never came up again. It continued to sleep in the living room, for the most part, though on warm summer nights it had a fondness for the young willow tree that had been a Christmas present from Sally. Professor Gottesman never learned whether it was male or female, nor how it nourished its massive, noisy body, nor how it managed its toilet facilities—a reticent man himself, he respected reticence in others. As a houseguest, the rhinoceros's only serious fault was a continuing predilection for hot baths (with Epsom salts, when it could get them.) But it always cleaned up after itself, and was extremely conscientious about not tracking mud into the house;

and it can be safely said that none of the Professor's visitors—even the rare ones who spent a night or two under his roof—ever remotely suspected that they were sharing living quarters with a rhinoceros. All in all, it proved to be a most discreet and modest beast.

The Professor had few friends, apart from Sally, and none whom he would have called on in a moment of bewildering crisis, as he had called on her. He avoided whatever social or academic gatherings he could reasonably avoid; as a consequence his evenings had generally been lonely ones, though he might not have called them so. Even if he had admitted the term, he would surely have insisted that there was nothing necessarily wrong with loneliness, in and of itself. "*I think*," he would have said—did often say, in fact, to Sally Lowry. "There are people, you know, for whom thinking is company, thinking is entertainment, parties, dancing even. The others, other people, they absolutely will not believe this."

"You're right," Sally said. "One thing about you, Gus, when you're right you're really right."

Now, however, the Professor could hardly wait for the time of day when, after a cursory dinner (he was an indifferent, impatient eater, and truly tasted little difference between a frozen dish and one that had taken half a day to prepare), he would pour himself a glass of wine and sit down in the living room to debate philosophy with a huge mortar-colored beast that always smelled vaguely incontinent, no matter how many baths it had taken that afternoon. Looking eagerly forward all day to anything was a new experience for him. It appeared to be the same for the rhinoceros.

As the animal had foretold, there was never the slightest suggestion in the papers or on television that the local zoo was missing one of its larger odd-toed ungulates. The Professor went there once or twice in great trepidation, convinced that he would be recognized and accused immediately of conspiracy in the rhinoceros's escape. But nothing of the sort happened. The yard where the rhinoceros had been kept was now occupied by a pair of despondent-looking African elephants; when Professor Gottesman made a timid inquiry of a guard, he was curtly informed that the zoo had never possessed a rhinoceros of any species. "Endangered species," the guard told him. "Too much red tape you have to go through to get one these days. Just not worth the trouble, mean as they are."

Professor Gottesman grew placidly old with the rhinoceros—that is to say, the Professor grew old, while the rhinoceros never changed in any way that he could observe. Granted, he was not the most observant of men, nor the most sensitive to change, except when threatened by it.

Nor was he in the least ambitious: promotions and pay raises happened, when they happened, somewhere in the same cloudily benign middle distance as did those departmental meetings that he actually had to sit through. The companionship of the rhinoceros, while increasingly his truest delight, also became as much of a cozily reassuring habit as his classes, his office hours, the occasional dinner and movie or museum excursion with Sally Lowry, and the books on French and German philosophy that he occasionally published through the university press over the years. They were indifferently reviewed, and sold poorly.

"Which is undoubtedly as it should be," Professor Gottesman frequently told Sally when dropping her off at her house, well across town from his own. "I think I am a good teacher—that, yes—but I am decidedly not an original thinker, and I was never much of a writer even in German. It does no harm to say that I am not an exceptional man, Sally. It does not hurt me."

"I don't know what exceptional means to you or anyone else," Sally would answer stubbornly. "To me it means being unique, one of a kind, and that's definitely you, old Gus. I never thought you belonged in this town, or this university, or probably this century. But I'm surely glad you've been here."

Once in a while she might ask him casually how his unicorn was getting on these days. The Professor, who had long since accepted the fact that no one ever saw the rhinoceros unless it chose to be seen, invariably rose to the bait, saying, "It is no more a unicorn than it ever was, Sally, you know that." He would sip his latte in mild indignation, and eventually add, "Well, we will clearly never see eye to eye on the Vienna Circle, or the logical positivists in general—it is a very conservative creature, in some ways. But we did come to a tentative agreement about Bergson, last Thursday it was, so I would have to say that we are going along quite amiably."

Sally rarely pressed him further. Sharp-tongued, solitary, and profoundly irreverent, only with Professor Gottesman did she bother to know when to leave things alone. Most often, she would take out her battered harmonica and play one or another of his favorite tunes—"Sweet Georgia Brown" or "Hurry on Down." He never sang along, but he always hummed and grunted and thumped his bony knees. Once he mentioned diffidently that the rhinoceros appeared to have a peculiar fondness for "Slow Boat to China." Sally pretended not to hear him.

In the appointed fullness of time, the university retired Professor Gottesman in a formal ceremony, attended by, among others, Sally Lowry, his sister Edith, all the way from Zurich, and the rhinoceros—the latter having spent all that day in the bathtub, in anxious preparation. Each of them assured him that he looked immensely distinguished as he was invested with the rank of *emeritus*, which allowed him to lecture as many as four times a year, and to be available to counsel promising graduate students when he chose. In addition, a special chair with his name on it was reserved exclusively for his use at the Faculty Club. He was quite proud of never once having sat in it.

"Strange, I am like a movie star now," he said to the rhinoceros. "You should see. Now I walk across the campus and the students line up, they line up to watch me totter past. I can hear their whispers—'Here he comes!' 'There he goes!' Exactly the same ones they are who used to cut my classes because I bored them so. Completely absurd."

"Enjoy it as your due," the rhinoceros proposed. "You were entitled to their respect then—take pleasure in it now, however misplaced it may seem to you." But the Professor shook his head, smiling wryly.

"Do you know what kind of star I am really like?" he asked. "I am like the old, old star that died so long ago, so far away, that its last light is only reaching our eyes today. They fall in on themselves, you know, those dead stars, they go cold and invisible, even though we think we are seeing them in the night sky. That is just how I would be, if not for you. And for Sally, of course."

In fact, Professor Gottesman found little difficulty in making his peace with age and retirement. His needs were simple, his pension and savings adequate to meet them, and his health as sturdy as generations of Swiss peasant ancestors could make it. For the most part he continued to live as he always had, the one difference being that he now had more time for study, and could stay up as late as he chose arguing about structuralism with the rhinoceros, or listening to Sally Lowry reading her new translation of Calvalcanti or Frescobaldi. At first he attended every conference of philosophers to which he was invited, feeling a certain vague obligation to keep abreast of new thought in his field. This compulsion passed quickly, however, leaving him perfectly satisfied to have as little as possible to do with academic life, except when he needed to use the library. Sally once met him there for lunch to find him feverishly rifling the ten Loeb Classic volumes of Philo Judaeus. "We were debating the concept of the logos last night," he explained to her, "and then the impossible beast rampaged off on a tangent involving Philo's locating the roots of Greek philosophy in the Torah: Forgive me, Sally, but I may be here for awhile." Sally lunched alone that day.

The Professor's sister Edith died younger than she should have. He grieved for her, and took much comfort in the fact that Nathalie never failed to visit him when she came to America. The last few times, she had brought a husband and two children with her—the youngest hugging a ragged but indomitable tiger named Charles under his arm. They most often swept him off for the evening; and it was on one such occasion, just after they had brought him home and said their good-byes, and their rented car had rounded the corner, that the mugging occurred.

Professor Gottesman was never quite sure himself about what actually took place. He remembered a light scuffle of footfalls, remembered a savage blow on the side of his head, then another impact as his cheek and forehead hit the ground. There were hands clawing through his pockets, low voices so distorted by obscene viciousness that he lost English completely, became for the first time in fifty years a terrified immigrant, once more unable to cry out for help in this new and dreadful country. A faceless figure billowed over him, grabbing his collar, pulling him close, mouthing words he could not understand. It was brandishing something menacingly in its free hand.

Then it vanished abruptly, as though blasted away by the sidewalk-shaking bellow of rage that was Professor Gottesman's last clear memory until he woke in a strange bed, with Sally Lowry, Nathalie, and several policemen bending over him. The next day's newspapers ran the marvelous story of a retired philosophy professor, properly frail and elderly, not only fighting off a pair of brutal muggers but beating them so badly that they had to be hospitalized themselves before they could be arraigned. Sally impishly kept the incident on the front pages for some days by confiding to reporters that Professor Gottesman was a practitioner of a long-forgotten martial-arts discipline, practiced only in ancient Sumer and Babylonia. "Plain childishness," she said apologetically, after the fuss had died down. "Pure self-indulgence. I'm sorry, Gus."

"Do not be," the Professor replied. "If we were to tell them the truth, I would immediately be placed in an institution." He looked sideways at his friend, who smiled and said, "What, about the rhinoceros rescuing you? I'll never tell, I swear. They could pull out my fingernails."

Professor Gottesman said, "Sally, those boys had been *trampled*, practically stamped flat. One of them had been *gored*, I saw him. Do you really think I could have done all that?"

"Remember, I've seen you in your wrath," Sally answered lightly and untruthfully. What she had in fact seen was one of the ace-of-clubs footprints she remembered in crusted mud on the Professor's front steps long ago. She said, "Gus. How old am I?"

The Professor's response was off by a number of years, as it always was. Sally said, "You've frozen me at a certain age, because you don't want me getting any older. Fine, I happen to be the same way about that rhinoceros of yours. There are one or two things I just don't want to know about that damn rhinoceros, Gus. If that's all right with you."

"Yes, Sally," Professor Gottesman answered. "That is all right."

The rhinoceros itself had very little to say about the whole incident. "I chanced to be awake, watching a lecture about Bulgarian icons on the Learning Channel. I heard the noise outside." Beyond that, it sidestepped all questions, pointedly concerning itself only with the Professor's recuperation from his injuries and shock. In fact, he recovered much faster than might reasonably have been expected from a gentleman of his years. The doctor commented on it.

The occurrence made Professor Gottesman even more of an icon himself on campus; as a direct consequence, he spent even less time there than before, except when the rhinoceros requested a particular book. Nathalie, writing from Zurich, never stopped urging him to take in a housemate, for company and safety, but she would have been utterly dumbfounded if he had accepted her suggestion. "Something looks out for him," she said to her husband. "I always knew that, I couldn't tell you why. Uncle Gustave is *somebody's* dear stuffed Charles."

Sally Lowry did grow old, despite Professor Gottesman's best efforts. The university gave her a retirement ceremony too, but she never showed up for it. "Too damn depressing," she told Professor Gottesman, as he helped her into her coat for their regular Wednesday walk. "It's all right for you, Gus, you'll be around forever. Me, I drink, I still smoke, I still eat all kinds of stuff they tell me not to eat—I don't even floss, for God's sake. My circulation works like the post office, and even my cholesterol has arthritis. Only reason I've lasted this long is I had this stupid job teaching beautiful, useless stuff to idiots. Now that's it. Now I'm a goner."

"Nonsense, nonsense, Sally," Professor Gottesman assured her vigorously. "You have always told me you are too mean and spiteful to die. I am holding you to this."

"Pickled in vinegar only lasts just so long," Sally said. "One cheery note, anyway—it'll be the heart that goes. Always is, in my family. That's good, I couldn't hack cancer. I'd be a shameless, screaming disgrace, absolutely no dignity at all. I'm really grateful it'll be the heart."

The Professor was very quiet while they walked all the way down to the little local park, and back again. They had reached the apartment complex where she lived, when he suddenly gripped her by the arms, looked straight into her face, and said loudly, "That is the best heart I ever knew, yours. I will not *let* anything happen to that heart."

"Go home, Gus," Sally told him harshly. "Get out of here, go home. Christ, the only sentimental Switzer in the whole world, and I get him. Wouldn't you just know?"

Professor Gottesman actually awoke just before the telephone call came, as sometimes happens. He had dozed off in his favorite chair during a minor intellectual skirmish with the rhinoceros over Spinoza's ethics. The rhinoceros itself was sprawled in its accustomed spot, snoring authoritatively, and the kitchen clock was still striking three when the phone rang. He picked it up slowly. Sally's barely audible voice whispered, "Gus. The heart. Told you." He heard the receiver fall from her hand.

Professor Gottesman had no memory of stumbling coatless out of the house, let alone finding his car parked on the street—he was just suddenly standing by it, his hands trembling so badly as he tried to unlock the door that he dropped his keys into the gutter. How long his frantic fumbling in the darkness went on, he could never say; but at some point he became aware of a deeper darkness over him, and looked up on hands and knees to see the rhinoceros.

"On my back," it said, and no more. The Professor had barely scrambled up its warty, unyielding flanks and heaved himself precariously over the spine his legs could not straddle when there came a surge like the sea under him as the great beast leaped forward. He cried out in terror.

He would have expected, had he had wit enough at the moment to expect anything, that the rhinoceros would move at a ponderous trot, farting and rumbling, gradually building up a certain clumsy momentum. Instead, he felt himself flying, truly flying, as children know flying, flowing with the night sky, melting into the jeweled wind. If the rhinoceros's huge, flat, three-toed feet touched the ground, he never felt it: nothing existed, or ever had existed, but the sky that he was and the bodiless power that he had become—he himself, the once and foolish old Professor Gustave Gottesman, his eyes full of the light of lost stars. He even forgot Sally Lowry, only for a moment, only for the least little time.

Then he was standing in the courtyard before her house, shouting and banging maniacally on the door, pressing every button under his hand. The rhinoceros was nowhere to be seen. The building door finally buzzed open, and the Professor leaped up the stairs like a young man, calling Sally's name. Her own door was unlocked; she often left it so absentmindedly, no matter how much he scolded her about it. She was in her bedroom, half-wedged between the side of the bed and the night table, with the telephone receiver dangling by her head. Professor Gottesman touched her cheek and felt the fading warmth.

"Ah, Sally," he said. "Sally, my dear." She was very heavy, but somehow it was easy for him to lift her back onto the bed and make a place for her among the books and papers that littered the quilt, as always. He found her harmonica on the floor, and closed her fingers around it. When there was nothing more for him to do, he sat beside her, still holding her hand, until the room began to grow light. At last he said aloud, "No, the sentimental Switzer will not cry, my dear Sally," and picked up the telephone.

The rhinoceros did not return for many days after Sally Lowry's death. Professor Gottesman missed it greatly when he thought about it at all, but it was a strange, confused time. He stayed at home, hardly eating, sleeping on his feet, opening books and closing them. He never answered the telephone, and he never changed his clothes. Sometimes he wandered endlessly upstairs and down through every room in his house; sometimes he stood in one place for an hour or more at a time, staring at nothing. Occasionally the doorbell rang, and worried voices outside called his name. It was late autumn, and then winter, and the house grew cold at night, because he had forgotten to turn on the furnace. Professor Gottesman was perfectly aware of this, and other things, somewhere.

One evening, or perhaps it was early one morning, he heard the sound of water running in the bathtub upstairs. He remembered the sound, and presently he moved to his living room chair to listen to it better. For the first time in some while, he fell asleep, and woke only when he felt the rhinoceros standing over him. In the darkness he saw it only as a huge, still shadow, but it smelled unmistakably like a rhinoceros that has just had a bath. The Professor said quietly, "I wondered where you had gone."

"We unicorns mourn alone," the rhinoceros replied. "I thought it might be the same for you."

"Ah," Professor Gottesman said. "Yes, most considerate. Thank you."

He said nothing further, but sat staring into the shadow until it appeared to fold gently around him. The rhinoceros said, "We were speaking of Spinoza."

Professor Gottesman did not answer. The rhinoceros went on, "I was very interested in the comparison you drew between Spinoza and Thomas Hobbes. I would enjoy continuing our discussion."

"I do not think I can," the Professor said at last. "I do not think I want to talk anymore."

It seemed to him that the rhinoceros's eyes had become larger and brighter in its own shadow, and its horn a trifle less hulking. But its stomach rumbled as majestically as ever as it said, "In that case, perhaps we should be on our way."

"Where are we going?" Professor Gottesman asked. He was feeling oddly peaceful and disinclined to leave his chair. The rhinoceros moved closer, and for the first time that the Professor could remember its huge, hairy muzzle touched his shoulder, light as a butterfly.

"I have lived in your house for a long time," it said. "We have talked together, days and nights on end, about ways of being in this world, ways of considering it, ways of imagining it as a part of some greater imagining. Now has come the time for silence. Now I think you should come and live with me."

They were outside, on the sidewalk, in the night. Professor Gottesman had forgotten to take his coat, but he was not at all cold. He turned to look back at his house, watching it recede, its lights still burning, like a ship leaving him at his destination. He said to the rhinoceros, "What is your house like?"

"Comfortable," the rhinoceros answered. "In honesty, I would not call the hot water as superbly lavish as yours, but there is rather more room to maneuver. Especially on the stairs."

"You are walking a bit too rapidly for me," said the Professor. "May I climb on your back once more?"

The rhinoceros halted immediately, saying, "By all means, please do excuse me."

Professor Gottesman found it notably easier to mount this time, the massive sides having plainly grown somewhat trimmer and smoother during the rhinoceros's absence, and easier to grip with his legs. It started on briskly when he was properly settled, though not at the rapturous pace that had once married the Professor to the night wind. For some while he could hear the clopping of cloven hooves far below him, but then they seemed to fade away. He leaned forward and said into the rhinoceros's pointed silken ear, "I should tell you that I have long since come to the conclusion that you are not after all an Indian rhinoceros, but a hitherto unknown species, somehow misclassified. I hope this will not make a difference in our relationship."

"No difference, good Professor," came the gently laughing answer all around him. "No difference in the world."

The Last and Only,
or,
Mr. Moscowitz becomes French

Once upon a time, there lived in California a Frenchman named George Moscowitz. His name is of no importance—there are old families in France named Wilson and Holmes, and the first president of the Third Republic was named MacMahon—but what was interesting about Mr. Moscowitz was that he had not always been French. Nor was he entirely French at the time we meet him, but he was becoming perceptibly more so every day. His wife, whose name was Miriam, drew his silhouette on a child's blackboard and filled him in from the feet up with tricolor chalk, adding a little more color daily. She was at mid-thigh when we begin our story.

Most of the doctors who examined Mr. Moscowitz agreed that his affliction was due to some sort of bug that he must have picked up in France when he and Mrs. Moscowitz were honeymooning there, fifteen years before. In its dormant stage, the bug had manifested itself only as a kind of pleasant Francophilia: on their return from France Mr. Moscowitz had begun to buy Linguaphone CDs, and to get up at six in the morning to watch a cable television show on beginner's French. He took to collecting French books and magazines, French music and painting and sculpture, French recipes, French folklore, French attitudes, and, inevitably, French people. As a librarian in a large university, he came in contact with a good many French exchange students and visiting professors, and he went far out of his way to make friends with them—Mr. Moscowitz, shy as a badger. The students had a saying among themselves that if you wanted to be French in that town, you had to clear it with Monsieur Moscowitz, who issued licenses and *cartes de séjour*. The joke was not especially unkind, because Mr. Moscowitz often had them to dinner at his home, and in his quiet delight in the very sound of their voices they found themselves curiously less bored with themselves, and with one another. Their companions at dinner were quite likely to be the ignorant Marseillais tailor who got all of Mr. Moscowitz's custom, or the Canuck coach of the soccer team, but there was something so touching in Mr. Moscowitz's assumption that all French-speaking people must be naturally at home together that professors and proletariat generally managed to find each other charming and valuable. And Mr. Moscowitz himself, speaking rarely, but sometimes smiling uncontrollably, like an exhalation of joy—he was a snob in that he preferred the culture and manners of another country to his own, and certainly a fool in that he could find wisdom in every foolishness uttered in French—he was marvelously happy then, and it was impossible for those around him to escape his happiness. Now and then he would address a compliment or a witticism to his wife, who would smile and answer softly, "*Merci*," or "*La-la*," for she knew that at such moments he believed without thinking about it that she too spoke French.

Mrs. Moscowitz herself was, as must be obvious, a patient woman of a tolerant humor, who greatly enjoyed her husband's enjoyment of all things French, and who believed, firmly and serenely, that this curious obsession would fade with time, to be replaced by bridge or chess, or—though she prayed not—golf. "At least he's dressing much better these days," she told her sister Dina, who lived in Scottsdale, Arizona. "Thank God you don't have to wear plaid pants to be French."

Then, after fifteen years, whatever it was that he had contracted in France, if that was what he had done, came fully out of hiding; and here stood Mr. Moscowitz in one doctor's office after another, French from his soles to his ankles, to his shins, to his knees, and still heading north for a second spring. (Mrs. Moscowitz's little drawing is, of course, only a convenient metaphor—if anything, her husband was becoming French from his bones out.) He was treated with drugs as common as candy and as rare as turtle tears by doctors ranging from Johns Hopkins specialists to a New Guinea shaman; he was examined by herbalists and honey-doctors, and by committees of medical men so reputable as to make illness in their presence seem almost criminal; and he was dragged to a crossroads one howling midnight to meet with a half-naked, foamy-chinned old man who claimed to be the son of Merlin's affair with Nimue, and a colonel in the Marine Reserves besides. This fellow's diagnosis was supernatural possession; his prescribed remedy would cost Mr. Moscowitz a black pig (and the pig its liver), and was impractical, but the idea left Mr. Moscowitz thoughtful for a long time.

In bed that night, he said to his wife, "Perhaps it is possession. It's frightening, yes, but it's exciting too, if you want the truth. I feel something growing inside me, taking shape as it crowds me out, and the closer I get to disappearing, the clearer it becomes. And yet, it is me too, if you understand—I wish I could explain to you how it feels—it is like, 'ow you say...."

"Don't say that," Mrs. Moscowitz interrupted with tears in her voice. She had begun to whimper quietly when he spoke of disappearing. "Only TV Frenchmen talk like that."

"*Excuse-moi, ma vieille.* The more it crowds me, the more it makes me feel like *me.* I feel a whole country growing inside me, thousands of years, millions of people, stupid, crazy, shrewd people, and all of them me. I never felt like that before, I never felt that there was anything inside me, even myself. Now I'm pregnant with a whole country, and I'm growing fat with it, and one day—" He began to cry himself then, and the two of them huddled small in their bed, holding hands all night long. He dreamed in French that night, as he had been doing for weeks, but he woke up still speaking it, and he did not regain his English until he had had his first cup of coffee. It took him longer each morning thereafter.

A psychiatrist whom they visited when Mr. Moscowitz's silhouette was French to the waist commented that his theory of possession by himself was a way of sidling up to the truth that Mr. Moscowitz was actually willing his transformation. "The unconscious is ingenious at devising methods of withdrawal," he explained, pulling at his fingertips as though milking a cow, "and national character is certainly no barrier to a mind so determined to get out from under the weight of being an American. It's not as uncommon as you might think, these days."

"*Qu'est-ce qu'il dit?*" whispered Mr. Moscowitz to his wife.

"I have a patient," mused the psychiatrist, "who believes that he is gradually being metamorphosed into a roc, such a giant bird as carried off Sindbad the Sailor to lands unimaginable and riches beyond comprehension. He has asked me to come with him to the very same lands when his change is complete."

"*Qu'est-ce qu'il dit? Qu'est-ce que c'est, roc?*" Mrs. Moscowitz shushed her husband nervously and said, "Yes, yes, but what about George? Do you think you can cure him?"

"I won't be around," said the psychiatrist. There came a stoop of great wings outside the window, and the Moscowitzes fled.

"Well, there it is," Mrs. Moscowitz said when they were home, "and I must confess I thought as much. You could stop this stupid change yourself if you really wanted to, but you don't want to stop it. You're withdrawing, just the way he said, you're escaping from the responsibility of being plain old George Moscowitz in the plain old United States. You're quitting, and I'm ashamed of you—you're copping out." She hadn't used the phrase since her own college days, at Vassar, and it made her feel old and even less in control of this disturbing situation.

"Cop-out, cop-out," said Mr. Moscowitz thoughtfully. "What charm! I love it very much, the American slang. Cop-out, copping out. I cop out, *tu* cop out, they all cop out...."

Then Mrs. Moscowitz burst into tears, and picking up her colored chalks, she scribbled up and down and across the neat silhouette of her husband until the chalk screamed and broke, and the whole blackboard was plastered red, white, and blue; and as she did this, she cried "I don't care, I don't care if you're escaping or not, or what you change into. I wouldn't care if you turned into a cockroach, if I could be a cockroach too." Her eyes were so blurred with tears that Mr. Moscowitz seemed to be sliding away from her like a cloud. He took her in his arms then, but all the comfort he offered her was in French, and she cried even harder.

It was the only time she ever allowed herself to break down. The next day she set about learning French. It was difficult for her, for she had no natural ear for language, but she enrolled in three schools at once—one for group study, one for private lessons, and the other online—and she worked very hard. She even dug out her husband's abandoned language CDs and listened to them constantly. And during her days and evenings, if she found herself near a mirror, she would peer at the plump, tired face she saw there and say carefully to it, *"Je suis la professeur. Vous êtes l'étudiante. Je suis française. Vous n'êtes pas française."* These were the first four sentences that the recordings spoke to her every day. It had occurred to her—though she never voiced the idea—that she might be able to will the same change that had befallen her husband on herself. She told herself often, especially after triumphing over her reflection, that she felt more French daily; and when she finally gave up the pretense of being transformed, she said to herself, "It's my fault. I want to change for him, not for myself. It's not enough." She kept up with her French lessons, all the same.

Mr. Moscowitz, on his part, was finding it necessary to take English lessons. His work in the library was growing more harassing every day: he could no longer read the requests filed by the students—let alone the forms and instructions on his own computer screen—and he had to resort to desperate guessing games and mnemonic systems to find anything in the stacks or on the shelves. His condition was obvious to his friends on the library staff, and they covered up for him as best they could, doing most of his work while a graduate student from the French department sat with him in a carrel, teaching him English as elementary as though he had never spoken it. But he did not learn it quickly, and he never learned it well, and his friends could not keep him hidden all the time. Inevitably, the Chancellor of the university interested himself in the matter, and after a series of interviews with Mr. Moscowitz—conducted in French, for the Chancellor was a traveled man who had studied at the Sorbonne—announced regretfully that he saw no way but to let Mr. Moscowitz go. "You understand my position, Georges, my old one," he said, shrugging slightly and twitching his mouth. "It is a damage, of course, well understood, but there will be much severance pay and a pension of the fullest." The presence of a Frenchman always made the Chancellor a little giddy.

"You speak French like a Spanish cow," observed Mr. Moscowitz, who had been expecting this decision and was quite calm. He then pointed out to the Chancellor that he had standing and to spare, and that he was not about to be gotten rid of so easily. Even in this imbecile country, an employee had his rights, and it was on the Chancellor's shoulders to find a reason for discharging him. He requested the Chancellor to show him a single university code, past or present, that listed change of nationality as sufficient grounds for terminating a contract; and he added that he was older than the Chancellor and had given him no encouragement to call him *tu*.

"But you're not the same man we hired!" cried the Chancellor in English.

"No?" asked Mr. Moscowitz when the remark had been explained to him. "Then who am I, please?"

The university would have been glad to settle the case out of court, and Mrs. Moscowitz pleaded with her husband to accept their offered terms, which were liberal enough; but he refused, for no reason that she could see but delight at the confusion and embarrassment he was about to cause, and a positive hunger for the tumult of a court battle. The man she had married, she remembered, had always found it hard to show anger even to his worst enemy, for fear of hurting his feelings; but she stopped thinking about it at that point, not wanting to make the Chancellor's case for him. "You are quite right, George," she told him, and then, carefully, "*Tu as raison, mon chou.*" He told her—as nearly as she could understand—that if she ever learned to speak French properly she would sound like a Basque, so she might as well not try. He was very rude to the Marseillais tailor these days.

The ACLU appointed a lawyer for Mr. Moscowitz, and, for all purposes but the practical, he won his case as decisively as Darrow defending Darwin. The lawyer laid great and tearful stress on the calamity (hisses from the gallery, where a sizeable French contingent grew larger every day) that had befallen a simple, ordinary man, leaving him dumb and defenseless in the midst of academic piranhas who would strip him of position, reputation, even statehood, in one pitiless bite. (This last was in reference to a foolish statement by the university counsel that Mr. Moscowitz would have some difficulty passing a citizenship test now, let alone a librarian's examination.) But his main defense was the same as Mr. Moscowitz's before the Chancellor: there was no precedent for such a situation as his client's, nor was this case likely to set one. If the universities wanted to write it into their common code that any man proved to be changing his nationality should summarily be discharged, then the universities could do that, and very silly they would look, too. ("What would constitute proof?" he wondered aloud, and what degree of change would it be necessary to prove? "Fifty percent? Thirty-three and one-third? Or just, as the French say, a *soupçon?*") But as matters stood, the university had no more right to fire Mr. Moscowitz for becoming a Frenchman than they would have if he became fat, or gray-haired, or two inches taller. The lawyer ended his plea by bowing deeply to his client and crying, "*Vive* Moscowitz!" And the whole courthouse rang and thundered then as Americans and French, judge and jury, counsels and bailiffs and the whole audience rose and roared, "*Vive* Moscowitz! *Vive* Moscowitz!" The Chancellor thought of the Sorbonne, and wept.

There were newspapermen in the courtroom, and by that last day there were television cameras. Mr. Moscowitz sat at home that night and leaned forward to stare at his face whenever it came on the screen. His wife, thinking he was criticizing his appearance, remarked, "You look nice. A little like Jean Gabin." Mr. Moscowitz grunted. "*Le camera t'aime,*" she said carefully. She answered the phone when it rang, which was often. Many of the callers had television shows of their own. The others wanted Mr. Moscowitz to write books.

Within a week of the trial, Mr. Moscowitz was a national celebrity, which meant that as many people knew his name as knew the name of the actor who played the dashing Gilles de Rais in a new television serial, and not quite as many as recognized the eleven-year-old Racine girl with a forty-inch bust, who sang Christian techno-rap. Mrs. Moscowitz saw him more often on television than she did at home—at seven on a Sunday morning he was invited to discuss post-existential film or France's relations with her former African colonies; at two o'clock he might be awarding a ticket to Paris to the winner of the daily *My Ex Will Hate This* contest; and at eleven PM, on one of the late-night shows, she could watch him speaking the lyrics to the internationally popular French song, "Je M'en Fous De Tout Ça," while a covey of teenage dancers yipped and jiggled around him. Mrs. Moscowitz would sigh, switch off the set, and sit down at the computer to study her assigned installment of the adventures of the family Vincent, who spoke basic French to one another and were always having breakfast, visiting aunts, or making lists. "Regard Helene," said Mrs. Moscowitz bitterly. "She is in train of falling into the quicksand again. Yes, she falls. Naughty, naughty Helene. She talks too much."

There was a good deal of scientific and political interest taken in Mr. Moscowitz as well. He spent several weekends in Washington, being examined and interviewed, and he met the President, briefly. The President shook his hand, and gave him a souvenir fountain pen and a flag lapel, and said that he regarded Mr. Moscowitz's transformation as the ultimate expression of the American dream, for it surely proved to the world that any American could become whatever he wanted enough to be, even if what he wanted to be was a snail-eating French wimp.

The scientists, whose lingering fear had been that the metamorphosis of Mr. Moscowitz had been somehow accomplished by the Russians or the Iranians, as a practice run before they turned everybody into Russians or Iranians, found nothing in Mr. Moscowitz either to enlighten or alert them. He was a small, suspicious man who spoke often of his rights, and might, as far as they could tell, have been born French. They sent him home at last, to his business manager, to his television commitments, to his endorsements, to his ghostwritten autobiography, and to his wife; and they told the President, "Go figure. Maybe this is the way the world ends, we wouldn't know. And it might not hurt to avoid crêpes for a while."

Mr. Moscowitz's celebrity lasted for almost two months—quite a long time, considering that it was autumn and there were a lot of other public novas flaring and dying on prime time. His highwater mark was certainly reached on the weekend that the officials of at least one cable network were watching one another's eyes to see how they might react to the idea of a George Moscowitz Show. His fortunes began to ebb on Monday morning—public interest is a matter of momentum, and there just wasn't anything Mr. Moscowitz could do for an encore.

"If he were only a *nice* Frenchman, or a *sexy* Frenchman!" the producers and the publishers and the ghostwriters and the A&R executives and the sponsors sighed separately and in conference. "Someone like Jean Reno or Charles Boyer, or Chevalier, or Jacques Pépin, or even Louis Jourdan—somebody charming, somebody with style, with manners, with maybe a little ho-*ho*, Mimi, you good-for-nothing little Mimi…"

But what they had, as far as they could see, was one of those surly frogs in a cloth cap who rioted in front of the American Embassy and trashed the Paris McDonald's. Once, on a talk show, he said, taking great care with his English grammar, "The United States is like a very large dog which has not been—*qu'est-ce que c'est le mot?*—housebro*ken*. It is well enough in its place, but its place is not on the couch. Or in the Mideast, or in Africa, or in a restaurant kitchen." The television station began to get letters. They suggested that Mr. Moscowitz go back where he came from.

So Mr. Moscowitz was whisked out of the public consciousness as deftly as an unpleasant report on what else gives mice cancer or makes eating fish as hazardous as bullfighting. His television bookings were cancelled; he was replaced by reruns, motivational speakers, old John Payne musicals, or one of the less distressing rappers. The contracts for his books and columns and articles remained unsigned, or turned out to conceal escape clauses, elusive and elliptical, but enforceable. Within a week of his last public utterance—"American women smell bad, they smell of fear and vomit and *l'ennui*"—George Moscowitz was no longer a celebrity. He wasn't even a Special Guest.

Nor was he a librarian anymore, in spite of the court's decision. He could not be discharged, but he certainly couldn't be kept on in the library. The obvious solution would have been to find him a position in the French department, but he was no teacher, no translator, no scholar; he was unqualified to teach the language in a junior high school. The Chancellor graciously offered him a departmental scholarship to get a degree in French, but he turned it down as an insult. "At least, a couple of education courses—" said the Chancellor. "Take them yourself," said Mr. Moscowitz, and he resigned.

"What will we do now, George?" asked his wife. "*Que ferons-nous?*" She was glad to have her husband back from the land of magic, even though he was as much a stranger to her now as he sometimes seemed to be to himself. ("What does a butterfly think of its chrysalis?" she wondered modestly, "Or of milkweed?") His fall from grace seemed to have made him kind again. They spent their days together now, walking, or reading Chateaubriand aloud; often silent, for it was hard for Mrs. Moscowitz to speak truly in French, and her husband could not mutter along in English for long without becoming angry. "Will we go to France?" she asked, knowing his answer.

"Yes," Mr. Moscowitz said. He showed her a letter. "The French government will pay our passage. We are going home." He said it many times, now with joy, now with a certain desperation. "We are going home."

The French of course insisted on making the news of Mr. Moscowitz's departure public in America, and the general American attitude was a curious mix of relief and chagrin. They were glad to have Mr. Moscowitz safely out of the way, but it was "doubtless unpleasant," as a French newspaper suggested, "to see a recognizable human shape insist on emerging from the great melting pot, instead of eagerly dissolving away." Various influences in the United States warned that Mr. Moscowitz was obviously a spy for some international conspiracy, but the President, who had vaguely liked him, said, "Well, good for him, great. Enjoy, baby." The government made up a special loose-leaf passport for Mr. Moscowitz, with room for other changes of nationality, just in case.

Mrs. Moscowitz, who made few demands on her husband, or anyone else, insisted on going to visit her sister Dina in Scottsdale before the move to France. She spent several days being taught to play video games by her nephew and enjoying countless tea parties with her two nieces, and sitting up late with Dina and her sympathetic husband, talking over all the ramifications of her coming exile. "Because that's the way I know I see it," she said, "in my heart. I try to feel excited—I really do try, for George's sake—but inside, inside..." She never wept or broke down at such points, but would pause for a few moments, while her sister fussed with the coffee cups and her brother-in-law looked away. "It's not that I'll miss that many people," she would go on, "or our life—well, George's life—around the university. Or the apartment, or all the things we can't take with us—that doesn't really matter, all that. Maybe if we had children, like you..." and she would fall silent again, but not for long, before she burst out, "But *me,* I'll miss *me!* I don't know who I'll be, living in France, but it'll be someone else, it won't ever be *me* again. And I did...I *did* like me the way I was, and so did George, no matter what he says now." But in time, as they knew she would, she would recover her familiar reliable calmness and decide, "Oh, it will be all right, I'm sure. I'm just being an old stick-in-the-mud. It *will* be an adventure, after all."

The French government sent a specially-chartered jet to summon the Moscowitzes; it was very grand treatment, Mrs. Moscowitz thought, but she had hoped they would sail. "On a boat, we would be nowhere for a few days," she said to herself, "and I do need to be nowhere first, just a little while." She took her books and CDs about the Vincent family along with her, and she drew a long breath and held onto Mr. Moscowitz's sleeve when the plane doors opened onto the black and glowing airfield, and they were invited to step down among the roaring people who had been waiting for two days to welcome them. "Here we go," she said softly. "*Allons-y.* We are home."

France greeted them with great pride and great delight, in which there was mixed not the smallest drop of humor. To the overwhelming majority of the French press, to the poets and politicians, and certainly to the mass of the people—who read the papers and the poems, and waited at the airport—it seemed both utterly logical and magnificently just that a man's soul should discover itself to be French. Was it not possible that all the souls in the world might be French, born in exile but beginning to find their way home from the cold countries, one by one? Think of all the tourists, the wonderful middle-aged tourists—where will we put them all? Anywhere, anywhere, it won't matter, for all the world will be France, as it should have been long ago, when our souls began to speak different languages. *Vive* Moscowitz then, *vive* Moscowitz! And see if you can get him to do a spread in Paris-Match, or on your television program, or book him for a few weeks at the Olympia. Got to make your money before Judgment Day.

But the government had not invited Mr. Moscowitz to France to abandon him to free enterprise—he was much too important for that. His television appearances were made on government time; his public speeches were staged and sponsored by the government; and he would never have been allowed, even had he wished, to endorse a soft drink that claimed that it made the imbiber twenty-two percent more French. He was not for rent. He traveled—or, rather, he was traveled—through the country, from Provence to Brittany, gently guarded, fenced round in a civilized manner; and throngs of people came out to see him. Then he was returned to Paris.

The government officials in charge of Mr. Moscowitz found a beautiful apartment in safe, quiet Passy for him and his wife, and let them understand that the rent would be paid for the rest of their lives. There was a maid and a cook, both paid for, and there was a garden that seemed as big as the Bois de Boulogne to the Moscowitzes, and there was a government chauffeur to take them wherever they wanted to go, whenever. And finally—for the government understood that many men will die without work—there was a job ready for Mr. Moscowitz when he chose to take it up, as the librarian of the Benjamin Franklin library, behind the Odeon. He had hoped for the Bibliothèque nationale, but he was satisfied with the lesser post. "We are home," he said to his wife. "Having one job or another—one thing or another—only makes a difference to those who are not truly at home. *Tu m'comprends?*

"*Oui,*" said Mrs. Moscowitz. They were forever asking each other that, *Do you understand me?* and they both always said *yes*. He spoke often of home and of belonging, she noticed; perhaps he meant to reassure her. For herself, she had come to realize that all the lists and journeys of the family Vincent would never make her a moment more French than she was, which was not at all, regardless. Indeed, the more she studied the language—the government had provided a series of tutors for her—the less she seemed to understand it, and she lived in anxiety that she and Mr. Moscowitz would lose this hold of one another, like children separated in a parade. Yet she was not as unhappy as she had feared, for her old capacity for making the best of things surfaced once again, and actually did make her new life as kind and rewarding as it could possibly have been, not only for her, but for those with whom she came in any sort of contact. She would have been very surprised to learn this last.

But Mr. Moscowitz himself was not happy for long in France. It was certainly no one's fault but his own. The government took the wisest care of him it knew—though it exhibited him, still it always remembered that he was a human being, which is hard for a government—and the people of France sent him silly, lovely gifts and letters of welcome from all across the country. In their neighborhood, the Moscowitzes were the reigning couple without really knowing it. Students gathered under their windows on the spring nights to sing to them, and the students' fathers, the butchers and grocers and druggists and booksellers of Passy, would never let Mrs. Moscowitz pay for anything when she went shopping. They made friends, good, intelligent, government-approved friends—and yet Mr. Moscowitz brooded more and more visibly, until his wife finally asked him, "What is it, George? What's the matter?"

"They are not French," he said. "All these people. They don't know what it *is* to be French."

"Because they live like Americans?" she asked gently. "George—" she had learned to pronounce it *Jhorj,* in the soft French manner—"everyone does that, or everyone will. To be anything but American is very hard these days. I think they do very well."

"They are not French," Mr. Moscowitz repeated. "I am French, but they are not French. I wonder if they ever were." She looked at him in some alarm. It was her first intimation that the process was not complete.

His dissatisfaction with the people who thought they were French grew more apparent every day. Friends, neighbors, fellow employees, and a wide spectrum of official persons passed in turn before his eyes; and he studied each one and plainly discarded them. Once he had been the kind of man who said nothing, rather than lie; but now he said everything he thought, which is not necessarily more honest. He stalked through the streets of Paris, muttering, "You are not French, none of you are—you are imposters! What have you done with my own people, where have they gone?" It was impossible for such a search to go unnoticed for long. Children as well as grown men began to run up to him on the street, begging, "*Monsieur Moscowitz, regardez-moi, je suis vraiment français!*" He would look at them once, speak or say nothing, and stride on. The rejected quite often wept as they looked after him.

There were some Frenchmen, of both high and low estate, who became furious with Mr. Moscowitz— who was *he*, a first generation American, French only by extremely dubious mutation, to claim that they, whose ancestors had either laid the foundations of European culture, or died, ignorant, in its defense, were not French? But in the main, a deep sadness shadowed the country. An inquisitor had come among them, an apostle, and they had been found wanting. France mourned herself, and began wondering if she had ever existed at all; for Mr. Moscowitz hunted hungrily through all recorded French history, searching for his lost kindred, and cried at last that from the days of the first paintings in the Dordogne caves, there was no evidence that a single true Frenchman had ever fought a battle, or written a poem, or built a city, or comprehended a law of the universe. "Dear France," he said with a kind of cold sorrow, "for all the Frenchmen who have ever turned your soil, you might have remained virgin and empty all these centuries. As far back in time as I can see, there has never been one, until now."

The President of France, a great man, his own monument in his own time, a man who had never wavered in the certainty that he himself was France, wrote Mr. Moscowitz a letter in which he stated: "We have always been French. We have been Gauls and Goths, Celts and Franks, but we have always been French. We, and no one else, have made France live. What else should we be but French?"

Mr. Moscowitz wrote him a letter in answer, saying, "You have inhabited France, you have occupied it, you have held it in trust if you like, and you have served it varyingly well—but that has not made you French, nor will it, any more than generations of monkeys breeding in a lion's empty cage will become lions. As for what else you may truly be, that you will have to find out for yourselves, as I had to find out."

The President, who was a religious man, thought of Belshazzar's Feast. He called on Mr. Moscowitz at his home in Passy, to the awe of Mrs. Moscowitz, who knew that ambassadors had lived out their terms in Paris without ever meeting the President face to face. The President said, "M. Moscowitz, you are denying us the right to believe in ourselves as a continuity, as part of the process of history. No nation can exist without that belief."

"Monsieur le Président, je suis désolée," answered Mr. Moscowitz. He had grown blue-gray and thin, bones hinting more and more under the once-genial flesh.

"We have done you honor," mused the President, "though I admit before you say it that we believed we were honoring ourselves. But you turn us into ghosts, *Monsieur* Moscowitz, homeless figments, and our grip on the earth is too precarious at the best of times for me to allow you to do this. You must be silent, or I will make you so. I do not want to, but I will."

Mr. Moscowitz smiled, almost wistfully, and the President grew afraid. He had a sudden vision of Mr. Moscowitz banishing him and every other soul in France with a single word, a single gesture; and in that moment's vision it seemed to him that they all went away like clouds, leaving Mr. Moscowitz to dance by himself in cobwebbed Paris on Bastille Day. The President shivered and cried out, "What is it that you want of us? What should we be? What is it, to be French, what does the stupid word mean?"

Mr. Moscowitz answered him. "I do not know, any more than you do. But I do not need to ask." His eyes were full of tears and his nose was running. "The French are inside me," he said, "singing and stamping to be let out, all of them, the wonderful children that I will never see. I am like Moses, who led his people to the Promised Land, but never set his own foot down there. All fathers are a little like Moses."

The next day, Mr. Moscowitz put on his good clothes and asked his wife to pack him a lunch. "With an apple, please," he said, "and the good Camembert, and a whole onion. Two apples." His new hat, cocked at a youthful angle, scraped coldly beside her eye when he kissed her. She did not hold him a moment longer than she ever had when he kissed her goodbye. Then Mr. Moscowitz walked away from her, and into legend.

No one ever saw him again. There were stories about him, as there still are; rumors out of Concarneau, and Sète, and Lille, from misty cities and yellow villages. Most of the tales concerned strange, magic infants, as marvelous in the families that bore them as merchildren in herring nets. The President sent out his messengers, but quite often there were no such children at all, and when there were they were the usual cases of crosseyes and extra fingers, webbed feet and cauls. The President was relieved, and said so frankly to Mrs. Moscowitz. "With all respectful sympathy, Madame," he told her, "the happiest place for your husband now is a fairy story. It is warm inside a myth, and safe, quite safe, and the company is of the best. I envy him, for I will never know such companions. I will get politicians and generals."

"And I will get his pension and his belongings," Mrs. Moscowitz said to herself. "And I will know solitude."

The President went on, "He was mad, of course, your husband, but what a mission he set himself! It was worthy of one of Charlemagne's paladins, or of your—" he fumbled through his limited stock of nonpartisan American heroes—"your Johnny Appleseed. Yes."

The President died in the country, an old man, and Mrs. Moscowitz in time died alone in Passy. She never returned to America, even to visit, partly out of loyalty to Mr. Moscowitz's dream, and partly because if there is one thing besides cheese that the French do better than any other people, it is the careful and assiduous tending of a great man's widow. She wanted for nothing to the end of her days, except her husband—and, in a very real sense, France was all she had left of him.

That was a long time ago, but the legends go on quietly, not only of the seafoam children who will create France, but of Mr. Moscowitz as well. In Paris and the provinces, anyone who listens long enough can hear stories of the American who became French. He wanders through the warm nights and the cold, under stars and streetlamps, walking with the bright purpose of a child who has slipped out of his parents' sight and is now free to do as he pleases. In the country, they say that he is on his way to see how his children are growing up, and perhaps there are mothers who lull their own children with that story, or warn them with it when they behave badly. But Parisians like to dress things up, and as they tell it, Mr. Moscowitz is never alone. Cyrano is with him, and St. Joan, Roland, D'Artagnan, and Villon—and there are others. The light of them brightens the road for Mr. Moscowitz to see his way.

But even in Paris there are people, especially women, who say that Mr. Moscowitz's only companion on his journey is Mrs. Moscowitz herself, holding his arm or running to catch up. And she deserves to be there, they will tell you, for she would have been glad of any child at all; and if he was the one who dreamed and loved France so much, still and all, she suffered.

Come Lady Death

This all happened in England a long time ago, when that George who spoke English with a heavy German accent and hated his sons was King. At that time there lived in London a lady who had nothing to do but give parties. Her name was Flora, Lady Neville, and she was a widow and very old. She lived in a great house not far from Buckingham Palace, and she had so many servants that she could not possibly remember all their names; indeed, there were some she had never even seen. She had more food than she could eat, more gowns than she could ever wear; she had wine in her cellars that no one would drink in her lifetime, and her private vaults were filled with great works of art that she did not know she owned. She spent the last years of her life giving parties and balls to which the greatest lords of England—and sometimes the King himself—came, and she was known as the wisest and wittiest woman in all London.

But in time her own parties began to bore her, and though she invited the most famous people in the land and hired the greatest jugglers and acrobats and dancers and magicians to entertain them, still she found her parties duller and duller. Listening to court gossip, which she had always loved, made her yawn. The most marvelous music, the most exciting feats of magic put her to sleep. Watching a beautiful young couple dance by her made her feel sad, and she hated to feel sad.

And so, one summer afternoon she called her closest friends around her and said to them, "More and more I find that my parties entertain everyone but me. The secret of my long life is that nothing has ever been dull for me. For all my life, I have been interested in everything I saw and been anxious to see more. But I cannot stand to be bored, and I will not go to parties at which I expect to be bored, especially if they are my own. Therefore, to my next ball I shall invite the one guest I am sure no one, not even myself, could possibly find boring. My friends, the guest of honor at my next party shall be Death himself!"

A young poet thought that this was a wonderful idea, but the rest of her friends were terrified and drew back from her. They did not want to die, they pleaded with her. Death would come for them when he was ready; why should she invite him before the appointed hour, which would arrive soon enough? But Lady Neville said, "Precisely. If Death has planned to take any of us on the night of my party, he will come whether he is invited or not. But if none of us are to die, then I think it would be charming to have Death among us—perhaps even to perform some little trick if he is in a good humor. And think of being able to say that we had been to a party with Death! All of London will envy us, all of England!"

The idea began to please her friends, but a young lord, very new to London, suggested timidly, "Death is so busy. Suppose he has work to do and cannot accept your invitation?"

"No one has ever refused an invitation of mine," said Lady Neville, "not even the King." And the young lord was not invited to her party.

▲▼▲

She sat down then and there and wrote out the invitation. There was some dispute among her friends as to how they should address Death. "His Lordship Death" seemed to place him only on the level of a viscount or a baron. "His Grace Death" met with more acceptance, but Lady Neville said it sounded hypocritical. And to refer to Death as "His Majesty" was to make him the equal of the King of England, which even Lady Neville would not dare to do. It was finally decided that all should speak of him as "His Eminence Death," which pleased nearly everyone.

Captain Compson, known both as England's most dashing cavalry officer and most elegant rake, remarked next, "That's all very well, but how is the invitation to reach Death? Does anyone here know where he lives?"

"Death undoubtedly lives in London," said Lady Neville, "like everyone else of any importance, though he probably goes to Deauville for the summer. Actually, Death must live fairly near my own house. This is much the best section of London, and you could hardly expect a person of Death's importance to live anywhere else. When I stop to think of it, it's really rather strange that we haven't met before now, on the street."

Most of her friends agreed with her, but the poet, whose name was David Lorimond, cried out, "No, my lady, you are wrong! Death lives among the poor. Death lives in the foulest, darkest alleys of this city, in some vile, rat-ridden hovel that smells of—" He stopped here, partly because Lady Neville had indicated her displeasure, and partly because he had never been inside such a hut or thought of wondering what it smelled like. "Death lives among the poor," he went on, "and comes to visit them every day, for he is their only friend."

Lady Neville answered him as coldly as she had spoken to the young lord. "He may be forced to deal with them, David, but I hardly think that he seeks them out as companions. I am certain that it is as difficult for him to think of the poor as individuals as it is for me. Death is, after all, a nobleman."

There was no real argument among the lords and ladies that Death lived in a neighborhood at least as good as their own, but none of them seemed to know the name of Death's street, and no one had ever seen Death's house.

"If there were a war," Captain Compson said, "Death would be easy to find. I have seen him, you know, even spoken to him, but he has never answered me."

"Quite proper," said Lady Neville. "Death must always speak first. You are not a very correct person, Captain," but she smiled at him, as all women did.

Then an idea came to her. "My hairdresser has a sick child, I understand," she said. "He was telling me about it yesterday, sounding most dull and hopeless. I will send for him and give him the invitation, and he in his turn can give it to Death when he comes to take the brat. A bit unconventional, I admit, but I see no other way."

"If he refuses?" asked a lord who had just been married.

"Why should he?" asked Lady Neville.

Again it was the poet who exclaimed amidst the general approval that it was a cruel and wicked thing to do. But he fell silent when Lady Neville innocently asked him, "Why, David?"

So the hairdresser was sent for, and when he stood before them, smiling nervously and twisting his hands to be in the same room with so many great lords, Lady Neville told him the errand that was required of him. And she was right, as she usually was, for he made no refusal. He merely took the invitation in his hand and asked to be excused.

He did not return for two days, but when he did he presented himself to Lady Neville without being sent for and handed her a small white envelope. Saying, "How very nice of you, thank you very much," she opened it and found therein a plain calling card with nothing on it except these words:

Death will be pleased to attend Lady Neville's ball.

"Death gave you this?" she asked the hairdresser eagerly. "What was he like?" But the hairdresser stood still, looking past her, and said nothing, and she, not really waiting for an answer, called a dozen servants to her and told them to run and summon her friends. As she paced up and down the room waiting for them, she asked again, "What is Death like?" The hairdresser did not reply.

When her friends came they passed the little card excitedly from hand to hand, until it had gotten quite smudged and bent from their fingers. But they all admitted that, beyond its message, there was nothing particularly unusual about it. It was neither hot nor cold to the touch, and what little odor clung to it was rather pleasant. Everyone said that it was a very familiar smell, but no one could give it a name. The poet said that it reminded him of lilacs but not exactly.

It was Captain Compson, however, who pointed out the one thing that no one else had noticed. "Look at the handwriting itself," he said. "Have you ever seen anything more graceful? The letters seem as light as birds. I think we have wasted our time speaking of Death as His This and His That. A woman wrote his note."

Then there was an uproar and a great babble, and the card had to be handed around again so that everyone could exclaim, "Yes, by God!" over it. The voice of the poet rose out the hubbub saying, "It is very natural, when you come to think of it. After all, the French say *la mort*. Lady Death. I should much prefer Death to be a woman."

"Death rides a great black horse," said Captain Compson firmly, "and wears armor of the same color. Death is very tall, taller than anyone. It was no woman I saw on the battlefield, striking right and left like any soldier. Perhaps the hairdresser wrote it himself, or the hairdresser's wife."

But the hairdresser refused to speak, though they gathered around him and begged him to say who had given him the note. At first they promised him all sorts of rewards, and later they threatened to do terrible things to him. "Did you write this card?" he was asked, and "Who wrote it, then? Was it a living woman? Was it really Death? Did Death say anything to you? How did you know it was Death? Is Death a woman? Are you trying to make fools of us all?"

Not a word from the hairdresser, not one word, and finally Lady Neville called her servants to have him whipped and thrown into the street. He did not look at her as they took him away, or utter a sound.

Silencing her friends with a wave of her hand, Lady Neville said, "The ball will take place two weeks from tonight. Let Death come as Death pleases, whether as a man or woman or strange, sexless creature."

She smiled calmly. "Death may well be a woman," she said. "I am less certain of Death's form than I was, but I am also less frightened of Death. I am too old to be afraid of anything that can use a quill pen to write me a letter. Go home now, and as you make your preparations for the ball see that you speak of it to your servants, that they may spread the news all over London. Let it be known that on this one night no one in the world will die, for Death will be dancing at Lady Neville's ball."

▲▼▲

For the next two weeks Lady Neville's great house shook and groaned and creaked like an old tree in a gale as the servants hammered and scrubbed, polished and painted, making ready for the ball. Lady Neville had always been very proud of her house, but as the ball drew near she began to be afraid that it would not be nearly grand enough for Death, who was surely accustomed to visiting in the homes of richer, mightier people than herself. Fearing the scorn of Death, she worked night and day supervising her servants' preparations. Curtains and carpets had to be cleaned, goldwork and silverware polished until they gleamed by themselves in the dark. The grand staircase that rushed down into the ballroom like a waterfall was washed and rubbed so often that it was almost impossible to walk on it without slipping. As for the ballroom itself, it took thirty-two servants working at once to clean it properly, not counting those who were polishing the glass chandelier that was taller than a man and the fourteen smaller lamps. And when they were done she made them do it all over, not because she saw any dust or dirt anywhere, but because she was sure that Death would.

As for herself, she chose her finest gown and saw to the laundering personally. She called in another hairdresser and had him put up her hair in the style of an earlier time, wanting to show Death that she was a woman who enjoyed her age and did not find it necessary to ape the young and beautiful. All the day of the ball she sat before her mirror, not making herself up much beyond the normal touches of rouge and eye shadow and fine rice powder, but staring at the lean old face she had been born with, wondering how it would appear to Death. Her steward asked her to approve his wine selection, but she sent him away and stayed at her mirror until it was time to dress and go downstairs to meet her guests.

Everyone arrived early. When she looked out of a window, Lady Neville saw that the driveway of her home was choked with carriages and fine horses. "It all looks like a funeral procession," she said.

The footman cried the names of her guests to the echoing ball-room. "Captain Henry Compson, His Majesty's Household Cavalry! Mr. David Lorimond! Lord and Lady Torrance!!" (They were the youngest couple there, having been married only three months before.) "Sir Roger Harbison! The Contessa della Candini!" Lady Neville permitted them all to kiss her hand and made them welcome.

She had engaged the finest musicians she could find to play for the dancing, but though they began to play at her signal, not one couple stepped out on the floor, nor did one young lord approach her to request the honor of the first dance, as was proper. They milled together, shin-ing and murmuring, their eyes fixed on the ballroom door. Every time they heard a carriage clatter up the driveway they seemed to flinch a little and draw closer together; every time the footman announced the arrival of another guest, they all sighed softly and swayed a little on their feet with relief.

"Why did they come to my party if they were afraid?" Lady Neville muttered scornfully to herself. "I am not afraid of meeting Death. I ask only that Death may be impressed by the magnificence of my house and the flavor of my wines. I will die sooner than anyone here, but I am not afraid."

Certain that Death would not arrive until midnight, she moved among her guests, attempting to calm them, not with her words, which she knew they would not hear, but with the tone of her voice as if they were so many frightened horses. But little by little, she herself was infected by their nervousness: whenever she sat down she stood up again immedi-ately, she tasted a dozen glasses of wine without finishing any of them, and she glanced constantly at her jeweled watch, at first wanting to hurry the midnight along and end the waiting, later scratching at the watch face with her forefinger, as if she would push away the night and drag the sun backward into the sky. When midnight came, she was standing with the rest of them, breathing through her mouth, shifting from foot to foot, lis-tening for the sound of carriage wheels turning in gravel.

▲▼▲

When the clock began to strike midnight, everyone, even Lady Neville and the brave Captain Compson, gave one startled little cry and then was silent again, listening to the tolling of the clock. The smaller clocks upstairs began to chime. Lady Neville's ears hurt. She caught sight of herself in the ballroom mirror, one gray face turned up toward the ceiling as if she were gasping for air, and she thought, "Death will be a woman, a hideous, filthy old crone as tall and strong as a man. And the most terrible thing of all will be that she will have my face." All the clocks stopped striking, and Lady Neville closed her eyes.

She opened them again only when she heard the whispering around her take on a different tone, one in which fear was fused with relief and a certain chagrin. For no new carriage stood in the driveway. Death had not come.

The noise grew slowly louder; here and there people were beginning to laugh. Near her, Lady Neville heard young Lord Torrance say to his wife, "There, my darling, I told you there was nothing to be afraid of. It was all a joke."

"I am ruined," Lady Neville thought. The laughter was increasing; it pounded against her ears in strokes, like the chiming of the clocks. "I wanted to give a ball so grand that those who were not invited would be shamed in front of the whole city, and this is my reward. I am ruined, and I deserve it."

Turning to the poet Lorimond, she said, "Dance with me, David." She signaled to the musicians, who at once began to play. When Lorimond hesitated, she said, "Dance with me now. You will not have another chance. I shall never give a party again."

Lorimond bowed and led her onto the dance floor. The guests parted for them, and the laughter died down for a moment, but Lady Neville knew that it would soon begin again. "Well, let them laugh," she thought. "I did not fear Death when they were all trembling. Why should I fear their laughter?" but she could feel a stinging at the thin lids of her eyes, and she closed them once more as she began to dance with Lorimond.

And then, quite suddenly, all the carriage horses outside the house whinnied loudly, just once, as the guests had cried out at midnight. There were a great many horses, and their one salute was so loud that everyone in the room became instantly silent. They heard the heavy steps of the footman as he went to open the door, and they shivered as if they felt the cool breeze that drifted into the house. Then they heard a light voice saying, "Am I late? Oh, I am so sorry. The horses were tired," and before the footman could re-enter to announce her, a lovely young girl in a white dress stepped gracefully into the ballroom doorway and stood there smiling.

She could not have been more than nineteen. Her hair was yellow, and she wore it long. It fell thickly upon her bare shoulders that gleamed warmly through it, two limestone islands rising out of a dark golden sea. Her face was wide at the forehead and cheekbones, and narrow at the chin, and her skin was so clear that many of the ladies there—Lady

Neville among them—touched their own faces wonderingly, and instantly drew their hands away as though their own skin had rasped their fingers. Her mouth was pale, where the mouths of other women were red and orange and even purple. Her eyebrows, thicker and straighter than was fashionable, met over dark, calm eyes that were set so deep in her young face and were so black, so uncompromisingly black, that the middle-aged wife of a middle-aged lord murmured, "Touch of a gypsy there, I think."

"Or something worse," suggested her husband's mistress.

"Be silent!" Lady Neville spoke louder than she had intended, and the girl turned to look at her. She smiled, and Lady Neville tried to smile back, but her mouth seemed very stiff. "Welcome," she said. "Welcome, my lady Death."

A sigh rustled among the lords and ladies as the girl took the old woman's hand and curtsied to her, sinking and rising in one motion, like a wave. "You are Lady Neville," she said. "Thank you so much for inviting me." Her accent was as faint and almost familiar as her perfume.

"Please excuse me for being late," she said earnestly. "I had to come from a long way off, and my horses are so tired."

"The groom will rub them down," Lady Neville said, "and feed them if you wish."

"Oh, no," the girl answered quickly. "Tell him not to go near the horses, please. They are not really horses, and they are very fierce."

She accepted a glass of wine from a servant and drank it slowly, sighing softly and contentedly. "What good wine," she said. "And what a beautiful house you have."

"Thank you," said Lady Neville. Without turning, she could feel every woman in the room envying her, sensing it as she could always sense the approach of rain.

"I wish I lived here," Death said in her low, sweet voice. "I will, one day."

Then, seeing Lady Neville become as still as if she had turned to ice, she put her hand on the old woman's arm and said, "Oh, I'm sorry, I'm so sorry. I am so cruel, but I never mean to be. Please forgive me, Lady Neville. I am not used to company, and I do such stupid things. Please forgive me."

Her hand felt as light and warm on Lady Neville's arm as the hand of any other young girl, and her eyes were so appealing that Lady Neville replied, "You have said nothing wrong. While you are my guest, my house is yours."

"Thank you," said Death, and she smile so radiantly that the musicians began to play quite by themselves, and with no sign from Lady

Neville. She would have stopped them, but Death said, "Oh, what lovely music! Let them play, please."

So the musicians played a gavotte, and Death, unabashed by eyes that stared at her in greedy terror, sang softly to herself without words, lifted her white gown slightly with both hands, and made hesitant little patting steps with her small feet. "I have not danced in so long," she said wistfully. "I'm quite sure I've forgotten how."

She was shy; she would not look up to embarrass the young lords, not one of whom stepped forward to dance with her. Lady Neville felt a flood of shame and sympathy, emotions she thought had withered in her years ago. "Is she to be humiliated at my own ball?" she thought angrily. "It is because she is Death; if she were the ugliest, foulest hag in all the world they would clamor to dance with her, because they are gentlemen and they know what is expected of them. But no gentleman will dance with Death, no matter how beautiful she is." She glance sideways at David Lorimond. His face was flushed, and his hands were clasped so tightly as he stared at Death that his fingers were like glass, but when Lady Neville touched his arm he did not turn, and when she hissed, "David!" he pretended not to hear her.

Then Captain Compson, gray-haired and handsome in his uniform, stepped out of the crowd and bowed gracefully before Death. "If I may have the honor," he said.

"Captain Compson," said Death, smiling. She put her arm in his. "I was hoping you would ask me."

This brought a frown from the older women, who did not consider it a proper thing to say, but for that Death cared not a rap. Captain Compson led her to the center of the floor, and there they danced. Death was curiously graceless at first—she was too anxious to please her partner, and she seemed to have no notion of rhythm. The Captain himself moved with the mixture of dignity and humor that Lady Neville had never seen in another man, but when he looked at her over Death's shoulder, she saw something that no one else appeared to notice: that his face and eyes were immobile with fear, and that, though he offered Death his hand with easy gallantry, he flinched slightly when she took it. And yet he danced as well as Lady Neville had ever seen him.

"Ah, that's what comes of having a reputation to maintain," she thought. "Captain Compson too must do what is expected of him. I hope someone else will dance with her soon."

But no one did. Little by little, other couples overcame their fear and slipped hurriedly out on the floor when Death was looking the other way, but nobody sought to relieve Captain Compson of his beautiful partner. They danced every dance together. In time, some of the men present began to look at her with more appreciation than terror, but when she returned their glances and smiled at them, they clung to their partners as if a cold wind were threatening to blow them away.

One of the few who stared at her frankly and with pleasure was young Lord Torrance, who usually danced only with his wife. Another was the poet Lorimond. Dancing with Lady Neville, he remarked to her, "If she is Death, what do these frightened fools think they are? If she is ugliness, what must they be? I hate their fear. It is obscene."

Death and the Captain danced past them at that moment, and they heard him say to her, "But if that was truly you that I saw in the battle, how can you have changed so? How can you have become so lovely?"

Death's laughter was gay and soft. "I thought that among so many beautiful people it might be better to be beautiful. I was afraid of frightening everyone and spoiling the party."

"They all thought she would be ugly," said Lorimond to Lady Neville. "I—I knew she would be beautiful."

"Then why have you not danced with her?" Lady Neville asked him. "Are you also afraid?"

"No, oh, no," the poet answered quickly and passionately. "I will ask her to dance very soon. I only want to look at her a little longer."

▲▼▲

The musicians played on and on. The dancing wore away the night as slowly as falling water wears down a cliff. It seemed to Lady Neville that no night had ever endured longer, and yet she was neither tired nor bored. She danced with every man there, except with Lord Torrance, who was dancing with his wife as if they had just met that night, and, of course, with Captain Compson. Once he lifted his hand and touched Death's golden hair very lightly. He was a striking man still, a fit partner for so beautiful a girl, but Lady Neville looked at his face each time she passed him and realized that he was older than anyone knew.

Death herself seemed younger than the youngest there. No woman at the ball danced better than she now, though it was hard for Lady Neville to remember at what point her awkwardness had given way to the liquid sweetness of her movements. She smiled and called to everyone who caught her eye—and she knew them all by name; she sang constantly, making up words to the dance tunes, nonsense words, sounds without meaning, and yet everyone strained to hear her soft voice without knowing why. And when, during a waltz, she caught up the trailing end of her gown to give her more freedom as she danced, she seemed to Lady Neville to move like a little sailing boat over a still evening sea.

Lady Neville heard Lady Torrance arguing angrily with the Contessa della Candini. "I don't care if she is Death, she's no older than I am, she can't be!"

"Nonsense," said the Contessa, who could not afford to be generous to any other woman. "She is twenty-eight, thirty, if she is an hour. And that dress, that bridal gown she wears—really!"

"Vile," said the woman who had come to the ball as Captain Compson's freely acknowledged mistress. "Tasteless. But one should know better than to expect taste from Death, I suppose." Lady Torrance looked as if she were going to cry.

"They are jealous of Death," Lady Neville said to herself. "How strange. I am not jealous of her, not in the least. And I do not fear her at all." She was very proud of herself.

Then, as unbiddenly as they had begun to play, the musicians stopped. They began to put away their instruments. In the sudden shrill silence, Death pulled away from Captain Compson and ran to look out of one of the tall windows, pushing the curtains apart with both hands. "Look!" she said, with her back turned to them. "Come and look. The night is almost gone."

The summer sky was still dark, and the eastern horizon was only a shade lighter than the rest of the sky, but the stars had vanished and the trees near the house were gradually becoming distinct. Death pressed her face against the window and said, so softly that the other guests could barely hear her, "I must go now."

"No," Lady Neville said, and was not immediately aware that she had spoken. "You must stay a while longer. The ball was in your honor. Please stay."

Death held out both hands to her, and Lady Neville came and took them in her own. "I've had a wonderful time," she said gently. "You cannot possibly imagine how it feels to be actually invited to such a ball as this, because you have given them and gone to them all your life. One is like another to you, but for me it is different. Do you understand me?" Lady Neville nodded silently. "I will remember this night forever," Death said.

"Stay," Captain Compson said. "Stay just a little longer." He put his hand on Death's shoulder, and she smiled and leaned her cheek against it. "Dear Captain Compson," she said. "My first real gallant. Aren't you tired of me yet?"

"Never," he said. "Please stay."

"Stay," said Lorimond, and he too seemed about to touch her. "Stay. I want to talk to you. I want to look at you. I will dance with you if you stay."

"How many followers I have," Death said in wonder. She stretched her hand toward Lorimond, but he drew back from her and then flushed in shame. "A soldier and a poet. How wonderful it is to be a woman. But why did you not speak to me earlier, both of you? Now it is too late. I must go."

"Please, stay," Lady Torrance whispered. She held on to her husband's hand for courage. "We think you are so beautiful, both of us do."

"Gracious Lady Torrance," the girl said kindly. She turned back to the window, touched it lightly, and it flew open. The cool dawn air rushed into the ballroom, fresh with rain but already smelling faintly of the London streets over which it had passed. They heard birdsong and the strange, harsh nickering of Death's horses.

"Do you want me to stay?" she asked. The question was put, not to Lady Neville, nor to Captain Compson, nor to any of her admirers, but to the Contessa della Candini, who stood well back from them all, hugging her flowers to herself and humming a little song of irritation. She did not in the least want Death to stay, but she was afraid that all the other women would think her envious of Death's beauty, and so she said, "Yes. Of course I do."

"Ah," said Death. She was almost whispering. "And you," she said to another woman, "do you want me to stay? Do you want me to be one of your friends?"

"Yes," said the woman, "because you are beautiful and a true lady."

"And you," said Death to a man, "and you," to a woman, "and you," to another man, "do you want me to stay?" And they all answered, "Yes, Lady Death, we do."

"Do you want me, then?" she cried at last to all them. "Do you want me to live among you and to be one of you, and not to be Death anymore? Do you want me to visit your houses and come to all your parties? Do you want me to ride horses like yours instead of mine, do you want me to wear the kind of dresses you wear, and say the things you would say? Would one of you marry me, and would the rest of you dance at my wedding and bring gifts to my children? Is that what you want?"

"Yes," said Lady Neville. "Stay here, stay with me, stay with us."

Death's voice, without becoming louder, had become clearer and older; too old a voice, thought Lady Neville, for such a young girl. "Be sure," said Death. "Be sure of what you want, be very sure. Do all of you want me to stay? For if one of you says to me, no, go away, then I must leave at once and never return. Be sure. Do you all want me?"

And everyone there cried with one voice, "Yes! Yes, you must stay with us. You are so beautiful that we cannot let you go."

"We are tired," said Captain Compson.

"We are blind," said Lorimond, adding, "especially to poetry."

"We are afraid," said Lord Torrance quietly, and his wife took his arm and said, "Both of us."

"We are dull and stupid," said Lady Neville, "and growing old uselessly. Stay with us, Lady Death."

And then Death smiled sweetly and radiantly and took a step forward, and it was as though she had come down among them from a very great height. "Very well," she said. "I will stay with you. I will be Death no more. I will be a woman."

▲▼▲

The room was full of a deep sigh, although no one was seen to open his mouth. No one moved, for the golden-haired girl was Death still, and her horses still whinnied for her outside. No one could look at her for long, although she was the most beautiful girl anyone there had ever seen.

"There is a price to pay," she said. "There is always a price. Some one of you must become Death in my place, for there must forever be Death in the world. Will anyone choose? Will anyone here become Death of his own free will? For only thus can I become a human girl."

No one spoke, no one spoke at all. But they backed slowly away from her, like waves slipping back down a beach to the sea when you try to catch them. The Contessa della Candini and her friends would have crept quietly out of the door, but Death smiled at them and they stood where they were. Captain Compson opened his mouth as though he were going to declare himself, but he said nothing. Lady Neville did not move.

"No one," said Death. She touched a flower with her finger, and it seemed to crouch and flex itself like a pleased cat. "No one at all," she said. "Then I must choose, and that is just, for that is the way I became Death. I never wanted to be Death, and it makes me so happy that you want me to become one of yourselves. I have searched a long time for people who would want me. Now I have only to choose someone to replace me and it is done. I will choose very carefully."

"Oh, we were so foolish," Lady Neville said to herself. "We were so foolish." But she said nothing aloud; she merely clasped her hands and stared at the young girl, thinking vaguely that if she had had a daughter she would have been greatly pleased if she resembled the lady Death.

"The Contessa della Candini," said Death thoughtfully, and that woman gave a little squeak of terror because she could not draw her breath for a scream. But Death laughed and said, "No, that would be silly." She said nothing more, but for a long time after that the Contessa burned with humiliation at not having been chosen to be Death.

"Not Captain Compson," murmured Death, "because he is too kind to become Death, and because it would be too cruel to him. He wants to die so badly." The expression on the Captain's face did not change, but his hands began to tremble.

"Not Lorimond," the girl continued, "because he knows so little about life, and because I like him." The poet flushed, and turned white, and then turned pink again. He made as if to kneel clumsily on one knee, but instead he pulled himself erect and stood as much like Captain Compson as he could.

"Not the Torrances," said Death, "never Lord and Lady Torrance, for both of them care too much about another person to take any pride in being Death." But she hesitated over Lady Torrance for a while, staring at her out of her dark and curious eyes. "I was your age when I became Death," she said at last. "I wonder what it will be like to be your age again. I have been Death for so long." Lady Torrance shivered and did not speak.

And at last Death said quietly, "Lady Neville."

"I am here," Lady Neville answered.

"I think you are the only one," said Death. "I choose you, Lady Neville."

Again Lady Neville heard every guest sigh softly, and although her back was to them all she knew that they were sighing in relief that neither themselves nor anyone dear to themselves had been chosen. Lady Torrance gave a little cry of protest, but Lady Neville knew that she would have cried out at whatever choice Death made. She heard herself say calmly, "I am honored. But was there no one more worthy than I?"

"Not one," said Death. "There is no one quite so weary of being human, no one who knows better how meaningless it is to be alive. And there is no one else here with the power to treat life"—and she smiled sweetly and cruelly—"the life of your hairdresser's child, for instance, as the meaningless thing it is. Death has a heart, but it is forever an empty heart, and I think, Lady Neville, that your heart is like a dry riverbed, like a seashell. You will be very content as Death, more so than I, for I was very young when I became Death."

She came toward Lady Neville, light and swaying, her deep eyes wide and full of the light of the red morning sun that was beginning to rise. The guests at the ball moved back from her, although she did not look at them, but Lady Neville clenched her hands tightly and watched Death come toward her with little dancing steps. "We must kiss each other," Death said. "That is the way I became Death." She shook her head delightedly, so that her soft hair swirled about her shoulders. "Quickly, quickly," she said. "Oh, I cannot wait to be human again."

"You may not like it," Lady Neville said. She felt very calm, though she could hear her old heart pounding in her chest and feel it in the tips of her fingers. "You may not like it after a while," she said.

"Perhaps not." Death's smile was very close to her now. "I will not be as beautiful as I am, and perhaps people will not love me as much as they do now. But I will be human for a while, and at last I will die. I have done my penance."

"What penance?" the old woman asked the beautiful girl. "What was it you did? Why did you become Death?"

"I don't remember," said the lady Death. "And you too will forget in time." She was smaller than Lady Neville, and so much younger. In her white dress she might have been the daughter that Lady Neville had never had, who would have been with her always and held her mother's head lightly in the crook of her arm when she felt old and sad. Now she lifted her head to kiss Lady Neville's cheek, and as she did so she whispered in her hear, "You will still be beautiful when I am ugly. Be kind to me then."

Behind Lady Neville the handsome gentlemen and ladies murmured and sighed, fluttering like moths in their evening dress, in their elegant gowns. "I promise," she said, and then she pursed her dry lips to kiss the soft, sweet-smelling cheek of the young Lady Death.

El Regalo

"You can't kill him," Mr. Luke said. "Your mother wouldn't like it." After some consideration, he added, "I'd be rather annoyed myself."

"But wait," Angie said, in the dramatic tones of a television commercial for some miraculous mop. "There's more. I didn't tell you about the brandied cupcakes—"

"Yes, you did."

"And about him telling Jennifer Williams what I got her for her birthday, and she pitched a fit, because she had two of them already—"

"He meant well," her father said cautiously. "I'm pretty sure."

"And then when he finked to Mom about me and Orlando Cruz, and we weren't doing *anything*—"

"Nevertheless. No killing."

Angie brushed sweaty mouse-brown hair off her forehead and regrouped. "Can I at least maim him a little? Trust me, he's earned it."

"I don't doubt you," Mr. Luke agreed. "But you're fifteen, and Marvyn's eight. Eight and a half. You're bigger than he is, so beating him up isn't fair. When you're...oh, say, twenty-three, and he's sixteen and a half— okay, you can try it then. Not until."

Angie's wordless grunt might or might not have been assent. She started out of the room, but her father called her back, holding out his right hand. "Pinky-swear, kid." Angie eyed him warily, but hooked her little finger around his without hesitation, which was a mistake. "You did that much too easily," her father said, frowning. "Swear by Buffy."

"What? You can't swear by a television show!"

"Where is that written? Repeat after me—'I swear by *Buffy the Vampire Slayer*—'"

"You really *don't* trust me!"

"'I swear by *Buffy the Vampire Slayer* that I will keep my hands off my baby brother—'"

"My baby brother, the monster! He's gotten worse since he started sticking that y in his name—"

"'—and I will stop calling him Ex-Lax—'"

"Come on, I only do that when he makes me really mad—"

"'—until he shall have attained the age of sixteen years and six months, after which time—'"

"After which time I get to pound him into marmalade. Deal. I can wait." She grinned; then turned self-conscious, making a performance of pulling down her upper lip to cover the shiny new braces. At the door, she looked over her shoulder and said lightly, "You are way too smart to be a father."

From behind his book, Mr. Luke answered, "I've often thought so myself." Then he added, "It's a Korean thing. We're all like that. You're lucky your mother isn't Korean, or you wouldn't have a secret to your name."

Angie spent the rest of the evening in her room, doing homework on the phone with Melissa Feldman, her best friend. Finished, feeling virtuously entitled to some low-fat chocolate reward, she wandered down the hall toward the kitchen, passing her brother's room on the way. Looking in—not because of any special interest, but because Marvyn invariably hung around her own doorway, gazing in aimless fascination at whatever she was doing, until shooed away—she saw him on the floor, playing with Milady, the gray, ancient family cat. Nothing unusual about that: Marvyn and Milady had been an item since he was old enough to realize that the cat wasn't something to eat. What halted Angie as though she had walked into a wall was that they were playing Monopoly, and that Milady appeared to be winning.

Angie leaned in the doorway, entranced and alarmed at the same time. Marvyn had to throw the dice for both Milady and himself, and the old cat was too riddled with arthritis to handle the pastel Monopoly money easily. But she waited her turn, and moved her piece—she had the silver top hat—very carefully, as though considering possible options. And she already had a hotel on Park Place.

Marvyn jumped up and slammed the door as soon as he noticed his sister watching the game, and Angie went on to liberate a larger-than-planned remnant of sorbet. Somewhere near the bottom of the container she finally managed to stuff what she'd just glimpsed deep in the part of her mind she called her "forgettery." As she'd once said to her friend Melissa, "There's such a thing as too much information, and it is not going to get me. I am never going to know more than I want to know about stuff. Look at the President."

For the next week or so Marvyn made a point of staying out of Angie's way, which was all by itself enough to put her mildly on edge. If she knew one thing about her brother, it was that the time to worry was when you didn't see him. All the same, on the surface things were peaceful enough, and continued so until the evening when Marvyn went dancing with the garbage.

The next day being pickup day, Mrs. Luke had handed him two big green plastic bags of trash for the rolling bins down the driveway. Marvyn had made enough of a fuss about the task that Angie stayed by the open front window to make sure that he didn't simply drop the bags in the grass, and vanish into one of his mysterious hideouts. Mrs. Luke was back in the living room with the news on, but Angie was still at the window when Marvyn looked around quickly, mumbled a few words she couldn't catch, and then did a thing with his left hand, so fast she saw no more than a blurry twitch. And the two garbage bags went dancing.

Angie's buckling knees dropped her to the couch under the window, though she never noticed it. Marvyn let go of the bags altogether, and they rocked alongside him—backwards, forwards, sideways, in perfect timing, with perfect steps, turning with him as though he were the star and they his backup singers. To Angie's astonishment, he was snapping his fingers and moonwalking, as she had never imagined he could do—and the bags were pushing out green arms and legs as the three of them danced down the driveway. When they reached the cans, Marvyn's partners promptly went limp and were nothing but plastic garbage bags again. Marvyn plopped them in, dusted his hands, and turned to walk back to the house.

When he saw Angie watching, neither of them spoke. Angie beckoned. They met at the door and stared at each other. Angie said only, "My room."

Marvyn dragged in behind her, looking everywhere and nowhere at once, and definitely not at his sister. Angie sat down on the bed and studied him: chubby and messy-looking, with an unmanageable sprawl of rusty-brown hair and an eyepatch meant to tame a wandering left eye. She said, "Talk to me."

"About what?" Marvyn had a deep, foggy voice for eight and a half— Mr. Luke always insisted that it had changed before Marvyn was born. "I didn't break your CD case."

"Yes, you did," Angie said. "But forget that. Let's talk about garbage bags. Let's talk about Monopoly."

Marvyn was utterly businesslike about lies: in a crisis he always told the truth, until he thought of something better. He said, "I'm warning you right now, you won't believe me."

"I never do. Make it a good one."

"Okay," Marvyn said. "I'm a witch."

When Angie could speak, she said the first thing that came into her head, which embarrassed her forever after. "You can't be a witch. You're a wizard, or a warlock or something." Like we're having a sane conversation, she thought.

Marvyn shook his head so hard that his eyepatch almost came loose. "Uh-uh! That's all books and movies and stuff. You're a man witch or you're a woman witch, that's it. I'm a man witch."

"You'll be a dead witch if you don't quit shitting me," Angie told him. But her brother knew he had her, and he grinned like a pirate (at home he often tied a bandanna around his head, and he was constantly after Mrs. Luke to buy him a parrot). He said, "You can ask Lidia. She was the one who knew."

Lidia del Carmen de Madero y Gomez had been the Lukes' house-keeper since well before Angie's birth. She was from Ciego de Avila in Cuba, and claimed to have changed Fidel Castro's diapers as a girl work-ing for his family. For all her years—no one seemed to know her age; certainly not the Lukes—Lidia's eyes remained as clear as a child's, and Angie had on occasion nearly wept with envy of her beautiful wrin-kled deep-dark skin. For her part, Lidia got on well with Angie, spoke Spanish with her mother, and was teaching Mr. Luke to cook Cuban food. But Marvyn had been hers since his infancy, beyond question or interference. They went to Spanish-language movies on Saturdays, and shopped together in the Bowen Street *barrio*.

"The one who knew," Angie said. "Knew what? Is Lidia a witch too?"

Marvyn's look suggested that he was wondering where their parents had actually found their daughter. "No, of course she's not a witch. She's a *santera*."

Angie stared. She knew as much about *Santeria* as anyone grow-ing up in a big city with a growing population of Africans and South Americans—which wasn't much. Newspaper articles and television spe-cials had informed her that *santeros* sacrificed chickens and goats and did...things with the blood. She tried to imagine Marvyn with a chicken, doing things, and couldn't. Not even Marvyn.

"So Lidia got you into it?" she finally asked. "Now you're a *santero* too?"

"Nah, I'm a witch, I told you." Marvyn's disgusted impatience was approaching critical mass.

Angie said, "Wicca? You're into the Goddess thing? There's a girl in my home room, Devlin Margulies, and she's a Wiccan, and that's all she talks about. Sabbats and esbats, and drawing down the moon, and the rest of it. She's got skin like a cheese-grater."

Marvyn blinked at her. "What's a Wiccan?" He sprawled suddenly on her bed, grabbing Milady as she hobbled in and pooting loudly on her furry stomach. "I already knew I could sort of mess with things—you remember the rubber duck, and that time at the baseball game?" Angie remembered. Especially the rubber duck. "Anyway, Lidia took me to meet this real old lady, in the farmers' market, she's even older than her, her name's Yemaya, something like that, she smokes this funny little pipe all the time. Anyway, she took hold of me, my face, and she looked in my eyes, and then she closed her eyes, and she just sat like that for so long!" He giggled. "I thought she'd fallen asleep, and I started to pull away, but Lidia wouldn't let me. So she sat like that, and she sat, and then she opened her eyes and she told me I was a witch, a *brujo*. And Lidia bought me a two-scoop ice-cream cone. Coffee and chocolate, with M&Ms."

"You won't have a tooth in your head by the time you're twelve." Angie didn't know what to say, what questions to ask. "So that's it? The old lady, she gives you witch lessons or something?"

"Nah—I told you, she's a big *santera*, that's different. I only saw her that one time. She kept telling Lidia that I had *el regalo*—I think that means the gift, she said that a lot—and I should keep practicing. Like you with the clarinet."

Angie winced. Her hands were small and stubby-fingered, and music slipped through them like rain. Her parents, sympathizing, had offered to cancel the clarinet lessons, but Angie refused. As she confessed to her friend Melissa, she had no skill at accepting defeat.

Now she asked, "So how do you practice? Boogieing with garbage bags?"

Marvyn shook his head. "That's getting old—so's playing board games with Milady. I was thinking maybe I could make the dishes wash themselves, like in *Beauty and the Beast*. I bet I could do that."

"You could enchant my homework," Angie suggested. "My algebra, for starters."

Her brother snorted. "Hey, I'm just a kid, I've got my limits! I mean, your homework?"

"Right," Angie said. "Right. Look, what about laying a major spell on Tim Hubley, the next time he's over here with Melissa? Like making his feet go flat so he can't play basketball—that's the only reason she likes him, anyway. Or—" her voice became slower and more hesitant "—what about getting Jake Petrakis to fall madly, wildly, totally in love with me? That'd be...funny."

Marvyn was occupied with Milady. "Girl stuff, who cares about all that? I want to be so good at soccer everybody'll want to be on my

team—I want fat Josh Wilson to have patches over both eyes, so he'll
leave me alone. I want Mom to order thin-crust pepperoni pizza every
night, and I want Dad to—"

"No spells on Mom and Dad, not ever!" Angie was on her feet, leaning menacingly over him. "You got that, Ex-Lax? You mess with them
even once, believe me, you'd better be one hella witch to keep me from
strangling you. Understood?"

Marvyn nodded. Angie said, "Okay, I tell you what. How about practicing on Aunt Caroline when she comes next weekend?"

Marvyn's pudgy pirate face lit up at the suggestion. Aunt Caroline
was their mother's older sister, celebrated in the Luke family for knowing everything about everything. A pleasant, perfectly decent person, her
perpetual air of placid expertise would have turned a saint into a serial
killer. Name a country, and Aunt Caroline had spent enough time there
to know more about the place than a native; bring up a newspaper story,
and without fail Aunt Caroline could tell you something about it that
hadn't been in the paper; catch a cold, and Aunt Caroline could recite the
maiden name of the top medical researcher in rhinoviruses' mother. (Mr.
Luke said often that Aunt Caroline's motto was, "Say something, and I'll
bet you're wrong.")

"Nothing dangerous," Angie commanded, "nothing scary. And nothing
embarrassing or anything."

Marvyn looked sulky. "It's not going to be any fun that way."

"If it's too gross, they'll know you did it," his sister pointed out. "I
would." Marvyn, who loved secrets and hidden identities, yielded.

During the week before Aunt Caroline's arrival, Marvyn kept so quietly to himself that Mrs. Luke worried about his health. Angie kept as
close an eye on him as possible, but couldn't be at all sure what he
might be planning—no more than he, she suspected. Once she caught
him changing the TV channels without the remote; and once, left alone
in the kitchen to peel potatoes and carrots for a stew, he had the peeler
do it while he read the Sunday funnies. The apparent smallness of his
ambitions relieved Angie's vague unease, lulling her into complacency
about the big family dinner that was traditional on the first night of a
visit from Aunt Caroline.

Aunt Caroline was, among other things, the sort of woman incapable
of going anywhere without attempting to buy it. Her own house was
jammed to the attic with sightseer souvenirs from all over the world:
children's toys from Slovenia, sculptures from Afghanistan, napkin rings
from Kenya shaped like lions and giraffes, legions of brass bangles,
boxes and statues of gods from India, and so many Russian *matryoshka*

dolls fitting inside each other that she gave them away as stocking-stuffers every Christmas. She never came to the table at the Lukes without bringing some new acquisition for approval; so dinner with Aunt Caroline, in Mr. Luke's words, was always Show and Tell time.

Her most recent hegira had brought her back to West Africa for the third or fourth time, and provided her with the most evil-looking doll Angie had ever seen. Standing beside Aunt Caroline's plate, it was about two feet high, with bat ears, too many fingers, and eyes like bright green marbles streaked with scarlet threads. Aunt Caroline explained rapturously that it was a fertility doll unique to a single Benin tribe, which Angie found impossible to credit. "No way!" she announced loudly. "Not for one minute am I even thinking about having babies with that thing staring at me! It doesn't even look pregnant, the way they do. No way in the world!"

Aunt Caroline had already had two of Mr. Luke's margaritas, and was working on a third. She replied with some heat that not all fertility figures came equipped with cannonball breasts, globular bellies and callipygous rumps—"Some of them are remarkably slender, even by Western standards!" Aunt Caroline herself, by anyone's standards, was built along the general lines of a chopstick.

Angie was drawing breath for a response when she heard her father say something in Korean behind her, and then her mother's soft gasp, "Caroline." But Aunt Caroline was busy explaining to her niece that she knew absolutely nothing about fertility. Mrs. Luke said, considerably louder, "Caroline, shut up, your doll!"

Aunt Caroline said, "What, what?" and then turned, along with Angie. They both screamed.

The doll was growing all the things Aunt Caroline had been insisting it didn't need to qualify as a fertility figure. It was carved from ebony, or from something even harder, but it was pushing out breasts and belly and hips much as Marvyn's two garbage bags had suddenly developed arms and legs. Even its expression had changed, from hungry slyness to a downright silly grin, as though it were about to kiss someone, anyone. It took a few shaky steps forward on the table and put its foot in the salsa.

Then the babies started coming.

They came pattering down on the dinner table, fast and hard, like wooden rain, one after another, after another, after another…perfect little copies, miniatures, of the madly smiling doll-thing, plopping out of it—*just like Milady used to drop kittens in my lap*, Angie thought absurdly. One of them fell into her plate, and one bounced into the soup, and a couple rolled into Mr. Luke's lap, making him knock his chair over trying to get out of the way. Mrs. Luke was trying to grab them all up at once, which wasn't possible, and Aunt Caroline sat where she was and shrieked. And the doll kept grinning and having babies.

Marvyn was standing against the wall, looking both as terrified as Aunt Caroline and as stupidly pleased as the doll-thing. Angie caught his eye and made a fierce signal, *enough, quit, turn it off,* but either her brother was having too good a time, or else had no idea how to undo whatever spell he had raised. One of the miniatures hit her in the head, and she had a vision of her whole family being drowned in wooden doll-babies, everyone gurgling and reaching up pathetically toward the surface before they all went under for the third time. Another baby car-omed off the soup tureen into her left ear, one sharp ebony fingertip drawing blood.

It stopped, finally—Angie never learned how Marvyn regained con-trol—and things almost quieted down, except for Aunt Caroline. The fer-tility doll got the look of glazed joy off its face and went back to being a skinny, ugly, duty-free airport souvenir, while the doll-babies seemed to melt away exactly as though they had been made of ice instead of wood. Angie was quick enough to see one of them actually dissolving into nothingness directly in front of Aunt Caroline, who at this point stopped screaming and began hiccupping and beating the table with her palms. Mr. Luke pounded her on the back, and Angie volunteered to practice her Heimlich maneuver, but was overruled. Aunt Caroline went to bed early.

Later, in Marvyn's room, he kept his own bed between himself and Angie, indignantly demanding, "What? You said not scary—what's scary about a doll having babies? I thought it was cute."

"Cute," Angie said. "Uh-huh." She was wondering, in a distant sort of way, how much prison time she might get if she actually murdered her brother. *Ten years? Five, with good behavior and a lot of psychiatrists? I could manage it.* "And what did I tell you about not embarrassing Aunt Caroline?"

"How did I embarrass her?" Marvyn's visible eye was wide with out-raged innocence. "She shouldn't drink so much, that's her problem. She embarrassed me."

"They're going to figure it out, you know," Angie warned him. "Maybe not Aunt Caroline, but Mom for sure. She's a witch herself that way. Your cover is blown, buddy."

But to her own astonishment, not a word was ever said about the episode, the next day or any other—not by her observant mother, not by her dryly perceptive father, nor even by Aunt Caroline, who might reasonably have been expected at least to comment at breakfast. A baffled Angie remarked to Milady, drowsing on her pillow, "I guess if a thing's weird enough, somehow nobody saw it." This explanation didn't satisfy her, not by a long shot, but lacking anything better she was stuck with it. The old cat blinked in squeezy-eyed agreement, wriggled herself into a more comfortable position, and fell asleep still purring.

Angie kept Marvyn more closely under her eye after that than she had done since he was quite small, and first showing a penchant for playing in traffic. Whether this observation was the cause or not, he did remain more or less on his best behavior, barring the time he turned the air in the bicycle tires of a boy who had stolen his superhero comic book to cement. There was also the affair of the enchanted soccer ball, which kept rolling back to him as though it couldn't bear to be with anyone else. And Angie learned to be extremely careful when making herself a sandwich, because if she lost track of her brother for too long, the sandwich was liable to acquire an extra ingredient. Paprika was one, Tabasco another; and Scotch Bonnet peppers were a special favorite. But there were others less hot and even more objectionable. As she snarled to a sympathetic Melissa Feldman, who had two brothers of her own, "They ought to be able to jail kids just for being eight and a half."

Then there was the matter of Marvyn's attitude toward Angie's attitude about Jake Petrakis.

Jake Petrakis was a year ahead of Angie at school. He was half-Greek and half-Irish, and his blue eyes and thick poppy-colored hair contrasted so richly with his olive skin that she had not been able to look directly at him since the fourth grade. He was on the swim team, and he was the president of the Chess Club, and he went with Ashleigh Sutton, queen of the junior class, rechristened "Ghastly Ashleigh" by the loyal Melissa. But he spoke kindly and cheerfully to Angie without fail, always saying *Hey, Angie*, and *How's it going, Angie?* and *See you in the fall, Angie, have a good summer.* She clutched such things to herself, every one of them, and at the same time could not bear them.

Marvyn was as merciless as a mosquito when it came to Jake Petrakis. He made swooning, kissing noises whenever he spied Angie looking at Jake's picture in her yearbook, and drove her wild by holding invented conversations between them, just loudly enough for her to hear. His increasing ability at witchcraft meant that scented, decorated, and misspelled love notes were likely to flutter down onto her bed at any moment, as were long-stemmed roses, imitation jewelry (Marvyn had limited experience and poor taste), and small, smudgy photos of Jake and Ashleigh together. Mr. Luke had to invoke Angie's oath more than once, and to sweeten it with a promise of a new bicycle if Marvyn made it through the year undamaged. Angie held out for a mountain bike, and her father sighed. "That was always a myth, about the gypsies stealing children," he said, rather wistfully. "It was surely the other way around. Deal."

Yet there were intermittent peaceful moments between Marvyn and Angie, several occurring in Marvyn's room. It was a far tidier place than Angie's room, for all the clothes on the floor and battered board game boxes sticking out from under the bed. Marvyn had mounted *National Geographic* foldout maps all around the walls, lining them up so perfectly that the creases were invisible; and on one special wall were prints and photos of a lot of people with strange staring eyes. Angie recognized Rasputin, and knew a few of the other names—Aleister Crowley, for one, and a man in Renaissance dress called Dr. John Dee. There were two women, as well: the young witch Willow, from *Buffy the Vampire Slayer*, and a daguerreotype of a black woman wearing a kind of turban folded into points. No Harry Potter, however. Marvyn had never taken to Harry Potter.

There was also, one day after school, a very young kitten wobbling among the books littering Marvyn's bed. A surprised Angie picked it up and held it over her face, feeling its purring between her hands. It was a dark, dusty gray, rather like Milady—indeed, Angie had never seen another cat of that exact color. She nuzzled its tummy happily, asking it, "Who are you, huh? Who could you ever be?"

Marvyn was feeding his angelfish, and didn't look up. He said, "She's Milady."

Angie dropped the kitten on the bed. Marvyn said, "I mean, she's Milady when she was young. I went back and got her."

When he did turn around, he was grinning the maddening pirate grin Angie could never stand, savoring her shock. It took her a minute to find words, and more time to make them come out. She said, "You went back. You went back in time?"

"It was easy," Marvyn said. "Forward's *hard*—I don't think I could ever get really forward. Maybe Dr. Dee could do it." He picked up the kitten and handed her back to his sister. It was Milady, down to the crooked left ear and the funny short tail with the darker bit on the end. He said, "She was hurting all the time, she was so old. I thought, if she could—you know—start over, before she got the arthritis...."

He didn't finish. Angie said slowly, "So where's Milady? The other one? I mean, if you brought this one...I mean, how can they be in the same world?"

"They can't," Marvyn said. "The old Milady's gone."

Angie's throat closed up. Her eyes filled, and so did her nose, and she had to blow it before she could speak again. Looking at the kitten, she knew it was Milady, and made herself think about how good it would be to have her once again bouncing around the house, no longer limping grotesquely and meowing with the pain. But she had loved the old cat all her life, and never known her as a kitten, and when the new Milady started to climb into her lap, Angie pushed her away.

"All right," she said to Marvyn. "All right. How did you get...back, or whatever?"

Marvyn shrugged and went back to his fish. "No big deal. You just have to concentrate the right way."

Angie bounced a plastic Wiffle ball off the back of his neck, and he turned around, annoyed. "Leave me alone! Okay, you want to know—there's a spell, words you have to say over and over and over, until you're sick of them, and there's herbs in it too. You have to light them, and hang over them, and you shut your eyes and keep breathing them in and saying the words—"

"I knew I'd been smelling something weird in your room lately. I thought you were sneaking takeout curry to bed with you again."

"And then you open your eyes, and there you are," Marvyn said. "I told you, no big deal."

"There you are where? How do you know where you'll come out? When you'll come out? Click your heels together three times and say there's no place like home?"

"No, dork, you just *know*." And that was all Angie could get out of him—not, as she came to realize, because he wouldn't tell her, but because he couldn't. Witch or no witch, he was still a small boy, with almost no real idea of what he was doing. He was winging it all, playing it all by ear.

Arguing with Marvyn always gave her a headache, and her history homework—the rise of the English merchant class—was starting to look good in comparison. She went back to her own bedroom and read two whole chapters, and when the kitten Milady came stumbling and squeaking in, Angie let her sleep on the desk. "What the hell," she told it, "it's not your fault."

That evening, when Mr. and Mrs. Luke got home, Angie told them that Milady had died peacefully of illness and old age while they were at work, and was now buried in the back garden. (Marvyn had wanted to make it a horrible hit-and-run accident, complete with a black SUV and half-glimpsed license plate starting with the letter Q, but Angie vetoed this.) Marvyn's contribution to her solemn explanation was to explain that he had seen the new kitten in a petshop window, "and she just looked so much like Milady, and I used my whole allowance, and I'll take care of her, I promise!" Their mother, not being a true cat person, accepted the story easily enough, but Angie was never sure about Mr. Luke. She found him too often sitting with the kitten on his lap, the two of them staring solemnly at each other.

But she saw very little evidence of Marvyn fooling any further with time. Nor, for that matter, was he showing the interest she would have expected in turning himself into the world's best second-grade soccer player, ratcheting up his test scores high enough to be in college by the age of eleven, or simply getting even with people (since Marvyn forgot nothing and had a hit list going back to day-care). She could almost always tell when he'd been making his bed by magic, or making the window plants grow too fast, but he seemed content to remain on that level. Angie let it go.

Once she did catch him crawling on the ceiling, like Spider-Man, but she yelled at him and he fell on the bed and threw up. And there was, of course, the time—two times, actually—when, with Mrs. Luke away, Marvyn organized all the shoes in her closet into a chorus line, and had them tapping and kicking together like the Rockettes. It was fun for Angie to watch, but she made him stop because they were her mother's shoes. What if her clothes joined in? The notion was more than she wanted to deal with.

As it was, there was already plenty to deal with just then. Besides her schoolwork, there was band practice, and Melissa's problems with her boyfriend; not to mention the endless hours spent at the dentist, correcting a slight overbite. Melissa insisted that it made her look sexy, but the suggestion had the wrong effect on Angie's mother. In any case, as far as Angie could see, all Marvyn was doing was playing with a new box of toys, like an elaborate electric train layout, or a top-of-the-line Erector set. She was even able to imagine him getting bored with magic itself after a while. Marvyn had a low threshold for boredom.

Angie was in the orchestra, as well as the band, because of a chronic shortage of woodwinds, but she liked the marching band better. You were out of doors, performing at parades and football games, part of the joyful noise, and it was always more exciting than standing up in a dark, hushed auditorium playing for people you could hardly see. "Besides," as she confided to her mother, "in marching band nobody really notices how you sound. They just want you to keep in step."

On a bright spring afternoon, rehearsing "The Washington Post March" with the full band, Angie's clarinet abruptly went mad. No "licorice stick" now, but a stick of rapturous dynamite, it took off on flights of rowdy improvisation, doing outrageous somersaults, back-flips, and cartwheels with the melody—things that Angie knew she could never have conceived of, even if her skill had been equal to the inspiration. Her bandmates, up and down the line, were turning to stare at her, and she wanted urgently to wail, "Hey, I'm not the one, it's my stupid brother, you know I can't play like that." But the music kept spilling out, excessive, absurd, unstoppable—unlike the march, which finally lurched to a disorderly halt. Angie had never been so embarrassed in her life.

Mr. Bishow, the bandmaster, came bumbling through the milling musicians to tell her, "Angie, that was fantastic—that was dazzling! I never knew you had such spirit, such freedom, such wit in your music!" He patted her—hugged her even, quickly and cautiously—then stepped back almost immediately and said, "Don't ever do it again."

"Like I'd have a choice," Angie mumbled, but Mr. Bishow was already shepherding the band back into formation for "Semper Fidelis" *and* "High Society," which Angie fumbled her way through as always, two bars behind the rest of the woodwinds. She was slouching disconsolately off the field when Jake Petrakis, his dark-gold hair still glinting damply from swimming practice, ran over to her to say, "Hey, Angie, cool," then punched her on the shoulder, as he would have done another boy, and dashed off again to meet one of his relay-team partners. And Angie went on home, and waited for Marvyn behind the door of his room.

She seized him by the hair the moment he walked in, and he squalled, "All right, let go, all right! I thought you'd like it!"

"Like it?" Angie shook him, hard. "*Like* it? You evil little ogre, you almost got me kicked out of the band! What else are you lining up for me that you think I'll *like*?"

"Nothing, I swear!" But he was giggling even while she was shaking him. "Okay, I was going to make you so beautiful, even Mom and Dad wouldn't recognize you, but I quit on that. Too much work." Angie grabbed for his hair again, but Marvyn ducked. "So what I thought, maybe I really could get Jake what's-his-face to go crazy about you. There's all kinds of spells and things for that—"

"Don't you dare," Angie said. She repeated the warning calmly and quietly. "Don't. You. Dare."

Marvyn was still giggling. "Nah, I didn't think you'd go for it. Would have been fun, though." Suddenly he was all earnestness, staring up at his sister out of one visible eye, strangely serious, even with his nose running. He said, "It is fun, Angie. It's the most fun I've ever had."

"Yeah, I'll bet," she said grimly. "Just leave me out of it from now on, if you've got any plans for the third grade." She stalked into the kitchen, looking for apple juice.

Marvyn tagged after her, chattering nervously about school, soccer games, the Milady-kitten's rapid growth, and a possible romance in his angelfish tank. "I'm sorry about the band thing, I won't do it again. I just thought it'd be nice if you could play really well, just one time. Did you like the music part, anyway?"

Angie did not trust herself to answer him. She was reaching for the apple juice bottle when the top flew off by itself, bouncing straight up at her face. As she flinched back, a glass came skidding down the counter toward her. She grabbed it before it crashed into the refrigerator, then turned and screamed at Marvyn, "Damn it, Ex-Lax, you quit that! You're going to hurt somebody, trying to do every damn thing by magic!"

"You said the D-word twice!" Marvyn shouted back at her. "I'm telling Mom!" But he made no move to leave the kitchen, and after a moment a small, grubby tear came sliding down from under the eye-patch. "I'm not using magic for everything! I just use it for the boring stuff, mostly. Like the garbage, and vacuuming up, and like putting my clothes away. And Milady's litter box, when it's my turn. That kind of stuff, okay?"

Angie studied him, marveling as always at his capacity for looking heartwrenchingly innocent. She said, "No point to it when I'm cleaning her box, right? Never mind—just stay out of my way, I've got a French midterm tomorrow." She poured the apple juice, put it back, snatched a raisin cookie and headed for her room. But she paused in the doorway, for no reason she could ever name, except perhaps the way Marvyn had moved to follow her and then stopped himself. "What? Wipe your nose, it's gross. What's the matter now?"

"Nothing," Marvyn mumbled. He wiped his nose on his sleeve, which didn't help. He said, "Only I get scared, Angie. It's scary, doing the stuff I can do."

"What scary? Scary how? A minute ago it was more fun than you've ever had in your life."

"It is!" He moved closer, strangely hesitant: neither witch, nor pirate nor seraph, but an anxious, burdened small boy. "Only sometimes it's like too much fun. Sometimes, right in the middle, I think maybe I should stop, but I can't. Like one time, I was by myself, and I was just fooling around...and I sort of made this *thing*, which was really interest-ing, only it came out funny and then I couldn't unmake it for the longest time, and I was scared Mom and Dad would come home—"

Angie, grimly weighing her past French grades in her mind, reached back for another raisin cookie. "I told you before, you're going to get yourself into real trouble doing crazy stuff like that. Just quit, before something happens by magic that you can't fix by magic. You want advice, I just gave you advice. See you around."

Marvyn wandered forlornly after her to the door of her room. When she turned to close it, he mumbled, "I wish I were as old as you. So I'd know what to do."

"Ha," Angie said, and shut the door.

Whereupon, heedless of French irregular verbs, she sat down at her desk and began writing a letter to Jake Petrakis.

Neither then nor even much later was Angie ever able to explain to anyone why she had written that letter at precisely that time. Because he had slapped her shoulder and told her she—or at least her music—was cool? Because she had seen him, that same afternoon, totally tangled up with Ghastly Ashleigh in a shadowy corner of the library stacks? Because of Marvyn's relentless teasing? Or simply because she was fifteen years old, and it was time for her to write such a letter to someone? Whatever the cause, she wrote what she wrote, and then she folded it up and put it away in her desk drawer.

Then she took it out, and put it back in, and then she finally put it into her backpack. And there the letter stayed for nearly three months, well past midterms, finals, and football, until the fateful Friday night when Angie was out with Melissa, walking and window-shopping in downtown Avicenna, placidly drifting in and out of every coffeeshop along Parnell Street. She told Melissa about the letter then, and Melissa promptly went into a fit of the giggles, which turned into hiccups and required another cappuccino to pacify them. When she could speak coherently, she said, "You ought to send it to him. You've got to send it to him."

Angie was outraged, at first. "No way! I wrote it for me, not for a test or a class, and damn sure not for Jake Petrakis. What kind of a dipshit do you think I am?"

Melissa grinned at her out of mocking green eyes. "The kind of dipshit who's got that letter in your backpack right now, and I bet it's in an envelope with an address and a stamp on it."

"It doesn't have a stamp! And the envelope's just to protect it! I just like having it with me, that's all—"

"And the address?"

"Just for practice, okay? But I didn't sign it, and there's no return address, so that shows you!"

"Right." Melissa nodded. "Right. That definitely shows me."

"Drop it," Angie told her, and Melissa dropped it then. But it was a Friday night, and both of them were allowed to stay out late, as long as they were together, and Avicenna has a lot of coffeeshops. Enough lattes and cappuccinos, with double shots of espresso, brought them to a state of cheerfully jittery abandon in which everything in the world was supremely, ridiculously funny. Melissa never left the subject of Angie's letter alone for very long—"Come on, what's the worst that could happen? Him reading it and maybe figuring out you wrote it? Listen, the really worst thing would be you being an old, old lady still wishing you'd told Jake Petrakis how you felt when you were young. And now he's married, and he's a grandfather, and probably dead, for all you know—"

"Quit it!" But Angie was giggling almost as much as Melissa now, and somehow they were walking down quiet Lovisi Street, past the gas station and the boarded-up health-food store, to find the darkened Petrakis house and tiptoe up the steps to the porch. Facing the front door, Angie dithered for a moment, but Melissa said, "An old lady, in a home, for God's sake, and he'll never know," and Angie took a quick breath and pushed the letter under the door. They ran all the way back to Parnell Street, laughing so wildly that they could barely breathe....

...and Angie woke up in the morning whispering *omigod, omigod, omigod*, over and over, even before she was fully awake. She lay in bed for a good hour, praying silently and desperately that the night before had been some crazy, awful dream, and that when she dug into her backpack the letter would still be there. But she knew dreadfully better, and she never bothered to look for it on her frantic way to the telephone. Melissa said soothingly, "Well, at least you didn't sign the thing. There's that, anyway."

"I sort of lied about that," Angie said. Her friend did not answer. Angie said, "Please, you have to come with me. Please."

"Get over there," Melissa said finally. "Go, now—I'll meet you."

Living closer, Angie reached the Petrakis house first, but had no intention of ringing the bell until Melissa got there. She was pacing back and forth on the porch, cursing herself, banging her fists against her legs, and wondering whether she could go to live with her father's sister Peggy in Grand Rapids, when the woman next door called over to tell her that the Petrakises were all out of town at a family gathering. "Left yesterday afternoon. Asked me to keep an eye on the place, cause they won't be back till sometime Sunday night. That's how come I'm kind of watching out." She smiled warningly at Angie before she went back indoors.

The very large dog standing behind her stayed outside. He looked about the size of a Winnebago, and plainly had already made up his mind about Angie. She said, "Nice doggie," and he growled. When she tried out "Hey, sweet thing," which was what her father said to all animals, the dog showed his front teeth, and the hair stood up around his shoulders, and he lay down to keep an eye on things himself. Angie said sadly, "I'm usually really good with dogs."

When Melissa arrived, she said, "Well, you shoved it under the door, so it can't be that far inside. Maybe if we got something like a stick or a wire clotheshanger to hook it back with." But whenever they looked toward the neighboring house, they saw a curtain swaying, and finally they walked away, trying to decide what else to do. But there was nothing; and after a while Angie's throat was too swollen with not crying for her to talk without pain. She walked Melissa back to the bus stop, and they hugged goodbye as though they might never meet again.

Melissa said, "You know, my mother says nothing's ever as bad as you thought it was going to be. I mean, it can't be, because nothing beats all the horrible stuff you can imagine. So maybe...you know..." but she broke down before she could finish. She hugged Angie again and went home.

Alone in her own house, Angie sat quite still in the kitchen and went on not crying. Her entire face hurt with it, and her eyes felt unbearably heavy. Her mind was not moving at all, and she was vaguely grateful for that. She sat there until Marvyn walked in from playing basketball with his friends. Shorter than everyone else, he generally got stepped on a lot, and always came home scraped and bruised. Angie had rather expected him to try making himself taller, or able to jump higher, but he hadn't done anything of the sort so far. He looked at her now, bounced and shot an invisible basketball, and asked quietly, "What's the matter?"

It may have been the unexpected froggy gentleness of his voice, or simply the sudden fact of his having asked the question at all. Whatever the reason, Angie abruptly burst into furious tears, the rage directed entirely at herself, both for writing the letter to Jake Petrakis in the first place, and for crying about it now. She gestured to Marvyn to go away, but—amazing her further—he stood stolidly waiting for her to grow quiet. When at last she did, he repeated the question. "Angie. What's wrong?"

Angie told him. She was about to add a disclaimer—"You laugh even once, Ex-Lax—" when she realized that it wouldn't be necessary. Marvyn was scratching his head, scrunching up his brow until the eyepatch danced; then abruptly jamming both hands in his pockets and tilting his head back: the poster boy for careless insouciance. He said, almost absently, "I could get it back."

"Oh, right." Angie did not even look up. "Right."

"I could so!" Marvyn was instantly his normal self again: so much for casualness and dispassion. "There's all kinds of things I could do."

Angie dampened a paper towel and tried to do something with her hot, tear-streaked face. "Name two."

"Okay, I will! You remember which mailbox you put it in?"

"Under the door," Angie mumbled. "I put it under the door."

Marvyn snickered then. *"Aww,* like a Valentine." Angie hadn't the energy to hit him, but she made a grab at him anyway, for appearance's sake. "Well, I could make it walk right back out the door, that's one way. Or I bet I could just open the door, if nobody's home. Easiest trick in the world, for us witches."

"They're gone till Sunday night," Angie said. "But there's this lady next door, she's watching the place like a hawk. And even when she's not, she's got this immense dog. I don't care if you're the hottest witch in the world, you do not want to mess with this werewolf."

Marvyn, who—as Angie knew—was wary of big dogs, went back to scratching his head. "Too easy, anyway. No fun, forget it." He sat down next to her, completely absorbed in the problem. "How about I…no, that's kid stuff, anybody could do it. But there's a spell…I could make the letter self-destruct, right there in the house, like in that old TV show. It'd just be a little fluffy pile of ashes—they'd vacuum it up and never know. How about that?" Before Angie could express an opinion, he was already shaking his head. "Still too easy. A baby spell, for beginners. I hate those."

"Easy is good," Angie told him earnestly. "I like easy. And you *are* a beginner."

Marvyn was immediately outraged, his normal bass-baritone rumble going up to a wounded squeak. "I am not! No way in the world I'm a beginner!" He was up and stamping his feet, as he had not done since he was two. "I tell you what—just for that, I'm going to get your letter back for you, but I'm not going to tell you how. You'll see, that's all. You just wait and see."

He was stalking away toward his room when Angie called after him, with the first glimmer both of hope and of humor that she had felt in approximately a century, "All right, you're a big bad witch king. What do you want?"

Marvyn turned and stared, uncomprehending.

Angie said, "Nothing for nothing, that's my bro. So let's hear it— what's your price for saving my life?"

If Marvyn's voice had gone up any higher, only bats could have heard it. "I'm rescuing you, and you think I want something for it? Julius

Christmas!" which was the only swearword he was ever allowed to get away with. "You don't have anything I want, anyway. Except maybe...."

He let the thought hang in space, uncompleted. Angie said, "Except maybe what?"

Marvyn swung on the doorframe one-handed, grinning his pirate grin at her. "I hate you calling me Ex-Lax. You know I hate it, and you keep doing it."

"Okay, I won't do it anymore, ever again. I promise."

"Mmm. Not good enough." The grin had grown distinctly evil. "I think you ought to call me O Mighty One for two weeks."

"What?" Now Angie was on her feet, misery briefly forgotten. "Give it up, Ex-Lax—two weeks? No chance!" They glared at each other in silence for a long moment before she finally said, "A week. Don't push it. One week, no more. And not in front of people!"

"Ten days." Marvyn folded his arms. "Starting right now." Angie went on glowering. Marvyn said, "You want that letter?"

"Yes."

Marvyn waited.

"Yes, O Mighty One." Triumphant, Marvyn held out his hand and Angie slapped it. She said, "When?"

"Tonight. No, tomorrow—going to the movies with Sunil and his family tonight. Tomorrow." He wandered off, and Angie took her first deep breath in what felt like a year and a half. She wished she could tell Melissa that things were going to be all right, but she didn't dare; so she spent the day trying to appear normal—just the usual Angie, aimlessly content on a Saturday afternoon. When Marvyn came home from the movies, he spent the rest of the evening reading *Hellboy* comics in his room, with the Milady-kitten on his stomach. He was still doing it when Angie gave up peeking in at him and went to bed.

But he was gone on Sunday morning. Angie knew it the moment she woke up.

She had no idea where he could be, or why. She had rather expected him to work whatever spell he settled on in his bedroom, under the stern gaze of his wizard mentors. But he wasn't there, and he didn't come to breakfast. Angie told their mother that they'd been up late watching television together, and that she should probably let Marvyn sleep in. And when Mrs. Luke grew worried after breakfast, Angie went to his room herself, returning with word that Marvyn was working intensely on a project for his art class, and wasn't feeling sociable. Normally she would never have gotten away with it, but her parents were on their way to brunch and a concert, leaving her with the usual instructions to feed and water the cat, use the twenty on the cabinet for something moderately healthy, and to check on Marvyn "now and then," which actually meant frequently. ("The day we don't tell you that," Mr. Luke said once, when she objected to the regular duty, "will be the very day the kid steals a kayak and heads for Tahiti." Angie found it hard to argue the point.)

Alone in the empty house—more alone than she felt she had ever been—Angie turned constantly in circles, wandering from room to room with no least notion of what to do. As the hours passed and her brother failed to return, she found herself calling out to him aloud. "Marvyn? Marvyn, I swear, if you're doing this to drive me crazy…O Mighty One, where are you? You get back here, never mind the damn letter, just get back!" She stopped doing this after a time, because the cracks and tremors in her voice embarrassed her, and made her even more afraid.

Strangely, she seemed to feel him in the house all that time. She kept whirling to look over her shoulder, thinking that he might be sneaking up on her to scare her, a favorite game since his infancy. But he was never there.

Somewhere around noon the doorbell rang, and Angie tripped over herself scrambling to answer it, even though she had no hope—almost no hope—of its being Marvyn. But it was Lidia at the door—Angie had forgotten that she usually came to clean on Sunday afternoons. She stood there, old and smiling, and Angie hugged her wildly and wailed, "Lidia, Lidia, *socorro*, help me, *ayúdame*, Lidia." She had learned Spanish from the housekeeper when she was too little to know she was learning it.

Lidia put her hands on Angie's shoulders. She put her back a little and looked into her face, saying, "*Chuchi, dime qué pasa contigo?*" She had called Angie *Chuchi* since childhood, never explaining the origin or meaning of the word.

"It's Marvyn," Angie whispered. "It's Marvyn." She started to explain about the letter, and Marvyn's promise, but Lidia only nodded and asked no questions. She said firmly, "*El Viejo puede ayudar.*"

Too frantic to pay attention to gender, Angie took her to mean Yemaya, the old woman in the farmer's market who had told Marvyn that he was a *brujo*. She said, "You mean *la santera*," but Lidia shook her head hard.

"No, no, *El Viejo*. You go out there, you ask to see *El Viejo. Solamente El Viejo. Los otros no pueden ayudarte.*"

The others can't help you. Only the old man. Angie asked where she could find *El Viejo*, and Lidia directed her to a *Santeria* shop on Bowen Street. She drew a crude map, made sure Angie had money with her, kissed her on the cheek and made a blessing sign on her forehead.

"*Cuidado, Chuchi*," she said with a kind of cheerful solemnity, and Angie was out and running for the Gonzales Avenue bus, the same one she took to school. This time she stayed on a good deal farther.

The shop had no sign, and no street number, and it was so small that Angie kept walking past it for some while. Her attention was finally caught by the objects in the one dim window, and on the shelves to right and left. There was an astonishing variety of incense, and of candles encased in glass with pictures of black saints, as well as boxes marked Fast Money Ritual Kit, and bottles of Elegua Floor Wash, whose label read "Keeps Trouble From Crossing Your Threshold." When Angie entered, the musky scent of the place made her feel dizzy and heavy and out of herself, as she always felt when she had a cold coming on. She heard a rooster crowing, somewhere in back.

She didn't see the old woman until her chair creaked slightly, because she was sitting in a corner, halfway hidden by long hanging garments like church choir robes, but with symbols and patterns on them that Angie had never seen before. The woman was very old, much older even than Lidia, and she had an absurdly small pipe in her toothless mouth. Angie said, "Yemaya?" The old woman looked at her with eyes like dead planets.

Angie's Spanish dried up completely, followed almost immediately by her English. She said, "My brother...my little brother...I'm supposed to ask for *El Viejo*. The old one, *viejo santero?* Lidia said." She ran out of words in either language at that point. A puff of smoke crawled from the little pipe, but the old woman made no other response.

Then, behind her, she heard a curtain being pulled aside. A hoarse, slow voice said, "*Quieres El Viejo?* Me."

Angie turned and saw him, coming toward her out of a long hallway whose end she could not see. He moved deliberately, and it seemed to take him forever to reach her, as though he were returning from another world. He was black, dressed all in black, and he wore dark glasses, even in the dark, tiny shop. His hair was so white that it hurt her eyes when she stared. He said, "Your brother."

"Yes," Angie said. "Yes. He's doing magic for me—he's getting something I need—and I don't know where he is, but I know he's in trouble, and I want him back!" She did not cry or break down—Marvyn would never be able to say that she cried over him—but it was a near thing.

El Viejo pushed the dark glasses up on his forehead, and Angie saw that he was younger than she had first thought—certainly younger than Lidia—and that there were thick white half-circles under his eyes. She never knew whether they were somehow natural, or the result of heavy makeup; what she did see was that they made his eyes look bigger and brighter—all pupil, nothing more. They should have made him look at least slightly comical, like a reverse-image raccoon, but they didn't.

"I know you brother," *El Viejo* said. Angie fought to hold herself still as he came closer, smiling at her with the tips of his teeth. "A *brujito*— little, little witch, we know. Mama and me, we been watching." He nodded toward the old woman in the chair, who hadn't moved an inch or said a word since Angie's arrival. Angie smelled a damp, musty aroma, like potatoes going bad.

"Tell me where he is. Lidia said you could help." Close to, she could see blue highlights in *El Viejo*'s skin, and a kind of V-shaped scar on each cheek. He was wearing a narrow black tie, which she had not noticed at first; for some reason, the vision of him tying it in the morning, in front of a mirror, was more chilling to her than anything else about him. He grinned fully at her now, showing teeth that she had expected to be yellow and stinking, but which were all white and square and a little too large. He said, "*Tu hermano está perdido.* Lost in Thursday."

"Thursday?" It took her a dazed moment to comprehend, and longer to get the words out. "Oh, God, he went back! Like with Milady—he went back to before I...when the letter was still in my backpack. The little showoff—he said forward was hard, coming forward—he wanted to show me he could do it. And he got stuck. Idiot, idiot, idiot!" *El Viejo* chuckled softly, nodding, saying nothing.

"You have to go find him, get him out of there, right now—I've got money." She began digging frantically in her coat pockets.

"No, no money." *El Viejo* waved her offering aside, studying her out of eyes the color of almost-ripened plums. The white markings under them looked real; the eyes didn't. He said, "I take you. We find you brother together."

Angie's legs were trembling so much that they hurt. She wanted to assent, but it was simply not possible. "No. I can't. I can't. You go back there and get him."

El Viejo laughed then: an enormous, astonishing Santa Claus *ho-ho-HO*, so rich and reassuring that it made Angie smile even as he was snatching her up and stuffing her under one arm. By the time she had recovered from her bewilderment enough to start kicking and fighting, he was walking away with her down the long hall he had come out of a moment before. Angie screamed until her voice splintered in her throat, but she could not hear herself: from the moment *El Viejo* stepped back into the darkness of the hallway, all sound had ended. She could hear neither his footsteps nor his laughter—though she could feel him laughing against her—and certainly not her own panicky racket. They could be in outer space. They could be anywhere.

Dazed and disoriented as she was, the hallway seemed to go soundlessly on and on, until wherever they truly were, it could never have been the tiny *Santeria* shop she had entered only—when?—minutes before. It was a cold place, smelling like an old basement; and for all its darkness, Angie had a sense of things happening far too fast on all sides, just out of range of her smothered vision. She could distinguish none of them clearly, but there was a sparkle to them all the same.

And then she was in Marvyn's room.

And it was unquestionably Marvyn's room: there were the bearded and beaded occultists on the walls; there were the flannel winter sheets that he slept on all year because they had pictures of the New York Mets ballplayers; there was the complete set of *Star Trek* action figures that Angie had given him at Christmas, posed just so on his bookcase. And there, sitting on the edge of his bed, was Marvyn, looking lonelier than anyone Angie had ever seen in her life.

He didn't move or look up until *El Viejo* abruptly dumped her down in front of him and stood back, grinning like a beartrap. Then he jumped to his feet, burst into tears and started frenziedly climbing her, snuffling, "Angie, Angie, Angie," all the way up. Angie held him, trying somehow to preserve her neck and hair and back all at once, while mumbling, "It's all right, it's okay, I'm here. It's okay, Marvyn."

Behind her, *El Viejo* chuckled, "Crybaby witch—little, little *brujito* crybaby." Angie hefted her blubbering baby brother like a shopping bag, holding him on her hip as she had done when he was little, and turned to face the old man. She said, "Thank you. You can take us home now."

El Viejo smiled—not a grin this time, but a long, slow shutmouth smile like a paper cut. He said, "Maybe we let *him* do it, yes?" and then he turned and walked away and was gone, as though he had simply slipped between the molecules of the air. Angie stood with Marvyn in her arms, trying to peel him off like a Band-Aid, while he clung to her with his chin digging hard into the top of her head. She finally managed to dump him down on the bed and stood over him, demanding, "What happened? What were you thinking?" Marvyn was still crying too hard to answer her. Angie said, "You just had to do it this way, didn't you? No silly little beginner spells—you're playing with the big guys now, right, O Mighty One? So what happened? How come you couldn't get back?"

"I don't know!" Marvyn's face was red and puffy with tears, and the tears kept coming while Angie tried to straighten his eyepatch. It was impossible for him to get much out without breaking down again, but he kept wailing, "I don't know what went wrong! I did everything you're supposed to, but I couldn't make it work! I don't know…maybe I forgot…." He could not finish.

"Herbs," Angie said, as gently and calmly as she could. "You left your magic herbs back—" she had been going to say "back home," but she stopped, because they *were* back home, sitting on Marvyn's bed in Marvyn's room, and the confusion was too much for her to deal with just then. She said, "Just tell me. You left the stupid herbs."

Marvyn shook his head until the tears flew, protesting, "No, I didn't, I didn't—look!" He pointed to a handful of grubby dried weeds scattered on the bed—Lidia would have thrown them out in a minute. Marvyn gulped and wiped his nose and tried to stop crying. He said, "They're really hard to find, maybe they're not fresh anymore, I don't know— they've always looked like that. But now they don't work," and he was wailing afresh. Angie told him that Dr. John Dee and Willow would both have been ashamed of him, but it didn't help.

But she also sat with him and put her arm around him, and smoothed his messy hair, and said, "Come on, let's think this out. Maybe it's the herbs losing their juice, maybe it's something else. You did everything the way you did the other time, with Milady?"

"I thought I did." Marvyn's voice was small and shy, not his usual deep croak. "But I don't know anymore, Angie—the more I think about it, the more I don't know. It's all messed up, I can't remember anything now."

"Okay," Angie said. "Okay. So how about we just run through it all again? We'll do it together. You try everything you do remember about— you know—moving around in time, and I'll copy you. I'll do whatever you say."

Marvyn wiped his nose again and nodded. They sat down cross-legged on the floor, and Marvyn produced the grimy book of paper matches that he always carried with him, in case of firecrackers. Following his directions Angie placed all the crumbly herbs into Milady's dish, and her brother lit them. Or tried to: they didn't blaze up, but smoked and smoldered and smelled like old dust, setting both Angie and Marvyn sneezing almost immediately. Angie coughed and asked, "Did that happen the other time?" Marvyn did not answer.

There was a moment when she thought the charm might actually be going to work. The room around them grew blurry—slightly blurry, granted—and Angie heard indistinct faraway sounds that might have been themselves hurtling forward to sheltering Sunday. But when the fumes of Marvyn's herbs cleared away, they were still sitting in Thursday—they both knew it without saying a word. Angie said, "Okay,

so much for that. What about all that special concentration you were telling me about? You think maybe your mind wandered? You pronounce
any spells the wrong way? Think, Marvyn!"

"I am thinking! I told you forward was hard!" Marvyn looked ready
to start crying again, but he didn't. He said slowly, "Something's wrong,
but it's not me. I don't think it's me. Something's *pushing*...." He brightened suddenly. "Maybe we should hold hands or something. Because of
there being two of us this time. We could try that."

So they tried the spell that way, and then they tried working it inside
a pentagram they made with masking tape on the floor, as Angie had
seen such things done on *Buffy the Vampire Slayer*, even though Marvyn
said that didn't really mean anything, and they tried the herbs again, in
a special order that Marvyn thought he remembered. They even tried it
with Angie saying the spell, after Marvyn had coached her, just on the
chance that his voice itself might have been throwing off the pitch or the
pronunciation. Nothing helped.

Marvyn gave up before Angie did. Suddenly, while she was trying
the spell over herself, one more time—some of the words seemed to
heat up in her mouth as she spoke them—he collapsed into a wretched
ball of desolation on the floor, moaning over and over, "We're finished,
it's finished, we'll never get out of Thursday!" Angie understood that
he was only a terrified little boy, but she was frightened too, and it
would have relieved her to slap him and scream at him. Instead, she
tried as best she could to reassure him, saying, "He'll come back for
us. He has to."

Her brother sat up, knuckles to his eyes. "No, he doesn't have to!
Don't you understand? He knows I'm a witch like him, and he's just
going to leave me here, out of his way. I'm sorry, Angie, I'm really sorry!"
Angie had almost never heard that word from Marvyn, and never twice
in the same sentence.

"Later for all that," she said. "I was just wondering—do you think we
could get Mom and Dad's attention when they get home? You think
they'd realize what's happened to us?"

Marvyn shook his head. "You haven't seen me all the time I've been
gone. I saw you, and I screamed and hollered and everything, but you
never knew. They won't either. We're not really in our house—we're just
here. We'll always be here."

Angie meant to laugh confidently, to give them both courage, but
it came out more of a hiccupy snort. "Oh, no. No way. There is no way
I'm spending the rest of my life trapped in your stupid bedroom. We're
going to try this useless mess one more time, and then...then I'll do

something else." Marvyn seemed about to ask her what else she could try, but he checked himself, which was good.

They attempted the spell more than one more time. They tried it in every style they could think of except standing on their heads and reciting the words backward, and they might just as well have done that, for all the effect it had. Whether Marvyn's herbs had truly lost all potency, or whether Marvyn had simply forgotten some vital phrase, they could not even recapture the fragile awareness of something almost happening that they had both felt on the first trial. Again and again they opened their eyes to last Thursday.

"Okay," Angie said at last. She stood up, to stretch cramped legs, and began to wander around the room, twisting a couple of the useless herbs between her fingers. "Okay," she said again, coming to a halt midway between the bedroom door and the window, facing Marvyn's small bureau. A leg of his red Dr. Seuss pajamas was hanging out of one of the drawers.

"Okay," she said a third time. "Let's go home."

Marvyn had fallen into a kind of fetal position, sitting up but with his arms tight around his knees and his head down hard on them. He did not look up at her words. Angie raised her voice. "Let's go, Marvyn. That hallway—tunnel-thing, whatever it is—it comes out right about where I'm standing. That's where *El Viejo* brought me, and that's the way he left when he…left. That's the way back to Sunday."

"It doesn't matter," Marvyn whimpered. "*El Viejo*…he's him! He's *him!*"

Angie promptly lost what little remained of her patience. She stalked over to Marvyn and shook him to his feet, dragging him to a spot in the air as though she were pointing out a painting in a gallery. "And you're Marvyn Luke, and you're the big bad new witch in town! You said it yourself—if you weren't, he'd never have bothered sticking you away here. Not even nine, and you can eat his lunch, and he knows it! Straighten your patch and take us home, bro." She nudged him playfully. "Oh, forgive me—I meant to say, O Mighty One."

"You don't have to call me that anymore." Marvyn's legs could barely hold him up, and he sagged against her, a dead weight of despair. "I can't, Angie. I can't get us home. I'm sorry…."

The good thing—and Angie knew it then—would have been to turn and comfort him: to take his cold, wet face between her hands and tell him that all would yet be well, that they would soon be eating popcorn with far too much butter on it in his real room in their real house. But she was near her own limit, and pretending calm courage for his sake was prodding her, in spite of herself, closer to the edge. Without looking at Marvyn, she snapped, "Well, I'm not about to die in last Thursday! I'm walking out of here the same way he did, and you can come with me or not, that's up to you. But I'll tell you one thing, Ex-Lax—I won't be looking back."

And she stepped forward, walking briskly toward the dangling Dr. Seuss pajamas...

...and into a thick, sweet-smelling grayness that instantly filled her eyes and mouth, her nose and her ears, disorienting her so completely that she flailed her arms madly, all sense of direction lost, with no idea of which way she might be headed; drowning in syrup like a trapped bee or butterfly. Once she thought she heard Marvyn's voice, and called out for him—"I'm here, I'm here!" But she did not hear him again.

Then, between one lunge for air and another, the grayness was gone, leaving not so much as a dampness on her skin, nor even a sickly after-taste of sugar in her mouth. She was back in the time-tunnel, as she had come to think of it, recognizing the uniquely dank odor: a little like the ashes of a long-dead fire, and a little like what she imagined moonlight might smell like, if it had a smell. The image was an ironic one, for she could see no more than she had when *El Viejo* was lugging her the other way under his arm. She could not even distinguish the ground under her feet; she knew only that it felt more like slippery stone than anything else, and she was careful to keep her footing as she plodded steadily forward.

The darkness was absolute—strange solace, in a way, since she could imagine Marvyn walking close behind her, even though he never answered her, no matter how often or how frantically she called his name. She moved along slowly, forcing her way through the clinging murk, vaguely conscious, as before, of a distant, flickering sense of sound and motion on every side of her. If there were walls to the time-tunnel, she could not touch them; if it had a roof, no air currents betrayed it; if there were any living creature in it besides herself, she felt no sign. And if time actually passed there, Angie could never have said. She moved along, her eyes closed, her mind empty, except for the formless fear that she was not moving at all, but merely raising and setting down her feet in the same place, endlessly. She wondered if she was hungry.

Not until she opened her eyes in a different darkness to the crow-ing of a rooster and a familiar heavy aroma did she realize that she was walking down the hallway leading from the *Santeria* shop to...wherever she had really been—and where Marvyn still must be, for he plainly had not followed her. She promptly turned and started back toward last Thursday, but halted at the deep, slightly grating chuckle behind her. She did not turn again, but stood very still.

El Viejo walked a slow full circle around her before he faced her, grinning down at her like the man in the moon. The dark glasses were off, and the twin scars on his cheeks were blazing up as though they had been slashed into him a moment before. He said, "I know. Before even I see you, I know."

Angie hit him in the stomach as hard as she could. It was like punching a frozen slab of beef, and she gasped in pain, instantly certain that she had broken her hand. But she hit him again, and again, screaming at the top of her voice, "Bring my brother back! If you don't bring him right back here, right now, I'll kill you! I will!"

El Viejo caught her hands, surprisingly gently, still laughing to himself. "Little girl, listen, listen now. *Niñita*, nobody else—nobody—ever do what you do. You understand? Nobody but me ever walk that road back from where I leave you, understand?" The big white half-circles under his eyes were stretching and curling like live things.

Angie pulled away from him with all her strength, as she had hit him. She said, "No. That's Marvyn. Marvyn's the witch, the *brujo*—don't go telling people it's me. Marvyn's the one with the power."

"Him?" Angie had never heard such monumental scorn packed into one syllable. *El Viejo* said, "Your brother nothing, nobody, we no bother with him. Forget him—you the one got the *regalo*, you just don't know." The big white teeth filled her vision; she saw nothing else. "I show you— me, *El Viejo*. I show you what you are."

It was beyond praise, beyond flattery. For all her dread and dislike of *El Viejo*, to have someone of his wicked wisdom tell her that she was like him in some awful, splendid way made Angie shiver in her heart. She wanted to turn away more than she had ever wanted anything—even Jake Petrakis—but the long walk home to Sunday was easier than breaking the clench of the white-haired man's malevolent presence would have been. Having often felt (and almost as often dismissed the notion) that Marvyn was special in the family by virtue of being the baby, and a boy—and now a potent witch—she let herself revel in the thought that the real gift was hers, not his, and that if she chose she had only to stretch out her hand to have her command settle home in it. It was at once the most frightening and the most purely, completely gratifying feeling she had ever known.

But it was not tempting. Angie knew the difference.

"Forget it," she said. "Forget it, buster. You've got nothing to show me."

El Viejo did not answer her. The old, old eyes that were all pupil continued slipping over her like hands, and Angie went on glaring back with the brown eyes she despaired of because they could never be as deep-set and deep green as her mother's eyes. They stood so—for how long, she never knew—until *El Viejo* turned and opened his mouth as though to speak to the silent old lady whose own stone eyes seemed not to have blinked since Angie had first entered the *Santeria* shop, a childhood ago. Whatever he meant to say, he never got the words out, because Marvyn came back then.

He came down the dark hall from a long way off, as *El Viejo* had done the first time she saw him—as she herself had trudged forever, only moments ago. But Marvyn had come a further journey: Angie could see that beyond doubt in the way he stumbled along, looking like a shadow casting a person. He was struggling to carry something in his arms, but she could not make out what it was. As long as she watched him approaching, he seemed hardly to draw any nearer.

Whatever he held looked too heavy for a small boy: it threatened constantly to slip from his hands, and he kept shifting it from one shoulder to the other, and back again. Before Angie could see it clearly, *El Viejo* screamed, and she knew on the instant that she would never hear a more terrible sound in her life. He might have been being skinned alive, or having his soul torn out of his body—she never even tried to tell herself what it was like, because there were no words. Nor did she tell anyone that she fell down at the sound, fell flat down on her hands and knees, and rocked and whimpered until the scream stopped. It went on for a long time.

When it finally stopped, *El Viejo* was gone, and Marvyn was standing beside her with a baby in his arms. It was black and immediately endearing, with big, bright, strikingly watchful eyes. Angie looked into them once, and looked quickly away.

Marvyn looked worn and exhausted. His eyepatch was gone, and the left eye that Angie had not seen for months was as bloodshot as though he had just come off a three-day drunk—though she noticed that it was not wandering at all. He said in a small, dazed voice, "I had to go back a really long way, Angie. Really long."

Angie wanted to hold him, but she was afraid of the baby. Marvyn looked toward the old woman in the corner and sighed; then hitched up his burden one more time and clumped over to her. He said, "Ma'am, I think this is yours?" Adults always commented on Marvyn's excellent manners.

The old woman moved then, for the first time. She moved like a wave, Angie thought: a wave seen from a cliff or an airplane, crawling along so slowly that it seemed impossible for it ever to break, ever to reach the shore. But the sea was in that motion, all of it caught up in that one wave;

and when she set down her pipe, took the baby from Marvyn and smiled, that was the wave too. She looked down at the baby, and said one word, which Angie did not catch. Then Angie had her brother by the arm, and they were out of the shop. Marvyn never looked back, but Angie did, in time to see the old woman baring blue gums in soundless laughter.

All the way home in a taxi, Angie prayed silently that her parents hadn't returned yet. Lidia was waiting, and together they whisked Marvyn into bed without any serious protest. Lidia washed his face with a rough cloth, and then slapped him and shouted at him in Spanish—Angie learned a few words she couldn't wait to use—and then she kissed him and left, and Angie brought him a pitcher of orange juice and a whole plate of gingersnaps, and sat on the bed and said, "What happened?"

Marvyn was already working on the cookies as though he hadn't eaten in days—which, in a sense, was quite true. He asked, with his mouth full, "What's *malcriado* mean?"

"What? Oh. Like badly raised, badly brought up—troublemaking kid. About the only thing Lidia didn't call you. Why?"

"Well, that's what that lady called…him. The baby."

"Right," Angie said. "Leave me a couple of those, and tell me how he got to be a baby. You did like with Milady?"

"Uh-huh. Only I had to go way, way, way back, like I told you." Marvyn's voice took on the faraway sound it had had in the *Santeria* shop. "Angie, he's so old."

Angie said nothing. Marvyn said in a whisper, "I couldn't follow you, Angie. I was scared."

"Forget it," she answered. She had meant to be soothing, but the words burst out of her. "If you just hadn't had to show off, if you'd gotten that letter back some simple, ordinary way—" Her entire chest froze solid at the word. "The letter! We forgot all about my stupid letter!" She leaned forward and snatched the plate of cookies away from Marvyn. "Did you forget? You forgot, didn't you?" She was shaking as had not happened even when *El Viejo* had hold of her. "Oh, God, after all that!"

But Marvyn was smiling for the first time in a very long while. "Calm down, be cool—I've got it here." He dug her letter to Jake Petrakis— more than a little grimy by now—out of his back pocket and held it out to Angie. "There. Don't say I never did nuttin' for you." It was a favorite phrase of his, gleaned from a television show, and most often employed when he had fed Milady, washed his breakfast dish, or folded his clothes. "Take it, open it up," he said now. "Make sure it's the right one."

"I don't need to," Angie protested irritably. "It's my letter—believe me, I know it when I see it." But she opened the envelope anyway and withdrew a single folded sheet of paper, which she glanced at...then *stared* at, in absolute disbelief.

She handed the sheet to Marvyn. It was empty on both sides.

"Well, you did your job all right," she said, mildly enough, to her stunned, slack-jawed brother. "No question about that. I'm just trying to figure out why we had to go through this whole incredible hooha for a blank sheet of paper."

Marvyn actually shrank away from her in the bed.

"I didn't do it, Angie! I swear!" Marvyn scrambled to his feet, standing up on the bed with his hands raised, as though to ward her off in case she attacked him. "I just grabbed it out of your backpack—I never even looked at it."

"And what, I wrote the whole thing in grapefruit juice, so nobody could read it unless you held it over a lamp or something? Come on, it doesn't matter now. Get your feet off your damn pillow and sit down."

Marvyn obeyed warily, crouching rather than sitting next to her on the edge of the bed. They were silent together for a little while before he said, "You did that. With the letter. You wanted it not written so much, it just *wasn't*. That's what happened."

"Oh, right," she said. "Me being the dynamite witch around here. I told you, it doesn't matter."

"It matters." She had grown so unused to seeing a two-eyed Marvyn that his expression seemed more than doubly earnest to her just then. He said, quite quietly, "You are the dynamite witch, Angie. He was after you, not me."

This time she did not answer him. Marvyn said, "I was the bait. I do garbage bags and clarinets—okay, and I make ugly dolls walk around. What's he care about that? But he knew you'd come after me, so he held me there—back there in Thursday—until he could grab you. Only he didn't figure you could walk all the way home on your own, without any spells or anything. I know that's how it happened, Angie! That's how I know you're the real witch."

"No," she said, raising her voice now. "No, I was just pissed-off, that's different. Never underestimate the power of a pissed-off woman, O Mighty One. But you...you went all the way back, on *your* own, and you grabbed *him*. You're going to be *way* stronger and better than he is, and he knows it. He just figured he'd get rid of the competition early on, while he had the chance. Not a generous guy, *El Viejo*."

Marvyn's chubby face turned gray. "But I'm *not* like him! I don't want to be like him!" Both eyes suddenly filled with tears, and he clung to his sister as he had not done since his return. "It was horrible, Angie, it was so horrible. You were gone, and I was all alone, and I didn't know what to do, only I had to do *something*. And I remembered Milady, and I figured if he wasn't letting me come forward I'd go the other way, and I was so scared and mad I just walked and walked and walked in the dark, until I...." He was crying so hard that Angie could hardly make the words out. "I don't want to be a witch anymore, Angie, I don't *want* to! And I don't want *you* being a witch either...."

Angie held him and rocked him, as she had loved doing when he was three or four years old, and the cookies got scattered all over the bed. "It's all right," she told him, with one ear listening for their parents' car pulling into the garage. "*Shh, shh,* it's all right, it's over, we're safe, it's okay, *shh*. It's okay, we're not going to be witches, neither one of us." She laid him down and pulled the covers back over him. "You go to sleep now."

Marvyn looked up at her, and then at the wizards' wall beyond her shoulder. "I might take some of those down," he mumbled. "Maybe put some soccer players up for a while. The Brazilian team's really good." He was just beginning to doze off in her arms, when suddenly he sat up again and said, "Angie? The baby?"

"What about the baby? I thought he made a beautiful baby, *El Viejo*. Mad as hell, but lovable."

"It was bigger when we left," Marvyn said. Angie stared at him. "I looked back at it in that lady's lap, and it was already bigger than when I was carrying it. He's starting over, Angie, like Milady."

"Better him than me," Angie said. "I hope he gets a kid brother this time, he's got it coming." She heard the car, and then the sound of a key in the lock. She said, "Go to sleep, don't worry about it. After what we've been through, we can handle anything. The two of us. And without witchcraft. Whichever one of us it is—no witch stuff."

Marvyn smiled drowsily. "Unless we really, *really* need it."

Angie held out her hand and they slapped palms in formal agreement. She looked down at her fingers and said, "*Ick!* Blow your *nose!*"

But Marvyn was asleep.

Julie's Unicorn

The note came with the entree, tucked neatly under the zucchini slices but carefully out of range of the seafood crepes. It said, in the unmistakable handwriting that any graphologist would have ascribed to a serial killer, "Tanikawa, ditch the dork and get in here." Julie took her time over the crepes and the spinach salad, finished her wine, sampled a second glass, and then excused herself to her dinner partner, who smiled and propped his chin on his fingertips, prepared to wait graciously, as assistant professors know how to do. She turned right at the telephones, instead of left, looked back once, and walked through a pair of swinging half-doors into the restaurant kitchen.

The heat thumped like a fist between her shoulder blades, and her glasses fogged up immediately. She took them off, put them in her purse and focused on a slender, graying man standing with his back to her as he instructed an earnest young woman about shiitake mushroom stew. Julie said loudly, "Make it quick, Farrell. The dork thinks I'm in the can."

The slender man said to the young woman, "Gracie, tell Luis the basil's losing its marbles, he can put in more oregano if he wants. Tell him to use his own judgment about the lemongrass—I like it myself." Then he turned, held out his arms and said, "Jewel. Think you strung it out long enough?"

"My dessert's melting," Julie said into his apron. The arms around her felt as comfortably usual as an old sofa, and she lifted her head quickly to demand, "God damn it, where have you been? I have had very strange phone conversations with some very strange people in the last five years, trying to track you down. What the hell happened to you, Farrell?"

"What happened to me? Two addresses and a fax number I gave you, and nothing. Not a letter, not so much as a postcard from East Tarpit-on-the-Orinoco, hi, marrying tribal chieftain tomorrow, wish you were here. But just as glad you're not. The story of this relationship."

Julie stepped back, her round, long-eyed face gone as pale as it ever got. Almost in a whisper, she asked, "How did you know? Farrell, how did you know?" The young cook was staring at them both in fascination bordering on religious rapture.

"What?" Farrell said, and now he was gaping like the cook, his own voice snagging in his throat. "You did? You got married?"

"It didn't last. Eight months. He's in Boston."

"That explains it." Farrell's sudden bark of laughter made Gracie the cook jump slightly. "By God, that explains it."

"Boston? Boston explains what?"

"You didn't want me to know," Farrell said. "You really didn't want me to know. Tanikawa, I'm ashamed of you. I am."

Julie started to answer him, then nodded toward the entranced young cook. Farrell said, "Gracie, about the curried peas. Tell Suzanne absolutely not to add the mango pickle until just before the peas are done, she always puts it in too early. If she's busy, you do it—go, go." Gracie, enchanted even more by the notion of getting her hands into actual food, fled, and Farrell turned back to face Julie. "Eight months. I've known you to take longer over a lithograph."

"He's a very nice man," she answered him. "No, damn it, that sounds terrible, insulting. But he is."

Farrell nodded. "I believe it. You always did have this deadly weakness for nice men. I was an aberration."

"No, you're my friend," Julie said. "You're my friend, and I'm sorry, I should have told you I was getting married." A waiter's loaded tray caught her between the shoulderblades just as a busboy stepped on her foot, and she was properly furious this time. "I didn't tell you because I knew you'd do exactly what you're doing now, which is look at me like that and imply that you know me better than anyone else ever possibly could, which is not true, Farrell. There are all kinds of people you don't even know who know things about me you'll never know, so just knock it off." She ran out of breath and anger more or less simultaneously. She said, "But somehow you've gotten to be my oldest friend, just by god-damn attrition. I missed you, Joe."

Farrell put his arms around her again. "I missed you. I worried about you. A whole lot. The rest can wait." There came a crash and a mad bellow from the steamy depths of the kitchen, and Farrell said, "Your dork's probably missing you too. That was the Table Fourteen dessert, sure as hell. Where can I call you? Are you actually back in Avicenna?"

"For now. It's always for now in this town." She wrote the address and telephone number on the back of the Tonight's Specials menu, kissed him hurriedly and left the kitchen. Behind her she heard another bellow, and then Farrell's grimly placid voice saying, "Stay cool, stay cool, big Luis, it's not the end of the world. Change your apron, we'll just add some more brandy. All is well."

It took more time than they were used to, even after more than twenty years of picking up, letting go and picking up again. The period of edginess and uncertainty about what questions to ask, what to leave alone, what might or might not be safe to assume, lasted until the autumn afternoon they went to the museum. It was Farrell's day off, and he drove Madame Schumann-Heink, his prehistoric Volkswagen van, over the hill from the bald suburb where he was condo-sitting for a friend and parked under a sycamore across from Julie's studio apartment. The building was a converted Victorian, miraculously spared from becoming a nest of suites for accountants and attorneys and allowed to decay in a decently tropical fashion, held together by jasmine and wisteria. He said to Julie, "You find trees, every time, shady places with big old trees. I've never figured how you manage it."

"Old houses," she said. "I always need work space and a lot of light, and only the old houses have it. It's a trade-off—plumbing for elbow room. Wait till I feed NMC." NMC was an undistinguished black and white cat who slept with six new kittens in a box underneath the tiny sink set into a curtained alcove. ("She likes to keep an eye on the refrigerator," Julie explained. "Just in case it tries to make a break for freedom.") She had shown up pregnant, climbing the stairs to scratch only at Julie's door, and sauntering in with an air of being specifically expected. The initials of her name stood for Not My Cat. Julie opened a can, set it down beside the box, checked to make sure that each kitten was securely attached to a nipple, briefly fondled a softly thrumming throat and told her, "The litter tray is two feet to your left. As if you care."

At the curb, gazing for a long time at Madame Schumann-Heink, she said, "This thing has become absolutely transparent, Joe, you know that. I can see the Bay right through it."

"Wait till you see her by moonlight," Farrell said. "Gossamer and cobwebs. The Taj Mahal of rust. Tell me again where the Bigby Museum is."

"North. East. In the hills. It's hard to explain. Take the freeway, I'll tell you where to turn off."

The Bigby City Museum had been, until fairly recently, Avicenna's nearest approach to a Roman villa. Together with its long, narrow reflecting pool and its ornamental gardens, it occupied an entire truncated hilltop from which, morning and evening, its masters—copper-mining kinglets—had seen the Golden Gate Bridge rising through the Bay mist like a Chinese dragon's writhing back. With the death of the last primordial Bigby, the lone heir had quietly sold the mansion to the city, set up its contents (primarily lesser works of the lesser Impressionists, a scattering of the Spanish masters, and the entire oeuvre of a Bigby who painted train stations) as a joint trust, and sailed away to a tax haven in the Lesser Antilles. Julie said there were a few early Brueghel oils and drawings worth the visit. "He was doing Bosch then—maybe forgeries, maybe not—and mostly you can't tell them apart. But with these you start seeing the real Brueghel, sort of in spite of himself. There's a good little Raphael too, but you'll hate it. An Annunciation, with *putti*."

"I'll hate it," Farrell said. He eased Madame Schumann-Heink over into the right-hand lane, greatly irritating a BMW, who honked at him all the way to the freeway. "Practically as much as I hate old whoever, the guy you married."

"Brian." Julie punched his shoulder hard. "His name is Brian, and he's a lovely, wonderful man, and I really do love him. We just shouldn't have gotten married. We both agreed on that."

"A damn Brian," Farrell said. He put his head out of the window and yelled back at the BMW, "She went and married a Brian, I ask you!" The BMW driver gave him the finger. Farrell said, "The worst thing is, I'd probably like him, I've got a bad feeling about that. Let's talk about something else. Why'd you marry him?"

Julie sighed. "Maybe because he was as far away from you as I could get. He's sane, he's stable, he's—okay, he's ambitious, nothing wrong with that—"

Farrell's immediate indignation surprised him as much as it did Julie. "Hey, I'm sane. All things considered. Weird is not wacko, there's a fine but definite line. And I'm stable as a damn lighthouse, or we'd never have stayed friends this long. Ambitious—okay, no, never, not really. Still cooking here and there, still playing a bit of obsolete music on obsolete instruments after hours. Same way you're still drawing cross sections of lungs and livers for medical students. What does old ambitious Brian do?"

"He's a lawyer." Julie heard herself mumbling, saw the corner of Farrell's mouth twitch, and promptly flared up again. "And I don't want to hear one bloody word out of you, Farrell! He's not a hired gun for corporations, he doesn't defend celebrity gangsters. He works for non-profits, environmental groups, refugees, gay rights—he takes on so many pro bono cases, half the time he can't pay his office rent. He's a better person than you'll ever be, Farrell. Or me either. That's the damn, damn trouble." Her eyes were aching heavily, and she looked away from him.

Farrell put his hand gently on the back of her neck. He said, "I'm sorry, Jewel." Neither of them spoke after that until they were grinding slowly up a narrow street lined with old sycamore and walnut trees and high, furry old houses drowsing in the late-summer sun.

Julie said, "I do a little word-processing, temp stuff," and then, in the same flat voice, "You never married anybody."

"Too old," Farrell said. "I used to be too young, or somebody was, I remember that. Now it's plain too late—I'm me, finally, all the way down, and easy enough with it, but I damn sure wouldn't marry me." He braked to keep from running over two cackling adolescents on skateboards, then resumed the lumbering climb, dropping Madame Schumann-Heink into second gear, which was one of her good ones. Looking sideways, he said, "One thing anyway, you're still the prettiest Eskimo anybody ever saw."

"Get out of here," she answered him scornfully. "You never saw an Eskimo that wasn't in some National Geographic special." Now she looked back at him, fighting a smile, and he touched her neck again, very lightly. "Well, I'm getting like that myself," she said. "Too old and too cranky to suit anybody but me. Turn right at the light, Joe."

The Bigby City Museum came upon them suddenly, filling the windshield just after the last sharp curve, as they rolled slightly downward into a graveled parking lot which had once been an herb garden. Farrell parked facing the Bay, and the two of them got out and stood silently on either side of Madame Schumann-Heink, staring away at the water glittering in the western sun. Then they turned, each with an odd, unspoken near-reluctance, to face the Museum. It would have been a beautiful building, Julie thought, in another town. It was three stories high, cream white, with a flat tile roof the color of red wine. Shadowed on three sides by cypress trees, camellia bushes softening the rectitude of the corners, a dancing-dolphin fountain chuckling in the sunny courtyard, and the white and peach rose gardens sloping away from the reflecting pool, it was a beautiful house, but one that belonged in Santa Barbara, Santa Monica or Malibu, worlds and wars, generations and elections removed from silly, vain, vainly perverse Avicenna. Farrell finally sighed and said, "Power to the people, hey," and Julie said, *"A bas les aristos,"* and they went inside. The ticketseller and the guest book were on the first floor, the Brueghels on the second. Julie and Farrell walked up a flowing mahogany stairway hung with watercolors from the Southwestern period of the train-station Bigby. On the landing Farrell looked around judiciously and announced, "Fine command of plastic values, I'll say that," to which Julie responded, "Oh, no question, but those spatio-temporal vortices, I don't know." They laughed together, joined hands and climbed the rest of the way.

There were ten or twelve other people upstairs in the huge main gallery. Most were younger than Farrell and Julie, with the distinct air of art students on assignment, their eyes flicking nervously from the Brueghels to their fellows to see whether anyone else had caught the trick, fathomed the koan, winkled out the grade points that must surely be hiding somewhere within those depictions of demon priests and creatures out of anchorite nightmares. When Julie took a small pad out of her purse, sat down on a couch and began copying certain corners and aspects of the paintings, the students were eddying silently toward her within minutes, just in case she knew. Farrell winked at her and wandered off toward a wall of train stations. Julie never looked up.

More quickly than she expected, he was back, leaning over her shoulder, his low voice in her hair. "Jewel. Something you ought to see. Right around the corner."

The corner was actually a temporary wall, just wide and high enough to hold three tapestries whose placard described them as "... mid-fifteenth century, artist unknown, probably from Bruges." The highest tapestry, done in the terrifyingly detailed millefleurs style, showed several women in a rich garden being serenaded by a lute-player, and Julie at first thought that Farrell—a lutanist himself—must have meant her to look at this one. Then she saw the one below.

It was in worse shape than the upper tapestry, badly frayed all around the edges and darkly stained in a kind of rosette close to the center, which showed a knight presenting a unicorn to his simpering lady. The unicorn was small and bluish-white, with the cloven hooves, long neck and slender quarters of a deer. The knight was leading it on a silvery cord, and his squire behind him was prodding the unicorn forward with a short stabbing lance. There was a soapbubble castle in the background, floating up out of a stylized broccoli forest. Julie heard herself say in a child's voice, "I don't like this."

"I've seen better," Farrell agreed. "Wouldn't have picked it as Bruges work myself." The lance was pricking the unicorn hard enough that the flesh dimpled around the point, and the unicorn's one visible eye, purple-black, was rolled back toward the squire in fear or anger. The knight's lady held a wreath of scarlet flowers in her extended right hand. Whether it was meant for the knight or the unicorn Julie could not tell.

"I wish you hadn't shown me this," she said. She turned and returned to the Brueghels, trying to recapture her focus on the sliver of canvas, the precise brushstroke, where the young painter could be seen to step away from his master. But time after time she was drawn back, moving blindly through the growing crowd to stare one more time at the shabby old imagining of beauty and theft before she took up her sketchpad again. At last she gave up any notion of work, and simply stood still before the tapestry, waiting patiently to grow numb to the unicorn's endless woven pain. The lady looked directly out at her, the faded smirk saying clearly, "Five hundred years. Five hundred years, and it is still going on, this very minute, all to the greater glory of God and courtly love."

"That's what you think," Julie said aloud. She lifted her right hand and moved it slowly across the tapestry, barely brushing the protective glass. As she did so, she spoke several words in a language that might have been Japanese, and was not. With the last syllable came a curious muffled jolt, like an underwater explosion, that thudded distantly through her body, making her step back and stagger against Farrell. He gripped her shoulders, saying, "Jewel, what the hell are you up to? What did you just do right then?"

"I don't know what you're talking about," she said, and for that moment it was true. She was oddly dizzy, and she could feel a headache coiling in her temples. "I didn't do anything, what could I do? What do you think I was doing, Joe?"

Farrell turned her to face him, his hands light on her shoulders now, but his dark-blue eyes holding her with an intensity she had rarely seen in all the years they had known each other. He said, "I remember you telling me about your grandmother's Japanese magic. I remember a night really long ago, and a goddess who came when you called her. It all makes me the tiniest bit uneasy."

The strange soft shock did not come again; the art students and the tourists went on drifting as drowsily as aquarium fish among the Brueghels; the figures in the tapestry remained exactly where they had posed for five centuries. Julie said, "I haven't done a damn thing." Farrell's eyes did not leave her face. "Not anything that made any difference, anyway," she said. She turned away and walked quickly across the gallery to examine a very minor Zurbaran too closely.

In time the notepad came back out of her purse, and she again began to copy those scraps and splinters of the Brueghels that held lessons or uses for her. She did not return to the unicorn tapestry. More time passed than she had meant to spend in the museum, and when Farrell appeared beside her she was startled at the stained pallor of the sky outside the high windows. He said, "You better come take a look. That was one hell of a grandmother you had."

She asked no questions when he took hold of her arm and led her— she could feel the effort it cost him not to drag her—back to the wall of tapestries. She stared at the upper one for a long moment before she permitted herself to understand.

The unicorn was gone. The knight and his squire remained in their places, silver cord hauling nothing forward, lance jabbing cruelly into helpless nothing. The lady went on smiling milkily, offering her flowers to nothingness. There was no change in any of their faces, no indication that the absence of the reason for their existence had been noticed at all. Julie stared and stared and said nothing.

"Let you out of my sight for five minutes," Farrell said. He was not looking at her, but scanning the floor in every direction. "All right, main thing's to keep him from getting stepped on. Check the corners—you do that side, I'll do all this side." But he was shaking his head even before he finished. "No, the stairs, you hit the stairs. If he gets down those stairs, that's it, we've lost him. Jewel, go!" He had not raised his voice at all, but the last words cracked like pine sap in fire.

Julie gave one last glance at the tapestry, hoping that the unicorn would prove not to be lost after all, but only somehow absurdly over-looked. But not so much as a dangling thread suggested that there had ever been any other figure in the frame. She said vaguely, "I didn't think it would work, it was just to be doing something," and sprang for the stairway.

By now the art students had been mostly replaced by nuzzling cou-ples and edgy family groups. Some of them grumbled as Julie pushed down past them without a word of apology; a few others turned to gape when she took up a position on the landing, midway between a lost-contact-lens stoop and a catcher's crouch, looking from side to side for some miniature scurry, something like a flittering dust-kitten with a tiny blink at its brow...But will it be flesh, or only dyed yarn? and will it grow to full size, now it's out of the frame? Does it know, does it know it's free, or is it hiding in my shadow, in a thousand times more danger than when there was a rope around its neck and a virgin grinning at it? Grandma, what have we done?

Closing time, nearly, and full dark outside, and still no trace of the unicorn. Julie's heart sank lower with each person who clattered past her down the stairs, and each time the lone guard glanced at her, then at Farrell, and then pointedly wiped his snuffly nose. Farrell comman-deered her notepad and prowled the floor, ostentatiously scrutinizing the Brueghels when he felt himself being scrutinized, but studying noth-ing but dim corners and alcoves the rest of the time. The museum lights were flicking on and off, and the guard had actually begun to say, "Five minutes to closing," when Farrell stopped moving, so suddenly that one

foot was actually in the air. Sideways-on to Julie, so that she could not
see what he saw, he slowly lowered his foot to the floor; very slowly
he turned toward the stair; with the delicacy of a parent maneuver-
ing among Legos, he navigated silently back to her. He was smiling as
carefully as though he feared the noise it might make.

"Found it," he muttered. "Way in behind the coat rack, there's a
water cooler on an open frame. It's down under there."

"So what are you doing down here?" Julie demanded. Farrell shushed
her frantically with his face and hands. He muttered, "It's not going
anywhere, it's too scared to move. I need you to distract the guard for a
minute. Like in the movies."

"Like in the movies." She sized up the guard: an overage rent-a-cop,
soft and bored, interested only in getting them out of the museum, lock-
ing up and heading for dinner. "Right. I could start taking my clothes
off, there's that. Or I could tell him I've lost my little boy, or maybe ask
him what he thinks about fifteenth-century Flemish woodcuts. What are
you up to now, Joe?"

"Two minutes," Farrell said. "At the outside. I just don't want the guy
to see me grabbing the thing up. Two minutes and gone."

"Hey," Julie said loudly. "Hey, it is not a thing, and you will not grab
it." She did lower her voice then, because the guard was glancing at his
watch, whistling fretfully. "Joe, I don't know if this has sunk in yet, but
a unicorn, a real unicorn, has been trapped in that miserable medieval
scene for five centuries, and it is now hiding under a damn water cooler
in the Bigby Museum in Avicenna, California. Does that begin to register
at all?"

"Trouble," Farrell said. "All that registers is me being in trouble
again. Go talk to that man."

Julie settled on asking with breathy shyness about the museum's
legendary third floor, always closed off to the public and rumored
variously to house the secret Masonic works of Rembrandt, Goya's
blasphemous sketches of Black Masses, certain Beardsley illustrations
of de Sade, or merely faded pornographic snapshots of assorted Bigby
mistresses. The guard's money was on forgeries: counterfeits donated to
the city in exchange for handsome tax exemptions. "Town like this, a
town full of art experts, specialists—well, you wouldn't want anybody
looking at that stuff too close. Stands to reason."

She did not dare look to see what Farrell was doing. The guard was
checking his watch again when he appeared beside her, his ancient
bomber jacket already on, her coat over his arm. "On our way," he
announced cheerfully; and, to the guard, "Sorry for the delay, we're

out of here." His free right hand rested, casually but unmoving, on the buttonless flap of his side pocket.

They did not speak on the stairs, nor immediately outside in the autumn twilight. Farrell walked fast, almost pulling her along, until they reached the van. He turned there, his face without expression for a very long moment before he took her hand and brought it to his right coat pocket. Through the cracked leather under her fingers she felt a stillness more vibrant than any struggle could have been: a waiting quiet, making her shiver with a kind of fear and a kind of wonder that she had never known and could not tell apart. She whispered, "Joe, can it—are you sure it can breathe in there?"

"Could it breathe in that damn tapestry?" Farrell's voice was rough and tense, but he touched Julie's hand gently. "It's all right, Jewel. It stood there and looked at me, and sort of watched me picking it up. Let's get on back to your place and figure out what we do now."

Julie sat close to him on the way home, her hand firmly on his coat-pocket flap. She could feel the startlingly intense heat of the unicorn against her palm as completely as though there were nothing between them; she could feel the equally astonishing sharpness of the minute horn, and the steady twitch of the five-century-old heart. As intensely as she could, she sent the thought down her arm and through her fingers: we're going to help you, we're your friends, we know you, don't be afraid. Whenever the van hit a bump or a pothole, she quickly pressed her hand under Farrell's pocket to cushion the legend inside.

Sitting on her bed, their coats still on and kittens meowling under the sink for their absent mother, she said, "All right, we have to think this through. We can't keep it, and we can't just turn it loose in millennial California. What other options do we have?"

"I love it when you talk like a CEO," Farrell said. Julie glared at him. Farrell said, "Well, I'll throw this out to the board meeting. Could you and your grandmother possibly put the poor creature back where you got it? That's what my mother always told me to do."

"Joe, we can't!" she cried out. "We can't put it back into that world, with people capturing it, sticking spears into it for the glory of Christian virginity. I'm not going to do that, I don't care if I have to take care of it for the rest of my life, I'm not going to do that."

"You know you can't take care of it." Farrell took her hands, turned them over, and placed his own hands lightly on them, palm to palm. "As somebody quite properly reminded me a bit back, it's a unicorn."

"Well, we can just set it free." Her throat felt dry, and she realized that her hands were trembling under his. "We'll take it to the wildest national park we can get to—national wilderness, better, no roads, people don't go there—and we'll turn it loose where it belongs. Unicorns live in the wilderness, it would get on fine. It would be happy."

"So would the mountain lions," Farrell said. "And the coyotes and the foxes, and God knows what else. A unicorn the size of a pork chop may be immortal, but that doesn't mean it's indigestible. We do have a problem here, Jewel." They were silent for a long time, looking at each other. Julie said at last, very quietly, "I had to, Joe. I just never thought it would work, but I had to try."

Farrell nodded. Julie was looking, not at him now, but at his coat pocket. She said, "If you put it on the table. Maybe it'll know we don't mean it any harm. Maybe it won't run away."

She leaned forward as Farrell reached slowly into his pocket, unconsciously spreading her arms to left and right, along the table's edge. But the moment Farrell's expression changed she was up and whirling to look in every direction, as she had done on the museum stair. The unicorn was nowhere to be seen. Neither was the cat NMC. The six kittens squirmed and squeaked blindly in their box, trying to suck each other's paws and ears.

Farrell stammered, "I never felt it—I don't know how…" and Julie said, "Bathroom, bathroom," and fled there, leaving him forlornly prowling the studio, with its deep, murky fireplace and antique shadows. He was still at it when she returned, empty-handed as he, and her wide eyes fighting wildness.

Very quietly, she said, "I can't find the cat. Joe, I'm scared, I can't find her."

NMC—theatrical as all cats—chose that moment to saunter grandly between them, purring in throaty hiccups, with the unicorn limp between her jaws. Julie's gasp of horror, about to become a scream, was choked off by her realization that the creature was completely unharmed. NMC had it by the back of the neck, exactly as she would have carried one of her kittens, and the purple eyes were open and curiously tranquil. The unicorn's dangling legs—disproportionately long, in the tapestry, for its deerlike body—now seemed to Julie as right as a peach, or the nautilus coil inside each human ear. There was a soft, curling tuft under its chin, less like hair than like feathers, matched by a larger one at the end of its tail. Its hooves and horn had a faint pearl shine, even in the dim light.

Magnificently indifferent to Farrell and Julie's gaping, NMC promenaded to her box, flowed over the side, and sprawled out facing the kittens, releasing her grip on the unicorn's scruff as she did so. It lay passively, legs folded under it, as the squalling mites scrimmaged across their mother's belly. But when Farrell reached cautiously to pick it up, the unicorn's head whipped around faster than any cat ever dreamed of striking, and the horn scored the side of his right hand. Farrell yelped, and Julie said wonderingly, "It wants to be there. It feels comforted with them."

"The sweet thing," Farrell muttered, licking the blood from his hand. The unicorn was shoving its way in among NMC's kittens now: as Julie and Farrell watched, it gently nudged a foster brother over to a nipple next down from the one it had chosen, took the furry tap daintily into its mouth, and let its eyes drift shut. Farrell said it was purring. Julie heard no sound at all from the thin blue-white throat, but she sat by the box long after Farrell had gone home, watching the unicorn's flanks rise and fall in the same rhythm as the kittens' breathing.

Surprisingly, the unicorn appeared perfectly content to remain indefinitely in Julie's studio apartment, living in an increasingly crowded cardboard box among six growing kittens, who chewed on it and slept on it by turns, as they chewed and slept on one another. NMC, for her part, washed it at least twice as much as she bathed any of the others ("To get rid of that nasty old medieval smell," Farrell said), and made a distinct point of sleeping herself with one forepaw plopped heavily across its body. The kittens were not yet capable of climbing out of the box—though they spent most of their waking hours in trying—but NMC plainly sensed that her foster child could come and go as easily as she. Yet, unlike its littermates, the unicorn showed no interest in going anywhere at all.

"Something's wrong," Farrell said after nearly a week. "It's not acting properly—it ought to be wild to get out, wild to be off about its unicorn business. Christ, what if I hurt it when I picked it up in the museum?" His face was suddenly cold and pale. "Jewel, I was so careful, I don't know how I could have hurt it. But I bet that's it. I bet that's what's wrong."

"No," she said firmly. "Not you. That rope around its neck, that man with the spear, the look on that idiot woman's face—there, there's the hurt, five hundred years of it, five hundred frozen years of capture. Christ, Joe, let it sleep as long as it wants, let it heal." They were standing together, sometime in the night, looking down at the cat box, and she gripped Farrell's wrist hard.

"I knew right away," she said. "As soon as I saw it, I knew it wasn't just a religious allegory, a piece of a composition. I mean, yes, it was that too, but it was real, I could tell. Grandma could tell." NMC, awakened by their voices, looked up at them, yawning blissfully, round orange eyes glowing with secrets and self-satisfaction. Julie said, "There's nothing wrong with it that being out of that damn tapestry won't cure. Trust me, I was an art major."

"Shouldn't it be having something beside cat milk?" Farrell wondered. "I always figured unicorns lived on honey and—I don't know. Lilies, morning dew. Tule fog."

Julie shook her head against his shoulder. "Serenity," she said. Her voice was very low. "I think they live on serenity, and you can't get much more serene than that cat. Let's go to bed."

"Us? Us old guys?" Farrell was playing absently with her black hair, fanning his fingers out through it, tugging very gently. "You think we'll remember how it's done?"

"Don't get cute," she said, harshly enough to surprise them both. "Don't get cute, Farrell, don't get all charming. Just come to bed and hold me, and keep me company, and keep your mouth shut for a little while. You think you can manage that?"

"Yes, Jewel," Farrell said. "It doesn't use the litter box, did you notice?"

▲▼▲

Julie dreamed of the unicorn that night. It had grown to full size and was trying to come into her bedroom, but couldn't quite fit through the door. She was frightened at first, when the great creature began to heave its prisoned shoulders, making the old house shudder around her until the roof rained shingles, and the stars came through. But in time it grew quiet, and other dreams tumbled between her and it as she slept with Farrell's arm over her, just as the unicorn slept with NMC.

In the morning, both of them late for work, unscrambling tangled clothing and exhuming a fossilized toothbrush of Farrell's ("All right, so I forgot to throw it out, so big deal!"), they nearly overlooked the unicorn altogether. It was standing—tapestry-size once again—at the foot of Julie's bed, regarding her out of eyes more violet than purple in the early light. She noticed for the first time that the pupils were horizontal, like those of a goat. NMC crouched in the doorway, switching her tail and calling plaintively for her strange foundling, but the unicorn had no heed for anyone but Julie. It lowered its head and stamped a mini-forefoot, and for all that the foot came down in a bright puddle of underwear it still made a sound like a bell ringing under the sea. Farrell and Julie, flurried as they were, stood very still.

The unicorn stamped a second time. Its eyes were growing brighter, passing from deep lavender through lilac, to blazing amethyst. Julie could not meet them. She whispered, "What is it? What do you want?"

Her only answer was a barely audible silver cry and the glint of
the fierce little horn as the unicorn's ears slanted back against its head.
Behind her Farrell, socks in hand, undershirt on backwards, murmured,
"Critter wants to tell you something. Like Lassie."

"Shut up, Farrell," she snapped at him; then, to the unicorn, "Please,
I don't understand. Please."

The unicorn raised its forefoot, as though about to stamp again.
Instead, it trotted past the bed to the rickety little dressing table that
Farrell had helped Julie put together very long ago, in another country.
Barely the height of the lowest drawer, it looked imperiously back at
them over its white shoulder before it turned, reared and stretched up
as far as it could, like NMC setting herself for a luxurious, scarifying
scratch. Farrell said, "The mirror."

"Shut up!" Julie said again; and then, "What?"

"The Cluny tapestries. *La Dame d la Licorne.* Unicorns like to look at
themselves. Your hand mirror's up there." Julie stared at him for only a
moment. She moved quickly to the dressing table, grabbed the mirror and
crouched down close beside the unicorn. It shied briefly, but immediately
after fell to gazing intently into the cracked, speckled glass with a curious air almost of puzzlement, as though it could not quite recognize itself.
Julie wedged the mirror upright against the drawer-pull; then she rose and
nudged Farrell, and the two of them hurriedly finished dressing, gulping
boiled coffee while the unicorn remained where it was, seemingly oblivi-
ous of everything but its own image. When they left for work, Julie looked
back anxiously, but Farrell said, "Let it be, don't worry, it'll stay where it
is. I took Comparative Mythology, I know these things."

True to his prediction, the unicorn had not moved from the mirror
when Julie came home late in the afternoon; and it was still in the same
spot when Farrell arrived after the restaurant's closing. NMC was beside
it, now pushing her head insistently against its side, now backing away
to try one more forlorn mother-call, while the first kitten to make it into
the wide world beyond the cat box was blissfully batting the tufted white
tail back and forth. The tail's owner paid no slightest heed to either of
them; but when Julie, out of curiosity, knelt and began to move the mirror away, the unicorn made a sound very like a kitten's hiss and struck
at her fingers, barely missing. She stood up calmly, saying, "Well, I'm for
banana cake, *Bringing Up Baby,* and having my feet rubbed. Later for
Joseph Campbell." The motion was carried by acclamation.

The unicorn stayed by the mirror that night and all the next day,
and the day after that. On the second day Julie came home to hear the
sweet rubber-band sound of a lute in her apartment, and found Farrell

sitting on the bed playing Dowland's "The Earl of Essex's Galliard." He looked up as she entered and told her cheerfully, "Nice acoustics you've got here. I've played halls that didn't sound half as good."

"That thing of yours about locks is going to get you busted one day," Julie said. The unicorn's eyes met hers in the hand mirror, but the creature did not stir. She asked, "Can you tell if it's listening at all?"

"Ears," Farrell said. "If the ears twitch even a bit, I try some more stuff by the same composer, or anyway the same century. Might not mean a thing, but it's all I've got to go by."

"Try Bach. Everything twitches to Bach."

Farrell snorted. "Forget it. Bourrees and sarabandes out the ying-yang, and not a wiggle." Oddly, he sounded almost triumphant. "See, it's a conservative little soul, some ways—it won't respond to anything it wouldn't have heard in its own time. Which means, as far as I can make out, absolutely nothing past the fifteenth century. Binchois gets you one ear. Dufay—okay, both ears, I'm pretty sure it was both ears. Machaut—ears and a little tail action, we're really onto something now. Des Pres, jackpot—it actually turned and looked at me. Not for more than a moment, but that was some look. That was a look."

He sighed and scratched his head. "Not that any of this is any help to anybody. It's just that I'll never have another chance to play this old stuff for an informed critic, as you might say. Somebody who knows my music in a way I never will. Never mind. Just a thought."

Julie sat down beside him and put her arm around his shoulders. "Well, the hell with unicorns," she said. "What do unicorns know? Play Bach for me."

Whether Farrell's music had anything to do with it or not, they never knew; but morning found the unicorn across the room, balancing quite like a cat atop a seagoing uncle's old steamer trunk, peering down into the quiet street below. Farrell, already up and making breakfast, said, "It's looking for someone."

Julie was trying to move close to the unicorn without alarming it. Without looking at Farrell, she murmured, "By Gad, Holmes, you've done it again. Five hundred years out of its time, stranded in a cat box in California, what else would it be doing but meeting a friend for lunch? You make it look so easy, and I always feel so silly once you explain—"

"Cheap sarcasm doesn't become you, Tanikawa. Here, grab your tofu scramble while it's hot." He put the plate into the hand she extended backwards toward him. "Maybe it's trolling for virgins, what can I tell you? All I'm sure of, it looked in your mirror until it remembered itself, and now it knows what it wants to do. And too bad for us if we can't figure it out. I'm making the coffee with a little cinnamon, all right?"

The unicorn turned its head at their voices; then resumed its patient scrutiny of the dawn joggers, the commuters and the shabby, ambling pilgrims to nowhere. Julie said, slowly and precisely, "It was woven into that tapestry. It began in the tapestry—it can't know anyone who's not in the tapestry. Who could it be waiting for on East Redondo Street?"

Farrell had coffee for her, but no answer. They ate their breakfast in silence, looking at nothing but the unicorn, which looked at nothing but the street; until, as Farrell prepared to leave the apartment, it bounded lightly down from the old trunk and was at the door before him, purposeful and impatient. Julie came quickly, attempting for the first time to pick it up, but the unicorn backed against a bookcase and made the hissing-kitten sound again. Farrell said, "I wouldn't."

"Oh, I definitely would," she answered him between her teeth. "Because if it gets out that door, you're going to be the one chasing after it through Friday-morning traffic." The unicorn offered no resistance when she picked it up, though its neck was arched back like a coiled snake's and for a moment Julie felt the brilliant eyes burning her skin. She held it up so that it could see her own eyes, and spoke to it directly.

"I don't know what you want," she said. "I don't know what we could do to help you if we did know, as lost as you are. But it's my doing that you're here at all, so if you'll just be patient until Joe gets back, we'll take you outside, and maybe you can sort of show us…" Her voice trailed away, and she simply stared back into the unicorn's eyes. When Farrell cautiously opened the door, the unicorn paid no attention; nevertheless, he closed it to a crack behind him before he turned to say, "I have to handle lunch, but I can get off dinner. Just don't get careless. It's got something on its mind, that one."

With Farrell gone, she felt curiously excited and apprehensive at once, as though she were meeting another lover. She brought a chair to the window, placing it close to the steamer trunk. As soon as she sat down, NMC plumped into her lap, kittens abandoned, and settled down for some serious purring and shedding. Julie petted her absently, carefully avoiding glancing at the unicorn, or even thinking about it; instead she bent all her regard on what the unicorn must have seen from her window. She recognized the UPS driver, half a dozen local joggers—each sporting a flat-lipped grin of agony suggesting that their Walkman headphones were too tight—a policewoman whom she had met on birdwatching expeditions, and the Frozen-Yogurt Man. The Frozen-Yogurt Man wore a grimy naval officer's cap the year around, along with a flapping tweed sport jacket, sweat pants and calf-length rubber boots. He had a thin yellow-brown beard, like the stubble of a burned-over wheatfield, and had never been seen, as far as Julie knew, without a frozen-yogurt cone in at least one hand. Farrell said he favored plain vanilla in a sugar cone. "With M&Ms on top. Very California."

NMC raised an ear and opened an eye, and Julie turned her head to see the unicorn once again poised atop the steamer trunk, staring down at the Frozen-Yogurt Man with the soft hairs of its mane standing erect from nape to withers. (Did it pick that up from the cats? Julie wondered in some alarm.) "He's harmless," she said, feeling silly but needing to speak. "There must have been lots of people like him in your time. Only then there was a place for them, they had names, they fit the world somewhere. Mendicant friars, I guess. Hermits."

The unicorn leaped at the window. Julie had no more than a second's warning: the dainty head lowered only a trifle, the sleek miniature hindquarters seemed hardly to flex at all; but suddenly—so fast that she had no time even to register the explosion of the glass, the unicorn was nearly through. Blood raced down the white neck, tracing the curve of the straining belly.

Julie never remembered whether she cried out or not, never remembered moving. She was simply at the window with her hands surrounding the unicorn, pulling it back as gently as she possibly could, praying in silent desperation not to catch its throat on a fang of glass. Her hands were covered with blood—some of it hers—by the time the unicorn came free, but she saw quickly that its wounds were superficial, already coagulating and closing as she looked on. The unicorn's blood was as red as her own, but there was a strange golden shadow about it: a dark sparkling just under or beyond her eyes' understanding. She dabbed at it ineffectually with a paper towel, while the unicorn struggled in her grasp. Strangely, she could feel that it was not putting forth its entire strength; though whether from fear of hurting her or for some other reason, she could not say.

"All right," she said harshly. "All right. He's only the Frozen-Yogurt Man, for God's sake, but all right, I'll take you to him. I'll take you wherever you want—we won't wait for Joe, we'll just go out. Only you have to stay in my pocket. In my pocket, okay?"

The unicorn quieted slowly between her hands. She could not read the expression in the great, bruise-colored eyes, but it made no further attempt to escape when she set it down and began to patch the broken window with cardboard and packing tape. That done, she donned the St. Vincent de Paul duffel coat she wore all winter, and carefully deposited the unicorn in the wrist-deep right pocket. Then she pinned a note on the door for Farrell, pushed two kittens away from it with her foot, shut it, said aloud, "Okay, you got it," and went down into the street.

The sun was high and warm, but a chill breeze lurked in the shade of the old trees. Julie felt the unicorn move in her pocket, and looked down to see the narrow, delicate head out from under the flap. "Back in there," she said, amazed at her own firmness. "Five hundred, a thousand years—don't you know what happens by now? When people see you?" The unicorn retreated without protest.

She could see the Frozen-Yogurt Man's naval cap a block ahead, bobbing with his shuffling gait. There were a lot of bodies between them, and she increased her own pace, keeping a hand over her pocket as she slipped between strollers and dodged coffeehouse tables. Once, sidestepping a skateboarder, she tripped hard over a broken slab of sidewalk and stumbled to hands and knees, instinctively twisting her body to fall to the left. She was up in a moment, unhurt, hurrying on.

When she did catch up with the Frozen-Yogurt Man, and he turned his blindly benign gaze on her, she hesitated, completely uncertain of how to approach him. She had never spoken to him, nor even seen him close enough to notice that he was almost an albino, with coral eyes and pebbly skin literally the color of yogurt. She cupped her hand around the unicorn in her pocket, smiled and said, "Hi."

The Frozen-Yogurt Man said thoughtfully, as though they were picking up an interrupted conversation, "You think they know what they're doing?" His voice was loud and metallic, not quite connecting one word with another. It sounded to Julie like the synthesized voices that told her which buttons on her telephone to push.

"No," she answered without hesitation. "No, whatever you're talking about. I don't think anybody knows what they're doing anymore."

The Frozen-Yogurt Man interrupted her. "I think they do. I think they do. I think they do." Julie thought he might go on repeating the words forever; but she felt the stir against her side again, and the Frozen-Yogurt Man's flat pink eyes shifted and widened. "What's that?" he demanded shrilly. "What's that watching me?"

The unicorn was halfway out of her coat pocket, front legs flailing as it yearned toward the Frozen-Yogurt Man.

Only the reluctance of passersby to make eye contact with either him or Julie spared the creature from notice. She grabbed it with both hands, forcing it back, telling it in a frantic hiss, "Stay there, you stay, he isn't the one! I don't know whom you're looking for, but it's not him." But the unicorn thrashed in the folds of cloth as though it were drowning.

The Frozen-Yogurt Man was backing away, his hands out, his face melting. Ever afterward, glimpsing him across the street, Julie felt chillingly guilty for having seen him so. In a phlegmy whisper he said, "Oh, no—oh, no, no, you don't put that thing on me. No, I been watching you all the time, you get away, you get away from me with that thing. You people, you put that chip behind my ear, you put them radio mice in my stomach you get away, you don't put nothing more on me, you done me enough." He was screaming now, and the officer's cap was tipping forward, revealing a scarred scalp the color of the sidewalk. "You done me enough! You done me enough!"

Julie fled. She managed at first to keep herself under control, easing away sedately enough through the scattering of mildly curious spectators; it was only when she was well down the block and could still hear the Frozen-Yogurt Man's terrified wailing that she began to run. Under the hand that she still kept in her pocket, the unicorn seemed to have grown calm again, but its heart was beating in tumultuous rhythm with her own. She ran on until she came to a bus stop and collapsed on the bench there, gasping for breath, rocking back and forth, weeping dryly for the Frozen-Yogurt Man.

She came back to herself only when she felt the touch of a cool, soft nose just under her right ear. Keeping her head turned away, she said hoarsely, "Just let me sit here a minute, all right? I did what you wanted. I'm sorry it didn't work out. You get back down before somebody sees you." A warm breath stirred the hairs on Julie's arms, and she raised her head to meet the hopeful brown eyes and all-purpose grin of a young golden retriever. The dog was looking brightly back and forth between her and the unicorn, wagging its entire body from the ears on down, back feet dancing eagerly. The unicorn leaned precariously from Julie's pocket to touch noses with it.

"No one's ever going to believe you," Julie said to the dog. The golden retriever listened attentively, waited a moment to make certain she had no more to confide, and then gravely licked the unicorn's head, the great red tongue almost wrapping it round. NMC's incessant grooming had plainly not prepared the unicorn for anything like this; it sneezed and took refuge in the depths of the pocket. Julie said, "Not a living soul."

The dog's owner appeared then, apologizing and grabbing its dangling leash to lead it away. It looked back, whining, and its master had to drag it all the way to the corner. Julie still huddled and rocked on the bus stop bench, but when the unicorn put its head out again she was laughing thinly. She ran a forefinger down its mane, and then laid two fingers gently against the wary, pulsing neck. She said, "Burnouts. Is that it? You're looking for one of our famous Avicenna loonies, none with less than a master's, each with a direct line to Mars, Atlantis, Lemuria, Graceland or Mount Shasta? Is that it?" For the first time, the unicorn pushed its head hard into her hand, as NMC would do. The horn pricked her palm lightly.

For the next three hours, she made her way from the downtown streets to the university's red-tiled enclave, and back again, with small side excursions into doorways, subway stations, even parking lots. She developed a peculiar cramp in her neck from snapping frequent glances at her pocket to be sure that the unicorn was staying out of sight. Whenever it indicated interest in a wild red gaze, storks'-nest hair, a shopping cart crammed with green plastic bags, or a droning monologue concerning Jesus, AIDS, and the Kennedys, she trudged doggedly after one more street apostle to open one more conversation with the moon. Once the unicorn showed itself, the result was always the same.

"It likes beards," she told Farrell late that night, as he patiently massaged her feet. "Bushy beards—the wilder and filthier, the better. Hair, too, especially that pattern baldness tonsure look. Sandals, yes, definitely—it doesn't like boots or sneakers at all, and it can't make up its mind about Birkenstocks. Prefers blankets and serapes to coats, dark hair to light, older to younger, the silent ones to the walking sound trucks—men to women, absolutely. Won't even stick its head out for a woman."

"It's hard to blame the poor thing," Farrell mused. "For a unicorn, men would be a bunch of big, stupid guys with swords and whatnot. Women are betrayal, every time, simple as that. It wasn't Gloria Steinem who wove that tapestry." He squeezed toes gently with one hand, a bruised heel with the other. "What did they do when they actually saw it?"

The unicorn glanced at them over the edge of the cat box, where its visit had been cause for an orgy of squeaking, purring and teething. Julie said, "What do you think? It was bad. It got pretty damn awful. Some of them fell down on their knees and started laughing and crying and praying their heads off. There were a couple who just sort of crooned and moaned to it—and I told you about the poor Frozen-Yogurt Man—and then there was one guy who tried to grab it away and run off with it. But it wasn't having that, and it jabbed him really hard. Nobody noticed, thank God." She laughed wearily, presenting her other foot for treatment. "The rest—oh, I'd say they should be halfway to Portland by now. Screaming all the way."

Farrell grunted thoughtfully, but asked no more questions until Julie was in bed and he was sitting across the room playing her favorite

Campion lute song. She was nearly asleep when his voice bumbled slowly against her half-dream like a fly at a window. "It can't know anyone who's not in the tapestry. There's the answer. There it is."

"There it is," she echoed him, barely hearing her own words. Farrell put down the lute and came to her, sitting on the bed to grip her shoulder.

"Jewel, listen, wake up and listen to me! It's trying to find someone who was in that tapestry with it—we even know what he looks like, more or less. An old guy, ragged and dirty, big beard, sandals—some kind of monk, most likely. Though what a unicorn would be doing anywhere near your average monk is more than I can figure. Are you awake, Jewel?"

"Yes," she mumbled. "No. Wasn't anybody else. Sleep." Somewhere very far away Farrell said, "We didn't see anybody else." Julie felt the bed sway as he stood up. "Tomorrow night," he said. "Tomorrow's Saturday, they stay open later on Saturdays. You sleep, I'll call you." She drifted off in confidence that he would lock the door carefully behind him, even without a key.

A temporary word-processing job, in company with a deadline for a set of views of diseased kidneys, filled up most of the next day for her. She was still weary, vaguely depressed, and grateful when she returned home to find the unicorn thoroughly occupied in playing on the studio floor with three of NMC's kittens. The game appeared to involve a good deal of stiff-legged pouncing, an equal amount of spinning and side-slipping on the part of the unicorn, all leading to a grand climax in which the kittens tumbled furiously over one another while the unicorn looked on, forgotten until the next round. They never came close to laying a paw on their swift littermate, and the unicorn in turn treated them with effortless care. Julie watched for a long time, until the kittens abruptly fell asleep.

"I guess that's what being immortal is like," she said aloud. The unicorn looked back at her, its eyes gone almost black. Julie said, "One minute they're romping around with you—the next, they're sleeping. Right in the middle of the game. We're all kittens to you."

The unicorn did a strange thing then. It came to her and indicated with an imperious motion of its head that it wanted to be picked up. Julie bent down to lift it, and it stepped off her joined palms into her lap, where—after pawing gently for a moment, like a dog settling in for the night—it folded its long legs and put its head down. Julie's heart hiccuped absurdly in her breast.

"I'm not a virgin," she said. "But you know that." The unicorn closed its eyes.

Neither of them had moved when Farrell arrived, looking distinctly irritated and harassed. "I left Gracie to finish up," he said. "Gracie. If I still have my job tomorrow, it'll be more of a miracle than any mythical beast. Let's go."

In the van, with the unicorn once again curled deep in Julie's pocket, Farrell said, "What we have to do is, we have to take a look at the tapestry again. A good long look this time."

"It's not going back there. I told you that." She closed her hand lightly around the unicorn, barely touching it, more for her own heartening than its reassurance. "Joe, if that's what you're planning—"

Farrell grinned at her through the timeless fast-food twilight of Madame Schumann-Heink. "No wonder you're in such good shape, all that jumping to conclusions. Listen, there has to be some other figure in that smudgy thing, someone we didn't see before. Our little friend has a friend."

Julie considered briefly, then shook her head. "No. No way. There was the knight, the squire, and that woman. That's all, I'm sure of it."

"Um," Farrell said. "Now, me, I'm never entirely sure of anything. You've probably noticed, over the years. Come on, Madame, you can do it." He dropped the van into first gear and gunned it savagely up a steep, narrow street. "We didn't see the fourth figure because we weren't looking for it. But it's there, it has to be. This isn't Comparative Mythology, Jewel, this is me."

Madame Schumann-Heink actually gained the top of the hill without stalling, and Farrell rewarded such valor by letting the old van freewheel down the other side. Julie said slowly, "And if it is there? What happens then?"

"No idea. The usual. Play it by ear and trust we'll know the right thing to do. You will, anyway. You always know the right thing to do, Tanikawa."

The casual words startled her so deeply that she actually covered her mouth for a moment: a classic Japanese mannerism she had left behind in her Seattle childhood.

"You never told me that before. Twenty years, and you never said anything like that to me." Farrell was crooning placatingly to Madame Schumann-Heink's brake shoes, and did not answer. Julie said, "Even if I did always know, which I don't, I don't always do it. Not even usually. Hardly ever, the way I feel right now."

Farrell let the van coast to a stop under a traffic light before he turned to her. His voice was low enough that she had to bend close to hear him. "All I know," he said, "there are two of us girls in this heap, and one of us had a unicorn sleeping in her lap a little while back. You work it out." He cozened Madame Schumann-Heink back into gear, and they lurched on toward the Bigby Museum.

A different guard this time: trimmer, younger, far less inclined to speculative conversation, and even less likely to overlook dubious goings-on around the exhibits.

Fortunately, there was also a university-sponsored lecture going on: it appeared to be the official word on the Brueghels, and had drawn a decent house for a Saturday night. Under his breath, Farrell said, "We split up. You go that way, I'll ease around by the Spanish stuff. Take your time."

Julie took him at his word, moving slowly through the crowd and pausing occasionally for brief murmured conversations with academic acquaintances. Once she plainly took exception to the speaker's comments regarding Brueghel's artistic debt to his father-in-law, and Farrell, watching from across the room, fully expected her to interrupt the lecture with a discourse of her own. But she resisted temptation; they met, as planned, by the three tapestries, out of the guard's line of sight, and with only a single bored-looking browser anywhere near them. Julie held Farrell's hand tightly as they turned to study the middle tapestry.

Nothing had changed. The knight and squire still prodded a void toward their pale lady, who went on leaning forward to drape her wreath around captive space. Julie imagined a bleak recognition in their eyes of knotted thread that had not been there before, but she felt foolish about that and said nothing to Farrell. Silently the two of them divided the tapestry into fields of survey, as they had done with the gallery itself when the unicorn first escaped. Julie took the foreground, scanning the ornamental garden framing the three human figures for one more face, likely dirty and bearded, perhaps by now so faded as to merge completely with the faded leaves and shadows. She was on her third futile sweep over the scene when she heard Farrell's soft hiss beside her.

"Yes!" he whispered. "Got you, you godly little recluse, you. I knew you had to be in there!" He grabbed Julie's hand and drew it straight up to the vegetable-looking forest surrounding the distant castle. "Right there, peeping coyly out like Julia's feet, you can't miss him."

But she could, and she did, for a maddening while; until Farrell made her focus on a tiny shape, a gray-white bulge at the base of one of the trees. Nose hard against the glass, she began at last to see it clearly: all robe and beard, mostly, but stitched with enough maniacal medieval detail to suggest a bald head, intense black eyes and a wondering expression. Farrell said proudly, "Your basic resident hermit. Absolutely required, no self-respecting feudal estate complete without one. There's our boy."

It seemed to Julie that the lady and the two men were straining their embroidered necks to turn toward the castle and the solitary form they had forgotten for five centuries. "Him?" she said. "He's the one?"

"Hold our friend up to see him. Watch what happens." For a while, afterward, she tried to forget how grudgingly she had reached into her coat pocket and slowly brought her cupped hand up again, into the light. Farrell shifted position, moving close on her right to block any possible glimpse of the unicorn. It posed on Julie's palm, head high, three legs splayed slightly for balance, and one forefoot proudly curled (*exactly like every unicorn I ever drew when I was young*, she thought). She looked around quickly—half afraid of being observed, half wishing it—and raised her hand to bring the unicorn level with the dim little figure of the hermit.

Three things happened then. The unicorn uttered a harsh, achingly plain cry of recognition and longing, momentarily silencing the Brueghel lecturer around the corner. At the same time, a different sound, low and disquieting, like a sleeper's teeth grinding together, seemed to come either from the frame enclosing the tapestry or the glass over it. The third occurrence was that something she could not see, nor ever after describe to Farrell, gripped Julie's right wrist so strongly that she cried out herself and almost dropped the unicorn to the gallery floor. She braced it with her free hand as it scrambled for purchase, the carpet-tack horn glowing like abalone shell.

"What is it, what's the matter?" Farrell demanded. He made clumsily to hold her, but she shook him away. Whatever had her wrist tightened its clamp, feeling nothing at all like a human hand, but rather as though the air itself were turning to stone—as though one part of her were being buried while the rest stood helplessly by. Her fingers could yet move, enough to hold the unicorn safe; but there was no resisting the force that was pushing her arm back down toward the tapestry foreground, back to the knight and the squire, the mincing damsel and the strangling garden. They want it. It is theirs. Give it to them. They want it.

"Fat fucking chance, buster," she said loudly. Her right hand was almost numb, but she felt the unicorn rearing in her palm, felt its rage shock through her stone arm, and watched from very far away as the bright horn touched the tapestry frame.

Almost silently, the glass shattered. There was only one small hole at first, popping into view just above the squire's lumpy face; then the cracks went spidering across the entire surface, making a tiny scratching sound, like mice in the walls. One by one, quite deliberately, the pieces of glass began to fall out of the frame, to splinter again on the hardwood floor.

With the first fragment, Julie's arm was her own once more, freezing cold and barely controllable, but free. She lurched forward, off-balance, and might easily have shoved the unicorn back into the garden after all. But Farrell caught her, steadying her hand as she raised it to the shelter of the forest and the face under the trees.

The unicorn turned its head. Julie caught the brilliant purple glance out of the air and tucked it away in herself, to keep for later. She could hear voices approaching now, and quick, officious footsteps that didn't sound like those of an art historian. As briskly as she might have shooed one of NMC's kittens from underfoot, she said, in the language that sounded like Japanese, "Go on, then, go. Go home."

She never actually saw the unicorn flow from her hand into the tapestry. Whenever she tried to make herself recall the moment, memory dutifully producing a rainbow flash or a melting movie-dissolve passage between worlds, irritable honesty told memory to put a sock in it. There was never anything more than herself standing in a lot of broken glass for the second time in two days, with a faint chill in her right arm, hearing Farrell's eloquently indignant voice denying to guards, docents and lecturers alike that either of them had laid a hand on this third-rate Belgian throw rug. He was still expounding a theory involving cool recycled air on the outside of the glass and warm condensation within as they were escorted all the way to the parking lot. When Julie praised his passionate inventiveness, he only growled, "Maybe that's the way it really was. How do I know?"

But she knew without asking that he had seen what she had seen: the pale shadow peering back at them from its sanctuary in the wood, and the opaline glimmer of a horn under the hermit's hand. Knight, lady and squire—one another's prisoners now, eternally—remained exactly where they were.

That night neither Farrell nor Julie slept at all. They lay silently close, peacefully wide-awake, companionably solitary, listening to her beloved Black-Forest-tourist-trash cuckoo clock strike the hours. In the morning Farrell said it was because NMC had carried on so, roaming the apartment endlessly in search of her lost nursling. But Julie answered, "We didn't need to sleep. We needed to be quiet and tell ourselves what happened to us. To hear the story."

Farrell was staring blankly into the open refrigerator, as he had been for some time. "I'm still not sure what happened. I get right up to the place where you lifted it up so it could see its little hermit buddy, and then your arm...I can't ever figure that part. What the hell was it that had hold of you?"

"I don't see how we'll ever know," she said. "It could have been them, those three—some force they were able to put out together that almost made me put the unicorn back with them, in the garden." She shivered briefly, then slipped past him to take out the eggs, milk and smoked salmon he had vaguely been seeking, and close the refrigerator door.

Farrell shook his head slowly. "They weren't real. Not like the unicorn. Even your grandmother couldn't have brought one of them to life on this side. Colored thread, that's all they were. The hermit, the monk, whatever—I don't know, Jewel."

"I don't know either," she said. "Listen. Listen, I'll tell you what I think I think. Maybe whoever wove that tapestry meant to trap a unicorn, meant to keep it penned up there forever. Not a wicked wizard, nothing like that, just the weaver, the artist. It's the way we are, we all want to paint or write or play something so for once it'll stay painted, stay played, stay put, so it'll still be alive for us tomorrow, next week, always. Mostly it dies in the night—but now and then, now and then, somebody gets it right. And when you get it right, then it's real. Even if it doesn't exist, like a unicorn, if you get it really right..."

She let the last words trail away. Farrell said, "Garlic. I bet you don't have any garlic, you never do." He opened the refrigerator again and rummaged, saying over his shoulder, "So you think it was the weaver himself, herself, grabbing you, from back there in the fifteenth century? Wanting you to put things back the way you found them, the way he had it—the right way?"

"Maybe." Julie rubbed her arm unconsciously, though the coldness was long since gone. "Maybe. Too bad for him. Right isn't absolutely everything."

"Garlic is," Farrell said from the depths of the vegetable bin. Emerging in triumph, brandishing a handful of withered-looking cloves, he added, "That's my Jewel. Priorities on straight, and a strong but highly negotiable sense of morality. The thing I've always loved about you, all these years."

Neither of them spoke for some while. Farrell peeled garlic and broke eggs into a bowl, and Julie fed NMC. The omelets were almost done before she said, "We might manage to put up with each other a bit longer than usual this time. Us old guys. I mean, I've signed a lease on this place, I can't go anywhere."

"Hand me the cayenne," Farrell said. "Madame Schumann-Heink can still manage the Bay Bridge these days, but I don't think I'd try her over the Golden Gate. Your house and the restaurant, that's about her limit."

"You'd probably have to go a bit light on the garlic. Only a bit, that's all. And I still don't like people around when I'm working. And I still read in the bathroom."

Farrell smiled at her then, brushing gray hair out of his eyes. "That's all right, there's always the litter box. Just don't you go marrying any Brians. Definitely no Brians."

"Fair enough," she said. "Think of it—you could have a real key, and not have to pick the lock every time. Hold still, there's egg on your forehead." The omelets got burned.

The Last Song of Sirit Byar

How much? *How* much to set down one miserable tale that will cost your chicken wrist an hour's effort at very most? Well, by the stinking armpits of all the gods, if I'd known there was that much profit in sitting in the marketplace scribbling other people's lives and feelings on bits of hide, I'd have spent some rainy afternoon learning to read and write myself. Twelve copper, we'll call it. *Twelve*, and I'll throw in a sweetener, because I'm a civilized woman under the grease and the hair. I promise not to break your nose, though it's a great temptation to teach you not to take advantage of strangers, even when they look like what I look like and speak your crackjaw tongue so outlandishly that you'd mimic me to my hog face if you dared. But no, no, sit back down, fair's fair, a bargain's a bargain. No broken nose. *Sit.*

Now. I want you to write this story, not for my benefit—am I likely to forget the only bloody man who ever meant more than a curse and a fart to me?—but for your own, and for those who yet sing the songs of Sirit Byar. Ah, *that* caught your ear, didn't it? Yes, yes, Sirit Byar, that one, the same who sang a king to ruin with a single mocking tune, and then charmed his way out of prison by singing ballads of brave lovers to the hangman's deaf-mute daughter. Sirit Byar, "the white *sheknath*," as they called him out of his hearing—the big, limping, white-haired man who could get four voices going on that antiquated eighteen-course *kiit* other men could hardly lift, let alone get so much as a jangle out of it. Sirit Byar, who could turn arrows with his music, call rock-*targs* to carry him over mountain rivers, make whiskery old generals dance like children. All trash, that, all marsh-goat shit, like every single other story they tell about him. Write this down. Are you writing?

Thirty years, more, he's been gone, and you'd think it a hundred listening to the shit wits who get his songs all wrong and pass them on to fools who never heard the man play. The *tales*, the things he's supposed to have said, the gods and heroes they tell you he sang for—believe it, he'd piss himself with laughing to hear such solemn dribble. And then he'd look at me and maybe I'd just catch the twitch at the right corner of his mouth, under the wine-stained white mustache, and he'd say in that barbarous south-coast accent he never lost, "What am I always telling you, big girl? Never bet on anything except human stupidity." And he'd have limped on.

I knew Sirit Byar from when I was eleven years old to his death, when I was just past seventeen. No, he didn't die in my arms—what are you, a bloody bard as well as a mincing scribbler? Yes, I *know* no one ever learned what became of him, I'll get to that part when I bloody well get to it. Don't gape at me like that or I'll pull your poxy ears off and send them to your mother, whatever kennel she's in. *Write*—we'll be all day at this if you keep on stopping to gape. Gods, what a town— back-country cousin-marriers, the lot of you. Just like home.

My name is Mircha Del. I was born around Davlo, that's maybe a hundred miles southwest of Fors na'Shachim. My father was a mountain farmer, clawing a little life from stone and sand, like everybody in this midden-heap. My mother had the good sense to run off as soon as she could after I was born. Never met her, don't know if she's alive or dead. My father used to say she was beautiful, but all you have to do is look at me for the facts of that. Probably the only woman he could get to live with him up there in those starvation hills, and even she couldn't stand it for long. No need to put all that in—this isn't about her, or about him either. Now he *did* die in my arms, by the way, if that interests you. Only time I can remember holding him.

At the age of eleven I had my full growth, and I looked just as hulking as I do now. My father once said I was meant for a man, which may be so, though I'd not have been any less ugly with balls and a beard. That's as may be, leave that out too. What matters is that I already had a man's strength, or near enough—enough anyway to get a crop in our scabby ground and to break a team of Karakosk horses—those big ones, the ones they raise on meat broth—to do our ploughing. And when our neighbor's idiot son—yes, a real idiot, who else would have been my playmate even when I was little?—got himself pinned under a fallen tree, they sent for me to lift it off him. He died anyway, mind you, but people took to calling me "the Davlo *sheknath*" for a while. I told Sirit Byar about that once, the likeness in our nicknames, and he just snorted. He said, "You hated it." I nodded. Sirit Byar said, "Me, too, always have," so maybe there was our real likeness. It made me feel better, anyway.

There used to be a tavern just outside Davlo, called the Miller's Joy. It's long gone now, but back then it was as lively a pothouse as you could find, with gaming most nights, and usually a proper brawl after, and every kind of entertainment from gamecocks to *shukri*-fighting, to real Leishai dancers, and sometimes even one of those rock-munching strongmen from down south. My father spent most of his evenings there, and many of his mornings as he got older, so I grew in the habit of walking down to Davlo to fetch him home—carry him, more times than not. And all that's the long way of telling you how I met Sirit Byar.

It happened that I tramped into the Miller's Joy one night to find my father—purely raging I was, too, because our lone miserable *rishu* was due to calve, and he'd sworn to be home this one night anyway. I delivered the calf myself, no trouble, but there could have been, and now I meant to scorch him for it before all his tavern mates. I could hear their racket a street away, and him bellowing and laughing in the middle of it. Wouldn't have been the first time I snatched him off a table and out the door for the cold walk home. Grateful he was for it most times, I think—it told him that someone yet cared where he was, and maybe it passed for love, how should I know? He was lonely with my mother gone, and too poor for drink and the whores both, so he made do with me yelling at him.

But that night there was another sound coming from the old den, and it stopped me in the street. First the fierce thump of a *kiit* strung with more and heavier courses than the usual, and then the voice, that voice—that harsh, hoarse, tender southern voice, always a breath behind the beat, that voice singing that first song, the first one I ever heard:

> *Face it,*
> *if you'd known what you know today,*
> *you'd have done the same stupid fucking thing*
> *anyway....*

Yes, you know it, don't you, even in my croak? Me, I didn't even know what I was hearing—I'd never heard anything like that music before, never heard a bard in my life. Bards don't come to Davlo. There's nothing for even a carnival jingler in Davlo, never mind someone like Sirit Byar. But there he was.

He looked up when I pushed the door open. There was a whole sprawl of drunken dirt farmers between us—a few listening to him where he sat cross-legged on a table with the *kiit* in his lap; most guzzling red ale and bawling their own personal songs—but Sirit Byar saw me. He looked straight across them to where I stood in the doorway: eleven years old, the size of a hay wagon and twice as ugly, and mucky as the floor of that taproom besides. He didn't smile or nod or anything, but just for a moment, playing a quick twirl on the *kiit* between verses, he said through the noise, "There you are, big girl." As though he'd been waiting. And then he went back to his song.

> *Face it,*
> *if she'd been fool enough to stay,*
> *you'd be the same mean, stupid bastard*
> *anyway....*

There was one man crying, doubled over his table, thumping his head on it and wailing louder than Sirit Byar was singing. And there was a miner from Grebak, just sitting silent, hands clasped together, pulling and squeezing at the big scabby knuckles. As for my father and the rest, it was drinking and fighting and puking all over their friends, like any other night at the Miller's Joy. The landlord was half-drunk himself, and he kept trying to throw out little Desh Jakani, the farrier, only he wouldn't go. The three barmaids were all making their own arrangements with anyone who could still stand up and looked likely to have two coppers left in his purse at closing time. But Sirit Byar kept looking at me through the noise and the stink and the flickering haze, and he sang:

> *Face it,*
> *if we all woke up gods one day,*
> *we'd still treat each other like garbage*
> *anyway....*

What did he look like? Well, the size of him was what I mostly saw that first night. Really big men are rare still in those Davlo hills—the diet doesn't breed them, not enough meat, and the country just hammers them low—and Sirit Byar was the biggest man I'd seen in my life. But I'm not talking about high or wide—get *this* down now—I'm talking about size. There was a color to him, even with his white hair and faded fisherman's tunic and trews; there was a purpose about him as he sat there singing that made everything and everyone in that roaring tavern small and dim and faraway, that's what I remember. And all he was, really, was a shaggy, rough-voiced old man—fifty anyway, surely—who sang dirty songs and called me "big girl." In a way, that's all he ever was.

The songs weren't *all* dirty, and they weren't all sad and mean, like that "Face It" one. That first night he sang "Grandmother's Ghost," which is just silly and funny, and he sang "The Sand Castles"—you know it?—and "The Ballad of Sailor Lal," which got even those drunken farmers thumping the tables and yelling out the chorus. And there was a song about a man who married the Fox in the Moon—that's still my favorite, though he never sang it much. I forgot about my father, I even forgot to sit down. I just stood in the doorway. with my mouth hanging open while Sirit Byar sang to me.

He really could set four voices against each other on that battered old *kiit*, that's no legend. Mostly for show, that was, for a finish—what I liked best was when he'd sing a line in one rhythm and the *kiit* would answer him back in another, and you couldn't believe they'd come out together at the end, even when you knew they would. Six years traveling with him, and I never got tired of hearing him do that thing with the rhythms.

The trouble started with "The Good Folk." It almost always did. That bloody song can stir things up even today, insulting everybody from great lords to shopkeepers, priests to bailiffs to the Queen's police; but back then, when it was new...sometimes back then you couldn't get halfway through it without starting a riot. I don't *think* Sirit Byar yet understood that, all those years ago in the Miller's Joy. Maybe he did. It'd have been just like him.

Anyway, he didn't get anything like halfway through "The Good Folk," not that night. As I recall it, he'd just sailed into the third stanza—no, no, it would have been the second, the one about the priests and what they do on the altars when everyone's gone home—when the man who'd been crying so loudly stood up, wiped his eyes, and knocked Sirit Byar clean off the table. Never saw the blow coming, no chance to ward it off—even so, he curled himself around the *kiit* as he fell, to keep it safe. The crying man went right at him, fists and feet, and he couldn't do much fighting back, not and protect the *kiit*. Then Kluj what's-his-name got into it—he'd jump anybody when he was down, that one—and then my bloody father, if you'll believe it, too blind drunk to know what was going on, just that it looked like fun. He and the crying man tripped each other up and rolled over Sirit Byar and right into the legs of the big miner's table, brought the whole thing down on themselves. Well, the miner, he started kicking at them with his lumpy boots, and *that* got Mouli Dja, my father's old drinking partner—"Drooly Mouli," people used to call him—anyway, that got *him* jumping in, yelling and swearing and chewing on the miner's knees. After that, it's not worth talking about, take my word for it. A little bleeding, a lot of snot, the rest plain mess. Tavern fights.

I told you I had near to my grown strength at eleven. I walked forward and yanked my father away from the crying man with one hand, while I peeled Mouli Dja off the miner with the other. Today I'd crack their idiot heads together and not think twice about it, but I was just a girl then, so I only dropped them in a corner on top of each other. Then I went back and started pulling people off Sirit Byar and stacking them somewhere else. Once I got them so they'd stay put, it went easier.

He wasn't much hurt. He'd been here before; he knew how to guard his head and his balls as well as the *kiit*. Anyway, that many people piling on, nothing serious ever gets done. Some blood in the white mustache, one eye closing and blackening. He looked up at me with the other one and said for the second time, "There you are, big girl." I held out my hand, but he got up without taking it.

Close to, he had a wild smell—furry, but like live fur, while it's still on the *shukri* or the *jarilao*. He was built straight up and down: wide shoulders, thick waist, thick short legs and neck. A heavy face, but not soft, not sagging—cheekbones you could have built a fence, a house with. Big eyes, set wide apart, half-hidden in the shadows of those cheekbones. Very quiet eyes, almost black, looking black because of the white hair. He never smiled much, but he usually looked about to.

"Time to go," he said, calm as you please, standing there in the ruins of a table and paying no mind to the people yelling and bleeding and falling over each other all around us. Sirit Byar said, "I was going to spend the night here, but it's too noisy. We'll find a shed or a fold somewhere."

And me? I just said, "I have to get my father home. You go on down the Fors road until you come to the little Azdak shrine, it'll be on the right. I'll meet you there." Sirit Byar nodded and turned away to dig his one sea-bag out from under Dordun the horse-coper, who was being strangled by some total stranger in a yellow hat. Funny, the things you remember. I can still see that hat, and it's been thirty years, more.

I did carry my father back to our farm—nothing out of the way in that, as I said. But then I had to sit him down on a barrel, bracing him so he wouldn't go all the way over, and tell him that I was leaving with Sirit Byar. And that was hard—first, because he was too drunk and knocked about to remember who any of us were; and second, because I couldn't have given him any sort of decent reason for becoming the second woman to leave him. He'd never been cruel to me, never used me the way half the farmers we knew used their daughters and laughed about it in the Miller's Joy. He'd never done me any harm except to sire me in that high, cold, lonely, miserable end of the world. And here I was, running away to follow a bard four, five times my age, a man I'd never seen or even heard of before that night. Oh, they'd be baiting him about it forever, Mouli Dja and the rest of his friends.

I don't think I tried to explain anything, finally. I just told him I'd not be helping him with the farming anymore, but that he wouldn't need to worry about feeding me either. He said nothing at all, but only kept blinking and blinking, trying to make his eyes focus on me. I never knew if he understood a word. I never knew what he felt when he woke up the next day and found me gone.

There wasn't much worth taking along. My knife, my tinder box, my good cloak. I had to go back for my lucky foreign coin—see here, this one that's never yet bought me a drink anywhere I've ever been. My father was already asleep, slumped on the barrel with his head against the wall. I put a blanket over him—he could have them both now—and I left a second time.

The Fors na'Shachim road runs straight the last mile or so to the Azdak shrine, and I could see Sirit Byar in the moonlight from a long way off. He wasn't looking around impatiently for me, but was kneeling before that ugly little heap of stones with the snaggletoothed Azdak face scratched into the top one. "Azdak" just means *stranger* in the tongue I grew up speaking. None of us ever knew the god's real name, or what he was good for, or who set up that shrine when my father was a boy. But we left it where it was, because it's bad luck not to, and some of us even worshipped it, because why not? Our own hill gods weren't worth shit, that was obvious, or they wouldn't have been scrabbling to survive in those hills like the rest of us. There was always the chance that a god who had journeyed this far might actually know something.

But Sirit Byar wasn't merely offering Azdak a quick nod and a marketing list. He was on his knees, as I said, with his big white head on a level with the god's, looking him in the eyes. His lips were moving, though I couldn't make out any words. As I reached him, he rose silently, picked up the *kiit* and his sea-bag, and started off on down the Fors road. I ran after him, calling, "My name is Mircha. Where are we going?"

Sirit Byar didn't even look at me. I asked him, "Why were you praying like that to Azdak? Is he your people's god?"

We tramped on a long way before Sirit Byar answered me. He said, "We know each other. His name is not Azdak, and I was not praying. We were talking."

"It'll rain before morning," I said. "I can smell it Where are we going?"

He just grunted, "Lesser Tichni or a hayloft, whichever comes first," and that was all he said until we were bedded down between two old donkeys in an old shed on very old straw. I was burrowing up to one of the beasts, trying to get warm, when Sirit Byar suddenly turned toward me and said, "You will carry the *kiit*. You can do that." And he was sound asleep, that fast. Me , I lay awake the rest of that night, partly because of the cold, but mostly because what I'd done was final-ly—*finally*, mind you—beginning to sink in. Here I was, already far-ther from home than ever I'd been, lying in moldy straw, listening to a strange man snoring beside me. Tell you how ignorant a lump I was back then, I thought snoring was just something my father did, nobody else. I wasn't frightened—I've never been frightened in my life, which is a great pity, by the way—but I was certainly confused, I'll say that. Nothing for it but to lie there and wait for morning, wondering how heavy the *kiit* would be to shoulder all day. It never once occurred to me that I could go home.

The *kiit* turned out to be bloody heavy, strong as I was, and bulky as a plough, which was worse. Those eighteen double courses made it impossible to get a proper grip on the thing—there was no comfortable way to handle it, except to keep shifting it around: now on my back, now hugged into my chest with both arms, now swinging loose in my hand, banging against everything it could reach. I was limping like Sirit Byar himself at the end of our first full day on the road.

So it began. We stopped at the first inn after sunset, and Sirit Byar played and sang for men dirtier and even more ugly-drunk than ever I'd seen in the Miller's Joy. It was a lesson to me, for that lot paid no atten-tion at all to "The Ballad of Sailor Lal," but whooped and cheered wildly for "The Good Folk," and made him sing it twice over so they could learn it themselves. You never know what they'll like or what they'll do, that's the only lesson there is.

Two nights and a ride on a tinker's cart later, we dined and slept in Fors na'Shachim—yes, at the black castle itself, with the Queen's ladies pouring our tea, and the chamber that Sirit Byar always slept in already made up for him. Four of the ladies were ordered to bathe me and find me something suitable to wear while the Queen had to look at me. I put up with the bath, but when they wanted to burn my clothes on the spot I threw one of the ladies across the room, so that took care of that. It quieted the giggling, besides. So I've had royalty concerning itself with what nightgown I should wear to bed, which is more than *you've* ever known, for all your reading and writing. They'd probably have bathed you, too.

And two days after that, we were on our way again, me back in the rags I'd practically been born in—they probably burned that borrowed dress and the nightgown—and Sirit Byar wearing what he always wore. They didn't sweeten *him* up to sing for the Queen, I can tell you. But he had gold coins in his pocket, thirty-six new strings on the *kiit*, a silk kerchief Herself had tied around his neck with her own fair hands, and he was limping off to sing his songs in every crossroads town between Fors and Chun for no more than our wretched meals and *dai*-beetle-ridden lodging. I was a silent creature myself in those days, but I had to ask him about that. I said, "She wanted you to stay. They did."

Sirit Byar just grunted. I went on, "You'd be a royal bard—you could have that palace room forever, the rest of your life. All you'd ever have to do is make up songs and sing them for the Queen now and then."

"I do that," Sirit Byar said. "Now and then. Don't dangle the *kiit* that way, it's scraping the road." He watched me as I struggled to balance the filthy thing on my shoulder, and for the first time since we'd met I saw him smile a very little.

"The singing is what matters, big girl," he said. "Not for whom." We walked a way without speaking, and then he continued. "To do what I do, I have to walk the roads. I can't ride. If I ride, the songs don't come. That's the way it is."

"And if you sleep in a bed?" I asked him. "And if you sing for people who aren't drunk and stupid and miserable?" I was eleven, and my feet hurt, and I could surely have done with a few more days in that black castle.

Sirit Byar said, "Give me that," and I handed him the *kiit*, glad to have it off my shoulder for a few minutes. I thought he was going to show me a better way of carrying it, but instead he retuned a few of the new strings—they won't hold their pitch the first day or two, drive you mad—and began to play as we walked. He played a song called "The Juggler."

No, you don't know that one. I've never yet met anyone who did. He hardly ever played it—maybe three times in the six years we were together, but I had it by heart the first time, as I always did with his songs. It's about a boy from a place about as wretched as Davlo, who teaches himself to juggle just because he's bored and lonely. And it turns out that he's good at it, a natural. He juggles everything around him—stones, food, tools, bottles, furniture, whatever's handy. People love him; they come miles to see him juggle, and by and by the King hears about it and wants him to live at the palace and be his personal juggler. But in the song the boy turns him down. He tells the King that once he starts juggling crowns and golden dishes and princesses, he'll never be able to juggle anything else again. He'll forget how it's done, he'll forget why he ever wanted to do it in the first place. So thank you, most honored, most grateful, but no. And it has the same last line at the end of every verse: *"Kings need jugglers, jugglers don't need kings...."* I can't sing it right, but that's how it went.

He sang it to me, right there, just the two of us walking along the road, and it's likely the most I ever learned about him at one time. Never any need to explain himself, not to me or anyone. I asked him that day if it bothered him when people didn't like his songs. Sirit Byar just shrugged his shoulders as though my question were a fly and he a horse trying to get rid of it. He said, "That's not my business. The Queen likes them; your father didn't. No business of mine either way."

He really didn't care. Set this down plain, if you botch all the rest, because it's what matters about him. As long as he could make his songs and get along singing them, he simply did not care where he slept, or what he ate, or whom he sang to. I can't tell you how much didn't matter to that man. When he had money he bought our meals with it, or more strings—that old *kiit* went through them like my father through red ale and black wine—or once in a while a night at an inn, for us to clean ourselves up a bit. When there was no money, there'd be food and lodging just the same, most often no worse. For a man who could go all day saying no more than half a dozen words, he had friends in places where I'd not have thought you could even find an enemy. The beggar woman in Rivni: we always stayed with her, just as regular as we stayed at the black castle, in the abandoned hen roost that was her home. The wind-witch in Leishai, where it's a respectable profession, because of the sailors. The two weavers near Sam—brothers, they were, and part-time body-snatchers besides. That bloody bandit in Cheth na'Deka—though that one always kept him up singing most of the night, demanding first this song, then that. And the shipchandler's wife of Arakli.

I'll always wonder about her, the chandler's wife. Her husband had a warehouse down near the river, and she used to let us sleep in it as long as we were careful to leave no least sign that we'd ever been there. She was a plain woman—dark, small, a bit plump, that's all I remember. Nice voice. And what there was between her and Sirit Byar I never knew, except that I got up to piss the one night and heard them outside. *Talking* they were, fool—talking they were, too softly for me to make out a word, sitting by the water, not even touching, with the moon's reflection flowing over their faces and the moon in Sirit Byar's white hair. And I pissed behind the warehouse, and I went back to sleep, and that's all.

We had a sort of regular route, if you want to call it that. Say Fors na'Shachim as a starting point—from there we'd work toward the coast through the Dungaurie Pass, strike Grannach Harbor and begin working north, with Sirit Byar singing in taverns, kitchens, great halls, and marketplaces in all the port towns as far as Leishai. Ah, the ports—the smell, salt and spice and tar, miles before you could even see the towns. The food waiting for us there in the stalls, on the barrows—fresh, fresh *courel, jeniak, boreen* soup with lots of catwort. Strings of little crackly *jai*-fish, two to a mouthful. And the light on the water, and children splashing in the shadows of the rotting pilings, and folk yelling welcome to their "white *sheknath*" in half a dozen tongues. The feeling that everything was possible, that you could go anywhere in the world from here, except back to Davlo. That was the best, better than the food, better than the smells. That feeling.

No, you'd think so, but he hardly ever sang sea-songs in the port towns. One, two, maybe, like "Captain Shallop and the Merrow" or "Dark Water Down"—otherwise he saved those for inland, where folk dream of far white isles and don't know what a merrow can do to you. In the ports he sang—oh, "Tarquentil's Hat," "The Old Priest and the Old God," "My One Sorrow," "The Ballad of the Captain's Mercy," "The Good Folk." Now *they* always loved "The Good Folk," the ports did, so there you are.

From Bitava we usually headed inland, still angling north, but no farther than Karakosk, ever. I've been told that he sang often in Corcorua; maybe, but not while I was with him. He'd no mind at all to limp across the Barrens, and he disliked most of the high northland anyway for its thin wine and its fat, stingy burghers. So I never saw anything loftier than the Durli Hills in those days, which suited me well enough—I've never been homesick for mountains a day in my life. We'd skirt the Durlis, begin bearing back south around Suk'hai, and fetch up in Fors again by Thieves' Day. A bath and a warm bed then—a few days of singing for the Queen and being made over by her ladies—and start all over again. So it was we lived for six years.

Duties? What were my *duties*? How daintily you do put it, to be sure, chicken-wrist. Well, I carried the *kiit*, and I brewed the tea and cooked our meals, when we had something to cook. A few times, mostly in Leishai, I ran off pickpockets he hadn't seen sliding alongside, and one night I broke the shoulder of a hatchet-swinging Bitava barber who'd taken a real dislike to "The Sand Castles." For the rest, I kept him mostly silent company, talked when he wanted talk, went round with the hat after he sang, and kept an eye out at all times for that wicked west-country liqueur they call Blue Death. Terrible shit, peel your gums right back, but he loved it, and it's hard to find much east of Fors. He drank it like water, whenever he could get it, but I can't remember seeing him drunk. Or maybe I did, maybe I saw him drunk a lot and didn't know it. There were things you never could tell about with Sirit Byar.

Once I asked him, "What would you do if you weren't a bard? If you just suddenly couldn't make up songs anymore?"

I thought I knew him well enough to ask, but he stopped in the road and gaped at me as though he'd never seen me before. That was the only time I ever saw him looking amazed, startled about anything. He mumbled, "You don't know."

I stared right back at him. I said, "Well, of course I don't know. I didn't know a bloody thing about being a bard, not how it is, you won't ever talk about that. All I know is what you like to eat, where you like to sit when you sing. Maybe you think that's all a hill girl from Davlo can understand. Maybe it is. You'll never know that either."

Sirit Byar smiled a real smile then, not the almost-smile he wore for everyone always. "Listen to the songs, big girl. It's all in the songs, everything I could tell you." We walked along a way after that, and by and by he said, "A bard always hoards one last song against the day when all the others go. It happens to every one of us, sooner or later—you wake up one morning and it's over, they've left you, they don't need you anymore. No warning. No warning when they flew into you, no warning when they fly away. That's why you always save that last song."

He cleared his throat, spat into the road, rubbed his nose, looked sideways at me. "But you have to be very careful, because a bard's last song has power. You never tell that song; you never sing it anywhere; you keep it for that day when it's the only song left to you. Because a last song is always *answered*." And after that he hardly talked at all for the rest of the day.

He taught me a little about playing the *kiit*, you know. I'm sure he did it just because he'd never found anyone besides him who could even handle the thing. I'm no musician—I can't do what he could do, but I know how he did it. Someday I'd like to show someone how he played, just so it won't die with me. Not that he'd have given one tiny damn, but I do.

Every so often we'd strike a song competition, a battle of bards, especially in the southwest—it's a tradition in that country to set poets a subject and start them outrhyming one another. Sirit Byar hated those things. He'd avoid even a town where we usually did well if he heard there was a contest going on there. Because once he was recognized, he never had a choice—they'd cancel the whole event if he didn't enter. He always won, but he was cranky for days afterward. Me, I liked the song tourneys—we ate well those days, and drank better, and some of the townsfolk's celebration of Sirit Byar was for me, too, or anyway it felt so. I was proud as any of the Queen's ladies to walk beside him in the street, holding the *kiit* so people could see the flowers woven in and out between its strings. And whenever Sirit Byar looked down through all the fuss and winked at me, bard to bard almost—well, you imagine how it was, chicken-wrist. You imagine this big freak's insides then.

No. Oh, no. Get *that* out of your head before it ever gets in, if you know what's good for you. I was eleven, lugging that *kiit*, for Sirit Byar, and then twelve and thirteen and fourteen, sleeping close for warmth in fields, barns, sheds, whores' cribs, and never in all that time. *Never.* Not once. It wouldn't have occurred to him.

It occurred to me, I'll tell you that. Yes, you can gape now, that's right, I'd be disappointed if you didn't. Listen to me now—I've had three, four times as many men as you've had women, for what that's worth. You think men care about soft skin, perfect teeth, adorable little noses? Not where I've been—not in the mines, not on the flatboats, the canal scows, not in the traders' caravans slinking through the Northern Barrens. Out there, I even get to say, "no, not now, piss off"—can you imagine *that* at least, chicken-wrist? Try.

I had my first while I was yet on the road with Sirit Byar. Not yet fourteen, me, and sneaking up on myself in every stock pond, every shiny pot, just on the off-hope that something might have changed since the last time. If I'd had a mother...aye, well, and what could the most loving mother have told me that the bottom of any kettle couldn't? What could Sirit Byar have said, who never looked in a glass from year's-end to year's-end? I truly doubt he remembered the color of his own eyes. Now me, I couldn't remember not knowing I was ugly enough to turn milk, curdle beer, and mark babies, but it hadn't mattered much at all until that boy at Limsatty Fair.

Ah, gods, that boy at the fair. I can still see him, thirty years gone, when I can't remember who pleased me last week. Pretty as you like, with lavender eyes, skin like brown cambric, bones in his face like kite-ribs. He was selling salt meat, if you'll believe it, and when Sirit Byar and I wandered by he looked at me for a moment, and looked politely away, so as not to stare. That's when I learned that I had a heart, chicken-wrist, because I felt such a pain in it that I couldn't believe I was still walking along and not falling dead on the spot. We were to make our camp in a field a mile from the fair, and I think I walked backward all the way. Sirit Byar had to grip me by the back of my smock and tow me like a bloody barge.

There was a little creek, and I was supposed to scoop some fish out of it for our dinner. Any hill child can do that, but instead I lay there on my stomach and cried as I've never cried in my life, before or since.

I didn't think it was ever going to stop. Leave that out. No. No, keep it in. What do I care?

Sirit Byar had probably been sitting by me for a long time before I felt his hand on my neck. He never touched me, you know, except to help me on the road, or to remind me about holding the damn *kiit* just so. Once, when I was sick with the white-mouth fever, he carried me and the *kiit* both for miles until we found a mad old woman who knew what to do. This was different, this was—I don't know, leave it, just leave it. He said, "Here."

He took off the Queen's silken kerchief he always wore around his neck and handed it to me so I could dry my eyes. Then he said, "Give me the *kiit*." I just stared at him, and he had to tell me again. "Give it to me, big girl."

He tuned it so carefully, you'd have thought he was getting ready to play at the black palace once again. Then he set his back against a tree, and began to sing. It wasn't a song I'd ever heard, and it didn't sound like one of his. The rhythm wasn't any I knew, the music was jags and slides and tangles, the words didn't make any sense. I told you, I had all his songs by heart the moment I heard them, but not that song. I do have a bit of it, like this:

> *If you hear not, hear me never—*
> *if you burn not, freeze forever—*
> *if you hunger not, starve in hell—*
> *if you will not, then you never shall....*

That line kept coming round and round again—*"If you will not, then you never shall."* It was a long song, and there was a thing about it made my skin fit all wrong on me. I lay where I was, sniffling away, while Sirit Byar kept singing, and the sun wandered down into twilight, slow as that song. At last I sat up and wiped my face with the Queen's kerchief, and remembered about our fish. I was moving myself back over to the creek when the music stopped, sudden as a door slam, and I turned and saw the salt-meat boy from the fair.

He was still so beautiful that it hurt to look at him, but something in his face was changed. Some kind of vague, puzzled anger, like someone who hasn't been blind long enough to get used to it. But he walked straight to me, and he took my hands and drew me to my feet, and we stood staring at each other for however long. When he began to lead me away, I turned to look back, but Sirit Byar was gone. I don't know what he had for dinner that night, nor where he slept.

Me, I slept warm on a cold hillside, as they say in the old ballads, and I woke just a minute or two before I should have. The salt-meat boy was up and scurrying into his clothes, and looking down at me with such bewilderment and such contempt—not for me, but for himself—as even I haven't seen again in my life. Then he fled, carrying his boots, and I lay there for a while longer, to give him time. I didn't cry.

Sirit Byar was at the creek, breakfasting on dry bread and cheese and the last of our sour Cape Dylee wine. There was enough laid out for two. Neither of us spoke a word until we were on our way again, bound for Derridow, I think. Finally I said, "The song brought him."

Sirit Byar grunted, looked away, mumbled something. I stopped right there on the road—he actually walked along a few steps before he realized I wasn't with him. I said, "Tell me why you sang that song. Tell me now."

He was a long time answering. We stood there and looked at each other almost the way I'd stood with that salt-meat boy, years and years ago it seemed. Finally Sirit Byar rubbed his hand across his mouth and muttered, "You're my big girl, and you were so sad."

And that was how I knew he liked me, you see. Two, almost three full years carrying his instrument, cooking his meals, grubbing up coins from tavern floors, and he'd never said. He turned right around then and started walking on, as fast as his limp would let him, and I hurried after him with the *kiit* banging the side of my knee. He wouldn't talk for a long time, not until a rain shower came up and we were huddled in the lee of a hayrick, waiting it out. I asked him, "How does it happen? The song making someone come to you."

Sirit Byar said, "Where I come from, there are songs for bringing game to the hunter—fish, birds. I just changed one a little for you."

I started to say, "Please, don't ever do that anymore," but I changed my mind halfway through. Whatever came of it, he gave me what I'd wanted most in all my life till then, and no blame to him if I woke from the dream too soon. So instead I asked, "Can you make other things happen with your songs?"

"Little things," Sirit Byar said. "The great ones who walked the roads before me—Sarani Elsu, K'lanikh-yara"—no, I never heard of them either, chicken-wrist—"*they* could sing changes, *they* could call rivers to them, they could call gods, lightning, the dead, not silly lovers." He patted my shoulder clumsily, I remember. He said, "All songs are magic, big girl. Some are more powerful than others, but all songs are always magic, always. You've seen me start our cooking fires in the rain—you remember the time I cured the farmer's dog that had eaten poison. My songs make little magics, that's all. They'll do for me."

Write that down, remember that he said just that. Remember it the next time you hear someone jabbering about Sirit Byar's great powers. *Little magics.* He never claimed anything more than that for himself. He never needed to.

Where was I? The rain let up, and we set out again, and presently Sirit Byar began singing a new song, one he hadn't yet finished, scrawling it in the air with one huge hand as we walked, the way he did. It ran so:

> *Long ago,*
> *before there were landlords*
> *long ago,*
> *before there were kings,*
> *there lived a lady*
> *made all out of flowers,*
> *made of honey and sunlight*
> *and such sweet things....*

Yes, of course you know it, that one got around everywhere—I've heard it as far north as Trodai, just last year. He sang it through for me the first time, the two of us shivering there in the rain, and when the sun came out, we walked on. Neither of us ever said another word about the salt-meat boy, as often as we came again to Limsatty Fair.

After that, something was a bit different between us. Closer, I don't know—maybe just easier. We talked more, anyway. I told Sirit Byar about the little scrap of a farm where I'd lived, and about how I'd chanced into the Miller's Joy that night, and that I was worried about my father—we hadn't been back to Davlo in three years. I asked after him whenever we met someone who'd passed through there, but for all I knew he might have died the day I left. I'd go days at a time without thinking of him at all, but I dreamed about him more and more.

Sirit Byar spoke sometimes of his south-coast town—not much bigger than Davlo, it sounded—and of his older sister, who raised him after their parents' deaths. Even now I can't imagine Sirit Byar having a family, having a sister. She set his leg herself when it got crushed between two skiffs and there wasn't even a witchwife for miles. She married there, and was killed in the Fishermen's Rebellion, and he never went back. Did you ever hear anyone sing that song of his, "Thou"? Most people think that song's about one god or another, but it's not; it's for his sister. He told me that.

Bedded down one night in the straw of a byre, with an old *rishu* and her calf for company, I asked him why he'd said that in the Miller's Joy when he first saw me—*"There you are, big girl."* How he knew that I was supposed to go with him and help him. Sirit Byar was sitting up across from me, fussing over a harmony on the *kiit* that never did satisfy him. He answered without looking up, "He told me. The one your folk call Azdak." I didn't understand him. Sirit Byar said, "When I came to Davlo. I saw him by the road, and we talked. He told me to watch for you."

"Azdak," I said. "Azdak. What would Azdak care about me?"

"He is the god of wanderers," Sirit Byar said. "He knows his own." The *kiit* wouldn't do a thing he wanted that evening, and he finally set it down gently in an empty manger. He went on, "Your Azdak told me you and I had a journey to make together. I didn't know what he meant then."

"Aye, and so we have, sure enough," I said. "Where's the mystery in that?"

Sirit Byar laughed. He said, "I don't think Azdak was talking about walking the roads, big girl. Gods likely don't bother much with such things."

"Well, they bloody should," I said, for he'd been limping worse than usual lately, and I'd had a stone bruise on my heel days on end. "He's no more use than our regular gods, if that's all he could tell you."

Sirit Byar shrugged. "I know only what he didn't mean, not what he did. That's how it is with gods." He stretched out on the far side of the *rishu*, wriggling himself down into the straw till all you could see of him was a big nose and a white mustache. He said, "Our real journey is yet to come," and was asleep.

Now whether it was the words or the way he said them that took hold of me, I couldn't tell you, but it was nightmare on nightmare after that—every time the damn *rishu* snuffled in her sleep, another monster turned up in mine. The last one must have been a pure beauty, because I woke up on Sirit Byar's chest, holding him tighter than ever I had the salt-meat boy. That wild, deep-woods smell of his was the most comforting thing in the wide world just then.

Well, there's comfort and comfort. I'll get this part over with quickly—no need to embarrass us both for twelve coppers. He held me for a while, petting my hair as though it might turn in his hand and bite him any minute. Then he started to put me by, gently as he could, but I wouldn't let him. I was saying, "It's dark, it's dark, you won't even see me, just this one time. Please." Like that.

Poor Sirit Byar, hey? The poor man, trying to get this whimpering hulk off him without hurting her brutish feelings. Ah, *that* one you can imagine, I can see it in your little pink eyes. Yes, well, I pushed him back down every time he sat up, and when he said, "Big girl, don't, no, you're too young," I kept on kissing him, saying, "I don't care, I won't tell anybody, please, I won't ever tell." Ah, poor, poor Sirit Byar.

He did the only thing he could do. He shoved me away, hard—big as he was, I was the stronger, but it's amazing what you can do when you're desperate, isn't it?—and jumped to his feet, panting as though we really had been doing it. For a moment he couldn't speak. He was backed into a far corner of the stall; he'd have to bolt past me to get out. I wasn't crying or laughing, or coming at him or anything, just standing there.

"Mircha," he said, and that was the only time but one he ever called me by my name. "Mircha, I can't. There's a lady."

A lady, mind you. Not a plain woman, a lady. "The bloody *hell* there is," I said. I don't think I screamed it, but who remembers? "Three years, almost, never out of each other's sight for ten minutes together, what bloody *lady*?"

"A long time," Sirit Byar said very softly. "A long, long time, big girl." The words were coming out of him one by one, two by two. He said, "I've not seen her since before you were born."

Never mind what I said to him then. If there's little enough in my life that warms me to remember, there's less that truly shames me, except for what I said to Sirit Byar in the next few moments. Just set it down that I asked him what he thought his great love was doing while he was wandering the land being forever faithful to her. Just set that much down—so—and let it alone.

Sirit Byar bore it all, big hands hanging open at his sides, and waited for me to run out of words and wind. Then he said, sounding very tired, "Her name is Jailly Doura. She is mad."

I sat down in the straw. Sirit Byar said, "Jailly Doura. There was a child. Her family married her to a man who took the child gladly, but it died." He swung his head left and right, the way he did sometimes, like an animal that can't find its old way out of a place. "It died," he said, "our child. She has been mad ever since, fifteen years it is. Jailly Doura."

Two *l*s in the name, are you getting it? I said, "Credevek. That place where the rich people live. We always walk wide of Credevek—you won't pass the city gates, let alone sing there."

"Once," Sirit Byar whispered. Slumped against the wall, gray as our old stone Azdak under the road-brown weathering, he looked like no one I'd ever seen. He said, "I sang once for her in Credevek."

"Once in fifteen years," I said. "We do better than that in Davlo. Well, maybe faithfulness is easier if you don't have to see the person. I wouldn't know." There was a calmness on me, just as new and strange as all those tears I'd shed over the salt-meat boy. I felt very old. I patted the straw beside me and said, "Come and sit. I won't attack you, I promise. Come *on*, then."

Fourteen, and ordering Sirit Byar about like a plough horse. But he came, and we sat close against each other, because the night had turned wickedly cold. Sirit Byar even laid his arm across my shoulders, and it was all right. Whatever happened, whatever it was took me for a little time, it never happened again. Not with him, not with anybody. I asked, "Did you know there was a baby?"

Sirit Byar nodded. After a while he said, "What could I have done? Her parents would have locked her away forever, rather than have her walking the roads with a moneyless, mannerless south-coast street singer. And here's a wealthy man waiting to marry her and take her to live in Credevek, and what's a street singer to do for a gently bred girl and a child?" He shivered suddenly, hard, I could feel it. He said, "I went away."

"What became of her?" He blinked at me. "I mean, after—afterward? Where is she now, who takes care of her?" In Davlo we had Mother Choy. She took in all our strays—animals, children, and the moontouched alike—and if the lot of them lived in rags, on scraps, and under rotting thatch, well, they were glad enough to get it. Sirit Byar said, "Jailly Doura's husband is a good man. Another would have sent her away, but she lives with him still, in a house just north of Credevek, and he looks after her himself. I have been to that house."

"Once," I said. Sirit Byar's hand tightened on my shoulder, hard, and his face clenched in the same way. I couldn't tell you which hurt me more. He said, "She would not come into the room. I sang all night for a dark doorway, and I could smell her, feel the air move against me when she moved, but she would not let me see her. I could not bear that. I could not bear to come back again."

I knew there was more. I knew him that well, anyway. Nothing to do but sit there in the stall, with the *rishu* snoring and her calf looking sleepily at us, and the air growing lighter and colder, both. And sure enough, in a year or two, Sirit Byar said, "I thought I could make her well. I was so sure."

He wasn't talking to me. I said, "All songs are magic, always. You told me that."

"So they are," Sirit Byar answered. "But my songs are for farmers' dogs, I told you that also. I learned that before you were born, in that house in Credevek." He turned to look at me, and his eyes were as old and weary as any I ever saw. He said, "The great ones, they could have

healed her. Sarani Elsu could have brought her back. *I—*" and he just
stopped, and his head went down.

I knew there wouldn't be another word this time, no matter how
long I waited for it. So after a while I said, "So you tried to sing her madness away, and it didn't work. And you never tried again. Fifteen years."

"Her husband told me not to come back," Sirit Byar mumbled. "I left
her worse off than before, what could I say to him? He is a good man,
what could I say?" He looked at me for an answer, but I didn't have one.
In a bit his head sagged forward again. I wriggled around until I could
get comfortable with his head resting on my arm, and then I just sat like
that until long into morning, while the old man slept and slept, and I
just sat.

And the next day, and the days after that, you'd think none of it had
ever happened. We walked the roads as usual, talking a bit more, as I've
said, but we never once talked about our night in the byre, and there
was never another bloody word about his Jailly Doura. Oh, I might have
asked, and he might have answered, but I didn't think I wanted to know
a thing more about her and him and their child than I already knew,
thank you very much. No, I wasn't *jealous*—please, do me a favor—but
I was fourteen and he was mine, that's all, whatever that means when
you're fourteen. He wasn't my father or my lover, he was just mine. And
if I *was* jealous, I had a bloody right to be, only I wasn't. Just big and
ugly, the same as always.

One thing different, though. At night, usually when he thought I
was asleep, he practiced a new song over and over. Or maybe it was
an old one, for all I could tell—he kept his voice so low and his south-
coast accent would get so thick that I couldn't make out one word in
ten. Even when I really was asleep, the slidey, whispery music always
filled my dreams full of faces I'd never seen, animals I didn't recognize.
It sounded like a lullaby people might sing in some other country; like
my lucky coin that's worth something somewhere, I've no doubt. Never
had dreams like that again.

We did get to Davlo that spring—Sirit Byar went out of his usual
way to make sure of it. There was nothing for him there. He didn't
bother with even a single night at the Miller's Joy, but stayed with a
farmer while I went on alone. I found Desh Jakani at his smithy, and he
told me that my father hadn't been into the Miller's Joy for more than a
month now, and that he'd been thinking seriously of going by our farm
any day to look in on him. "Never the same man after you ran away," he
told me. "The spirit just went out of him, everybody says so." My father
hadn't had much spirit in him to begin with, and Desh Jakani was a liar

born, but all the same I scrambled up that mountain track as though a rock-*targ* were after me, really thankful that I'd come home when I had, and wishing with all my heart that I were anywhere, anywhere else in the world.

The way had disappeared completely. I'd always kept things cut back at least a little, but everything—the path, the pasture, our few poor fields—everything was smothered in foxweed, ice-berry brambles and *drumak*. I looked for our *rishu* and the two Karakosk horses, but they were gone. The door of the house hung on one hinge. My father squatted naked in the doorway.

He wasn't mad, like Sirit Byar's Jailly Doura, or even very drunk. He knew me right away, but he didn't care. I picked him up—all cold bones, he was—and carried him into the house. No point in going into what it looked like; it was just the house of a man who'd given up long ago. When I left? Like enough. Likely Desh Jakani was right about that, after all.

My father never spoke a single word during the two days I stayed with him. I put him to bed, and I made soup for him—I'm no cook, and proud of it, but I can make decent soup—and managed to get some of it down his throat, while I told him all about my travels with Sirit Byar, the things I'd seen with him, the people I'd met, the songs I'd learned. I think I sang him every song I knew of Sirit Byar's during those two days, including "The Good Folk," the one that started the brawl in the Miller's Joy so long ago. He listened. I don't know what he heard, because his eyes never changed, but he was listening, I know that much.

I even told him about the salt-meat boy. That was on the morning of the third day, when I was holding him steady on the chamber pot. That's when he died, trust my father. Not a sound, not a whimper, not the tiniest fart—he was just dead in my arms, just like that. I buried him at the doorstep, because that's the way we do in Davlo, and left the door open for the animals and the creeping vines, and walked down into town one last time to join Sirit Byar.

What? What? You should see the look on your little face—you can't wait to know if we ever went to Credevek together, ever tried a second time to sing Jailly Doura back from wherever her poor ragged mind had been roaming all this long time. Well, let me tell you, for the next two years, Sirit Byar saw to it that we didn't go anywhere near Suk'hai, let alone Credevek. He'd have us veering back south as early as Chun, never mind who expected him where, or what bounty he might be passing up. When I asked, he only grunted that he was getting too old to trudge that far uphill, and anyway, those folk were all too tightfisted to make the extra miles worthwhile. Wasn't my place to argue with him, even if I'd been of a mind to. I wasn't.

Those were good years, those last two we had together. My strength had caught up with my size, and I could have carried the *kiit* all day by a couple of fingers. We tramped every road between Cape Dylee and Karakosk, between Grannach Harbor and Derridow, him writing his new songs in the air as we went, and me eyeing every pretty boy in every town square as boldly as though I were some great wild beauty who'd been the one to do the choosing all her life. There wasn't one of them as beautiful as my salt-meat boy, and they didn't all come bleating after me by night—no fear about that—but I'll tell you one thing, Sirit Byar never had to sing anybody to my bed again, no bloody fear about *that*, either. You're almost sweet when you blush, chicken-wrist, do you know that? Almost.

Yes. Yes, yes, we did go to Credevek together.

It was my doing, if you want to know. I won't say he'd never have gone without me; all I *will* say is that he hadn't been back there for— what's that make it?—seventeen years, so you figure it out. What put it into my head, that's another story. I wanted to see her, I know that. It started as a notion, just a casual wondering what she looked like, but then I couldn't get it out of my head; it kept growing stronger and stronger. And maybe I wanted to see him, too, see him with her, just to know. Just to find out what it was I wanted to know. Maybe that was it, who remembers?

So that last morning, after we'd been to Chun—I remember it was Chun, because that was one place where Sirit Byar did sing "The Juggler" in public—and came once more to the Fors na'Shachim crossroads, I said to him, as casually as I could, "That peddler yesterday, the man we traded with for the new kettle? He spoke of trouble on the Fors road. I meant to tell you."

Sirit Byar shrugged. "Bandits." One fairy tale's true, anyway—there wasn't a high-toby in the country would have laid a hand on Sirit Byar or lifted a single copper from him. They used to come out of the woods sometimes, bashful as marsh-goats, and travel along with us a little way, hanging back to encourage him to try over a new song as though they weren't there. They couldn't make him out, you see. I think they felt he was somehow one of them, but they couldn't have said why. That's what I think.

"Plague," I told him. "Fire-plague, broken out all down the Fors road between here and Dushant. He said the only safe route south was the Snowhawk's Highway. It's a good road—we can follow it as far as Cheth na'Vaudry and then cut west to Fors. We could do that."

Sirit Byar looked at me for a long time. Did he know I was lying? I've no more idea than you have. What *I* knew was that fire-plague hits the south coast, his country, at least once every ten years; people die in hundreds, thousands sometimes. He said at last, "We would have to pass through Credevek."

I didn't answer him. We stood silent at the crossroads, listening to insects, birds, the wind in the dry leaves. Then Sirit Byar said, "Azdak." Not another word. He took the *kiit* from my hand and set off toward Credevek without looking back. Limp or no limp, I had to trot to catch up with him.

So there's how we came to Credevek, which is a strange place, all grand lawns, high stone houses, cobblestone streets, servants coming and going on their masters' errands. No beggars. No tinkers, no peddlers. A few farm carts, a few children. *Quiet.* The quiet sticks to your skin in that town.

Sirit Byar marched straight down the main street of Credevek, with me trailing after him, not knowing what to do or even how to walk if I wasn't carrying the *kiit*. People came to their windows to stare at us, but no one recognized Sirit Byar, and he never looked this way or that. Straight through the town until the paved streets and the stone houses fell away, nothing much after but meadowland gone to seed, a few pastures, and the brown Durli Hills in the distance. And one big wooden house snugged down into the shadows between two foothills—you could miss it if you didn't look sharp. Sirit Byar said, "If we travel by night, we will reach the Snowhawk's Highway before noon tomorrow."

I said, "That's where they live, isn't it? That's where Jailly Doura lives."

Sirit Byar nodded. "If she lives still." He turned to look at me, and suddenly he reached out to put his hand on the side of my neck, right here. My hair, the roots of my hair, just went cold with it. He said, "Between that house and where we stand, there's our journey. That's what the god of wanderers was saying to me. Whatever happens in that house, this is why we met, you and I. I would never be here, but for you. Thank you, Mircha."

I didn't know what to say. I just said, "Well, I wanted to get out of Davlo, that's all." I tried to take the *kiit* back—I mean, it was my *job*, carrying it, from the first day—but he wouldn't let me. He swung it to his shoulder and we started on our journey.

And it was a longer journey than it looked, I can tell you. By noon, which is when we should have reached the house in the foothills, it hardly seemed any closer than when we'd first seen it. Barely this side of sunset, it was, before we'd done with trudging through empty, stony defiles and turned up a last steep road that ran between two huge boulders. There was a man waiting there. He was short and old, and the little that was left of his hair was as white as Sirit Byar's, and if he wasn't exactly fat, he looked soft as porridge, and about that color. But he faced us proudly, blocking our way like one of those boulders himself. He said, "Sirit Byar. I thought it would be today."

Now. I have to tell the rest slowly. I have to be careful, remember it right, so you can set it down exactly the way it was. Sirit Byar said, "Aung Jatt," and nothing more. He just stood looking down at the other man, the way the high, shadowed house looked down on us three. Aung Jatt didn't take any notice of me, which is difficult. He said to Sirit Byar, "You cannot see her. I will not allow it."

"It has been seventeen years," Sirit Byar began, but Aung Jatt interrupted him.

"And if it had been fifty, she'd still not be healed of you, healed of your music. I told you never to return here, Sirit Byar." You know how, when you grip something too tightly, it starts shivering and slipping in your hand? Aung Jatt's voice was like that.

Sirit Byar said only, "I must sing for her once more."

"Oh, aye, once more," the old man answered him. "And when you have sung your songs of love and ghosts, dragons and sailors, and gone your way again, who will stay behind to piece what's left of her into some kind of human shape *once more*?" He mimicked Sirit Byar's deep, hoarse voice so bitterly that I giggled. I couldn't help it. Aung Jatt never took his eyes off Sirit Byar.

"She did not know me for three years after you were here," he whispered. "Three years. What possessed me to let her listen to you? What made me imagine that the music of the father might keep her from trying to follow the child? For three years, she wept in the dark and ate what I pushed under her door—for two years more, she said no word but the child's name, over and over and over. For five years after that—" He made himself stop; you could hear his throat clicking and grinding. Sirit Byar waited, blinking in the setting sun.

"Seventeen years," Aung Jatt said presently. "There are times even now when she takes me for you, do you know that?" He grinned like a dead man. "You might think that would hurt me, and in a way it does, because then she sometimes tries to kill me. I must always be watchful."

Sirit Byar closed his eyes, shook his head, and started to move around Aung Jatt, up the road toward the house beyond. Aung Jatt stopped him with a palm gently against his chest. He said, "But she has stopped calling for the child. Most often she sleeps through the night, and it has been some while since I had to feed her. And she hates you far more than I do, Sirit Byar."

You couldn't be sure, because the sunlight was slanting off the windows, but I thought I saw someone moving in the house, just for a moment, the way you can see a feeling flicker across someone's eyes and gone again. Aung Jatt went on, "She hates you because she knows—she *knows*—that the child would still be alive if you had defied her parents and stayed with her. I know better, but there." He chuckled and patted Sirit Byar's chest with his fingertips. He said, "Did I tell you when you were here before that it was a boy? I'm growing old, I forget things."

Sirit Byar said, without looking at me, "Come on, big girl," and put Aung Jatt out of his way with one arm. Aung Jatt made no protest this time. He was still smiling a little as he watched us step past him—I say *us*, but he never saw me, not for a minute. He didn't follow, and he didn't speak again until we were on the stone steps that led to the front door. Then he called after us, "Beware, Sirit Byar! The second floor is her domain—when you are there with her, you are in the moon. The servants will not ever climb the stair, and should she come down, they scuttle away into corners like beetles until she passes. Beware of her, Sirit Byar!"

I heard Sirit Byar's scornful grunt next to me—after six years, there wasn't a grunt or a snort of his I couldn't translate. But I wasn't scornful, I'll tell you that much. I said I've never been frightened, and it's true, but madmen—madwomen—make me uneasy, if you like. Madwomen in the dark make me very uneasy. Sirit Byar pushed the door open. Just before we went inside, I looked back at Aung Jatt. He was standing exactly where we had left him, and he was laughing without making a sound.

It was a fine, proud house, certainly—and remember, I've slept in a palace. Felt bigger inside than outside somehow, and it felt *soft*, too—lots of thick Tahi'rak rugs and drapes and those buttery cushions they sew in Fors out of traders' old saddle-blankets. Hardly an inch of floor or wall showing: the whole place was made like a cradle, like a special box you keep something precious and breakable in. Servants slipped past us without a word, or anyway their shadows did, for I couldn't hear their footsteps, nor our own, come to that. I couldn't hear the front door swing shut, or any sound from the outside once it had. What I did hear was someone breathing. It wasn't Sirit Byar, and it wasn't me—I don't think either of us had breathed since we came through that door. Sirit Byar touched my shoulder and nodded me left, toward the stair. You'd expect a house like this to have a grand spiral stairway, but this was just a narrow little one, not room enough for the two of us to go abreast.

Sirit Byar had to hold the *kiit* tight against his side to keep it from hitting the railing. I followed him, not thinking too much, not feeling anything, because why not? Where else was I to go right then?

It was different on the second floor. Deepsea cold, it was, and thick with twilight, old, stale, mushy twilight filling our eyes and ears and nostrils, like when you get smothered in the bedding when you're asleep, and then that's all you can dream. The breathing was all around us now, no louder, but quickening, eager. There wasn't another sound anywhere in the world. Sirit Byar stopped on the landing. Clearly, loudly even, he said, "Jailly Doura."

The breathing never faltered. Sirit Byar said again, "Jailly Doura. I am here."

No answer. Where we stood, I could make out a chair, a wall, another chair, a gray face floating in the air, the gray mouth of a corridor. Sirit Byar looked left and right, trying to guess where the breathing might be coming from. My eyes were growing used to the dimness now—I saw that the floating face was a painting hanging on the wall, and I saw other paintings, and lamps and braziers as tall as me, taller, all unlit, and a great dark chandelier swinging overhead. The corridor lay straight ahead of us, with high double doors on either hand. Sirit Byar said, "This way," and went forward like a man moving in his own house in full day. I hurried after him, I didn't want to be left behind, left alone in the moon.

He never looked at any of the doors, only strode along until the corridor bent right and opened out into a kind of—what?—well, like an indoor courtyard, I suppose. There must have been an opening to the sky somewhere, because the twilight was more watery here, but I still couldn't see as far as the walls of the place, and the little warm night wind I felt on my face now and then made me wonder if it *had* any walls. There were a couple of benches, and there were pale statues in alcoves—and, of all the bloody things, a tree, set right into the floor, right in the middle of the room. A *sesao*, I think, or it might have been a red *mouri*, what do I know about trees? I certainly don't know how Aung Jatt ever watered and nourished the thing, but its trunk disappeared in darkness, and its branches reached out almost as far as the bench where Sirit Byar had calmly sat down and begun tuning the *kiit*. I stood. I wanted my feet under me in that house, I knew that much.

The breathing still sounded so close I thought I could feel it sometimes, and yet I couldn't even be sure where it was coming from. Sirit Byar looked up into the tree branches and said, "Do you remember this song, Jailly Doura?" He touched the *kiit* with the heel of his hand, to get a sort of deep sigh out of all the strings, and began to sing.

I knew the song. So do you—if there's one song of Sirit Byar's that the wind carried everywhere, and that clung where it landed like a cocklebur, it was "Where's My Shoe?" Right, that funny, ridiculous song about a man who keeps losing things—his shoe, his wig, his spectacles, his false teeth, his balls, his wife—and that's the way people sing it in the taverns. But the melody's a sad one, if you whistle it over slowly, and people don't always sing the very last verses, because those are about misplacing your faith, your heart. Nobody ever sang it the way Sirit Byar sang it that night, quiet and gentle, with the *kiit* bouncing happily along, running circles all around the words. I can't listen to it now, never, not since that time.

He spoke to the tree again, saying, "Do you remember? You always liked that song—listen to this now." And his voice, that damn fisherman's growl of his, sounded like a boy's voice, and you'd have thought he'd never trusted anyone with his songs before.

He sang "The Woodcutter's Wife" next, that odd thing about an old woman who doesn't want to die without hearing someone, anyone, say, "You're my dear friend, and I love you." Anyway, she goes from her husband to her children, then to her brothers and sisters, and finally hears the words from a tired village whore, who'll say anything for money. And yet, when she does say it for money, somehow it comes out true, and the old woman dies happy. Not a song I'd choose, was it me trying to woo a madwoman out of her tree, but he knew what he was doing. About songs, he always knew what he was doing.

I think it was "The Good Folk" next, and then "The Old Priest and the Old God." By then it had gotten so dark in that strange courtyard that I couldn't see the tree, let alone Sirit Byar. He took flint and steel out of one pocket, a candle end from the other, and made a little sputtering light that he stood up on the bench beside him. He sang the song about the lady made out of flowers, and he sang "Thou," the one he wrote for his sister, and even my favorite, the one about the man and the Fox in the Moon. Never moved from where he sat in his tatter of candlelight, no more than I did. I just stood very still and listened to him singing, old song on new, one after another. I could hear Jailly Doura's heart beating somewhere near, as well as her breathing, both quick as a bird's— or a *shukri's*—and one time I was sure I could smell her, like faraway water. Twice Sirit Byar asked, "Will you show yourself, Jailly Doura?" but no chance of that. So he just sang on to someone he couldn't see, making his magic, drawing her in through the dark, so slowly, the way you can sometimes charm a dream into letting you remember it. That's magic, too.

Then he sang the lullaby. The one he'd been practicing every night for two years. I remember a bit of it, just a little.

> *Don't fall asleep,*
> *don't close your eyes—*
> *everything happens at night.*
> *Don't you sleep—*
> *as soon as you slumber,*
> *the sun starts to ripen,*
> *the flowers tell stories....*

She made a sound. Not a moan, not a cry, not anything with a name or a shape. Just put down that she tried very hard not to make it. It came out of her anyway.

When she hit him, she knocked the *kiit* out of his hands. That time he couldn't save it—rugs or no rugs, I heard it crack and split, heard eighteen double courses yowl against stone. I just caught a lightning flash of her in the candlelight: matted gray hair flying, eyes like gashes in dead flesh, gaunt arms flailing out of control, beating her own head as much as Sirit Byar's. Something bright flickered in her hands against his throat. The candle fell over and went out.

The darkness was so heavy, I felt myself bending under it. I said, "Jailly Doura, don't hurt him. Please, don't hurt him." I could hear the *kiit* strings still thrashing and jangling faintly, but nothing more, not even the dreadful *breathing*. Nothing more until Sirit Byar began to sing again.

> *Don't you sleep—*
> *the marsh-goats are singing,*
> *the fish are all dancing,*
> *the river asks riddles....*

You couldn't have told that he was singing past a dagger, or a broken piece of glass, or whatever she had been saving for him all this long while. He sounded the way he always did—gruff and south coast, and a little slower than the beat, and not caring about anything in the world but the song. He might have been back in the Miller's Joy, sitting on a table, singing it to fighting, bawling sots; he might have been trying it over to himself as we trudged down some evening road looking for a place to sleep. He sounded like Sirit Byar.

He sang it through to the end, the lullaby, so I knew she hadn't killed him yet, but that was all I did know. I couldn't see anything, I couldn't hear anything, except the footsteps beginning to shuffle slowly toward me. They dragged a little, as though she'd somehow taken on Sirit Byar's limp. I'd have run—all bloody *right*, of course I'd have run, that's just good sense, that's different from fear—but in that crushing dark the steps were coming from everywhere, the way the breathing had been at first. My knees wouldn't hold me up. I sat down and waited.

Close to, she didn't smell like a distant river at all, but like any old hill woman, like my father. She smelled lifelong tired, lifelong dirty, she smelled of clothes sweated in and slept in until they've just *died*, you understand me? I know that smell; I was born and raised to it, and I'd smell just like that now if I hadn't run off with Sirit Byar. What chilled my bowels was the notion that a wealthy madwoman, prowling a grand house among terrified servants, should smell like home.

When I felt her standing over me, with the stiff, cold ends of that hair trailing across the back of my neck, I said loudly, "I am Mircha Del, of Davlo. You should know that if you're going to kill me." Then I just sat there, feeling out with my skin for whatever she had in her hand.

Her breath on my cheek was raw and old and stagnant, a sick animal's breath. I closed my eyes, even in the darkness, the way you do when you're hoping the *sheknath* or the rock-*targ* will think you're dead. I was ready for her teeth, for her long, jagged nails, but the next thing I felt was her arms around me.

She rocked me, chicken-wrist. Jailly Doura held me in her sad, skinny arms and bumped me back and forth against her breast, pushing and tugging on me as though she were trying to loosen a tree stump in the ground. Likely she didn't remember at all how you rock somebody, but then I don't remember anybody ever rocking me in my life, except her, so I wouldn't ever have known the right way. I did have an idea that it was supposed to be more comfortable, but it wasn't bad. And the breath wasn't so awful, either, when you got used to it, nor that hair all down my face. What was bad was the little whimpering sound, so soft that I didn't truly hear it but felt it in my body, the broken crooning that never quite became tears but just shivered and shivered on the edge. That was bad, but I kept my eyes closed tight and helped her rock me, and Sirit Byar began to sing again.

It doesn't matter what he sang. I know some of the songs in my bones to this day—bloody well *should*, after all—and there were others I'd never heard before and never will again, no matter. What matters is that he sang all night long, sitting by his shattered *kiit*, with a madwoman's grieving for his only applause. Jailly Doura went on rocking me in her arms, and Sirit Byar sang about merrows and farmwives and wandering Narsai tinkers, and I'll be damned if I didn't fall off to sleep—only a little, only for a moment now and then—as though they were really my parents putting me to bed, just the way they did every night. And stone Azdak only knows what Aung Jatt thought was going on upstairs.

Dawn came suddenly, or maybe I'd been dozing again. It was like staring through rain, but I could see the courtyard around us—there were walls, of course, and a few narrow windows, and the tree wasn't *that* big—and I could see Sirit Byar, looking a bit smaller than usual himself, and white as his own hair in that rainy light. Jailly Doura was still holding me, but not rocking anymore, and sometime in the night she'd stopped making that terrible silent sound. If I turned my head very slowly and carefully, I could see most of one side of her face—a thin, lined, worn face it was, but the nose was strong and the mouth wasn't a dead slash at all, but full and tender. Her hair was a forsaken birds' nest, thick with mess—well, about like mine, as you can see. Her eyes were closed.

Sirit Byar stood up. His voice was a rag of itself, but he spoke out loudly, not to Jailly Doura this time, nor to me, but to *someone*. I couldn't tell where he was looking, what he was seeing. He said, "This is my last song. Take it. I make this bargain of my own will. I, Sirit Byar." He stood silent for a moment, and then he nodded once, slowly, as though he'd had his reply. Oh, chicken-wrist, I can still see him.

I'm not going to sing you the whole song, that last one. I could, but I'm not going to. This one dies with me, it's supposed to. But this is the ending:

> *Merchant, street girl, beggar, yeoman,*
> *king or common, man or woman,*
> *only two things make us human—*
> *sorrow and love, sorrow and love....*
>
> *Songs and fame are vain endeavor—*
> *only two things fail us never,*
> *only two things last forever—*
> *sorrow and love, sorrow and love....*

By the time he finished, it was light enough that I could see Aung Jatt standing in the courtyard entrance. Behind me Jailly Doura stirred and sighed, and as I turned my head she opened her eyes again. But they weren't the same eyes. They were gray and wide and full of surprise, curiosity, whatever you want—they were a young woman's eyes in a tired grown face. Maybe I had eyes like that when I was first traveling with Sirit Byar, but I doubt it. She said softly, just the way he'd said it to me, "There you are."

And Sirit Byar answered her, "Here I am."

Careful now, both of us, chicken-wrist, you and me. Jailly Doura looked down at me in her arms and said—said *what*? She said, "Are you my daughter, little one?"

"No," I said. "No, no, I'm not. I wish I were."

Then I was horribly afraid that I might have lost her again, saying that, driven her right back to where she'd been, but she only smiled and touched my lips and whispered, "Ah, I know. I was just hoping for a moment, one last, last time. Never mind. You have a sweet face."

I do not have a sweet face. There are ugly people who have sweet faces, much good may it do them in this world. I have the face I want, a dirty, mean, wild animal's face that makes people leave me alone. Fine. Fine, I wouldn't have it different. But if ever I wanted in my life to have sweetness that somebody could see, it would have been then. I stood up, cramped and cranky, and helped Jailly Doura to rise.

She was small, really, a tiny gray barefoot person in a mucky ruin of a gown that must have cost someone a few gold *lotis* a long time ago, and that a beggar wouldn't have wiped his nose on now. She was as shaky on her feet as a newborn marsh-goat, but she wasn't mad. I looked over toward Aung Jatt, trying to beckon him over to her, but he was staring at Sirit Byar, who had stumbled down to one knee. Jailly Doura was by him before I was. She knelt before him and took his face between her hands. "Not so soon," she said. I remember that. She said, "Not so soon, I'll not have it. I will not, my dear, no. Do you hear me, Sirit Byar?"

You see, she knew better than I what he'd done. He had given up his last song to the gods, the Other Folk, whatever you people call them. And a bard's last song has power, a last song is always answered, as this one was—but what becomes of the bard when the song is over? Sirit Byar's face was a shrunken white mask, but his eyes were open and steady. He said, "Forgive me, Jailly Doura."

"Not if you leave us," she answered him. "Not if you dare leave now." But there was no anger in her voice, and no hope either. Sirit Byar made that half-grunt, half-snort sound that he always made when people were being a little too much for him. He said, "Well, forgive me or no, you are well, and I've done what was for me to do. Now I'm weary."

I wanted to touch him. I wanted to hold him the way Jailly Doura had held me all night, but I just stood with my fingers in my mouth, like a scared baby. Sirit Byar smiled his almost-smile at me and whispered, "I'm sorry the *kiit* broke, big girl. I wanted you to have it. Good-bye."

And he was gone, so. Aung Jatt closed his eyes himself, and began to weep. I remember. Jailly Doura didn't, and I didn't, but old Aung Jatt cried and cried.

I buried him myself, and the shards of the *kiit* with him, under the threshold of the house, as I'd done with my father. The others wanted to help me, but I wouldn't let them. When I was finished, I scratched a picture of Azdak, god of wanderers, on the stone stair, and I walked away. So now you know where Sirit Byar lies.

There's no more worth the telling. Aung Jatt and Jailly Doura wanted me to stay with them as long as I liked, forever, but I only passed a few days at the house with them. What I mostly remember is washing and washing Jailly Doura's long gray-black hair in her bath, as the Queen's ladies used to do with me, four of them at a time to hold me in the tub. I always hated it, and I've not put up with it since, but it's different when you're doing it for someone else. You don't wash fifteen, sixteen years of lunatic despair away in three days, but by the time I left, Jailly Doura could anyway peep in a mirror and start to recognize the handsome, dignified mistress of a great house, with servants underfoot like *dai-beetles* and a husband who looked at her like sunrise. I don't begrudge it—whatever was hers she'd paid double-dear price for it, and double again. But I'd have liked Sirit Byar to see her this way, even once.

When I left, she walked with me down to the two great stones where we'd first met Aung Jatt, a hundred years ago. She didn't bother with saying, "Come back and visit us," and I didn't bother promising. Instead she took both my hands and swung them, the way children do, and she just said, "I would have been proud if you had been my daughter."

I didn't know how to answer. I kissed her hands, which I've never done with anybody except the Queen, and you have to do that. Then I swung Sirit Byar's old sea-bag to my shoulder, and I started off alone. I didn't look back, but Jailly Doura called after me, "So would *he* have been proud. Remember, Mircha Del."

And I have remembered, and that's why the fit took me to have someone set it all down, the only true tale of Sirit Byar you're ever likely to hear. No, I told you I don't want it; what good's your scribble to me? I can't read it—and besides, I was there. Keep it for yourself, keep it for anyone who wants to know a little of what he was. Bad enough they mess up his songs, let them get *something* the right way round, anyway. Farewell, my chicken-wrist—here's your twelve coppers, and another for the sweet way you blush. There's an ore barge tied up at Grebak, waiting for a good woman to handle the sweep, if I'm there by tomorrow eve.

Lila the Werewolf

Lila Braun had been living with Farrell for three weeks before he found out she was a werewolf. They had met at a party when the moon was a few nights past the full, and by the time it had withered to the shape of a lemon Lila had moved her suitcase, her guitar, and her Ewan MacColl records two blocks north and four blocks west to Farrell's apartment on Ninety-eighth Street. Girls sometimes happened to Farrell like that.

One evening, Lila wasn't in when Farrell came home from work at the bookstore. She had left a note on the table, under a can of tuna fish. The note said that she had gone up to the Bronx to have dinner with her mother, and would probably be spending the night there. The coleslaw in the refrigerator should be finished before it went bad.

Farrell ate the tuna fish and gave the coleslaw to Grunewald. Grunewald was a half-grown Russian wolfhound, the color of sour milk. He looked like a goat, and had no outside interests except shoes. Farrell was taking care of him for a girl who was away in Europe for the summer. She sent Grunewald a tape recording of her voice every week.

Farrell went to a movie with a friend, and to the West End afterward for beer. Then he walked home alone under the full moon, which was red and yellow. He reheated the morning coffee, played a record, read through a week-old "News Of The Week In Review" section of the Sunday Times, and finally took Grunewald up to the roof for the night, as he always did. The dog had been accustomed to sleep in the same bed with his mistress, and the point was not negotiable. Grunewald mooed and scrabbled and butted all the way, but Farrell pushed him out among the looming chimneys and ventilators and slammed the door. Then he came back downstairs and went to bed.

He slept very badly. Grunewald's baying woke him twice; and there was something else that brought him half out of bed, thirsty and lonely, with his sinuses full and the night swaying like a curtain as the figures of his dream scurried offstage. Grunewald seemed to have gone off the air—perhaps it was the silence that had awakened him. Whatever the reason, he never really got back to sleep.

He was lying on his back, watching a chair with his clothes on it becoming a chair again, when the wolf came in through the open window. It landed lightly in the middle of the room and stood there for a moment, breathing quickly, with its ears back. There was blood on the wolf's teeth and tongue, and blood on its chest.

Farrell, whose true gift was for acceptance, especially in the morning, accepted the idea that there was a wolf in his bedroom and lay quite still, closing his eyes as the grim, black-lipped head swung towards him. Having once worked at a zoo, he was able to recognize the beast as a Central European subspecies: smaller and lighter-boned than the northern timber wolf variety, lacking the thick, ruffy mane at the shoulders and having a more pointed nose and ears. His own pedantry always delighted him, even at the worst moments.

Blunt claws clicking on the linoleum, then silent on the throw rug by the bed. Something warm and slow splashed down on his shoulder, but he never moved. The wild smell of the wolf was over him, and that did frighten him at last to be in the same room with that smell and the Miro prints on the walls. Then he felt the sunlight on his eyelids, and at the same moment he heard the wolf moan softly and deeply.

The sound was not repeated, but the breath on his face was suddenly sweet and smoky, dizzyingly familiar after the other. He opened his eyes and saw Lila. She was sitting naked on the edge of the bed, smiling, with her hair down.

"Hello, baby," she said. "Move over, baby. I came home."

Farrell's gift was for acceptance. He was perfectly willing to believe that he had dreamed the wolf; to believe Lila's story of boiled chicken and bitter arguments and sleeplessness on Tremont Avenue; and to forget that her first caress had been to bite him on the shoulder, hard enough so that the blood crusting there as he got up and made breakfast might very well be his own. But then he left the coffee perking and went up to the roof to get Grunewald. He found the dog sprawled in a grove of TV antennas, looking more like a goat than ever, with his throat torn out. Farrell had never actually seen an animal with its throat torn out.

The coffeepot was still chuckling when he came back into the apartment, which struck him as very odd. You could have either werewolves or Pyrex nine-cup percolators in the world, but not both, surely. He told Lila, watching her face. She was a small girl, not really pretty, but with good eyes and a lovely mouth, and with a curious sullen gracefulness that had been the first thing to speak to Farrell at the party. When he told her how Grunewald had looked, she shivered all over, once.

"Ugh!" she said, wrinkling her lips back from her neat white teeth. "Oh baby, how awful. Poor Grunewald. Oh, poor Barbara." Barbara was Grunewald's owner.

"Yeah," Farrell said. "Poor Barbara, making her little tapes in Saint-Tropez." He could not look away from Lila's face.

She said, "Wild dogs. Not really wild, I mean, but with owners. You hear about it sometimes, how a pack of them get together and attack children and things, running through the streets. Then they go home and eat their Dog Yummies. The scary thing is that they probably live right around here. Everybody on the block seems to have a dog. God, that's scary. Poor Grunewald."

"They didn't tear him up much," Farrell said. "It must have been just for the fun of it. And the blood. I didn't know dogs killed for the blood. He didn't have any blood left."

The tip of Lila's tongue appeared between her lips, in the unknowing reflex of a fondled cat. As evidence, it wouldn't have stood up even in old Salem; but Farrell knew the truth then, beyond laziness or rationalization, and went on buttering toast for Lila. Farrell had nothing against werewolves, and he had never liked Grunewald.

He told his friend Ben Kassoy about Lila when they met in the Automat for lunch. He had to shout it over the clicking and rattling all around them, but the people sitting six inches away on either hand never looked up. New Yorkers never eavesdrop. They hear only what they simply cannot help hearing.

Ben said, "I told you about Bronx girls. You better come stay at my place for a few days."

Farrell shook his head. "No, that's silly. I mean, it's only Lila. If she were going to hurt me, she could have done it last night. Besides, it won't happen again for a month. There has to be a full moon."

His friend stared at him. "So what? What's that got to do with anything? You going to go on home as though nothing had happened?"

"Not as though nothing had happened," Farrell said lamely. "The thing is, it's still only Lila, not Lon Chaney or somebody. Look, she goes to her psychiatrist three afternoons a week, and she's got her guitar lesson one night a week, and her pottery class one night, and she cooks eggplant maybe twice a week. She calls her mother every Friday night, and one night a month she turns into a wolf. You see what I'm getting at? It's still Lila, whatever she does, and I just can't get terribly shook about it. A little bit, sure, because what the hell. But I don't know. Anyway, there's no mad rush about it. I'll talk to her when the thing comes up in conversation, just naturally. It's okay."

Ben said, "God damn. You see why nobody has any respect for liberals anymore? Farrell, I know you. You're just scared of hurting her feelings."

"Well, it's that too," Farrell agreed, a little embarrassed. "I hate confrontations. If I break up with her now, she'll think I'm doing it because she's a werewolf. It's awkward, it feels nasty and middle-class. I should have broken up with her the first time I met her mother, or the second time she served the eggplant. Her mother, boy, there's the real werewolf, there's somebody I'd wear wolfsbane against, that woman. Damn, I wish I hadn't found out. I don't think I've ever found out anything about people that I was the better for knowing."

Ben walked all the way back to the bookstore with him, arguing. It touched Farrell, because Ben hated to walk. Before they parted, Ben suggested, "At least you could try some of that stuff you were talking about, the wolfsbane. There's garlic, too—you put some in a little bag and wear it around your neck. Don't laugh, man. If there's such a thing as werewolves, the other stuff must be real, too. Cold iron, silver, oak, running water—"

"I'm not laughing at you," Farrell said, but he was still grinning. "Lila's shrink says she has a rejection thing, very deep-seated, take us years to break through all that scar tissue. Now if I start walking around wearing amulets and mumbling in Latin every time she looks at me, who knows how far it'll set her back? Listen, I've done some things I'm not proud of, but I don't want to mess with anyone's analysis. That's the sin against God." He sighed and slapped Ben lightly on the arm. "Don't worry about it. We'll work it out, I'll talk to her."

But between that night and the next full moon, he found no good, casual way of bringing the subject up. Admittedly, he did not try as hard as he might have: it was true that he feared confrontations more than he feared werewolves, and he would have found it almost as difficult to talk to Lila about her guitar playing, or her pots, or the political arguments she got into at parties. "The thing is," he said to Ben, "it's sort of one more little weakness not to take advantage of. In a way."

They made love often that month. The smell of Lila flowered in the bedroom, where the smell of the wolf still lingered almost visibly, and both of them were wild, heavy zoo smells, warm and raw and fearful, the sweeter for being savage. Farrell held Lila in his arms and knew what she was, and he was always frightened; but he would not have let her go if she had turned into a wolf again as he held her. It was a relief to peer at her while she slept and see how stubby and childish her fingernails were, or that the skin around her mouth was rashy because she had been snacking on chocolate. She loved secret sweets, but they always betrayed her.

It's only Lila after all, he would think as he drowsed off. Her mother used to hide the candy, but Lila always found it. Now she's a big girl, neither married nor in graduate school, but living in sin with an Irish musician, and she can have all the candy she wants. What kind of a werewolf is that. Poor Lila, practicing *Who killed Davey Moore? Why did he die?...*

▲▼▲

The note said that she would be working late at the magazine, on layout, and might have to be there all night. Farrell put on about four feet of Telemann laced with Django Reinhardt, took down *The Golden Bough*, and settled into a chair by the window. The moon shone in at him, bright and thin and sharp as the lid of a tin can, and it did not seem to move at all as he dozed and woke.

Lila's mother called several times during the night, which was interesting. Lila still picked up her mail and most messages at her old apartment, and her two roommates covered for her when necessary, but Farrell was absolutely certain that her mother knew she was living with him. Farrell was an expert on mothers. Mrs. Braun called him Joe each time she called and that made him wonder, for he knew she hated him. Does she suspect that we share a secret? Ah, poor Lila.

The last time the telephone woke him, it was still dark in the room, but the traffic lights no longer glittered through rings of mist, and the cars made a different sound on the warming pavement. A man was saying clearly in the street, "Well, *I'd* shoot'm. *I'd* shoot'm." Farrell let the telephone ring ten times before he picked it up.

"Let me talk to Lila," Mrs. Braun said.

"She isn't here." What if the sun catches her, what if she turns back to herself in front of a cop, or a bus driver, or a couple of nuns going to early Mass? "Lila isn't here, Mrs. Braun."

"I have reason to believe that's not true." The fretful, muscular voice had dropped all pretense of warmth. "I want to talk to Lila."

Farrell was suddenly dry-mouthed and shivering with fury. It was her choice of words that did it. "Well, I have reason to believe you're a suffocating old bitch and a bourgeois Stalinist. How do you like them apples, Mrs. B?" As though his anger had summoned her, the wolf was standing two feet away from him. Her coat was dark and lank with sweat, and yellow saliva was mixed with the blood that strung from her jaws. She looked at Farrell and growled far away in her throat.

"Just a minute," he said. He covered the receiver with his palm. "It's for you," he said to the wolf. "It's your mother." The wolf made a pitiful sound, almost inaudible, and scuffed at the floor. She was plainly exhausted. Mrs. Braun pinged in Farrell's ear like a bug against a lighted window. "What, what? Hello, what is this? Listen, you put Lila on the phone right now. Hello? I want to talk to Lila. I know she's there."

Farrell hung up just as the sun touched a corner of the window. The wolf became Lila. As before, she only made one sound. The phone rang again, and she picked it up without a glance at Farrell. "Bernice?" Lila always called her mother by her first name. "Yes—no, no—yeah, I'm fine. I'm all right, I just forgot to call. No, I'm all right, will you listen? Bernice, there's no law that says you have to get hysterical. Yes, you are." She dropped down on the bed, groping under her pillow for cigarettes. Farrell got up and began to make coffee.

"Well, there was a little trouble," Lila was saying. "See, I went to the zoo, because I couldn't find—Bernice, I know, I *know*, but that was, what, three months ago. The thing is, I didn't think they'd have their horns so soon. Bernice, I had to, that's all. There'd only been a couple of cats and a—well, sure they chased me, but I—well, Momma, Bernice, what did you want me to do? Just what did you want me to do? You're always so dramatic—why do I shout? I shout because I can't get you to listen to me any other way. You remember what Dr. Schechtman said—what? No, I told you, I just forgot to call. No, that is the reason, that's the real and only reason. Well, whose fault is that? What? Oh, Bernice. Jesus Christ, Bernice. All right, *how* is it Dad's fault?"

She didn't want the coffee, or any breakfast, but she sat at the table in his bathrobe and drank milk greedily. It was the first time he had ever seen her drink milk. Her face was sandy-pale, and her eyes were red. Talking to her mother left her looking as though she had actually gone ten rounds with the woman. Farrell asked, "How long has it been happening?"

"Nine years," Lila said. "Since I hit puberty. First day, cramps; the second day, this. My introduction to womanhood." She snickered and spilled her milk. "I want some more," she said. "Got to get rid of that taste."

"Who knows about it?" he asked. "Pat and Janet?" They were the two girls she had been rooming with.

"God, no. I'd never tell them. I've never told a girl. Bernice knows, of course, and Dr. Schechtman—he's my head doctor. And you now. That's all." Farrell waited. She was a bad liar, and only did it to heighten the effect of the truth. "Well, there was Mickey," she said. "The guy I told you about the first night, you remember? It doesn't matter. He's an acidhead in Vancouver, of all places. He'll never tell anybody."

He thought: I wonder if any girl has ever talked about me in that sort of voice. I doubt it, offhand. Lila said, "It wasn't too hard to keep it a secret. I missed a lot of things. Like I never could go to the riding camp, and I still want to. And the senior play, when I was in high school. They picked me to play the girl in *Liliom*, but then they changed the evening, and I had to say I was sick. And the winter's bad, because the sun sets so early. But actually, it's been a lot less trouble than my goddamn allergies." She made a laugh, but Farrell did not respond.

"Dr. Schechtman says it's a sex thing," she offered. "He says it'll take years and years to cure it. Bernice thinks I should go to someone else, but I don't want to be one of those women who runs around changing shrinks like hair colors. Pat went through five of them in a month one time. Joe, I wish you'd say something. Or just go away."

"Is it only dogs?" he asked. Lila's face did not change, but her chair rattled, and the milk went over again. Farrell said, "Answer me. Do you only kill dogs, and cats, and zoo animals?"

The tears began to come, heavy and slow, bright as knives in the morning sunlight. She could not look at him; and when she tried to speak she could only make creaking, cartilaginous sounds in her throat. "*You* don't know," she whispered at last. "You don't have any idea what it's like."

"That's true," he answered. He was always very fair about that particular point.

He took her hand, and then she really began to cry. Her sobs were horrible to hear, much more frightening to Farrell than any wolf noises. When he held her, she rolled in his arms like a stranded ship with the waves slamming into her. I always get the criers, he thought sadly. My girls always cry, sooner or later. But never for me.

"Don't leave me!" she wept. "I don't know why I came to live with you—I knew it wouldn't work—but don't leave me! There's just Bernice and Dr. Schechtman, and it's so lonely. I want somebody else, I get so lonely. Don't leave me, Joe. I love you, Joe. I love you."

She was patting his face as though she were blind. Farrell stroked her hair and kneaded the back of her neck, wishing that her mother would call again. He felt skilled and weary, and without desire. I'm doing it again, he thought. "I love you," Lila said. And he answered her, thinking, I'm doing it again. That's the great advantage of making the same mistake a lot of times. You come to know it, and you can study it and get inside it, really make it yours. It's the same good old mistake, except this time the girl's hang-up is different. But it's the same thing. I'm doing it again.

▲▼▲

The building superintendent was thirty or fifty: dark, thin, quick, and shivering. A Lithuanian or a Latvian, he spoke very little English. He smelled of black friction tape and stale water, and he was strong in the twisting way that a small, lean animal is strong. His eyes were almost purple, and they bulged a little, straining out—the terrible eyes of a herald angel stricken dumb. He roamed the basement all day, banging on pipes and taking the elevator apart.

The superintendent met Lila only a few hours after Farrell did; on that first night, when she came home with him. At the sight of her the little man jumped back, dropping the two-legged chair he was carrying. He promptly fell over it, and did not try to get up, but cowered there, clucking and gulping, trying to cross himself and make the sign of the horns at the same time. Farrell started to help him, but he screamed. They could hardly hear the sound.

It would have been merely funny and embarrassing, except for the fact that Lila was equally frightened of the superintendent, from that moment. She would not go down to the basement for any reason, nor would she enter or leave the house until she was satisfied that he was nowhere near. Farrell had thought then that she took the superintendent for a lunatic.

"I don't know how he knows," he said to Ben. "I guess if you believe in werewolves and vampires, you probably recognize them right away. I don't believe in them at all, and I live with one."

He lived with Lila all through the autumn and the winter. They went out together and came home, and her cooking improved slightly, and she gave up the guitar and got a kitten named Theodora. Sometimes she wept, but not often. She turned out not to be a real crier.

She told Dr. Schechtman about Farrell, and he said that it would probably be a very beneficial relationship for her. It wasn't, but it wasn't a particularly bad one either. Their lovemaking was usually good, though it bothered Farrell to suspect that it was the sense and smell of the Other that excited him. For the rest, they came near being friends. Farrell had known that he did not love Lila before he found out that she was a werewolf, and this made him feel a great deal easier about being bored with her.

"It'll break up by itself in the spring," he said, "like ice."

Ben asked, "What if it doesn't?" They were having lunch in the Automat again. "What'll you do if it just goes on?"

"It's not that easy." Farrell looked away from his friend and began to explore the mysterious, swampy innards of his beef pie. He said, "The trouble is that I know her. That was the real mistake. You shouldn't get to know people if you know you're not going to stay with them, one way or another. It's all right if you come and go in ignorance, but you shouldn't know them."

A week or so before the full moon, she would start to become nervous and strident, and this would continue until the day preceding her transformation. On that day, she was invariably loving, in the tender, desperate manner of someone who is going away; but the next day would see her silent, speaking only when she had to. She always had a cold on the last day, and looked grey and patchy and sick, but she usually went to work anyway.

Farrell was sure, though she never talked about it, that the change into wolf shape was actually peaceful for her, though the returning hurt. Just before moonrise she would take off her clothes and take the pins out of her hair, and stand waiting. Farrell never managed not to close his eyes when she dropped heavily down on all fours; but there was a moment before that when her face would grow a look that he never saw at any other time, except when they were making love. Each time he saw it, it struck him as a look of wondrous joy at not being Lila anymore.

"See, I know her," he tried to explain to Ben. "She only likes to go to color movies, because wolves can't see color. She can't stand the Modern Jazz Quartet, but that's all she plays the first couple of days afterward. Stupid things like that. Never gets high at parties, because she's afraid she'll start talking. It's hard to walk away, that's all. Taking what I know with me."

Ben asked, "Is she still scared of the super?"

"Oh, God," Farrell said. "She got his dog last time. It was a Dalmatian— good-looking animal. She didn't know it was his. He doesn't hide when he sees her now, he just gives her a look like a stake through the heart. That man is a really classy hater, a natural. I'm scared of him myself." He stood up and began to pull on his overcoat. "I wish he'd get turned on to her mother. Get some practical use out of him. Did I tell you she wants me to call her Bernice?"

Ben said, "Farrell, if I were you, I'd leave the country. I would."

They went out into the February drizzle that sniffled back and forth between snow and rain. Farrell did not speak until they reached the corner where he turned towards the bookstore. Then he said very softly, "Damn, you have to be so careful. Who wants to know what people turn into?"

May came, and a night when Lila once again stood naked at the window, waiting for the moon. Farrell fussed with dishes and garbage bags and fed the cat. These moments were always awkward. He had just asked her, "You want to save what's left of the rice?" when the telephone rang.

It was Lila's mother. She called two and three times a week now. "This is Bernice. How's my Irisher this evening?"

"I'm fine, Bernice," Farrell said. Lila suddenly threw back her head and drew a heavy, whining breath. The cat hissed silently and ran into the bathroom.

"I called to inveigle you two uptown this Friday," Mrs. Braun said. "A couple of old friends are coming over, and I know if I don't get some young people in we'll just sit around and talk about what went wrong with the Progressive Party. The Old Left. So if you could sort of sweet-talk our girl into spending an evening in Squaresville—"

"I'll have to check with Lila." She's *doing* it, he thought, that terrible woman. Every time I talk to her, I sound married. I see what she's doing, but she goes right ahead anyway. He said, "I'll talk to her in the morning." Lila struggled in the moonlight, between dancing and drowning.

"Oh," Mrs. Braun said. "Yes, of course. Have her call me back." She sighed. "It's such a comfort to me to know you're there. Ask her if I should fix a fondue?"

Lila made a handsome wolf: tall and broad-chested for a female, moving as easily as water sliding over stone. Her coat was dark brown, showing red in the proper light, and there were white places on her breast. She had pale green eyes, the color of the sky when a hurricane is coming. Usually she was gone as soon as the changing was over, for she never cared for him to see her in her wolf form. But tonight she came slowly towards him, walking in a strange way, with her hindquarters almost dragging. She was making a high, soft sound, and her eyes were not focusing on him.

"What is it?" he asked foolishly. The wolf whined and skulked under the table, rubbing against his leg. Then she lay on her belly and rolled and as she did so the sound grew in her throat until it became an odd, sad, thin cry; not a hunting howl, but a shiver of longing turned into breath. "Jesus, don't do that!" Farrell gasped. But she sat up and howled again, and a dog answered her from somewhere near the river. She wagged her tail and whimpered.

Farrell said, "The super'll be up here in two minutes flat. What's the matter with you?" He heard footsteps and low frightened voices in the apartment above them. Another dog howled, this one nearby, and the wolf wriggled a little way towards the window on her haunches, like a baby, scooting. She looked at him over her shoulder, shuddering violently. On an impulse, he picked up the phone and called her mother.

Watching the wolf as she rocked and slithered and moaned, he described her actions to Mrs. Braun. "I've never seen her like this," he said. "I don't know what's the matter with her."

"Oh, my God," Mrs. Braun whispered. She told him.

When he was silent, she began to speak very rapidly. "It hasn't happened for such a long time. Schechtman gives her pills, but she must have run out and forgotten—she's always been like that, since she was little. All the thermos bottles she used to leave on the school bus, and every week her piano music—"

"I wish you'd told me before," he said. He was edging very cautiously towards the open window. The pupils of the wolf's eyes were pulsing with her quick breaths.

"It isn't a thing you tell people!" Lila's mother wailed in his ear. "How do you think it was for me when she brought her first little boyfriend—" Farrell dropped the phone and sprang for the window. He had the inside track, and he might have made it, but she turned her head and snarled so wildly that he fell back. When he reached the window, she was already two fire-escape landings below, and there was eager yelping waiting for her in the street.

Dangling and turning just above the floor, Mrs. Braun heard Farrell's distant yell, followed immediately by a heavy thumping on the door. A strange, tattered voice was shouting unintelligibly beyond the knocking. Footsteps crashed by the receiver and the door opened.

"My dog, my dog!" the strange voice mourned. "My dog, my dog, my dog!"

"I'm sorry about your dog," Farrell said. "Look, please go away. I've got work to do."

"I got work," the voice said. "I know my work." It climbed and spilled into another language, out of which English words jutted like broken bones. "Where is she? Where is she? She kill my dog."

"She's not here." Farrell's own voice changed on the last word. It seemed a long time before he said, "You'd better put that away."

Mrs. Braun heard the howl as clearly as though the wolf were running beneath her own window: lonely and insatiable, with a kind of gasping laughter in it. The other voice began to scream. Mrs. Braun caught the phrase *silver bullet* several times. The door slammed; then opened and slammed again.

▲▼▲

Farrell was the only man of his own acquaintance who was able to play back his dreams while he was having them: to stop them in mid-flight, no matter how fearful they might be—or how lovely—and run them over and over studying them in his sleep, until the most terrifying reel became at once utterly harmless and unbearably familiar. This night that he spent running after Lila was like that.

He would find them congregated under the marquee of an apartment house, or romping around the moonscape of a construction site: ten or fifteen males of all races, creeds, colors, and previous conditions of servitude; whining and yapping, pissing against tires, inhaling indiscriminately each other and the lean, grinning bitch they surrounded. She frightened them, for she growled more wickedly than coyness demanded, and where she snapped, even in play, bone showed. Still they tumbled on her and over her, biting her neck and ears in their turn; and she snarled but she did not run away.

Never, at least, until Farrell came charging upon them, shrieking like any cuckold, kicking at the snuffling lovers. Then she would turn and race off into the spring dark, with her thin, dreamy howl floating behind her like the train of a smoky gown. The dogs followed, and so did Farrell, calling and cursing. They always lost him quickly, that jubilant marriage procession, leaving him stumbling down rusty iron ladders into places where he fell over garbage cans. Yet he would come upon them as inevitably in time, loping along Broadway or trotting across Columbus Avenue towards the Park; he would hear them in the tennis courts near the river, breaking down the nets over Lila and her moment's Ares. There were dozens of them now, coming from all directions. They stank of their joy, and he threw stones at them and shouted, and they ran.

And the wolf ran at their head, on sidewalks and on wet grass; her tail waving contentedly, but her eyes still hungry, and her howl growing ever more warning than wistful. Farrell knew that she must have blood before sunrise, and that it was both useless and dangerous to follow her. But the night wound and unwound itself, and he knew the same things over and over, and ran down the same streets, and saw the same couples walk wide of him, thinking he was drunk.

Mrs. Braun kept leaping out of a taxi that pulled up next to him; usually at corners where the dogs had just piled by, knocking over the crates stacked in market doorways and spilling the newspapers at the subway kiosks. Standing in broccoli, in black taffeta, with a front like a ferry-boat—yet as lean in the hips as her wolf-daughter—with her plum-colored hair all loose, one arm lifted, and her orange mouth pursed in a bellow, she was no longer Bernice but a wronged fertility goddess getting set to blast the harvest. "We've got to split up!" she would roar at Farrell, and each time it sounded like a sound idea. Yet he looked for her whenever he lost Lila's trail, because she never did.

The superintendent kept turning up too, darting after Farrell out of alleys or cellar entrances, or popping from the freight elevators that load through the sidewalk. Farrell would hear his numberless passkeys clicking on the flat piece of wood tucked into his belt.

"You see her? You see her, the wolf, kill my dog?" Under the fat, ugly moon, the Army .45 glittered and trembled like his own mad eyes.

"Mark with a cross." He would pat the barrel of his gun and shake it under Farrell's nose like a maraca. "Mark with a cross, bless by a priest. Three silver bullets. She kill my dog."

Lila's voice would come sailing to them then, from up in Harlem or away near Lincoln Center, and the little man would whirl and dash down into the earth, disappearing into the crack between two slabs of sidewalk. Farrell understood quite clearly that the superintendent was hunting Lila underground, using the keys that only superintendents have to take elevators down to the black sub-sub-basements, far below the bicycle rooms and the wet, shaking laundry rooms, and below the furnace rooms, below the passages walled with electricity meters and roofed with burly steam pipes; down to the realms where the great dim water mains roll like whales, and the gas lines hump and preen, down where the roots of the apartment houses fade together, and so along under the city, scrabbling through secret ways with silver bullets, and his keys rapping against the piece of wood. He never saw Lila, but he was never very far behind her.

Cutting across parking lots, pole-vaulting between locked bumpers, edging and dancing his way through fluorescent gaggles of haughty children; leaping uptown like a salmon against the current of the theatre crowds; walking quickly past the random killing faces that floated down the night tide like unexploded mines, and especially avoiding the crazy faces that wanted to tell him what it was like to be crazy—so Farrell pursued Lila Braun, of Tremont Avenue and CCNY, in the city all night long. Nobody offered to help him, or tried to head off the dangerous-looking bitch bounding along with the delirious gaggle of admirers streaming after her; but then, the dogs had to fight through the same clenched legs and vengeful bodies that Farrell did. The crowds slowed Lila down, but he felt relieved whenever she turned towards the emptier streets. *She must have blood soon, somewhere.*

Farrell's dreams eventually lost their clear edge after he played them back a certain number of times, and so it was with the night. The full

moon skidded down the sky, thinning like a tatter of butter in a skil-
let, and remembered scenes began to fold sloppily into each other. The
sound of Lila and the dogs grew fainter whichever way he followed.
Mrs. Braun blinked on and off at longer intervals; and in dark doorways
and under subway gratings, the superintendent burned like a corposant,
making the barrel of his pistol run rainbow. At last he lost Lila for good,
and with that it seemed that he woke.

It was still night, but not dark, and he was walking slowly home on
Riverside Drive through a cool, grainy fog. The moon had set, but the
river was strangely bright: glittering grey as far up as the Bridge, where
headlights left shiny, wet paths like snails. There was no one else on the
street. "Dumb broad," he said aloud. "The hell with it. She wants to mess
around, let her mess around." He wondered whether werewolves could
have cubs, and what sort of cubs they might be. Lila must have turned
on the dogs by now, for the blood. Poor dogs, he thought. They were all
so dirty and innocent and happy with her.

"A moral lesson for all of us," he announced sententiously. "Don't
fool with strange, eager ladies, they'll kill you." He was a little hysterical.
Then, two blocks ahead of him, he saw the gaunt shape in the grey light
of the river; alone now, and hurrying. Farrell did not call to her, but as
soon as he began to run, the wolf wheeled and faced him. Even at that
distance, her eyes were stained and streaked and wild. She showed all
the teeth on one side of her mouth, and she growled like fire.

Farrell trotted steadily towards her, crying, "Go home, go home! Lila,
you dummy, get on home, it's morning!" She growled terribly, but when
Farrell was less than a block away she turned again and dashed across
the street, heading for West End Avenue. Farrell said, "Good girl, that's
it," and limped after her.

In the hours before sunrise on West End Avenue, many people
came out to walk their dogs. Farrell had done it often enough with poor
Grunewald to know many of the dawn walkers by sight, and some to
talk to. A fair number of them were whores and homosexuals, both of
whom always seem to have dogs in New York. Quietly, almost always
alone, they drifted up and down the Nineties, piloted by their small,
fussy beasts, but moving in a kind of fugitive truce with the city and
the night that was ending. Farrell sometimes fancied that they were all
asleep, and that this hour was the only true rest they ever got.

He recognized Robie by his two dogs, Scone and Crumpet. Robie
lived in the apartment directly below Farrell's, usually unhappily. The
dogs were horrifying little homebrews of Chihuahua and Yorkshire
terrier, but Robie loved them.

Crumpet, the male, saw Lila first. He gave a delighted yap of welcome and proposition (according to Robie, Scone bored him, and he liked big girls anyway) and sprang to meet her, yanking his leash through Robie's slack hand. The wolf was almost upon him before he realized his fatal misunderstanding and scuttled desperately in retreat, meowing with utter terror.

Robie wailed, and Farrell ran as fast as he could, but Lila knocked Crumpet off his feet and slashed his throat while he was still in the air. Then she crouched on the body, nuzzling it in a dreadful way.

Robie actually came within a step of leaping upon Lila and trying to drag her away from his dead dog. Instead, he turned on Farrell as he came panting up, and began hitting him with a good deal of strength and accuracy. "Damn you, damn you!" he sobbed. Little Scone ran away around the corner, screaming like a mandrake.

Farrell put up his arms and went with the punches, all the while yelling at Lila until his voice ripped. But the blood frenzy had her, and Farrell never imagined what she must be like at those times. Somehow she had spared the dogs who had loved her all night, but she was nothing but thirst now. She pushed and kneaded Crumpet's body as though she were nursing.

All along the avenue, the morning dogs were barking like trumpets. Farrell ducked away from Robie's soft fists and saw them coming; tripping over their trailing leashes, running too fast for their stubby legs. They were small, spoiled beasts, most of them, overweight and short-twinded, and many were not young. Their owners cried unmanly pet names after them, but they waddled gallantly towards their deaths, barking promises far bigger than themselves, and none of them looked back.

She looked up with her muzzle red to the eyes. The dogs did falter then, for they knew murder when they smelled it, and even their silly, nearsighted eyes understood vaguely what creature faced them. But they knew the smell of love too, and they were all gentlemen.

She killed the first two to reach her—a spitz and a cocker spaniel—with two snaps of her jaws. But before she could settle down to her meal, three Pekes were scrambling up to her, though they would have had to stand on each other's shoulders. Lila whirled without a sound, and they fell away, rolling and yelling but unhurt. As soon as she turned, the Pekes were at her again, joined now by a couple of valiant poodles. Lila got one of the poodles when she turned again. Robie had stopped beating on Farrell, and was leaning against a traffic light, being sick. But other people were running up now: a middle-aged black man, crying; a plump youth in a plastic car coat and bedroom slippers, who kept whimpering, "Oh God, she's eating them, look at her, she's really eating them!"; two lean, ageless girls in slacks, both with foamy beige hair. They all called wildly to their unheeding dogs, and they all grabbed at Farrell and shouted in his face. Cars began to stop.

The sky was thin and cool, rising pale gold, but Lila paid no attention to it. She was ramping under the swarm of little dogs; rearing and spinning in circles, snarling blood. The dogs were terrified and bewildered, but they never swerved from their labor. The smell of love told them that they were welcome, however ungraciously she seemed to receive them. Lila shook herself, and a pair of squealing dachshunds, hobbled in a double harness, tumbled across the sidewalk to end at Farrell's feet. They scrambled up and immediately towed themselves back into the maelstrom. Lila bit one of them almost in half, but the other dachshund went on trying to climb her hindquarters, dragging his ripped comrade with him. Farrell began to laugh.

The black man said, "You think it's funny?" and hit him. Farrell sat down, still laughing. The man stood over him, embarrassed, offering Farrell his handkerchief. "I'm sorry, I shouldn't have done that," he said. "But your dog killed my dog."

"She isn't my dog," Farrell said. He moved to let a man pass between them, and then saw that it was the superintendent, holding his pistol with both hands. Nobody noticed him until he fired; but Farrell pushed one of the foamy-haired girls, and she stumbled against the superintendent as the gun went off. The silver bullet broke a window in a parked car.

The superintendent fired again while the echoes of the first shot were still clapping back and forth between the houses. A Pomeranian screamed that time, and a woman cried out, "Oh my God, he shot Borgy!" But the crowd was crumbling away, breaking into its individual components like pills on television. The watching cars had sped off at the sight of the gun, and the faces that had been peering down from windows disappeared. Except for Farrell, the few people who remained were scattered halfway down the block. The sky was brightening swiftly now.

"For God's sake, don't let him!" the same woman called from the shelter of a doorway. But two men made shushing gestures at her, saying, "It's all right, he knows how to use that thing. Go ahead, buddy."

The shots had at last frightened the little dogs away from Lila. She crouched among the twitching splotches of fur, with her muzzle wrinkled back and her eyes more black than green. Farrell saw a plaid rag that had been a dog jacket protruding from under her body. The superintendent stooped and squinted over the gun barrel, aiming with grotesque care, while the men cried to him to shoot. He was too far from the werewolf for her to reach him before he fired the last silver bullet, though he would surely die before she died. His lips were moving as he took aim.

Two long steps would have brought Farrell up behind the superintendent. Later he told himself that he had been afraid of the pistol, because that was easier than remembering how he had felt when he looked at Lila. Her tongue never stopped lapping around her dark jaws; and even as she set herself to spring, she lifted a bloody paw to her mouth. Farrell thought of her padding in the bedroom, breathing on his face. The superintendent grunted and Farrell closed his eyes. Yet even then he expected to find himself doing something.

Then he heard Mrs. Braun's unmistakable voice. *"Don't you dare!"* She was standing between Lila and the superintendent: one shoe gone, and the heel off the other one; her knit dress torn at the shoulder, and her face tired and smudgy. But she pointed a finger at the startled superintendent, and he stepped quickly back, as though she had a pistol, too.

"Lady, that's a wolf," he protested nervously. "Lady, you please get, get out of the way. That's a wolf, I go shoot her now."

"I want to see your license for that gun." Mrs. Braun held out her hand. The superintendent blinked at her, muttering in despair. She said, "Do you know that you can be sent to prison for twenty years for carrying a concealed weapon in this state? Do you know what the fine is for having a gun without a license? The fine is Five. Thousand. Dollars." The men down the street were shouting at her, but she swung around to face the creature snarling among the little dead dogs.

"Come on, Lila," she said. "Come on home with Bernice. I'll make tea and we'll talk. It's been a long time since we've really talked, you know? We used to have nice long talks when you were little, but we don't anymore." The wolf had stopped growling, but she was crouching even lower, and her ears were still flat against her head. Mrs. Braun said, "Come on, baby. Listen, I know what—you'll call in sick at the office and stay for a few days. You'll get a good rest, and maybe we'll even look around a little for a new doctor, what do you say? Schechtman hasn't done a thing for you, I never liked him. Come on home, honey. Momma's here, Bernice knows." She took a step towards the silent wolf, holding out her hand.

The superintendent gave a desperate, wordless cry and pumped forward, clumsily shoving Mrs. Braun to one side. He leveled the pistol point-blank, wailing, "My dog, my dog!" Lila was in the air when the gun went off, and her shadow sprang after her, for the sun had risen. She crumpled down across a couple of dead Pekes. Their blood dabbled her breasts and her pale throat.

Mrs. Braun screamed like a lunch whistle. She knocked the superintendent into the street and sprawled over Lila, hiding her completely
from Farrell's sight. "Lila, Lila," she keened to her daughter, "poor baby,
you never had a chance. He killed you because you were different, the
way they kill everything different." Farrell approached her and stooped
down, but she pushed him against a wall without looking up. "Lila, Lila,
poor baby, poor darling, maybe it's better, maybe you're happy now. You
never had a chance, poor Lila."

The dog owners were edging slowly back and the surviving dogs
were running to them. The superintendent squatted on the curb with his
head in his arms. A wary, muffled voice said, "For God's sake, Bernice,
would you get up off me? You don't have to stop yelling, just get off."

When she stood up, the cars began to stop in the street again. It
made it very difficult for the police to get through. Nobody pressed
charges, because there was no one to lodge them against. The killer
dog—or wolf, as some insisted—was gone; and if she had an owner, he
could not be found. As for the people who had actually seen the wolf
turn into a young girl when the sunlight touched her; most of them managed not to have seen it, though they never really forgot. There were a
few who knew quite well what they had seen, and never forgot it either,
but they never said anything. They did, however, chip in to pay the
superintendent's fine for possessing an unlicensed handgun. Farrell gave
what he could.

Lila vanished out of Farrell's life before sunset. She did not go
uptown with her mother, but packed her things and went to stay with
friends in the Village. Later he heard that she was living on Christopher
Street; and later still, that she had moved to Berkeley and gone back to
school. He never saw her again.

"It had to be like that," he told Ben once. "We got to know too much
about each other. See, there's another side to knowing. She couldn't look
at me."

"You mean because you saw her with all those dogs? Or because she
knew you'd have let that little nut shoot her?" Farrell shook his head.

"It was that, I guess, but it was more something else, something I
know. When she sprang, just as he shot at her that last time, she wasn't
leaping at him. She was going straight for her mother. She'd have got her
too, if it hadn't been sunrise."

Ben whistled softly. "I wonder if her old lady knows."

"Bernice knows everything about Lila," Farrell said.

Mrs. Braun called him nearly two years later to tell him that Lila
was getting married. It must have cost her a good deal of money and

ingenuity to find him (where Farrell was living then, the telephone line was open for four hours a day), but he knew by the spitefulness in the static that she considered it money well spent.

"He's at Stanford," she crackled. "A research psychologist. They're going to Japan for their honeymoon."

"That's fine," Farrell said. "I'm really happy for her, Bernice." He hesitated before he asked, "Does he know about Lila? I mean, about what happens—?"

"Does he know?" she cried. "He's proud of it—he thinks it's wonderful! It's his field!"

"That's great. That's fine. Goodbye, Bernice. I really am glad."

And he was glad, and a little wistful, thinking about it. The girl he was living with here had a really strange hangup.

What Tune the Enchantress Plays

Ah, *there* you are. I was beginning to wonder.

No, no. come in, do—it's your lair, after all. Tidy, too, for a demon. I'd do something about those bones, myself, and whatever *that* is, over in the corner, that smelly wet thing. But each to his taste, I say; you probably wouldn't think much of my notions of décor, either. Gods know, my mother doesn't.

Ah-ah-*ah*, no bolting—don't embarrass us both on such a pleasant evening. Sit down, and let's chat a little, you and I, like the old friends we practically are. Well, we might as well be, don't you think, as long as it's taken me to track you here. You're very good, you know. *Sit.*

Now.

You're good, as I said, but as shortsighted with it as all your kind. Whatever possessed you to come to Kalagira, when you could have been happily ravaging Coraic, or the fat, juicy villages around Chun? Didn't you know about Kalagira?

Forgive me—that was most rude, and foolish as well. Why expect a demon to be aware of one small southern province, tucked away beyond the Pass of Soshali, when so few humans are? Let me enlighten you, then. Kalagira is a country of *majkes*: witches like my grandmother, sorceresses like my mother...and the occasional enchantress, like me. There are certain differences worth note, but we will come to that. There is time.

There is time, until moonset.

At moonset I will sing to you, as I sang you here—oh, yes, that was my song you followed, with its whispers of blood and rapine, its bait of helpless victims, so close. At moonset I will sing another song, and you will go wherever it is that such as you go, when ended in this world.

Meanwhile, we will talk, because it amuses me, because it passes the time, and for one other reason. I shall tell you of my first encounter with a creature like you. Perhaps it will amuse you in your turn.

Well, it was not quite like you, really, that first demon of mine. If *demon* is what it truly was—it was larger, and rather more...majestic, excuse me, and definitely more powerful—but I run ahead of myself. Bide, Breya Drom, bide. The moon is still high.

Well, then.

Not all Kalagira women are witches or sorceresses—far from it—but there has been no male with such power born here in the entire history of the province, as far back as the old tales tell us, or the chronicles go. What is known, and known well, is that if the men of Kalagira cannot themselves work magic, still they are its *carriers*, if you understand me. A Kalagira *maj* who marries a local man will invariably find the knack— as we call it—making itself felt in all of her girl children; while one who weds Outside will see it come to an end in her own line, never to reappear. For that reason, Kalagira magic stays in Kalagira. In the oldest and most powerful families, it may have run true for five, six, seven generations, or even more. This can lead to old rivalries at times, old grudges.

Do you have males and females, your kind? I've never been certain. Well out of it, if you don't, but it's the sort of thing I wonder about in the early mornings, when I'm trying not to wake.

Do you have parents? Do you have children?

No?

Then attend, please, for these details matter. My mother's name is Willalou. In her time she was the most powerful sorceress in Kalagira, though today she spends her time gardening and translating the later poems of Lenji. My father is Dunreath, the potter. They live together in the house he built for my mother. She was powerful enough to have brought it into being with a chant and a gesture—a single scribing in the air—but he would never allow it, and she was wise enough to leave such matters entirely to him. You may not know this, being a demon, but it is not easy, in Kalagira or anywhere else, for a proud, skilled man to be with a woman like my mother. But they loved each other, always, and they have lived well together.

One evening, when I was perhaps five years old, my father brought home a small boy.

He brought him home under his arm, squirming and snarling like a trapped *shukri*. I remember as though it were yesterday: the fire smoking, and the smell of wet wool; the rain—little more than a mist—sighing against the windows, and my mother rising from her loom, saying, "Dunreath?" And me, asking loudly—quite loudly, I fear—"What is *that?* Papa, what is *that?*"

"It's not a that, dear," my father answered wearily. "It's a he—a very dirty he—but I can't tell you his name, because he won't say." He looked at my mother and raised his bushy eyebrows slightly. I loved his eyebrows.

"His name is Lathro," my mother said. "Lathro Baraquil." The boy's eyes widened, but his mouth remained almost invisible, so tightly was it shut. "He lives with his Aunt Yunieska and her son Pashak, and he needs a bath. He needs two baths." My father put the boy down; my mother held out her hand, and he went with her, mutely still, but obediently. My mother had that effect on people.

I heard them talking that night, and was surprised when my father asked, "How did you know he was Yunieska's boy?" Didn't he realize that Mother was magic, and knew everything?

"He's her nephew," my mother answered. "I've seen him in the street now and then, filthier even than this sometimes. That woman has no business with a child, none."

"Cleans up well enough," my father said. "I had no idea he's got freckles."

My mother laughed softly. "He's very brave, too. He *looked* at me when I put him in the tub—Dunreath, I don't think he's ever had a bath in his life, not an all-over one. He must have thought I was going to drown him, but he gave me that *look,* and then he stepped into the tub like a prince. There's definitely somebody under all that dirt."

"I wasn't planning on keeping him," my father said quickly. "I just thought maybe you could clean him up a little, find him something to eat, and shoo him off home. I'll clean the tub."

My mother did not answer for a time, and then not directly. She said only, "I'm going to speak to Yunieska the next time I see her." The way she said *speak* made me giggle, but it made me shiver a little as well.

That was how Lathro came.

He stayed two days, that first time, hardly saying a word he didn't have to, but behaving with a kind of silent grace and courtesy that must have been natural to him; he certainly couldn't have learned it from his aunt and his cousin. On the third day he got into a fight with my older brother Jadrilja, and disappeared for very nearly a month, which is difficult in a small village like ours.

But then he came back.

I found him myself this time, standing in front of our house, balanced on one bare foot and scratching it with the toes of the other. He looked at me, looked away, and mumbled the first words he ever addressed directly to me, "I come for a wash."

Jadrilja was more than ready to pick up his debate with Lathro where our father had halted it, but that didn't happen for a good day and a half; and by that time I had noticed that Lathro Baraquil's brown eyes stood forth with a rich warmth disconcerting in that fierce little face. My own eyes are green, like my mother's; my father's are almost black, like those of all the men in his family. I had never seen eyes like Lathro Baraquil's eyes. I still haven't.

So it began, long and long before either of us was aware that anything was beginning. It was much like inviting a wary, untrusting feral animal first into the yard, then a little way up onto the veranda; then into the house, if only by leaving the door ajar for the creature to choose as it will. First Lathro came, as he said, only for a bath, and once in a great while for my mother to trim his thatch of thick brown hair. Then he began to arrive, more and more, at dinnertime, for my mother to stuff him like a Thieves' Day piglet. She was not a particularly good cook, no more than I—magic never provided a proper meal for anyone—but Lathro never complained.

And in time he began to come for me.

I knew it, accepted it, and gave it no further thought beyond our pleasure in being together. We wandered, raced, climbed trees, told each other stories; squabbled on many occasions, made up quickly, and often fell asleep on a hillside or under a tree, piled together as warmly and innocently as puppies. And when Lathro fought with one or another of my brothers—he simply could not keep from it—they had me to deal with as well. Utterly disloyal, but there you are.

Was I aware that one of us was heir to power such as the other could never possibly know, merely by virtue of being born the right sex? I suppose I must have been, but I cannot recall it making the least bit of difference or discord between us. It might well have done so, as the years passed, if I had paid the heed I should have to my mother's grimly patient attempts to instruct me in shapeshifting, in spirit-summoning, thaumaturgy, rhymes and songs of lore, and all the other arts I was condemned to master. But surely even a demon can see that I was fatally happy as I was. I had my mother for any magic I needed, my father for those moments when I was sad for no reason that I could put a name to...and for all the rest I had Lathro Baraquil.

We must have seemed a strange pair to many, even as children. I was considered beautiful from my earliest youth, while for his part Lathro grew up plain—beautifully, beguilingly plain—and stubby with it, being no taller than I, ever. His best features, to the outside eye, would have been that tumbly brown hair that I loved to comb (useless as the effort was), and those brown eyes, kind for all the wide wildness they held.

He grew up strong as well, much stronger than could be imagined at sight. At fifteen he was working at Jarg's smithy, handling such tasks as holding the back of a haywagon up for as long a time as it took Jarg to replace a wheel or improvise an axle. I recall seeing him turn with his bare hands a frozen bolt that old Jarg couldn't budge with a sledge-hammer and a bucket of grease. Lathro hurt his right hand badly doing that once, and I healed it on the spot in a way my mother had taught me when I happened to be actually paying attention. I was proud of myself then.

If my parents thought us too close in those days, I never knew about it. My belief is that they still saw us as children, and Lathro as family, or the very next thing to it. At all events, they made no objection to the hours we spent together, and the only time my mother ever became annoyed with us was they day when I saw five of the village boys harassing a blind madman, snatching away his crutch so that he fell, and then breaking it over his shoulders. I ran to tell Lathro, who came down on them like a storm out of the Northern Barrens. Two or three of them went limping around on crutches themselves for some while.

Unhappily, these very ones happened to be the sons of the wealthiest merchants in our village. Their fathers descended on Jarg, insisting that Lathro be discharged immediately; and from his Aunt Yunieska they demanded he be given swift and merciless punishment. I can still see their puffy, bearded faces, red as vultures' pates, and hear their voices splitting with fury, and the spittle flying. As I can still feel Lathro's firm, gentle hand in mine as we looked on.

My mother put a stop to it all, as I knew she would the moment I saw her approaching. The merchants fell silent before her gaze, and I realized—for the first time, really—that they were dreadfully afraid of her.

She said to the merchants, "If I had seen what your sons were at, I can assure you, there would not be one of them who got away from there on less than four legs. Quite possibly six." I had never heard her voice sound like that. She said, "Count yourselves fortunate, and go away. Now."

They went away, and my mother turned on me before I could cheer her triumph. "Child, what on earth possessed you to place Lathro in such jeopardy, doing your work for you? You know who you are—you could have run those boys into the next shire with three words I taught you long ago. You are a stupid, stupid girl, and I am ashamed of you."

I hung my head. I muttered, "I am ashamed too, Mother. But I was afraid. I did not think. I ask your forgiveness."

"Breya is *not* stupid," Lathro said. "She is *not.*"

As angry as my mother was, that took more courage than attacking those five fools. My mother ignored him, seemingly, but her voice softened. She said, "My daughter, after me you are already the most powerful woman in Kalagira, whether you know it or not, and there will come a time when you will be far more powerful than I. Others can afford not to think; you never can, or you will do great damage. Do you understand what I am saying to you, Breya Drom? And why I say it?"

I nodded. I whispered, "Yes."

My mother turned to Lathro, and she actually smiled slightly. "Boy," she said, "inhumanly dirty and hungry small boy, you cannot conquer all the cruelty in the world by yourself. Not even you." She patted his cheek then, and turned away. Over her shoulder, she added, "But there's no harm in trying. I'll say that for you."

Was it with that last light glance that she understood what was between us, Lathro and me? I will never know, and she will certainly never tell me. Not even now.

What I do know, for always, is that on that very same day, Lathro Baraquil kissed me for the first time.

It was a clumsy kiss, as unruly as his hair, and it stumbled blindly over my face for what felt like a lifetime before it found my mouth. I was just as awkward: the two of us like blind newborn kittens, scrambling through a forest of fur toward the nipple—toward life. It was so sweet that I wept as though my heart were breaking, and poor Lathro was terrified, thinking that he had somehow hurt me or frightened me. But I reassured him.

And where to from there? What did we whisper, what did we promise each other? What gift did we exchange to seal our troth? And again, what did my mother know before we did? No business of any demon's.

When the time finally came to speak I never told my mother, "Lathro Baraquil has my heart." I was much too clever for that, well knowing that she could have crumbled the notion like stale bread with a few gently scornful words, and blown the fragments away with a look or a gesture. What I said was, "Lathro is my heart," which was the truth.

But Willalou my mother was more clever than I by far. She embraced me immediately—not the least moment of hesitation, mind—and cried out, "My dear, my Breya, I am so happy for you—*so* happy!" Thus she caused me to lower my guard, to ease my anxiety regarding her reaction to my news; and, indeed, *almost* to miss her wistful little sideways murmur, "But a bit sad for myself..."

I didn't miss it, nor was I meant to. With a suddenly lurching heart, I demanded, "Sad? Why should you be sad?"

My mother smiled valiantly. "I'm sorry, darling. Do forgive an old woman her self-indulgence." She sighed deeply, perfectly. "It's terrible of me, but I have to say it, forgive me. It's the children, you see."

I wasn't prepared. I was ready for a lot of things that she might say, but not that. I said indignantly, "Children? And why should there not be children?"

Oh, Mother. Clever, clever Mother. No sorcery of any sort: not even that thing she did with the fingers of her left hand, out of sight by her side, to change someone's mind. No, she merely let her eyes fill slowly, and stepped back, still with her hands tight on my arms, and she whispered, "My dear, my dear, didn't he tell you?"

This time it was no lurch, but a freezing drop, as though through a gallows trapdoor. "Tell me *what?*"

"He didn't tell you he was from Outside? He really didn't tell you? He was very little when they came here, Yunieska and Pashak. From Chun, I think, although it's hard to remember...maybe I mean Oun, I'm not sure. But anyway."

I said, "I don't care." She didn't hear me. I couldn't hear myself.

She drew me close now, saying, "Darling, darling, you mustn't blame the boy. Think how frightened he must have been at the thought of telling you that if you married him you could never have children of...our sort. I certainly don't blame him, and you *mustn't.*"

"I don't," I said, louder this time. "Oh, I don't." Then I ran away. I could feel her looking after me—one always can with *our sort*—but she did not call, and I did not look back.

Lathro was not at the smithy—I could tell that from a good distance by the silence of the forge. I hurried on by, and found him mucking out Dree Shandriladze's livery stable, as I had thought he would be. No one ever accused my Lathro of not knowing the meaning of real work.

He looked up as I entered the stable, and I could have wept without shame for the pure joy and welcome in his eyes. The next moment, I did weep, for he raised a hand in warning, saying, "Wait, Moon Fox—" such was always his pet name for me—"wait only a moment, while I make this midden-heap fit for your feet." Then, after laying down every board and bit of sacking he could find, he strode to me anyway, scooped me high in his arms, and carried me over to the nest of straw bales he had made for us when he began working there. We held each other, and I breathed his breath and burrowed my way under his arm, and asked, "When did you know?"

He had no idea what I meant. Lathro never lied, not to anyone. I told him the truth of his Outside birth, and of his coming to Kalagira as an infant, and he took it in as flesh parts before the candor of an arrow: I even heard the soft gasp as it went home. Then I made him make love with me, there, for the very first time, with half a dozen coach horses looking on, because it was all I knew to do to comfort him.

In time, when we could at last distinguish the beating of his heart from my own, he said, "Breya. You have to leave me."

I stared at him. There was no answer in me. He said, "You come from a great line of *majkes*, and you will grow to be the greatest of all that line, as your mother said. Am I to be the cause of that line ending with you? I love you better than that, Breya Drom."

"And I love you better than my grandchildren," I answered him. "What have they ever done for me?" I meant to make him laugh, but clearly failed. I went on, "I am not responsible to my *line*, Lathro. I am responsible for my *life*—our life together. For the rest of it, I could be as happy here, right here with you, as anywhere else in the world. I would never ask for more than this—cleaning stables, rubbing down horses, currying them, loving in their good smell. This is happiness for me, Lathro, don't you understand?"

He quieted me with a finger across my lips. "Beloved, this is contentment, nothing more. I haven't your education, but I know the difference. I am no one, son of nothing, and always will be. But magic is part of what you are—you could no more abandon it than step out of that beautiful tea-colored skin you wear so well. And with no daughters to pass it on to, and they to theirs—"

"What if I married someone else, but only had sons? The magic would end then just as surely."

"But at least they would be Kalagira men, such children, able to pass the knack to their own daughters if fate so willed. Ours could not."

"It wouldn't matter!" I tried to hush him with kisses, but he put me aside. "Yes, it would, Breya. Yes, you would live in joy with me anywhere—a stable, a woodcutter's shack, a swineherd's one-room hovel— I know that, how could I not know that? And you would never think for a moment of envying the life of another person on this earth, or of using power to make us more than we already were together." He kissed my fingers then, slowly, one by one. He said, "But children...grandchildren...great-grandchildren...all without magic, never to have it, none of them—look at me, Breya, and tell me you would not ever regret your choice. No, straight at me, there's my girl. Tell me now."

Unlike Lathro, I am a very good liar. Daughter of Willalou, how should I not be? What is all magic but lying, a grandly ruthless reshaping of reality to our purposes? I lied you here, did I not, singing to you of slaughter, luring you with your own hunger? But I could not lie to Lathro in that moment. I wanted him to be wrong, with all my heart…but I was not certain, so I lowered my eyes and turned away.

"There's my girl," he said again, and there was more love and understanding in his voice than I could bear. I took my leave of him as soon as I could, and he did not try to keep me, though I wanted him to. Love as we might, I was a long time forgiving him for knowing me.

We did not see each other for some while after that. My doing.

Nor did I have much to do with my mother and father. I stayed in my own quarters, speaking to no one, eating hardly at all, creating small, spiteful enchantments that shame me today, for their pettiness as much as their malice; and generally *sulking*—I can find no kinder word for my behavior, and I have tried. Something was so, and its so-ness stood between me and my heart's desire; and though I willed it not to be so, it was more powerful than my will.

I did much of my sulking in one shuttered storeroom, perhaps because of its particular air of dank misery, perhaps merely because my parents always knew where I was, and what I was doing, and could come and find me there doing it, if they really wanted to. Only they had better not try.

Dunreath chanced on me when he came into the storeroom looking for the ingredients to a glaze he had not used in years. He might well have missed me, huddled silent in a corner as I was; but, blundering in the darkness, he stumbled over me, letting out a yelp of startlement. He is a big, absent-minded sort of man, my father, happiest at his wheel and kiln; but he does know about love, and at a glance he had my measure.

"Child," he said, awkward as a troll at a tea-party. "Child, Breya, don't, please. Don't cry, Breya." And he patted my hair with his rough potter's hand.

I wasn't crying then, for a wonder, but that clumsy touch opened the sluicegates in earnest. I fell on his chest, wailing loudly and wildly enough to deafen the dead. My father held me, whispering whatever lame comfort he could, stroking my neck and shoulders as though I were clay to be petted and kneaded into life.

"Girl, don't weep so," he begged me. "Don't weep, I can't bear it. I like the boy myself, always did, and if you want him so much, you should have him, that's the way *I* look at it. To hell with our line, we've known magic long enough. Your mother would have married *me* if I'd been born Outside, everybody knows that. What bloody difference, hey?"

Is there giving in marriage among demons? If that is so, then maybe— just maybe—you understand something about my father's loyalty. If I knew anything about Willalou, it's that she would never have married a man who was not from Kalagira. My mother loved Dunreath more than anyone, but she loved her heritage more, for good or ill. And Dunreath knew it, but loved her enough not to say so. There is more magic in this world than magicians dream.

"I wish men could be *majkes*," I told him when I finally stopped crying. "I *do*, I wish I could give Lathro my knack. He'd be so good—he'd know the right way to use the power, and I don't, and I don't *care* that I don't. Mother's determined to make me into a great enchantress, but it's not what I want. Doesn't what *I* want matter to *anybody?* Can't I ever be ordinary and happy, like a man?"

"No, love," my father answered me. "No, you can't be—and if you could be, you wouldn't like it." He went back to holding me then, and I went back to weeping. At some point he said, "Breya, you're a hawk, born to soar, born for the heights. You were never meant for the barnyard."

And I remember wailing, "I'm not a bird—I'm human, I'm *me!*" and running away to find Lathro, with my heart wild in my throat and my eyes blind with loneliness and dread.

By instinct, I looked for him neither in the smithy nor the stable, but at the moribund *dika* tree that had been our meeting place since we were children. It was dying then, and it is still stubbornly dying now; but our pet superstition was that our presence—and, in time, our love—was all that kept it putting out the occasional blossom or pale sprig of leaves. It is where I would have gone.

But he was not there, under the tree. He had vanished completely, from the village and from my days, leaving not a trace of his passage.

There are certain obvious advantages to being a *maj* of any sort. One is the ability to track down almost anyone you really set out to find. But nothing that I tried worked. And even Willalou, when I went to her, finally threw up her hands and said, "Daughter, wherever he may be, he has passed beyond my reach. Which is a worry by itself, as much as his being gone."

"Yes," I said. "How thoughtless of him." If my words sound harsh and unfilial…well, remember that I was trying not to shatter into very small fragments. I said, "I will find him, Mother."

My mother said, "You will not."

I stared at her. Dunreath had spoiled me shamelessly, with no slightest regard to its effect on my future character; and while Willalou was sterner, I had known all my life that her *no* truly meant *not now, don't bother me, try me again in a day or two.* But in this moment her lips were thinner, her eyes harder, than I had ever seen them. Protest dried up in my own mouth, and I actually backed away from her.

She said, "Wherever that boy has run off to is no fit place for you. Not as you are, gifted beyond my imagining, and vulnerable as a newborn. You have disregarded my instruction all your life, shirked every lesson you could manage to avoid, studied nothing you found boring— and where are you now? Not only would you be useless in any peril when I am not by to rescue you, but you are utterly powerless to aid the one you claim to love. Tell me I am wrong, my daughter. I want to hear you tell me I am wrong."

She had never spoken so to me in my life. There was nothing for me to say; and if there had been, I would have known better than to say it. I waited in silence, staring down at the intricacies of my sandal straps, until she finally ran out of rage and breath more or less together. She said, "So. Now, at bloody last, we begin."

And so, indeed, it began: that insanely intensive course of training in everything that should have been woven into my bones and brain before ever I had need of them. My mother was absolutely pitiless, driving me without rest for either of us, constantly humiliating me to tears, whether over the nursery-simple rhymes that can confer invisibility, locate water in a desert, or heal a fatal wound; or when I, for the hundredth time, tangled up one of her fiendishly complicated invocations with another that was almost identical. She drilled me endlessly in the doggerel chants, phrases, and rituals of a dozen languages, all seemingly unrelated, that could, even so, be fitted together in a remarkable number of different ways to produce strikingly varied results. We battled through the night many a time, I and this terrible woman with my mother's face: me with my mind turning to watery curds, and she haranguing me without cease, barking, "I taught you that when you were seven years old—or I thought I had—you should know it in your sleep. Where is your head?" To this day, I still hate that contemptuous question with no answer. "Where is your head?" over and over. "*Where is your head?*"

Fortunately I learn quickly, when I learn at all; fortunately also, I have an ear for music. This is crucial for an enchantress, as it is not for a witch or a sorceress, since so much of our power lies in song. My mother has a perfectly good voice, but much preferred to recite her spells in a decidedly flat, plain manner—always while *moving*, letting her body sing the magic. But if I could not sing, I might as well be a witch in a cave, growling my incantations over a greasy, smoky fire. (Meaning no disrespect to Grandmother, who was actually a cheerful, sociable soul, like most witches.) As it was, Willalou sang me hoarse, day on day, night on night. "No, do it *again*—can't you hear where you lose the rhythm? *Where is your head?*"

Five endless months. Nearly six. I am grateful beyond words that the memory blurs. It was coming on autumn when my mother finally announced, with no preamble, "Well, I've done what I could. You're still the poorest excuse for a proper enchantress I've ever seen, but at least I'm not quite so feared that you'll put a spell on yourself, or call something you don't want when you're trying to summon Lathro." She paused for a moment, and then added quietly, her voice that of the mother I knew for the first time in forever, "Which, by the way, would *not* do. Do not ever try to bring that boy of yours to you by magic, despite all temptation. Do you understand me, Breya?"

Her eyes were dark with urgency, as I have only rarely seen them. I said, "I understand your meaning, mother. But not your reason. Why not?"

My mother hesitated again, longer this time. She said finally, her voice uncharacteristically muffled, almost mumbling, "Because it will alert the Being he has gone to seek. And may have found by now."

I gaped at her. She went on, increasingly defensive, "He came to me the very day before he ran off. He wanted me to know—though he swore me not to tell you—that he was away in search of a creature he had heard tell of, powerful enough to change fate and make *maj* of an ordinary man." She paused a third time. "Even a man of Kalagira. He thought such a change might help him carry magic for you, even Outside born, and would not listen when I warned him of the terrible price the Being would claim."

There is a difference between being truly speechless and not having the air to make the sound come out. I felt as though I had been struck in the stomach, having had no warning and no chance to brace myself. I said stupidly, "A creature."

"A Being," my mother said. "It was old when your grandmother was not yet born, and its power is not of this world. I believe, if it so chose—"

"A *maj*." My voice was rising slowly, like floodwaters. "You think Lathro has gone to this—thing—to be magicked into the knack, so that he and I might perhaps have..." My mother nodded, looking guiltier by the minute. I whispered, "And you tell me this *now?*"

"It would have done no good before. You would have hared off straight after him, and you no more suited for such a quest than a— a *chicken!*"

"All this time," I said. I was cold with fury, shaking uncontrollably. "All these days wasted going over and over this stupid spell, that baby rhyme, the Three Theories—"

"—which you should have *learned* as a baby—"

"And all the time, Lathro going further and further away, *disappearing...*" I couldn't speak anymore; it was language disappearing now. I turned and walked out of the house. My mother said nothing, and did not follow.

I left the next morning on Belgarth, the warhorse my father had accepted in payment for a great floral vase, so huge as to require three handles, that he had created for a lord's wedding. Belgarth was getting on by then, and grown fat with inactivity; but I had learned to ride on his king's couch of a back, and we were fond of each other. Besides, he always smelled wonderful, like a dew-damp hayfield warming in the morning sun, and his chestnut hide set off my coloring to perfection. And yes, *majkes* do indeed think about such things, like anyone else.

Dunreath made no objection to my taking his horse, but he looked so wretched that it hurt my heart, and I would have turned back then, if I could have. When he held me, I whispered, "I'm sorry," which I could not say to Willalou, even when she held my stirrup while I mounted, and we bade each other farewell. Nor did she ask forgiveness for what she had said and done, but only stood at Belgarth's head, tall and beautiful and dry-eyed, looking straight at me. She said, "I have no counsel for you, and only one suggestion. Accept it or not, as you choose."

I waited, not speaking. My mother said, "All I know of this Being that you and Lathro seek, is that it is in some way bound to running water. Look for it near rivers, brooks, the smallest streams, search where running water is used by men—in mills, in tanneries, canals, weirs. And if you go north, towards Chun—remember, Lathro may have been born there—seek out a river town called Mulleary, and a woman named Dragine. We were acquainted long ago. If anyone in the land knows where this Being can be found, it will be Dragine." The way she held my gaze with her own was as near to an embrace as makes no matter. "Goodbye, then, my daughter," and she stood aside to let Belgarth pass.

I did not look back as I rode away.

I had never been beyond the borders of Kalagira, nor even close to them. I had never been away from home for longer than three days. Yet here I was, journeying alone into what, for me, was wilderness: the country roads winding more or less towards Chun, so ill-kept and overgrown that half a dozen bandits could be crouched within arm's-reach and you not know—and beyond those, the bare hills surrounding Fors na' Shachim and the Queen's black castle. Belgarth wasn't much concerned with scenery—he's all for tiltyards, short, lumbering charges with murderous clashes at the end of them—and he wasn't happy with stony little roads overhung with brambly vines. Yet he strode on gallantly all

the same, a warhorse ever, war or no. There would have been little forage for him, in the normal way; but I made certain to bring rich grass
to birth unseasonably, wherever we made camp, and water pooling out
of stones. And yes, it *was* my mother who finally hammered that smallest charm into me—and yes, I *should* have learned it at the same time I
learned to dress myself.

It seemed the most practical thing—grudge it as I might—to follow
Willalou's suggestion and seek out the Dragine woman. I had no notion
of what a Being—and did that signify demon, lamia, *yaroth,* or some
other monster?—powerful enough to turn a mortal man into a *maj* might
look or be like, and if there was someone who did I had many questions
to ask. I heeded my mother's hint about running water as well, and set
out to trace the course of everything flowing south of Fors na' Shachim.
Of course it was a completely absurd notion—was that a laugh? Does
your kind actually make a sound to express amusement?—but I was
frightened for my man, and certain that nothing was beyond one as
much in love as I.

Yes, that *is* a laugh-sound, isn't it? But as dark and distorted as
you are.

Often I let Belgarth choose our road—why not, since all horses, left
to themselves, will go toward the smell of water, and all paths were the
same to me so long as they headed eventually toward Chun? Meanwhile
I practiced my spells, like any novice, as we covered the country foot by
plodding foot: singing to mark earth and stone and the air itself, to keep
us from wandering in circles or unwittingly doubling back on our trail.

As for what I would do when I at last saw Lathro Baraquil's face,
I had forced myself, days and miles back, to banish such imaginings
altogether. I might—or might not, even after Willalou's improvised dis-
ciplines—be a match for the Being I sought; but even if I were, that
was no guarantee Lathro would choose to return home with me when
I found him. What if he had not yet found the Being, but insisted on
continuing the search? Or what if he had already become a *maj* and considered himself far too grand now for a scab-kneed childhood playmate?
Too many unknown factors; nothing to do but trudge on, singing.

We kept almost entirely to the mountains: since so many of the
streams and rivers of this region spring up there, it did seem to improve
the odds at least somewhat. But we might as well have been seeking
roses in the Northern Barrens, for I encountered no smallest trace of
Lathro, nor of the Being I was hunting so steadfastly. I learned not a
thing from the rare traveler, and nothing at all in any of the few villages in which I stabled Belgarth and passed the night. Yet I could not

rid myself of the *awareness* of both of them, the conviction that they were somewhere nearby, whatever my training, my observations, or my inborn senses told me to the contrary. The heart is not the infallible guide it claims to be, but it does get a few things right now and then.

The nights were turning seriously chilly, and Belgarth was even showing early suggestions of a winter coat, when we followed a swift, restless little river into a town called, not Mulleary, but Mul*deary*, rather larger than any we had come across in some while. I asked if a woman named Dragine lived there, and was told that she was visiting in a distant village, but would return in two days' time. Belgarth and I spent those days doing little else but eating and sleeping. I had been running for nearly two months on nothing but vague memories of rest, real meals and a proper bed; and for all that happened in Muldeary, I will remember it as the town in which I *slept*. And took baths.

Dragine arrived at dawn of the second day, walking briskly out of a dust storm that drifted away when she told it to. She was a tiny creature with a face like a spiderweb and hair so black you could hardly see it, if you understand me. I caught up with her crossing Beggars' Square, where the homeless of Muldeary are fed every morning, and began to introduce myself, but she kept striding on without even looking at me until I said, "I am Willalou's daughter. Willalou of Kalagira."

Dragine stopped in her tracks then, and I saw her eyes for the first time. I had expected them to be as black as her hair, but they were a tawny brownish yellow, or yellowish brown. She peered at me—I suppose I should say 'up at me,' small as she was, but somehow it felt as though our eyes were on a level—and she said, "I know your mother." Her voice sounded like sand blowing against the sides of an empty house.

"Yes," I said. "She told me not to leave Muldeary until I had seen you." She started to turn away, and I grabbed at flattery to hold her attention, adding, "She speaks well of you."

Dragine said, "You are a liar," but she said it indifferently, as though she were already tired of me. "I never could abide your mother, and she never had anything but contempt for me. Why are you still bothering me?"

"Because my mother told me you had knowledge to fit my need." Dragine did not reply, but she did not walk away, either, or turn her strange eyes from mine. We stood there together in Beggars' Square, and I told her about Lathro Baraquil.

Her expression never changed, nor did her tone. She looked me up and down for a time, then shrugged very slightly and said, "Come to my house tonight. Ten minutes to midnight, no sooner." She never mentioned where her house could be found, nor did I think then to ask her for directions. Whatever she actually might be—witch, sorceress like my mother, or even a true enchantress—in her presence I had trouble thinking at all.

I took Belgarth out for a fast trot, bordering on a canter, and spent the rest of the day searching for someone willing to tell me where Dragine lived. It was an interesting experience: none of them recoiled in obvious terror at the idea of revealing her location, and yet somehow I came away from none of them with an exact address. In the end I had to employ a finding spell, which is so childishly simple that it always gives me a headache. But I was there precisely at the appointed time, and I came on foot, to show respect, though it meant a long walk.

It was an ordinary house she lived in, neither a mansion nor a hovel: it might well have been the home of an honest and energetic farmwife, one who spent great amounts of time scrubbing and polishing worn kitchen flagstones that would never come quite clean. I remember that it smelled of old fires, and that the river ran near enough that I could see its banks from the front yard, and hear its rambling chatter as I stood on the threshold.

Lathro Baraquil opened the door to me.

Do your folk have hearts? Do they serve another purpose, as ours do, besides hurrying the impatient blood along through your veins, if you even *have* veins? Mine stopped—just for an instant, but completely—and then it surged to the size of Belgarth, so that my chest could not nearly contain it, and with a cry the Queen must have heard in Fors na' Shachim I threw myself into Lathro's arms. I think we mortals must each be allowed one moment like that in our lives. I don't believe we are constructed to withstand two.

For the sake of accuracy, however, I must admit that I threw myself against Lathro's arms, not into them. He made no effort to embrace me, but only stood still, looking not into my eyes but over my shoulder, his own eyes empty as eggshells of feeling. He did not know me at all; and what stood in his place, in his clothes—I had made him that shirt; *made* it, not conjured it—I could never possibly know.

He did not recoil, nor thrust me away. He stood still, staring over my shoulder at the night, with every treasured bump and bone and angle of him turned foreign, after years of being as much my own as his. I babbled his name, but it had no more effect than the sound of the stream. Nothing in him knew me.

Beyond him Dragine waited, her face as unreadable as ever, but her eyes glowing like the eyes of a hunting *shukri*. She said, "He has been here for some while, waiting for the Being to be called. I myself, however, have been waiting for you."

I pushed past Lathro to confront her, demanding, "What have you done to him? Tell me now, or I will kill you where you stand!" Eighteen and gently bred up, can you imagine me saying such a thing to anyone? I have not even said it to you, although the moon is on its way to setting.

In her voice of blowing sand, Dragine answered me, "That would be wrong and foolish of you, since it was not I who set this spell upon him."

I could not respond. I simply stared. Dragine said, "It happens with humans. They often desire something so greatly, for so long, that with the proper push they cannot remember why they craved it in the first place. So it is with your man—he was in this state when he found his way here. Only if he came from where you did, I suspect there was little *finding* on his path. He has been here quite some time." She paused, watching me take that in, and then went on, "In the end, it is your doing, even more than his."

"*My* doing?" The absurdity of the claim outraged me, but it frightened me as well. "How can it have been my doing?"

Dragine pointed at Lathro, standing completely motionless, not even blinking. "When you told him that you two could never marry, because of his being an Outsider, what did you *think* he would do? You say you have known him since childhood—what did you *think?*"

I could hear my mother's "*Where is your head?*" under my own whispered reply. "I never told him that. I would never have..."

"No? Well, someone did." Dragine's yellow teeth bared their tips in a smile of mean delight. "And that same someone directed him straight here, to me. What do you think of that, Breya Drom, daughter of Willalou?"

There was a taste of copper in my mouth, and a distant braying in my ears. I said, "My mother set Lathro searching for you? I don't believe it." But I did, I did, even before Dragine answered me.

"I would never dream of lying to you—I am enjoying the truth far too much, little witch-girl." She was beginning to laugh, like a sandstorm gathering strength.

Strangely, the contempt in the word *witch-girl* cleared my head, leaving me more coldly, stubbornly rational than I had been since I left home. I said, as haughtily as I was able, "I am no witch, but an enchantress, as you well know, and the daughter of one who could crumble you and a dozen like you into her soup." The laughter grew until I could actually feel the sand against my skin, like tiny blades. Beside me, Lathro showed no reaction at all, his entire attention focused on nothing

I could see or imagine. His eyes had not met mine squarely since he had opened Dragine's door to me. I said again, "Tell me why you hate my mother so. Because she doesn't know, I'm sure."

"You think not?" Dragine's laughter did not return; rather, she looked at me with something almost like pity. "She told you nothing she did not *have* to tell you, did she then? Nothing?"

I had no answer for her. With no further word, she turned and led me—and silent, obedient Lathro too—through the house to a curious place I'd not noticed from outside: neither a room nor a yard nor a veranda, but a plain high-walled space open in part to the sky. The walls were white and bare. There were no chairs, or even cushions, to sit on; the only distinguishing feature of the area was a small pool, ringed round with large stones, carefully arranged. There was no moon that night, but the stars were reflected thickly in the pool, darting like bright fish, as the current from some hidden inlet stirred the surface. I could see my shadow in it, but not my face.

Dragine squatted on her heels, and gestured to me to do the same. She did not look at Lathro, who stood by, hands folded in front of him, staring away at nothing. She said, "I was born in Kalagira. I grew up with your mother. Did she tell you *that*, at least?" I shook my head. "Well, so it was. And as you and this one here—" she jerked a gaunt finger at Lathro—"have been to each other, so was I with your father. Dunreath the potter." When she spoke his name she closed her eyes, barely for longer than a blink, but I saw.

"Were you promised?" I could not imagine her young with Dunreath—the bitter spider-lines gone, the tawny eyes innocently yearning—but my folk take handfasting seriously, and I had to know.

Dragine looked at me for a long, cold time before she replied. "Breathe easy, witch-girl, your father never deceived me. We were close to promising—he even spoke of it, a time or two—but I was shy still. I was shy…" Her voice had grown soft when she spoke of Dunreath, almost wistful; but it turned to blowing sand again with her next words. "Then came your mother."

Oh, perhaps you can see it; perhaps you can take my word for my young father's first sight of a maiden Willalou. Dragine must have seen the vision in my face, for she said, "Aye, there was never a day when I could match her for beauty. Nor for power, either…not then."

The last two words were uttered in a near-animal growl, and I could hardly catch them, but I did. I said, "And now?"

Dragine smiled fully for the first time, granting me, as though by a flash of lightning, an instant's glimpse of the girl who had had every reason to believe that Dunreath belonged to her, with her. She said, "I was not born a *maj*, or to a gifted line. There has never been so much as the feeblest barnyard witch in my family, search as far back as you will. How should my potter not have been drawn to such a face, such a gift, as Willalou's? No, I blame him not at all, your father."

"But my mother must take the blame for everything," I said, "every misfortune that has befallen you since you lost Dunreath to her. Even before then, am I wrong?"

"I blame her for being exactly what she is, no more: for knowing that what is not hers is hers to take. Do you feel that unjust, witch-girl? Too bad. I also honor her for making me what I am." The smile thinned, curling into the newest of new moons. "The Being your foolish man seeks draws no line between one sex and another. It responds simply to desire. To need."

"Such as yours," I said, and she nodded. I said, "But it could not bring my father back to you. He loved my mother on sight, loves her still. Nothing could have changed that."

"The Being gave me a greater gift." Dragine's voice was surprisingly gentle, almost dreamy. "Shall I show you?"

She raised both arms, crossed them at the wrists, pointed at me with both pairs of middle and index fingers, and spoke a rhyme that Willalou had drummed into my head so hard, so often, that I knew to drop flat on my belly as two gouts of fire, shaped like dragon heads, leaped from Dragine's fingertips and shot past me, hissing like full-sized wyrms. Ordinarily such sendings burst within seconds, harmless as Thieves' Day crackers; but these doubled on their sizzling trails and came racing for me again. There were eyes in those tiny fire-faces, and they saw me.

But I know a rhyme worth two of that, and I sang it, rising to a crouch—sang it back at Dragine, not at the dragon-heads, and they promptly popped like milkweed seedpods, and were gone.

I stood up slowly, glancing sideways at Lathro as I did so. He had not moved, nor did he appear to have noticed what had taken place. I said loudly to Dragine, "*That* was what your Being taught you? *That* was worth a slice of your soul? You ought to ask for your payment back."

Dragine was breathing hard: deep animal inhalations—such as you breathe now, in the darkness, waiting for the moon to be gone. She said, "The Being has no interest in souls. What it took in payment for my new power was my ability to love, for which I had no more use in any case, nor ever would. I have no complaints. See now!"

And with those last words—and a few others—she Shifted, and on the instant it was a great *sheknath* who stood in her place: hindquarters higher than the mighty bowed forelegs, jaws and chest and shoulders still muddy from digging out its most recent meal. It rose on its hind legs and roared at me, but I sang my mother's favorite old lullaby, and it dropped down and promptly went to sleep. Dragine was some little while regaining her true shape, and she was not pleased when she finally managed it.

"I will not fight with you," she declared. "I did not summon you for that, but to watch you lose your man to a fantasy, as I lost mine. It lasts longer than destruction, grief does. As you will learn."

Whereupon she made a sign before Lathro's face. The eager life came back into his brown eyes to break my heart, but he never looked at me, only asking Dragine, "Is it time? Has the Being come at last?"

"Soon, boy," she answered him soothingly. "Very soon now." Her eyes were full of triumph as she looked back at me, saying, "You see how it is? He has no care for you, nor for anything but his desire. The memory of Willalou's daughter has vanished, making you a ghost to him, and any dream of your future together just that, a dream, long slipped away with the morning. Nor will being made a *maj*—oh, yes, the Being will certainly grant his wish—bring him home to you, no more than I will ever have your father back. So here we both are, abandoned forever by our loves—" and this time the smile was as joyously murderous as a rock-*targ*'s skull-baring grin, just before it strikes for the throat or the contents of your stomach—"and all of it, *all,* due to the devices of the clever, wicked woman from whose wickedness you spring. Do you understand me at last, witch-girl?"

"No," I said. "I will not. I will not understand you." Rather than listen further to her, or to myself, I turned desperately to Lathro, saying, "Love, love, here I am, your Moon-Fox, your Breya. Can't you see me, don't you know me at all?" I even shook him a little, grasping his shoulders, to no avail.

His eyes were warm and alive, as I have said, but I was not in them. Whoever he saw standing before him, shrilling like a locust, it was not I. He spoke for the first time, saying, with some wonder in his voice, "You are so pretty. I never imagined the Being would be pretty."

I choked on my own sudden tears, and Dragine laughed in purest delight, sounding almost like a happy child. "Nay, she's no Being, boy, she can give you nothing you need, my word on it. Come, we'll call now, you and I."

She moved to the edge of the pool, spread her hands over the starfish shimmering in its depths, and spoke to them too rapidly for me to catch more than a few of the words. They were in a tongue I had heard my mother speak: it is very old, and there are some bad stories about its origins. Lathro joined in the calling, briefly and stumblingly, as Dragine's voice rose to a kind of shrill croon, not loud, but *high,* high enough that it disappeared at the end, like a lark or a falcon climbing out of sight. I wanted to cover my ears, but I didn't. A moment later I very nearly covered my eyes, because the surface of the pool gradually began to swirl counterclockwise, right to left, gaining speed until the sound of its spinning echoed Dragine's uncanny wail. It no longer looked like water: first it was black stone—then starlit spiraling diamond—and finally it was jeweled smoke, sparkling pale-blue smoke, whirling slowly into shape, like clay on my father's wheel. A figure began to rise out of the little pool.

It was man-shaped, but not a man. I never did determine what it was, or even what it chose to resemble, so sinuously and playfully did it sport from form to smoky near-form. At one moment it might have been a sort of hornless goat, dancing on its hind legs; but step closer to the pool, or consider it from another angle—or simply *wait*—and it seemed an enormous head, with black wriggly-wet things like eels where its teeth should have been, and that head was dancing too. Or let a small pewter cloud hide a star or two, and behold then a dead tree, its skeletal boughs aswarm with glittering, watchful stone eyes; or again you might suddenly be staring at a great almost-butterfly, burning as it whirled, yet never consumed, though its blaze dazzled even Dragine's eyes. She turned from it to stare at me, and though she said nothing, yet I heard her in my mind, her silent laughter echoing within me.

"She arranged it all, witch-girl. She set your man all afire to get rid of him...then set you to find him, after training you up to face the Being who comes when I call, as she well knows. A Being who has more power than she ever dreamed of having, for all her hopes, all her craving..."

When the Being spoke out of its flaming, shifting whirlwind, it addressed itself directly to me. Through all its constant transformations its voice remained the same: a deep, deep buzzing that I heard along my spine and in my cheekbones more than in my ears. "There will be no confrontation between us, Breya Drom, because there is no reason for such a thing. You have already lost any battle there could be."

"Have I, then?" Compared to that voice, I sounded to myself like a little girl refusing to go to bed. But I was profoundly weary, and deeply frightened, and more stubbornly angry than either. I said, "Whatever battles my mother had in mind, she will have to find someone else to fight them. All I came for was Lathro Baraquil."

"And all *he* came for, he has already found." The Being extended what was momentarily a hand toward Lathro, and he *hungered* toward it—that is the best word I can find—reaching out with his whole self, but I pushed his hand away before they could meet.

"We are going home," I said. "Lathro and I."

The Being chuckled. It had slowed its spinning—a dizzying effect by itself—and was regarding me out of a single eye in the flat face of a creature a bit like a furry fish. It buzzed. "Tell *him* that, girl." Lathro looked as though he were about to jump into the pool: not to gain any gift from the Being, but to join with it, to become part of it, as he had been part of me so long ago. The Being said to him, "Ask and have, Lathro Baraquil."

Behind me Dragine laughed once, a single bark, bruising my ears. "Yes! Ask and have, boy. Ask and have!"

And suddenly it was all too much for me—too much and too little at the same time. All of it, all: Lathro's dream of carrying magic...Willalou's shameless machinations...Dragine's vengefulness...my own idiot journey in pursuit of my useless fantasies...the Being's benign disregard... even being called *witch-girl* one time too many. Suddenly I wanted no further part of it, even if it cost me my one love. "Do what you will," I said aloud, though none seemed to hear me. "Do what you please, I'm done." And I turned my back on the lot of them, and I walked away.

Nor did I turn again, not until I heard the Being's insect-whirr once more, "Ask and have of me, Lathro Baraquil," and Lathro's voice, that I had first heard mumbling *I come for a wash*, saying now, loudly and boldly, "Then I ask for the full powers and abilities of a true *maj*, and I ask further—"

But by then I was singing.

I have no memory of making that decision, or of choosing the charm I sang. It has only happened so for me once or twice, since. What I do remember is that Lathro went mute on the instant, and that Dragine whirled, wrinkled lips drawn back, furiously chanting a counterspell that I warded off easily with a gesture. That made me overconfident— I was young, after all—and I was not prepared when the Being struck at me with...with what? A spell, was it? A cantrip of some sort? A hex, even? Did the Being know any of those words, did it think in those terms? No matter: my brain was too occupied with careening from one side of the universe to the other, and I could not find my legs and arms. There was a howling in my head.

I stood up—somebody did, anyway—and saw that the Being had flowed into the form of something that might have set out to be a claw-footed, stinking *churfa*, and changed its mind halfway along, for the worse. It said, "Give over, Breya Drom. Go your way and leave me to mine, and your man to the way he has chosen. What he pays to walk it may not be what Dragine paid—but in any case, he is lost to you. Give over, child. Go home."

I might have done just that, had Dragine not squalled at that moment, "And tell your mother we are quits when you get there." Her face was as savagely satisfied as though she had been making love all night long.

Lathro was silent still, but not staring worshipfully at the Being now. He was looking directly toward me, and it seemed to me that there was at least *something* like recognition in his face—something surfacing that was near to being my Lathro. I dared not think any further than that.

Not that there was time for it, since I had no illusions that the Being's words meant truce; they certainly didn't to me. Lathro was coming home with me, whether he wanted to or not—his desires had just become completely irrelevant. Dragine aimed a second spell at me: a spiteful thing that would likely have cost me a few years in beetle shape, had she managed it, but I batted it back at her like a featherball, such as children play with, and kept my attention focused on the Being. Willalou may indeed have decoyed me to its den and its acolyte to destroy it; my only concern now was to keep it from destroying me. Nothing in my body was working properly, except my blood, and that was up and raging. I took a deep breath, began walking directly towards the Being, and I sang as I went.

Not until I began that song had I truly known I was an enchantress, for all my proud disdain. Do you understand me, huddling there, as far from me as the walls of your lair will let you, with your red eyes counting the minutes until the moon is gone? It was one of the many things I had never bothered to learn, you see. I knew who my mother was, for good or ill, and that my power descended from her, and from my mothers before her. I knew that Willalou was a sorceress, and that a sorceress thinks about magic—with great care, in most cases. But an enchantress *is* magic, *is* what she does: an enchantress dwells in a place, not without thought, but beyond it, somewhere on some other side. And I hadn't known that, for all my mother's harping on how much greater than herself I was born to be. Some things cannot be known, only experienced.

With that song, with those charmed notes leaping up out of me like children—for all I knew at the time, the only children I was ever likely to have—I came of age.

The Being had reverted to the whirling cone of pale-blue smoke that I had first seen rising out of the pool. I felt its enormous blasts of heat and energy hammering at me, and I know most of them connected somewhere, but it did not seem to matter, it seemed to be happening very far off, to someone else. The song I sang was our family's ancient war chant: few beyond the family have ever heard it, and nobody sings it but us. I knew the Being could not have heard it before.

The song built up momentum, like a sling whirled round and round the head until you at last let go. When I did, with the last stanza, the recoil—there is no other word—lifted me and hurled me across that open space, helpless as a new-hatched canary in a cloudburst. It slammed me first into a white wall, then tumbled me straight into Dragine's pool. I seem to remember the water tasting somehow burned, but I could be wrong. I was drowning at the time.

It was a shallow little pool, but you can drown just as easily in inches as in fathoms, and I wasn't even conscious enough to lift my head out of the water. Lathro it was who picked me up, and then put me down carefully and dried my wet clothes as best he could. He whispered "*Moon Fox...Moon Fox,*" over and over as he did so.

The Being itself was out of the pool, stumbling near me—almost over me, as I sat up—on absurdly pink pigeon feet far too small for the hulking, unwieldy form it appeared to have been trapped in by my song. I cannot adequately describe that shape: it had something of flesh to it, but more was quite simply wooden, or almost wooden...and there was, about the face, if that is what it was, a sort of...No. No. All I know is that it was dying, and blind, and that I felt sorry for it, for the Being, whatever it had so nearly cost Lathro and me. And when it managed to buzz out, "*I have had my price, all the same...*" before it toppled and crashed down, there were tears in my eyes. I did not understand what it had told me, not then.

Lathro took my hand without speaking. I said, "Well, there goes your chance at magic. Perhaps you'll forgive me one day."

Dragine was on her knees beside the fallen Being. After a moment she reached out slowly to touch the blind face, that face that I cannot portray any more than I could the look in her eyes. Lathro took my own face between his hands, as of old, this time so gently and timorously that I could barely feel it. He said, "The question is whether you can forgive me. I only wanted to be a proper match for you, Breya."

I stopped him, and not gently. "And just exactly what have you been to me since we were five years old? Can you honestly imagine me partnered with anyone else in the entire world? Anyone?"

"No. No, I never could, you know that. But then our children—"

"Bugger the children!" I picked that word up from Dunreath when I was quite small, and he was having a bad day with his pots and jugs. "If my line's knack comes to an end with me—well, so it does. Too many *majkes* in the family, anyway, and not enough blacksmiths."

Bruised and hurting everywhere, I was yet holding him so hard that I was having as much trouble breathing as he was. I said, "Home. We are going home now."

Strangely—or perhaps not—Dragine showed me no rancor for having caused the end of the Being; indeed, she showed nothing at all, but only crouched on her heels by the great dead thing, still touching it now and again. Once, when she looked up and saw me staring, as I could not help doing, she said in her desert voice, "It was my friend. Go away."

So we took the road home to Kalagira, the two of us astride Belgarth, who carries double easily, though he complains vigorously in the mornings. It took us a long time, but we didn't mind. There's little to tell of that passage, except for a moment I do like to remember, when I suggested proudly to Lathro that he had but to say the word and I could surely make our journey a great deal easier for everyone involved, and perhaps even eliminate it altogether. What's the good of being an enchantress, after all, if you can't show off for your beloved once in a while?

But Lathro refused. He said—and I have it still in my head, word for firm word—"Breya Drom, through my foolishness we have already missed too much of our time together in this world, and risked all. I will not lose another minute of you, another second, for good or ill, ever again."

When we reached my home, I asked Lathro to stable Belgarth for me, and he nodded understandingly. "You'll want some time alone with your mother. Of course." I watched him walk away with the old horse, and felt my heart floating after him. Then I left my shoes at the door, and went in.

She was practicing on her *kiit* in her workroom; I could hear the music as I came along the corridor. Her hands are not quite big enough for the full-sized instrument she insists on using, but she plays well all the same—I loved to have her play me to sleep when I was small.

She spoke to me before I had even reached her workroom. "Welcome, daughter. Welcome, my pride." No one catches Willalou unaware: and what I now was she would have sensed two villages away.

She put down the *kiit* and came swiftly to enfold me, but I held her off with a raised hand. How strange that did feel, evading my mother's embrace for the first time in my life. I could hear the comforting old sound of Dunreath's wheel going, deep in his own studio, and was desperately glad that he was not present. I said, "We talk."

She stood straight now, as always, and looked into my eyes and shrugged slightly. She said, "I did what was necessary. No more, and no less."

"I think not," I said. "I think bloody not."

"The Being is dead. There will be no others, and so no witches or sorceresses who should never have been *majkes*, not ever. Dragine had no power in her before her desperate bargain, and she is broken now, no danger to anyone. You did these things, not I, and it is a little late for qualms and regrets. As though you had any need of them."

I had to fight off the appeal of her smile, exactly as I had had to deal with Dragine's spells, except that this was much harder, and took much more of me. I said, "You manipulated everything. *Everything.* You goaded Lathro into running off to make himself worthy of me, thinking that would be the end of him—and then you put me through that whole charade of *training*—"

"Charade?" My mother spat the word out, genuinely furious; no elegant playacting here. "I saved your life, ungrateful idiot! You would be dead now—or worse, much worse—if I had not forced you to become what you were supposed to be, what I had come to despair of your ever bothering to be. I made you an enchantress, my daughter, which was more than your inheritance or your own nature could have done, and what matter if I used all the world to do it. Will you give me the lie, then?"

Rage can often make plain, homely people beautiful, or almost so. It does not have the same effect on beautiful ones like my mother. I said, "It was poor Dragine, and the Being itself, who made me an enchantress. You made me a tool." I fell silent for a moment, because my own anger suddenly had me by the throat, and I could barely breathe with it. "And I could have stood that—I could have endured it all and still trusted you, and loved you—but for the look of my Lathro when he opened Dragine's door and did not know me."

My mother had the grace not to speak. My mother has a great deal of grace.

"You ensorcelled my love," I said. "You *dared*," and how I got that word out, I will never know. "Lathro was under your spell from the moment he left this house and set off to find the Being, as you had charged him, bidding him forget me. But you had not counted on the strength of his love; he was throwing off the charm before ever I defeated the Being." I actually smiled at her then, so proud I was of Lathro. "You should have known better, Mother."

There was no surrender in Willalou, no smallest yielding; I would never have expected any. "When I was training you, I knew that it might one day come to this—that if you survived the trials for which I was preparing you, you would return with mastery enough to punish me for deceiving you. Do it, then. I did what I did, and unlike you I regret none of it. Do as you choose, Breya. Don't dally, girl, *do* it."

I think she may very well have expected death, but I could not do that to Dunreath. So I did something else instead.

She never lowered her eyes from mine as I sang three words that stripped her power from her, leaving her as mortal as my father, as vulnerable to the world as Lathro's first kiss had made me feel. She took a single long breath—then went back to her chair, picked up the *kiit,* and began to play again.

We have not spoken since.

And, yes, if it could possibly interest a demon, I regret that. But it was to be expected, for the Being's last words were spoken truly. I did pay a price that night in Muldeary: I lost my mother. At need an enchantress can deceive anyone or anything but herself, but no spell in my throat could ever hide the truth of Willalou from me, no matter how much I may sometimes wish it.

So here I sit now, in your lair, watching the moon over your spine-crested shoulder, and feeling the quickening inside me. Not even Lathro knows yet, but I am with child. Actually, I think I am with children, for I can already sense the doubleness, though it is too soon for them to be much more than two breaths. Daughters, I hope, though *majkes* they will not be, neither of them. They are Lathro's children. That is magic enough.

The moon is down and gone, and it has come time for me to sing you to your end—or, for all I know, your beginning—in some demon afterworld. It seems a pity, after having spent this night telling you things I have never spoken of to another human, but there it is. You can only be what you are, with that nasty fixation of yours on other people's livers and hearts...and I can only be myself. It has cost me what it has cost me, but I am an enchantress, which is different from a witch or a sorceress, and I have more lives to guard than just the two I carry. You do understand? I would truly prefer to think so.

Goodbye, demon. Goodbye.

Uncle Chaim and Aunt Rifke and the Angel

My Uncle Chaim, who was a painter, was working in his studio—as he did on every day except Shabbos—when the blue angel showed up. I was there.

I was usually there most afternoons, dropping in on my way home from Fiorello LaGuardia Elementary School. I was what they call a "latchkey kid," these days. My parents both worked and traveled full-time, and Uncle Chaim's studio had been my home base and my real playground since I was small. I was shy and uncomfortable with other children. Uncle Chaim didn't have any kids, and didn't know much about them, so he talked to me like an adult when he talked at all, which suited me perfectly. I looked through his paintings and drawings, tried some of my own, and ate Chinese food with him in silent companionship, when he remembered that we should probably eat. Sometimes I fell asleep on the cot. And when his friends—who were mostly painters like himself—dropped in to visit, I withdrew into my favorite corner and listened to their talk, and understood what I understood. Until the blue angel came.

It was very sudden: one moment I was looking through a couple of the comic books Uncle Chaim kept around for me, while he was trying to catch the highlight on the tendons under his model's chin, and the next moment there was this angel standing before him, actually *posing,* with her arms spread out and her great wings taking up almost half the studio. She was not blue herself—a light beige would be closer—but she wore a blue robe that managed to look at once graceful and grand, with a white undergarment glimmering beneath. Her face, half-shadowed by a loose hood, looked disapproving.

I dropped the comic book and stared. No, I *gaped,* there's a difference. Uncle Chaim said to her, "I can't see my model. If you wouldn't mind moving just a bit?" He was grumpy when he was working, but never rude.

"*I* am your model," the angel said. "From this day forth, you will paint no one but me."

"I don't work on commission," Uncle Chaim answered. "I used to, but you have to put up with too many aggravating rich people. Now I just paint what I paint, take it to the gallery. Easier on my stomach, you know?"

His model, the wife of a fellow painter, said, "Chaim, who are you talking to?"

"Nobody, nobody, Ruthie. Just myself, same way your Jules does when he's working. Old guys get like that." To the angel, in a lower voice, he said, "Also, whatever you're doing to the light, could you not? I got some great shadows going right now." For a celestial brightness was swelling in the grubby little warehouse district studio, illuminating the warped floor boards, the wrinkled tubes of colors scattered everywhere, the canvases stacked and propped in the corners, along with several ancient rickety easels. It scared me, but not Uncle Chaim. He said. "So you're an angel, fine, that's terrific. Now give me back my shadows."

The room darkened obediently. "*Thank* you. Now about *moving…*" He made a brushing-away gesture with the hand holding the little glass of Scotch.

The model said, "Chaim, you're worrying me."

"What, I'm seventy-six years old, I'm not entitled to a hallucination now and then? I'm seeing an angel, you're not—this is no big deal. I just want it should move out of the way, let me work." The angel, in response, spread her wings even wider, and Uncle Chaim snapped, "Oh, for God's sake, shoo!"

"It is for God's sake that I am here," the angel announced majestically. "The Lord—Yahweh—I Am That I Am—has sent me down to be your muse." She inclined her head a trifle, by way of accepting the worship and wonder she expected.

From Uncle Chaim, she didn't get it, unless very nearly dropping his glass of Scotch counts as a compliment. "A muse?" he snorted. "I don't need a muse—I got models!"

"That's it," Ruthie said. "I'm calling Jules, I'll make him come over and sit with you." She put on her coat, picked up her purse, and headed for the door, saying over her shoulder, "Same time Thursday? If you're still here?"

"I got more models than I know what to do with," Uncle Chaim told the blue angel. "Men, women, old, young—even a cat, there's one lady always brings her cat, what am I going to do?" He heard the door slam, realized that Ruthie was gone, and sighed irritably, taking a larger swallow of whiskey than he usually allowed himself. "Now she's upset, she thinks she's my mother anyway, she'll send Jules with chicken soup and an enema." He narrowed his eyes at the angel. "And what's this, how I'm only going to be painting you from now on? Like Velázquez stuck painting royal Hapsburg imbeciles over and over? Some hope you've got! Listen, you go back and tell—" he hesitated just a trifle—"tell whoever sent you that Chaim Malakoff is too old not to paint what he likes, when he likes, and for who he likes. You got all that? We're clear?"

It was surely no way to speak to an angel; but as Uncle Chaim used to warn me about everyone from neighborhood bullies to my fourth-grade teacher, who hit people, "You give the bastards an inch, they'll walk all over you. From me they get *bupkes, nichevo,* nothing. Not an inch." I got beaten up more than once in those days, saying that to the wrong people.

And the blue angel was definitely one of them. The entire room suddenly filled with her: with the wings spreading higher than the ceiling, wider than the walls, yet somehow not touching so much as a stick of charcoal; with the aroma almost too impossibly haunting to be borne; with the vast, unutterable beauty that a thousand medieval and Renaissance artists had somehow not gone mad (for the most part) try-ing to ambush on canvas or trap in stone. In that moment, Uncle Chaim confided later, he didn't know whether to pity or envy Muslims their ancient ban on depictions of the human body.

"I thought maybe I should kneel, what would it hurt? But then I thought, *what would it hurt?* It'd hurt my left knee, the one had the arthritis twenty years, that's what it would hurt." So he only shrugged a little and told her, "I could manage a sitting on Monday. Somebody cancelled, I got the whole morning free."

"Now," the angel said. Her air of distinct disapproval had become one of authority. The difference was slight but notable.

"*Now,*" Uncle Chaim mimicked her. "All right, already—Ruthie left early, so why not?" He moved the unfinished portrait over to anoth-er easel, and carefully selected a blank canvas from several propped against a wall. "I got to clean off a couple of brushes here, we'll start. You want to take off that thing, whatever, on your head?" Even I knew perfectly well that it was a halo, but Uncle Chaim always told me that you had to start with people as you meant to go on.

"You will require a larger surface," the angel instructed him. "I am not to be represented in miniature."

Uncle Chaim raised one eyebrow (an ability I envied him to the point of practicing—futilely—in the bathroom mirror for hours, until my parents banged on the door, certain I was up to the worst kind of no good). "No, huh? Good enough for the Persians, good enough for Holbein and Hilliard and Sam Cooper, but not for you? So okay, so we'll try this one…" Rummaging in a corner, he fetched out his biggest canvas, dusted it off, eyed it critically—"Don't even remember what I'm doing with anything this size, must have been saving it for you"—and finally set it up on the empty easel, turning it away from the angel. "Okay, Malakoff's rules. Nobody—*nobody*—looks at my painting till I'm done. Not angels, not Adonai, not my nephew over there in the corner, that's David, Duvidl—not even my wife. Nobody. Understood?"

The angel nodded, almost imperceptibly. With surprising meekness, she asked, "Where shall I sit?"

"Not a lot of choices," Uncle Chaim grunted, lifting a brush from a jar of turpentine. "Over there's okay, where Ruthie was sitting—or maybe by the big window. The window would be good, we've lost the shadows already. Take the red chair, I'll fix the color later."

But sitting down is not a natural act for an angel: they stand or they fly; check any Renaissance painting. The great wings inevitably get crumpled, the halo always winds up distinctly askew; and there is simply no way, even for Uncle Chaim, to ask an angel to cross her legs or to hook one over the arm of the chair. In the end they compromised, and the blue angel rose up to pose in the window, holding herself there effortlessly, with her wings not stirring at all. Uncle Chaim, settling in to work—brushes cleaned and Scotch replenished—could not refrain from remarking, "I always imagined you guys sort of hovered. Like hummingbirds."

"We fly only by the Will of God," the angel replied. "If Yahweh, praised be His name—" I could actually *hear* the capital letters— "withdrew that mighty Will from us, we would fall from the sky on the instant, every single one."

"Doesn't bear thinking about," Uncle Chaim muttered. "Raining angels all over everywhere—falling on people's heads, tying up traffic—"

The angel looked, first startled, and then notably shocked. "I was speaking of *our* sky," she explained haughtily, "the sky of Paradise, which compares to yours as gold to lead, tapestry to tissue, heavenly choirs to the bellowing of feeding hogs—"

"All *right* already, I get the picture." Uncle Chaim cocked an eye at her, poised up there in the window with no visible means of support, and then back at his canvas. "I was going to ask you about being an angel, what it's like, but if you're going to talk about us like that—badmouthing the *sky*, for God's sake, the whole *planet*."

The angel did not answer him immediately, and when she did, she appeared considerably abashed and spoke very quietly, almost like a scolded schoolgirl. "You are right. It is His sky, His world, and I shame my Lord, my fellows and my breeding by speaking slightingly of any part of it." In a lower voice, she added, as though speaking only to herself, "Perhaps that is why I am here."

Uncle Chaim was covering the canvas with a thin layer of very light blue, to give the painting an undertone. Without looking up, he said, "What, you got sent down here like a punishment? You talked back, you didn't take out the garbage? I could believe it. Your boy Yahweh, he always did have a short fuse."

"I was told only that I was to come to you and be your model and your muse," the angel answered. She pushed her hood back from her face, revealing hair that was not bright gold, as so often painted, but of a color resembling the night sky when it pales into dawn. "Angels do not ask questions."

"Mmm." Uncle Chaim sipped thoughtfully at his Scotch. "Well, one did, anyway, you believe the story."

The angel did not reply, but she looked at him as though he had uttered some unimaginable obscenity. Uncle Chaim shrugged and continued preparing the ground for the portrait. Neither one said anything for some time, and it was the angel who spoke first. She said, a trifle hesitantly, "I have never been a muse before."

"Never had one," Uncle Chaim replied sourly. "Did just fine."

"I do not know what the duties of a muse would be," the angel confessed. "You will need to advise me."

"What?" Uncle Chaim put down his brush. "Okay now, wait a minute. *I* got to tell you how to get into my hair, order me around, probably tell me how I'm not painting you right? Forget it, lady—you figure it out for yourself, I'm working here."

But the blue angel looked confused and unhappy, which is no more natural for an angel than sitting down. Uncle Chaim scratched his head and said, more gently, "What do I know? I guess you're supposed to stimulate my creativity, something like that. Give me ideas, visions, make me see things, think about things I've never thought about." After a pause, he added, "Frankly, Goya pretty much has that effect on me already. Goya and Matisse. So that's covered, the stimulation—maybe you could just tell them, *him*, about that…"

Seeing the expression on the angel's marble-smooth face, he let the sentence trail away. Rabbi Shulevitz, who cut his blond hair close and wore shorts when he watered his lawn, once told me that angels are supposed to express God's emotions and desires, without being troubled by any of their own. "Like a number of other heavenly dictates," he murmured when my mother was out of the room, "that one has never quite functioned as I'm sure it was intended."

They were still working in the studio when my mother called and ordered me home. The angel had required no rest or food at all, while Uncle Chaim had actually been drinking his Scotch instead of sipping it (I never once saw him drunk, but I'm not sure that I ever saw him entirely sober), and needed more bathroom breaks than usual. Daylight gone, and his precarious array of 60-watt bulbs proving increasingly unsatisfactory, he looked briefly at the portrait, covered it, and said to the angel, "Well, *that* stinks, but we'll do better tomorrow. What time you want to start?"

The angel floated down from the window to stand before him. Uncle Chaim was a small man, dark and balding, but he already knew that the angel altered her height when they faced each other, so as not to overwhelm him completely. She said, "I will be here when you are."

Uncle Chaim misunderstood. He assured her that if she had no other place to sleep but the studio, it wouldn't be the first time a model or a friend had spent the night on that trundle bed in the far corner. "Only no peeking at the picture, okay? On your honor as a muse."

The blue angel looked for a moment as though she were going to smile, but she didn't. "I will not sleep here, or anywhere on this earth," she said. "But you will find me waiting when you come."

"Oh," Uncle Chaim said. "Right. Of course. Fine. But don't change your clothes, okay? Absolutely no changing." The angel nodded.

When Uncle Chaim got home that night, my Aunt Rifke told my mother on the phone at some length, he was in a state that simply did not register on her long-practiced seismograph of her husband's moods. "He comes in, he's telling jokes, he eats up everything on the table, we snuggle up, watch a little TV, I can figure the work went well today. He doesn't talk, he's not hungry, he goes to bed early, tosses and tumbles around all night...okay, not so good. Thirty-seven years with a person, wait, you'll find out." Aunt Rifke had been Uncle Chaim's model until they married, and his agent, accountant and road manager ever since.

But the night he returned from beginning his portrait of the angel brought Aunt Rifke a husband she barely recognized. "Not up, not down, not happy, not *not* happy, just...*dazed*, I guess that's the best word. He'd start to eat something, then he'd forget about it, wander around the apartment—couldn't sit still, couldn't keep his mind on anything, had trouble even finishing a sentence. One sentence. I tell you, it scared me.

I couldn't keep from wondering, *is this how it begins?* A man starts acting strange, one day to the next, you think about things like that, you know?" Talking about it, even long past the moment's terror, tears still started in her eyes.

Uncle Chaim did tell her that he had been visited by an angel who demanded that he paint her portrait. *That* Aunt Rifke had no trouble believing, thirty-seven years of marriage to an artist having inured her to certain revelations. Her main concern was how painting an angel might affect Uncle Chaim's working hours, and his daily conduct. "Like actors, you know, Duvidl? They *become* the people they're doing, I've seen it over and over." Also, blasphemous as it might sound, she wondered how much the angel would be paying, and in what currency. "And saying we'll get a big credit in the next world is not funny, Chaim. *Not* funny."

Uncle Chaim urged Rifke to come to the studio the very next day to meet his new model for herself. Strangely, that lady, whom I'd known all my life as a legendary repository of other people's lives, stories and secrets, flatly refused to take him up on the offer. "I got nothing to wear, not for meeting an angel in. Besides, what would we talk about? No, you just give her my best, I'll make some *rugelach.*" And she never wavered from that position, except once.

The blue angel was indeed waiting when Uncle Chaim arrived in the studio early the next morning. She had even made coffee in his ancient glass percolator, and was offended when he informed her that it was as thin as rain and tasted like used dishwater. "Where I come from, no one ever *makes* coffee," she returned fire. "We command it."

"That's what's wrong with this crap," Uncle Chaim answered her. "Coffee's like art, you don't order coffee around." He waved the angel aside, and set about a second pot, which came out strong enough to widen the angel's eyes when she sipped it. Uncle Chaim teased her— "Don't get stuff like *that* in the Green Pastures, huh?"—and confided that he made much better coffee than Aunt Rifke. "Not her fault. Woman was raised on decaf, what can you expect? Cooks like an angel, though."

The angel either missed the joke or ignored it. She began to resume her pose in the window, but Uncle Chaim stopped her. "Later, later, the sun's not right. Just stand where you are, I want to do some work on the head." As I remember, he never used the personal possessive in referring to his models' bodies: it was invariably "turn the face a little," "relax the shoulder," "move the foot to the left." Amateurs often resented it; professionals tended to find it liberating. Uncle Chaim didn't much care either way.

For himself, he was grateful that the angel proved capable of holding a pose indefinitely, without complaining, asking for a break, or needing the toilet. What he found distracting was her steadily emerging interest in talking and asking questions. As requested, her expression never changed and her lips hardly moved; indeed, there were times when he would have sworn he was hearing her only in his mind. Enough of her queries had to do with his work, with how he did what he was doing, that he finally demanded point-blank, "All those angels, seraphs, cherubim, centuries of them—all those Virgins and Assumptions and whatnot—and you've never once been painted? Not one time?"

"I have never set foot on earth before," the angel confessed. "Not until I was sent to you."

"Sent to me. Directly. Special Delivery, Chaim Shlomovitch Malakoff—one angel, totally inexperienced at modeling. Or anything else, got anything to do with human life." The angel nodded, somewhat shyly. Uncle Chaim spoke only one word. "*Why?*"

"I am only eleven thousand, seven hundred and twenty-two years old," the angel said, with a slight but distinct suggestion of resentment in her voice. "No one tells me a *thing*."

Uncle Chaim was silent for some time, squinting at her face from different angles and distances, even closing one eye from time to time. Finally he grumbled, more than half to himself, "I got a very bad feeling that we're both supposed to learn something from this. Bad, bad feeling." He filled the little glass for the first time that day, and went back to work.

But if there was to be any learning involved in their near-daily meetings in the studio, it appeared to be entirely on her part. She was ravenously curious about human life on the blue-green ball of damp dirt that she had observed so distantly for so long, and her constant questioning reminded a weary Uncle Chaim—as he informed me more than once—of me at the age of four. Except that an angel cannot be bought off, even temporarily, with strawberry ice cream, or threatened with loss of a bedtime story if she can't learn to take "I don't *know!*" for an answer. At times he pretended not to hear her; on other occasions, he would make up some patently ridiculous explanation that a grandchild would have laughed to scorn, but that the angel took so seriously that he was guiltily certain he was bound to be struck by lightning. Only the lightning never came, and the tactic usually did buy him a few moments peace—until the next question.

Once he said to her, in some desperation, "You're an angel, you're supposed to know everything about human beings. Listen, I'll take you out to Bleecker, MacDougal, Washington Square, you can look at the books, magazines, TV, the classes, the beads and crystals…it's all about how to get in touch with angels. Real ones, real angels, never mind that stuff about the angel inside you. Everybody wants some of that angel wisdom, and they want it bad, and they want it right now. We'll take an afternoon off, I'll show you."

The blue angel said simply, "The streets and the shops have nothing to show me, nothing to teach. You do."

"No," Uncle Chaim said. "No, no, no, no, *no*. I'm a painter—that's all, that's it, that's what I know. Painting. But you, you sit at the right hand of God—"

"He doesn't have hands," the angel interrupted. "And nobody exactly *sits*—"

"The point I'm making, you're the one who ought to be answering questions. About the universe, and about Darwin, and how everything really happened, and what is it with God and shellfish, and the whole business with the milk and the meat—*those* kinds of questions. I mean, I should be asking them, I know that, only I'm working right now."

It was almost impossible to judge the angel's emotions from the expressions of her chillingly beautiful porcelain face; but as far as Uncle Chaim could tell, she looked sad. She said, "I also am what I am. We angels—as you call us—we are messengers, minions, lackeys, knowing only what we are told, what we are ordered to do. A few of the Oldest, the ones who were there at the Beginning—Michael, Gabriel, Raphael— *they* have names, thoughts, histories, choices, powers. The rest of us, we tremble, we *hide* when we see them passing by. We think, *if those are angels, we must be something else altogether,* but we can never find a better word for ourselves."

She looked straight at Uncle Chaim—he noticed in some surprise that in a certain light her eyes were not nearly as blue as he had been painting them, but closer to a dark sea-green—and he looked away from an anguish that he had never seen before, and did not know how to paint. He said, "So okay, you're a low-class angel, a heavenly grunt, like they say now. So how come they picked you to be my muse? Got to mean *something*, no? Right?"

The angel did not answer his question, nor did she speak much for the rest of the day. Uncle Chaim posed her in several positions, but the unwonted sadness in her eyes depressed him past even Laphroaig's ability to ameliorate. He quit work early, allowing the angel—as he would never have permitted Aunt Rifke or me—to potter around the studio, putting it to rights according to her inexpert notions, organizing brushes, oils, watercolors, pastels and pencils, fixatives, rolls of canvas, bottles of tempera and turpentine, even dusty chunks of rabbit skin glue, according to size. As he told his friend Jules Sidelsky, meeting for their traditional weekly lunch at a Ukrainian restaurant on Second Avenue, where the two of them spoke only Russian, "Maybe God could figure where things are anymore. Me, I just shut my eyes and pray."

Jules was large and fat, like Diego Rivera, and I thought of him as a sort of uncle too, because he and Ruthie always remembered my birthday, just like Uncle Chaim and Aunt Rifke. Jules did not believe in angels, but he knew that Uncle Chaim didn't necessarily believe in them either, just because he had one in his studio every day. He asked seriously, "That helps? The praying?" Uncle Chaim gave him a look, and Jules dropped the subject. "So what's she like? I mean, as a model? You like painting her?"

Uncle Chaim held his hand out, palm down, and wobbled it gently from side to side. "What's not to like? She'll hold any pose absolutely forever—you could leave her all night, morning I guarantee she wouldn't have moved a muscle. No whining, no bellyaching—listen, she'd make Cinderella look like the witch in that movie, the green one. In my life I never worked with anybody gave me less *tsuris.*"

"So what's with—?" and Jules mimicked his fluttering hand. "I'm waiting for the *but,* Chaim."

Uncle Chaim was still for a while, neither answering nor appearing to notice the steaming *varyniki* that the waitress had just set down before him. Finally he grumbled, "She's an angel, what can I tell you? Go reason with an angel." He found himself vaguely angry with Jules, for no reason that made any sense. He went on, "She's got it in her head she's supposed to be my muse. It's not the most comfortable thing sometimes, all right?"

Perhaps due to their shared childhood on Tenth Avenue, Jules did not laugh, but it was plainly a near thing. He said, mildly enough, "Matisse had muses. Rodin, up to here with muses. Picasso about had to give them serial numbers—I think he married them just to keep them straight in his head. You, me...I don't see it, Chaim. We're not muse types, you know? Never were, not in all our lives. Also, Rifke would kill you dead. Deader."

"What, I don't know that? Anyway, it's not what you're thinking." He grinned suddenly, in spite of himself. "She's not that kind of girl, you ought to be ashamed. It's just she wants to help, to inspire, that's what muses do. I don't mind her messing around with *my* mess in the studio—I mean, yeah, I mind it, but I can live with it. But the other day—"

he paused briefly, taking a long breath—"the other day she wanted to give me a haircut. A haircut. It's all right, go ahead."

For Jules was definitely laughing this time, spluttering tea through his nose, so that he turned a bright cerise as other diners stared at them. "A haircut," he managed to get out, when he could speak at all clearly. "An angel gave you a haircut."

"No, she didn't *give* me a haircut," Uncle Chaim snapped back crossly. "She wanted to, she offered—and then, when I said *no, thanks,* after awhile she said she could play music for me while I worked. I usually have the news on, and she doesn't like it, I can tell. Well, it wouldn't make much sense to her, would it? Hardly does to me anymore."

"So she's going to be posing *and* playing music? What, on her harp? That's true, the harp business?"

"No, she just said she could command the music. The way they do with coffee." Jules stared at him. "Well, *I* don't know—I guess it's like some heavenly Muzak or something. Anyway, I told her no, and I'm sorry I told you anything. Eat, forget it, okay?"

But Jules was not to be put off so easily. He dug down into his *galushki poltavski* for a little time, and then looked up and said with his mouth full, "Tell me one thing, then I'll drop it. Would you say she was beautiful?"

"She's an angel," Uncle Chaim said.

"That's not what I asked. Angels are all supposed to be beautiful, right? Beyond words, beyond description, the works. So?" He smiled serenely at Uncle Chaim over his folded hands.

Uncle Chaim took so long to answer him that Jules actually waved a hand directly in front of his eyes. "Hello? Earth to Malakoff—this is your wakeup call. You in there, Chaim?"

"I'm there, I'm there, stop with the kid stuff." Uncle Chaim flicked his own fingers dismissively at his friend's hand. "Jules, all I can tell you, I never saw anyone looked like her before. Maybe that's beauty all by itself, maybe it's just novelty. Some days she looks eleven thousand years old, like she says—some days...some days she could be younger than Duvidl, she could be the first child in the world, first one ever." He shook his head helplessly. "I don't *know,* Jules. I wish I could ask Rembrandt or somebody. Vermeer. Vermeer would know."

Strangely, of the small corps of visitors to the studio—old painters like himself and Jules, gallery owners, art brokers, friends from the neighborhood—I seemed to be the only one who ever saw the blue angel as anything other than one of his unsought acolytes, perfectly happy to stretch canvases, make sandwiches and occasionally pose, all for the gift of a growled thanks and the privilege of covertly studying him at work. My memory is that I regarded her as a nice-looking older lady with wings, but not my type at all, I having just discovered Alice Faye. Lauren Bacall, Lizabeth Scott and Lena Horne came a bit later in my development.

I knew she was an angel. I also knew better than to tell any of my own friends about her: we were a cynical lot, who regularly got thrown out of movie theatres for cheering on the Wolf Man and booing Shirley Temple and Bobby Breen. But I was shy with the angel, and—I guess—she with me, so I can't honestly say I remember much either in the way of conversation or revelation. Though I am still haunted by one particular moment when I asked her, straight out, "Up there, in heaven—do you ever see Jesus? Jesus Christ, I mean." We were hardly an observant family, any of us, but it still felt strange and a bit dangerous to say the name.

The blue angel turned from cleaning off a palette knife and looked directly at me, really for the first time since we had been introduced. I noticed that the color of her wings seemed to change from moment to moment, rippling constantly through a supple spectrum different from any I knew; and that I had no words either for her hair color, or for her smell. She said, "No, I have never seen him."

"Oh," I said, vaguely disappointed, Jewish or not. "Well—uh—what about his mother? The—the Virgin?" Funny, I remember that *that* seemed more daringly wicked than saying the other name out loud. I wonder why that should have been.

"No," the angel answered. "Nor—" heading me off—"have I ever seen God. You are closer to God now, as you stand there, than I have ever been."

"That doesn't make any sense," I said. She kept looking at me, but did not reply. I said, "I mean, you're an angel. Angels live with God, don't they?"

She shook her head. In that moment—and just for that moment—her richly empty face showed me a sadness that I don't think a human face could ever have contained. "Angels live alone. If we were with God, we would not be angels." She turned away, and I thought she had finished speaking. But then she looked back quite suddenly to say, in a voice that did not sound like her voice at all, being lower than the sound I knew, and almost masculine in texture, "*Dark and dark and dark...so empty... so dark...*"

It frightened me deeply, that one broken sentence, though I couldn't have said why: it was just so dislocating, so completely out of place—even the rhythm of those few words sounded more like the hesitant

English of our old Latvian rabbi than that of Uncle Chaim's muse. He didn't hear it, and I didn't tell him about it, because I thought it must be me, that I was making it up, or I'd heard it wrong. I was accustomed to thinking like that when I was a boy.

"She's got like a dimmer switch," Uncle Chaim explained to Aunt Rifke; they were putting freshly-washed sheets on the guest bed at the time, because I was staying the night to interview them for my Immigrant Experience class project. "Dial it one way, you wouldn't notice her if she were running naked down Madison Avenue at high noon, flapping her wings and waving a gun. Two guns. Turn that dial back the other way, all the way...well, thank God she wouldn't ever do that, because she'd likely set the studio on fire. You think I'm joking. I'm not joking."

"No, Chaim, I know you're not joking." Rifke silently undid and remade both of his attempts at hospital corners, as she always did. She said, "What I want to know is, just where's that dial set when you're painting her? And I'd think a bit about that answer, if I were you." Rifke's favorite cousin Harvey, a career social worker, had recently abandoned wife and children to run off with a beautiful young dope dealer, and Rifke was feeling more than slightly edgy.

Uncle Chaim did think about it, and replied, "About a third, I'd say. Maybe half, once or twice, no more. I remember, I had to ask her a couple times, turn it down, please—go work when somebody's *glowing* six feet away from you. I mean, the moon takes up a lot of space, a little studio like mine. Bad enough with the wings."

Rifke tucked in the last corner, smoothed the sheet tight, faced him across the bed and said, "You're never going to finish this one, are you? Thirty-seven years, I know all the signs. You'll do it over and over, you'll frame it, you'll hang it, you'll say, *okay, that's it, I'm done*—but you won't be done, you'll just start the whole thing again, only maybe a different style, a brighter palette, a bigger canvas, a smaller canvas. But you'll never get it the way it's in your head, not for you." She smacked the pillows fluffy and tossed them back on the bed. "Don't even bother arguing with me, Malakoff. Not when I'm right."

"So am I arguing? Does it look like I'm arguing?" Uncle Chaim rarely drank at home, but on this occasion he walked into the kitchen, filled a glass from the dusty bottle of *grappa*, and turned back to his wife. He said very quietly, "Crazy to think I could get an angel right. Who could paint an angel?"

Aunt Rifke came to him then and put her hands on his shoulders. "My crazy old man, that's who," she answered him. "Nobody else. God would know."

And my Uncle Chaim blushed for the first time in many years. I
didn't see this, but Aunt Rifke told me.

Of course, she was quite right about that painting, or any of the
many, many others he made of the blue angel. He was never satisfied
with any of them, not a one. There was always *something* wrong, something missing, something there but *not* there, glimpsed but gone. "Like
that Chinese monkey trying to grab the moon in the water," Uncle Chaim
said to me once. "That's me, a Chinese monkey."

Not that you could say he suffered financially from working with
only one model, as the angel had commanded. The failed portraits
that he lugged down to the gallery handling his paintings sold almost
instantly to museums, private collectors and corporations decorating
their lobbies and meeting rooms, under such generic titles as *Angel in
the Window, Blue Wings, Angel with Wineglass,* and *Midnight Angel.*
Aunt Rifke banked the money, and Uncle Chaim endured the unveilings
and the receptions as best he could—without ever looking at the paintings themselves—and then shuffled back to his studio to start over. The
angel was always waiting.

I was doing my homework in the studio when Jules Sidelsky visited
at last, lured there by other reasons than art, beauty or deity. The blue
angel hadn't given up the notion of acting as Uncle Chaim's muse, but
never seemed able to take it much beyond making a tuna salad sandwich,
or a pot of coffee (at which, to be fair, she had become quite skilled),
summoning music, or reciting the lost works of legendary or forgotten
poets while he worked. He tried to discourage this habit; but he did learn
a number of Shakespeare's unpublished sonnets, and was able to write
down for Jules three poems that drowned with Shelley off the Livorno
coast. "Also, your boy Pushkin, his wife destroyed a mess of his stuff
right after his death. My girl's got it all by heart, you believe that?"

Pushkin did it. If the great Russian had been declared a saint, Jules
would have reported for instruction to the Patriarch of Moscow on the
following day. As it was, he came down to Uncle Chaim's studio instead,
and was at last introduced to the blue angel, who was as gracious as
Jules did his bewildered best to be. She spent the afternoon declaiming
Pushkin's vanished verse to him in the original, while hovering tirelessly
upside down, just above the crossbar of a second easel. Uncle Chaim
thought he might be entering a surrealist phase.

Leaving, Jules caught Uncle Chaim's arm and dragged him out of his
door into the hot, bustling Village streets, once his dearest subject before
the coming of the blue angel. Uncle Chaim, knowing his purpose, said,
"So now you see? Now you see?"

"I see." Jules's voice was dark and flat, and almost without expression. "I see you got an angel there, all right. No question in the world about that." The grip on Uncle Chaim's arm tightened. Jules said, "You have to get rid of her."

"*What?* What are you *talking* about? Just finally doing the most important work of my life, and you want me...?" Uncle Chaim's eyes narrowed, and he pulled forcefully away from his friend. "What is it with you and my models? You got like this once before, when I was painting that Puerto Rican guy, the teacher, with the big nose, and you just couldn't stand it, you remember? Said I'd stolen him, wouldn't speak to me for weeks, *weeks,* you remember?"

"Chaim, that's not true—"

"And so now I've got this angel, it's the same thing—worse, with the Pushkin and all—"

"Chaim, damn it, I wouldn't care if she were Pushkin's sister, they played Monopoly together—"

Uncle Chaim's voice abruptly grew calmer; the top of his head stopped sweating and lost its crimson tinge. "I'm sorry, I'm sorry, Jules. It's not I don't understand, I've been the same way about other people's models." He patted the other's shoulder awkwardly. "Look, I tell you what, anytime you want, you come on over, we'll work together. How about that?"

Poor Jules must have been completely staggered by all this. On the one hand he knew—I mean, even *I* knew—that Uncle Chaim never invited other artists to share space with him, let alone a model; on the other, the sudden change can only have sharpened his anxiety about his old friend's state of mind. He said, "Chaim, I'm just trying to tell you, whatever's going on, it isn't good for you. Not her fault, not your fault. People and angels aren't supposed to hang out together—we aren't built for it, and neither are they. She really needs to go back where she belongs."

"She can't. Absolutely not." Uncle Chaim was shaking his head, and kept on shaking it. "She got *sent* here, Jules, she got sent to *me*—"

"By whom? You ever ask yourself that?" They stared at each other. Jules said, very carefully, "No, not by the Devil. I don't believe in the Devil any more than I believe in God, although he always gets the good lines. But it's a free country, and I *can* believe in angels without swallowing all the rest of it, if I want to." He paused, and took a gentler hold on Uncle Chaim's arm. "And I can also imagine that angels might not be exactly what we think they are. That an angel might lie, and still be an angel. That an angel might be selfish—jealous, even. That an angel might just be a little bit out of her head."

In a very pale and quiet voice, Uncle Chaim said, "You're talking about a fallen angel, aren't you?"

"I don't know what I'm talking about," Jules answered. "That's the God's truth." Both of them smiled wearily, but neither one laughed. Jules said, "I'm dead serious, Chaim. For your sake, your sanity, she needs to go."

"And for my sake, she can't." Uncle Chaim was plainly too exhausted for either pretense or bluster, but there was no give in him. He said, "*Landsmann,* it doesn't matter. You could be right, you could be wrong, I'm telling you, it doesn't matter. There's no one else I want to paint anymore—there's no one else I *can* paint, Jules, that's just how it is. Go home now." He refused to say another word.

In the months that followed, Uncle Chaim became steadily more silent, more reclusive, more closed-off from everything that did not directly involve the current portrait of the blue angel. By autumn, he was no longer meeting Jules for lunch at the Ukrainian restaurant; he could rarely be induced to appear at his own openings, or anyone else's; he frequently spent the night at his studio, sleeping briefly in his chair, when he slept at all. It had been understood between Uncle Chaim and me since I was three that I had the run of the place at any time; and while it was still true, I felt far less comfortable there than I was accustomed, and left it more and more to him and the strange lady with the wings.

When an exasperated—and increasingly frightened—Aunt Rifke would challenge him, "You've turned into Red Skelton, painting nothing but clowns on velvet—Margaret Keane, all those big-eyed war orphans," he only shrugged and replied, when he even bothered to respond, "You were the one who told me I could paint an angel. Change your mind?"

Whatever she truly thought, it was not in Aunt Rifke to say such a thing to him directly. Her only recourse was to mumble something like, "Even Leonardo gave up on drawing cats," or "You've done the best anybody could ever do—let it go now, let *her* go." Her own theory, differing somewhat from Jules's, was that it was as much Uncle Chaim's obsession as his model's possible madness that was holding the angel to earth. "Like Ella and Sam," she said to me, referring to the perpetually quarrelling parents of my favorite cousin Arthur. "Locked together, like some kind of punishment machine. Thirty years they hate each other, cats and dogs, but they're so scared of being alone, if one of them died—" she snapped her fingers—"the other one would be gone in a week. Like that. Okay, so not exactly like that, but like that." Aunt Rifke wasn't getting a lot of sleep either just then.

She confessed to me—it astonishes me to this day—that she prayed more than once herself, during the worst times. Even in my family, which still runs to atheists, agnostics and cranky anarchists, Aunt Rifke's unbelief was regarded as the standard by which all other blasphemy had to be judged, and set against which it invariably paled. The idea of a prayer from her lips was, on the one hand, fascinating—how would Aunt Rifke conceivably address a Supreme Being?—and more than a little alarming as well. Supplication was not in her vocabulary, let alone her repertoire. Command was.

I didn't ask her what she had prayed for. I did ask, trying to make her laugh, if she had commenced by saying, "To Whom it may concern..." She slapped my hand lightly. "Don't talk fresh, just because you're in fifth grade, sixth grade, whatever. Of course I didn't say that, an old Socialist Worker like me. I started off like you'd talk to some kid's mother on the phone, I said, 'It's time for your little girl to go home, we're going to be having dinner. You better call her in now, it's getting dark.' Like that, polite. But not fancy."

"And you got an answer?" Her face clouded, but she made no reply. "You didn't get an answer? Bad connection?" I honestly wasn't being fresh: this was my story too, somehow, all the way back, from the beginning, and I had to know where we were in it. "Come *on*, Aunt Rifke."

"I got an answer." The words came slowly, and cut off abruptly, though she seemed to want to say something more. Instead, she got up and went to the stove, all my aunts' traditional *querencia* in times of emotional stress. Without turning her head, she said in a curiously dull tone, "*You* go home now. Your mother'll yell at me."

My mother worried about my grades and my taste in friends, not about me; but I had never seen Aunt Rifke quite like this, and I knew better than to push her any further. So I went on home.

From that day, however, I made a new point of stopping by the studio literally every day—except Shabbos, naturally—even if only for a few minutes, just to let Uncle Chaim know that someone besides Aunt Rifke was concerned about him. Of course, obviously, a whole lot of other people would have been, from family to gallery owners to friends like Jules and Ruthie; but I was ten years old, and feeling like my uncle's only guardian, and a private detective to boot. A guardian against *what*? An angel? Detecting *what*? A portrait? I couldn't have said for a minute, but a ten-year-old boy with a sense of mission definitely qualifies as a dangerous flying object.

Uncle Chaim didn't talk to me anymore while he was working, and I really missed that. To this day, almost everything I know about painting—about *being* a painter, every day, all day—I learned from him, grumbled out of the side of his mouth as he sized a canvas, touched up a troublesome corner, or stood back, scratching his head, to reconsider a composition or a subject's expression, or simply to study the stoop of a shadow. Now he worked in bleak near-total silence; and since the blue angel never spoke unless addressed directly, the studio had become a far less inviting place than my three-year-old self had found it. Yet I felt that Uncle Chaim still liked having me there, even if he didn't say anything, so I kept going, but it was an effort some days, mission or no mission.

His only conversation was with the angel—Uncle Chaim always chatted with his models; paradoxically, he felt that it helped them to concentrate—and while I honestly wasn't trying to eavesdrop (except sometimes), I couldn't help overhearing their talk. Uncle Chaim would ask the angel to lift a wing slightly, or to alter her stance somewhat: as I've said, sitting remained uncomfortable and unnatural for her, but she had finally been able to manage a sort of semi-recumbent posture, which made her look curiously vulnerable, almost like a tired child after an adult party, playing at being her mother, with the grownups all asleep upstairs. I can close my eyes today and see her so.

One winter afternoon, having come tired, and stayed late, I was half-asleep on a padded rocker in a far corner when I heard Uncle Chaim saying, "You ever think that maybe we might both be dead, you and me?"

"We angels do not die," the blue angel responded. "It is not in us to die."

"I told you, lift your chin," Uncle Chaim grunted. "Well, it's built into *us,* believe me, it's mostly what we do from day one." He looked up at her from the easel. "But I'm trying to get you into a painting, and I'll never be able to do it, but it doesn't matter, got to keep trying. The head a *little* bit to the left—no, that's too much, I said a *little.*" He put down his brush and walked over to the angel, taking her chin in his hand. He said, "And you... whatever you're after, you're not going to get that right, either, are you? So it's like we're stuck here together—and if we *were* dead, maybe this is hell. Would we know? You ever think about things like that?"

"No." The angel said nothing further for a long time, and I was dozing off again when I heard her speak. "You would not speak so lightly of hell if you had seen it. I have seen it. It is not what you think."

"*Nu?*" Uncle Chaim's voice could raise an eyebrow itself. "So what's it like?"

"*Cold.*" The words were almost inaudible. "So cold...so lonely...so *empty.* God is not there...no one is there. No one, no one, no one...no one..."

It was that voice, that other voice that I had heard once before, and I have never again been as frightened as I was by the murmuring terror in her words. I actually grabbed my books and got up to leave, already framing some sort of gotta-go to Uncle Chaim, but just then Aunt Rifke walked into the studio for the first time, with Rabbi Shulevitz trailing behind her, so I stayed where I was. I don't know a thing about ten-year-olds today; but in those times one of the major functions of adults was to supply drama and mystery to our lives, and we took such things where we found them.

Rabbi Stuart Shulevitz was the nearest thing my family had to an actual regular rabbi. He was Reform, of course, which meant that he had no beard, played the guitar, performed Bat Mitzvahs and interfaith marriages, invited local priests and imams to lead the Passover ritual, and put up perpetually with all the jokes told, even by his own congregation, about young, beardless, terminally tolerant Reform rabbis. Uncle Chaim, who allowed Aunt Rifke to drag him to *shul* twice a year, on the High Holidays, regarded him as being somewhere between a mild head cold and mouse droppings in the pantry. But Aunt Rifke always defended Rabbi Shulevitz, saying, "He's smarter than he looks, and anyway he can't help being blond. Also, he smells good."

Uncle Chaim and I had to concede the point. Rabbi Shulevitz's immediate predecessor, a huge, hairy, bespectacled man from Riga, had smelled mainly of rancid hair oil and cheap peach *schnapps*. And he couldn't sing "Red River Valley," either.

Aunt Rifke was generally a placid-appearing, *hamishe* sort of woman, but now her plump face was set in lines that would have told even an angel that she meant business. The blue angel froze in position in a different way than she usually held still as required by the pose. Her strange eyes seemed almost to change their shape, widening in the center and somehow *lifting* at the corners, as though to echo her wings. She stood at near-attention, silently regarding Aunt Rifke and the rabbi.

Uncle Chaim never stopped painting. Over his shoulder he said, "Rifke, what do you want? I'll be home when I'm home."

"So who's rushing you?" Aunt Rifke snapped back. "We didn't come about you. We came the rabbi should take a look at your *model* here." The word burst from her mouth trailing blue smoke.

"What look? I'm working, I'm going to lose the light in ten, fifteen minutes. Sorry, Rabbi, I got no time. Come back next week, you could say a *barucha* for the whole studio. Goodbye, Rifke."

But my eyes were on the Rabbi, and on the angel, as he slowly approached her, paying no heed to the quarreling voices of Uncle Chaim and Aunt Rifke. Blond or not, "Red River Valley" or not, he was still magic in my sight, the official representative of a power as real as my disbelief. On the other hand, the angel could fly. The Chassidic wonder-*rebbes* of my parents' Eastern Europe could fly up to heaven and share the Shabbos meal with God, when they chose. Reform rabbis couldn't fly.

As Rabbi Shulevitz neared her, the blue angel became larger and more stately, and there was now a certain menacing aspect to her divine radiance, which set me shrinking into a corner, half-concealed by a dusty drape. But the rabbi came on.

"Come no closer," the angel warned him. Her voice sounded deeper, and slightly distorted, like a phonograph record when the Victrola hasn't been wound tight enough. "It is not for mortals to lay hands on the Lord's servant and messenger."

"I'm not touching you," Rabbi Shulevitz answered mildly. "I just want to look in your eyes. An angel can't object to that, surely."

"The full blaze of an angel's eyes would leave you ashes, impudent man." Even I could hear the undertone of anxiety in her voice.

"That is foolishness." The rabbi's tone continued gentle, almost playful. "My friend Chaim paints your eyes full of compassion, of sorrow for the world and all its creatures, every one. Only turn those eyes to me for a minute, for a very little minute, where's the harm?"

Obediently he stayed where he was, taking off his hat to reveal the black *yarmulke* underneath. Behind him, Aunt Rifke made as though to take Uncle Chaim's arm, but he shrugged her away, never taking his own eyes from Rabbi Shulevitz and the blue angel. His face was very pale. The glass of Scotch in his left hand, plainly as forgotten as the brush in his right, was beginning to slosh over the rim with his trembling, and I was distracted with fascination, waiting for him to drop it. So I wasn't quite present, you might say, when the rabbi's eyes looked into the eyes of the blue angel.

But I heard the rabbi gasp, and I saw him stagger backwards a couple of steps, with his arm up in front of his eyes. And I saw the angel turning away, instantly; the whole encounter couldn't have lasted more than five seconds, if that much. And if Rabbi Shulevitz looked stunned and frightened—which he did—there is no word that I know to describe the expression on the angel's face. No words.

Rabbi Shulevitz spoke to Aunt Rifke in Hebrew, which I didn't know, and she answered him in swift, fierce Yiddish, which I did, but only insofar as it pertained to things my parents felt were best kept hidden from me, such as money problems, family gossip and sex. So I missed most of her words, but I caught anyway three of them. One was *shofar,* which is the ram's horn blown at sundown on the High Holidays, and about which I already knew two good dirty jokes. The second was *minyan*, the number of adult Jews needed to form a prayer circle on special occasions. Reform *minyanim* include women, which Aunt Rifke always told me I'd come to appreciate in a couple of years. She was right.

The third word was *dybbuk.*

I knew the word, and I didn't know it. If you'd asked me its meaning, I would have answered that it meant some kind of bogey, like the Invisible Man, or just maybe the Mummy. But I learned the real meaning fast, because Rabbi Shulevitz had taken off his glasses and was wiping his forehead, and whispering, "*No. No. Ich vershtaye nicht...*"

Uncle Chaim was complaining, "What the hell *is* this? See now, we've lost the light already, I *told* you." No one—me included—was paying any attention.

Aunt Rifke—who was never entirely sure that Rabbi Shulevitz *really* understood Yiddish—burst into English. "It's a *dybbuk,* what's not to understand? There's a *dybbuk* in that woman, you've got to get rid of it! You get a *minyan* together, right now, you get rid of it! Exorcise!"

Why on earth did she want the rabbi to start doing pushups or jumping-jacks in this moment? I was still puzzling over that when he said, "That woman, as you call her, is an angel. You cannot...Rifke, you do not exorcise an angel." He was trembling—I could see that—but his voice was steady and firm.

"You do when it's possessed!" Aunt Rifke looked utterly exasperated with everybody. "I don't know how it could happen, but Chaim's angel's got a *dybbuk* in her—" she whirled on her husband—"which is why she makes you just keep painting her and painting her, day and night. You finish—really finish, it's done, over—she might have to go back out where it's not so nice for a *dybbuk,* you know about that? Look at her!" and she pointed an orange-nailed finger straight in the blue angel's face. "*She* hears me, *she* knows what I'm talking about. You know what I'm talking, don't you, Miss Angel? Or I should say, Mister *Dybbuk?* You tell me, okay?"

I had never seen Aunt Rifke like this; she might have been possessed herself. Rabbi Shulevitz was trying to calm her, while Uncle Chaim fumed at the intruders disturbing his model. To my eyes, the angel looked more than disturbed—she looked as terrified as a cat I'd seen backed against a railing by a couple of dogs, strays, with no one to call them away from tearing her to pieces. I was anxious for her, but much more so for my aunt and uncle, truly expecting them to be struck by lightning, or turned to salt, or something on that order. I was scared for the rabbi as well, but I figured he could take care of himself. Maybe even with Aunt Rifke.

"A *dybbuk* cannot possibly possess an angel," the rabbi was saying. "Believe me, I majored in Ashkenazic folklore—wrote my thesis on Lilith, as a matter of fact—and there are no accounts, no legends, not so much as a single *bubbemeise* of such a thing. *Dybbuks* are wandering spirits, some of them good, some malicious, but all houseless in the universe. They cannot enter heaven, and Gehenna won't have them, so they take refuge within the first human being they can reach, like any parasite. But an angel? Inconceivable, take my word. Inconceivable."

"In the mind of God," the blue angel said, "nothing is inconceivable."

Strangely, we hardly heard her; she had almost been forgotten in the dispute over her possession. But her voice was that other voice—I could see Uncle Chaim's eyes widen as he caught the difference. That voice said now, "She is right. I am a *dybbuk.*"

In the sudden absolute silence, Aunt Rifke, serenely complacent, said, "Told you."

I heard myself say, "Is she bad? I thought she was an angel."

Uncle Chaim said impatiently, "What? She's a model."

Rabbi Shulevitz put his glasses back on, his eyes soft with pity behind the heavy lenses. I expected him to point at the angel, like Aunt Rifke, and thunder out stern and stately Hebrew maledictions, but he only said, "Poor thing, poor thing. Poor creature."

Through the angel's mouth, the *dybbuk* said, "Rabbi, go away. Let me alone, let me be. I am warning you."

I could not take my eyes off her. I don't know whether I was more fascinated by what she was saying, and the adults having to deal with its mystery, or by the fact that all the time I had known her as Uncle Chaim's winged and haloed model, someone else was using her the way I played with my little puppet theatre at home—moving her, making up things for her to say, perhaps even putting her away at night when the studio was empty. Already it was as though I had never heard her strange, shy voice asking a child's endless questions about the world, but only this grownup voice, speaking to Rabbi Shulevitz. "You cannot force me to leave her."

"I don't want to force you to do anything," the rabbi said gently. "I want to help you."

I wish I had never heard the laughter that answered him. I was too young to hear something like that, if anyone could ever be old enough. I cried out and doubled up around myself, hugging my stomach, although what I felt was worse than the worst bellyache I had ever wakened with in the night. Aunt Rifke came and put her arms around me, trying to soothe me, murmuring, half in English, half in Yiddish, "Shh, shh, it's all right, *der rebbe* will make it all right. He's helping the angel, he's getting rid of that thing inside her, like a doctor. Wait, wait, you'll see, it'll be all right." But I went on crying, because I had been visited by a monstrous grief not my own, and I was only ten.

The *dybbuk* said, "If you wish to help me, rabbi, leave me alone. I will not go into the dark again."

Rabbi Shulevitz wiped his forehead. He asked, his tone still gentle and wondering, "What did you do to become...what you are? Do you remember?"

The *dybbuk* did not answer him for a long time. Nobody spoke, except for Uncle Chaim muttering unhappily to himself, "Who needs this? Try to get your work done, it turns into a *ferkockte* party. Who needs it?" Aunt Rifke shushed him, but she reached for his arm, and this time he let her take it.

The rabbi said, "You are a Jew."

"I was. Now I am nothing."

"No, you are still a Jew. You must know that we do not practice exorcism, not as others do. We heal, we try to heal both the person possessed and the one possessing. But you must tell me what you have done. Why you cannot find peace."

The change in Rabbi Shulevitz astonished me as much as the difference between Uncle Chaim's blue angel and the spirit that inhabited her and spoke through her. He didn't even look like the crew cut, blue-eyed, guitar-playing, basketball-playing (well, he tried) college-student-dressing young man whose idea of a good time was getting people to sit in a circle and sing "So Long, It's Been Good to Know You" or "Dreidel, Dreidel, Dreidel" together. There was a power of his own inhabiting him, and clearly the *dybbuk* recognized it. It said slowly, "You cannot help me. You cannot heal."

"Well, we don't know that, do we?" Rabbi Shulevitz said brightly. "So, a bargain. You tell me what holds you here, and I will tell you, honestly, what I can do for you. *Honestly.*"

Again the *dybbuk* was slow to reply. Aunt Rifke said hotly, "What is this? What *help?* We're here to expel, to get rid of a demon that's taken over one of God's angels, if that's what she really is, and enchanted my husband so it's all he can paint, all he can think about painting. Who's talking about *helping* a demon?"

"The rabbi is," I said, and they all turned as though they'd forgotten I was there. I gulped and stumbled along, feeling like I might throw up. I said, "I don't think it's a demon, but even if it is, it's given Uncle Chaim a chance to paint a real angel, and everybody loves the paintings, and they buy them, which we wouldn't have had them to sell if the—the *thing*—hadn't made her stay in Uncle Chaim's studio." I ran out of breath, gas and show-business ambitions all at pretty much the same time, and sat down, grateful that I had neither puked nor started to cry. I was still grandly capable of both back then.

Aunt Rifke looked at me in a way I didn't recall her ever doing before. She didn't say anything, but her arm tightened around me. Rabbi Shulevitz said quietly, "Thank you, David." He turned back to face the angel. In the same voice, he said, "Please. Tell me."

When the *dybbuk* spoke again, the words came one by one—two by two, at most. "A girl...There was a girl...a young woman..."

"*Ai,* how not?" Aunt Rifke's sigh was resigned, but not angry or mocking, just as Uncle Chaim's, "*Shah,* Rifkela" was neither a dismissal nor an order. The rabbi, in turn, gestured them to silence.

"She wanted us to marry," the *dybbuk* said. "I did too. But there was time. There was a world...there was my work...there were things to see...to taste and smell and do and *be*...It could wait a little. She could wait..."

"Uh-huh. Of course. You could *die* waiting around for some damn man!"

"*Shah,* Rifkela!"

"But this one did not wait around," Rabbi Shulevitz said to the *dybbuk.* "She did not wait for you, am I right?"

"She married another man," came the reply, and it seemed to my ten-year-old imagination that every tortured syllable came away tinged with blood. "They had been married for two years when he beat her to death."

It was my Uncle Chaim who gasped in shock. I don't think anyone else made a sound.

The *dybbuk* said, "She sent me a message. I came as fast as I could. I *did* come," though no one had challenged his statement. "But it was too late."

This time we were the ones who did not speak for a long time. Rabbi Shulevitz finally asked, "What did you do?"

"I looked for him. I meant to kill him, but he killed himself before I found him. So I was too late again."

"What happened then?" That was me, once more to my own surprise. "When you didn't get to kill him?"

"I lived. I wanted to die, but I lived."

From Aunt Rifke—how not? "You ever got married?"

"No. I lived alone, and I grew old and died. That is all."

"Excuse me, but that is *not* all." The rabbi's voice had suddenly, startlingly, turned probing, almost harsh. "That is only the beginning." Everyone looked at him. The rabbi said, "So, after you died, what did happen? Where did you go?"

There was no answer. Rabbi Shulevitz repeated the question. The *dybbuk* responded finally, "You have said it yourself. Houseless in the universe I am, and how should it be otherwise? The woman I loved died because I did not love her enough—what greater sin is there than that? Even her murderer had the courage to atone, but I dared not offer my own life in payment for hers. I chose to live, and living on has been my punishment, in death as well as in life. To wander back and forth in a cold you cannot know, shunned by heaven, scorned by purgatory... do you wonder that I sought shelter where I could, even in an angel? God himself would have to come and cast me out again, Rabbi—you never can."

I became aware that my aunt and uncle had drawn close around me, as though expecting something dangerous and possibly explosive to happen. Rabbi Shulevitz took off his glasses again, ran his hand through his crewcut, stared at the glasses as though he had never seen them before, and put them back on.

"You are right," he said to the *dybbuk*. "I'm a rabbi, not a *rebbe*—no Solomonic wisdom, no magical powers, just a degree from a second-class seminary in Metuchen, New Jersey. You wouldn't know it." He drew a deep breath and moved a few steps closer to the blue angel. He said, "But this *gornisht* rabbi knows anyway that you would never have been allowed this refuge if God had not taken pity on you. You must know this, surely?" The *dybbuk* did not answer. Rabbi Shulevitz said, "And if God pities you, might you not have a little pity on yourself? A little forgiveness?"

"Forgiveness..." Now it was the *dybbuk* who whispered. "Forgiveness may be God's business. It is not mine."

"Forgiveness is everyone's business. Even the dead. On this earth or under it, there is no peace without forgiveness." The rabbi reached out then, to touch the blue angel comfortingly. She did not react, but he winced and drew his hand back instantly, blowing hard on his fingers, hitting them against his leg. Even I could see that they had turned white with cold.

"You need not fear for her," the *dybbuk* said. "Angels feel neither cold nor heat. You have touched where I have been."

Rabbi Shulevitz shook his head. He said, "I touched you. I touched your shame and your grief—as raw today, I know, as on the day your love died. But the cold...the cold is yours. The loneliness, the endless guilt over what you should have done, the endless turning to and fro in empty darkness...none of that comes from God. You must believe me, my friend." He paused, still flexing his frozen fingers. "And you must come forth from God's angel now. For her sake and your own."

The *dybbuk* did not respond. Aunt Rifke said, far more sympathetically than she had before, "You need a *minyan*, I could make some calls. We'd be careful, we wouldn't hurt it."

Uncle Chaim looked from her to the rabbi, then back to the blue angel. He opened his mouth to say something, but didn't.

The rabbi said, "You have suffered enough at your own hands. It is time for you to surrender your pain." When there was still no reply, he asked, "Are you afraid to be without it? Is that your real fear?"

"It has been my only friend!" the *dybbuk* answered at last. "Even God cannot understand what I have done so well as my pain does. Without the pain, there is only me."

"There is heaven," Rabbi Shulevitz said. "Heaven is waiting for you. Heaven has been waiting a long, long time."

"*I am waiting for me!*" It burst out of the *dybbuk* in a long wail of purest terror, the kind you only hear from small children trapped in a nightmare. "You want me to abandon the one sanctuary I have ever found, where I can huddle warm in the consciousness of an angel and sometimes—for a little—even forget the thing I am. You want me to be naked to myself again, and I am telling you *no, not ever, not ever, not ever*. Do what you must, Rabbi, and I will do the only thing I can." It paused, and then added, somewhat stiffly, "Thank you for your efforts. You are a good man."

Rabbi Shulevitz looked genuinely embarrassed. He also looked weary, frustrated and older than he had been when he first recognized the possession of Uncle Chaim's angel. Looking vaguely around at us, he said, "I don't know—maybe it *will* take a *minyan*. I don't want to, but we can't just..." His voice trailed away sadly, too defeated even to finish the sentence.

Or maybe he didn't finish because that was when I stepped forward, pulling away from my aunt and uncle, and said, "He can come with me, if he wants. He can come and live in me. Like with the angel."

Uncle Chaim said, "*What?*" and Aunt Rifke said, "*No!*" and Rabbi Shulevitz said, "*David!*" He turned and grabbed me by the shoulders, and I could feel him wanting to shake me, but he didn't. He seemed to be having trouble breathing. He said, "David, you don't know what you're saying."

"Yes, I do," I said. "He's scared, he's so scared. I know about scared."

Aunt Rifke crouched down beside me, peering hard into my face. "David, you're ten years old, you're a little boy. This one, he could be a thousand years, he's been hiding from God in an angel's body. How could you know what he's feeling?"

I said, "Aunt Rifke, I go to school. I wake up every morning, and right away I think about the boys waiting to beat me up because I'm small, or because I'm Jewish, or because they just don't like my face, the way I look at them. Every day I want to stay home and read, and listen to the radio, and play my All-Star Baseball game, but I get dressed and I eat breakfast, and I walk to school. And every day I have to think how I'm going to get through recess, get through gym class, get home without running into Jay Taffer, George DiLucca. Billy Kronish. I know all about not wanting to go outside."

Nobody said anything. The rabbi tried several times, but it was Uncle Chaim who finally said loudly, "I got to teach you to box. A little Archie Moore, a little Willie Pep, we'll take care of those *mamzers.*" He looked ready to give me my first lesson right there.

When the *dybbuk* spoke again, its voice was somehow different: quiet, slow, wondering. It said, "Boy, you would do that?" I didn't speak, but I nodded.

Aunt Rifke said, "Your mother would *kill* me! She's hated me since I married Chaim."

The *dybbuk* said, "Boy, if I come...outside, I cannot go back. Do you understand that?"

"Yes," I said. "I understand."

But I was shaking. I tried to imagine what it would be like to have someone living inside me, like a baby, or a tapeworm. I was fascinated by tapeworms that year. Only this would be a spirit, not an actual physical thing—that wouldn't be so bad, would it? It might even be company, in a way, almost like being a comic-book superhero and having a secret identity. I wondered whether the angel had even known the *dybbuk* was in her, as quiet as he had been until he spoke to Rabbi Shulevitz. Who, at the moment, was repeating over and over, "No, I can't permit this. This is *wrong*, this can't be allowed. No." He began to mutter prayers in Hebrew.

Aunt Rifke was saying, "I don't care, I'm calling some people from the *shul*, I'm getting some people down here right *away!*" Uncle Chaim was gripping my shoulder so hard it hurt, but he didn't say anything. But there was really no one in the room except the *dybbuk* and me. When I think about it, when I remember, that's all I see.

I remember being thirsty, terribly thirsty, because my throat and my mouth were so dry. I pulled away from Uncle Chaim and Aunt Rifke, and I moved past Rabbi Shulevitz, and I croaked out to the *dybbuk*, "Come on, then. You can come out of the angel, it's safe, it's okay." I remember thinking that it was like trying to talk a cat down out of a tree, and I almost giggled.

I never saw him actually leave the blue angel. I don't think anyone did. He was simply standing right in front of me, tall enough that I had to look up to meet his eyes. Maybe he wasn't a thousand years old, but Aunt Rifke hadn't missed by much. It wasn't his clothes that told me—he wore a white turban that looked almost square, a dark-red vest sort of thing and white trousers, under a gray robe that came all the way to the ground—it was the eyes. If blackness is the absence of light, then those were the blackest eyes I'll ever see, because there was no light in those eyes, and no smallest possibility of light ever. You couldn't call them sad: *sad* at least knows what *joy* is, and grieves at being exiled from joy. However old he really was, those eyes were a thousand years past sad.

"Sephardi," Rabbi Shulevitz murmured. "Of course he'd be Sephardi."

Aunt Rifke said, "You can see through him. Right through."

In fact he seemed to come and go: near-solid one moment, cobweb and smoke the next. His face was lean and dark, and must have been a proud face once. Now it was just weary, unspeakably weary—even a ten-year-old could see that. The lines down his cheeks and around the eyes and mouth made me think of desert pictures I'd seen, where the earth gets so dry that it pulls apart, cracks and pulls away from itself. He looked like that.

But he smiled at me. No, he smiled *into* me, and just as I've never seen eyes like his again, I've never seen a smile as beautiful. Maybe it couldn't reach his eyes, but it must have reached mine, because I can still see it. He said softly, "Thank you. You are a kind boy. I promise you, I will not take up much room."

I braced myself. The only invasive procedures I'd had any experience with then were my twice-monthly allergy shots and the time our doctor had to lance an infected finger that had swollen to twice its size. Would possession be anything like that? Would it make a difference if you were sort of inviting the possession, not being ambushed and taken over, like in *Invasion of the Body Snatchers*? I didn't mean to close my eyes, but I did.

Then I heard the voice of the blue angel.

"There is no need." It sounded like the voice I knew, but the *breath* in it was different—I don't know how else to put it. I could say it sounded stronger, or clearer, or maybe more musical; but it was the breath, the free breath. Or maybe that isn't right either, I can't tell you—I'm not even certain whether angels breathe, and I knew an angel once. There it is.

"Manassa, there is no need," she said again. I turned to look at her then, when she called the *dybbuk* by his name, and she was smiling herself, for the first time. It wasn't like his; it was a faraway smile at something I couldn't see, but it was real, and I heard Uncle Chaim catch his breath. To no one in particular, he said, "*Now* she smiles. Never once, I could never once get her to smile."

"Listen," the blue angel said. I didn't hear anything but my uncle grumbling, and Rabbi Shulevitz's continued Hebrew prayers. But the *dybbuk*—Manassa—lifted his head, and the endlessly black eyes widened, just a little.

The angel said again, "Listen," and this time I did hear something, and so did everyone else. It was music, definitely music, but too faint with distance for me to make anything out of it. But Aunt Rifke, who loved more kinds of music than you'd think, put her hand to her mouth and whispered, "*Oh*."

"Manassa, listen," the angel said for the third time, and the two of them looked at each other as the music grew stronger and clearer. I can't describe it properly: it wasn't harps and psalteries—whatever a psaltery is, maybe you use it singing psalms—and it wasn't a choir of soaring heavenly voices, either. It was almost a little scary, the way you feel when you hear the wild geese passing over in the autumn night. It made me think of that poem of Tennyson's, with that line about *the horns of Elfland faintly blowing.* We'd been studying it in school.

"It is your welcome, Manassa," the blue angel said. "The gates are open for you. They were always open."

But the *dybbuk* backed away, suddenly whimpering. "I cannot! I am afraid! They will see!"

The angel took his hand. "They see now, as they saw you then. Come with me, I will take you there."

The *dybbuk* looked around, just this side of panicking. He even tugged a bit at the blue angel's hand, but she would not let him go. Finally he sighed very deeply—lord, you could feel the dust of the tombs in that sigh, and the wind between the stars—and nodded to her. He said, "I will go with you."

The blue angel turned to look at all of us, but mostly at Uncle Chaim. She said to him, "You are a better painter than I was a muse. And you taught me a great deal about other things than painting. I will tell Rembrandt."

Aunt Rifke said, a little hesitantly, "I was maybe rude. I'm sorry." The angel smiled at her.

Rabbi Shulevitz said, "Only when I saw you did I realize that I had never believed in angels."

"Continue not to," the angel replied. "We rather prefer it, to tell you the truth. We work better that way."

Then she and the *dybbuk* both looked at me, and I didn't feel even ten years old; more like four or so. I threw my arms around Aunt Rifke and buried my face in her skirt. She patted my head—at least I guess it was her, I didn't actually see her. I heard the blue angel say in Yiddish, "*Sei gesund,* Chaim's Duvidl. You were always courteous to me. Be well."

I looked up in time to meet the old, old eyes of the *dybbuk*. He said, "In a thousand years, no one has ever offered me freely what you did." He said something else, too, but it wasn't in either Hebrew or Yiddish, and I didn't understand.

The blue angel spread her splendid, shimmering wings one last time, filling the studio—as, for a moment, the mean winter sky outside seemed to flare with a sunset hope that could not have been. Then she and Manassa, the *dybbuk,* were gone, vanished instantly, which makes me think that the wings aren't really for flying. I don't know what other purpose they could serve, except they did seem somehow to enfold us all and hold us close. But maybe they're just really decorative. I'll never know now.

Uncle Chaim blew out his breath in one long, exasperated sigh. He said to Aunt Rifke, "I never did get her right. You know that."

I was trying to hear the music, but Aunt Rifke was busy hugging me, and kissing me all over my face, and telling me not ever, *ever* to do such a thing again, what was I thinking? But she smiled up at Uncle Chaim and answered him, "Well, she got *you* right, that's what matters." Uncle Chaim blinked at her. Aunt Rifke said, "She's probably telling Rembrandt about you right now. Maybe Vermeer, too."

"You think so?" Uncle Chaim looked doubtful at first, but then he shrugged and began to smile himself. "Could be."

I asked Rabbi Shulevitz, "He said something to me, the *dybbuk,* just at the end. I didn't understand."

The rabbi put his arm around me. "He was speaking in old Ladino, the language of the Sephardim. He said, '*I will not forget you.*'" His smile was a little shaky, and I could feel him trembling himself, with everything over. "I think you have a friend in heaven, David. Extraordinary Duvidl."

The music was gone. We stood together in the studio, and although there were four of us, it felt as empty as the winter street beyond the window where the blue angel had posed so often. A taxi took the corner too fast, and almost hit a truck; a cloud bank was pearly with the moon's muffled light. A group of young women crossed the street, singing. I could feel everyone wanting to move away, but nobody did, and nobody spoke, until Uncle Chaim finally said, "Rabbi, you got time for a sitting tomorrow? Don't wear that suit."

Salt Wine

All right, then. First off, this ain't a story about some seagoing candytrews dandy Captain Jack, or whatever you want to call him, who falls in love with a mermaid and breaks his troth to a mortal woman to live with his fish-lady under the sea. None of that in this story, I can promise you; and our man's no captain, but a plain blue-eyed sailorman named Henry Lee, AB, who starts out good for nowt much but reefing a sail, holystoning a deck, taking a turn in the crow's-nest, talking his way out of a tight spot, and lending his weight to the turning of a capstan and his voice to the bellowing of a chanty. He drank some, and most often when he drank it ended with him going at it with one or another of his mates. Lost part of an ear that way off Panama, he did, and even got flogged once for pouring grog on the captain. But there was never no harm in Henry Lee, not in them days. Anybody remembers him'll tell you that.

Me name's Ben Hazeltine. I remember Henry Lee, and I'll tell you why.

I met Henry Lee when we was both green hands on the *Mary Brannum,* out of Cardiff, and we stayed messmates on and off, depending. Didn't always ship out together, nowt like that—just seemed to happen so. Any road, come one rainy spring, we was on the beach together, out of work. Too many hands, not enough ships—you get that, some seasons. Captains can take their pick those times, and Henry Lee and I weren't neither one anybody's first pick. Isle of Pines, just south of Cuba—devil of a place to be stranded, I'll tell you. Knew we'd land a berth sooner or later—always had before—only we'd no idea when, and both of us hungry enough to eat a seagull, but too weak to grab one. I'll tell you the God's truth, we'd gotten to where we was looking at bloody starfish and those Portygee man-o'-war jellies and wondering… well, there you are, that's how bad it were. I've been in worse spots, but not many.

Now back then, there was mermaids all over the place, like you don't see so much today. Partial to warm waters, they are—the Caribbean, Mediterranean, the Gulf Stream—but I've seen them off the Orkneys, and even off Greenland a time or two, that's a fact. What's *not* a fact is the singing. Combing their hair, yes; they're women, after all, and that's what women do, and how you going to comb your hair out underwater? But I never heard one mermaid sing, not once.

And they ain't all beautiful—stop a clock, some of them would.

Now, what you *didn't* see much of in the old times, and don't hardly be seeing at all these days, was mer*men*. Merrows, some folk call them. Ugly as fried sin, the lot: not a one but's got a runny red nose, nasty straggly hair—red too, mostly, I don't know why—stumpy green teeth sticking up and out every which way, skin like a crocodile's arse. You get a look at one of those, it don't take much to figure why your mermaid takes to hanging around sailors. Put me up against a merrow, happen even *I* start looking decent enough, by and by.

Any road, like I told you, Henry Lee and I was pretty well down to eating our boots—or we would have been if we'd had any. We was stumbling along the beach one morning, guts too empty to growl, look-ing for someone to beg or borrow from—or maybe just chew up on the spot, either way—when there's a sudden commotion out in the water, and someone screaming for help. Well, I knew it were a merrow straight-away, and so did Henry Lee—you can't ever mistake a merrow's creaky, squawky voice, once you've heard it—and when we ran to look, we saw he had a real reason to scream. Big hammerhead had him cornered against the reef, circling and circling him, the way they do when they're working up to a strike. No, I tell a lie, I misremember—it were a tiger shark, not a hammerhead. Hammer, he swims in big packs, he'll stay out in the deep water, but your tiger, they'll come right in close, right into the shallows. And they'll leave salmon or tuna to go after a merrow. Just how they are.

Now merrows are tough as they're unsightly, you don't never want to be disputing a fish or a female with a merrow. But to a tiger shark, a merrow's a nice bit of Cornish pasty. This one were flapping his arms at the tiger, hitting out with his tail—worst thing he could have done; they'll go for the tail first thing, that's the good part. I says to Henry Lee, I says, "Look sharp, mate—might be summat over for us." Sharks is real slapdash about their meals, and we was *hungry*.

But Henry Lee, he gives me just the one look, with his eyes all big and strange—and then rot me if he ain't off like a pistol shot, diving into the surf and heading straight for the reef and that screaming merrow. Ain't too many sailors can really swim, you know, but Henry Lee, he were a Devon man, and he used to say he swam before he could walk. He had a knife in his belt—won it playing euchre with a Malay pirate—and I could see it glinting between his teeth as he slipped through them waves like a dolphin, which is a shark's mortal enemy, you know. Butt 'em in the side, what they do, in the belly, knock 'em right out of the water. I've seen it done.

That tiger shark never knew Henry Lee were coming till he were on its back, hanging on like a jockey and stabbing everywhere he could reach. Blood enough in the water, I couldn't hardly see anything—I could just hear that merrow, still screeching his ugly head off. Time I caught sight of Henry Lee again, he were halfway back to shore, grinning at me around that bloody knife, and a few fins already slicing in to finish off their mate, ta ever so. I practically dragged Henry Lee out of the water, 'acos of he were bleeding too—shark's hide'll take your own skin off, and his thighs looked like he'd been buggering a hedgehog.

"Barking mad," I told him. "Barking, roaring, *howling* mad! God's frigging *teeth,* you ought to be put somewhere you can't hurt yourself—aye, nor nobody else. What in frigging Jesus' frigging name *possessed* you, you louse-ridden get?"

See, it weren't that we was all such mates back then, me and Henry Lee, it were more that I thought I *knew* him—knew what he'd do when, and what he wouldn't; knew what I could trust him for, and what I'd better see to meself. There's times your life can depend on that kind of knowing—weren't for that, I wouldn't be here, telling this. I says it again, "What the Christ possessed you, Henry bleeding Lee?"

But he'd already got his back to me, looking out toward the reef, water still roiling with the sharks fighting for leftovers. "Where's that merrow gone?" he wanted to know. "He was just there—where's he got to?" He was set to swim right back out there, if I hadn't grabbed him again.

"Panama by now, if he's got the sense of a weevil," says I. "More sense than you, anyway. What kind of bloody idiot risks his life for a bloody merrow?"

"An idiot who knows how a merrow can reward you!" Henry Lee turned back around to face me, and I swear his blue eyes had gone black and wild as the sea off Halifax. "Didn't you never hear about that? You save a merrow's life, he's bound to give you all his treasure, all the plunder he's ever gathered from shipwrecks, sea fights—everything he's got in his cave, it's the rule. He don't have no choice, it's the *rule!*"

I couldn't help it, I were laughing before he got halfway through. "Aye, Henry Lee," I says. "Aye, I've heard that story, and you know where I heard it? At me mam's tit, that's where, and at every tit since, and every mess where I ever put me feet under the table. Pull the other one, chum, that tale's got long white whiskers on it." Wouldn't laugh at him so today, but there you are. I were younger then.

Well, Henry Lee just gave me that look, one more time, and after that he didn't speak no more about merrows and treasures. But he were up all that night—we slept on the beach, y'see, and every time I roused, the fool were pacing the water's edge, this way and that, gaping out into the bloody black, plain waiting for that grateful merrow to show up with his arms full of gold and jewels and I don't know what, all for him, along of being saved from the sharks. *"Rule,"* thinks I. "Rule, me royal pink bum," and went back to sleep.

But there's treasure and there's treasure—depends how you look at it, I reckon. Very next day, Henry Lee found himself a berth aboard a whaler bound home for Boston and short a foremast hand. He tried to get me signed on too, but…well, I knew the captain, and the captain remembered me, so that were the end of that. You'd not believe the grudges some of them hold.

Me, I lucked onto a Spanish ship, a week or ten days later—she'd stopped to take on water, and I got talking with the cook, who needed another messboy. I've had better berths, but it got me to Málaga—and after that, one thing led to another, and I didn't see Henry Lee again for six or seven years, must have been, the way it happens with seamen. I thought about him often enough, riding that tiger shark to rescue that merrow who were going to make him rich, and I asked after him any time I met an English hand, or a Yankee, but never a word could anyone tell me—not until I rounded a fruitstall in the marketplace at Velha Goa, and almost ran over him!

How *I* got there's no great matter—I were a cook meself by then, on a wallowing scow of an East Indiaman, and trying to get some greens and fresh fruit into the crew's hardtack diet, if just to sweeten the farts in the fo'c'sle. As for why I were running, with a box of mangoes in me arms…well, that don't figure in this story neither, so never you mind.

Henry Lee looked the same as I remembered him—still not shaving more than every three days, I'd warrant, still as blue-eyed an innocent as ever cracked a bos'un's head with a beer bottle. Only change in him I could see, he didn't look like a sailor no more. Hard to explain; he were dressing just the same as ever—singlet, blue canvas pants, same rope-sole shoes, even the very same dirty white cap he always wore—but *summat* was different about him. Might have been the way he walked—he'd lost that little roll we all have, walked like he'd not been to sea in his life. Aye, might have been that.

Well, he give a great whoop to see me, and he grabbed hold of me, mangoes and all, and dragged me off into a dark little Portygee tavern—smelled of dried fish and fried onions, I remember, and cloves under it all. They knew him there—landlord patted his back, kissed him on the cheek, brought us some kind of mulled ale, and left us alone. And Henry Lee sat there with his arms folded and grinned at me, not saying a word, until I finally told him he looked like a blasted old hen, squatting over one solitary egg, and it likely rotten at that. "Talk or be damned to you," I says. "The drink's not good enough to keep me from walking out of this fleapit."

Henry Lee burst out laughing then, and he grabbed both me hands across the table, saying, "Ah, it's just so grand to see you, old Ben, I don't know what to say first, I swear I don't."

"Tell about the money, mate," I says, and didn't he stare *then?* I says, "Your clothes are for shite, right enough, but you're walking like a man with money in every pocket—you talk like your mouth's full of money, and you're scared it'll all spill out if you open your lips too wide. Now, last time I saw you, you hadn't a farthing to bless yourself with, so let's talk about that, hey? That merrow turn up with his life savings, after all?" And *I* laughed, because I'd meant it as a joke. I did.

Henry Lee didn't laugh. He looked startled, and then he leaned so close I could see where he'd lost a side tooth and picked up a scar right by his left eyebrow—made him look younger, somehow, those things did, along with that missing bit of ear—and he dropped his voice almost to a whisper, no matter there wasn't a soul near us. "No," says he, "no, Ben, he did better than that, a deal better than that. He taught me the making of salt wine."

Aye, that's how I looked at him—exactly the way you're eyeing me now. Like I'm barking mad, and Jesus and the saints wouldn't have me. And the way you mumbled, *"Salt wine?"*—I said it just the same as you, tucking me head down like that, getting me legs under me, in case things turned ugly. I did it true. But Henry Lee only sat back and grinned again. "You heard me, Ben," he says. "You heard me clear enough."

"Salt wine," I says, and different this time, slowly. "Salt wine...that'd be like pickled beer? Oysters in honey, that kind of thing, is it? How about bloody fried marmalade, then?" Takes me a bit of time to get properly worked up, mind, but foolery will do it. "Whale blubber curry," I says. "Boiled nor'easter."

For answer, Henry Lee reaches into those dirty canvas pants and comes up with a cheap pewter flask, two for sixpence in any chandlery. Doesn't say one word—just hands it to me, folds his hands on the table and waits. I take me time, study the flask—got a naked lady and a six-point buck on one side, and somebody in a flying chariot looks like it's caught fire on the other. I start to say how I don't drink much wine—never did, not Spanish sherry, nor even port, nor none of that Frenchy slop—but Henry Lee flicks one finger to tell me I'm to shut me gob and taste. So that's what I did.

All right, this is the hard part to explain. Nor about merrows, nor neither the part about some bloody fool jumping on the back of a tiger shark—the part about the wine. Because it *were* wine in that flask, and it *were* salty, and right there's where I run aground on a lee shore, trying to make you taste and see summat you never will, if your luck holds. *Salt wine*—not red nor neither white, but gray-green, like the deep sea, and smelling like the sea, filling your head with the sea, but wine all the same. *Salt wine....*

First swallow, I lost meself. I didn't think I were ever coming back.

Weren't nothing like being drunk. I've downed enough rum, enough brandy, dropped off to sleep in enough jolly company and wakened in enough stinking alleys behind enough shebeens to know the difference. This were more...this were like I'd fallen overboard from me, from meself, and not a single boat lowered to find me. But it didn't matter none, because *summat* were bearing me up, *summat* were surging under me, big and fast and wild, as it might have been a dolphin between me legs, tearing along through the sea—or the air, might be we were flying, I'd not have known—carrying somebody off to somewhere, and who it was I can't tell you now no more than I could have then. But it weren't me, I'll take me affydavy on that. I weren't there. I weren't anywhere or anybody, and just then that were just where I wanted to be.

Just then...Aye, you give me a choice just then, happen I might have chosen...But I'd just had that one swallow, after all, so in a bit there I were, me as ever was, back at that tavern table with Henry Lee, and him still grinning like a dog with two tails, and he says to me, "Well, Ben?"

When I can talk, I ask him, "You can make this swill yourself?" and when he nods, "Then I'd say your merrow earned his keep. Not half bad."

"Best *you* ever turned into piss," Henry says. I don't say nowt back, and after a bit, he leans forward, drops his voice way down again, and says, "It's our fortune, Ben. Yours and mine. I'm swearing on my mother's grave."

"If the dollymop's even got one," I says, because of course he don't know who his mam was, no more than I know mine. They just dropped us both and went their mortal ways, good luck to us all. I tell him, "Never mind the swearing, just lay out what you mean by *our fortune*. I didn't save no merrow—fact, I halfway tried to save *you* from trying to save him. He don't owe me nowt, and nor do you." And I'm on me feet and ready to scarper—just grab up those mangoes and walk. Ain't a living soul thinks I've got no pride, but I bloody do.

But Henry Lee's up with me, catching ahold of me arm like an octopus, and he's saying, "No, no, Ben, you don't understand. I need you, you have to help me, sit down and *listen*." And he pulls and pushes me back down, and leans right over me, so close I can see the scar as cuts into his hairline, where the third mate of the *Boston Annie* got him with a marlinspike, happened off the Azores. He says, "I can make it, the salt wine, but I need a partner to market it for me. I've got no head for business—I don't know the first thing about selling. You've got to ship it, travel with it, be my factor. Because I can't do this without you, d'you see, Ben?"

"No, I don't see a frigging thing," I says in his face. "I'm no more a factor than you're a bloody nun. What I am's a seacook, and it's past time I was back aboard me ship, so by your leave—"

Henry Lee's still gripping me arm so it *hurts*, and I can't pry his fingers loose. "Ben, *listen!*" he fair bellows again. "This is Goa, not the City of London—the Indians won't ever deal honestly with a Britisher who doesn't have an army behind him—why should they?—and the Portuguese bankers don't trust me any more than I'd trust a single one of them not to steal the spots off a leopard and come back later for the whiskers. There's a few British financiers, but *they* don't trust anyone who didn't go to Eton or Harrow. Now you're a lot more fly than you ever let on, I've always known that—"

"Too kind," I says, but he don't hear.

He goes on, "You're the one who always knew when we were being cheated—by the captain, by the company, by the lady of the house, didn't matter. Any *souk* in the world, any marketplace, I always let you do the bargaining—*always*. You'd haggle forever over a penny, a peseta, a single anna—and you'd get your price every time. Remember? I surely remember."

"Ain't nothing like running a business," I tell him. "What you're talking about is responsibility, and I never been responsible for nowt but the job I were paid to do right. I like it that way, Henry Lee, it suits me. What you're talking about—"

"I'm talking about a *future*, Ben. Spend your whole life going from berth to berth, ship to ship—where are you at the end of it? Another rotting hulk, like all the rest, careened on the beach, and no tide ever coming again to float you off. I'm offering you the security of a decent roof over your head, good meals on your table, and a few teeth left in your mouth to chew them with." He lets go of me then, but his blue eyes don't. He says, "I'd outfit you, I'd pay your way, and I'd give you one-third of the profits—ah, hell, make it forty, forty percent, what do you say? It'll be worth it to me to sleep snug a'nights, knowing my old shipmate's minding the shop and putting the cat out. What do you say, Ben? Will you do it for me?"

I look at him for a good while, not saying nowt. I remember him one time, talking a drunken gang of Yankee sailors out of dropping us into New York harbor for British spies—wound up buying us drinks, they did, which bloody near killed us anyway. And Piraeus—God's teeth, Piraeus—when the fool put the comehither on the right woman at the wrong time, and there we was, locked in a cellar for two days and nights, while her husband and his mates went on and on, just upstairs, about how to slaughter us so we'd remember it. Henry Lee, he finally got them persuaded that I were carrying some sort of horrible disease, rot your cods off, you leave it long enough, make your nose fall into your soup. They pushed the cellar key under the door and was likely in Istanbul, time we got out of that house. Me, I didn't stop feeling me nose for another two days.

So I know what Henry Lee can do, talking, and I sniff all around his words, like a fox who smells the bait and knows the trap's there, somewhere, underneath. I keep telling him, over and over, "Henry Lee, I never been no better than you with figures—I'd likely run you bankrupt inside of a month." Never stops him—he just grins and answers back, "I'm bankrupt already, Ben. I'm not swimming in boodle, like you thought—I've gone and sunk all I own into a thousand cases of salt wine. Nothing more to lose, you see—there's no way you can make anything any the worse. So what do you say now?"

I don't answer, but I up with that naked-lady flask, and I take another swallow. This time I know what's coming, and I set meself for it, but the salt wine catches me up again, lifts me and tosses me like before, same as if I was a ship with me mainmast gone, and the waves doing what they like with me. No, it's not like before—I don't lose Ben Hazeltine, nor I don't forget who I am. What happens, I *find* summat. I find *everything*. I can't rightly stand up proper, 'acos I don't know which way up *is*, and I feel the eyes rocking in me head, and I'm dribbling wine like I've not done since I were a babby…but for a minute, two minutes—no more, I couldn't have stood no more—everything in the world makes sense to me. For one minute, I'm the flyest cove in the whole world.

Then it's gone—gone, thank God or Old Horny, either one—and I'm back to old ordinary, and Henry Lee's watching me, not a word, and when I can talk I say, "There's more. I know you, and I know there's

more. You want me to come in with you, Henry Lee, you tell me the part
you're not telling me. Now."

He don't answer straight off—just keeps looking at me out of those
nursery-blue eyes. I decide I'd best help him on a bit, so I say, "Right,
then, don't mind if we do talk about merrows. Last time I saw you, you
was risking your life for the ugliest one of them ugly buggers, and him
having to hand over every farthing he'd got sewn into his underwear,
because that's the frigging rule, right? So when did that happen, hey? We
never seen him again, far as *I* know."

"He found me," Henry Lee says. "Took him a while, but he caught
up with me in Port of Spain. It's important to them, keeping their word,
though you wouldn't think so." He keeps cracking his knuckles, the way
he always used to do when he weren't sure the captain were swallowing his tale about why we was gone three days in Singapore. "I had it
wrong," he says, "that rule thing. I expected he'd come with his whole
fortune in his arms, but all the merrow has to bring you is the thing
that's most precious to him in the world. The most precious thing in the
world to that merrow I saved—I call him Gorblimey, that's as close as I
can get to his name—the most precious thing to him was that recipe for
salt wine. It's only some of them know how to make it, and they've never
given it to a human before. I'm the only one."

Me head's still humming like a honey tree, only it's swarming with
the ghosts of all the things I knew for two minutes. Henry Lee goes on,
"He couldn't write it down for me—they can't read or write, of course,
none of them, I'd never thought about that—so he made me learn it by
heart. All that night, over and over, the two of us, me hiding in a lifeboat,
him floating in the ship's shadow, over and over and *over,* till I couldn't
have remembered my own name. He was so afraid I'd get it wrong."

"How would you know?" I can't help asking him. "Summat like that
wine, how could you tell if it *were* wrong, or gone bad?"

Henry Lee bristles up at me, the way he'd have his ears flat back if
he was a cat. "I make it exactly the way Gorblimey taught me—*exactly.* There's no chance of any mistake, Gorblimey himself wouldn't know
whether I made it or he did. Get that right out of your headpiece, Ben, and
just tell me if you'll help me. *Now,*" he growls, mimicking me to the life.
He'd land in the brig, anyway once every voyage, imitating the officers.

Now, I'm not blaming nobody, you may lay to that. I'm not even
blaming the salt wine, although I could. What I done, I done out of me
own chuckleheadedness, not because I was drunk, not because Henry
Lee and me'd been shipmates. No, it were the money, and that's the
God's truth—just the money. He were right, you can live on a seacook's

pay, but that's all you *can* do. Can't retire, and maybe open a little seaside inn—can't marry, can't live nowhere but on a bloody ship...no, it's no life, not without the needful, and there's not many can afford to be too choosy how they come by it. I says, "Might do, Henry Lee. Forty percent. Might do. *Might*."

Henry Lee just lit up all at once, one big *wooosh*, like a Guy Fawkes bonfire. "Ah, Ben. Ah, Ben, I knew you'd turn up trumps, old growly truepenny Ben. You won't be sorry, my old mate," and he claps me on the shoulder, near enough knocking me over. "I promise you won't be sorry."

So I left that Indiaman tub looking for another cook, and I signed on right there as Henry Lee's factor—his partner, his first mate, his right hand, whatever you like to call it. Took us a hungry year or so to get our feet under us, being just the two, but the word spread faster than you might have supposed. Aye, that were the thing about that salt wine—there were them as took to it like a Froggie to snails, and another sort couldn't even abide the *look* of it in the bottle. I were with that lot, and likely for the same reason—not 'acos it were nasty, but 'acos it were too good, too *much*, more than a body could thole, like the Scots say. I never touched it again after that second swig, never once, not in all the years I peddled salt wine fast as Henry Lee could make it. Not for cheer, not for sorrow, not even for a wedding toast when Henry Lee married, which I'll get to by and by. Couldn't thole it, that's all, couldn't risk it no more. Third time might eat me up, third time might make me disappear. I stayed faithful to rum and mother's-ruin, and let the rest go, for once in me fool life.

Year and a half, we had buyers wherever ships could sail. London, Liverpool, Marseilles, Hamburg, Amsterdam, Buenos Aires, Athens, New York, Naples...we did best in seaports, always. I didn't travel everywhere the wine went; we hired folk in time, me and Henry Lee, and we even bought a ship of our own. Weren't no big ship, not so's you'd take notice, but big enough for what we put aboard her, which was the best captain and crew anyone could ask for. That were me doing—Henry Lee wanted to spend more on a fancier ship, but I told him it weren't how many sails that mattered, but the hands on the halyards. And he listened to me, which he mostly did...aye, you couldn't never call him stupid, poor sod. I'll say that, anyway.

Used to look out for that merrow, Henry Lee's Gorblimey, times I were keeping the wine company on its way. Not that I'd likely have known him from any other of the ones I'd see now and again, chasing the flying fish or swimming along with the porpoises—even nastier, they looked, in the middle of those creatures—but I'd ponder whiles if he knew what were passing above his head, and what he'd be thinking about it if he did. But Henry Lee never spoke word about merrows nor mermaids, none of all that, not if he could help it. Choused him, whiles, I did, telling him he were afeard Gorblimey'd twig how well we was getting on, and come for his own piece, any day now. That'd rouse him every time, and he'd snap at me like a moray, so I belayed that. Might could be I shouldn't have, but who's to say? Who's to say now?

He'd other matters on his mind by then, what with building himself a slap-up new house on the seafront north of Velha Goa. Palace and a half, it were, to me own lookout, with two floors and two verandas and *four* chimneys—four chimneys, in a country where you might be lighting a fire maybe twice a year. But Henry Lee told me, never mind: didn't the grandest place in that Devon town where he were born have four chimneys, and hadn't he always wanted to live just so in a house just like that one? Couldn't say nowt much to that, could I? Me that used to stare hours into the cat's-meat shop window back home, 'cause I got it in me head the butcher were me da? He weren't, by the by, but you see?

But I did speak a word or two when Henry Lee up and got wed. Local girl, Julia Caterina and about five other names I disremember, with a couple of *da*s in between, like the Portygee nobs do. Pretty enough, she were, with dark brown hair for two or three, brown eyes to crack your heart, and a smile to make a priest give up Lent. Aye, and though she started with nobbut *hello* and *goodbye* and *whiskey-soda* in English, didn't she tackle to it till she shamed me, who never mastered no more than a score of words in her tongue, and not one of them fit for her ears. Good-tempered with it, too—though she fought her parents bareknuckle and toe to toe, like Figg or Mendoza, until they let her toss over the grandee they'd promised her to, all for the love of a common Jack Tar, that being what he still were in their sight, didn't matter how many Bank of England notes he could wave at them. "She's a lady," I says, "for all she's a Portygee, and you're no more a gentleman than that monkey in your mango tree. Money don't make such as us into gentlemen, Henry Lee. All it does, it makes us rich monkeys. You know that, same as me."

"I'm plain daft over her, Ben," says he, like I'd never spoke at all. "Can't eat, can't sleep, can't do a thing but dream about having her near me all the time. Nothing for it but the altar."

"Speaking of altars," says I, "you'll have to turn Papist, and there's not one of her lot'll ever believe you mean it, no more than I would. And never mind her family—what about her friends, what about that whole world she's been part of since the day she were born? You reckon to sweep her up and away from all that, or try to ease yourself into it and hope they won't twig what you are? Which is it to be, then, hey?"

"I don't know, Ben," says Henry Lee, real quiet. "I don't know any-thing anymore." He said me name, but he weren't talking to me—maybe to that monkey, maybe to the waves out beyond the seawall. "The one thing I've got a good hold on, when I'm with her, it's like coming home. First time I saw her, it came over me, I've been gone a long time, and now I'm home."

Well, you can't talk sense to nobody in a state like that, so I wished them luck and left them to it. Aye, and I even danced at the wed-ding, sweating like a hog in a new silk suit, Chinee silk, and kicking the bride's shins with every turn. Danced with the mother-in-law too, with her crying on me shoulder the while, how she'd lost her poor angel forever to this soulless brute of an English *merchant,* which no matter he'd converted, he weren't no real Catholic, nor never would be. I tried to get *her* shins, that one, but she were quick, I'll say that for her.

So there's Henry Lee and his pretty new missus, and him so happy staying home with her, hosting grand gatherings just for folk to look at her, he weren't no use for nowt else, save telling me how happy he were. Oh, he still brewed up the salt wine himself—wouldn't trust me nor no other with the makings—but for the rest of it, I were near enough run-ning the business without him. Took in the orders, paid the accounts, kept the books, supervised the packing and the shipping, every case, every bloody bottle. Even bought us a second ship—found her and bar-gained for her, paid cash down, all on me own hook. Long way from the Isle of Pines, hey?

Like I say, I didn't make all the voyages. Weren't any degree necessary for me to make none on 'em, tell the truth—and besides I were getting on, and coming to like the land more than I ever thought I would. But I never could shake me taste for the Buenos Aires run. I knew some women there, and a few men too…aye, that's a fine town, Buenos. A man could settle in that town, and I were thinking about it then.

So we're three days from landfall, and I'm on deck near sunset, taking the air and keeping a lookout for albatrosses. No finer bird than an albatross, you can keep your eagles. A quiet, quiet evening—wide red sky streaked with a bit of green, fine weather tomorrow. You can hear the gulls' wings, and fish jumping now and then, and the creaking of the strakes, and sometimes even the barrels of salt wine shifting down in the hold. Then I hear footsteps behind me, and I turn and see the bos'un's mate coming up on deck. Can't think of his name right now—a short, wide man, looked like a wine barrel himself, but tough as old boots. Monkey Sucker, that's it, that's what they called him. Because he liked to drink his rum out of a cocoanut, you see. Never see no one doing that, these days.

He weren't looking too hearty, old Monkey Sucker. Red eyes and walking funny, for a start, like his legs didn't belong to him, but I put that down to him nipping at the bung down below. Now I already told you, I never again laid lip to that salt wine from that first day to this, but folk that liked it, why, they'd be waiting on the docks when we landed, ready to unload the cargo themselves right on the spot. And half the crew was the same way, run yourself blind barmy trying to keep them out of the casks. Well, we done the practical, Henry Lee and me: we rigged the hold to keep all but the one barrel under lock and key. That one we left out and easy tapped, and it'd usually last us there and back, wherever we was bound. But this Monkey Sucker...no, he weren't just drunk, I saw that on second glance. Not drunk. I wish it *had* been that, for he weren't a bad sort.

"Mr. Hazeltine," he says to me. "Well, Mr. Hazeltine." Kept on saying me name like we'd just met, and he were trying to get a right fix on it. His voice didn't sound proper, neither, but it kept cracking and bleating—like a boy's voice when it's changing, you know. And there were summat bad wrong with his nose and his mouth.

"Monk," I says back, "you best get your arse below decks before the captain claps eyes on you. You look worse than a poxy bumboy on Sunday morning." The light's going fast now, but I can make out that his face is all bad swole up and somehow *twisty*-like, and there's three lines like welts on both sides of his neck. He's got his arms wrapped around himself, holding himself *tight*, the way you'd think he were about to birth four thousand babies at one go, like some fish do it. And he keeps mumbling me name, over and over, but he's not looking at me, not once, he's looking at the rail on the starboard side. Aye, I should have twigged to that straightaway, I know. I didn't, that's all.

Suddenly he says, "Water." Clear as clear, no mistake about it. "Water," and he points over the side. Excited, bobbing on his toes, like a nipper at Brighton. Third time, "*Water*," and at least I were the first to bawl, "Man overboard!" there's that. In the midst of all the noise and garboil, with everyone tumbling on deck to heave to, and the captain yelling at everyone to lower a boat, with the bos'un crazy trying to lower *two*, 'acos he and Monkey Sucker was old mates...in the midst of it all, I saw Monkey Sucker in the sea. I *saw* him, understand? He weren't splashing around, waving and screaming for help, and he weren't treading water neither. No, he's trying to swim, calm as can be—only he's trying to swim like a fish, laying himself flat in the water and *wriggling* his legs together, same as if he had a tail, understand? Only he didn't have no tail, and he sank like that, straight down, straight down. They kept that boat out all night, but they never did find him.

We reported the death to the customs people in Buenos Aires, and I sent word to Henry Lee back in Goa. The captain and the mates kept asking the crew about why Monkey Sucker had done it, scragged himself that way—were it the drink got him? Were it over some dockside bint? Did he owe triple interest on some loan to Silas Barker or Icepick Neddie Frey? Couldn't get no answer, not one, that made no sense to them, nor to me neither.

Heading home, every barrel gone, hold full of Argentine wheat for ballast, now it's me turn to chat up the crew, on night watch or in the mess. I go at it like a good 'un, but there's not a soul can tell me anything I don't know.

I were first ashore before dawn at Velha Goa—funny to think of that fine Mandovi River all silted up today, whole place left to the snakes and the kites—and if I didn't run all the way to Henry Lee's house, may I never piss again. Man at the door to let me in, another man to take me hat and offer me a glass. I didn't take it.

I bellow for Henry Lee, and here he comes, rushing downstairs in his shirtsleeves, one shoe off and one on. "Ben, what is it? What's happened? Is it the ship?" Because he never could get used to having two ships of his own—always expected one or t'other to sink or burn, or be taken by the Barbary pirates. I didn't say nowt, just grabbed him by the arm and hauled him off into the room he calls the library. Shut the door, turn around, look into his frighted blue eyes. "It ain't the ship, Henry Lee," I tell him. "It's the hands."

"The hands," he says. "I don't understand."

"And it ain't the hands," I say, "it's the buyers. And it ain't the buyers." I take a breath, wish God'd put a noggin of rum in me fist right now, but there ain't no God. "It's the wine."

Henry Lee shakes his head. He reaches for a bottle on the sideboard, pours himself a drink. Salt wine, it is—I knock it out of his hand, so it splashes on his fancy rug, and now I'm whispering, because if I shout everything comes apart. "It's the wine, Henry Lee. You know it, and now I know."

That about him knowing, that was a guess, and now I'm the one looking away, 'acos of I don't want to find out I'm right. And because it's hard to say the bloody words, either way. "The salt wine," I says. "It frigging well killed a man, this time out, and I'm betting it's done it before."

"No," Henry Lee says. "No, Ben, that's not possible." But I look straight back at him, and I know what he's fighting not to think.

"Maybe he didn't mean no harm, your Gorblimey," I go on. "Maybe he'd no notion what his old precious gift would do to human beings. Maybe it depends on how much of it you drink, or how often." So still in that fine house, I can hear his Julia Caterina turning in the bed upstairs, murmuring into her pillow. I say, "Old Monkey Sucker, he never could keep away from the cask in the hold, maybe that's why...why it happened. Maybe if you don't drink too much."

"No," Henry Lee answers me, and his voice is real quiet too. "That wouldn't make sense, Ben. I drink salt wine every day. A lot of it."

He's always got a flask of the creature somewhere about him, true enough, and you won't see him go too long without his drop. But there's no sign of any change, not in his face, nor in his skin, nor his teeth—and that last time Monkey Sucker said "water" I could see his teeth had got all sprawled out-like, couldn't hardly close his mouth. But Henry Lee just went on looking like Henry Lee, except a little bit grayer, a bit wearier, a bit more pulled-down, like, the way quitting the sea will do to you. No merrow borning there, not that I could see.

"Well, then," says I, "it's not the amount of wine. But it *is* the wine. Tell me that's not so, and I'll believe you, Henry Lee. I will."

Because I never knew him lie to me. Might take his time getting around to telling me some things, but he wouldn't never lie outright. But he just shook his head again, and looked down, and he heaved a sigh sounded more like a death rattle. Says, "It could be. It could be. I don't know, Ben."

"You know," I says. "How long?" He don't answer, don't say nowt for a while—he just turns and turns in a little tight circle, this way and that, like a bear at a baiting. Finally he goes on, mumbling now, like he'd as soon I didn't hear. "The Tagus, last year, that time I took Julia Caterina to Lisbon. A man on the riverbank, he just *tumbled*...I didn't get a really good look, I couldn't be sure what I was seeing, I swear, Ben." I can't make no sound. Henry Lee grabs me hands, wrings them between his until they hurt. "Ben, it's like you said, maybe Gorblimey didn't know himself—"

I pull me hands free, and for a minute I have to close me eyes, 'acos if I was on a ship I'd be seasick. I hear meself saying, "Maybe he didn't. But we do. We know now."

"No, we don't! It still mightn't be the wine—it could be any number of things." He takes a deep, deep breath, plunges on. "Even if—even if that's so, obviously it's just a few, a very few, not one in a thousand, if even...I mean, you don't see it happening everywhere, it's just—it's like the way some folk can't abide shellfish, the way cheese gripes your gut, Ben, every time. It's got to be so with the salt wine."

"Even one," I says. It catches in me throat and comes out a whisper, so I can't tell if he's heard. We stand there, looking at each other, like we're waiting to be introduced. Henry Lee reaches for me hand again, but I step away. Henry Lee starts to say summat, but then he don't. There's blood in me mouth, I can taste it.

"I done bad things, Henry Lee," I says at last. "I know where I'm going when I go, and none to blame but me. I know who's waiting for me there, too—some nights I see their faces all around the room, plain as I now see you. But in me life I never done nothing, *nothing*...I got to get out of your house, Henry Lee."

And I'm for the door, because I can't look at him no more. He calls after me—once, twice—and I think he's bound sure to try and drag me back, maybe to gull me into seeing things his way, maybe just not to be alone. But he don't, and I walk on home along the seafront, a deal slower than I came. And when I get there—it were a plain little house, nobbut the one servant, and him not living in, because I can't abide folk around me when I rise—when I got there, I drank meself to sleep with me whole stock of good Christian rum. And in the morning I went to see Henry Lee's lawyer—*our* lawyer—Portygee-Goan, he were, name of Andres Furtado, near enough—and I started working an old fool name of Ben Hazeltine loose from the salt wine business. It took me some while.

Cost me a few bob, too, I don't mind saying. We'd made an agreement long back, Henry Lee and me, that if ever I wanted to sell me forty percent, he'd have to buy me out, will-he, nil-he. But I didn't want no more of that salt wine money—couldn't swallow the notion, no more than I could have swallowed a single mouthful of the stuff ever again after that second time.

So by and by, all what you call the legalities was taken care of, and there was I, on the beach again, in a manner of speaking. But at least I'd saved a bit—wouldn't last forever, but leastways I could bide me time finding other work, and not before the mast, neither. Too old to climb the rigging, too used to proper dining to go back to cooking in burned pots and rusty pannikins in some Grand Banks trawler's galley—aye, and far too fast-set in me ways of doing things to be taking orders from no captain hadn't seen what I've seen in this world. "Best bide ashore awhile, Ben Hazeltine," I says to meself, "and see who might be needing what you yet can do. There'll be someone," I says, "as there always is," and I'd believe it, too, days on end. But I'd been used to a lot of things regular, not only me meals. Henry Lee, he were one of them, him and his bloody salt wine. Not that I'd have gone back working for the fool—over the side meself first, and I can't swim no better than poor old Monkey Sucker. But still.

So when Henry Lee's young wife shows up at me door, all by herself, no husband, no servants, just her parasol and a whole great snowy spill of lace down her front, I asked her in like she were me long-lost baby sister. We weren't close, didn't know each other much past the salon and the dining room, but she were pretty and sweet, and I liked her the best I could. Like I tried to tell Henry Lee, I don't belong in the same room with no lady. Even when it's me own room.

Any road, she come in, and she sat down, and she says, "Mr. Ben, my husband, he miss you very much." Never knew a woman quicker off the mark and to the point than little Mrs. Julia Caterina Five-other-names Lee. I can still see her, sitting in me best company chair, with her little fan and her hands in her lap, and that bit of a smile that she could never quite hide. Henry Lee said it were a nervous thing with her mouth, and that she were shamed by it, but I don't know.

"We're old partners, him and me," I answers her. "We was sailors together when we was young. But I'm done working with him, no point in pretending otherwise. You're wasting your time, ma'am, I have to tell you. He shouldn't ought to have sent you here."

"Oh, he did not sent me," she says quickly. "I come—how is it?—on my ownsome? And no, I do not imagine you to come back for him, I would not ask you such a thing, not for him. But you...I think for you this would be good." I gawk at her, and she smiles a real smile now. She says, "You come to us alone—no friend, no woman, never. I think you are lonely."

Not in me life. Nobody in me *life* has ever spoke that word about me. Nobody. Not me, not nobody, never. I can't do nothing but sit there and gawp. She goes on, "He has not many friends either, my Enrique. You, me—maybe one of my brothers, maybe the *abogao,* the lawyer. Not so many, eh?" And she puts out her hands toward me, a little way. Not for me to take them—more like giving me summat. She says, "I do not know what he have done to make you angry. So bad?"

I can't talk—it ain't in me just then, looking at those hands, at her face. I nod, that's all.

No tears, no begging, no trying to talk me round. She just nods herself, and gets up, and I escort her out to where her coachman's waiting. Settling back inside, she holds out one hand, but this time it's formal, it's what nobby Portygee ladies do. I kissed her mother's hand at the wedding, so I've got the trick of it—more like a breath, it is, more like you're smelling a flower. For half a minute, less, we're looking straight into each other's eyes, and I see the sadness. Maybe for Henry Lee, maybe for me—I never did know. Maybe it weren't never there.

But afterwards I couldn't stop thinking about her. I don't mean *her*, not like that, wouldn't have occurred to me. I mean what she said, and the way she looked at me, and her coming to see me by herself, which you won't never see no Portygee lady doing, high nor low. And saying that thing about me being lonely—true or not ain't the point. It were her *saying* it, and how I felt to hear her. I plain wanted to hear her again, is all.

But I didn't. It would have meant seeing Henry Lee, and I weren't no way up to that. I talked to him in me head every time I saw one or t'other of our ships slipping slow out of the harbor in the morning sun, sails filling and the company pennant snapping atop the mizzenmast. And her hold full of poison. I had time enough on me hands to spend with sailors ashore, and shillings enough to buy another round of what's-your-fancy, and questions enough to keep them talking and me mind unsettled. Because most of them hadn't noticed nothing—no shipmates turning, no buyers swimming out to sea, no changelings whispering to them from the dark water. But there was always a couple, two or even three who'd seen *summat* they'd as soon not have seen, and who'd have to down more than a few jars of the best before they'd speak about it even to each other. Aye, I knew *that* feeling, none better.

They wasn't all off our ships, neither. Velha were still a fair-sized port then, not like it is now, and there was traders and packets and merchantmen in from everywhere, big and small. I were down the harbor pretty regular, any road, sniffing after work—shaming, me age, but there you are—and I talked with whoever'd stay for it, officers and foremast hands alike. Near as I could work it out, Henry Lee were right, in his way—however much of the salt wine were going down however many throats all over the world, couldn't be more than almost nobody affected beyond waking next day with a bad case of the whips and jingles. Like he'd said to me, *just a few, a very few,* and what difference to old Ben Hazeltine? No lookout of mine no more, I were clear out of that whole clamjamfry altogether, and nobody in the world could say I weren't. Not one single soul in the world.

Only I'd been in it, you see. Right up to me whiskers in it, year on year—grown old in it, I had. Call it regret, call it guilt, call it what you like, all I knew was I'd sleep on straw in the workhouse and live on slops and sermons before I'd knock on Henry Lee's door again. Even to have *her* look at me one more time, the way she looked in me house, in me best chair. I've made few promises in me life, and kept less, but I made that one then, made it to meself. Suppose you could call it a vow, like, if that suits you.

And I kept that one. It weren't easy, whiles, what with me not finding nobbut portering to do, or might be pushing a barrow for a day or two, but I held to that vow right up to the day when one of Henry Lee's men come to say his master were in greatest need of me—put it just like that, "greatest need"—and would I please come right away, *please.* Tell the truth, I mightn't have come for Henry Lee himself, but that servant, trying to be so calm and proper, with his eyes so frantic…Goanese Konkany, he were, name of Gopi.

I didn't run there, like I'd last done—didn't even ride in the carriage he'd sent for me. I walked, and I took me own time about it, too, and I thought on just what I'd say, and what he'd do when I said it, and what I'd do then. And before I knew, I were standing on the steps of that fine house, with no butler waiting but Henry Lee himself, with both hands out to drag me inside. "Ben," he keeps saying, "ah, Ben, Ben, Ben." Like Monkey Sucker again, saying *Mr. Hazeltine, Mr. Hazeltine,* over and over.

He looked old, Henry Lee did. Hair gone gray—face slumped in like he'd lost all his teeth at once—shoulders bent to break your heart, the way you'd think he'd been stooping in a Welsh coal mine all his life. And the blue eyes of him…I only seen such eyes one time before, on a donkey that knew it were dying, and just wanted it over with. All I could think to say were, "You shouldn't never have left the sea, Henry Lee— not never." But I didn't say it.

He turned away and started up that grand long stair up to the second floor and the bedrooms, with his footsteps sounding like clods falling on a coffin. And I followed after, wishing the stair'd never end, but keep us climbing on and on for always, never getting where we had to go, and I wished I'd never left the sea neither.

I smelled it while we was still on the stair. It ain't a *bad* smell, considering: it's cold and clean, like the wind off Newfoundland or when you're just entering the Kattegat, bound for Copenhagen. Aye…aye, you could say it's a fishy smell, too, if you care to, which I don't. I'd smelled it before that day, and I've smelled it since, but I don't never smell it without thinking about her, *Señora* Julia Caterina Five-names Lee, Missus Henry Lee. Without seeing her there in the big bed.

He'd drawn every curtain, so you had to stand blind and blinking for a few minutes, till your eyes got used to the dark. She were lying

under a down quilt—me wedding gift to the bride, Hindoo lady up in
Ponda sewed it for me—but just as we came in she shrugged it off, and
you could see her bare as a babby to the waist. Henry Lee, he rushes forward to pull the quilt back up, but she turns her head to look up at him,
and he stops where he stands. She makes a queer little sound—hear it
outside your window at night, you'd think it were a cat wanting in.

"She can talk still," says Henry Lee, desperate-like, turning to me.
"She was talking this morning." I stare into Julia Caterina's pretty brown
eyes—huge now, and steady going all greeny-black—and I want to tell
Henry Lee, oh, she'll talk all right, no fear. Mermaids *chatter*, believe
me—talk both your lugs off, they will, you give them the chance.
Mermaids gets lonely.

"She drank so *little*," Henry Lee keeps saying. "She didn't really like
any wine, French or Portuguese, or...ours. She only drank it to be polite,
when we had guests. Because it was our business, after all. She understood about business." I look down at the quilt where it's covering her
lower parts, and I look back at Henry Lee, and he shakes his head. "No,
not yet," he whispers. *No tail yet,* is what he meant—*she's still got legs*—
but he couldn't say it, no more than me. Julia Caterina reaches up for
him, and he sits by her on the bed and kisses both her hands. I can just
see the half-circle outlines beginning just below her boobies, very faint
against the pale skin. *Scales....*

"How long?" Henry Lee asks, looking down into her face, like he's
asking her, not me.

"You'd know better than me," I tells him straight. "I only seen one
poor sailor, maybe cooked halfway. And no women."

Henry Lee closes his eyes. "I never..." I can't hardly hear him. He
says, "I never...only that one time on the river, in the dark. I never saw."

"Aye, made sure of that didn't you?" I says. "You'll know next time."

He does look at me then, and his mouth makes one silent word—
don't. After a bit he gets so he can breathe out, "Aren't I being punished
enough?"

"Not nearly," I says. But Julia Caterina makes that sound again, and
all on a sudden I'm so rotten sorry for her and Henry Lee I can't barely
speak words meself. Nowt to do but rest me hand on his shoulder, while
he sits there by his wife, and her *turning* under his own hands. Time we
leave that sea-smelling room, it's dark outside, same as in.

And I didn't stir out of that house for the next nineteen days. Seems
longer to me betimes, remembering—shorter too, other times, short as
loving a wall and a barmaid—but nineteen days it were, with all the
curtains drawn, every servant long fled, bar Gopi, him who'd come for

me. That one, he stayed right along, went on shopping and cooking and sweeping; and if the smell and the closed rooms and us whispering up and down the stair—aye, and the sounds Henry Lee made alone in the night—if it all ever frighted him, he never said. A good man.

Like I figured, she never lost speech. I'd hear them talking hours on end, her and Henry Lee—always in the Portygee, of course, so's I couldn't make out none of it, which was good. Weren't for me to know what Henry Lee was saying to his wife, and her changing into a mermaid along of him getting rich. He tried to tell me some of their talk, but I didn't want to hear it then, and I've forgot it all now—made bleeding sure of *that*. I already know enough as I shouldn't, ta ever so.

Nineteen days. Nineteen mornings rising with me head so full of that sea-smell—stronger every day—I couldn't hardly swallow nowt but maybe porridge, couldn't never drink nowt but water. Nineteen nights lying awake hour on hour in one of the servants' garrets—I put meself there, 'acos I don't dream in them little cubbies the way I do in big echoey rooms such as Henry Lee had for his guests. I don't like dreaming, to this day I don't, and I liked it less then. Never closed me eyes until I had to, in that dark house.

Seventeenth night...seventeenth night, I've just finally gotten to sleep when Henry Lee wakes me, shaking me like the house is afire. I come up fighting and cursing—can't help it, always been that way—and I welt him a rouser on the earhole, but he drags me out of the bed and bundles me down to their room with a blanket around me shoulders. I keep pulling away from him, 'acos I know what I'm going to see, but he won't let go. His blue eyes look like he's been crying blood.

He'd covered her with every damp towel and rag in the house, but she'd thrown them all off...and there it is, there, laying out on the sheets that Henry Lee changes with his own hands every day, and Gopi takes to the *dhobi-wallah* for washing. There it is.

Everything's gone. Legs, feet, belly, all of it, *everything,* gone as though there'd never been nothing below her waist but that tail, scales flickering and glittering like wet emeralds in the candlelight. Look at it one way, it's a wonderful thing, that tail. It's the longest part of a mermaid or a merrow, and even when it's not moving at all, like hers wasn't just then, I swear you can see it *breathing* by itself, if you stand still and look close. In and out, slow, only a little, but you can see. It's them and it's *not* them, and that's all I'm going to say.

Now and then she'd twitch it a bit, flip the finny end some—getting used to it, like, having a tail. Each time she did that, Henry Lee'd draw his breath sharp, but all he said to me as we stood by the bed, he said, "It's made her more beautiful, Ben, hasn't it?" And it had that. She'd always had a good face, Julia Caterina, but the change had shaped it over, same as it had shaped her body. There was a wildness mixed in with the old sweetness now—mermaids is animals, some ways—and it had turned her, *whetted* her, into summat didn't have no end to how beautiful it could be. I told you early on, they ain't all beautiful, but even the ugly ones…see now, people got ends, people got *limits*—mermaids don't. Mermaids got no limits, except the sea.

She said his name, and her voice were different too—higher, yes, but mainly *clearer*, like all the clouds had blown off it. If that voice called for you, even soft, you'd hear it a long way. Henry Lee picked her up in his arms and put his cheek against hers, and she held onto him, and that tail tried to hold him too, bumping hard against his legs. I thought to slip out of there unnoticed, me and me blanket, but then Henry Lee said, quiet-like, "We could…I suppose we could put her in the water tonight, couldn't we, Ben?"

Well, I turned round on that fast, telling him, "Not near!" I pointed at the three double lines on both sides of her neck, so faint they were, still barely visible in her skin. "The gill slits ain't opened yet—drop her in a bathtub, she'd likely drown. Happen they might never open, I don't know. I'm telling you straight, I never seen this—I don't *know!*"

She looked at me then, and she smiled a little, but it weren't her smile. I leaned closer, and she said in English, so softly Henry Lee didn't hear, "Unbind my hair."

They don't all have long golden hair, that's just nursery talk. I seen one off Porto Rico had a mane red as sunset clouds, and I seen a fair old lot with thick dark hair like Julia Caterina's. But I never touched none of them before. It weren't me place to touch her neither, and Henry Lee standing by, too, but I done it anyway, like it were the hair asking me to do it, and not her. First twitch, it all come right down over me hands, ripe and heavy and *hot*—hot like I'd spilled cooking oil on meself, the way it clings and keeps burning, and water makes it worse. Truth, for a minute I thought me hands *was* ablaze—seemed like I could *see* them burning like fireships through that black swirly tangle wouldn't let them go. I yelled out then—I ain't shamed none to admit it, I know what I felt—and I snatched me hands right back, and of course there weren't a mark on them. And I looked into her eyes, and they was green and gray and green again, like the salt wine, and she laughed. She knew I were frighted and hurting, and she laughed and laughed.

I thought there were nothing left of her then—all gone, the little Portygee woman who'd sat in me chair and said something nobody else never said to me before. But then the eyes was hers again, all wide with fear and love, and she reached out for Henry Lee like she really were drowning. Aye, that were the worst of it, some way, those last two days, 'acos of one minute she'd be hissing like a cat, did he try to touch her or pet her, flopping away from him, the way you'd have thought he were her worst enemy in the world. Next minute, curled small in his arms, trembling all over, weeping dry-eyed, the way mermaids do, and him singing low to her in Portygee, sounded like nursery rhymes. Never saw him blubbing himself, not one tear.

She didn't stay in the bed much no more, but managed to get around the room using her arms and her tail—practicing-like, you see. Wouldn't eat nothing, no matter Henry Lee cozened her with the freshest fish and crab, mussels just out of the sea. Sometimes at first she'd take a little water, but by and by she'd show her teeth and knock the cup out of his hand. Mermaids don't drink, no more nor fish do.

They don't sleep, neither—not what you'd call sleeping—so there'd be one of us always by her, him or me, for fear she'd do herself a mischief. We wasn't doing much sleeping then ourselves, by then, so often enough we'd find ourselves side by side, not talking, just watching her while she watched the sea through the window and the moon ripened in the trees. The one time we ever did talk about it, he said to me, "You were right, Ben. I haven't been punished nearly enough for what I've done."

"Some get punished too much," I says, "and some not at all. Don't seem to make much difference, near as I can tell."

Henry Lee shakes his head. "You got out the moment you knew we might have harmed even one person. I stayed on. I'll never be quits for this, Ben."

I don't have no answer, except to tell him about a thing I did long ago that I'm still being punished for meself. I'd never told nobody before, and I'm not about to tell you now. I just did it to maybe help Henry Lee a little, which it didn't. He patted me back and squeezed me shoulder a little bit, but he didn't say no more, and nor did I. We sat together and watched Julia Caterina in the moonlight.

Come that nineteenth night, the moon rose full to bursting, big and bright and yellow as day, with one or two red streaks, like an egg gone bad, laying down a wrinkly-gold path you could have walked on to the horizon…or swum down, as the case might be. Julia Caterina went wild at the sight, beating at the window the way you'd have thought she were a moth trying to get to the candle. It come to me, she'd waited for this moon the same way the turtles wait to come ashore and lay their eggs in the light—the way those tiny fish I disremember flood over the beaches at high tide, millions of them, got to get those eggs buried *fast*, before the next wave sweeps them back out to sea. Now it were like the moon were waiting for her, and she knew the way there.

"Not yet," Henry Lee says, desperate-like, "not yet—*they*'ve not..." He didn't finish, but I knew he were talking about the pale lines on her neck, darker every day, but still not opened into proper gill slits. But right as he spoke, right then, those same lines swelled and split and flared red, and that sudden, they was there, making her more a fish than the tail ever could, because now she didn't need the land at all, or the air. Aye, now she could stay under water all the time, if she wanted. She were ready for the sea, and she knew it, no more to say.

Henry Lee carried her in his arms all the way down from his grand house—*their* house until two nights ago—to the water's edge, nobody to see nowt, just a couple of fishing boats anchored offshore. A dugout canoe, too, which you still used to see in them days. She wriggled out of his arms there, turning in the air like a cat, and a little wave splashed up in her face as she landed, making her laugh and splash back with her tail. Henry Lee were drenched right off, top to toe, but you could see he didn't know. Julia Caterina—her as had been Julia Caterina—she swam round and round, rolling and diving and admiring all she could do in the water. There's nothing *fits* the sea like a mermaid—not fish, not seals, dolphins, whales, nothing. There in the moonlight, the sea looked happy to be with her.

I can't swim, like I told you—I just waded in a few steps to watch her playing so. All on a sudden—for all the world like she'd heard a call from somewhere—she did a kind of a swirling cartwheel, gave a couple of hard kicks with that tail, and like *that*, she's away, no goodbye, clear of the shore, leaving her own foxfire trail down the middle of that moonlight path. I thought she were gone then, gone forever, and I didn't waste no time in gawping, but turned to see to Henry Lee. He were standing up to his knees in the water, taking his shirt off.

"Henry Lee," I says. "Henry Lee, what the Christ you doing?" He don't even look over at me, but throws the shirt back toward the shore and starts unbuttoning his trews. Bought from the only bespoke gentlemen's tailor in Velha Goa, those pants, still cost you half what you'd pay in Lisbon. Henry Lee just drops them in the water. Goes to work getting rid of his smallclothes, kicking off his soaked shoes, while I'm yapping at him about catching cold, pneumonia. Henry Lee smiles at me. Still got most all his teeth, which even the Portygee nobs can't say they do, most of them. He says, "She'll be lonely out there."

I said summat, must have. I don't recall what it were. Standing there naked, Henry Lee says, "She'll need me, Ben."

"She's got all she needs," I says. "You can't go after her."

"I promised I'd make it up to her," he says. "What I did. But there's no way, Ben, there's no way."

He moves on past me, walking straight ahead, water rising steady. I stumble and scramble in front of him, afeared as I can be, but he's not getting by. "You can't make it up," I tells him. "Some things, you can't ever make up—you live with them, that's all. That's the best you can do." He's taller by a head, but I'm bigger, wider. He's not getting by.

Henry Lee stops walking out toward the deep. Confused-like, shaking his head some, starts to say me name...then he looks over me shoulder and his eyes go wide, with the moon in them. "She's there," he whispers, "she came back for me. There, right *there.*" And he points, straining on his toes like a nipper sees the Dutch-biscuit man coming down the street.

I turn me head, just for an instant, just to see where he's pointing. *Summat* glimmers in the shadow of the dugout, diving in and out of the moonlight, and maybe it's a dolphin, and maybe it's Henry Lee's wife, turning for one last look at her poor husband who'd driven both of their lives on the rocks. Didn't know then, don't know now. All I'm sure of is, the next minute I'm sitting on me arse in water up to me chin, and Henry Lee's past me and swimming straight for that glimmer—long, raking Devonshire strokes, looking like he could go on forever if he had to. And bright as the night was, I lost sight of him—and her too, *it,* whatever it were—before he'd reached that boat. Bawled for him till me voice went—even tried to go after him in the dugout—but he were gone. They were gone.

His body floated in next afternoon. Gopi found it, sloshing about in the shallows.

Her family turned over every bit of ground around that house of Henry Lee's, looking for where he'd buried her. I'm dead sure they believe to this day that he killed Julia Caterina and then drowned himself, out of remorse or some such. They was polite as pie whenever we met, no matter they couldn't never stand one solitary thing about me—but after she disappeared only times I saw them was at a *feria,* where they'd always cut me dead. I didn't take it personal.

The will left stock and business to the family, but left both ships to me. I sold one of them for enough money to get meself to Buenos Aires, like I'd been wanting, and start up in the freighting trade, convoying everything from pianos to salt beef, rum to birdseed, tea to railroad ties...whatever you might want moved from *here* to *there.* Got two young partners do most of the real work these days, but I still go along with a shipment, times, just to play I'm still a foremast hand—plain Able-bodied Seaman, same as Henry Lee. The way it was when we didn't know what he died knowing. What I'll die knowing.

He left me the recipe for salt wine, too. I burned it. I'd wanted to buy up the stock and pour every bottle into the sea—giving it back to the merrows, you could say—but the family wouldn't sell, not to me. Heard they sold it to a German dealer, right after I left Goa, and he took it all home to Berlin with him. Couldn't say, meself.

I seen her a time or two since. Once off the Hebrides—leastways, I'm near about sure it was her—and once in the Bay of Biscay. That time she came right up to the ship, calling to me by name, quiet-like. She hung about most of the night, calling, but I never went to the rail, 'acos I couldn't think of nothing to say.

Two Hearts

My brother Wilfrid keeps saying it's not fair that it should all have happened to me. Me being a girl, and a baby, and too stupid to lace up my own sandals properly. But *I* think it's fair. I think everything happened exactly the way it should have done. Except for the sad parts, and maybe those too.

I'm Sooz, and I am nine years old. Ten next month, on the anniversary of the day the griffin came. Wilfrid says it was because of me, that the griffin heard that the ugliest baby in the world had just been born, and it was going to eat me, but I was *too* ugly, even for a griffin. So it nested in the Midwood (we call it that, but its real name is the Midnight Wood, because of the darkness under the trees), and stayed to eat our sheep and our goats. Griffins do that if they like a place.

But it didn't ever eat children, not until this year.

I only saw it once—I mean, once *before*—rising up above the trees one night, like a second moon. Only there wasn't a moon, then. There was nothing in the whole world but the griffin, golden feathers all blazing on its lion's body and eagle's wings, with its great front claws like teeth, and that monstrous beak that looked so huge for its head…. Wilfrid says I screamed for three days, but he's lying, and I *didn't* hide in the root cellar like he says either, I slept in the barn those two nights, with our dog Malka. Because I knew Malka wouldn't let anything get me.

I mean my parents wouldn't have, either, not if they could have stopped it. It's just that Malka is the biggest, fiercest dog in the whole village, and she's not afraid of anything. And after the griffin took Jehane, the blacksmith's little girl, you couldn't help seeing how frightened my father was, running back and forth with the other men, trying to organize some sort of patrol, so people could always tell when the griffin was coming. I know he was frightened for me and my mother, and doing everything he could to protect us, but it didn't make me feel any safer, and Malka did.

But nobody knew what to do, anyway. Not my father, nobody. It was bad enough when the griffin was only taking the sheep, because almost everyone here sells wool or cheese or sheepskin things to make a living. But once it took Jehane, early last spring, that changed everything. We sent messengers to the king—three of them—and each time the king sent someone back to us with them. The first time, it was one knight, all by himself. His name was Douros, and he gave me an apple. He rode away into the Midwood, singing, to look for the griffin, and we never saw him again.

The second time—after the griffin took Louli, the boy who worked for the miller—the king sent five knights together. One of them did come back, but he died before he could tell anyone what happened.

The third time an entire squadron came. That's what my father said, anyway. I don't know how many soldiers there are in a squadron, but it was a lot, and they were all over the village for two days, pitching their tents everywhere, stabling their horses in every barn, and boasting in the tavern how they'd soon take care of that griffin for us poor peasants. They had musicians playing when they marched into the Midwood—I remember that, and I remember when the music stopped, and the sounds we heard afterward.

After that, the village didn't send to the king anymore. We didn't want more of his men to die, and besides they weren't any help. So from then on all the children were hurried indoors when the sun went down, and the griffin woke from its day's rest to hunt again. We couldn't play together, or run errands or watch the flocks for our parents, or even sleep near open windows, for fear of the griffin. There was nothing for me to do but read books I already knew by heart, and complain to my mother and father, who were too tired from watching after Wilfrid and me to bother with us. They were guarding the other children too, turn and turn about with the other families—*and* our sheep, *and* our goats— so they were always tired, as well as frightened, and we were all angry with each other most of the time. It was the same for everybody.

And then the griffin took Felicitas.

Felicitas couldn't talk, but she was my best friend, always, since we were little. I always understood what she wanted to say, and she understood me, better than anyone, and we played in a special way that I won't ever play with anyone else. Her family thought she was a waste of food, because no boy would marry a dumb girl, so they let her eat with us most of the time. Wilfrid used to make fun of the whispery quack that was the one sound she could make, but I hit him with a rock, and after that he didn't do it anymore.

I didn't see it happen, but I still see it in my head. She *knew* not to go out, but she was always just so happy coming to us in the evening.

And nobody at her house would have noticed her being gone. None of them ever noticed Felicitas.

The day I learned Felicitas was gone, that was the day I set off to see the king myself.

Well, the same *night*, actually—because there wasn't any chance of getting away from my house or the village in daylight. I don't know what I'd have done, really, except that my Uncle Ambrose was carting a load of sheepskins to market in Hagsgate, and you have to start long before sunup to be there by the time the market opens. Uncle Ambrose is my best uncle, but I knew I couldn't ask him to take me to the king—he'd have gone straight to my mother instead, and told her to give me sulphur and molasses and put me to bed with a mustard plaster. He gives his *horse* sulphur and molasses, even.

So I went to bed early that night, and I waited until everyone was asleep. I wanted to leave a note on my pillow, but I kept writing things and then tearing the notes up and throwing them in the fireplace, and I was afraid of somebody waking, or Uncle Ambrose leaving without me. Finally I just wrote, *I will come home soon.* I didn't take any clothes with me, or anything else, except a bit of cheese, because I thought the king must live somewhere near Hagsgate, which is the only big town I've ever seen. My mother and father were snoring in their room, but Wilfrid had fallen asleep right in front of the hearth, and they always leave him there when he does. If you rouse him to go to his own bed, he comes up fighting and crying. I don't know why.

I stood and looked down at him for the longest time. Wilfrid doesn't look nearly so mean when he's sleeping. My mother had banked the coals to make sure there'd be a fire for tomorrow's bread, and my father's moleskin trews were hanging there to dry, because he'd had to wade into the stockpond that afternoon to rescue a lamb. I moved them a little bit, so they wouldn't burn. I wound the clock—Wilfrid's supposed to do that every night, but he always forgets—and I thought how they'd all be hearing it ticking in the morning while they were looking everywhere for me, too frightened to eat any breakfast, and I turned to go back to my room.

But then I turned around again, and I climbed out of the kitchen window, because our front door squeaks so. I was afraid that Malka might wake in the barn and right away know I was up to something, because I can't ever fool Malka, only she didn't, and then I held my breath almost the whole way as I ran to Uncle Ambrose's house and scrambled right into his cart with the sheepskins. It was a cold night, but under that pile of sheepskins it was hot and nasty-smelling, and there wasn't anything to do but lie still and wait for Uncle Ambrose. So I mostly thought about Felicitas, to keep from feeling so bad about leaving home and everyone. That was bad enough—I never really *lost* anybody close before, not *forever*—but anyway it was different.

I don't know when Uncle Ambrose finally came, because I dozed off in the cart, and didn't wake until there was this jolt and a rattle and the sort of floppy grumble a horse makes when *he's* been waked up and doesn't like it—and we were off for Hagsgate. The moon was setting early, but I could see the village bumping by, not looking silvery in the light, but small and dull, no color to anything. And all the same I almost began to cry, because it already seemed so far away, though we hadn't even passed the stockpond yet, and I felt as though I'd never see it again. I would have climbed back out of the cart right then, if I hadn't known better.

Because the griffin was still up and hunting. I couldn't see it, of course, under the sheepskins (and I had my eyes shut, anyway), but its wings made a sound like a lot of knives being sharpened all together, and sometimes it gave a cry that was dreadful because it was so soft and gentle, and even a little sad and *scared*, as though it were imitating the sound Felicitas might have made when it took her. I burrowed deep down as I could, and tried to sleep again, but I couldn't.

Which was just as well, because I didn't want to ride all the way into Hagsgate, where Uncle Ambrose was bound to find me when he unloaded his sheepskins in the marketplace. So when I didn't hear the griffin anymore (they won't hunt far from their nests, if they don't have to), I put my head out over the tailboard of the cart and watched the stars going out, one by one, as the sky grew lighter. The dawn breeze came up as the moon went down.

When the cart stopped jouncing and shaking so much, I knew we must have turned onto the King's Highway, and when I could hear cows munching and talking softly to each other, I dropped into the road. I stood there for a little, brushing off lint and wool bits, and watching Uncle Ambrose's cart rolling on away from me. I hadn't ever been this far from home by myself. Or so lonely. The breeze brushed dry grass against my ankles, and I didn't have any idea which way to go.

I didn't even know the king's name—I'd never heard anyone call him anything but *the king*. I knew he didn't live in Hagsgate, but in a big castle somewhere nearby, only nearby's one thing when you're riding in a cart and different when you're walking. And I kept thinking about my family waking up and looking for me, and the cows' grazing sounds made me hungry, and I'd eaten all my cheese in the cart. I wished I had a penny with me—not to buy anything with, but only to toss up and let it tell me if I should turn left or right. I tried it with flat stones, but I never could find them after they came down. Finally I started off going left, not for any reason, but only because I have a little silver ring on my left hand that my mother gave me. There was a sort of path that way too, and I thought maybe I could walk around Hagsgate and then I'd think about what to do after that. I'm a good walker. I can walk anywhere, if you give me time.

Only it's easier on a real road. The path gave out after awhile, and I had to push my way through trees growing too close together, and then through so many brambly vines that my hair was full of stickers and my arms were all stinging and bleeding. I was tired and sweating, and almost crying—*almost*—and whenever I sat down to rest bugs and things kept crawling over me. Then I heard running water nearby, and that made me thirsty right away, so I tried to get down to the sound. I had to crawl most of the way, scratching my knees and elbows up something awful.

It wasn't much of a stream—in some places the water came up barely above my ankles—but I was so glad to see it I practically hugged and kissed it, flopping down with my face buried in it, the way I do with Malka's smelly old fur. And I drank until I couldn't hold any more, and then I sat on a stone and let the tiny fish tickle my nice cold feet, and felt the sun on my shoulders, and I didn't think about griffins or kings or my family or anything.

I only looked up when I heard the horses whickering a little way upstream. They were playing with the water, the way horses do, blowing bubbles like children. Plain old livery-stable horses, one brownish, one grayish. The gray's rider was out of the saddle, peering at the horse's left forefoot. I couldn't get a good look—they both had on plain cloaks, dark green, and trews so worn you couldn't make out the color—so I didn't know that one was a woman until I heard her voice. A nice voice, low, like Silky Joan, the lady my mother won't ever let me ask about, but with something rough in it too, as though she could scream like a hawk if she wanted to. She was saying, "There's no stone I can see. Maybe a thorn?"

The other rider, the one on the brown horse, answered her, "Or a bruise. Let me see."

That voice was lighter and younger-sounding than the woman's voice, but I already knew he was a man, because he was so tall. He got down off the brown horse and the woman moved aside to let him pick up her horse's foot. Before he did that, he put his hands on the horse's head, one on each side, and he said something to it that I couldn't quite hear. *And the horse said something back.* Not like a neigh, or a whinny, or any of the sounds horses make, but like one person talking to another. I can't say it any better than that. The tall man bent down then, and he took hold of the foot and looked at it for a long time, and the horse didn't move or switch its tail or anything.

"A stone splinter," the man said after a while. "It's very small, but it's worked itself deep into the hoof, and there's an ulcer brewing. I can't think why I didn't notice it straightaway."

"Well," the woman said. She touched his shoulder. "You can't notice everything."

The tall man seemed angry with himself, the way my father gets when he's forgotten to close the pasture gate properly, and our neighbor's black ram gets in and fights with our poor old Brimstone. He said, "I can. I'm supposed to." Then he turned his back to the horse and bent over that forefoot, the way our blacksmith does, and he went to work on it.

I couldn't see what he was doing, not exactly. He didn't have any picks or pries, like the blacksmith, and all I'm sure of is that I *think* he was singing to the horse. But I'm not sure it was proper singing. It sounded more like the little made-up rhymes that really small children chant to themselves when they're playing in the dirt, all alone. No tune, just up and down, *dee-dah, dee-dah, dee...*boring even for a horse, I'd have thought. He kept doing it for a long time, still bending with that hoof in his hand. All at once he stopped singing and stood up, holding something that glinted in the sun the way the stream did, and he showed it to the horse, first thing. "There," he said, "there, that's what it was. It's all right now."

He tossed the thing away and picked up the hoof again, not singing, only touching it very lightly with one finger, brushing across it again and again. Then he set the foot down, and the horse stamped once, hard, and whinnied, and the tall man turned to the woman and said, "We ought to camp here for the night, all the same. They're both weary, and my back hurts."

The woman laughed. A deep, sweet, slow sound, it was. I'd never heard a laugh like that. She said, "The greatest wizard walking the world, and your back hurts? Heal it as you healed mine, the time the tree fell on me. That took you all of five minutes, I believe."

"Longer than that," the man answered her. "You were delirious, you wouldn't remember." He touched her hair, which was thick and pretty, even though it was mostly gray. "You know how I am about that," he said. "I still like being mortal too much to use magic on myself. It spoils it somehow—it dulls the feeling. I've told you before."

The woman said "*Mmphh,*" the way I've heard my mother say it a thousand times. "Well, *I've* been mortal all my life, and some days...."

She didn't finish what she was saying, and the tall man smiled, the way you could tell he was teasing her. "Some days, what?"

"Nothing," the woman said, "nothing, nothing." She sounded irritable for a moment, but she put her hands on the man's arms, and she said in a different voice, "Some days—some early mornings—when the wind smells of blossoms I'll never see, and there are fawns playing in the misty orchards, and you're yawning and mumbling and scratching your head, and growling that we'll see rain before nightfall, and probably hail as well...on such mornings I wish with all my heart that we could both live forever, and I think you were a great fool to give it up." She laughed again, but it sounded shaky now, a little. She said, "Then I remember things I'd rather not remember, so then my stomach acts up, and all sorts of other things start *twingeing* me—never mind what they are, or where they hurt, whether it's my body or my head, or my heart. And then I think, *no, I suppose not, maybe not.*" The tall man put his arms around her, and for a moment she rested her head on his chest. I couldn't hear what she said after that.

I didn't think I'd made any noise, but the man raised his voice a little, not looking at me, not lifting his head, and he said, "Child, there's food here." First I couldn't move, I was so frightened. He *couldn't* have seen me through the brush and all the alder trees. And then I started remembering how hungry I was, and I started toward them without knowing I was doing it. I actually looked down at my feet and watched them moving like somebody else's feet, as though they were the hungry ones, only they had to have me take them to the food. The man and the woman stood very still and waited for me.

Close to, the woman looked younger than her voice, and the tall man looked older. No, that isn't it, that's not what I mean. She wasn't young at all, but the gray hair made her face younger, and she held herself really straight, like the lady who comes when people in our village are having babies. She holds her face all stiff too, that one, and I don't like her much. This woman's face wasn't beautiful, I suppose, but it was a face you'd want to snuggle up to on a cold night. That's the best I know how to say it.

The man...one minute he looked younger than my father, and the next he'd be looking older than anybody I ever saw, older than people are supposed to *be*, maybe. He didn't have any gray hair himself, but he did have a lot of lines, but that's not what I'm talking about either. It was the eyes. His eyes were green, green, *green*, not like grass, not like emeralds—I saw an emerald once, a gypsy woman showed me—and not anything like apples or limes or such stuff. Maybe like the ocean, except I've never seen the ocean, so I don't know. If you go deep enough into the woods (not the Midwood, of course not, but any other sort of woods), sooner or later you'll always come to a place where even the *shadows* are green, and that's the way his eyes were. I was afraid of his eyes at first.

The woman gave me a peach and watched me bite into it, too hungry to thank her. She asked me, "Girl, what are you doing here? Are you lost?"

"No, I'm not," I mumbled with my mouth full. "I just don't know where I am, that's different." They both laughed, but it wasn't a mean, making-fun laugh. I told them, "My name's Sooz, and I have to see the king. He lives somewhere right nearby, doesn't he?"

They looked at each other. I couldn't tell what they were thinking, but the tall man raised his eyebrows, and the woman shook her head a bit, slowly. They looked at each other for a long time, until the woman said, "Well, not nearby, but not so very far, either. We were bound on our way to visit him ourselves."

"Good," I said. "Oh, *good*." I was trying to sound as grown-up as they were, but it was hard, because I was so happy to find out that they could take me to the king. I said, "I'll go along with you, then."

The woman was against it before I got the first words out. She said to the tall man, "No, we couldn't. We don't know how things are." She looked sad about it, but she looked firm, too. She said, "Girl, it's not you worries me. The king is a good man, and an old friend, but it has been a long time, and kings change. Even more than other people, kings change."

"I have to see him," I said. "You go on, then. I'm not going home until I see him." I finished the peach, and the man handed me a chunk of dried fish and smiled at the woman as I tore into it. He said quietly to her, "It seems to me that you and I both remember asking to be taken along on a quest. I can't speak for you, but I begged."

But the woman wouldn't let up. "We could be bringing her into great peril. You can't take the chance, it isn't right!"

He began to answer her, but I interrupted—my mother would have slapped me halfway across the kitchen. I shouted at them, "I'm *coming* from great peril. There's a griffin nested in the Midwood, and he's eaten Jehane and Louli and—and my Felicitas—" and then I *did* start weeping, and I didn't care. I just stood there and shook and wailed, and dropped the dried fish. I tried to pick it up, still crying so hard I couldn't see it, but the woman stopped me and gave me her scarf to dry my eyes and blow my nose. It smelled nice.

"Child," the tall man kept saying, "child, don't take on so, we didn't know about the griffin." The woman was holding me against her side, smoothing my hair and glaring at him as though it was his fault that I was howling like that. She said, "Of course we'll take you with us, girl dear—there, never mind, of course we will. That's a fearful matter, a griffin, but the king will know what to do about it. The king eats griffins for breakfast snacks—spreads them on toast with orange marmalade and gobbles them up, I promise you." And so on, being silly, but making me feel better, while the man went on pleading with me not to cry. I finally stopped when he pulled a big red handkerchief out of his pocket, twisted and knotted it into a bird-shape, and made it fly away. Uncle Ambrose does tricks with coins and shells, but he can't do anything like that.

His name was Schmendrick, which I still think is the funniest name I've heard in my life. The woman's name was Molly Grue. We didn't leave right away, because of the horses, but made camp where we were instead. I was waiting for the man, Schmendrick, to do it by magic, but he only built a fire, set out their blankets, and drew water from the stream like anyone else, while she hobbled the horses and put them to graze. I gathered firewood.

The woman, Molly, told me that the king's name was Lír, and that they had known him when he was a very young man, before he became king. "He is a true hero," she said, "a dragonslayer, a giantkiller, a rescuer of maidens, a solver of impossible riddles. He may be the greatest hero of all, because he's a good man as well. They aren't always."

"But you didn't want me to meet him," I said. "Why was that?"

Molly sighed. We were sitting under a tree, watching the sun go down, and she was brushing things out of my hair. She said, "He's old now. Schmendrick has trouble with time—I'll tell you why one day, it's a long story—and he doesn't understand that Lír may no longer be the man he was. It could be a sad reunion." She started braiding my hair around my head, so it wouldn't get in the way. "I've had an unhappy feeling about this journey from the beginning, Sooz. But *he* took a notion that Lír needed us, so here we are. You can't argue with him when he gets like that."

"A good wife isn't supposed to argue with her husband," I said. "My mother says you wait until he goes out, or he's asleep, and then you do what you want."

Molly laughed, that rich, funny sound of hers, like a kind of deep gurgle. "Sooz, I've only known you a few hours, but I'd bet every penny I've got right now—aye, and all of Schmendrick's too—that you'll be arguing on your wedding night with whomever you marry. Anyway, Schmendrick and I aren't married. We're together, that's all. We've been together quite a long while."

"Oh," I said. I didn't know any people who were together like that, not the way she said it. "Well, you *look* married. You sort of do."

Molly's face didn't change, but she put an arm around my shoulders and hugged me close for a moment. She whispered in my ear, "I wouldn't marry him if he were the last man in the world. He eats wild radishes in bed. *Crunch, crunch, crunch,* all night—*crunch, crunch, crunch.*" I giggled, and the tall man looked over at us from where he was washing a pan in the stream. The last of the sunlight was on him, and those green eyes were bright as new leaves. One of them winked at me, and I *felt* it, the way you feel a tiny breeze on your skin when it's hot. Then he went back to scrubbing the pan.

"Will it take us long to reach the king?" I asked her. "You said he didn't live too far, and I'm scared the griffin will eat somebody else while I'm gone. I need to be home."

Molly finished with my hair and gave it a gentle tug in back to bring my head up and make me look straight into her eyes. They were as gray as Schmendrick's were green, and I already knew that they turned darker or lighter gray depending on her mood. "What do you expect to happen when you meet King Lír, Sooz?" she asked me right back. "What did you have in mind when you set off to find him?"

I was surprised. "Well, I'm going to get him to come back to my village with me. All those knights he keeps sending aren't doing any good at all, so he'll just have to take care of that griffin himself. He's the king. It's his job."

"Yes," Molly said, but she said it so softly I could barely hear her. She patted my arm once, lightly, and then she got up and walked away to sit by herself near the fire. She made it look as though she was banking the fire, but she wasn't really.

We started out early the next morning. Molly had me in front of her on her horse for a time, but by and by Schmendrick took me up on his, to spare the other one's sore foot. He was more comfortable to lean against than I'd expected—bony in some places, nice and springy in others. He didn't talk much, but he sang a lot as we went along, sometimes in languages I couldn't make out a word of, sometimes making up silly songs to make me laugh, like this one:

Soozli, Soozli,
speaking loozli,

you disturb my oozli-goozli.
Soozli, Soozli,
would you choozli
to become my squoozli-squoozli?

He didn't do anything magic, except maybe once, when a crow kept diving at the horse—out of meanness; that's all, there wasn't a nest anywhere—making the poor thing dance and shy and skitter until I almost fell off. Schmendrick finally turned in the saddle and *looked* at it, and the next minute a hawk came swooping out of nowhere and chased that crow screaming into a thornbush where the hawk couldn't follow. I guess that was magic.

It was actually pretty country we were passing through, once we got onto the proper road. Trees, meadows, little soft valleys, hillsides covered with wildflowers I didn't know. You could see they got a lot more rain here than we do where I live. It's a good thing sheep don't need grazing, the way cows do. They'll go where the goats go, and goats will go anywhere. We're like that in my village, we have to be. But I liked this land better.

Schmendrick told me it hadn't always been like that. "Before Lír, this was all barren desert where nothing grew—*nothing,* Sooz. It was said that the country was under a curse, and in a way it was, but I'll tell you about that another time." People *always* say that when you're a child, and I hate it. "But Lír changed everything. The land was so glad to see him that it began blooming and blossoming the moment he became king, and it has done so ever since. Except poor Hagsgate, but that's another story too." His voice got slower and deeper when he talked about Hagsgate, as though he weren't talking to me.

I twisted my neck around to look up at him. "Do you think King Lír will come back with me and kill that griffin? I think Molly thinks he won't, because he's so old." I hadn't known I was worried about that until I actually said it.

"Why, of course he will, girl." Schmendrick winked at me again. "He never could resist the plea of a maiden in distress, the more difficult and dangerous the deed, the better. If he did not spur to your village's aid himself at the first call, it was surely because he was engaged on some other heroic venture. I'm as certain as I can be that as soon as you make your request—remember to curtsey properly—he'll snatch up his great sword and spear, whisk you up to his saddlebow, and be off after your griffin with the road smoking behind him. Young or old, that's always been his way." He rumpled my hair in the back. "Molly overworries. That's *her* way. We are who we are."

"What's a curtsey?" I asked him. I know now, because Molly showed me, but I didn't then. He didn't laugh, except with his eyes, then gestured for me to face forward again as he went back to singing.

> *Soozli, Soozli,*
> *you amuse me,*
> *right down to my solesli-shoesli.*
> *Soozli, Soozli,*
> *I bring newsli—*
> *we could wed next stewsli-Tuesli.*

I learned that the king had lived in a castle on a cliff by the sea when he was young, less than a day's journey from Hagsgate, but it fell down—Schmendrick wouldn't tell me how—so he built a new one somewhere else. I was sorry about that, because I've never seen the sea, and I've always wanted to, and I still haven't. But I'd never seen a castle, either, so there was that. I leaned back against his chest and fell asleep.

They'd been traveling slowly, taking time to let Molly's horse heal, but once its hoof was all right we galloped most of the rest of the way. Those horses of theirs didn't look magic or special, but they could run for hours without getting tired, and when I helped to rub them down and curry them, they were hardly sweating. They slept on their sides, like people, not standing up, the way our horses do.

Even so, it took us three full days to reach King Lír. Molly said he had bad memories of the castle that fell down, so that was why this one was as far from the sea as he could make it, and as different from the old one. It was on a hill, so the king could see anyone coming along the road, but there wasn't a moat, and there weren't any guards in armor, and there was only one banner on the walls. It was blue, with a picture of a white unicorn on it. Nothing else.

I was disappointed. I tried not to show it, but Molly saw. "You wanted a fortress," she said to me gently. "You were expecting dark stone towers, flags and cannons and knights, trumpeters blowing from the battlements. I'm sorry. It being your first castle, and all."

"No, it's a *pretty* castle," I said. And it *was* pretty, sitting peacefully on its hilltop in the sunlight, surrounded by all those wildflowers. There was a marketplace, I could see now, and there were huts like ours snugged up against the castle walls, so that the people could come inside for protection, if they needed to. I said, "Just looking at it, you can see that the king is a nice man."

Molly was looking at me with her head a little bit to one side. She said, "He is a hero, Sooz. Remember that, whatever else you see, whatever you think. Lír is a hero."

"Well, I know *that*," I said. "I'm sure he'll help me. I am."

But I wasn't. The moment I saw that nice, friendly castle, I wasn't a bit sure.

We didn't have any trouble getting in. The gate simply opened when Schmendrick knocked once, and he and Molly and I walked in through the market, where people were selling all kinds of fruits and vegetables, pots and pans and clothing and so on, the way they do in our village. They all called to us to come over to their barrows and buy things, but nobody tried to stop us going into the castle. There were two men at the two great doors, and they did ask us our names and why we wanted to see King Lír. The moment Schmendrick told them his name, they stepped back quickly and let us by, so I began to think that maybe he actually was a great magician, even if I never saw him do anything but little tricks and little songs. The men didn't offer to take him to the king, and he didn't ask.

Molly was right. I *was* expecting the castle to be all cold and shadowy, with queens looking sideways at us, and big men clanking by in armor. But the halls we followed Schmendrick through were full of sunlight from long, high windows, and the people we saw mostly nodded and smiled at us. We passed a stone stair curling up out of sight, and I was sure that the king must live at the top, but Schmendrick never looked at it. He led us straight through the great hall—they had a fireplace big enough to roast three cows!—and on past the kitchens and the scullery and the laundry, to a room under another stair. *That* was dark. You wouldn't have found it unless you knew where to look. Schmendrick didn't knock at that door, and he didn't say anything magic to make it open. He just stood outside and waited, and by and by it rattled open, and we went in.

The king was in there. All by himself, the king was in there.

He was sitting on an ordinary wooden chair, not a throne. It was a really small room, the same size as my mother's weaving room, so maybe that's why he looked so big. He was as tall as Schmendrick, but he seemed so much *wider*. I was ready for him to have a long beard, spreading out all across his chest, but he only had a short one, like my father, except white. He wore a red and gold mantle, and there was a real golden crown on his white head, not much bigger than the wreaths we put on our champion rams at the end of the year. He had a kind face, with a big old nose, and big blue eyes, like a little boy. But his eyes were so tired and heavy, I didn't know how he kept them open. Sometimes he didn't. There was nobody else in the little room, and he peered at the three of us as though he knew he knew us, but not *why*. He tried to smile.

Schmendrick said very gently, "Majesty, it is Schmendrick and Molly, Molly Grue." The king blinked at him.

"Molly with the cat," Molly whispered. "You remember the cat, Lír."

"Yes," the king said. It seemed to take him forever to speak that one word. "The cat, yes, of course." But he didn't say anything after that, and we stood there and stood there, and the king kept smiling at something I couldn't see.

Schmendrick said to Molly, "*She* used to forget herself like that." His voice had changed, the same way it changed when he was talking about the way the land used to be. He said, "And then you would always remind her that she was a unicorn."

And the king changed too then. All at once his eyes were clear and shining with feeling, like Molly's eyes, and he *saw* us for the first time. He said softly, "Oh, my friends!" and he stood up and came to us and put his arms around Schmendrick and Molly. And I saw that he had been a hero, and that he was still a hero, and I began to think it might be all right, after all. Maybe it was really going to be all right.

"And who may this princess be?" he asked, looking straight at me. He had the proper voice for a king, deep and strong, but not frightening, not mean. I tried to tell him my name, but I couldn't make a sound, so he actually knelt on one knee in front of me, and he took my hand. He said, "I have often been of some use to princesses in distress. Command me."

"I'm not a princess, I'm Sooz," I said, "and I'm from a village you wouldn't even know, and there's a griffin eating the children." It all tumbled out like that, in one breath, but he didn't laugh or look at me any differently. What he did was ask me the name of my village, and I told him, and he said, "But indeed I know it, madam. I have been there. And now I will have the pleasure of returning."

Over his shoulder I saw Schmendrick and Molly staring at each other. Schmendrick was about to say something, but then they both turned toward the door, because a small dark woman, about my mother's age, only dressed in tunic, trews and boots like Molly, had just come in. She said in a small, worried voice, "I am so truly sorry that I was not here to greet His Majesty's old companions. No need to tell me your illustrious names—my own is Lisene, and I am the king's royal secretary, translator, and protector." She took King Lír's arm, very politely and carefully, and began moving him back to his chair.

Schmendrick seemed to take a minute getting his own breath back. He said, "I have never known my old friend Lír to need any of those services. Especially a protector."

Lisene was busy with the king and didn't look at Schmendrick as she answered him. "How long has it been since you saw him last?" Schmendrick didn't answer. Lisene's voice was quiet still, but not so nervous. "Time sets its claw in us all, my lord, sooner or later. We are none of us that which we were." King Lír sat down obediently on his chair and closed his eyes.

I could tell that Schmendrick was angry, and growing angrier as he stood there, but he didn't show it. My father gets angry like that, which is how I knew. He said, "His Majesty has agreed to return to this young person's village with her, in order to rid her people of a marauding griffin. We will start out tomorrow."

Lisene swung around on us so fast that I was sure she was going to start shouting and giving everybody orders. But she didn't do anything like that. You could never have told that she was the least bit annoyed or alarmed. All she said was, "I am afraid that will not be possible, my lord. The king is in no fit condition for such a journey, nor certainly for such a deed."

"The king thinks rather differently." Schmendrick was talking through clenched teeth now.

"Does he, then?" Lisene pointed at King Lír, and I saw that he had fallen asleep in his chair. His head was drooping—I was afraid his crown was going to fall off—and his mouth hung open. Lisene said, "You came seeking the peerless warrior you remember, and you have found a spent, senile old man. Believe me, I understand your distress, but you must see—"

Schmendrick cut her off. I never understood what people meant when they talked about someone's eyes actually flashing, but at least green eyes can do it. He looked even taller than he was, and when he pointed a finger at Lisene I honestly expected the small woman to catch fire or maybe melt away. Schmendrick's voice was especially frightening because it was so quiet. He said, "Hear me now. I am Schmendrick the Magician, and I see my old friend Lír, as I have always seen him, wise and powerful and good, beloved of a unicorn."

And with that word, for a second time, the king woke up. He blinked once, then gripped the arms of the chair and pushed himself to his feet. He didn't look at us, but at Lisene, and he said, "I will go with them. It is my task and my gift. You will see to it that I am made ready."

Lisene said, "Majesty, no! Majesty, I beg you!"

King Lír reached out and took Lisene's head between his big hands, and I saw that there was love between them. He said, "It is what I am for. You know that as well as *he* does. See to it, Lisene, and keep all well for me while I am gone."

Lisene looked so sad, so *lost*, that I didn't know what to think, about her or King Lír or anything. I didn't realize that I had moved back against Molly Grue until I felt her hand in my hair. She didn't say anything, but it was nice smelling her there. Lisene said, very quietly, "I will see to it."

She turned around then and started for the door with her head lowered. I think she wanted to pass us by without looking at us at all, but she couldn't do it. Right at the door, her head came up and she stared at Schmendrick so hard that I pushed into Molly's skirt so I couldn't see her eyes. I heard her say, as though she could barely make the words come out, "His death be on your head, magician." I think she was crying, only not, the way grown people do.

And I heard Schmendrick's answer, and his voice was so cold I wouldn't have recognized it if I didn't know. "He has died before. Better that death—better this, better *any* death—than the one he was dying in that chair. If the griffin kills him, it will yet have saved his life." I heard the door close.

I asked Molly, speaking as low as I could, "What did he mean, about the king having died?" But she put me to one side, and she went to King Lír and knelt in front of him, reaching up to take one of his hands between hers. She said, "Lord...Majesty...friend...dear friend—remember. Oh, please, please *remember.*"

The old man was swaying on his feet, but he put his other hand on Molly's head and he mumbled, "Child, Sooz—is that your pretty name, Sooz?—of course I will come to your village. The griffin was never hatched that dares harm King Lír's people." He sat down hard in the chair again, but he held onto her hand tightly. He looked at her, with his blue eyes wide and his mouth trembling a little. He said, "But you must remind me, little one. When I...when I lose myself—when I lose *her*—you must remind me that I am still searching, still waiting...that I have never forgotten her, never turned from all she taught me. I sit in this place...I *sit*...because a king has to sit, you see...but in my mind, in my poor mind, I am always away with *her....*"

I didn't have any idea what he was talking about. I do now.

He fell asleep again then, holding Molly's hand. She sat with him for a long time, resting her head on his knee. Schmendrick went off to make sure Lisene was doing what she was supposed to do, getting everything ready for the king's departure. There was a lot of clattering and shouting already, enough so you'd have thought a war was starting, but nobody came in to see King Lír or speak to him, wish him luck or anything. It was almost as though he wasn't really there.

Me, I tried to write a letter home, with pictures of the king and the castle, but I fell asleep like him, and I slept the rest of that day and all night too. I woke up in a bed I couldn't remember getting into, with Schmendrick looking down at me, saying, "Up, child, on your feet. You started all this uproar—it's time for you to see it through. The king is coming to slay your griffin."

I was out of bed before he'd finished speaking. I said, "Now? Are we going right now?"

Schmendrick shrugged his shoulders. "By noon, anyway, if I can finally get Lisene and the rest of them to understand that they are *not* coming. Lisene wants to bring fifty men-at-arms, a dozen wagonloads of supplies, a regiment of runners to send messages back and forth, and every wretched physician in the kingdom." He sighed and spread his hands. "I may have to turn the lot of them to stone if we are to be off today."

I thought he was probably joking, but I already knew that you couldn't be sure with Schmendrick. He said, "If Lír comes with a train of followers, there will be no Lír. Do you understand me, Sooz?" I shook my head. Schmendrick said, "It is my fault. If I had made sure to visit here more often, there were things I could have done to restore the Lír Molly and I once knew. My fault, my thoughtlessness."

I remembered Molly telling me, "Schmendrick has trouble with time." I still didn't know what she meant, nor this either. I said, "It's just the way old people get. We have old men in our village who talk like him. One woman, too, Mam Jennet. She always cries when it rains."

Schmendrick clenched his fist and pounded it against his leg. "King Lír is *not* mad, girl, nor is he senile, as Lisene called him. He is *Lír*, Lír still, I promise you that. It is only here, in this castle, surrounded by good, loyal people who love him—who will love him to death, if they are allowed— that he sinks into...into the condition you have seen." He didn't say anything more for a moment; then he stooped a little to peer closely at me. "Did you notice the change in him when I spoke of unicorns?"

"Unicorn," I answered. "One unicorn who loved him. I noticed."

Schmendrick kept looking at me in a new way, as though we'd never met before. He said, "Your pardon, Sooz. I keep taking you for a child. Yes. One unicorn. He has not seen her since he became king, but he is what he is because of her. And when I speak that word, when Molly or I say her name—which I have not done yet—then he is recalled to himself." He paused for a moment, and then added, very softly, "As we had so often to do for her, so long ago."

"I didn't know unicorns had names," I said. "I didn't know they ever loved people."

"They don't. Only this one." He turned and walked away swiftly, saying over his shoulder, "Her name was Amalthea. Go find Molly, she'll see you fed."

The room I'd slept in wasn't big, not for something in a castle. Catania, the headwoman of our village, has a bedroom nearly as large, which I know because I play with her daughter Sophia. But the sheets I'd been under were embroidered with a crown, and engraved on the headboard was a picture of the blue banner with the white unicorn. I had slept the night in King Lír's own bed while he dozed in an old wooden chair.

I didn't wait to have breakfast with Molly, but ran straight to the little room where I had last seen the king. He was there, but so changed that I froze in the doorway, trying to get my breath. Three men were bustling around him like tailors, dressing him in his armor: all the padding underneath, first, and then the different pieces for the arms and legs and shoulders. I don't know any of the names. The men hadn't put his helmet on him, so his head stuck out at the top, white-haired and big-nosed and blue-eyed, but he didn't look silly like that. He looked like a giant.

When he saw me, he smiled, and it was a warm, happy smile, but it was a little frightening too, almost a little terrible, like the time I saw the griffin burning in the black sky. It was a hero's smile. I'd never seen one before. He called to me, "Little one, come and buckle on my sword, if you would. It would be an honor for me."

The men had to show me how you do it. The swordbelt, all by itself, was so heavy it kept slipping through my fingers, and I did need help with the buckle. But I put the sword into its sheath alone, although I needed both hands to lift it. When it slid home it made a sound like a great door slamming shut. King Lír touched my face with one of his cold iron gloves and said, "Thank you, little one. The next time that blade is drawn, it will be to free your village. You have my word."

Schmendrick came in then, took one look, and just shook his head. He said, "This is the most ridiculous...It is four days' ride—perhaps five—with the weather turning hot enough to broil a lobster on an iceberg. There's no need for armor until he faces the griffin." You could see how stupid he felt they all were, but King Lír smiled at him the same way he'd smiled at me, and Schmendrick stopped talking.

King Lír said, "Old friend, I go forth as I mean to return. It is my way."

Schmendrick looked like a little boy himself for a moment. All he could say was, "Your business. Don't blame me, that's all. At *least* leave the helmet off."

He was about to turn away and stalk out of the room, but Molly came up behind him and said, "Oh, Majesty—Lír—how grand! How beautiful you are!" She sounded the way my Aunt Zerelda sounds when she's carrying on about my brother Wilfrid. He could mess his pants and jump in a hog pen, and Aunt Zerelda would still think he was the best, smartest boy in the whole world. But Molly was different. She brushed those tailors, or whatever they were, straight aside, and she stood on tiptoe to smooth King Lír's white hair, and I heard her whisper, "I wish *she* could see you."

King Lír looked at her for a long time without saying anything. Schmendrick stood there, off to the side, and he didn't say anything either, but they were together, the three of them. I wish that Felicitas and I could have been together like that when we got old. Could have had time. Then King Lír looked at *me*, and he said, "The child is waiting." And that's how we set off for home. The king, Schmendrick, Molly, and me.

To the last minute, poor old Lisene kept trying to get King Lír to take some knights or soldiers with him. She actually followed us on foot when we left, calling, "Highness—Majesty—if you will have none else, take me! Take me!" At that the king stopped and turned and went back to her. He got down off his horse and embraced Lisene, and I don't know what they said to each other, but Lisene didn't follow anymore after that.

I rode with the king most of the time, sitting up in front of him on his skittery black mare. I wasn't sure I could trust her not to bite me, or to kick me when I wasn't looking, but King Lír told me, "It is only peaceful times that make her nervous, be assured of that. When dragons charge her, belching death—for the fumes are more danger-ous than the flames, little one—when your griffin swoops down at her, you will see her at her best." I still didn't like her much, but I did like the king. He didn't sing to me, the way Schmendrick had, but he told me stories, and they weren't fables or fairytales. These were real, true stories, and he knew they were true because they had all happened to him! I never heard stories like those, and I never will again. I know that for certain.

He told me more things to keep in mind if you have to fight a dragon, and he told me how he learned that ogres aren't always as stupid as they look, and why you should never swim in a mountain pool when the snows are melting, and how you can *sometimes* make friends with a troll. He talked about his father's castle, where he grew up, and about how he met Schmendrick and Molly there, and even about Molly's cat, which he said was a little thing with a funny crooked ear. But when I asked him why the castle fell down, he wouldn't exactly say, no more than Schmendrick would. His voice became very quiet and faraway. "I forget things, you know, little one," he said. "I try to hold on, but I do forget."

Well, I knew *that*. He kept calling Molly Sooz, and he never called me anything but *little one,* and Schmendrick kept having to remind him where we were bound and why. That was always at night, though. He was usually fine during the daytime. And when he did turn confused again, and wander off (not just in his mind, either—I found him in the woods one night, talking to a tree as though it was his father), all you had to do was mention a white unicorn named Amalthea, and he'd come to himself almost right away. Generally it was Schmendrick who did that, but I brought him back that time, holding my hand and telling me how you can recognize a pooka, and why you need to. But I could never get him to say a word about the unicorn.

Autumn comes early where I live. The days were still hot, and the king never would take his armor off, except to sleep, not even his helmet with the big blue plume on top, but at night I burrowed in between Molly and Schmendrick for warmth, and you could hear the stags belling everywhere all the time, crazy with the season. One of them actually charged King Lír's horse while I was riding with him, and Schmendrick was about to do something magic to the stag, the same way he'd done with the crow. But the king laughed and rode straight at him, right *into* those horns. I screamed, but the black mare never hesitated, and the stag turned at the last moment and ambled out of sight in the brush. He was wagging his tail in circles, the way goats do, and looking as puzzled and dreamy as King Lír himself.

I was proud, once I got over being frightened. But both Schmendrick and Molly scolded him, and he kept apologizing to me for the rest of the day for having put me in danger, as Molly had once said he would. "I forgot you were with me, little one, and for that I will always ask your pardon." Then he smiled at me with that beautiful, terrible hero's smile I'd seen before, and he said, "But oh, little one, the remembering!" And that night he didn't wander away and get himself lost. Instead he sat happily by the fire with us and sang a whole long song about the adventures of an outlaw called Captain Cully. I'd never heard of him, but it's a really good song.

We reached my village late on the afternoon of the fourth day, and Schmendrick made us stop together before we rode in. He said, directly to me, "Sooz, if you tell them that this is the king himself, there will be nothing but noise and joy and celebration, and nobody will get any rest with all that carrying-on. It would be best for you to tell them that we have brought King Lír's greatest knight with us, and that he needs a night to purify himself in prayer and meditation before he deals with your griffin." He took hold of my chin and made me look into his green, green eyes, and he said, "Girl, you have to trust me. I always know what I'm doing—that's my trouble. Tell your people what I've said." And Molly touched me and looked at me without saying anything, so I knew it was all right.

I left them camped on the outskirts of the village, and walked home by myself. Malka met me first. She smelled me before I even reached Simon and Elsie's tavern, and she came running and crashed into my legs and knocked me over, and then pinned me down with her paws on my shoulders, and kept licking my face until I had to nip her nose to make her let me up and run to the house with me. My father was out with the flock, but my mother and Wilfrid were there, and they grabbed me and nearly strangled me, and they cried over me—rotten, stupid Wilfrid too!—because everyone had been so certain that I'd been taken and eaten by the griffin. After that, once she got done crying, my mother spanked me for running off in Uncle Ambrose's cart without telling anyone, and when my father came in, he spanked me all over again. But I didn't mind.

I told them I'd seen King Lír in person, and been in his castle, and I said what Schmendrick had told me to say, but nobody was much cheered by it. My father just sat down and grunted, "Oh, aye—another great warrior for our comfort and the griffin's dessert. Your bloody king won't ever come here his bloody self, you can be sure of that." My mother reproached him for talking like that in front of Wilfrid and me, but he went on, "Maybe he cared about places like this, people like us once, but he's old now, and old kings only care who's going to be king after them. You can't tell me anything different."

I wanted more than anything to tell him that King Lír *was* here, less than half a mile from our doorstep, but I didn't, and not only because Schmendrick had told me not to. I wasn't sure what the king might look like, white-haired and shaky and not here all the time, to people like my father. I wasn't sure what he looked like to me, for that matter. He was a lovely, dignified old man who told wonderful stories, but when I tried to imagine him riding alone into the Midwood to do battle with a griffin, a griffin that had already eaten his best knights…to be honest, I couldn't do it. Now that I'd actually brought him all the way home with me, as I'd set out to do, I was suddenly afraid that I'd drawn him to his death. And I knew I wouldn't ever forgive myself if that happened.

I wanted so much to see them that night, Schmendrick and Molly and the king. I wanted to sleep out there on the ground with them, and listen to their talk, and then maybe I'd not worry so much about the morning. But of course there wasn't a chance of that. My family would hardly let me out of their sight to wash my face. Wilfrid kept following me around, asking endless questions about the castle, and my father took me to Catania, who had me tell the whole story over again, and agreed with him that whomever the king had sent this time wasn't likely to be any more use than the others had been. And my mother kept feeding me and scolding me and hugging me, all more or less at the same time. And then, in the night, we heard the griffin, making that soft, lonely, horrible sound it makes when it's hunting. So I didn't get very much sleep, between one thing and another.

But at sunrise, after I'd helped Wilfrid milk the goats, they let me run out to the camp, as long as Malka came with me, which was practically like having my mother along. Molly was already helping King Lír into his armor, and Schmendrick was burying the remains of last night's dinner, as though they were starting one more ordinary day on their journey to somewhere. They greeted me, and Schmendrick thanked me for doing as he'd asked, so that the king could have a restful night before he—

I didn't let him finish. I didn't know I was going to do it, I swear, but I ran up to King Lír, and I threw my arms around him, and I said, "Don't go! I changed my mind, don't go!" Just like Lisene.

King Lír looked down at me. He seemed as tall as a tree right then, and he patted my head very gently with his iron glove. He said, "Little one, I have a griffin to slay. It is my job."

Which was what I'd said myself, though it seemed like years ago, and that made it so much worse. I said a second time, "I changed my mind! Somebody else can fight the griffin, you don't have to! You go home! You go home *now* and live your life, and be the king, and everything…." I was babbling and sniffling, and generally being a baby, I know that. I'm glad Wilfrid didn't see me.

King Lír kept petting me with one hand and trying to put me aside with the other, but I wouldn't let go. I think I was actually trying to pull his sword out of its sheath, to take it away from him. He said, "No, no, little one, you don't understand. There are some monsters that only a king can kill. I have always known that—I should never, never have sent those poor men to die in my place. No one else in all the land can do this for you and your village. Most truly now, it is my job." And he kissed my hand, the way he must have kissed the hands of so many queens. He kissed my hand too, just like theirs.

Molly came up then and took me away from him. She held me close, and she stroked my hair, and she told me, "Child, Sooz, there's no turning back for him now, or for you either. It was your fate to bring this last cause to him, and his fate to take it up, and neither of you could have done differently, being who you are. And now you must be as brave as he is, and see it all play out." She caught herself there, and changed it. "Rather, you must wait to learn how it has played out, because you are certainly not coming into that forest with us."

"I'm coming," I said. "You can't stop me. Nobody can." I wasn't sniffling or anything anymore. I said it like that, that's all.

Molly held me at arm's length, and she shook me a little bit. She said, "Sooz, if you can tell me that your parents have given their permission, then you may come. Have they done so?"

I didn't answer her. She shook me again, gentler this time, saying, "Oh, that was wicked of me, forgive me, my dear friend. I knew the day we met that you could never learn to lie." Then she took both of my hands between hers, and she said, "Lead us to the Midwood, if you will, Sooz, and we will say our farewells there. Will you do that for us? For me?"

I nodded, but I still didn't speak. I couldn't, my throat was hurting so much. Molly squeezed my hands and said, "Thank you." Schmendrick came up and made some kind of sign to her with his eyes, or his eyebrows, because she said, "Yes, I know," although he hadn't said a thing. So she went to King Lír with him, and I was alone, trying to stop shaking. I managed it, after a while.

The Midwood isn't far. They wouldn't really have needed my help to find it. You can see the beginning of it from the roof of Ellis the baker's house, which is the tallest one on that side of the village. It's always dark, even from a distance, even if you're not actually in it. I don't know if that's because they're oak trees (we have all sorts of tales and sayings about oaken woods, and the creatures that live there) or maybe because of some enchantment, or because of the griffin. Maybe it was different before the griffin came. Uncle Ambrose says it's been a bad place all his life, but my father says no, he and his friends used to hunt there, and he actually picnicked there once or twice with my mother, when they were young.

King Lír rode in front, looking grand and almost young, with his
head up and the blue plume on his helmet floating above him, more
like a banner than a feather. I was going to ride with Molly, but the king
leaned from his saddle as I started past, and swooped me up before him,
saying, "You shall guide and company me, little one, until we reach the
forest." I was proud of that, but I was frightened too, because he was so
happy, and I knew he was going to his death, trying to make up for all
those knights he'd sent to fight the griffin. I didn't try to warn him. He
wouldn't have heard me, and I knew that too. Me and poor old Lisene.

He told me all about griffins as we rode. He said, "If you should
ever have dealings with a griffin, little one, you must remember that
they are not like dragons. A dragon is simply a dragon—make yourself
small when it dives down at you, but hold your ground and strike at
the underbelly, and you've won the day. But a griffin, now…a griffin is
two highly dissimilar creatures, eagle and lion, fused together by some
god with a god's sense of humor. And so there is an eagle's heart beating in the beast, and a lion's heart as well, and you must pierce them
both to have any hope of surviving the battle." He was as cheerful as
he could be about it all, holding me safe on the saddle, and saying
over and over, the way old people do, "Two hearts, never forget that—
many people do. Eagle heart, lion heart—eagle heart, lion heart. *Never*
forget, little one."

We passed a lot of people I knew, out with their sheep and goats,
and they all waved to me, and called, and made jokes, and so on. They
cheered for King Lír, but they didn't bow to him, or take off their caps,
because nobody recognized him, nobody knew. He seemed delighted
about that, which most kings probably wouldn't be. But he's the only
king I've met, so I can't say.

The Midwood seemed to be reaching out for us before we were anywhere near it, long fingery shadows stretching across the empty fields,
and the leaves flickering and blinking, though there wasn't any wind. A
forest is usually really noisy, day and night, if you stand still and listen
to the birds and the insects and the streams and such, but the Midwood
is always silent, silent. That reaches out too, the silence.

We halted a stone's throw from the forest, and King Lír said to me,
"We part here, little one," and set me down on the ground as carefully as
though he was putting a bird back in its nest. He said to Schmendrick,
"I know better than to try to keep you and Sooz from following—" he
kept on calling Molly by my name, every time, I don't know why—"but
I enjoin you, in the name of great Nikos himself, and in the name of our
long and precious friendship…." He stopped there, and he didn't say

anything more for such a while that I was afraid he was back to forgetting who he was and why he was there, the way he had been. But then he went on, clear and ringing as one of those mad stags, "I charge you in *her* name, in the name of the Lady Amalthea, not to assist me in any way from the moment we pass the very first tree, but to leave me altogether to what is mine to do. Is that understood between us, dear ones of my heart?"

Schmendrick hated it. You didn't have to be magic to see that. It was so plain, even to me, that he had been planning to take over the battle as soon as they were actually facing the griffin. But King Lír was looking right at him with those young blue eyes, and with a little bit of a smile on his face, and Schmendrick simply didn't know what to do. There wasn't anything he *could* do, so he finally nodded and mumbled, "If that is Your Majesty's wish." The king couldn't hear him at all the first time, so he made him say it again.

And then, of course, everybody had to say goodbye to me, since I wasn't allowed to go any further with them. Molly said she knew we'd see each other again, and Schmendrick told me that I had the makings of a real warrior queen, only he was certain I was too smart to be one. And King Lír...King Lír said to me, very quietly, so nobody else could hear, "Little one, if I had married and had a daughter, I would have asked no more than that she should be as brave and kind and loyal as you. Remember that, as I will remember you to my last day."

Which was all nice, and I wished my mother and father could have heard what all these grown people were saying about me. But then they turned and rode on into the Midwood, the three of them, and only Molly looked back at me. And I think *that* was to make sure I wasn't following, because I was supposed just to go home and wait to find out if my friends were alive or dead, and if the griffin was going to be eating any more children. It was all over.

And maybe I would have gone home and let it be all over, if it hadn't been for Malka.

She should have been with the sheep and not with me, of course—that's her job, the same way King Lír was doing his job, going to meet the griffin. But Malka thinks I'm a sheep too, the most stupid, aggravating sheep she ever had to guard, forever wandering away into some kind of danger. All the way to the Midwood she had trotted quietly alongside the king's horse, but now that we were alone again she came rushing up and bounced all over me, barking like thunder and knocking me down, hard, the way she does whenever I'm not where she wants me to be. I always brace myself when I see her coming, but it never helps.

What she does then, before I'm on my feet, is take the hem of my smock in her jaws and start tugging me in the direction she thinks I should go. But this time...this time she suddenly got up, as though she'd forgotten all about me, and she stared past me at the Midwood with all the white showing in her eyes and a low sound coming out of her that I don't think she knew she could make. The next moment, she was gone, racing into the forest with foam flying from her mouth and her big ragged ears flat back. I called, but she couldn't have heard me, baying and barking the way she was.

Well, I didn't have any choice. King Lír and Schmendrick and Molly all had a choice, going after the Midwood griffin, but Malka was my dog, and she didn't know what she was facing, and I *couldn't* let her face it by herself. So there wasn't anything else for me to do. I took an enormous long breath and looked around me, and then I walked into the forest after her.

Actually, I ran, as long as I could, and then I walked until I could run again, and then I ran some more. There aren't any paths into the Midwood, because nobody goes there, so it wasn't hard to see where three horses had pushed through the undergrowth, and then a dog's tracks on top of the hoofprints. It was very quiet with no wind, not one bird calling, no sound but my own panting. I couldn't even hear Malka anymore. I was hoping that maybe they'd come on the griffin while it was asleep, and King Lír had already killed it in its nest. I didn't think so, though. He'd probably have decided it wasn't honorable to attack a sleeping griffin, and wakened it up for a fair fight. I hadn't known him very long, but I knew what he'd do.

Then, a little way ahead of me, the whole forest exploded.

It was too much noise for me to sort it out in my head. There was Malka absolutely *howling*, and birds bursting up everywhere out of the brush, and Schmendrick or the king or someone was shouting, only I couldn't make out any of the words. And underneath it all was something that wasn't loud at all, a sound somewhere between a growl and that terrible soft call, like a frightened child. Then—just as I broke into the clearing—the rattle and scrape of knives, only much louder this time, as the griffin shot straight up with the sun on its wings. Its cold golden eyes *bit* into mine, and its beak was open so wide you could see down and down the blazing red gullet. It filled the sky.

And King Lír, astride his black mare, filled the clearing. He was as huge as the griffin, and his sword was the size of a boar spear, and he shook it at the griffin, daring it to light down and fight him on the ground. But the griffin was staying out of range, circling overhead to get a good look at these strange new people. Malka was utterly off her head, screaming and hurling herself into the air again and again, snapping at the griffin's lion feet and eagle claws, but coming down each time without so much as an iron feather between her teeth. I lunged and caught her in the air, trying to drag her away before the griffin turned on her, but she fought me, scratching my face with her own dull dog claws, until I had to let her go. The last time she leaped, the griffin suddenly stooped and caught her full on her side with one huge wing, so hard that she couldn't get a sound out, no more than I could. She flew all the way across the clearing, slammed into a tree, fell to the ground, and after that she didn't move.

Molly told me later that that was when King Lír struck for the griffin's lion heart. I didn't see it. I was flying across the clearing myself, throwing myself over Malka, in case the griffin came after her again, and I didn't see anything except her staring eyes and the blood on her side. But I did hear the griffin's roar when it happened, and when I could turn my head, I saw the blood splashing along *its* side, and the back legs squinching up against its belly, the way you do when you're really hurting. King Lír shouted like a boy. He threw that great sword as high as the griffin, and snatched it back again, and then he charged toward the griffin as it wobbled lower and lower, with its crippled lion half dragging it out of the air. It landed with a saggy thump, just like Malka, and there was a moment when I was absolutely sure it was dead. I remember I was thinking, very far away, *this is good, I'm glad, I'm sure I'm glad.*

But Schmendrick was screaming at the king, "Two hearts! *Two hearts!*" until his voice split with it, and Molly was on me, trying to drag me away from the griffin, and *I* was hanging onto Malka—she'd gotten so *heavy*—and I don't know what else was happening right then, because all I was seeing and thinking about was Malka. And all I was feeling was her heart not beating under mine.

She guarded my cradle when I was born. I cut my teeth on her poor ears, and she never made one sound. My mother says so.

King Lír wasn't seeing or hearing any of us. There was nothing in the world for him but the griffin, which was flopping and struggling lopsidedly in the middle of the clearing. I couldn't help feeling sorry for it, even then, even after it had killed Malka and my friends, and all the sheep and goats too, and I don't know how many else. And King Lír must have felt the same way, because he got down from his black mare and went straight up to the griffin, and he spoke to it, lowering his sword until the tip was on the ground. He said, "You were a noble and terrible adversary—surely the last such I will ever confront. We have accomplished what we were born to do, the two of us. I thank you for your death."

And on that last word, the griffin had him.

It was the eagle, lunging up at him, dragging the lion half along, the way I'd been dragging Malka's dead weight. King Lír stepped back, swinging the sword fast enough to take off the griffin's head, but it was faster than he was. That dreadful beak caught him at the waist, shearing through his armor the way an axe would smash through piecrust, and he doubled over without a sound that I heard, looking like wetwash on the line. There was blood, and worse, and I couldn't have said if he was dead or alive. I thought the griffin was going to bite him in two.

I shook loose from Molly. She was calling to Schmendrick to *do* something, but of course he couldn't, and she knew it, because he'd promised King Lír that he wouldn't interfere by magic, whatever happened. But I wasn't a magician, and I hadn't promised anything to anybody. I told Malka I'd be right back.

The griffin didn't see me coming. It was bending its head down over King Lír, hiding him with its wings. The lion part trailing along so limply in the dust made it more fearful to see, though I can't say why, and it was making a sort of cooing, purring sound all the time. I had a big rock in my left hand, and a dead branch in my right, and I was bawling something, but I don't remember what. You can scare wolves away from the flock sometimes if you run at them like that, determined.

I can throw things hard with either hand—Wilfrid found *that* out when I was still small—and the griffin looked up fast when the rock hit it on the side of its neck. It didn't like that, but it was too busy with King Lír to bother with me. I didn't think for a minute that my branch was going to be any use on even a half-dead griffin, but I threw it as far as I could, so that the griffin would look away for a moment, and as soon as it did I made a little run and a big sprawling dive for the hilt of the king's sword, which was sticking out under him where he'd fallen. I knew I could lift it because of having buckled it on him when we set out together.

But I couldn't get it free. He was too heavy, like Malka. But I wouldn't give up or let go. I kept pulling and pulling on that sword, and I didn't feel Molly pulling at *me* again, and I didn't notice the griffin starting to scrabble toward me over King Lír's body. I did hear Schmendrick, sounding a long way off, and I thought he was singing one of the nonsense songs he'd made up for me, only why would he be doing something like that just now? Then I did finally look up, to push my sweaty hair off my face, just before the griffin grabbed me up in one of its claws, yanking me away from Molly to throw me down on top of King Lír. His armor was so cold against my cheek, it was as though the armor had died with him.

The griffin looked into my eyes. That was the worst of all, worse than the pain where the claw had me, worse than not seeing my parents and stupid Wilfrid anymore, worse than knowing that I hadn't been able to save either the king or Malka. Griffins can't talk (dragons do, but only to heroes, King Lír told me), but those golden eyes were saying into my eyes, "Yes, I will die soon, but you are all dead now, all of you, and I will pick your bones before the ravens have mine. And your folk will remember what I was, and what I did to them, when there is no one left in your vile, pitiful anthill who remembers your name. So I have won." And I knew it was true.

Then there wasn't anything but that beak and that burning gullet opening over me.

Then there was.

I thought it was a cloud. I was so dazed and terrified that I really thought it was a white cloud, only traveling so low and so fast that it smashed the griffin off King Lír and away from me, and sent me tumbling into Molly's arms at the same time. She held me tightly, practically smothering me, and it wasn't until I wriggled my head free that I saw what had come to us. I can see it still, in my mind. I see it right now.

They don't look *anything* like horses. I don't know where people got that notion. Four legs and a tail, yes, but the hooves are split, like a deer's hooves, or a goat's, and the head is smaller and more—*pointy*— than a horse's head. And the whole body is different from a horse, it's like saying a snowflake looks like a cow. The horn looks too long and heavy for the body, you can't imagine how a neck that delicate can hold up a horn that size. But it can.

Schmendrick was on his knees, with his eyes closed and his lips moving, as though he was still singing. Molly kept whispering, "Amalthea... Amalthea..." not to me, not to anybody. The unicorn was facing the griffin across the king's body. Its front feet were skittering and dancing a little, but its back legs were setting themselves to charge, the way rams do. Only rams put their heads down, while the unicorn held its head high, so that the horn caught the sunlight and glowed like a seashell. It gave a cry that made me want to dive back into Molly's skirt and cover my ears, it was so raw and so...*hurt*. Then its head did go down.

Dying or not, the griffin put up a furious fight. It came hopping to meet the unicorn, but then it was out of the way at the last minute, with its bloody beak snapping at the unicorn's legs as it flashed by. But each time that happened, the unicorn would turn instantly, much quicker than a horse could have turned, and come charging back before the griffin could get itself braced again. It wasn't a bit fair, but I didn't feel sorry for the griffin anymore.

The last time, the unicorn slashed sideways with its horn, using it like a club, and knocked the griffin clean off its feet. But it was up before the unicorn could turn, and it actually leaped into the air, dead lion half and all, just high enough to come down on the unicorn's back, raking with its eagle claws and trying to bite through the unicorn's neck, the way it did with King Lír. I screamed then, I couldn't help it, but the unicorn reared up until I thought it was going to go over backwards, and it flung the griffin to the ground, whirled and drove its horn straight through the iron feathers to the eagle heart. It trampled the body for a good while after, but it didn't need to.

Schmendrick and Molly ran to King Lír. They didn't look at the griffin, or even pay very much attention to the unicorn. I wanted to go to Malka, but I followed them to where he lay. I'd seen what the griffin had done to him, closer than they had, and I didn't see how he could still be alive. But he was, just barely. He opened his eyes when we kneeled beside him, and he smiled so sweetly at us all, and he said, "Lisene? Lisene, I should have a bath, shouldn't I?"

I didn't cry. Molly didn't cry. Schmendrick did. He said, "No, Majesty. No, you do not need bathing, truly."

King Lír looked puzzled. "But I smell bad, Lisene. I think I must have wet myself." He reached for my hand and held it so hard. "Little one," he said. "Little one, I know you. Do not be ashamed of me because I am old."

I squeezed his hand back, as hard as I could. "Hello, Your Majesty," I said. "Hello." I didn't know what else to say.

Then his face was suddenly young and happy and wonderful, and he was gazing far past me, reaching toward something with his eyes. I felt a breath on my shoulder, and I turned my head and saw the unicorn. It was bleeding from a lot of deep scratches and bites, especially around its neck, but all you could see in its dark eyes was King Lír. I moved aside so it could get to him, but when I turned back, the king was gone. I'm nine, almost ten. I know when people are gone.

The unicorn stood over King Lír's body for a long time. I went off after a while to sit beside Malka, and Molly came and sat with me. But Schmendrick stayed kneeling by King Lír, and he was talking to the unicorn. I couldn't hear what he was saying, but I could tell from his face that he was asking for something, a favor. My mother says she can always tell before I open my mouth. The unicorn wasn't answering, of course—they can't talk either, I'm almost sure—but Schmendrick kept at it until the unicorn turned its head and looked at him. Then he stopped, and he stood up and walked away by himself. The unicorn stayed where she was.

Molly was saying how brave Malka had been, and telling me that she'd never known another dog who attacked a griffin. She asked if Malka had ever had pups, and I said, yes, but none of them was Malka. It was very strange. She was trying hard to make me feel better, and I was trying to comfort her because she couldn't. But all the while I felt so cold, almost as far away from everything as Malka had gone. I closed her eyes, the way you do with people, and I sat there and I stroked her side, over and over.

I didn't notice the unicorn. Molly must have, but she didn't say anything. I went on petting Malka, and I didn't look up until the horn came slanting over my shoulder. Close to, you could see blood drying in the shining spirals, but I wasn't afraid. I wasn't anything. Then the horn touched Malka, very lightly, right where I was stroking her, and Malka opened her eyes.

It took her a while to understand that she was alive. It took me longer. She ran her tongue out first, panting and panting, looking so *thirsty*. We could hear a stream trickling somewhere close, and Molly went and found it, and brought water back in her cupped hands. Malka lapped it all up, and then she tried to stand and fell down, like a puppy. But she kept trying, and at last she was properly on her feet, and she tried to lick my face, but she missed it the first few times. I only started crying when she finally managed it.

When she saw the unicorn, she did a funny thing. She stared at it for a moment, and then she bowed or curtseyed, in a dog way, stretching out her front legs and putting her head down on the ground between them. The unicorn nosed at her, very gently, so as not to knock her over again. It looked at me for the first time...or maybe I really looked at *it* for the first time, past the horn and the hooves and the magical whiteness, all the way into those endless eyes. And what they did, somehow, the unicorn's eyes, was to free me from the griffin's eyes. Because the awfulness of what I'd seen there didn't go away when the griffin died, not even when Malka came alive again. But the unicorn had all the world in her eyes, all the world I'm never going to see, but it doesn't matter, because now I *have* seen it, and it's beautiful, and I was in there too. And when I think of Jehane, and Louli, and my Felicitas who could only talk with her eyes, just like the unicorn, I'll think of them, and not the griffin. That's how it was when the unicorn and I looked at each other.

I didn't see if the unicorn said goodbye to Molly and Schmendrick, and I didn't see when it went away. I didn't want to. I did hear Schmendrick saying, "A dog. I nearly kill myself singing her to Lír, calling her as no other has *ever* called a unicorn—and she brings back, not him, but the dog. And here I'd always thought she had no sense of humor."

But Molly said, "She loved him too. That's why she let him go. Keep your voice down." I was going to tell her it didn't matter, that I knew Schmendrick was saying that because he was so sad, but she came over and petted Malka with me, and I didn't have to. She said, "We will escort you and Malka home now, as befits two great ladies. Then we will take the king home too."

"And I'll never see you again," I said. "No more than I'll see him."

Molly asked me, "How old are you, Sooz?"

"Nine," I said. "Almost ten. You know that."

"You can whistle?" I nodded. Molly looked around quickly, as though she were going to steal something. She bent close to me, and she whispered, "I will give you a present, Sooz, but you are not to open it until the day when you turn seventeen. On that day you must walk out away from your village, walk out all alone into some quiet place that is special to you, and you must whistle like this." And she whistled a little ripple of music for me to whistle back to her, repeating and repeating it until she was satisfied that I had it exactly. "Don't whistle it anymore," she told me. "Don't whistle it aloud again, not once, until your seventeenth birthday, but keep whistling it inside you. Do you understand the difference, Sooz?"

"I'm not a baby," I said. "I understand. What will happen when I do whistle it?"

Molly smiled at me. She said, "Someone will come to you. Maybe the greatest magician in the world, maybe only an old lady with a soft spot for valiant, impudent children." She cupped my cheek in her hand. "And just maybe even a unicorn. Because beautiful things will always want to see you again, Sooz, and be listening for you. Take an old lady's word for it. Someone will come."

They put King Lír on his own horse, and I rode with Schmendrick, and they came all the way home with me, right to the door, to tell my mother and father that the griffin was dead, and that I had helped, and you should have seen Wilfrid's face when they said *that*! Then they both hugged me, and Molly said in my ear, "Remember—not till you're seventeen!" and they rode away, taking the king back to his castle to be buried among his own folk. And I had a cup of cold milk and went out with Malka and my father to pen the flock for the night.

So that's what happened to me. I practice the music Molly taught me in my head, all the time, I even dream it some nights, but I don't ever whistle it aloud. I talk to Malka about our adventure, because I have to talk to *someone*. And I promise her that when the time comes she'll be there with me, in the special place I've already picked out. She'll be an old dog lady then, of course, but it doesn't matter. Someone will come to us both.

I hope it's them, those two. A unicorn is very nice, but they're my friends. I want to feel Molly holding me again, and hear the stories she didn't have time to tell me, and I want to hear Schmendrick singing that silly song:

> *Soozli, Soozli,*
> *speaking loozli,*
> *you disturb my oozli-goozli.*
> *Soozli, Soozli,*
> *would you choozli*
> *to become my squoozli-squoozli...?*

I can wait.

Giant Bones

Boy, call me in to you just once more, and you will regret it until you're very, very old. I'll not tell you again, the *jejebhai*'s due any hour now—twins, by the look of it—and if I'm not with her she's like as not to smother one while she's dropping the other, crazy as she is. So I haven't the bloody time to tell you tales, nor smooth your blanket, nor bring you water. If your mother were here, as she bloody should be, instead of being off in Chun nursing your aunt because the idiot woman didn't have sense enough to leave red *kalyars* alone in the wet season, then she could play games with you all night, for all of me. But if I climb up to this loft again tonight, it will be with a willowy switch in my hand. Do you understand me?

What? *What* under your bed? Rock-*targs*? There's never been a single rock-*targ* in this flat-arse farmland, you know that as well as I do. They're mountain creatures; they won't come below the snowline to feast on a fat caravan, never mind squeezing themselves under one scrawny little boy's bed. There aren't any even in our high country, come to that. The giants ran them all out, they're still afraid of the giants, even now.

What? No, there aren't any giants under your bed, either. The giants are gone, too, long and long since. Haven't been any since your great-great-great-grandfather's time, I can tell you that for a fact. Go to sleep, if you know what's good for you.

Now what's he crying about? Because there aren't any giants? Is that it? Boy, there are times...*what?* Oh now, don't you start *that* again, do you hear me? You are *not* too small, I never said that, that was your Uncle Tavdal, and he's a fool. But a tall fool, just as you'll be, stop stewing over it. You're small for your age, yes, but so were your sisters Rii and Sardur, whatever they say now. So was Jadamak—he didn't even start getting his growth until he was well older than you, there's another fact for you. And I'll tell you something more—

What? Be quiet, I thought that was the *jejebhai* bleating....

No, I guess not. Not that it would mean much if it were—she's just like you, call and call and carry on, and when you get there, nothing but big eyes and feeling a bit lonesome. Wouldn't surprise me at all if she decided not to drop them till dawn, like last time. Spiteful animal, always was. Like your aunt.

How do I know you'll be tall? Well, let *me* ask a question for a change—have you ever seen a short one in our family? Think about it, name me one—uncles, cousins, second cousins, distant as you like. No? Hah? No, and you won't either, I don't care how far you look. Every one of us is big, man or woman, wise or brainless. It's how we are, the same as those Mundrakathis down by the canal, all with those pale, pale skins and the men with their extra little fingers. Only with us it's a bit different, there's a bit more to it. Ask your mother sometime, she'll tell you.

I said your *mother*. No. No, absolutely not, I'm going back down to the barn this minute. Besides, your mother's the one to ask about things like that. She's the one who tells stories, sings the old wisdom songs, passes things on when it's time. I'm just the one who takes care of the beasts. Fair enough—we both push the plow. I'm going now, that's all.

No, I said *no!* Give it up, boy, before you really rouse me. I can't afford to lose even one *jejebhai* kid, let alone two, not with the price of vegetables gone so low it's hardly worth hauling them to market. Good night, good-bye, and go to bloody sleep!

Because I *do* know, there's why! Because of your three-times-great-grandfather and the giants of Torgry Mountain, there's why! Nine years old, she should have told you by now, and I'll tell her so when she comes home, if she ever does. Instead of leaving it for me.

All right. All *right*, then—but one squall from the barn and your mother tells you the rest, is that a bargain? And you'll keep to it, like a grown man? No fussing, no sniveling? Mind, now.

Well. I've not told stories much—I don't know where you're supposed to start, or what's important to put in. So I'm just going to begin with your great-great-great-grandfather, only I can't keep calling him that all through, so I'll call him Grandfather Selsim. I think that was his name, or close enough to it. No one's really sure.

Grandfather Selsim was the first of our lot to come into this country. He didn't mean to, not as far as I ever learned, being no farmer but a coppersmith by trade, aye, a tinker if you like, and horsedealer as well betimes, tell the truth. But he was living in the north, beyond the mountains, when times were hard and land was dear. And that was good for the tinker, you see, because folk were mending and making do in those days, not buying all new like your aunt in Chun and that fat maggot she married. But it wasn't such a fine thing for the horsedealer, no, nor for anyone with even a few dreams of settling somewhere and might be starting a family. I was up north myself one time, working, before we had this place, before you were born. Never liked it much.

So one morning Grandfather Selsim just up and says, "Well, that's it, I'm surely done here," and he jumped on the ugly-tempered, leg-biting *churfa* he always rode and headed straight south. No notion where he was bound, no friends or relations beyond Rhyak, everything he owned sold fast and cheap to feed him along the way. Just going south, traveling by the sun and the mountains dead ahead. And that was your great-great-great-grandfather Selsim.

Did you hear anything just then? Tell me if you did, mind, because I'll know. There's a sound she makes when the kid...no, no, nothing yet.

I hate this. Where was I?

Grandfather Selsim, he'd been here and there enough to know that mountains aren't ever as close as they look, but for all that he was near to being out of food by the time he reached the northern foothills. Oh, he did some tinkerwork along the way for a meal or two, and he likely even begged when it came to it. There's those in the family wouldn't ever admit to that, but I say you do what's to do. All we know, we mightn't be here tonight, you and I and them, too, if Grandfather Selsim had been ashamed to beg. And maybe he was thinking about us all, that far back, hey? Who knows?

You've never been anywhere near a mountain, so I suppose I'd better tell you about being in the mountains. It's cold, that's one thing—maybe not all the time, but most always. And the roads are bad, when there are any roads, and you spend hours just crawling, scrambling, scuttling along on all fours. And all the while you're doing that, the air's growing thin and thinner, till you feel too weak to scratch your head and breathing doesn't do you any good at all. And there are the rock-*targs*.

You don't even know what a rock-*targ* looks like, do you? All that carrying on about them being under your bed, and you don't even know....You remember when your cousin Bai killed that *lourijakh* that climbed on the roof, trying to get in? Well, those are a little like rock-*targs*, only not as big, of course, not nearly as big. And the rock-*targs*' faces look more human somehow, and they can almost talk—not really talk, but it makes it worse. You don't ever find many of them in one spot, but in those days they were still scattered over Torgry Mountain and that whole northern range. Because of the *kagi*, there used to be a lot of wild *kagi* up on the high crags. But it doesn't matter—they're always hungry, always hunting. And they'd rather eat people. Your *lourijakh* doesn't care, he'll eat anything, but a rock-*targ* can smell you a mile upwind, and he'll leave a fresh kill to come after you. No, I can't tell you why, how do I know? It's just the way they are.

In those days your Grandfather Selsim didn't know much more about rock-*targs* than you do. No reason he should have—I told you, they don't come down into the low country, thank the gods for *something* anyway. And mountain folk don't usually see them either, unless it's too late. Oh, they stay out of sight, but they're there.

What? I'm scaring you now? Well, there's just no pleasing you, is there? First you're at me and at me to tell you all about giants and rock-*targs* and how I know you're going to be as tall as the rest of us—next minute, there you are, head under the blanket, just carrying on. Shall I leave off the story, then? I'd just as soon, it's a deal more work than I expected. Your mother does it all so easily, every night, I don't know how she does it. You go off to sleep then, and I'll bed down with the *jejebhai*. Sooner or later she's bound to give in and drop those...what? No. Well.

Your Grandfather Selsim, he didn't know how high the mountains were, nor what grew or moved in them, nor what was on the other side. Some of the foothill folk gave him work to do, and a little food for doing it, and when he asked them the best way across the range, everyone said there wasn't any pass but the one over Torgry Mountain. Not that it was a real pass, nothing even like a real pass, but I'll get to that. Now, today, you can flank the range, just go all the way around—it takes forever, but you can do it. But back then, no road, only that mountain track. And your Grandfather Selsim never was much for going around things, people always say that.

Naturally everyone warned him about the rock-*targs*. They all said he'd best wait for winter, when the beasts get a bit sluggish, and you can see them better against the snow, so you've some sort of a chance to escape. But you can't cross the bloody range in winter—not then, not today—so what difference? And all those people told your Grandfather Selsim first one thing and then another about what rock-*targs* look like and what they do, so by and by he understood that not a one of them knew one thing for certain. So he said to the *churfa* as he set off again, "Well, we'll just go carefully, you and I, mind our manners and keep our wits about us, and might be we'll jog along all right. Carried us this far, anyway, manners and wits."

But I think what he really put his faith in was the big old *dasko* knife he had from his father: the real South Island make, it was, double-edged and so long that it stuck out a bit at both ends of his blanket roll. I haven't seen one of those in years—what? No, we don't still have it.

I'll tell you why in a minute. Do you interrupt your mother all the time, every night, when she's telling you a story? I don't know how she does it.

Right, right. Up went your Grandfather Selsim into the high country, with that mean little scribble of a road twitching and jiggling underfoot, until suddenly there wasn't any road, and it wasn't plain high country anymore, it was pure Torgry Mountain, and he had to dismount and lead the *churfa*, even with those clawed feet they have. And from there on your great-great-great probably learned a deal about mountains in a very short time. How you're always thirsty, doesn't matter how cold it is, because the thin air dries the water right out of you. How you can climb for hours, and then look down and you'd swear you're hardly any higher than when you started out, except that back down there the sun's so bright you can see the shadows on the ground, and where you are it's gray and windy as—as what?—as your Uncle Tavdal. And how there's nothing like mountain quiet, and how sounds and smells are all so clear they almost hurt, and how they seem so much closer than they really are. Which is not good if you're listening for monsters and winding their lairs. And you can't mistake the rock-*targ* scent, even if you've never seen one. Even if you don't know the bloody name of whatever smells like that, you know.

Oh, no. You'll just get frightened again if I tell you—I'm not going through that a second time, thanks ever so kindly. Besides, I've only sniffed a few places where they'd been long before, and that's nothing like what your Grandfather Selsim had in his throat. I'll tell you this much—just that shadow of a smell and I was pissing down my legs, each time. Oh, you like that, that's funny, is it? Well, then you can just laugh yourself sick thinking what the fresh stink probably did to Grandfather Selsim. All I know is that the *churfa* screamed like a demon in foal, the way they do, then pulled its reins right out of Grandfather Selsim's grasp and ran off back the way they'd come.

Well, what do you *think* he did? With the beast carrying everything he owned in the world? Of course, he went after it, and a good thing, too. Not that he caught up, but at least he did chance on the blanket roll—yes, yes, *dasko* knife and all—tangled in the brush that must have snatched it off the *churfa*'s back. So he'd sleep warm, whatever, and maybe having the big knife was some comfort to him. That first day or two, anyway.

Far as anyone knows, nothing at all worried him those two days, except for the little matter of something to eat. I'm sure lower down he dug up some of those *tanku* roots you can't stand, and then higher up he probably found some wild mountain radishes. They aren't real radishes, but you can eat them raw, so your Grandfather Selsim can't have gone too hungry on Torgry. Come nightfall, he must have slept in the open, had to have the sense not to go into a cave. Late spring, it could have been worse.

But by the third day he'd have climbed above the snowline.

Now I'm not saying that everything changes the moment you take the first step into the first snowdrift. The birds don't stop singing, and things still grow—although by now you're down mostly to shrubs and cloudberries and wizeny little *sulsawi*-trees—and you don't see skeletons lying around everywhere and rock-*targs* jumping out at you from every direction. It's not like that. It's just the quiet gets quieter—well, it just *does*—and it gets colder as you go higher, and the shadows move quicker over the snow. Sometimes you see a flock of *kagi* away off on a ridge, all blue and ripply horned and so pretty. Only, all the time you're watching them, you keep knowing what else is watching, too, and watching you, and choosing.

Rock-*targs* hunt by day. Get safely past sundown, you'll be all right until morning. Story has it they're afraid of the moon, but I couldn't say. Anyway, your Grandfather Selsim would have been moving right on up Torgry Mountain, nearing dusk of that first day, probably some pleased with himself for managing as well as he was doing, alone, on foot, all his provisions gone. He couldn't have known it, but another good day would have seen him to the summit, and an easy enough journey down from there. And if it had happened so, who knows where we'd all be? Or who? Hey?

I don't know just where or when the rock-*targ* came across the snowfield at your grandfather. One thing I know, he never heard it coming, because you don't; they can move like smoke, no mind how big they are. Only reason he wasn't killed in that first rush, it seems he turned for some reason—a bird, maybe a cloud red-gold with the sun behind it—and the thing's charge ripped his left shoulder open, spun him, and knocked him twenty feet away, all over blood and next to unconscious, surely. He carried that scar the rest of his life, Grandfather Selsim, and the arm never worked right again. The eye, too. It caught his left eye, some way.

I told you, I've never seen a rock-*targ* close to, myself, and I don't expect you'll ever meet anyone who has. But one thing people do say, when they're over you, gobbling their almost-talk and ready to tear you apart, their faces slide right up and back, straight back, showing the whole skull beneath. Now I can't tell you how that could be, I can't imagine it, and it's likely not true. But that's what people say.

When the creature came at him again, your Grandfather Selsim had just strength and wit enough to drag out his *dasko* knife and hold it on his belly, point up. They always go for the belly first, that's a fact anyway. And the rock-*targ* snatched the knife away from him and bit it in half! Right in half. And I know this is true, because I've seen the two pieces—your Uncle Lenelosi has them now, you can see them when we visit next. What? Because he's older than I am, will you hush? Yes, I'm sure we'll get them when Uncle Lenelosi dies. Will you *hush*?

I won't say your Grandfather Selsim gave himself up for lost, but I certainly don't know what else he could have done, what with that thing blotting out the sky, its triple row of fangs becoming another kind of sky. Their spit burns if it gets on you, did you know that? He carried a few of those scars to his grave, too, I've been told.

And then.

Then a pair of hands as big as—as big as, I don't know, big as two plows they must have looked to Grandfather Selsim—took hold of the rock-*targ*, one at the back of its human neck, one wrapped right around those hindquarters that were already curling off the ground to rip your grandfather's belly clean out of his body. For a moment he saw it hanging up there, looking little and foolish, too bewildered even to snap its jaws. The hands shook it once; they shook it the way your mother snaps a sheet still wet from the river before she hangs it out on the line. Your grandfather heard the creature's back break, just before he fainted. Or maybe he fainted just afterward, when the big hands reached down for him.

However it happened, your Grandfather Selsim didn't remember another thing until he was suddenly wide awake and hurting everywhere as he'd never hurt in his life. Somebody'd neatly bound up his shoulder with his own torn shirt, and he was lying in a heap of leaves, looking up with his one good eye into what he thought were trees, great ragged trees with dark moons floating in their branches. It took him a long, long while to understand that those weren't moons but huge bearded faces, not just bearded but swallowed up in mucky black hair that wasn't really like a beard at all. And the size of them...well, they weren't nearly as big as trees, but close enough, close enough. Nobody knows, not anymore, but from what I've been told I'd guess they'd have been between twelve and maybe fourteen feet tall. Now your Uncle Tavdal, he says they couldn't have been that tall, says bones wouldn't carry bodies that heavy. Your Uncle Tavdal is a fool.

They were talking to each other, the faces were. Grandfather Selsim could feel the words, not so much hear them, right through his body, thumping and thrumming in his bones. Because their voices were so deep, you see. At first he figured they were like rock-*targs* that way, just imitating the cries of the things they killed. But then he got to realizing that the words made sentences, and that they sounded a little like the same dialect the foothill folk used, only with strange grumbles and gurgles mixed in. And after another really long time, the sentences even started to make some sense. They were about him. The hairy faces were trying to decide what to do about him.

He couldn't tell them apart, of course, not then, not at all. What he *could* tell was that most of them were for getting rid of him, doing him in—what? Well, how should I know? Likely just by leaving him there to starve or freeze or bleed to death. Maybe by stepping on his head, all right? I can't believe you ask your mother so many questions.

Why did the giants want to kill him? Well, I was getting to that, if you hadn't interrupted. Best your Grandfather Selsim could make out, they were afraid he would tell the other humans about them. It didn't matter whether he meant them any harm—once humans know about you, you come to harm, that's how it is. Well, *I'm* not saying that, that's how those giants felt. And maybe it's so. I'm not saying.

They were the last ones, you see, the giants of Torgry Mountain, and they knew they were the last. "Giants know when giants go," that's something people always say your Grandfather Selsim always said. The odd thing, the funny thing, is that in those days it was the rock-*targs* that kept this lot of giants from being discovered. People were that afraid of the rock-*targs*, they wouldn't ever cross the mountain except in winter, and not many then. Now I don't know if the giants knew that the rock-*targs* were protecting them, just by being there, being what they were. Wouldn't have made any difference, chances are.

But that all comes later. Meanwhile, your Grandfather Selsim was lying there, looking away high at those great dark shaggy faces, hoping even one giant would speak for keeping him, though he couldn't think why they should want to. For the babies to teethe on, maybe, the way you chewed that stuffed *sheknath* I made you to pieces. He just lay still and hurt, and hoped.

And one giant did speak for him. Right when he was giving himself up a second time, one giant did speak out.

He was the biggest and hairiest of them, and smelled the worst. Your grandfather felt him saying to the others, "I will keep this little one. It was I who killed the rock-*targ*, so this one belongs to me, and it is my choice to keep him. No more talk."

And there it stuck, though they kept at it until your grandfather had to roll himself up in a ball and cover his ears. Well, you think what a roomful of giants shouting and arguing would feel like if it was all booming around in *your* body. It went on a good long while, too.

But all the booming and bellowing didn't make any difference. That biggest giant seemed to be someone really grand among them, because the others couldn't shift him an inch, and they couldn't say no to him either. So at last they gave up, they wandered off one by one, rumbling away like thunderheads, and were gone into the trees like *that*. Took him the longest while to get used to it, your Grandfather Selsim, the way those great crashing things could just not be there, disappear without a sound when they wanted to.

Well, he figured he might as well stand up as not, so he grabbed on to a low-hanging branch and pulled himself up on his feet. He was a small-made man, your grandfather—now this is important, why do you think I'm telling you this bloody story?—and they say he stood about knee-high to that creature that looked down at him, not saying a thing with the others gone, watching him silently out of its shadowy black eyes. Your Grandfather Selsim got tired of that in a hurry, and he tilted his head back and bawled, "Can you hear me?"

No answer. He tries again, loud as he can—*"Do you understand me?"* Nothing more aggravating than someone staring at you and not speaking. I don't care who it is.

Then the giant laughed at him. They say your grandfather had to hang on hard to that branch to keep from falling, because the ground shivered under his feet, but maybe that's just talk. Maybe it's just he was so amazed at the notion of those faces even smiling, let alone laughing like that. The giant slapped his legs—must have sounded like trees snapping when it's so cold the sap freezes—and dropped down, squatting, leaning in close. Your Grandfather Selsim didn't back away. The giant said, keeping his voice as low as he could, "My name is Dudrilashashek"—or something like that, your grandfather wasn't ever really sure. "Do you have a name, little one?"

"Of course I have a name!" your grandfather yelled up into that face. "Why wouldn't I have a name?"

"No need to shout," the giant answered—he was almost whispering himself, but with every word he spoke your grandfather's hair blew straight back. "There are so many of you, and you swarm around so, squeaking and chittering. How are we to know if you all have proper names? If you think of yourselves as yourselves?"

Well, your grandfather lost no time in setting *him* right, and you can believe me about that. Yes, we have names, and mine is Selsim— yes, we know who we are—yes, we have real conversations with each other—yes, we love, and we weep, and we laugh and suffer and endure as much as any bloody giants. He couldn't be sure if his impudence was making this giant angry, but he was too angry to care. Because he was telling him about *us*, about all of us, not just this one family. About all of us, at the top of his voice.

When he was through, or maybe when he just ran out of wind, the giant Dudrilashashek kept squatting there, still three, four feet taller than he was, staring at him and very slowly beginning to smile. Your grandfather used to say that all the giants had really beautiful white teeth, when you could see them through the tangly, greasy hair. Didn't smile much, though, none of them, but when they did smile, you noticed it.

"There," the giant said, "I was right, I *knew* I was right. Who would have thought you little ones had anything inside you but blind insect energy? Absolutely amazing. Oh, I knew I was right to insist on keeping you with us. Amazing."

"Keep me?" asked your Grandfather Selsim. "What are you talking about?" And now, now he was frightened as he hadn't been before, not when he was looking right into the rock-*targ*'s maw, not even when he knew the giants were quarrelling about whether he should live or die. "Why keep me? What for?"

"Why, to study, of course," Dudrilashashek answered him. "For we are a thoughtful folk, and pay all the attention we can to everything that crosses our lives—rock-*targs* or the tiniest waterbugs, it is all one to us. It is what we were put here for, we Qu'alo—to study, to consider, to turn over logs and stones and ideas equally, to learn what lies underneath. For that, and that alone, we were made."

What? That was what they called themselves, the Qu'alo. Means "The Proper People," if I remember it right. They never thought they were giants, by the way. They just thought humans were stunted.

Well now, between one thing and another, your Grandfather Selsim had had a really bad day. He put his hands on his hips, and he leaned back and shouted up into that giant's face, "You've made the wrong choice, big one! You can kill me, but you can't keep me here to be bloody *studied*! If I'm a bug, very well then—you just try guarding a bug every single minute of the day and night. This bug will be through your fat, clumsy fingers, down the road and long gone before you take your next bath. Which had better be pretty soon, by the way." Oh, he was definitely in a mood, and just getting warmed up, too.

But Dudrilashashek still didn't get angry. No, he kept on smiling that huge sweet smile, and he said back to your grandfather, "Please, little friend, if I seem callous, forgive me—it is merely that I am so *glad* of you. It is a lonely affair, being the only creatures in the world aware both of the world and of ourselves in it. Would you be offended now if I picked you up, just for a closer look? Being most careful, I promise."

Well, you can imagine Grandfather Selsim took his time over that one. He didn't think he was going to like being scooped up like a baby, like a pet, dangling between those immense hands, or flat on his back with his legs in the air, rocked in the curve of an elbow bigger than himself. Still, Dudrilashashek had asked very politely, considering he didn't have to, and your grandfather always appreciated politeness, especially from giants. So he said, "All right, but gently does it, then. And no upside-down business, understood?"

And Dudrilashashek answered him, "My word on it," and lifted him as carefully as he'd promised, one hand giving him a place to stand, the other steadying him with two fingers, so lightly your grandfather hardly felt the grip at all. The giant raised him up until their eyes were on a level and stared at him, just clucking with fascination, like your Aunt Kelya when she hasn't seen you for a while. "Look at that!" he kept saying, "you have fingernails almost like ours," and again, "Look at *that*— why, I think you could grow a beard like a real Qu'alo, if you fancied." Your Grandfather Selsim didn't know whether to fall down in his hand laughing, or to stand there and gape for realizing that everyone thinks they're the only Proper People in the world.

He didn't do either one. He kept his balance, and his dignity, pretty much, and he let Dudrilashashek sniff him all over without saying a word. Oh, there's another thing about giants, by the way—they heard better than they saw, what with all that hair, and they could smell another Qu'alo a mile away and know who he was, and what he'd had for breakfast, and how he was feeling right then. Of course, anyone else could smell *them* a good long way off, too, so much good it did them, hey? But your grandfather said he grew accustomed to the Qu'alo stink by and by—said he didn't even notice it after a time. And why not, hey? When you think what I've had to get used to with your mother's people.

What? No, I don't suppose he ever did know what he smelled like to them.

Well, when Dudrilashashek was done sniffing Grandfather Selsim, he said to him, "Now, if you don't mind, my brothers and sisters will do the same. Tedious for you, I'm sure, but the ritual has to be performed, if you are to stay with us. I'll bring you to them, shall I?"

"Indeed, you'll not," answered your grandfather—still a good bit cheekier than you or I would have spoken to a giant, I daresay. He said,

"I'm quite tired, not to mention hungry and thirsty, and I hurt a good deal, and my left eye doesn't work. This is because I've recently been chewed on by a rock-*targ*. I'm very grateful to you for saving my life, but I don't want to be smelled over anymore just now, and I'm not planning to stay a day longer than I have to. I want to lie down somewhere. If *you* wouldn't mind."

But Dudrilashashek replied, "I am sorry, this is more important, though I'm sure it can't seem so to you. The others must get your scent in their nostrils as soon as I do, in order that we may know you all in the same way, at the same time. For us, smell is so changeable, so easily affected by feelings, fears, health, age, diet, and endless other matters, that one of us might meet you only a few days from now and not know you at all. Which could be a very unhappy thing, for both of you. No, this *must* be done at once—forgive me, little friend."

And with that, he tightened his grip on your grandfather—oh, just slightly, but quite enough—and marched off into the woods calling for his friends and relations. They had a funny way of calling each other, a kind of hollow, hooty sound, not loud, but it seemed to carry forever. I've heard it said that when Grandfather Selsim was an old man, there were times when he would sit up in the middle of the night and swear he heard the Qu'alo calling to him, out on Torgry Mountain, so far away. They were all gone by then, and he knew it better than anyone, but even so. Wait, wait, you'll see.

Anyway. Nothing for it. Your grandfather had to stand in Dudrilashashek's vast palm for an hour or more, while the other Qu'alo came one at a time to touch and stare and smell him, just to be absolutely sure they'd know him again. Big foreheads, big cheekbones, small underslung chins, he said they all had, and the younger ones' hair was grayish-brownish, not really black. He was too weary to notice anything more then, or even to try telling the females from the males. When it was over at last, Dudrilashashek took him to a cave where they brought their sick ones, changed the bandage on his shoulder, fed him a soup of wild leeks and mushrooms out of a bowl he could have bathed in, and personally tucked him up in a sweet-smelling bed of green spring boughs. "There," he said, proud as proud. "Sleep now, and when you wake, I am sure much will look different to you."

Grandfather Selsim was already asleep, near enough, but he managed to mumble, "I'll not be staying long. As soon as I can travel decently, I'll be on my way. Rock-*targs* or no."

Old Dudrilashashek didn't contradict him, only nodded seriously and said, in that voice that always seemed to be coming right out of

Grandfather Selsim's own insides, "When you are healed, we will talk of this. Sleep now."

"Giants or no," your grandfather whispered, and slept for two days.

Yes, indeed, he certainly did have to piss something terrible when he woke up, thank you very much, I'd have forgotten. *And* he had to have some more soup, *and* he had to wash himself, *and* he had to have his shoulder looked at and tended. Dudrilashashek said he was coming along very well, and lucky with it, because a rock-*targ* bite usually poisons up and kills you just as dead. But whatever the Qu'alo had put on it, the great ragged gash was already knitting as nicely as you please, not a sign of infection. He still couldn't see a thing out of his left eye, but it wasn't hurting him very much, and Dudrilashashek told him that in time he'd have at least some vision back. For now he was to rest and grow strong, and not think of anything else. Especially not about leaving.

Your Grandfather Selsim looked straight at that giant—as straight as he could with one eye gone, anyway—and he said firmly, "Three days. Three days, and maybe two. It's nothing to do with you and your tribe— I never stay anywhere any longer than that. I am a tinker and a traveler, and I must be getting along. That's what I do, get along."

But the giant shook his head, looking solemn and regretful, and answered him, "It cannot be, little friend. The others will not have it, and I can command them only so far. In return for your life, I have already promised that you would be kept with us always, for fear of your leading a swarm of your folk to bedevil us here. I myself believe you'd do no such thing, but they'll not hear of chancing it. Your pardon, Shelshim"—don't laugh, that was the only way the Qu'alo could ever say his name—"but I can see that you wish the truth. This is the truth."

"If I promised them," your grandfather said. "If I give my word. Where I come from, we set great store by keeping one's word. I could swear on anything you hold sacred." Dudrilashashek just looked sadder and sadder. Grandfather Selsim said, "I'll run away. You know that, too."

"Please," the old giant said, and they say he was that upset, his enormous face was rippling and trembling all over, just like that disgusting pink dessert your Aunt Kelya makes every Winter-Farewell feast. He said, "Please, Shelshim, don't, I beg you. We are so good at hunting and tracking, at smelling out on an entire mountainside the one plant we desire to eat—and we are so dreadfully clumsy with these fingers of ours, sometimes. It would be terrible for us all, now that we know you, if you were accidentally harmed in being retaken. Or if the rock-*targs* found you before we did." *No,* they didn't call them that, of course not, they had their own word. No, I don't *know* what it was. Quiet.

Now your Grandfather Selsim never could abide being threatened, and he answered right off, "I'd rather die this minute with a rock-*targ* at my throat than live forever as the Qu'alo's pet human, with never a breath nor one single step to call my own. It won't do, Dudrilashashek. There's no one born who can keep me anywhere I don't want to be." And with that he turned painfully over and went back to sleep for another day. It's said that the giant watched over him all that time. Yes, I'm sure he had to go piss, too, at some point. Thank you.

So there's the way matters stood, and when your Grandfather Selsim woke again, it was time again for him to learn a great deal in a hurry. Tinkers are good at that, have to be. For one thing, he learned that the Qu'alo didn't have any one special place—a cave, or a clearing, or maybe a flat rock—where they lived together, or where they might be used to gathering, like the meeting hall in our village. The Qu'alo roamed Torgry Mountain as they chose, alone or with one or two others, no more. They spent most of their days looking for food, because it's hard to keep that big of a body properly stoked when you don't eat meat, or even fish, no more than a *rishu* does. Well, grubs, they ate grubs and bugs sometimes. They nested wherever night found them, usually in a *sum'yadi* tree, because of those being the only ones big enough to hold them and thick-dark enough to hide them. And they could go days, weeks at a time without seeing another of their kind, never give a thought to it. But each one of them always knew where all the rest were, same way you know where your fingers or your toes are. Don't ever have to think about it, do you? Same with the Qu'alo, exactly.

What? Can't you listen for even one minute when I'm telling you something? No, he certainly *didn't* run off the first chance he got, as he'd sworn. It took him a good sight longer than he'd expected to get over his wounds—even after his shoulder had healed and he was starting to notice a few things out of the side of that left eye, he still ached where he hadn't been wounded, still moved timidly, looking behind him every other step he took. It'll do that to you, a rock-*targ* attack, people say. You know you're really dead, even if nobody else knows. You keep expecting the thing to come back and claim you.

Dudrilashashek looked after him for a while, showing him how to find the wild berries and roots and such stuff that the Qu'alo lived on, and where the best streams were, and the safe caves to sleep in. Very considerate giant, that one—he knew a human couldn't sleep the way the giants did, practically tying the *sum'yadi* branches in knots to make a bed. Your grandfather paid attention, not like some of us. He paid more attention to the way the Qu'alo did things than he ever had to any-thing before. Because his life depended on it right then, and he knew that, if he didn't know much else yet.

Mind you, it took him the longest while to tell one of them from another, except for Dudrilashashek. All of them huge, all of them cov-ered with hair, all of them stinking to shame a *churfa*...it wasn't until after Dudrilashashek had left him on his own, more or less, that he began to know some of the other Qu'alo. And that was only because he was still afraid of being by himself, afraid of some rock-*targ* finding him alone. If those giants wanted to study him like a book or a bug, that was all right, that was fine—just so they bore him company and didn't leave him where the rock-*targs* could get him.

Two or three of the Qu'alo never spoke a word, not ever. You looked in those black eyes, your Grandfather Selsim said—like undersea caves, they were, once you looked past all the black hair—and you knew the Qu'alo really were a thoughtful people, they thought about things all the time. Only they weren't like your Uncle Tavdal—they didn't think talk-ing was the same as thinking, you understand? Just got in the way, more than likely. That's how they were, mostly.

Not all of them, though. There were a pair of brothers named some-thing like Calijostylakomo and Galijostylakomo—and not a word out of you, those were their *names*, and that's all there is to that. Your grand-father called them Cali and Gali, and he could always tell those two apart because Cali never could grow a beard as thick as the other giants' beards, and it bothered him. Or maybe that was Gali, I couldn't say. Anyway, they were young, which is maybe why they talked a bit more than the others. And they were mischievous, at least for giants. They liked to wrestle—Grandfather Selsim used to climb a tree to stay out of the way, and even that was risky. And sometimes, instead of bedding down at sunset like the other Qu'alo, they'd go off together and spend the whole night hunting rock-*targs*. Used to bait them out of their lairs and roll boulders down on them.

There was another one he was friendly with, a woman of the Qu'alo—her name was Yriadvele, more or less. Now they were even shyer than the rest of the giants, the women were, and the only rea-son Grandfather Selsim ever exchanged two words with her is that he once fell into a trap, a pit that Cali and Gali had dug to catch rock-*targs* in, and he was just lucky that they were young and too lazy to bother with putting poisoned stakes at the bottom. This Yriadvele heard his cries, and she came and scooped him out of there, quick as that. And afterward he somehow had a claim on her, the way it can happen. She'd pop him up on her shoulder and off they'd go for a long walk in the forest, or out on the open mountainside, toward evening, with no chance of travelers seeing them. I used to carry you like that, you remember?

Your grandfather didn't talk much about her for years, not until he was really getting on, that's what I was told. He said he could always tell Yriadvele from the others because she had a grayish sort of mantle up around her shoulders. The hair, I mean, that's because she was still young. Anyway, they'd talk for hours on end, your Grandfather Selsim and this enormous woman-creature who was so hairy and so stinking that after a time he didn't notice any of that at all. Truth of it is, he came to think she was pretty, in a way, with her huge black eyes and really delicate little ears—and he said she was graceful, too, moving that body silently among the trees. Like the rest of them, if she didn't want you to see her, you didn't see her. But when she was there, she was *there*, the trees and the mountain boulders all faded into air around her. Now that's exactly what your grandfather said, word for word, just the way I had it from my own grandfather.

What did they talk about? Well, she'd ask him how human beings lived, what they ate, where they slept, and what they did when they were sick, and about clothes, and about how they felt about being such small creatures in such a big world. And games, playing games, she never did understand about that. The Qu'alo didn't play, you see, they didn't have a notion of what the word meant. She asked him to tell her about the games over and over.

She didn't talk at all like Dudrilashashek. No, I don't know why, and your grandfather never did either. He used to wonder sometimes if she was maybe simple, but how do you tell with a giant? Once she said, slow and halting, sometimes a minute or two between the words, "When we sleep, sometimes we see a story, we are in the story. You?"

"Dreams," your grandfather said. "Yes, we dream, we see stories, too. Like you, just the same."

But Yriadvele turned her great head slowly to look straight into his eyes, and her own so dark you couldn't see yourself in them, nor the sky behind you, nor a green leaf or a bit of sun. She said, "With us, the same story every night. Always. The rock-*targs*. Our brothers."

Your grandfather must have just stared at her. She said, "Made at the same time, rock-*targs* and we Qu'alo. Looked the same once, lived together, the same people. But we changed, slowly, slowly, left them, lost them. So now, every night we live, the dream, every night, how it was once. The gods punish us for changing."

No, what do you think, of course I don't know if that's true or not. It's what the Qu'alo believed, that's all. Your Grandfather Selsim never said whether *he* believed it, but he did say it sounded just like the gods.

Do you know what she thought was the funniest thing in the world? Telling jokes—I mean the *idea* of telling jokes. It took a while for her to believe that humans would spend time making up stories and repeating them to each other just to make each other laugh. But once she did take hold of it—why, then it became hers, her own joke, and she might start giggling to herself at the thought of it, any time at all, the way you hear thunder back of the hills on a hot night. He'd find her that way sometimes, your grandfather, playing with her special joke. And sometimes she'd start in *really* laughing, no warning. He said the ground would tremble, blossoms and leaves would be coming down everywhere, birds would pop right off their nests, and your bones would buzz for an hour afterward. That's what it was like when the Qu'alo laughed.

One time he asked if the giants had families, the way humans do. He hardly ever saw more than two Qu'alo together, couldn't be sure how many of them there were on Torgry Mountain, and he certainly couldn't even guess which ones might be children. She didn't answer him, she didn't speak at all until the next day. Just about the time he'd forgotten his question, she said, "Once, now not." Her voice was so soft he couldn't feel it in his body, the way he always did. She said it three times. "Once. Once. Once."

He didn't try to escape until he'd been with the Qu'alo two months, or maybe three, and by then he'd almost forgotten he was supposed to be their prisoner. They never caged or fenced or tethered him; he never saw them following him, watching him, not like that, nothing like that. He could wander any place he liked, stay out of sight of any Qu'alo as long as he felt like it. But the night he walked off through the deepest woods, not going near the trail he'd been traveling when the rock-*targ* jumped him, but veering, angling, first this way, then that, sidling toward the summit—do you know, he hadn't gone more than a mile when it was old Dudrilashashek filling his path, saying gently, "No, no, little one, I am sorry. Come, I will take you back, come now." Just as though he were no older than you, and walking in his sleep.

That was how it was every time he tried to slip away from the Qu'alo, to turn back to his interrupted journey, back into his own ordinary tinker's life. Never a reproach, never a threat, but always some huge creature suddenly *there* in front of him without a sound. Now and then it would be Yriadvele herself, and *she'd* simply pick him up and carry him, holding him straight out between her two hands, not on her shoulder, the way she did when they were off somewhere. That was how it was for eighteen years.

Eighteen years, that's right, that's how long he lived with the Qu'alo. Eating what they ate, sleeping when they slept, browsing in the shadows the day long, same as they did. Sounds like the most boring life you ever heard of, doesn't it? Well, it likely would have been just that for you or me, but it was something different for your Grandfather Selsim. Because after a time, might have been a few years, they say he started to think the thoughts of the Qu'alo, do you understand what I'm saying to you? Big thoughts, old thoughts, turning in his mind, the way you see a big fish come up in the evening and heave over at the surface with the sunset on his silver belly, and just slide away back down again. Long, strange, slow thoughts, take even a Qu'alo forever to get them right. Maybe you have to live that way to think that way. After a while, maybe that's all you want to do in the world. No, you don't understand, boy, and I don't either. What I *know* is, your Grandfather Selsim spent eighteen years of his life with those stinking giants, and after the first three years, four years, he stopped trying to escape. He'd have stayed with them the rest of his life, if he could, and you wouldn't be here, nor me either. You think about that a little bit.

The winters? Yes, the mountain winters were hard, but Dudrilashashek taught him the Qu'alo trick for that. Do you know what they used to do when the leaves fell, when the streams all froze, when everything they ate was under two feet of snow? Do you know what the Qu'alo did? Why, they went to sleep, there's what they did. They'd find empty rock-*targ* caves—well, maybe they weren't always empty when they found them, but pretty soon after—and they'd pile together, two or three or four of them, and just sleep it out like that. And if it turned warm for a little, they might get up and wander around, dig under the snow for a nibble, then go back to sleep. People can do that, too, if they learn the trick. Your grandfather did. I think you should try it sometime.

Why couldn't he stay with them? Well, that's the story, isn't it? That's what we're getting to now.

It was Yriadvele who came for him when that first giant died. It was late on a summer afternoon, getting on for sundown. She just said, "Dead. With me," so he went with her, sitting on her shoulder like always. She wouldn't say who it was, nor even tell him his age—he was afraid a rock-*targ* might finally have gotten Cali or Gali. Well, he asked her, what was it he died of, then? That was when she looked sideways at him and said, "Qu'alo. Being Qu'alo." And what *that* meant, he had no idea.

They were in a clearing, all of them, gathered around the dead one. They had him laid out on a sort of scaffold thing—you know the way the Nounouris put their dead people up high in the trees? The Qu'alo did something like that except this platform wasn't any higher than about so, about my chest, and the body was mostly covered with fresh-cut branches that smelled sweet. Grandfather Selsim couldn't see the face, but he could see every one of the giants he knew to talk to, so he felt better. We can't help that, that's the way we are. As long as it's no one we know.

That was when he noticed how few of them there really were—no more than fifteen or sixteen, counting the children. And only about three of those, there's another thing. Now you're a farmer's son, you imagine they're *rishus* or *jejebhais* and work it out in your head, go on. Right—you can't keep up a herd of anything breeding at that rate, not a chance in the world. The Qu'alo were dying off, they were already doomed, almost on purpose. The way I've seen it happen sometimes.

Well, I have, and so have you, if you'll think about it. You remember that time when that whole flock of *makhyabs* over at the Jutt place, when he was going to get rich off those thousands and thousands of bright-red eggs they were going to lay—you remember when they all died, every one of them, almost overnight, and Bala Jutt came weeping for me to come look at the bodies and tell him what could have gone wrong. You were small, but you remember? Right, well, those *makhyabs* died because they didn't like Bala Jutt, and they didn't like the way he kept them, and they decided that living like that simply wasn't worth it. I don't mean they held a meeting and took a vote. I mean they just *decided*. Same with the Qu'alo. Not just the same, but the same.

Why? Well, if your Grandfather Selsim never knew, I certainly don't, and maybe the Qu'alo didn't know either, not in words. I don't think they ever put anything important into words, even to themselves. Just hush and listen.

Anyway, your Grandfather Selsim was most likely thinking about things like that when Yriadvele started to dance. He heard the heavy double thump behind him, and when he whirled around he saw her, stepping hard and slow, back and forth, one foot to the other. Then she was stamping, faster, making the platform with the body on it tremble, and then her arms began to lift away from her sides, as though she were getting ready to fly. Her eyes weren't looking at him or at anything, and her face was just as dark and hidden as always.

Then the others started in. Fifteen giants, stamping the ground all together. So now it was the trees shaking, and the ground *bouncing* like the skin on a drum, and people say the setting sun was bouncing, too, in the sky. I don't suppose it was what we'd call dancing—most of them just kept jumping up and down and waving their big arms around—but your grandfather said Yriadvele was turning and swaying, bending to touch the earth, kneeling, straightening, reaching out like for something nobody else could see.

The way he told it, the frightening part was the *quiet*, not the noise. Underneath the noise, those tremendous feet booming on the ground, underneath it was still as could be, silent all the way down. And when they suddenly stopped, all of them together—oh, *that* quiet was too much for him, he backed away until he bumped into a tree, and then he hid behind it. But they weren't looking at him, not Yriadvele, none of them. They were looking at the dead Qu'alo on the scaffold thing.

This is what they did.

I was just thinking, I don't know if I should be telling you this. If you start having nightmares, your mother will—what? Ah, don't tell me that—you had one just last week, woke me up yelling about *shukris* all over you, chewing you to bits. You don't remember, no, of course not. Your mother does. I think maybe you ought to go to sleep now.

All right, all right, just quiet *down*! Couldn't hear the *jejebhai* having triplets with you carrying on like that. Be *quiet*, I'll tell you the rest of it. Only if you do have a bad dream, I don't want to know anything about it. Me or anyone, that's agreed? Gods, how did I get *into* this?

So. This is what they did, then. They walked by him one at a time, the dead one, and each of them bowed his head and sniffed at him, really deeply, the same way they'd smelled your grandfather over, so carefully. It took a long time, because they were saying good-bye, not hello, and it was full dark when they all sat down to eat him.

You heard me. They ate him. They'd already cleaned him, same way you would with a fish, and now they built a big fire to see by—that was the first time your grandfather knew they could do that, they never had before—and they sat down together and ate that dead Qu'alo all gone. Only time he ever saw them eat meat, too. Don't make those silly faces—I'm telling you, that's what they did. It took them till dawn.

Listen to me, stop making those *faces*. Do you know what your Grandfather Selsim said about it? He said it was beautiful, somehow it was the most beautiful thing he ever saw. They sat around that scaffold in the dark, those huge creatures, and they talked, their voices not just low but soft, sad, gentle, a way he'd never heard them. He couldn't make out a word, even sitting close, but he knew they were talking about their friend. And at the same time they were eating him, they were praising him and honoring him and loving him, you understand? It wasn't like people gobbling and grunting over their dinner—it was different, it was beautiful. That's exactly what your grandfather said.

It took all night, I told you that. And at the end of it, with the morning rolling up over the trees, there wasn't a thing left on the platform but these long, clean bones shining there. Yes, sure, the skull too, what do you think? Nothing but giant bones, and they buried those in a special place, your grandfather never would say where. And that was what the Qu'alo did when a Qu'alo died.

The way old Dudrilashashek explained to your grandfather, "It is our way of keeping the one who dies with us forever. The flesh is unimportant, and passes through us, but what remains—our lives, our thoughts, our memories, our time in the world—the very last of the Qu'alo will contain all that, contain us all, every one ever. And when that last one is gone..." Your Grandfather Selsim said he shrugged so slowly, so heavily that it was like watching a whole mountain range being born and dying, all in one motion. Dudrilashashek said, "Well," and nothing more.

Eighteen years, then. Eighteen years, your Grandfather Selsim lived on Torgry Mountain with the Qu'alo, and one by one he watched them go. Never a wound or an injury, never a sickness that he could see—they just died, one or two a year. Young ones, old, he didn't ever learn to tell much difference, except for the few he'd become a little friendly with: Jalayakudrilak, who could tell you weeks ahead what the weather was going to be; Tudoguraj, who loved to sing, imagine a giant chirping and twittering away like a tree full of hatchlings; and there was one called Rumirideyol, the only Qu'alo who refused to kill rock-*targs* if she could avoid it, and wept afterward when she couldn't. Cali and Gali went together—your grandfather was glad of that. He was the one who found them, lying side by side, one brother's head on the other's shoulder, and not a mark on them. One by one.

Mind now, this is going to sound really silly, and I don't want one solitary snicker out of you. When you're down to just a handful of giants, it gets hard to do what you have to do with your dead. Are you laughing? You'd better not be laughing. The Qu'alo managed all right, but it was harder and sadder for them each time they came to sit around that brush-covered ceremonial platform. When Dudrilashashek went, your grandfather cried. He liked that old windbag of a giant, he missed him till the day he died himself. He even wanted to take part in the—you know, what they did—but Yriadvele wouldn't let him. She said it wasn't right, not while one Qu'alo lived, so that was that. But she let him dance with them, his little hops and thumps like the ghost of the dead one's dance. And he always helped to bury the great, shining bones.

Couldn't he have escaped, with so few giants to watch him? Well, of course, he could have, they were a long way past caring about that. But he didn't want to—by then he belonged with them, can you understand that? He didn't want to leave them, they were his family by then, some way. That's all I know, that's all I can tell you.

And finally there wasn't a Qu'alo left but Yriadvele. After eighteen years. They stayed very close together now, the giant woman and your grandfather—he said they even slept together, with him under her arm like a baby bird. She didn't seem likely to die any minute, but neither had the others, so he wasn't going to take chances. That winter, in the cave they'd been using for so long, he slept dreaming that spring had come and she wouldn't wake, he dreamed that over and over, waking himself up each time to make sure she was still breathing. Then he'd go back to sleep and dream it again. Like you when you're waiting for your birthday.

And it came true, that dream, near as makes no difference. Oh, she woke when it was time, but not completely, never all the way. She couldn't walk at all the first day or two, and your Grandfather Selsim had to forage for her. But there was no chance he could find enough food to fill a twelve-foot giant, especially one who hadn't eaten all winter. Maybe it would have been all right if she'd been able to feed herself, I don't know. He said even when she could walk she hardly ate a thing, but she was thirsty all the time and mostly stayed by a stream which had just wakened up itself. Her eyes were the color of cobwebs, not black as they should be, and her coat had that flat, staring, sticky look to it you don't ever want to see on a *rishu*, a *jejebhai*, even a miserable *dhrush-indi*. She didn't say a word, and your grandfather didn't know what to do except stay with her.

And finally she said to him, "You take me there."

"No," he said. "No, there's no need, there's nothing wrong with you, you're just still sleepy. You need to eat more, that's all."

But she put her hands on him in a way she never had done before. She touched his shoulders, and his face, and she took his head between those hands that could have crushed it like a rotten old *chouka* nut. Her poor streaked eyes were looking straight into his, and whatever she saw there, it made her smile a little. He'd never seen her smile at him just like that before, not in eighteen years.

"Time, Shelshim," she said. "Time, friend."

He said it took all day to get where they were going. She wasn't walking very well, and he couldn't support her, and he couldn't do much for her when she fell. Must have been like a tree going down, except a tree doesn't make a sound when it's hurt, and it can't clutch and scrabble and claw itself back up again. Once she tumbled into a ravine and lay there so long without moving he thought she really was dead, but when he climbed down to her, she opened her eyes, grabbed out to catch a root or a branch and started over. Come sundown, they were standing by that rickety scaffold where all her people before had rested one last time. She was staring down at it, holding herself as straight as she could, but her head was rolling on her neck, and she smelled wrong. The last day or so, that good Qu'alo stink had all faded, just thinned out and blown away. Now she just smelled like any old animal.

He said, "I can't do it, you know I can't. Even if I could make myself do it, I'm a human, I'm too small. It'd take me forever." He laughed a little, saying it, hoping she'd laugh, too.

"Bones, Shelshim," she said. Her voice was such a whisper that he couldn't feel it in his body anymore; she actually had to pick him up one last time, bring him close to hear. "*Bones*, Shelshim. Cover me, leave me, you come back sometime. Please, Shelshim."

He didn't understand. He said, "To bury your bones. Of course I'll do that for you. I can do that."

She shook him then—not hard, nothing like the way they did with the rock-*targs*, but his head still jolted back and forth and his arms flapped around, weak as she was. "Eat," she said. "The bones, eat. Not gone, so, not gone. Keep us, Shelshim."

And those were the last words Yriadvele ever spoke to him. She lay down on the platform, and your grandfather covered her with the softest new boughs and twigs and leaves he could find, and she just nodded when he had it right, and closed her eyes. He sat by her all that day and night, but he couldn't tell when she died.

There wasn't anything he could do for her, not then, so he went away and he waited, the way she told him to. I can't tell you how long—how long does it take insects, little animals, to strip away the rotting flesh from a twelve-foot giant? Weeks, months, most of a year? All I know is, as long as it took, your Grandfather Selsim lived alone on the mountain top, same way he'd lived for eighteen years. Except now he slept in the giants' old nests for the comfort of the smell, and safety from the rock-*targs*, and he said he talked a lot to imaginary human beings, because he needed the practice after such a time of thinking Qu'alo thoughts in Qu'alo silence. And he thought about the world he almost remembered, and about what Yriadvele had asked of him, and whenever it was that he finally went back to the scaffold and pulled away the dead branches, there were the bones, and he knew what to do with them. You're making faces again, stop it.

Your grandfather took Yriadvele's bones, one by one, and he ground them up as fine as he could, stone against flat stone, and he ate them. No, I don't know how long it took him, what they tasted like. I don't know if he just ate them or drank them in water, or sprinkled them over some nice kami leaves. All I'm sure of is that he ate Yriadvele's bones, all of them, and then he stood up from there and he walked back to the trail over Torgry Mountain, and on down the other side, and he kept walking. And in time he came to this flat, hazy country where we live today, and settled to farming, and married and started our family, all that time ago. And that's the end of the story, and I'm in the barn, and you're asleep, good night.

What? Well, I told you, that's why we're all tall, that's why I know you'll be tall soon enough. *Now* do you understand me? We're whatever's left of the Qu'alo, you and me and the rest of our family—they're in *our* bones now, because of your Grandfather Selsim and his giant friend. Mind, we just got a bit of their height, that's all; we didn't get the hairiness or the stink—the gods do get something right once in a while. And if any of us got any of those great, slow, wonderful thoughts, I surely haven't noticed it. But maybe those are inside *you*, who knows? Who knows what a little boy who can't keep his eyes open to ask any more questions is thinking, hey? Good night, then, good night.

What? In ten years, that's when I'll have the strength to tell you another story. Most exhausting work I ever did. I swear I don't know how your mother manages every night. And that bloody *jejebhai's* going to wait till I'm finally asleep, I know that much for certain. Good night, boy. Let go of my hand. Good *night*.

King Pelles the Sure

Once there was a king who dreamed of war. His name was Pelles.

He was a gentle and kindly monarch, who ruled over a small but wealthy and completely tranquil kingdom, beloved alike by noble and peasant, despite the fact that he had no queen, and so no heir except a brother to ensure an orderly succession. Even so, he was the envy of mightier kings, whose days were so full of putting down uprisings, fighting off one another's invasions, and wiping out rebellious villages that they never knew a single moment of comfort or security. King Pelles—and his people, and his land—knew nothing else.

But the king dreamed of war.

"Nobody is ever remembered for living out a dull, placid, uneventful life," he would say to his Grand Vizier, whom he daily compelled to play at toy soldiers with him on the parlor floor. "Peace is all very well—a fine thing, certainly—but do you ever hear ballads about King Herman the Peaceful? Do you ever listen to bards chanting the deeds of King Leslie the Calm, or read great national epics about King James the Docile, King William the Diplomatic? You do not!"

"There was Ethelred the Unready," suggested the Grand Vizier, whose back hurt from crouching over the carpet battlefield every afternoon. "Meaning unready for conflict or crusade, unwilling to slaughter needlessly. And King Charles the Good—"

"But it is Charles the Hammer who lives in legend," King Pelles retorted. "William the Conqueror—Erik Bloodaxe—Alfonso the Avenger—Selim the Valiant—Ivan the Terrible. Our own schoolchildren know *those* names…and why not," he added bitterly, "since we don't have any heroes of our own. How can we, when nobody ever even raids us, or bothers to challenge us over land or resources, or attempts to annex us, to swallow our little realm whole, as has happened to so many such lands in our time? Sometimes I feel as though I should send out a dozen heralds to proclaim our need of an enemy. I *do*, Vizier."

"No, sire," said the Grand Vizier earnestly. "No, truly, you don't want to do anything like that. I promise you, you don't." He straightened up, rubbing his back and smoothing out his robe of office. He said, "Sire, Majesty, if I may humbly suggest it, you would do well—as would every soul dwelling on this soil that we call home—to appreciate what you see as our insignificance. There is an old saying that there is no country as unhappy as one that needs heroes. Trust me when I say in my turn that our land's happiness is your greatest victory in this life, and that you will never know another to equal it. Nor should you try, for that would show you both greedy and ungrateful, and offend the gods. I urge you to leave well enough alone."

Having spoken so, the Grand Vizier braced himself for an angry response, or at least a petulant one, being a man in late middle age who had served other kings. He was both astonished and alarmed to realize that King Pelles had hardly heard him, so caught up was he in romantic visions of battle. "It would have to be in self-defense, of course," the king was saying dreamily. "We have no interest in others' treasure or territory—we're not that sort of nation. If someone would only try to invade us by crafty wiles, such as filling a wooden horse with armed soldiers and leaving it invitingly outside the gates of our capital city. Then we could set it afire and roast them all—"

He caught sight of the horrified expression on the Grand Vizier's face, and added hurriedly, "Not that we ever *would,* of course, certainly not, I was just speculating."

"Of course, sire," murmured the Grand Vizier. But his breath was turning increasingly short and painful, as King Pelles went on.

"Or if they should come by sea, slipping into our port on a foggy night, we would be ready with a corps of young men trained to swim out with braces and augurs and sink their ships. And if they struck by air, perhaps dropping silently from the sky in dark balloons, our archers could shoot all them down with fire-arrows. Or if we could induce them to tunnel under the castle walls—oh, *that* would be good, if they tunneled—then we could..."

The Grand Vizier coughed, as delicately as he could manage it, given the panicky constriction of his throat. He said, "Your Highness, meaning absolutely no disrespect, you have never seen war—"

"Exactly, exactly!" King Pelles broke in. "How can one know the true meaning of peace, who has no experience of its undoubtedly horrid counterpart? Can you answer me that, Vizier?"

"Majesty, I have known that experience," the Grand Vizier replied quietly. "It was far from here, in a land I traveled to as a boy. I shared it with many brave and dear and young friends, who are all dead now—as I should have been, but for the courtesy of the gods, and the enemy's poor aim. You have missed nothing, my lord."

He seemed to have grown older as he spoke, and the king—who may have been foolish, but who was not a fool—saw, and answered him equally gently. "I understand what you are telling me, good Vizier. But this would be only a little war, truly—no more enduring or consuming than one of our delightful carpet clashes. A *manageable* war—a demonstration, one might say, just to let our rivals see that our people are not to be trifled with. In case they were thinking about trifling. Do you see the difference, Vizier? Between this war and yours?"

With another king, the Grand Vizier would have considered long and carefully before risking the truth. With King Pelles, he had no such fears, but he also knew his man well enough to recognize when hearing the truth would make no smallest difference to what the king decided to do. So he said only, "Well, well, be sure to employ great precision in choosing your foe—"

"*Our* foe," King Pelles corrected him. "Our *nation's* foe."

"*Our* foe," the Grand Vizier agreed. "We must, whatever else we do, select the weakest enemy available—"

"But that would be dishonorable!" the king protested. "Ignoble! Unsporting!" He was decidedly upset.

The Grand Vizier was firm in this. "We are hardly a nation at all; we are more like a shire or a county with an army. A distinctly small army. A more powerful adversary would destroy us—that is simply a fact, my king. You cannot *manage* a war without attention to facts."

He was hoping that his sardonic emphasis on the notion of managing such a capricious thing as war might deter King Pelles from the whole fancy, but it did not. After a silence, the king finally sighed and said, "Well. If that is what a war is, so be it. Consider our choices, Vizier, and make your recommendation." He added then, rather quickly, "But do arrange for a *gracious* war, if you possibly can. Something... something a little *tidy*. With songs in it, you know."

The Grand Vizier said, "I will do what I can."

As it turned out, he did tragically better than he meant. Perhaps because King Pelles had never wanted to know it, he truly had no notion of how deeply his land was hated for its prosperity on the one hand and coveted on the other. The Grand Vizier had hoped to engineer a very brief war for the king, quickly over, with minimum damage, disruption or inconvenience to everyone involved, and easily succeeded in tempting their little country's nearest neighbor to invade (in the traditional style, as it happens, by marching across borders). But his plan went completely out of control in a matter of hours. Wise enough to lure a weaker country into a foolish attack, he was as innocent, in his own way, as his king, never having considered that other lands might be utterly delighted to join with the lone aggressor he had bargained for. An alliance of territories which normally despised each other formed swiftly, and King Pelles's land came under siege from all sides.

Actually, it was no war at all, but a massacre, a butchery. There was a good deal of death, which was something else the king had never seen. He was still shaking and crying from the horror of it, and the pity, and his terrible shame, when the Grand Vizier disguised them both as peasant women and set them scurrying out the back way as the flaming castle came down, seeming to melt and dissolve like so much pink candy floss. King Pelles looked back and wept anew for his home, and for his country; and the Grand Vizier remembered the words of Boabdil's mother when the Moorish king looked back in tears from the mountain pass at lost Spain behind him. *"Weep not like a woman for the kingdom you could not defend like a man."* But then he thought that defending things like men was what had gotten them into this catastrophe in the first place, and decided to say nothing.

The king and his Grand Vizier scrambled day on wretched day across the trampled, smoking land, handicapped somewhat by their long skirts and heavy muddy boots, but running like a pair of aging thieves all the same. No one stopped them, or even looked at them closely, although there were mighty rewards posted everywhere for their heads, and they really looked very little like peasant women, even on their best days. But the country was in such havoc, with so many others—displaced, homeless, penniless, mad with terror and loss—fleeing in every direction, that no one had the time or the inclination to concern themselves with the identities of their poor companions on the road. The soldiers of the alliance were too busy looting and burning, and those whose homes were being looted and burned were too busy not being in them. King Pelles and the Grand Vizier were never once recognized.

One evening, dazed as a child abruptly awakened from a happy dream, the king finally asked where they were bound.

"I have relatives in the south country beyond those hills you see," the Grand Vizier told him. "A cousin and her husband—they have a farm. It has been a long time since I last saw them, and I cannot entirely remember where they live. But they will take us in, I am sure of it."

King Pelles sighed like the great Moor. "Better your family than mine. *My* cousins—my own brother—would demand a bribe, and then turn us over to the conquerors anyway. They are bad people, the lot of them." He huddled deeper into his ragged blanket, shrugging himself closer to their tiny fire. "But I am the worst by far," he added, "the worst, there is no comparison. I deserve whatever becomes of me."

"You did not know, sire," the Grand Vizier offered in attempted solace. "That is the worst that can be said of you, that you did not know."

"But you did, you *did*, and you tried to warn me, and I refused to listen to you. And you obeyed my orders, and now you share my fate, and my people's innocent lives lie in ruins, and it is my doing, and there is no atoning for it." The king rocked back and forth, then stretched on the ground in his blanket, as though he were trying to bury himself where he lay, whimpering again and again, "No atoning, no atoning." He hurt himself doing this, for the ground was shingly and rock-strewn. The Grand Vizier knew he would see the bruises in the morning.

"You were a good king," the Vizier said. "You meant well."

"*No!*" The word came out as a scream of agony. "I *never* meant well! I meant glory for myself—nothing less or more than that. And I knew it, I *knew* it, I knew it at the time, and still I had to go ahead, had to play out my toy battle with soft, breakable human bodies, breakable human souls. *No atoning...*"

There was nothing for the Grand Vizier then, but to say, as to a child, "Go to sleep, Your Majesty. What's done is done, and one of us is as guilty as the other. And even so, we must sleep."

But he himself slept poorly—perhaps even worse than King Pelles— in the barns and the empty cattle byres and the caves; and the king's piteous murmurings as he dreamed were hardly of any help. There was always the smell of smoke, from one direction or another; at times there would come noises in the night, which might as easily have been restless cows as pursuing spies or soldiers, but there was never any way for the Vizier to make certain of either. All he allowed himself to think about was the need to guide the king safely to shelter from one night to the next—further than that, his imagining dared not go, if he meant to sleep at all. *And even if we find my cousin—what was her husband's name again?—even if we do find their farm, what then?*

By great good fortune, they did find the Grand Vizier's cousin, whose name was Nerissa—her husband's name was Antonio—and were welcomed as though they had last visited only days ago, or a week at most. The little farm was a crowded place, since Nerissa and Antonio, with no children of their own, had gladly taken in their widowed friend Clara and her four, who ranged in age from six to seventeen years. Nevertheless, they received King Pelles and the Grand Vizier unhesitatingly: as Antonio said, "No farm was ever the worse for more hands in the fields, nor more faces around the dinner table. And whoever noticed the smudged and sunburned face of a farmworker who wasn't one himself? Have no fear—you are safe with us. In these times, there is no safety but family."

So it was that he who had been the king of all the land and he who had been its most powerful dignitary became nothing more than hands in the fields, and were grateful. Neither was young, but they worked hard and long all the same, and proudly kept even with Antonio and the others when it came time to bring the harvest home. And every evening, King Pelles told stories about wise animals and clever magicians to Clara's children, and later the Grand Vizier conducted an informal history lesson for the older ones, in which their mother often joined. Still an attractive woman, she had clear brown skin and dark, amused eyes which were increasingly attentive, as time passed, to whatever the Vizier said or did. Antonio and Nerissa saw this, and were glad of it, as was the king. "Your cousin has wasted his life on my foolishness," he said to Nerissa. "I am so happy that she will give it back to him."

When the Grand Vizier could do it without feeling intrusive, he listened—with the back of his head, perhaps, or the back of his mind—to the king's fairytales. They were not like any he had ever heard, and they fascinated and alarmed him at the same time. Few had what he would have considered happy endings, especially as a child—the gallant prince frequently failed to arrive in time to rescue the princess from the dragon, more often than not the poison was not counteracted, the talking cat could not always preserve his master from his own stupidity. Endings changed, as well, with each telling, and characters wandered from one story into a different one, often changing their natures as they did so. On occasion grief flowed into overwhelming joy, though that outcome was never something you might want to bet on. The Grand Vizier constantly expected the children to become frightened or upset, but they listened in obvious absorption, the younger ones crowding each other on the king's lap, and all four nodding silently from time to time, as children do to express trust in the tale.

Maybe it is the way he tells them, the Grand Vizier thought more than once, for King Pelles always had a special voice at those times, different than the way he spoke in the fields or at evening table. It was a low voice, with a calmness in it that—as the Vizier knew—had grown directly from suffering and remorse, and seemed to draw the children's confidence whether or not the words were understood.

Yet content as King Pelles was in his new life, fond of Clara's children as he was, warmed far deeper than his bones by being a true part of a family for the first time…even so, he still wept in his sleep, whispering brokenly, "*No atoning…*" The Grand Vizier heard him every night.

Winter was always hard in that kingdom, even in the south country, but the Grand Vizier was profoundly glad of it. The snow and mud closed the roads, for one thing: there would be no further pursuit of the king for a time, and who knew what might happen, or have happened, by spring? What news reached the farm suggested that a group of the king's former advisors had banded together to install a ruler of their choosing, and thus restore at least their notion of order to the kingdom, but the Vizier could not discover his name, nor learn any further details of the story. But he allowed himself to be somewhat hopeful, to imagine that perhaps—just *perhaps*—the hunt might have dwindled away, and that the king's existence might have become completely unimportant to the new regime. For the first time in his long career of service, the Grand Vizier dreamed a small dream for himself.

But with the thawing of the roads, with the tinkling dissolution of the icicles that had fringed the farmhouse's gables for many months, with the first tentative sounds of the frogs who had slept in the deep beds of the frozen streams all winter…the soldiers came marching. With the first storks, they came.

Martine, Clara's younger daughter, was playing by the awakening pond one afternoon, and heard their boots and the rattle of their mail before they had rounded the bend in the road. She, like all the others, had been told over and over that if she ever saw even one soldier she must run straight to the house and warn her mother's special friend, and the other one as well, the storyteller. She never waited to see these, but was up and away at the first sound, and through the front door in a muddy flash, crying, "They're here! They're here!"

Antonio had long since prepared a hiding-place for King Pelles and the Grand Vizier in case of just such an emergency. It lay under the floor of his own bedroom, so cunningly made and so close-fit that it was impossible to tell which boards might turn on hinges, or how to make them open, even if you knew. The two men were down there, motionless in the dark, well before the soldiers had reached the farmhouse; until the first fist hammered on the front door, the only sound they heard was the beating of each other's hearts.

The soldiers were polite, as soldiers go. They trampled no chickens, broke nothing in the house, and kept their hands off Antonio's fresh stock of winter ale, last of the season. Filling the kitchen with their size and the noise of their bodies, they treated Nerissa and Clara with truly remarkable courtesy; and their captain offered boiled sweets to the children clustered behind them, even responding with a good-humored chuckle when little Martine kicked his shin. Nor did they ask a single question concerning guests, or visitors, or new-hired laborers. Indeed, they were so amiable and considerate, by contrast with what the family had expected, that it took Nerissa a moment longer than it should have to realize that they had not been sent for the king and the Grand Vizier at all.

They had come for her husband.

"You see, ma'am," the Captain explained, as three of his men laid hold of Antonio, who had bolted too late for the back door, "the war just keeps going *on*. Wars, I mean. It's chaos, madness, really it is, ever since that idiot Pelles started the whole thing. Everyone turning against everyone else—whole regiments changing sides, generals selling out their own troops—mutiny over *there*, rebellion *here*, betrayal *that* way, corruption *this* way…and what's a poor soldier to do but follow his orders, no matter who's giving them today? And my orders all winter have been to round up every single warm body, which means every able, breathing male with both legs under him, and ship them straightaway to the front. And so that's what I do."

"The front," Nerissa said numbly. "Which front? Where is the battle?"

The Captain spread his arms in dramatic frustration. "Well, I don't know *which* front, do I? As many of them as there are these days? Somebody else tells me that when we get there. Very sorry to be snatching away your breadwinner, ma'am—'pon my soul, I am—but there it is, you see, and I put it to you, what's a poor soldier to do?" He turned irritably toward the soldiers struggling with Antonio. "*Hold* him, blast you! What's the bloody matter with you?"

In the moment that his gaze was not on her, Nerissa reached for her favorite butchering knife. Behind her, Clara's hand closed silently on a cleaver. Only Martine saw, and drew breath to scream more loudly than she ever had in her short life. But the Captain was never to know how close he was to death in that moment, because just then King Pelles walked alone into the kitchen.

He wore his royal robes, and his crown as well, which the children had never seen in all the time he had lived with them. Nodding pleasantly at the soldiers, he said to the Captain, "Let the man go. You will have a much richer prize to show your general than some poor farmer."

The Captain was dumb with amazement, turning all sorts of colors as he gaped at the king. His men, thoroughly astounded themselves, eased their grip on Antonio, who promptly burst free and headed for the door a second time. Some would have given chase, but King Pelles snapped out again, "Let him go!" and it was a king's order, prisoner or no. The men fell back.

"We weren't looking for you, sir," the Captain said, almost meekly. "We thought you were dead."

"Well, how much better for you that I'm not," the king replied briskly. "There will be a bonus involved, surely, and you certainly should be able to trade me to one side or another—possibly all of them, if you manage it right. I know all about managing," he added, in a somewhat different voice.

A young officer just behind the captain demanded, "Where is the Grand Vizier? He was seen with you on the road."

King Pelles shrugged lightly and sighed. "And that was where he died, on the way here, poor chap. I buried him myself." He turned back to the Captain. "Where are you supposed to take me, if I may ask?"

"To the new king," the Captain muttered in answer. "To King Phoebus."

"To my brother?" It was the king's turn to be astonished. "My brother is king now?"

"As of three days ago, anyway. When I left headquarters, he was." The Captain spread his arms wide again. "What do *I* know, these days?"

Even in his happiest moments on Nerissa and Antonio's farm, the king had never laughed as he laughed now, with a kind of delight no less rich for being ironic. "Well," he said finally. "Well, by all means, let us go to my brother. Let us go to King Phoebus, then—and on the way, perhaps we might talk about managing." He removed his crown, smiling as he handed it to the Captain. "There you are. Can't be king if you don't have a crown, you know."

Nerissa and Clara stood equally as stunned as the men who cautiously laid hands on the unresisting King Pelles; but the two youngest children set up a wail of angry protest when they began leading him away. They clung to his legs and wept, and neither the Captain nor their mother could part them from him. That took the king himself, who finally turned to put his arms around them, calling each by name, and saying, "Remember the stories. My stories will always be with you." He embraced the two women, saying to Clara in a low voice, "Take care of him, as he took care of me." Then he went away with the soldiers, eyes clear and a smile on his face.

If the Captain had looked back, he might well have seen the Grand Vizier, who came wandering into the kitchen a moment later, nursing a large bruise on his cheekbone, and another already forming on his jaw. Clara flew to him, as he said dazedly, "He hit me. I wouldn't let him surrender himself alone, so then he...Call them back—I'm his Vizier, he can't go without me. Call them back."

"Hush," Clara said, holding him. "Hush."

In time the long night of wars, rebellions, and retaliations of every sort slowly gave way at least to truces born of simple exhaustion, and reliable news became easier to come by, even for wary hillfolk like themselves. Thus the Grand Vizier was able to discover that the king's brother Phoebus had quite quickly been overthrown, very likely while the soldiers were still on the road with their captive. But further he could not go. He never found out what had become of King Pelles, and after some time he came to realize that he did not really want to.

"As long as we don't know anything certainly," he said to his family, "it is always possible that he might still be alive. Somewhere. I cannot speak for anyone else, but that is the only way I can live with his sacrifice."

"Perhaps sacrifice was the only way he could live," suggested his wife. The Grand Vizier turned to her in some surprise, and Clara smiled at him. "I heard him in the night too," she said.

"*I* hear his stories," young Martine said importantly. "I close my eyes when I get into bed, and he tells me a story."

"Yes," said the Grand Vizier softly. "Yes, he tells me stories too."

Vanishing

Jansen knew perfectly well that when Arl asked him to drive her to the clinic for her regular prenatal checkup, it meant that every single one of his daughter's usual rides was unavailable. She had already told him that it wouldn't be necessary for him to wait; that Elly, her mother, would be off work by the time the examination was done, and could bring her home. They drove down to Klamath Falls in silence, except for his stiffly-phrased questions about the health of the child she was carrying, and the state of her preparations for its arrival. Once he asked when she expected her husband back, but her reply was such a vague mumble that he missed the sense of it completely. Now and then he glanced sideways at her, but when she met his eyes with her own fierce, stubborn brown ones, he looked away.

When they parked at the clinic, he said, "I'll come in with you."

"You don't have to," Arl said. "I told you."

"Yeah, I know what you told me. But it's my grandson in there"—he pointed at her heavily rounded belly—"and I'm entitled to know how he's getting on. Let's go."

Arl did not move. "Dad, I really don't want you in there."

Jansen consciously kept his voice low and casual. "Tell you what, I don't care." He got out of the car, walked around to the passenger side, and opened the door. Arl sat where she was for a moment, giving him the *I just dare you* face he'd known since her childhood; but then she sighed abruptly and pushed herself to her feet, ignoring his offered hand, and plodded ahead of him to the clinic. Jansen followed closely, afraid that she might fall, the walkway being wet with recently melted snow. He would have taken her arm, but he knew better.

This one would rather die than forgive me. Gracie almost has, Elly might—someday—but Arl? Not ever.

In the clinic they sat one chair apart after she signed in. Jansen pretended to be browsing through *Sports Illustrated* until Arl disappeared with the Ob-Gyn nurse. He lowered the magazine to his lap then, and simply stared straight ahead at the gray world beyond the window. A sticky-faced child, running by, kicked his ankle and kept going, leaving its pursuing mother to apologize; a young couple sitting next to him argued in savagely-controlled whispers over the exact responsibility for a sexually-transmitted disease. Jansen froze it all out and asked himself for the hundredth useless time why he shouldn't sell the shop—or just close it and leave, the way people were walking away from their own homes these days. Walk away and put some daylight between himself and trouble. Hanging around sure as hell wasn't doing him any good, and alimony checks didn't care whether you mailed them from Dallas or down the block. Neither did Elly and the girls, not so you'd notice. At least in Dallas he could be warm while he was lonely. He let his eyelids drift shut as he tried to imagine being somewhere else, being *someone* else, and failed miserably in the attempt. Eyes closed, all the screw-ups and disappointments just seemed to press in closer than ever.

Shit, he thought. *All of it, all of it.* And then, *At least the little rugrat quit zooming around. That's something.*

The magazine slid from his relaxed fingers, but he didn't hear it hit the floor, and when he opened his eyes to reach down and pick it up he saw that he wasn't in the waiting room anymore.

He wasn't in Klamath Falls anymore, either. It was night, and he was on the Axel-Springer-Strasse. Instantly alert, he knew where he was, and never thought for a second that he was dreaming. Despite shock, beyond the uncertainties and anxieties of age, he knew that after more than forty-five years he was back at the Wall. The Wall that didn't exist anymore.

Kreuzberg district, West Berlin, between Checkpoint Charlie and the checkpoint at Heinrich-Heine-Strasse, just past where the Zimmerstrasse runs out and the barbed wire and barriers start zigzagging west...

There it was, directly before him, just *there*, lit by streetlamps—not the graffiti-covered reinforced concrete of the *Grenzmauer 75* that had been hammered to bits by the joyously triumphant "woodpeckers," East and West, when Germany was reunited, and the pieces sold off for souvenirs, but the crude first version he had patrolled in 1963, a gross lump haphazardly thrown together from iron supports, tangles of barbed wire, and dirty gray cement building blocks the East German workers had pasted in place with slaps of mortar no one bothered to smooth. Jansen said softly, "No." He put his fingers to his mouth, like a child, shaking his head hard enough that his neck hurt, hoping desperately to make the clinic waiting-room materialize around him; but the Wall stayed where it was, and so did he.

He was sitting, he realized, in the doorway of a building he did not want to think about; had, in fact, refused to think about for many years.

The old ironwork of the entrance was hard and cold against his shoulders as he pushed away from it and struggled to his feet.

Everything around him was familiar, his memory somehow fresher for so rarely having been examined. To his right the Wall angled sharply, blocking the road and continuing along the Kommandantenstrasse, while across from him he could see, just barely, the top of the eastern guard tower that looked down on the Death Strip, that deadly emptiness between the eastern inner fence and the Wall, where the VoPos and Russians would fire on anyone trying to make it across to West Berlin.

Jansen turned from the Wall and took a few hesitant paces along the street. Most of it had actually belonged to East Germany—the Wall had been built several meters inside the formal demarcation line between East and West, so in some places any West Berliner who stepped too close was in danger of being arrested by East German guards; but elsewhere, in the West Berlin suburbs and beyond, there had been small family gardens growing literally in the shadow of the Wall, and even a little fishing going on. Jansen had always admired the Germans' make-do adaptiveness.

Here in the city's urban heart, however, the buildings and shops and little businesses displayed a jumble of conditions, some still unrepaired nearly twenty years after the Allies had bombed and blasted their way into Berlin. Aside from the pooling glow of the streetlamps, Jansen could see no slightest sign of life. All the windows were dark, no smoke rose from any chimneys, and there was no one else in the street. The world was as hushed as though it had stopped between breaths. Beneath the unnaturally starless, cloudless black of the night sky there was not so much as a pigeon searching for crumbs, or a stray dog trotting freely.

Jansen moved on in the silence, confused and wary.

A few buildings past the Zimmerstrasse he couldn't take it any more. Feeling overwhelmed in the empty quiet, he knocked at the next door he came to, and waited, struggling to bring back what little German he had ever had. *Sprechen Sie Englische?*, of course. He'd used that one a lot, and found enough Germans who did to get by. But there was also *Wo bin ich?*—"where am I?" and *Was ist los?*—"what is happening?"— and *Bitte, ich bin verloren*—"please, I'm lost." They all seemed entirely appropriate to his situation.

When no one responded, he knocked again, harder; then tried the next door, with the same result, and then the three doors after that, each one in turn. Nothing. Yet he had no sense of the city being abandoned, evacuated; even the front window of the little shop where he and Harding had taken turns buying sausages and cheese for lunch was still crowded with its mysterious, wondrous wares. He saw his dark reflection in the shop window, and recognized his daily grizzled self: lean-faced and thin-mouthed, with deep-set, distant eyes...*no change there*, he thought: an old man caught, somehow, in this younger Jansen's place.

He might have graduated from knocking to shouting, except for what he discovered at the next intersection.

Ernie Hamblin—one of the traffic section MPs quartered with Jansen in the Andrews Barracks—had gotten a big laugh out of Jansen getting turned around and lost, twice, in his first week on duty, all because the two streets that met here had four different names, one for each direction of the compass. Jansen looked to the right, up the Kochstrasse, and saw nothing unusual when compared with his memory. Straight ahead—as Axel-Springer-Strasse became the Lindenstrasse—looked wrong, but in the darkness he couldn't quite make out why. To the left though, down the Oranienstrasse, there was nothing.

Literally nothing. No street, no houses, no streetlamps...only the same endless black as the sky, extending both outward and downward without the slightest hint of change. He walked as close to the road's sharp edge as he dared, trying to make sense of what he wasn't seeing, but could not. It wasn't a cliff face or a pit: it was simply emptiness, darkness vast and implacable, an utter end to the world, as if God had shrugged, shaken His head and walked away in the middle of the Third Day. The ground that should have been there was gone. The city that should have been built on it was gone and worse than gone, carved away with absolute, unhuman precision. Looking out and away at that edge, where it floated rootless in the black sky, Jansen could see buildings that had been neatly sliced in half, as though by some cosmic guillotine, their truncated interiors looking pitifully like opened dollhouses.

After a while Jansen realized that the edge had a shape; and that it matched, block for receding block, the cartoon lightning jag that was the corresponding section of the Wall. In the face of that understanding, rational thought was impossible. He turned and ran, and didn't notice anything at all until he stopped, out of breath and shaking, in front of the same doorway where he'd come back to this place.

It was open.

▲▼▲

Jansen stood for a long time at the foot of the narrow stair, looking up into the shadows and becoming more aware with every passing moment that the last thing he wanted to do was go even one step further, because that would commit himself irrevocably to whatever reality lay in wait at the top. When he did finally begin to climb, his body felt like the body of someone heavier than he, someone older, and even more weary.

The second floor stairs creaked on the sixth and eleventh steps, exactly as he remembered. All the interior doors were closed, blocking out the light from the street, so by the time he reached the fourth landing he was feeling his way, palms and fingers rasping over the rough burned wood and ragged wallpaper. The Berlin Brigade may have sworn by spotless uniforms and occupied fancy officers' quarters, but they took their OPs—their observation posts—largely as they found them. Jansen counted right-hand doorframes, stopping when he got to the third. His hand found the familiar shape of the brass doorknob, turned it, and eased the door open, grateful to see light again, even if it wasn't very strong this high above the streetlamps.

The first thing his eyes registered was the neatly folded khaki sweater on the one old armchair in the room. *Just where I left it...transferred to Stuttgart on half an hour's notice, never did get back here.* Then he saw the folding chair placed carefully on its handmade wooden riser, in front of the open window, and the crude signatures and battalion numbers and obscenities scratched into the walls, including six-inch high letters that said T HE "40" HIRED gUNS. Next to that was a blocky '50s-vintage German wall telephone, its cord dangling above a beaten-up oil heater. On the cheap metal table in the corner were a couple of paperbacks—Mickey Spillane, Erle Stanley Gardner—and some torn candy bar wrappers. *Harding,* he thought. *Three crap mysteries from the PX every week, like clockwork, along with half their Baby Ruths and Mounds. Good as gold or cigarettes when it came to bartering with the street kids.*

Jansen picked up the Spillane book, opened it, and realized that it was completely blank inside its lurid cover. He frowned, then dropped the empty book and lifted the wall telephone's absurdly light-blue handset. He held it to his ear, and the result was exactly what he expected: no dial tone, no static sputter—nothing but the dark silence of a long-dead line. He jiggled the hook, which was pointless but irresistible, and then hung up, a little harder than he perhaps needed to do.

After that he moved to the window, easing gently down into the folding chair positioned before it, because the dream-prop wooden riser under its legs was obviously just as flimsy as the one he'd teetered on so many times back in the real West Berlin. All he needed were his old binoculars and some wet-eared short-time 1st Lieutenant bitching at him and it would be like he'd never left. Except, of course, that there had been a couple of Germanys then, and as he looked out across the street he could see that the world was just as gone on the GDR side of the Wall as on this one. Ahead of him lay the Death Strip he had looked down upon every day for almost two years, the pale gravel raked over the flat ground between the crude outer Wall, topped with Y-shaped iron trees supporting a cloud of barbed wire, and the even cruder inner wall on the other side of the ramshackle watchtower. But the VoPo barracks he knew from before, the decaying and abandoned pre-War buildings that should have been there, were not; and as he looked from right to left, as far as he could see, sharp-edged blackness traced a line that paralleled the Wall itself. Spotting one or two of the old Russian T-62 tanks would have been a strange but distinct comfort right now, but of course there weren't any.

The telephone rang.

Jansen spun in his chair and the riser gave way beneath his shifting weight with a sharp crack, spilling him heavily to the ground. His back twisted, muscles on the lower left side spasming, and his right knee flared red with pain. *Fuck. Real enough to hurt like a son of a bitch!*

The phone rang a second time, then a third ring, a fourth. It took him that long to struggle back to his feet and hitch straight-legged over to it, his right knee still not trustworthy.

He put his hand on the receiver. It seemed to buzz like a rattlesnake in his fingers, and he held onto it for a second before he could make himself pick it up and put it to his ear.

He said, "Who is this?"

An instant of silence; then a sudden burst of surprised laughter. "So who should it be, *bulvan*?" The accent was Russian, as was the gruff timbre of the voice. Even the laughter was Russian. "Come to the window, so I can see you again. I am wondering if you are the Rawhide or the Two-Gun Kid."

Jansen said, "For God's sake, who are you? *Where* are you?"

"Come look. I will turn on light."

Jansen moved stiffly back to the window, the receiver cord just long enough to stretch. Stepping over the fallen chair, he put his free hand on the windowsill and leaned down to look out. A hundred yards away, toward the far side of the Death Strip, the lights inside the East German guard tower were blinking on and off. As he watched, the pattern stopped and the lights stayed on, allowing him to see a bundled-up figure pointing one forefinger at him, sighting along it like a pistol.

Into the handset, Jansen said, "You?"

"*Garazhi*, Rawhide. Me. So good to see you again." The distant figure executed a clumsy bow.

"Why are you calling me that?" Jansen's mouth was so dry it pained him.

The chuckle came through the receiver again. "The glorious Soviet army was not nearly as efficient as your leaders liked to believe. Knew only the names of your officers, no one else. But from first day we looked across at each other, I had to call you *something*. I was learning English from comic books—very big on black market, you see, the westerns with horses and guns and silly hats, so I called you *Rawhide Kid* and that short man—"

"Roscoe Harding."

"Really? For us he was *Two-Gun Kid*, and your mostly night fellows, *Kid Colt* and *Tex Hopalong*. Very satisfying, very shoot-'em-up. We had many such jokes."

"You don't want to know what we called you."

Another laugh. "Possibly not. But what name should I give you now, Rawhide? We are both older, I see, and it does not suit."

"My name's Jansen. Henry Jansen. Listen, you, whatever your name is—"

"Leonid," said the voice in his ear. "Leonid Leonidovich Nikolai Gavrilenko."

"That's a mouthful."

"True. But we are such old acquaintances, you must call me *Lyonya*. Or not, as you prefer. I do not presume." He paused, then said, "Welcome back to the Wall, my friend Jansen. Henry."

"Look behind you." Jansen kept his voice deliberately flat, but he could feel himself struggling not to panic. "This place isn't real."

"*Da, temnyi*. The darkness. I have seen."

Jansen said, "What the hell is going on? I can't be here. I was in a clinic waiting room with my daughter. She's seven months pregnant, and her husband's run off somewhere. She'll need me." Even as he spoke the words, he tasted their untruth in the back of his mouth. Arl had never had a chance to need him, and wouldn't know how to begin now, even if he wasn't who he was. But the Russian was impressed, or sounded so.

"Lucky man, Henry. I congratulate you, to have someone needing you. A good life, then? Since we saw each other last?"

"No," Jansen said. "Not so good. But I have to get back to it right now. Arl—my daughter—she won't know where I am. Hell, *I* don't know where I am."

"That is, I think, what we should be finding out. We put our thinking caps on, you and I." A certain growling bemusement had entered the Russian's voice. "Do Americans still say that? It cannot be accident, this place. Something is happening to us, *something* has brought us here. Have looked, but seen no one but you. So I think now, yes, after all, we must meet in person, do you not agree? At last, meet. With thinking caps."

As absolutely as Jansen wanted to leave the room, the deep suspicion that had been born in him here—never to abate fully—had its own hold. "I'm not sure that's a good idea, *tovarich.*"

"No one is using that word anymore." Gavrilenko's voice was flat, without rancor or any sort of nostalgia. "Except the comedians. A comedy word now. Listen, Jansen, we don't give it up so fast! It is not good to be in this place alone, surely, whatever it is. That is why I called you. Old place, old face from old place, old time—this cannot be coincidence."

Jansen frowned. "Maybe, maybe not. But that's another thing. How did you know this number? Nobody was supposed to have it but the commander and the NCOIC. They didn't even give it to us! Some kraut spy sneak it out to you? Was that another one of the *jokes?*"

"You are not thinking, Henry."

"Fuck you, Gavrilenko. Why should I trust a single goddamn thing you say? I want to go home!"

There was a long silence.

He threw the receiver down, grabbed the empty window frame with both hands and stuck his head out into the night. "Do you hear me, you fucking Russian asshole? I want to go home! *I have to go home!*"

He saw the woman then, entering the Death Strip from somewhere just beyond and to the right of the watchtower. She walked quickly, looking from side to side, shoulders tense, head forward. She wore a faded light-brown coat, a transparent kerchief over her hair, and flat, rundown shoes. In one hand she carried what looked like a small duffel bag.

Oh God, oh no, Jansen thought. *Not this, not this, not again.*

The Russian had seen her too. Even at this distance Jansen clearly heard him shouting in Russian, and then in German. But she kept coming on, and suddenly Jansen understood that she was a ghost. He had never seen one before, but there was no doubt in his mind.

As the woman came even with Gavrilenko's tower she began to run, racing toward the Wall. Halfway there a battery of searchlights came on, so bright they were blinding to Jansen's dark-adjusted eyes. *Automatic, self-activated, never did figure where the trip must be. Maybe they moved it around, be just like them...*

And then the firing started.

He couldn't tell where it was coming from: there were no snipers shooting from jeeps or gun-trucks, and in the guard tower there was only the Russian—yelling and screaming, yes, but without any weapon in his hands. Yet real bullets were somehow crackling and spitting all around the woman's churning legs, kicking up little spouts in the neatly-raked gravel like pettish children scuffling their feet. It wasn't happening exactly as it had happened, though. Back then there had been alarms, VoPos and West Berliners shouting—Harding too, right in Jansen's ear—dogs barking, engines revving, the mixed sounds of panic and hope and adrenaline-spiked fear. Here, after Gavrilenko stopped shouting, there was only the spattering echo of gunfire as the woman dodged left and right between the concrete obstacles. *I couldn't have done anything.*

I couldn't!

The two paired hooks of a ship's ladder sailed over the Wall between two of the iron Ys, under the barbed wire, catching among the irregular concrete blocks and mortar. On the other side, out of his sight, the ghost pulled the ladder taut—Jansen could see the hooks shift, almost coming loose before catching. The woman climbed rapidly: in another moment her head topped the Wall, and she pulled a pair of clippers from her waistband and swiftly opened a gap in the barbed wire barrier. Then she braced herself with her hands and looked directly into Jansen's eyes.

She was twenty-three, or so he'd been told, though at the time he had thought she looked older. Now she seemed incredibly young to him, younger than Arl, even, but her plain little face was as gray as the Wall, and her eyes were an inexpressive pale-blue. They were not in the least accusatory or reproachful, but once they had hold of Jansen, he could not look away. He wanted to speak, to explain, to apologize, but that was impossible. The nameless dead woman held him with eyes that neither glittered nor burned, nor even judged him, but would not let go. Jansen stood as motionless as she, squeezing the window frame so hard that he lost feeling in his fingers.

Then a single shot cracked his heart and the woman was suddenly slammed forward, her body twisting so that she fell across the top of the Wall, her left foot kicking one of the ladder hooks loose. She rolled partway onto her side, lifting her head for a moment, and again he saw her eyes. When they finally closed and freed him, he began to cry silently.

How long he stood weeping, he couldn't say. Gavrilenko did not call out to him across the gap, and there were no other sounds anywhere in the world. Jansen was still staring at the body on the Wall when—exactly as though a movie were being run in reverse—the dead woman sat up, crawled backwards to the ladder, reattached the dangling hook, and began descending as she had come. This time she did not look at him at all, and as her head dropped almost out of view the barbed wire knitted itself together.

He watched for a time, but she did not reappear.

The receiver felt as heavy as a barbell when he finally lifted the telephone. He could hear Gavrilenko breathing hoarsely on the line, waiting for him. "The Friedrichstrasse," Jansen said. "Checkpoint Charlie. I'll meet you there."

▲▼▲

It had never taken Specialist 4 Henry Jansen—20 years old, of the 385th Military Police Battalion, specially attached to the 287th Military Police Company—more than eight minutes to cover the four and a half blocks from the Axel-Springer-Strasse observation post to Checkpoint Charlie. The 66-year-old Jansen, kidnapped by the past and all but completely disoriented, took longer, partly because of his knee, but mostly due to mounting fear and bewilderment. The guillotine dark was constantly visible over the Wall that flanked him on his right, and to his left it waited at the end of every side street. Passing the t-intersections he couldn't help but stop and stare.

He consciously attempted to hold his shoulders as straight and swaggering as those of that young MP from Wurtsboro, but despite the effort his head kept lowering between his shoulders, like a bull trying to catch up with the dancing *banderilleros,* jabbing their maddening darts into him from all sides. The further he went into this unreal slice of an empty Berlin, the deeper the *banderillos* seemed to drive into his weary spirit.

I couldn't have helped her. I couldn't have helped, I couldn't... She lay there two hours, she bled to death right in front of me, and there wasn't anything I could do. Harding wouldn't let me go to her, anyway, and he outranked me.

But that thought didn't ease him, no more than it ever had. Why should he expect it to help now, in this false place and timeless time, this cage of memories?

By the time he reached Checkpoint Charlie he was sweating coldly, though not from exertion.

The checkpoint was a long, low shack set in the middle of the Friedrichstrasse, with a barrier of stacked sandbags arrayed facing the "Worker and Farmer Paradise" gate on the East German side. Just past the shack he could see the *imbiss* stand where he and his buddies had grabbed coffee, sodas, and sandwiches while on duty, and also the familiar hulk of a massive apartment building, abandoned and empty both then and now.

Someone was standing at the checkpoint, thoughtfully studying the guard shack, but it was not Gavrilenko. Jansen could tell that even from a distance. This stranger was a tall man with thinning blonde hair—probably American, to judge by his neat but casual dress—who looked to be in his middle to late 40s. When the man turned and caught sight of Jansen he looked first utterly astonished, and then profoundly grateful to see another human being. He hurried forward, actually laughing with relief. "Well, thank *God*. I'd just about come to believe I was the only living creature in Berlin! Glad to see there's two of us."

He had the faintest of German accents, hiding shyly under the broad, flat vowels of the Midwest. When he got to Jansen he put out a hand, which Jansen took somewhat cautiously.

"Hi," the tall man said. "My name's Ben. Ben Richter."

"I'm Henry Jansen." He let go of Richter's hand. "This isn't Berlin, though. It's not anywhere."

"No," the stranger agreed. "But it's not a dream, either. I know it's not a dream." He peered closely and anxiously into Jansen's face. "Do you have *any* idea what's happened to us?"

"Don't fall asleep in a Planned Parenthood clinic, I'll tell you that much," Jansen said. "That's where I was."

"I was trying *not* to fall asleep," Richter answered. "I was driving home from a business meeting, and my eyelids kept dropping shut. Just a few seconds at a time, but it's terrifying, the way your head suddenly snaps awake, and you *know* you're just about to crash into someone. Couldn't figure it out. I wasn't tired when I started out, got plenty of rest the night before. Weird." He seemed suddenly alarmed. "Do you think my car just went on, with no driver?"

Jansen felt his face grow cold, almost numb. "Couldn't tell you." After a pause, he added, "Ben, was it?"

"Actually, it's Bernd, but everyone's always called me Ben, since I started school. Kids just decide, don't they?"

Jansen said, "I knew somebody named Richter when I was in junior high. You got any relatives in Wurtsboro, New York?"

The tall man laughed slightly. "I don't know if I've got any relatives *anywhere*. Not in the States, for sure."

"Forget it. Guess I'm just looking for connections."

Richter grinned. "Not exactly surprising, given the circumstances."

"We're not alone," Jansen told him. "There's at least one more of us, anyway, a Russian. Name's Gavrilenko. We spotted each other across the Wall. He was supposed to meet me here—I don't know what's keeping him." After a moment, he added, "Don't know how *he* got here; I mean, if he was asleep or not."

Richter asked hesitantly, "Did you and your friend—uh, the Russian—did you have any luck figuring this out?"

Jansen thought of the running dead woman, and the barbed wire mending itself. Even now some things were too crazy for him to say straight out.

"It has to be something to do with the Wall. Right? Has to. I mean, it's what's *here*." He watched for a reaction, but saw none. "And Gavrilenko and me, we were both on the Wall a couple of years after it went up. Nineteen sixty-three, sixty-four—kids, both of us. He was a guard over there, I was an MP over here. Never got above Specialist 4, so I did some of everything. Pulled patrol, hauling drunk GIs out of bars, clubs, like that. A little checkpoint duty right here"—he gestured around him—"but mostly I was in an observation post over on the Axel-Springer-Strasse. That's how we knew each other back then, two strangers waving across the Wall in the mornings." He realized that he was now talking much too fast, and consciously slowed his speech. "Long ago, all that crap. You wouldn't be interested—you weren't even born then."

"Yes, I was," Richter said quietly. He said nothing more for a few moments, studying Jansen out of chestnut-brown eyes set in an angular, thoughtful face. "There's a Marriott there now, you know, at that corner. In the real world, I mean. Right where the Wall was."

"How do you know that?"

"I've stayed there. My wife's German, so we visit. And I've got a little business going." He looked around slowly, then shrugged. "Weird. Only seen it like this in pictures. Maybe you can tell me about it?"

Jansen blinked. "Tell you about *what?*"

"Berlin in those days. When you were a kid MP—probably a couple of years out of high school, right?" He did not wait for Jansen's answering nod. "See, I was born in Berlin, but I wasn't raised here. Didn't come back until the Wall fell in eighty-nine—just felt I had to, somehow—and that's how I met Annaliese." The smile was simultaneously proud and tender. "We live in St. Paul. Three boys, a girl, and an Irish setter. I mean, how bourgeois American can you get?"

"Wouldn't know," Jansen said. "Wish I knew what's keeping Gavrilenko."

"Listen, let's sit down somewhere, okay? While we wait for your Russian friend."

Richter walked around the guard shack and hoisted himself up onto the top row of sandbags. Jansen followed him, and he and Richter sat

with their legs dangling, looking straight ahead, both of them unconsciously kicking their heels against the sandbags' brown canvas. The
tall man was the first to speak. "Hard to believe these were for real. Not
exactly a lot of protection."

"Better than nothing," Jansen said. "I wasn't in the Army then, but in
October of '61, a few months after the Wall went up, there was an all-day
standoff right here between our guys—Fortieth Armor, Sixth Infantry—
and about thirty Russian tanks. See, we were set to show them that we
could still drive anywhere we wanted in the GDR, and they were going
to show *us* that those days were *over*. And you better believe there were
dogfaces crouching behind these same sandbags, locked and loaded and
ready to start World War Three, just say the word. I saw the pictures in
the Wurtsboro paper."

Richter shrugged. "I've read about the standoff. Seems a little ridiculous, frankly. Awful lot of chestbeating for something that didn't even
last a day."

"True. But it *could* have been worse. Ask me, the Russkies came
out on top, any way you slice it—from that point on they handed out a
lot of shit here, every crossing, and it may have been small shit, but we
couldn't give it back since we had orders to play nice. Well...not all of
them. That's not fair. Mainly it was the generals who were trouble, the
big ones who gave the orders and made asses of themselves when they'd
come into West Berlin. The men were okay. Russkies, Krauts, they were
okay. Even some of the VoPos."

"Ah. The *Volkspolizei.*"

"Just like us MPs, only with more training and a *lot* more fire-
power." Jansen chuckled in his throat. "We had a big snowball fight with
a bunch of VoPos one time." He paused, reflecting. "Couldn't make a
decent snowball for shit, most of them. Always wondered about that."

Richter cocked his head slightly to the side, considering Jansen med-
itatively. "So you actually had fun, too. It wasn't all confrontations with
tanks and going into bars after drunken soldiers."

"Trick was to keep from staying *in* the bars *with* the drunken soldiers," Jansen told him. "The city was booming with bars, with clubs,
a couple new ones opening every week. Some you'd go to for the beer,
some for the great music—one time I heard Nat King Cole and Les Paul
and Mary Ford on the same night. Two-buck tickets! Some places, you'd
take a young lady, some others you'd go to *find* a young lady. Yeah, we
had a lot of fun in Berlin. Nineteen, twenty-year-old kids with guns and
money, never been away from home before, never drunk anything stronger than Pabst? We had fun."

Jansen studied Richter. The man's expression was an odd mixture of wistfulness and something deeper, something impatient beyond his interest in Jansen's surfacing memories. For his part, Jansen had not talked this much to anyone in a very long while, and he'd never shared these stories, not even with Elly or the kids. Sharing would have meant deliberately remembering everything, which even the drinking couldn't deal with. Here, though, that self-imposed restriction was as pointless as the rest of it.

"There was a game we used to play," he said. "Worked best in the winter too, only we didn't need snow for this one, we needed ice." He pointed ahead of them, toward a broad white line painted on the ground. "That's the border, near as anybody could figure. Ground got good and icy, you'd take a run and throw yourself down, and *slide*, like you're sliding into a base, only you're sliding right into the GDR." He laughed outright at the memory. "Then you'd get up and run right back across the line, safe in the good old American Sector. The Krauts used to watch us and just laugh themselves silly."

Richter said musingly, almost to himself, "All those good times... and all the things going on just under the surface." Jansen frowned, not understanding. Richter went on. "More than a hundred thousand people tried to escape into West Berlin from East Germany in the twenty-eight years the Wall sealed it off. Did you know that, Henry?"

"Knew it was a lot," Jansen said. "Didn't know it was that many—thought the big rush was all before the Wall."

"It was. But another hundred thousand, afterwards. Most went to jail. Maybe five thousand made it through. And a lot died. But you were here. You know that."

Her dark hair, her pale-blue eyes, the little sound she made at the last, dying...

"Yeah. I do."

Richter had turned away, looking toward the point where the blackness slashed down forever on the East German apartment buildings. But his voice was clear and precise as he said, "Different organizations have different estimates. When the Wall fell, when Germany was reunited, the East German state wasn't in any hurry to release records that made them look like the killers they were. We've had to build up a database one case at a time, literally. One escape attempt at a time. One body at a time. Counting the heart attacks, the wounds that turned fatal on the other side of the Wall, the ones who just disappeared forever, the babies smothered trying to keep them quiet. Officially—you check the encyclopedia articles, the tourist handouts—only 136 people died. But we're figuring twelve hundred, minimum. Not that we'll ever be able to prove half of them." His voice was calm and almost expressionless, utterly dispassionate.

"*We,*" Jansen said. "Who's *we?*"

Richter laughed suddenly, warmly, with a touch of embarrassment as faint as his accent. "I'm sorry. I forget not everyone is as obsessed with this as I am. *We* is the August 13 Society—I do fundraising for them in the States, and volunteer work for them when I'm here...I mean, *there.* Real Berlin. We're actually trying to document every case where people died trying to cross, not just the Wall, but the entire East-West border— to memorialize them, make them real for everybody. So they won't be forgotten again."

Jansen nodded, but did not respond.

Richter said presently, "What I can't figure out is the connection between all three of us—you and me and our absent Russian. Before you showed up I thought I'd driven into a rail, that maybe I was dead and this was Hell; or else maybe I'd stroked out and was in a coma somewhere while my imagination played really bad games with me. But those two possibilities would exclude you, so cross them off the whiteboard...which leaves nothing. I've never before met either one of you, and you were both long gone from Berlin by the time I came back. So what's the link?"

"What's if it's just...I don't know, random. Coincidence."

"I don't buy that. I'm a mathematician, Henry. Anyway I *was* a math-ematician, before I put together my little software company. This place may be impossible, but the odds against a common pattern when two of the three of us have an obvious connection? Maybe not totally impos-sible...let's just say *highly* unlikely."

Jansen said, "We sort of have the Wall in common. But it isn't the same. You obviously know a lot about it, what with this Society thing you do. But it's not like you ever served here. You didn't live with it every day, like us. You weren't ever *on* the Wall—"

"No," Richter agreed. "I wasn't."

To Jansen's eye, Richter seemed suddenly tense and hesitant, like someone trying to avoid making up his mind.

"Well," Jansen spoke up. "What is it? You going to shoot that bird or let it fly?"

The tall man nodded. "Interesting choice of words."

"My stupid mouth is half the reason I'm divorced. What'd I say this time?"

Richter hopped off the sandbags and walked a few steps before answering. When he did, his voice was dry and tight. "My mother was a Berliner."

"Yeah, you said you were born here. So?"

"*East* Berlin, Henry. She died on the Wall."

Jansen wanted to run again, like before, but his legs wouldn't get him down off the barrier. If he couldn't run, maybe he could scream? *Not your hell, maybe, you poor bastard. Definitely mine.*

When he finally found words, they surprised him. "You don't sound like you're sure."

Richter turned and looked at him oddly. Jansen wondered if something unheard in his voice had given him away. He was about to speak again when the tall man finally answered.

"The records are all scrambled—when there are records at all—and they mostly don't have names in them, just scraps of facts and description. An address here, an occupation there, a set of initials, shorthand reports of a thousand disconnected, meaningless conversations...it's a jigsaw puzzle with most of the pieces missing. I've been digging through the archives for a long time, learning how to read what's there *and* what's been omitted." His mouth tightened. "She died on the Wall, all right. The pieces of the picture are there."

"But you aren't certain."

"If you're asking me whether I have the *Stasi*-stamped file folder to prove it, no." Bitterness colored Richter's voice, and something Jansen couldn't begin to put a name to. He watched as the tall man stared fiercely at the ragged fringe of East German buildings that were visible from here.

"I never knew her," Richter continued. "My step-parents were friends with my mother, and they brought me with them when they got out of East Germany in 1960. It was her idea. She wasn't well—pregnancy and childbirth had been rough—and anyway she knew it would be easier for them, because they'd had a baby who died and they still had the right papers. The idea was that my mother would make it out on her own when she got better, and we'd all be in America together." His faint smile was small and young. "Only they built the Wall, and things didn't work out. She never showed up. One letter made it: nothing else. The Bruckners raised me on their own, in Wisconsin. They were good people. I can't complain."

"What about your father? Where the hell was he?" Unsummoned, there was a vision of Arl in Jansen's head, crying into Elly's arms because Larry had left without so much as a note two days after the little pink dot on the dipstick changed everything.

"Apparently I'm the by-product of a little too much Pilsner at a college party. She never told anyone his name, not even the Bruckners, not even with all the pressure of being nineteen and pregnant in a police state where social pressure favored abortion. All I know about *der fehlende vater* is that he must have been tall and blonde, because according to my step-parents nobody in my mother's family was. It had to come from somewhere."

The woman at the Wall. Got to be his mother. Goddamit, goddamit, tell him what you saw, you stupid fucking coward...but maybe I don't have to. Maybe, maybe if I just shut up he'll talk about something else.

Where the hell's Gavrilenko?

At the same moment, Richter said "Enough with my sob story. I seriously don't think your Russian's coming. Let's go find him." He started off without looking back.

"Hold up," Jansen said, easing down off the sandbags. His knee had stiffened while he was sitting. "Old guy, here. Anyway, maybe we shouldn't be in such a hurry."

Richter stopped and looked at him quizzically. "Why not?"

Tell him you saw his mother. Tell him you saw her die. Twice.

"No reason." Jansen stared into Richter's eyes. How could he have missed how much they looked like hers? "It's just...what if we take a different route than he does, coming here, and we miss each other?"

"Then we'll come back. Anyway, there's not a whole lot of *there* over there. Come on," Richter said, and this time his grin was a young boy's. "It's not icy, but I bet we can imagine we're sliding across the line."

▲▼▲

The Wall on this side ran behind houses that looked like an abandoned stage or movie set: if the west side looked as though every inhabitant had suddenly left town, but might return at any second, here the air of a forced and permanent evacuation was glaringly inescapable. Doors and windows were not merely boarded over, but bricked up as well; many buildings had been demolished, and the rubble—often topped with barbed wire—left in place, to block any passage to the Wall. There were warnings, genuine or not, of minefields—Richter translated the signs for Jansen—and the whole effect was of desertion and neglect. The two men walked close together, automatically speaking in low voices and moving at a pace tailored to accommodate Jansen's slower steps.

Chickenshit. You could walk faster. You're just afraid of getting there.

Jansen asked presently, "You got into it, this August thing, because of your mom?" But Richter shook his head.

"Not exactly, not the way you mean. My step-parents wanted me to grow up to be a good American, so I was assimilated as hell. They told me about my mom—her name was Zinzi, by the way—but not much else, not until I was older. I definitely had the American habit of not thinking about the past very much, and certainly not some faraway European past that might as well have been in an old library book, as far as I was concerned. My head was all forward, all the time. I went to a good college, studied math and computer programming, got naturalized, taught for a while. I was an assistant professor of Mathematics at the University of Wisconsin when I came to Berlin to drink dark beer and knock down my own piece of the Wall and wound up meeting Annaliese instead. Hah. Hey, I never asked—you married?"

"Already told you I was divorced. Twice, actually."

"Oh. Sorry."

"Don't be. Just the ways things are." Jansen felt his heart thudding harder in his chest. "My first ex used to say I was a coconut in a world of bananas. I can hurt people just bumping into them."

"Colorful. Any kids?"

"Two daughters. They hate my guts too, but the pregnant one hates me worse. So there's a bright spot."

Richter stopped walking and turned to face Jansen. "Even if things righteously suck with your kids, I'm sure you remember when they were little. So maybe you'll get this. When Jacob—my son—when Jacob turned six months old, the same age I was when I was brought to America...I remember, I looked down at him in my arms, burping bubbles and trying to eat my shirt buttons, and I tried to imagine what Zinzi Richter would have said if she could have seen him, her first grandchild. And I thought how lucky I was to be able to tell him everything my step-parents had told me about her, even if it wasn't all that much. Then I started thinking about all the people who wouldn't ever know what happened to their grandparents or their parents, and I'd read about the August 13 Society, and one thing led to another. I'd started up my company by then—we do case management software for big legal firms—and our code was pretty useful for what the Society does, so I had an in. And here I am." He smiled crookedly, spreading his hands.

"Makes sense," Jansen said.

"You should tell Jacob that. He thinks I'm crazy. My mother really is just a page in a scrapbook to him. He's going to be fifteen next June, and what *he* likes about coming over here is that he's tall enough now to get away with telling the local girls he's really seventeen."

They started on again, both of them unconsciously keeping to the right side of the road, away from the darkness they could see on the other side of the decayed and empty buildings. To Jansen it definitely seemed closer here, which bothered him. He thought of the suddenly open door back on the Axel-Springer-Strasse, and the words *herding us* passed through his mind.

Richter said, "You can tell I'm nervous, because I'm talking too much."

That surprised Jansen. "You don't *act* nervous."

"Quaking in my Nikes. Not the slightest sign of danger since I showed up here, but this place is really starting to creep me out. Hence the talking."

"So talk," Jansen said firmly. "Tell me more about your kids."

"I'd rather listen. Tell me what you do."

Jansen grunted, waved the question away.

"No, seriously."

"Nothing important. I remodel stuff. Kitchens and bathrooms, mostly. One-man gang, hire extra help when I have to. Been doing it more or less since I left the Army."

"That's good work," Richter said. "You do your job, and then when you're finished, when you look at what you've done, you get to see that you've made something better, made it work, made it beautiful. There's pride in that. You're a lucky man."

"Gavrilenko called me that too," Jansen said slowly. "I don't think I'm so fucking lucky." Richter regarded him curiously. Jansen said, "I'm good with my hands, with wood and tile and plastic piping, but that's it. Sinks and toilets, cabinets and countertops? Sure. People? Forget it. My exes, my kids, they're all right about me. Since I got back from Germany, I can't think of one damn thing that's gone right, except work. Not one damn thing in forty years."

Richter said, "It's the Wall." Jansen looked up in surprise. "People I work with—former refugees, their families—they tell a story that one guy who didn't make it over put a curse on the Wall with his dying breath. He made it so even if you escape, even with the Wall down and gone, there's still a curse that follows you in your life. Because you got out and he didn't."

Jansen thought *nobody ever gets out*. But what he said was, "No offense, but that's bullshit. Anyway, I didn't have anything to escape from. I did my time, got rotated to Stuttgart and then stateside. Period."

They walked a little way further in silence before Richter continued. "Maybe. But people tell stories like that because they mean something. And you said yourself that your troubles started here. It wasn't all snowball fights, Henry."

"Crap. I was a kid."

"Which makes it better how?" Richter's tone had shifted, the hint of impatience becoming more pronounced. "Jesus Christ, man, you *know* I've been through the East German records fifty-seven times. I'm the guy with the damn database. So why are you dancing with me like this? Even on the official record there are at least three or four deaths that correlate with the time you must have been here. Fechter, he's the most famous, but there were others. And at least twenty, thirty more the Society is researching. Are you telling me none of that ever touched you, that you never saw anything? If not, then why the hell are you here? *What's our connection?*"

Jansen was shaking his head before Richter was halfway finished. "That's not it! It *can't* be it."

"*What* can't be it?"

Jansen started to turn away, but Richter squared off on him. The tall man's hands came down on Jansen's shoulders, and they were bigger hands than Jansen had noticed. He said nothing. He only waited.

Oh, God.

Jansen said tonelessly, "You can't put this on me."

"I didn't," Richter answered. "But you can take it off."

"Shit!" For just a moment Jansen couldn't breathe.

Richter's eyes were hot behind a face suddenly flattened into an unyielding mask. "I'm not an idiot. You've been wanting to tell me something since we were back at the sandbags. Spill."

"I—I don't know who it was. Just some girl, some woman...I never knew her name." Jansen heard the sirens and shouting, the gunfire; only by Richter's lack of reaction did he understand that the blaring cacophony was all in his head. "But I'll never forget what happened. Fuck, I still dream it."

Richter nodded him on.

"It was 1963. I was almost out, just screwing around on duty in the observation post, joking with Harding about making a midnight run to clip a little barbed wire off as a souvenir, something to take home with me. Then his eyes went all spooky and he said 'Fuck me Lord,' just like that, quiet as if we were in a library...and I saw what he was seeing. This woman—"

"Wait a sec. That was the Axel-Springer-Strasse OP?"

Jansen nodded.

Richter bored in. "July or November?"

"July. I wasn't here in November."

"Tell me what she looked like."

Jansen felt himself snapping. "Don't make me do this!"

"*Tell* me."

"You have to hear me say it? It was your mother! Of *course* it was your mother. She had your goddamn eyes, you bastard, and she came out of nowhere on the far side of the Death Strip, and maybe she would have made it if she were a little faster, or maybe she wouldn't, I don't know, I only know it was like they were *playing* with her, like they could have cut her down at any time, but they waited until she was half-way over the top. Then somebody took her out with a single shot and she lay there on top of the wall for two hours, *two fucking hours*, bleeding out, never making a sound until the end, and the whole time I...the whole time..."

He turned his head, unable to bear looking into Richter's face.

"I wanted to go to her. Harding wouldn't let me. I did call the NCOIC and scream for a doctor, for help, for somebody, but nobody came. Nobody came. It was just me and Harding, and he wouldn't look. But for the whole two hours I did. I saw her die."

Richter's hands closed once, briefly. They seemed to sink past flesh and muscle to leave their fingerprints in his bones; yet, strangely, Jansen felt no pain at all. When Richter let go and lifted them away, something iron went with them that Jansen never tried to name.

"Yes," Richter said without expression. "I thought that might have been the one." He turned away.

"That's not all," Jansen said to the tall man's stiffened back.

Richter slowed down, but didn't stop.

"Here's the thing." Jansen had to raise his voice as the other man moved away. "You fell asleep in your car, and you woke up here in this theater set, but you didn't get to see the play. Me, I had to watch it all over again. So did Gavrilenko, from his guard tower. The run, the bullets, her death on top of the Wall. Everything. Do you hear me? *I saw your mother die all over again*...and when it was over I saw her climb back down, just like she was getting ready for another show. *That's* why Gavrilenko and I were supposed to meet. I don't know why I'm here, I swear to God I don't, but whatever I've done wrong in my life I can't possibly deserve having to see that again—and you don't want to see it either. Trust me on that!"

Richter stood still and said nothing for what felt to Jansen like a very long time, but which was certainly only seconds. Then he heard Zinzi Richter's son say, simply, "Huh," and had to hurry to catch up with the tall man as he walked, with quickening strides, toward the darkness.

▲▼▲

The guard tower had looked considerably more impressive and ominous from a dingy room in a crumbling apartment house across from the Wall than it did at close range. At once splintery-new and yet already rickety, it had far more of an agricultural air than a military one, looking somewhere between a flattened silo and a hayloft. Jansen felt that there should have been a weathervane on its squared-off roof.

Richter stopped in his tracks so suddenly that Jansen bumped into his back before he could halt himself. At the foot of the tower stairs stood the ghost of Zinzi Richter.

Ashen, slender, with dark auburn hair limp against her skull, as though with sweat, she paid absolutely no attention either to Jansen or to her staring son. All her concentration was directed up the single flight of rusted metal steps to the doorway where a big old man stood hugging himself as he rocked erratically against the doorframe. Zinzi Richter made no attempt to go up to him, but simply stood waiting at the foot of the stair.

"That's her," Richter whispered. "The Bruckners had one photo. Oh my God."

As though she had put on her Sunday best for the occasion, the ghost looked as clear and solid as any human being whose heart still jumped in the cage of her ribs, still ordered blood out to her fingertips and back through her throat and her thighs. Richter took a step toward her, but this time it was Jansen's hand clamping hard on his arm. Jansen said softly, "Wait. She's here for *him*."

Through binoculars—the closest acquaintance he had ever had with Leonid Leonidovich Gavrilenko over the Wall—Jansen had always seen the Russian as bull-featured and powerfully built, with an undomesticated mass of heavy black hair that stood up crazily on either side of his broad, high-boned face when he pulled off his knit woolen cap. The man he saw now had none of that force, nothing of that implicit swagger: he only slumped against the doorframe, his lips moving as though in prayer. Jansen thought, *He's old;* and then, *No, I'm old, and I don't look like that. What's happened to him?*

"That's why he didn't come to the checkpoint. He can't come down," Jansen said to Richter. "*She's* there, and he's afraid of her."

Richter ignored him. He pulled away from Jansen's grip and approached the ghost of Zinzi Richter, plainly trying not to run to her. He said, "Mother, it's me, I'm your son. I'm Bernd." He tried to take her hands in his, but she did not move, or look at him, or respond in any way. She stayed where she was, looking up the stair at Gavrilenko.

Jansen said, "Ben." A strange calmness was upon him, as though for the first time in his life he actually knew what to do. He said, "Ben, we have to go up there."

Richter turned to him, so determinedly *not* crying that Jansen felt tears starting in his own eyes. "I can touch her—I didn't know you could touch ghosts. But she doesn't see me, she doesn't even know I'm here. I don't understand."

"She's waiting for Gavrilenko," Jansen said. "She'll wait forever, if she has to. You want to find out what all this is about, we have to bring him to her. Now."

The last word snapped out in a tone that surprised him; he hardly recognized his own voice. But it seemed to help Ben, who managed to get hold of himself and follow Jansen as the older man started up the guard tower stairs. *Well, I did make it to corporal before it was all over. Might have made sergeant if I'd stayed in. Things I could have been.* Jansen looked back once at the ghost. She had not stirred at all from her position, nor changed the direction of her gaze. *Holy shit, the Russian's treed, is what it is. She's got him treed.* He could not control a swift shiver.

Near the top of the stair he looked away from the tower and saw the darkness closing in, pitilessly paring away everything that was not itself.

The guardroom door was open. Gavrilenko backed away as Jansen and Richter came in, still seemingly holding himself together with both arms. In a rough, throaty grumble, a ghost itself of the striding peasant vigor Jansen had heard over the phone, the Russian said, "Unavoidably detained, Rawhide. Trouble on the range, I am afraid."

"You have to come down to her, Gavrilenko," Jansen said. "It's time."

"Is time, is time." Something of the jovial telephone derision flickered in the Russian's gruff voice. "Now you are sounding like a priest come to walk me to firing squad. No, Rawhide, I do not go with you. I stay here until she goes away. I can stay here." He rose shakily to his full height, arms firmly folded across his chest.

"Leonid," Jansen said. "That woman down there—the man with me is her son. Talk to him."

Gavrilenko turned to face Richter. His still-powerful face had gone grayish-white, making the beard stubble stand out starkly, like the last stalks of a gleaned-over wheat field.

"Her son..." Gavrilenko did not move, nor take his eyes from Richter's face for a long moment; then, to Jansen's astonishment, he began to smile. His teeth were remarkably white, unusual for an East European of his generation. He drew a short breath and recited, in the classic half-chanting Russian style, "*After the first death, there is no other.* Mr. Dylan Thomas, English poet."

When there was no response, Gavrilenko repeated, "*He* understood. Shakespeare, Pushkin, they did not understand so well as Mr. Dylan Thomas." He seemed unable to take his eyes from Richter. He said suddenly, "Your mother—I knew her." The smile drew his lips flat against the good white teeth. "This one—" he jerked a thumb at Jansen—"he only sees her dying, no more. But I...*I* saw her living—she was good at living, Zinzi. Only a short time, we had, but we made of it what we can. *Could*—what we *could*. You see, I forget my English so soon." The wide smile still clung to his lips, fading only slowly, like the shape of a cloud.

Richter's face was also taut, but his eyes remained steady and composed. He said quietly, "You were not my father."

Gavrilenko sighed. It was a long, slow sigh, almost theatrically Russian, and its wordless tone carried the suggestion of sorrow at once too deep to be born, and too hopeless to be worth bothering with. "No, I am not your father—that was some student, she told me, gone off to the West before she even knew she was pregnant. But I could have been. For three weeks, I could have been."

It was not said boastingly or mockingly, but was somehow part of the sigh. Jansen thought about Arl's vanished husband and had to shake free of a sudden spasm of pure rage. "You helped her plan that run, didn't you? Had to be someone who knew the triggers, the timing."

"I do more, Rawhide. I show her the weak places, I show where the big searchlights are, where the VoPos hide—everything I know, she knows." His voice had taken on the same singsong quality as when he quoted the Thomas line. "She had a little money, not so much. I spread it among the VoPos, everybody getting something—so when she runs we are all turning into very bad shots, you understand? No big deal, everybody getting something." He clasped his big hands at the waist, like a child set to recite at school. To Richter he said, "I do all that for Zinzi Richter, for your mother. Because she was funny, and I liked her, you know? Also, I was young."

"Because you were screwing her and taking her money," Richter said harshly. "You used her."

"So? She is using me too." Gavrilenko appeared genuinely indignant. "You think she sleeps with me out of love? *Chort*—she knows what she does, and so did I. She comes to me, straight to bed, down payment, right? Was a bargain, and both kept our word." He laughed abruptly. "Like I said, young."

Jansen said, "Something obviously went wrong."

Gavrilenko was silent for a long time. He did not turn away from them, but he ceased to look directly at Richter, and his glances at Jansen had become defiantly despairing. He said finally, "The Stasi, Stasi, KGB—eyes everywhere, even when you know they have eyes. The day she makes her run...suddenly, no VoPos I recognize, no VoPos I pay money to, whole new crowd. Stasi agents, every one—I know this. What to do? I want to warn her, but I am on duty, they have made sure I have no chance. You understand?" He was glaring at them both now, looking more like an old bull than ever. "You understand? I had no chance!"

After a moment he shrugged, long and deliberately. "Also no choice." Now he clearly forced himself to meet Richter's eyes, and the physical effort was visible on his face. He repeated doggedly, "No choice."

Richter's silence was more than Jansen could bear. He had to speak. "So you shot her. She trusted you, and you killed her."

"*They were watching me!*" It sounded as though Gavrilenko's throat was tearing from the words. "All of them, firing wide, missing and missing, *watching,* looking like this—" he mimicked someone stealing covert side-glances—"waiting for *me* to shoot and miss, so they know I am traitor. Her or me, and what would *you* do, brave Rawhide?" He was breathing like a runner whose strength has ended before his race. "Sweet, funny little Zinzi, nice girl—you tell me what you would do, eh? I wait."

Neither Jansen nor Richter responded, nor did they look at each other. For his part, the constant image in Jansen's mind of Zinzi Richter's doomed attempt to reach her baby kept being replaced by one of his own daughters. Outside the guardroom door, the edged darkness was slicing in closer, while through the window, in a strangely dizzying sweep, he could see back across the Death Strip and the Wall to the apartment where he had spent much of two years staring at this very room.

"I wait," Gavrilenko repeated, and this time it was not a mocking challenge. This time it was soft and urgent, almost plaintive, as though he really did want an answer, was in desperate need of any reply at all, For a third time he said, "I wait to be told what I should have done. Speak, wise Americanski friends."

"That's a comedy word," Jansen said. "Nobody uses that anymore."

Then Richter answered him at last, his words falling like the muffled strokes of an old clock. He said, "Mr. Gavrilenko, I have to thank you. If your guilt were not so great, if you had just been an agent, a VoPo, who shot my mother and went off to lunch, it would never have dragged you here to see her again. It would never have called to Henry's guilt, or to my own guilt for being born, and causing her death...her stupid, stupid, needless death." For those few words there was a sound in his voice like claws on stone, and his hands kept opening and closing at his sides.

"You can't think that," Jansen said. "She could have died the exact same way, even if you hadn't been born. Believe me, you do *not* want to spend your life thinking—"

Richter cut him off. "What I think is not important. We're here, and this has got to be why we're here. What we *do* now is what matters. We go down to my mother, to look into her face. All three of us. This is not a request."

He looked sharply at Jansen, who nodded. But Gavrilenko backed away, shaking his head, saying, "No, *no*, I cannot, will not, *no,* never possible." He wailed and struggled frantically when Jansen and Richter caught hold of his flailing arms and literally dragged him out of the guard room. Old and ill, half-mad or not—his eyes were rolling as wildly as those of a terrified stallion—he was still stronger than either of them alone, and their cramped passage down the guard tower's stairway was a battle. Jansen had a bloody nose by the time they had the Russian near ground-level, and Richter's shirt was splitting down the back seam. Through it all, Gavrilenko wailed and cursed in an absurd and piteous mix of Russian, German, and English, going utterly limp at the last, which meant hauling him the final few steps like a side of beef or bale of hay, until they were finally able to dump him at Zinzi Richter's feet and step back, breathless and exhausted.

The ghost saw them.

On her plain, unremarkable little face the joy of Richter's presence, his existence—the *fact* of him—leaped up like a flame in dry grass. Seeing this recognition, the tall man took her hands between his, bowed over them, and began to cry, almost soundlessly. She drew her hands free and held him close; but over his shoulder her eyes met Jansen's, and he actually staggered back a pace, shaken by the depth of the sorrow and sympathy—sorrow specifically for him—that he read there. He heard himself saying aloud, in absurd embarrassment, "Hey, it hasn't been as bad as all that. Really." But it had been, it had been, and she knew.

Then she gently released her son, and knelt down beside Gavrilenko, where he lay on his face, hands covering his eyes. With her own hands on his upper arms, she silently coaxed him to face her. Gavrilenko screamed once—not loudly, but in a tone of pure terror, and of resignation to terror as well, like a rabbit unresisting in the clutches of a horned owl. He scrambled to a sitting position, his hands now flat on the ground

beside him, face dazed and alien. The ghost commanded his eyes as she
had Jansen's—how long ago?—holding them in thrall to her own, seeing
through them and past them, down into uttermost Gavrilenko, his body
shaking with the need to hide his eyes again but unable to do so. He
whimpered now and then; and still clung to himself.

By and by he began to speak. "After first death, really is no other.
You and me, Henry—you remember us? Two tired, lonely, nervous
boys in uniform, pretending to be men, doing job..." He rose slowly
to his feet. "I kill so many people since then—you know? Easy, really. *Easy.* Killings, I am telling you honestly, but no *deaths*...not after
her." He did meet Zinzi Richter's quiet eyes then, though again Jansen
saw the physical shock spread through his body. He said, "Different,
you understand?"

Jansen asked, "You stayed in the army? No...what, you were KGB?"

"Oh, please, no KGB anymore," Gavrilenko reproved him. "In new
democratic Russia, FSB—execute you with new democratic pistol. No,
Henry, I did my time in private enterprise. Big capitalist, all American
values, even before it was common. You would be proud."

"The Mafia." Richter's voice was tight and thick, for all its evenness.
"You worked for the Russian Mafia. You killed people for them."

Gavrilenko grinned at him like a skull. "Kill for the Mafia, kill for
Mother Russia—what difference? I was an independent contractor, just
like American plumber." He nodded toward Jansen. "I went here, I went
there, fix the sink, the toilet, go home, rest tired feet, watch the TV." He
spoke directly to Zinzi Richter now, to no one else in the world. He said,
"This is your blessing. You made me so."

Something he couldn't guess at made Jansen look away, and he fancied that he could actually see the darkness moving in around them if he
watched it closely enough. From where they stood, nothing was visible
now but the tower, the Wall in one direction, and the dark wall itself in
the other...and after studying it, when he looked again on Gavrilenko he
saw something that he could not have been expected to recognize, yet
felt he should have seen from the moment he and Richter had entered
the guardroom. With a sudden surge of wonder and pity, he whispered,
"Leonid. You're like her..." He was trembling, and it was hard to get
words out, or to remember what words were.

Gavrilenko shook his head slowly, heavily. "Not like her. She is long
dead, forever young, forever innocent. While Leonid Leonidovich Nikolai
Gavrilenko lies in Petersburg hospital, Walther PPK bullet in coward's
brain." He grimaced in bitter disgust. "So many heads, so many bullets, one to a customer...only Gavrilenko, pig-drunk, old, sick, shaking

with fear, cannot even kill himself decently...coward, coward, pathetic..."
There were a few more words, all Russian.

The ghost of Zinzi Richter spoke then, without making a sound.
Picking up her blue duffel bag, she looked at the three of them and
mouthed a single word, rounding it out with great care and precision.
Jansen could not read her lips, but Richter nodded. His mother gestured
broadly, intensely with her free arm: pointing first toward the crouching,
stalking darkness, then toward the Wall, unmistakably inviting them all
to run with her while there was still time. She mouthed the silent word
a second time.

Jansen and Richter both sensed Gavrilenko's decision before he even
turned. They clutched at his arms, but he broke free with a frantic,
wordless cry and dashed away from them, lunging and stumbling back
toward the East Germany of their memories. Richter, quicker off the
mark than Jansen, almost caught him at the inner wall; astonishingly,
the old Russian hurled himself at it like a gymnast, leaping to catch the
top, and was up and over it and straight into the darkness without hesi-
tating. He vanished instantly, like a match-flame blown out, leaving no
sound or glance behind him.

Richter stopped, staring at the edge.

Jansen joined him, and they stood together in silence for some minutes. The darkness, if it did not retreat, at least advanced no further.
Jansen said finally, "You really think it was him that brought us here? It
wasn't your mother?"

"I have no idea," Richter said, turning away from the void. "Maybe
we all did it."

Jansen looked at the ghost of Zinzi Richter, waiting for them by the
guard tower, forming for a third time the word he could not understand.
"What *is* that?" he demanded of Richter. "What's that she's saying?"

Richter smiled. *"Freiheit. German for freedom."*

Abruptly Zinzi Richter turned and began to run, heading once again
for the Death Strip, and Richter ran after her, his face as bright and
determined as the face of any small boy racing with his mother. Jansen
came panting in the rear, no better conditioned than the average sixty-
six-year-old kitchen remodeler, but resolved not to be left behind in
this place, to find his way back to a maternity clinic in Klamath Falls,
Oregon. *Arl...Arl...I'll be right there...*

The spotlights came on, and the gunfire began.

Crossing the Death Strip, Jansen placed his feet exactly in Zinzi
Richter's tracks, as her son was doing, and hunched down as low as he
could, even as the rifle shots kicked up gravel close enough to sting his

face and twitch at his shirt. He tried to shut the awareness out of his consciousness. *Real bullets? Memories of bullets? Ghost bullets, fired by ghosts back in 1963—God!* And then, despite a sudden blossoming fear of dying where he didn't belong, a single thought consumed him. *It's not enough to follow. I've got to get there first.*

Just as Gavrilenko's old legs and big old hands had taken him over the inner wall without assistance, so Jansen's legs, when called upon, somehow responded with speed that did not belong to him, and never had. He passed up a surprised Richter and forcefully crowded past Zinzi Richter as she set her ladder's hooks, stopping only long enough to pull the wire cutters from her duffel before starting to climb. Up the shaking rungs, atop the Wall, he worked faster than she could have, snapping wires real enough to tear his face and hands in half a dozen places. Then they were there with him, the mother and the son, and he swept them before him through the gap he had created, holding their hands as they eased themselves over the other side. He turned his back on the gunfire, covering both his charges with the width of his own torso, breath pulled deep into his lungs as if he could somehow expand to shield not just these two, but everything in the world. He felt their fingers slip away from his and he smiled.

The rifle fire kept up, but Jansen didn't move, thinking *shit, if the Krauts didn't fire in damn platoons, they'd never hit anybody.*

He heard the one sharp crack they say you never hear, and closed his eyes.

▲▼▲

Arl, hugely pregnant and wheezing with the effort, was trying to keep him from falling out of bed in what must be the clinic's emergency ward. There were half a dozen beds around him, most empty, a couple with curtains drawn around them and nurses coming and going. Jansen caught himself, scrambled crabwise back onto the bed, said, "What the Christ?" and tried to sit up. Arl pushed him back down, hard.

"No, you don't—you stay *put,* old man." There was relief in her voice—he caught that, having looked long for such things—but also the same dull rancor and plain dislike that colored their every conversation, even the most casual. "You're staying right here until Dr. Chaudhry comes."

"What happened? The baby?"

"The baby's all right. I'm all right too, thanks." That wasn't just him, he knew; everybody asked about the baby first, and it was starting to piss her off as she neared her term. She said, "They found you on the floor in the waiting room. They thought it might be a stroke."

"Oh, Jesus. I just fell asleep, that's all. Been staying up too late watching old movies. I'm fine, shit's sake." He looked at his hands and wrists, saw no barbed-wire wounds, and started to get up, but she pushed him down again, and he could feel the real fury in her hands.

"You *stay* there, damn it. A lot of people think they're just fine after a stroke, and they get on their feet, take a few steps, and *bang,* gone for good this time." Her face was sweaty with effort and anger; but he saw fear there as well, and heard it in her voice. "On good days I can just about stand you, and on the bad ones...God, do you have any *idea?"*

"Yes," Jansen said. "Matter of fact."

Arl drew a long breath. "But when I saw you..." Her voice caught, and she started again. "I realized right there, I am not ready to have you gone, I'm *not.* Not you too, it's too damn *much,* do you understand me? Don't you dare die on me, not now. Not fucking *now."*

Jansen found her hand on the bed, and put his hand over it. She did not respond, but she did not pull the hand away. "You look like me," he said. "Gracie's all Elly, but you've got my chin, and my nose, and my cheekbones. Must have really hated that, huh?"

The smile was thin and elusive, but it was a smile. "I hated my whole face. Most girls do, but I had reasons." She looked down at their hands together. "I even hated my hands, because they're too much like yours. I'm okay with them now, though, more or less."

Jansen said, "You're like me. That's what you hate." Her eyes widened in outrage, and she jerked away, but he held tightly to her hand. "What I mean, you're like the *good* me. The best of me. The me I was supposed to be, before things...just happened. You understand what I'm saying?"

Arl was beginning to frown in an odd way, staring at him. "You sure you haven't had a stroke? I wish the doctor'd get here. You talked while you were out, I couldn't make anything out of it, except it was really weird. Like you were having a weird dream."

"Not a stroke," Jansen said. "Not a dream." He did not try to sit up again, but kept his eyes fixed on her. He said, "Just someplace I needed to be. Don't ask me about it right now, and I won't ask you about stuff you don't want to tell me, okay?" She did not reply, but her hand turned slightly under his, and a couple of fingers more or less intertwined. "And I promise I won't die until you're finished yelling at me. Fair?"

Arl nodded. "But this doesn't mean I actually like you. Just so you know that."

"Fair," Jansen said again. He did withdraw his hand from hers now.

Dr. Chaudhry came in, a brisk young Bengali with a smile that was not brisk, but thoughtful, almost dreamy. He sat down on the opposite side of the bed from Arl and said, "Well, I hear that you have been frightening your good daughter quite badly. Not very considerate, Mr. Jansen."

"I'm not a very considerate person," Jansen said. "My family could tell you."

"This is something you must change right away," Dr. Chaudhry said, trying to look severe and not succeeding. "You are going to be a grandfather, you know. You will have responsibilities."

"Yeah," Jansen said. He looked up at the lights on the ceiling then, and let Dr. Chaudhry count his pulse.

.

The Tale of Junko and Sayuri

In Japan, very, very, long ago, when almost anybody you met on the road might turn out to be a god or a demon, there was a young man named Junko. That name can mean "genuine" in Japanese, or "pure," or "obedient," and he was all of those things then. He served the great *daimyo* Lord Kuroda, lord of much of southern Honshu, as Chief Huntsman, and was privileged to live in the lord's castle itself, rather than in any of the outer structures, the *yagura*. In addition, he was handsome and amiable, and all the ladies of the court were aware of him. But he had no notion of this, which only added to his charm. He was a very serious young man.

He was also a commoner, born of the poorest folk in a poor village, which meant that he had not the right even to a family name, nor even to be called Junko-*san* as a mark of respect. In most courts of that time, he would never have been permitted to look straight into the eyes of a samurai, let alone to live so intimately among them. But the Lord Kuroda was an unusual man, with his own sense of humor, his own ideas of what constituted a samurai, and with a doubtless lamentable tendency to treat everyone equally. This was generally blamed on his peculiar horoscope.

Now at this time, it often seemed as though half of Japan were forever at war with the other half. The mighty private armies of the *daimyos* marched and galloped up and down the land, leaving peasant villages and great fortresses alike smoldering behind them as they pleased. The *shogun* at Kyoto might well issue his edicts from time to time, but the shogunate had not then the power that it was to seize much later; so for the most part his threats went unheeded, and no peace treaty endured for long. The Lord Kuroda held himself and his own people aside from war as much as he could, believing it tedious, pointless and utterly impractical, but even he found it wise to keep an army of retainers. And the poor in other less fortunate prefectures replanted and built their houses again, and said among themselves that Buddha and the *kami*— the many gods of Shinto—alike slept.

One cold winter, when game was particularly scarce, Junko went out hunting for his master. Friends would gladly have come with him, but everyone knew that Junko preferred to hunt alone. He was polite about it, as always, but he felt that the other courtiers made too much noise and frightened away the winter-white deer and rabbits and wild pigs that he was stalking. He himself moved as quietly—even pulling a sledge behind him—as any fish in a stream, or any bird in the air, and he never came home empty-handed.

On this day, as Amaterasu, the sun, was drowsing down the western sky, Junko also was starting back to the Lord Kuroda's castle. His sledge was laden with a fat stag, and a pig as well, and Junko knew that another kill would load the sledge too heavily for his strength. All the same, he could not resist loosing one last arrow at a second wild pig that had broken the ice on a frozen stream, and was greedily drinking there, ignoring everything but the water. It was too good a chance to pass up, and Junko stood very still, took a deep breath—then let it out, just a little bit, as archers will do—and let his arrow fly.

It may have been that his hands were cold, or that the pig moved slightly at the last moment, or even that the growing twilight deceived Junko's eye, though that seems unlikely. At all events, he missed his mark—the arrow hissed past the pig's left ear, sending the animal off in a panicky scramble through the brush, out of sight and range in an instant—but he hit *something.* Something at the very edge of the water gave a small, sad cry, thrashed violently in the weeds there for a moment, and then fell silent and still.

Junko frowned, annoyed with himself; he had been especially proud of the fact that he never needed more than one arrow to bring down his prey. Well, whatever little creature he had accidentally wounded, it was his duty to put it quickly out of its pain, since an honorable man should never inflict unnecessary suffering. He went forward carefully, his boots sinking into the wet earth.

He found it lying half-in, half-out of the stream: an otter, with his arrow still in his flank. It was conscious, but not trying to drag itself away—it only looked at him out of dazed dark eyes and made no sound, not even when he knelt beside it and drew his knife to cut its throat. It looked at him—nothing more.

"It would be such a pity to ruin such fur with blood," he thought. "Perhaps I could make a tippet out of it for my master's wife." He put the knife away slowly and lifted the otter in his arms, preparing to break its neck with one swift twist. The otter's sharp teeth could surely have taken off a finger through the heavy mittens, but it struggled not at all, though Junko could feel the captive heart beating wildly against him. When he closed his free hand on the creature's neck, the panting breath, so softly desperate, made his wrist tingle strangely.

"So beautiful," he said aloud in the darkening air. He had never had any special feeling about animals: they were good to eat or they weren't good to eat, though he did rather admire the shimmering grace of fish and the cool stare of a fox. But the otter, hurt and helpless between his hands, made him feel as though he were the one wounded, somehow. "Beautiful," he whispered again, and very carefully and slowly he began to withdraw the arrow.

When Junko arrived back at his lord's castle, it was full dark and the otter lay under his shirt, warm against his belly. He delivered his kill, to be taken off to the great kitchens, gravely accepted the thanks due him, and hurried away to the meager quarters granted him at the castle as soon as it was correct to do so. There he laid the otter on a ragged old cloak that his sister had given him when he was a boy, and knelt beside the creature to study it in lamplight. The wound was no worse than it had been, and no better, though the blood had stopped flowing. He gave the otter water in a little clay dish, but it sniffed feebly at it without drinking; when he put his hand gently on the arrow-wound, he could feel the fever already building.

"Well," he said to the otter, "all I know to do is to treat you as I did my little brother, the time he fell on the ploughshare. No biting, now." With his dagger, he trimmed the oily brown fur around the injury; with a rag dipped in hot *nihonshu,* which others call *sake,* he cleaned the area over and over; and with herbal infusions whose use he had learned from his mother's mother, he did his best to draw the infection. Through it all the otter never stirred or protested, but watched him steadily as he labored to undo the damage he had caused. He sang softly now and then, old nonsensical children's songs, hardly knowing he was doing it, and now and then the otter cocked an ear, seeming to listen.

When he was done he offered the water again, and this time the otter drank from the dish, cautiously, never taking its eyes from him, but deeply even so. Junko then lifted it in the old cloak and set all upon his own *tatami* mat, saying, "I cannot bind your wound properly, but healing in open air is best, anyway. And now you should sleep." He covered the otter with his coat, then lay down near it on the *tatami* and quickly fell asleep himself. The otter was awake longer than he, its wide eyes darker than the darkness.

In the morning the gash in the otter's flank smelled far less of fever, and the little animal was clearly hungry. Knowing that otters eat mainly

fish, along with such things as frogs and turtles, Junko dressed hurriedly
and went to a river that was near the castle (the better for the *daimyo* to
keep an eye on the boats that went up and down between the distant cities), and there he caught and cleaned several small fish and brought them
back to his quarters. The otter devoured them all, groomed its fur with
great care—spending half an hour on its exposed wound alone—and
then fell back to sleep for the rest of the day, much of which Junko spent
studying it, sitting crosslegged beside his *tatami*. He was completely
captivated to learn that the otter snored—very daintily and delicately,
through its diamond-shaped nose—and that it smelled only slightly of
fish, even after its meal, and much more of spring-warmed earth, as
deep in winter as they were. He touched its front claws and realized that
they were almost as hard as armor.

When a highly-placed serving woman suggested through another
servant that she might possibly enjoy his company for tea, Junko made
the most courteous apology he could, and went on staring at the otter
on his sleeping mat. Towards evening the little creature woke up and lay
considering him in its turn, out of eyes much brighter and clearer than
they had been. He spoke to it then, saying, "I am very sorry that I hurt
you. I hope you are better today." The otter licked its whiskers without
taking its eyes from his.

During the days that passed, Junko told no one about the otter: neither the Lord Kuroda nor his wife, the Lady Hara, nor even his closest
friend, the horsemaster Akira Yamagata, who might have been expected
to understand his fascination. He fed and cared for the otter every day,
cleaned and aired out his quarters himself, and saw the arrow-wound
closing steadily from the inside, as every soldier knows is the proper
way of healing. And the otter lay patiently under his hands as he tended
it, and shared his *tatami* at night; and if it did not purr, or arch itself
back against his hands, as a cat will, when he stroked its beautiful, rich
fur, nevertheless it never drew away from the contact, but looked constantly into his eyes, as though it would have spoken to him if it could.
He fell into the habit of talking to it himself, more and more, and he
named it Sayuri, because men have to name things, and Sayuri was his
sister's name.

One morning he told the otter, "My lord will have me guide a hunt
meeting with the Lord Sugihara, down on holiday from Osaka. I am not
looking forward to it, because neither trusts the other for an instant,
and it could all become very wearying, though certainly educational.
But when I return, however late it may be, I will take you back to your
stream and release you there. You are fully recovered now, and a castle

is no place for a wild creature like yourself. Stay well and warm until I come back."

The meeting between the two lords was indeed tiresome, and the hunt itself extremely unsatisfactory; but it had at least the virtue of taking less time than he would have expected, so the sun was still in the sky when Junko climbed the stair to his quarters. He went slowly, remembering his promise to the otter, and finding himself curiously reluctant to keep it. "It will be lonely," he thought. "I will miss...what is it that I will miss?" He could not say, but he knew that it was a real thing. So he sighed and went on to his quarters and opened the door.

The otter was gone.

In its place there stood, waiting for him, the most beautiful young woman he had ever seen. She stood barely higher than his heart, wearing a blue and white kimono, and her face was the dawn shade of a tea-rose, and as perfectly boned and structured as the kites that children were competing with every spring even then. Junko stood gaping at her, not even trying to speak.

"Yes," she said quietly, smiling with small white teeth at his bewilderment. "I am indeed that otter you shot, and then nursed back to health so tenderly. I am quite well now, as you see."

"But," said Junko. "But."

The young woman smiled more warmly as he stumbled among words, finding only that one. "This is my true form, but I take other shapes from time to time, as I choose. And it is so pleasant to be an otter—even as they hunt and mate, and raise their children, and struggle to survive, they seem to be having such a joyful time of it. Don't you think so, my lord?"

Junko said, "But" again, that being the only word he was quite master of. The woman came toward him, her long, graceful fingers toying with the knot of the *obi* at her waist.

"I could not return to my own form until today," she explained to him, "because I was wounded, which always keeps me from changing. I might very well have died an otter, but for your devoted care. It is only proper that I make you some little recompense, surely?"

She seemed so hesitant herself that the last words came out a shy question. But the *obi* had already fallen to the floor.

Later, in the night, propped on her elbow and looking at him with eyes even darker than the otter's eyes, she said, "You have never lain so with a woman, have you?"

Junko blushed in the darkness. "Not exactly. I mean, of course there were...No."

The young woman was silent for a time. Then she said, "Well, I will tell you something, since you have been so honest with me. Nor will I lie to you—I have mated, made love, yes, but never in this form. Only as a deer, or a wildcat, or even as a snow monkey, in the northern mountains. Never as a human being, until now."

"And you *are* human?" Junko asked her. "Forgive me, but are you sure you are not an animal who can change into a woman?" For there are all sorts of legends in Japan about such creatures. Especially foxes.

She chuckled against his shoulder. "I am altogether human, I promise you." After a moment, she added, "You named me Sayuri. I like that name. I will keep it."

"But you must have a name of your own, surely? Everyone has a name."

"Not I, never." She put a finger on his lips to forestall further questioning. "Sayuri will suit me very well."

And the beautiful young woman who had been an otter suited Junko very well herself. He presented her formally as his fiancée to the Lord Kuroda the next day, and then to the full court. He was awkward at it, certainly, never having been schooled in such regions of etiquette; but all were charmed by the young woman's grace and modesty, even so, despite the fact that she could offer nothing in the way of family history or noble lineage. Indeed, Lord Kuroda's wife, the Lady Hara, immediately requested her as one of her ladies-in-waiting. So all went well there, and Junko—still as dazed by his sudden fortune as the otter had been by his arrow—was proud and happy in a way that he had never known in all his life.

He and Sayuri were married in short order by the Shinto priest Yukiyasa, the same who had married Lord Kuroda to Lady Hara, which everyone agreed was good luck, and were given new quarters in the castle—modest still, but more fitting for so singular a couple. More, his master, as a wedding gift, saw to it that Junko was given proper hunting equipment to replace the battered bow and homemade arrows with which he had first arrived at court. There were those present at the ceremony who bit their lips in envy of such favor to a commoner; but Junko, in his desire that everyone share in his joy, noticed none of this. The Lord Kuroda did.

Early on the morning after their wedding, when few were yet awake, Junko and his bride walked in the castle garden, in the northeast corner, where the stream entered, and which was known as the Realm of the Blue Dragon. The days were cold still, but they walked close together and were content, saying very little. But the stream made Junko think of the strange and nearly fatal way in which he had met his Sayuri, and he asked her then, "Beloved, do you think you would ever be likely to change into an otter again? For I hurt you by mischance, but there are many people who trap otters for their fur, and I would be afraid for you."

Sayuri's laughter was like the sound of the water flowing beside them, as she answered him. "I think not, my lord. There are more risks involved with that form—including marriage—than I had bargained for." Then she turned a serious face to her new husband, holding his arm tightly. "But I would grieve were I forbidden to change shape ever again. It is a part of whatever I am, you must know that."

"'Whatever I am,'" Junko repeated slowly, and for a moment it seemed as though the back of his neck was colder than it should be, even on a winter morning. "But you assured me that you were altogether human. Those were your words."

"And I am, I am certain I am!" Sayuri stopped walking and turned him to face her. "But what else am I? No name but the one you gave me…no childhood that I can recall, except in flashes, like lightning, here and gone…no father or mother to present me at my own wedding…far more memories of the many animals I have been than of the woman I know I am. There *must* be more to me than I can see in your eyes, or in the jeweled hand mirror that was the Lady Hara's gift. Do you understand, husband?"

There were tears on her long black eyelashes, and though they did not fall, they reassured Junko in a curious way, since animals cannot weep. He put his arms around her to comfort her, saying, "Do as you will, as you need to do, my wife. I ask only that you protect yourself from all injury, since you cannot regain your human form then, and anything could happen to you. Will you promise me that?"

Then Sayuri laughed, and shook her head so that the teardrops flew, and she said, "I swear that and more. You will never again share your sleeping mat with anything furred, or with any more than two legs." And Junko joined in her laughter, and they went on with their walk, all the way across the garden to the southwest corner, which is still called the Realm of the White Tiger.

So they lived quite happily together for some years at the court of the *daimyo* Lord Kuroda. Junko served his master with the same perfect loyalty as ever, and went on providing more game than any other huntsman for the castle kitchens; while Sayuri continued to be much favored by the Lady Hara, joining her in her favorite arts of music, brush-painting, and especially *ikebana,* the spreading new discipline of flower-arrangement. So skilled was she at this latter, in fact, that Lady Hara often sought her assistance in planning the decorations for a poetry recital in her own quarters, or even for a feast on the green summer island in the stream. Watching the two of them pacing slowly by the water together, the fringes of the great lady's parasol touching his otter-wife's thick and fragrant hair, Junko was so proud that it pained him, and made it hard to breathe.

And if, now and then, he awoke in the night to find the space beside him still warm but empty, or heard a rustle in the trees outside, or a sigh of the grass, that he was huntsman enough to know was no bird, no doe teaching her fawn to strip bark from Lord Kuroda's plum trees, he learned to turn over and go back to sleep, and ask no questions in the morning. For Sayuri was most often back by dawn, or very soon thereafter—always in human shape, as she had promised him—usually chilled beyond the bone and needing to be warmed. And Junko would warm her and never ask her to say where—and what—she had been.

She did not always leave the castle: mouse and bat were among her favorite forms, and between those two she knew everything that was taking place within its walls. More than once she shocked Junko by informing him that this or that high-ranking retainer was slipping into dusty alcoves with this or that servant girl; he learned before Lord Kuroda that the Lady Hara was again with child, but that it would be best the *daimyo* not know, since this one too would not live to be born. Animals know these things. As an owl, she might glide silently over the forest at night, and tell him if the deer had shifted their grazing grounds, as they did from time to time, or were lying up in a new place. In fox-shape, she warned of an approaching forest fire without ever seeing a flame; Junko roused the castle and gained great praise and credit thereby. He wanted earnestly to explain that all honor was due to his wife Sayuri, but this was impossible, and she seemed more than content with his gratitude and their somewhat unlikely happiness. So they lived, and the time passed.

One night it happened that she returned to their bed shivering, not with cold, nor with fear—there were several cats in the castle—but, as he slowly realized, with anger, which was not something he was used to from Sayuri. She might be by turns as calm and thoughtful as a fox, as playful as an otter, as gentle as a deer, fiercely passionate as any mink or marten, or as curious and mischievous as a red-faced snow monkey. All these moods and humors he had come in time to understand—but anger was a new thing entirely. He held her, and asked simply, "What is it, my love?"

At first she would not speak, or could not; but by and by, when the trembling passed a little, she whispered, "I was in the kitchen,"—by this Junko knew that she had been in mouse-shape—"and the cooks were

talking late over their own meal. And one said it was a shame that you
had been passed over for the lord's private guard in favor of Yasunari
Saito, since you had surely earned promotion a dozen times over. But
another cook said,"—the words were choking her again—"that it made
no difference, because you were a commoner with no surname, and that
it was miraculous that you were even in Lord Kuroda's home, let alone
his retinue. *Miraculous*—after all you have done for them!" The tears of
rage came then.

"Well, well," Junko said, stroking her hair, "that must have been
Aoki. He has never liked me, that one, and it wouldn't matter to him if
I had a dozen surnames. For the rest of it, things are the way they are,
and that is...well, the way it is. Don't cry, please, Sayuri. I am grateful for
what I have, and most grateful for you. Don't cry."

But later, when she had at last fallen asleep on his chest, he could
not help brooding—only a little—about the unfairness of Saito's promotion. *Unfair* was not a word Junko had allowed himself even to think
since he was quite small, and still learning the way things were, but it
seemed to slither in his mind, and he could not get to grips with it, or
make it go away. It was long before he slept again.

As has been said, the Lord Kuroda was a wise man, though not at
all handsome, who saw more at a single dinner than many were likely to
see in a week or a month. Riding out hunting one day, with Junko at his
elbow, and they two having drawn a little apart from their companions,
he said to him briefly and directly, "Saito is a fool, but his advancement
was necessary, since I may well need his father's two hundred and fifty
samurai one day." Junko bowed his head without answering. Lord Kuroda
continued, "But it means nothing to me that you bring no warriors with
you—nothing but your strength and your faithfulness. The next opening
in my guard you shall fill."

With that he spurred ahead, doubtless to avoid Junko's stammering
thanks. Junko was too overcome to be much of a hand at the hunt that
afternoon; but while the others teased and derided him for this, Lord
Kuroda only winked gravely.

Of course Sayuri was overjoyed at the news of the lord's promise,
and she and Junko celebrated it with *nihonshu* and love, and then
shochu, which is brewed from rice and sweet potatoes and a few other
things. And afterward it was her turn to lie awake in the night, with
her husband in her arms, and her mind perhaps full of small-animal
thoughts. And perhaps not; who knows? It was all so long ago.

But it was at most a month before the horse of the samurai Daisuke
Ikeda shied at a rabbit underfoot, reared, fell backwards and crushed

his rider. There was much sorrow at court, for Ikeda was the oldest of the *daimyo*'s guard, and a well-liked man; but there was also a space in the guard to fill, and Lord Kuroda was as good as his word. Within days, Junko was wearing his master's livery, for all the world as though he were as good as Ikeda, or anyone else, and riding at his side on a fine, proud young stallion. And however many at court may have thought this highly unsuitable, no one said a word about it.

Junko also grieved for Ikeda, who had been kind to him. But his delight in his new position was muted, more than he would have expected, by his odd disquiet concerning that rabbit. Riding in the rear, as befit a commoner (it had been a formal procession, meant to impress a neighboring lord), he had seen the animal shoot from its hole, seemingly as blindly as though red-eyed Death were on its heels; and he had never known Ikeda's wise old horse to panic at an ambush, much less a rabbit. One worrisome thought led to another, and that to a third, until finally he brought them all to his wife. He had grown much in the habit of doing this.

Sayuri sat crosslegged on the proper new bed that the Lord Kuroda had given them to replace their worn *tatami*, and she listened attentively to Junko's fears, saying nothing until he was finished. Then she replied simply, "Husband, I was not the rabbit—I was the weasel just behind it, chasing it out of its burrow into the horse's path. Can you look at your own new horse—at your beautiful new livery—at this bed of ours—and say I have done wrong?"

"But Ikeda is dead!" Junko cried in horror. "Ask rather how I can look at his widow, at his children, at my master—at myself in the mirror now! Oh, I wish you had never told me this, Sayuri!"

"Then you should not have asked me," she answered him. "The weasel never meant for the good Ikeda to be killed—though he was old and should have retired from the guard long ago. The weasel only wanted the rabbit." She beckoned Junko to sit beside her, saying, "But is a wife not supposed to concern herself with the advancement of her husband's fortunes? I was told otherwise by the priest who married us." She put her arms around Junko. "Come, my love, take the good luck with the regrettable, and say as many prayers for Ikeda's repose as will comfort you." She laughed then: the joyous childlike giggle that never failed to melt even the sternest heart. "Although I think that *I* am more skilled at that than any prayer."

But Junko paced the castle all night, and wandered the grounds like a spirit; it was dawn before he could at last reassure himself that what she had told him was both sound and sensible. Ikeda's death had clearly been an accident, after all, and there was nothing in the least shameful in making the best of even such a tragedy. Sayuri's shapeshifting had brought about great good for him, however unintentional; let him give thanks for such a wife and, as he rode proudly beside the Lord Kuroda, bless the wandering arrow that had found an otter instead of a wild pig. "She is my luck," he thought often. "I should have given her that name, *luck*, instead of *little lily*."

But he did, indeed, pray often at the family shrine erected for Daisuke Ikeda.

Now in time Junko came to realize that, while he had certainly been honored far beyond his origins in becoming part of Lord Kuroda's private guard, he had also attained a kind of limit beyond which he had no chance of rising. Above the guard stood his master's counselors and ministers: some of them higher in rank than others, some higher in a more subtle manner, unspoken and unwritten. In any case, their world was far out of reach for a nameless commoner, no matter how graciously favored by his lord. He would always be exactly what he was—unlike Sayuri, who could at least become different animals in her search for her true nature. And, understanding this, for the first time in his life Junko began to admit aloud that the world was unjust.

"Look at Nakamura," he would say resentfully to his wife over the teacups. "Not only does he review the guard when Lord Kuroda is away or indisposed—Nakamura, who barely knows a lance from a chopstick—he advises my master on diplomacy, when he has never been north of the Inland Sea in his life. And Hashimoto—Finance Minister Hashimoto, if you please—Hashimoto holds the position for no other reason than that he is Lady Hara's second cousin on her father's side. It is not correct, Sayuri. It is not *right*."

Sayuri smiled and nodded, and made tea. She had become celebrated among the ladies-in-waiting for the excellence and delicacy of her *gyukuro* green tea.

And a few weeks later, Minister Shiro Nakamura, who loved to stroll alone in the castle gardens before dawn, to catch the first scent of the awakening flowers, was found torn in pieces by what could only have been a wolf. There were never many wolves in Japan, even then, but there was no question of the killer in this case: the great paw-prints in the soft earth were so large that Junko suggested that the animal might well have come from Hokkaido, where the wolves were notably larger. "But how could a wolf ever find its way from Hokkaido Island so far south to Honshu?" he asked himself in the night. "And why should it do so?" He was very much afraid that he knew the answer.

The hunt that was immediately organized after the discovery of Minister Nakamura's still-warm body found no wolf of any species, but it did find blood in one of the paw prints, and on the blade of the antique dagger that Nakamura always carried. Sayuri was not at home when Junko returned; nor did she appear for several days, and even then she looked pale and faint, and spoke little. Junko made the excuse of illness to the Lady Hara, who sent medicines and dainties, plainly hoping that Sayuri's reported condition might betoken a new godchild. For his part, he asked no questions of his wife, knowing that she would tell him the truth. She always did.

It took more time, and a great deal of courteously muffled scandal and outrage at court before Junko ascended into the ranks of Lord Kuroda's advisors. He did not replace Minister Nakamura, but a station was created for him: that of Minister to the Lower Orders. When Junko's first speechless gratitude began to be replaced by stumbling bewilderment, Lord Kuroda explained to him, thus: "By now, my friend, you should know that I am not one of those nobles who believe that the commoners have no reason to exist, except that we give them the privilege of serving us. Quite a few, in fact,"—and here he named a good eight or ten of the castle servants, ending with Junko himself—"show evidence of excellent sense, excellent judgment." He paused, looking straight into Junko's eyes. "And where there is judgment, there will be opinions."

By this Junko understood that he had been chosen to be a liaison— what some might call a spy—between the *daimyo* and all those who were not nobles, priests or samurai. The notion offended him deeply, but he had not attained his unusually favored position by showing offense. He merely bowed deeply to the Lord Kuroda, and replied that he would do his best to give satisfaction. The Lord Kuroda looked long into his eyes without responding.

So Junko, surname or no, became the first commoner ever accepted into a world his class had long been forbidden even to dream of entering. His and Sayuri's quarters were changed once again for rooms that seemed to him larger than his entire native village; they were assigned a servant of their own, and a new bed that, as Sayuri giggled, was "like a great snowdrift. I am certain we will yet find a bear sleeping out the winter with us." The haughtiness of Lord Kuroda's other counselors, and the sense that their servant despised them, seemed a small price to pay at the time.

Out of respect and gratitude to his master, Junko served him well as Minister to the Lower Orders. He provoked no disloyal or rebellious conversations, but only listened quietly to the talk of the stables, the kitchens, the deep storerooms and the barracks. What he thought Lord Kuroda should know, he reported faithfully; what seemed to him to be no one's business but the speakers' remained where he heard it. And Lord Kuroda appreciated his discreet ability to tell the difference, and told him so, even calling him Junko-*san* in private. And once—not very long before at all—that would have been more than enough.

But again he had collided with an invisible barrier. Precisely because the post had been invented especially for him, there was no precedent for promotion, nor any obvious position for him to step into whenever it should become vacant. Those who had always been kindly and amiable to Junko the castle's chief huntsman, now looked with visible contempt on Junko the Minister, Junko the jumped-up pet of the Lord Kuroda. Those below him took great pleasure in observing his frustration and discomfort; when they dared, they murmured as they passed him, "Did you think you were better than we are? Did you really believe they would let you become one of *them?* Then you were a fool—and now you are no one. No one."

Junko never spoke of his unhappiness to Lord Kuroda, but he expressed it once to his friend Akira Yamagata. The horsemaster, being a silent man, much more at ease with beasts than people, replied shortly, "Let demons fly away with them all. You cannot win with such folk; you cannot ever be even with them in their minds. Serve your master, and you cannot go wrong. Any horse will tell you that."

As for Sayuri, she simply listened, and arranged fresh flowers everywhere in their quarters, and made green *gyokuro* tea. When she walked with Junko in the castle gardens, and he asked her whether she felt herself any nearer to perceiving her true nature, she most often replied, "My husband, I know more and more what I am *not*—but as to what I *am*..." and her voice would trail away, leaving the thought unfinished. Then she would add, quickly and softly, "But human—that, yes. I know I am human."

Now the most clever and ambitious of the Lord Kuroda's counselors, recently become Minister of Waterways and Fisheries, was a man named Mitsuo Kondo. Perhaps because he was little older than Junko, only now approaching his middle years, he went well out of his way to show his scorn for a commoner, though never in the presence of the *daimyo*. In the same way, Junko responded humbly to Kondo's poorly-veiled insults; while at home he confided to his wife that he often dreamed of wringing the man's thin neck, as he had so often done with chickens in his childhood. "Being of low birth, I am naturally acquainted with barnyards," he remarked bitterly to Sayuri.

It happened that on a warm night of early summer, Junko woke thirsty to an empty bed—he was quite used to this by now—and was still thirsty when he had drunk the last remaining green tea. Setting off to find water, barefooted and still drowsy, he had just turned into a corridor that led to the kitchens, when he heard the scraping of giant claws on a weathered *sugi*-wood floor, and flattened himself against the wall so hard that the imprint of the molding remained on his skin for hours afterward.

A huge black bear was lumbering down a passageway just ahead. It must surely have smelled his terror—or, as he imagined, heard the frantic beating of his heart—for it hesitated, then rose on its hind legs, turning toward him to sniff the air, growling softly. He saw the deep yellow-white chevron on the creature's breast, as well as the bright blood on its horrific fangs and claws, and he smelled both the blood and the raw, wild, strangely sweet odor of the beast itself. Even armed he might not be the creature's match; weaponless, he knew this was the moment of his death. But then the bear's great bulk dropped to the floor again, turning away, and his forgotten breath hissed between his teeth as the animal moved slowly on out of his sight, still growling to itself.

Junko did not go back to his quarters that night, but sat shivering where he was until dawn, tracing a trail of dead moss between two floorboards over and over with his forefinger. Then at last he slipped warily back into the new bed where Sayuri had laughingly imagined a bear keeping them company. She was sound asleep, not even stirring at his return. Junko lay still himself, studying her hands: one partly under her head, one stretched out on the pillow. There was no blood on any of the long fingers he loved to watch moving among her flowers. This was not as reassuring to him as it might once have been.

The hunt for Minister Kondo went on for days. The blood trail was washed away by a sudden summer rain, except for the track leading from his private offices, and there were other indications that he had been carried off by some great animal, or something even worse. For all his dislike of Kondo, Junko took a leading part in the hunt—as did Lord Kuroda himself—from its earliest moments to the very last, when it was silently agreed that the Minister's body would never be found. Lord Kuroda commanded ten days of mourning, and had a shrine created in Minister Kondo's memory on his own summer island. It is still there, though no one today knows whom it was meant to honor.

Even after the proper period of remembrance had passed, the empty place among the *daimyo*'s counselors remained unfilled for some considerable while. Few had liked Kondo any more than Junko did; all had

feared his ambition, his gifts, and his evil tongue, and many were happy
that he was gone, however horrified they may have been at the manner
of his departure. But Lord Kuroda was clearly grieved—and, more than
that, suspicious, though of what even he could not precisely say. Wolves
and bears were common enough in Honshu in those days, but not in
Honshu gardens and palaces; nor was the loss of three important members of his court, each under such curious circumstances, something
even a mighty *daimyo* could easily let pass. The tale had already spread
through the entire province, from bands of half-naked beggars huddled
muttering under bridges to courts as great as his own. There was even a
delicate message from the Shogun in Kyoto. Lord Kuroda brooded long
over the proper response.

Junko came to feel his master's contemplative eyes on him even
when he was not in Lord Kuroda's presence. At length, to ease his mind,
he went directly to the *daimyo* and asked him, "Lord, have I done wrong?
I pray you tell me if this is so." For he knew his own silent part in the
three deaths, and he was afraid for his wife Sayuri.

But Lord Kuroda answered him gently, "Your pardon, loyal Junko,
if I have caused you to be more troubled than we all are, day on day. I
think you know that I have often considered your country astuteness to
be of more plain practical aid to me than the costly education of many
a noble. Now I wonder whether you might have any least counsel to
offer me regarding the terrible days through which we are passing." He
permitted himself a very small, sad chuckle. "Because, just as everyone
in my realm knows his station, my own task is to provide each of them
with wisdom, assurance and security. And I have none to offer them, no
more than they. Do you understand me, Junko?"

Then Junko was torn in his heart, for he had never lost his fondness
for the Lord Kuroda, and it touched him deeply to see the *daimyo* so dis-
tressed. But he shook his head and murmured only, "These are indeed
dark times, my lord, and there is nothing that would honor my unworthy
self more than to offer you any candle to light your way. But in all truth,
I have no guidance for you, except to offer sacrifice and pay the priests
well. Who but they can read the intentions of the *kami*?"

"Apparently the gods' intentions were for my priests to leave me," the
Lord Kuroda replied. "Half of them ran off when Minister Nakamura's
body was discovered, and you yourself have seen the rest vanishing day
by day since Kondo's has *not* been discovered. In a little the only priest
left to me will be my old Yukiyasa." He sighed deeply, and turned from
Junko, saying, "No matter, my friend. I had no business to place my own
yoke upon your shoulders. Go to your bed and your life, and think no

more of this. But know that I am grateful…grateful." And as he shuffled away, disappearing from sight among his bodyservants, it seemed to Junko for the first time that his master was an old man.

He repeated the conversation to Sayuri, generally satisfied with the way he had responded to the *daimyo*'s queries, but adding in some annoyance, "I expected him to offer me Kondo's position, but he never mentioned it. It will surely come, I am certain."

Sayuri had grown increasingly silent since the night of the black bear, more and more keeping to their quarters, avoiding her many friends and interests, shirking her duty to the Lady Hara when she dared; most often taking refuge in sleep, where she twitched and whimpered as Junko had never known her to do. Now, without looking at him, she said, "Yes. It will come."

And so it did, in good time, and with little competition, whether direct or stealthy, for rising to high rank at the court of Lord Kuroda more and more clearly involved risking a terrible end. There was no one who openly connected the deaths with the steady advancement of the peasant Junko—Junko-*san* now, to all, by special order—nor, certainly, with his charming and modest wife—but there were some who pondered, and one in particular who pondered deeply. This was Yukiyasa.

Yukiyasa was the Shinto priest who had married Sayuri to Junko. As the Lord Kuroda had predicted, he was the only priest who had not fled the court, and the only person who seemed able to rouse Sayuri from her melancholic torpor. Out of his hearing, he was called the Turtle, partly due to his endlessly wrinkled face and neck, but also because of his bright black eyes that still missed nothing—not the smallest change in the flowing of the sea or the angle of the wind, not the slightest trembling of the eyelashes of a woman fearing to show fear for her husband far away in battle. If age had slowed his step, it seemed to have quickened his perceptions: he could smell rain two days off, identify a Mongolian plover before others could be sure it was even a bird, and hear a leaf's fall or a fieldmouse's squeak through the castle walls. But he did look more and more like a turtle every season.

Junko instinctively avoided the old priest as much as he could, keeping clear of the *inari* shrine he maintained, except for the *Shogatsu Matsuri,* the New Year's festival. But Yukiyasi visited with Sayuri almost daily—in her quarters, if she did not come to the shrine—reading to her from the *Kojiki* and the *Nihon shoki,* teasing and provoking her until she had no choice but to smile, often remarking that she should one day consider becoming a Shinto priest herself. She always changed the subject, but the notion made her thoughtful, all the same.

"Today he said that I understood the way of the gods," she reported to Junko one spring evening. "What do you suppose he meant by that?"

They were walking together in the Realm of the Blue Dragon, still their favorite part of the castle gardens, and Junko's attention was elsewhere at the moment, contemplating the best use of the numerous waterways and fisheries that ran through the Lord Kuroda's vast domain. Now, his notice returning to his wife, he said, "The *kami* have always been shapeshifters; look at the foxes your friend's shrine celebrates. Perhaps he senses…" He did not finish the sentence.

Sayuri's grip on his arm tightened enough to hurt him. "No," she said in a small voice. "No, that cannot be, cannot. I change no longer. Never again." Her face had gone paler than the moon.

"The bear?" He had never meant to ask her, and immediately wished he could take back the question. But she answered him straightforwardly, almost in a rush, as the melting snows had quickened the measure even of Lord Kuroda's gentle stream.

"I was so frightened to be the bear. I didn't like it at all. It was a terrible thing."

"A terrible thing that you were—or a terrible thing you did?" He could not keep his own words from tumbling out.

"Both," she whispered, *"both."* She was crying now, but she resisted strongly when Junko tried to hold her. "No, no, you mustn't, it is too dangerous. I am sorry, so sorry, I so wish your arrow had killed me. Then Ikeda would be alive, and Nakamura, and Kondo—"

"And I would still be what I was born," Junko interrupted her. "Junko the hunter, lower than any cook—because a cook is at least an artist, while a huntsman is a butcher—Junko, with his peasant ways and peasant accent, barely tolerable just as long as he keeps to his place. If it were not for you, my otter, my wolf—"

"No!" She twisted away from him, and actually ran a few paces off before she turned to stare at him in real horror. It was long before she spoke again, and then she said quietly, "We have quite traded places, have we not, my husband? You were the one who grieved for the poor victims of my shape-changing, and it was I who laughed at your foolish concern and prided myself upon the improvements I brought to your fortunes, as a good wife should do. And now…" She faltered for a little, still looking at him as though *he* were the strange animal she had never seen before. "Now you turn out to be the shapeshifter, after all, and I the soft fool who'll have none of it, no more. Not even for love of you—and I loved you when I was an otter—not even for the sake of at last learning my own being, my own soul. That can go undiscovered forever, and

welcome, and I will remain Sayuri, your wife, no more and no less. And I will tend three graves, and pray at the shrine, and live as I can with what I have done. That is how it will be."

"'That is how it will be,'" Junko mimicked her. "And I? I am to rise no higher at this court, where the old men despise me and the young ones plot against me—all because you have suddenly turned nun?" He moved toward her, his eyes narrowing. "Yukiyasa," he said slowly. "It's the Turtle, isn't it? That horrible antique, with his foul-smelling robes and his way of shooting his head out and blinking at people. It's Yukiyasa who has put all this into your head, I know it. I swear, if I really *could* change my shape—"

But Sayuri covered his mouth with her hand, crying, "Don't! Don't ever say that, I beg you! You have no idea what that is like, what that *is*, or you would never say such a thing." In that moment, the look in her beautiful dark eyes made Junko think of the black bear rising on its hind legs and turning to sniff the air for him, and he was afraid of her. He did not move, nor did he try to speak, until she took her hand away.

Then he said, not mockingly this time, but as soothingly as he knew how, "Well, we have come a very long way together—too long a way for us to turn on each other now. I ask pardon for my thoughtlessness and my stupidity, and I promise never to speak of...what we will not speak of, ever again. Such advancement as I can win on my own, that will I do, and be well satisfied with my own nature, and my own fate. Will that content you, my wife?"

"That will content me, husband," she whispered after a little. She did not resist when Junko put his arms around her, but he could feel the fear in her body, and so he added lightly, "And I promise also never to say another word concerning your Turtle, for I know how much his wisdom and kindness mean to you. Not a word—not even if you were indeed to become a priest, as he wishes you to do. So." He stroked her hair, as she had always liked him to do. "Shall we go on with our walk?"

And Sayuri laughed for the first time in a long while, and she nodded and put her arm through his, and they walked on together.

But it was not true; though, to do him justice, Junko tried earnestly, for a while, to believe it so. Even while taking his new post as Minister of Waterways and Fisheries with all seriousness—descended as he was from river people who had manned weirs, dams and sluices throughout Honshu and Shikoku for generations—he could not help coveting another position: that of Masanori Morioka, Chief Minister for Dealing with Barbarians. This ranked just under the Lord Kuroda himself—in another country, Morioka would have been called Prime Minister—and where the *daimyo* was aging visibly, Morioka was only a year or two older than Junko himself. Far more important, he came of high samurai family, and, since Lord Kuroda and the Lady Hara had no children, he might already have been chosen to succeed his lord when the time came. Junko was increasingly certain of this: the Lord Kuroda was no one to leave his lands in chaos while his relatives went to war over so rich a prize. It must be Murioka; there could be no doubt of it.

In the past, this would have mattered little to the Junko whose only concern was whether the rains had brought enough new grass for the deer, and if the snow monkeys' unusually thick coats might foretell an evil winter. But it mattered now to this Junko, and—again to be fair— he did his best to conceal his jealousy from his wife. In this he failed, because he talked in his sleep almost every night, and Sayuri's heart shivered to decipher his mumblings and his whispered rants. She would lie as close to him as she could then, hoping somehow to absorb his aching resentment into her own body, and wishing once again, deeply and dearly, that she had died an otter.

As the Lord Kuroda grew more frail, and Morioka steadily assumed a greater share of the *daimyo*'s responsibilities, Junko's anger and envy became more and more plain to see, and not only by his wife. Lady Hara spoke of it with some disquiet to Sayuri; and Akira, the taciturn horsemaster, told Junko that he needed to ride out more, and to spend more time in the company of horses than of courtiers, and less time fretting over childish matters that he could not control in any case. And it was Lord Kuroda himself, having summoned Junko to him in private, who was the one to ask, "Have I done wrong, then? What troubles you, Junko-*san*?" For he always showed a tenderness toward Junko that made certain spiteful folk grumble that the *daimyo* had fathered him in secret on a peasant woman.

Then Junko, for a moment, was ashamed of his bitterness, and he knelt before Lord Kuroda and put his hands between the hard old hands that trembled only a little, even now, and he whispered, "Never have I had anything from you but goodness beyond my worth. But would that I enjoyed the opportunity to serve you that others have earned—perhaps through ability, perhaps...not."

By this Lord Kuroda knew that he was speaking of Masanori Morioka. He responded with unaccustomed sternness, "Minister of Waterways and Fisheries you are, and I would never permit even Morioka to trespass on a single one of the duties and privileges that your honorable service has won for you. But we must always remember that all barbarians believe themselves to be civilized, and dealing with such people while keeping the dangerous truth from them requires a subtlety that few possess. You are not one of them, Junko-*san*."

He smiled at Junko then, leaning stiffly forward to raise him to his feet. "Nor am I, not really. It is a matter of training from one's childhood, my friend—learning to sense and walk, even in the dark, the elusive balance between humility and servility, candor and courtesy, power and the appearance of power. Masanori Morioka is far better at this game than I ever was, even when I was young. Let the worst come, I will have no fears for my realm in his hands."

With those words, the worst had indeed come to Junko; with those words Morioka was doomed. Yet he managed to keep his answer calm and slow, saying merely, "In his hands? Is it so decided, lord?"

"It is so decided," his master replied.

Junko drew himself to his full height and bowed deeply, holding his arms rigid at his sides. "Then I also must retire from the court, since Minister Morioka and I dislike each other too greatly to work together after you are gone. While you remain, so will I."

But the Lord Kuroda smiled then: not widely, which was not his way, but with a certain sad warmth that was new to his kind, ugly face. He responded only, "In that case I will stay alive just as long as it befits me to do so," and with a small flick of his fingers gave Junko leave to withdraw.

On the way to his quarters, he briefly encountered Morioka, who bowed mockingly to him, saying nothing until Junko had returned the bow and passed on. Then he called after him, "And how go the mighty consultations with our *daimyo?*" for he knew where Junko had been, and he had his own envy of the Lord Kuroda's feeling for Junko.

"As well as your great battles," Junko answered him, and Morioka scowled like a demon-mask, since he had never borne arms for Lord Kuroda or any other, and everyone at court knew *that*. So they went on to their separate destinations; and Junko, reaching home, flung himself down on the bed and wept with a terrifying ferocity. Nor could he stop: it was as though the tears of rage that had been building and swelling within him since his stoic childhood had finally surged out of his control, and were very likely to flood him as the cyclones still did every year to his family's sliver of farmland. He was all water, and all bitterness, and nothing beyond, ever.

He continued biting the bedclothes to muffle his weeping, but Sayuri heard him just the same, and came to him. At first she drew back in something close to fear of such violent anguish; but in a little she sat on the edge of the bed and put her hand timidly on his shoulder, saying, "Husband, I cannot bear to see you so. What in this world can possibly be such an immeasurable grief to you? Speak to me, and if I cannot help you, I will at least share your sorrow. Share it with me now, I beg you."

And she said all else that good wives—and good husbands, as well—say at such moments; and after a long while Junko lifted his head to face her. His eyes and nose and mouth were all clotted with tears, and he looked as children look who have been punished for no reason they can understand. But behind the tears Sayuri saw a hot and howling anger that would have turned him to a beast then and there, if it could have done. In a thick, shaking voice he told her what the Lord Kuroda had told him, ending by saying, more quietly now, "You see, it was all for nothing, after all. All of it, for nothing."

Sayuri thought at first that he was speaking of his long, difficult climb up from his poor peasant birth to the castle luxury where they sat together on a bed whose sheets were of Chinese silk. But Junko, his voice gone wearily flat and almost toneless, went on, "Everything you did for me, for us—Ikeda, Nakamura, Kondo—it was all wasted, they might just as well have been spared. Yes—they might as well have remained alive."

"Yes," Sayuri repeated dazedly. "They might have remained alive." But then she shook off the confused stupor that his words had brought about, and she gripped his wrists, saying, "But Junko-*san*, no, I never killed for your sake. I was a bear, a wolf, a weasel after a rabbit—I was hungry, not human. In those beast forms I did not even know who those men were!"

"Did you not?" the fierce question came back at her. "Be honest with yourself, my wife. Did the wolf never know for a moment that tearing out the throat of Isamu Nakamura would benefit a certain peasant who dreamed of becoming a counselor to a *daimyo*? What of the bear—surely the bear must have known that carrying off the previous Minister of Waterways and Fisheries would open the way—"

"*No!* No, it is not true!" Still holding his wrists tightly, she shook him violently. "The animals were innocent—*I* was innocent! It was coincidence, nothing more—"

"*Was it?*" They stared at each other for a moment longer, before Sayuri released Junko's wrists and he turned away, shaking his head. "It doesn't matter, it is of no importance. Whatever was true then, you will take no more shapes, and I...I will stay not one day after Lord Kuroda is gone. We will retire to my home village, and I will be a big man there, and you the most beautiful and accomplished woman. And why not?— we deserve it. And they will give us the very grandest house they possess, in my honor, and it will be smaller than this one room, and smell of old men. And why not? We have served the great *daimyo* faithfully and well, and we deserve it all."

And saying this, he walked away, leaving Sayuri alone to bite her knuckles and make small sounds without tears.

The old priest Yukiyasa found her so when he came to read to her, since she had not appeared at the shrine. Having performed her wedding, he regarded her therefore as his daughter and his responsibility, and he lifted her face and looked long at her, asking no questions. Nor did she speak, but placed one hand over his dry, withered hand and they stood in silence, until her mind was a little eased. Then she said, in a voice that sounded as ancient as his, "I have done evil, and may do so again. Can you help me, Turtle?" For he knew perfectly well what he was called, but she was the only one permitted to address him by that name.

Yukiyasa said, "Often and often does evil result where nothing but good was meant. I am sure this is true in your case."

But Sayuri answered, "What I intended—even if it was not quite I who intended it—is of no importance. What I did is what matters."

The priest peered at her, puzzled as he had not been in a very long time, and yet with a curious sense that he might do best to remain so. He continued, "I have many times thought that in this world far more harm is wrought by foolish men than by wicked ones. Perhaps you were foolish, my daughter. Are you also vain enough to imagine yourself the only one?"

That won him a fragment of a smile, coming and going so swiftly that it might have been an illusion, and perhaps was. But Yukiyasa was encouraged, and he said further, "You *were* foolish, then," not making a question of it. "Well, so. I myself have done such things as I would never confess to you—not because they were evil, but because they were so *stupid*—"

Sayuri said, "I change into animals. People have died."

Yukiyasa did not speak for a long time, but he never took his eyes from Sayuri's eyes. Finally he said quietly, "Yes, I see them," and he did not say whether he meant wolves or bears, or Daisuke Ikeda, Minister Shiro Nakamura or Minister Mitsuo Kondo. He said, "The *kami* did this to you before you were born. It is your fate, but it is not your fault."

"But what *I* did is my fault!" she cried. "Death is death, killing is killing!" She paused to catch her breath and compose herself, and then went on in a lower tone. "My husband thinks that I killed those men to remove them from his path to power in the court. I say *no, no, it was the animals, not me*—but what if it is true? What if that is exactly what happened? What should I do then, Turtle, please tell me? Turtle, please!"

The old man took her hands between his own. "Even if every word is true, you are still blameless. Listen to me now. I have studied the way of the *kami* all my life, and I am no longer sure that there is even such a thing as blame, such a thing as sin. You did what you did, and you are being punished for it now, as we two stand here. The *kami* are never punished. This is the one thing I know, daughter, with all my years and all my learning. The *kami* are never punished, and we always are."

Then he kissed Sayuri on the forehead, and made her lie down, and recited to her from the *Kojiki* until she fell asleep, and he went away.

Passing the courtyard where the *daimyo*'s soldiers trained, he noticed Junko watching an exercise, but plainly not seeing it. The old priest paused beside him for a time, observing Junko's silent discomfort in his presence without enjoying it. When Junko finally bowed and started away—still without speaking, discourteous as that was—Yukiyasa addressed him, saying, "I will give you my advice, though you do not want it. Whether for a good reason or a bad one, it would be a terrible mistake for you ever again to order your wife, in words or in your thoughts, to become so much as a squirrel or a sparrow. A good reason or a bad one. Do you understand me?"

Then Junko turned and strode back to him, his face white, but his eyes wide with anger, and his voice a low hiss. "I do *not* understand you. I do not know what you are talking about. My wife is no shapeshifter, but if she were, I would never make such a request of her. Never, I have *sworn* to her that I would never—"

He halted, realizing what he had said. Yukiyasa looked at him for a long moment before he repeated, "In words or in thoughts," and walked slowly on to the shrine where he lived. Junko stared after him, but did not follow.

But by this time he was too far lost in envy of Masanori Morioka to give more than the briefest consideration to the Shinto priest's warning. True to his promise to her, he held himself back from urging Sayuri to remember, in so many words, that there was no future for them in a court commanded by Morioka. Even so, he found one way or another to put it into her mind every day; and every night he awoke well before dawn, hoping to find her gone, as had happened so many times in their life together. But she continued to slumber the night through, though often enough she wakened him with her twitching and moaning, which once would have moved him instantly to soothe and comfort her. Now he only turned over with a disappointed grunt and drowsed off again. He had always had the gift of sleep.

Finally, on a night of early autumn, his desire was granted. The moon was high and small, leaves were stirring softly in a warm breeze, and the space beside him was empty. Junko smiled in the darkness and rose quickly to follow. Then he hesitated, partly from fear of just what he might overtake; partly because it would clearly be better to be aroused by running feet in the corridors and the dreadful news about Minister Morioka. But it was impossible for even him to close his eyes now, so he donned a kimono and paced their quarters from one end to the other, impatiently pushing fragile screens aside, cursing when he tripped over pairs of Sayuri's *geta*, and listening for screams.

But there was no sound beyond the soft creaking of the night, and finally the silence became more than he could endure. Telling himself that Sayuri, in whatever form, would surely know him, he drew a long breath and stepped out into the corridor.

Standing motionless as his eyes grew accustomed to the darkness, he saw and heard nothing, but he smelled...or almost smelled...no, he had no words for what he smelled. The wild odor of the bloody-mouthed black bear was lodged in his throat yet, as was the scent of the wolf fur clutched in the dead fingers of Minister Nakamura. But this was a cold smell, like that of a great serpent, and there was another underneath, even colder—*burned bone,* Junko thought, though that made no sense at all; and then, even more absurdly, *bone flames.* He turned to look back at the entrance to his quarters, but it seemed already far away, receding as he watched, like a sail on the sea.

There was no choice but to go on. He wished that he had brought a sword or a *tanto* dagger, but only samurai were permitted to carry such weapons; and for all his kindly respect and affection, the Lord Kuroda had never made any exception for Junko. When he was in Morioka's place, he would change *that.* He moved ahead, step by step, cautiously feeling his way between splashes of moonlight.

Masanori Morioka's quarters were located a floor above his own—closer to the *daimyo's,* which was something else to brood about, and tend to later. He started up the stair, anxious neither to alert nor alarm anyone, and beginning to wonder—all was still *so* quiet—whether he had misread Sayuri's absence. What if she had merely gone scurrying in mouse-shape, as she had once been fond of doing, skittering in the castle rafters as a bat, or even roving outside as any sort of small night thing? How would it look if he were surprised wandering himself where he had no reason to be at such an hour? He paused, very nearly of a mind to turn back...and yet the serpent-smell had grown stronger with each step, and so near now that he felt as though he were the creature exuding it: as though the coldly burning bones were, in some way, his own.

Another step, and another after, moving sideways now without realizing that he was doing so, the serpent-smell pressing on him like a smothering blanket, making his breath come shorter and shallower. Once he lurched to one knee, twice into the wall, unsure now of whether he was stumbling upstairs or down...then he did hear the scream.

It was a woman's scream, not a man's. And it came, not from Minister Morioka's quarters, but from those of the Lord Kuroda and the Lady Hara.

For an instant, Junko was too stupefied to be afraid; it was as though the strings of his mind had been cut, as well as those of his petrified body. Then he uttered a wordless cry that he himself never heard, and sprang toward the *daimyo*'s rooms, kicking off his slippers when they skidded on the polished floors.

Lady Hara screamed again, as Junko burst through the rice-paper door, stumbling over the wreckage of shattered *tansu* chests and *shoji* screens. He could not see her or Lord Kuroda at first: the vast figure in his path seemed to draw all light and shape and color into itself, so that nothing was real except the towering horns, the cloven hooves, the sullen gleam of the reptilian scales from the waist down, the unbearable stench of simmering bone...

"Ushi-oni!" He heard it in his mind as an insect whisper. Lord Kuroda was standing between his wife and the demon, legs braced in a fighting stance, *wakizashi* sword trembling in his old hand. The *ushi-oni* roared like a landslide and knocked the sword across the room. Lord Kuroda drew his one remaining weapon, the *tanto* he carried always in his belt. The *ushi-oni* made a different sound that might have been laughter. The dagger fell to the floor.

Junko said, "Sayuri."

The great thing turned at his voice, as the black bear had done, and he saw the nightmare cow-face, and the rows of filthy fangs crowding the slack, drooling lips. And—as he had seen it in the red eyes of the bear—the unmistakable recognition.

"My wife," Junko said. "Come away."

The *ushi-oni* roared again, but did not move, neither toward him, nor toward Lord Kuroda and Lady Hara. Junko said, "Come. I never meant this. I never meant this."

Out of the corner of his eye, Junko saw the *daimyo* moving to recover his fallen dagger. But the *ushi-oni*'s attention was all on Junko, the mad yellow-white eyes had darkened to a dirty amber, and the claws on its many-fingered hands had all withdrawn slightly. Junko faced it boldly, all unarmed as he was, saying again, "Come away, Sayuri. We do not belong here, you and I."

He knew that if he turned his head he would see a blinking, quaking Minister Morioka behind him in the ruined doorway, but for that he cared nothing now. He took a few steps toward the *ushi-oni,* halting when it growled stinking fire and backed away. Junko did not speak further, but only reached out with his eyes. *We know each other.*

He was never to learn whether the monster that had been—that *was*—his wife would have come to him, nor what would have been the result if it had. Lady Hara, suddenly reaching the limit of her body's courage, uttered a tiny sigh, like a child falling asleep, and collapsed to the floor. The *ushi-oni* began to turn toward her, and at that moment the Lord Kuroda lunged forward and struck with all the strength in his old arm. The *tanto* buried itself to the coral-ornamented hilt in the right side of the demon.

The *ushi-oni*'s howl shook the room and seemed to split Junko's head, bringing blood even from his eyes, as well as from his ears and nose. A great scaled paw smashed him down as the creature roared and reeled in its death agony, trampling everything it had not already smashed to splinters, dragging ancient scrolls and brush paintings down from the walls, crushing the Lord Kuroda family shrine underfoot. The *ushi-oni* bellowed unceasingly, the sound slamming from wall back to broken wall, and everyone hearing it bellowed with the same pain, bleeding like Junko and like him holding, not their heads and faces, but their hearts. When the demon fell, and was silent, the sound continued on forever.

But even forever ends, and there came a time when Junko pulled himself to his feet. He found himself face to face with Minister Morioka, pale as a grubworm, gabbling like an infant, walking as though he had just learned how. Others were in the room now, all shouting, all brandishing weapons, all keeping their distance from the great, still thing on the floor. He saw the Lord Kuroda, far away across the ruins, bending over Lady Hara, carefully and tenderly lifting her to her feet while staring strangely at Junko. Whatever his face, as bloody as Junko's own, revealed, it was neither anger nor outrage, but Junko looked away anyway.

The *ushi-oni* had not moved since its fall, but its eyes were open, unblinking, darkening. Junko knelt beside it without speaking. The fanged cow-lips twitched slightly, and a stone whisper reached his ear and no other, shaping two words. *"My nature..."* There were no more words, and no sound in the room.

Junko said, "She was my wife."

No one answered him, not until the Lord Kuroda said, "No." Junko realized then that the expression in his master's eyes was one of deepest pity. Lord Kuroda said, "It is not possible. An *ushi-oni* may take on another shape if it wishes, being a demon, but in death it returns to its true being, always. You see that this has not occurred here."

"No," Junko answered him, "because this *was* Sayuri's natural form. This is what she was, but she did not know it, no more than I. I swear that she did not know." He rose, biting his lower lip hard enough to bring more blood to his mouth, and faced the *daimyo* directly. He said, "This was my doing. All of it. The weasel, the wolf, the bear—she meant only to help me, and I...I did not want to know." He looked around at the shattered room filled with solemn people in nightrobes and armor. "Do you understand? Any of you?"

The Lord Kuroda's compassionate manner had taken on a shade of puzzlement; but the Lady Hara was nodding her elegant old head. Behind Junko, Minister Morioka had at last found language, though his stammering voice retained none of its normal arrogance. He asked timidly, "How could an *ushi-oni* not know what it was? How could such a monster ever marry a human being?"

"Perhaps because she fell in love," the Lady Hara said quietly. "Love makes one forget many things."

"I cannot speak for my wife," Junko replied. "For myself, there are certain things I will remember while I live, which I beg will not be long." He turned his eyes to Minister Morioka. "I wanted her to kill you. I never said it in those words—*never*—but I made very sure she knew that I wanted you out of my way, as she had removed three others. I ask your pardon, and offer my head. There can be no other atonement."

Then the Minister shrank back without replying, for while he had no objection to the death penalty, he greatly preferred to see it administered by someone else. But the Lord Kuroda asked in wonder, "Yet the *ushi-oni* came here, to these rooms, not to Minister Morioka's quarters. Why should she—*it*—have done so?"

Junko shook his head. "That I cannot say. I know only that I am done with everything." He walked slowly to retrieve the *daimyo*'s sword, brought it to him, and knelt again, baring his neck without another word.

Lord Kuroda did not move or speak for a long time. The Lady Hara put her hand on his arm, but he did not look at her. At last he set the *wakizashi* back in its lacquered sheath, the soft click the only sound in the ravaged room, which seemed to have turned very cold since the fall of the *ushi-oni*. He touched Junko's shoulder, beckoning him to rise.

"Go in peace," he said without expression, "if there is any for you. No harm will come to you, since it will be known that you are still under the protection of the Lord Kuroda. Farewell...Junko-*san*."

A moment longer they stared into one another's eyes; then Junko bowed to his master and his master's lady, turned like a soldier, and walked away, past smashed and shivered *tengu* furniture, past Minister Morioka—who would not look at him—through the crowd of gaping, muttering retainers, and so out of the Lord Kuroda's castle. He did not return to his quarters for any belongings, but went away barefoot, clad only in his kimono, and he looked back only once, when he smelled the smoke and knew that the servants were already burning the body of the *ushi-oni* that was also his wife Sayuri. Then he went on.

And no one ever would have known what became of him, if the old priest Yukiyasa had not been the patient, inquisitive man that he was. Some years after the disappearance of Minister Junko, the commoner who had ridden at the right hand of a *daimyo* for a little while, Yukiyasa left his Shinto shrine in the care of a disciple, picked up his staff and his begging bowl, and set off on a trail long since grown cold. But it was not the first such trail that he had followed in his life, and he possessed the curious patience of the very old, that is perhaps the closest mortal approach to immortality. The journey was a trying one, but many peasant families were happy to please the gods by offering him lodging, and peasants have long memories. It took the priest less time than one might have expected to track Junko to a village that barely merited the title, on a brook that was called a river by the people living there. For that matter, Junko himself was not known in the village by his rightful name, but as Toru, which is *wayfarer*. Yukiyasa found him at the brook in the late afternoon, lying flat on his belly, fishing for salmon by the oldest method there is, which is tickling them slowly and gently, until they fall asleep, and then scooping them into a net. There were already six fish on the grass beside him.

Junko was coaxing a seventh salmon to the bank, and did not look up or speak when the old priest's shadow fell over him. Not until he had landed the last fish did he say, "I knew it was you, Turtle. I could always smell you as far as the summer island."

Yukiyasa took no offense at this, but only chuckled as he sat down. "The incense does cling. Others have mentioned it."

Neither spoke for some time, but each sat considering the other. To the priest's eye, Junko looked brown and healthy enough, but notably older than he should have. His face was thinner, his hair had turned completely white, and there was an air about him, not so much of loneliness as of solitude, as though what lived inside him had left no room for another living being, or even a living thought. *He chose a good name,* Yukiyasa thought. "You do well here, my son?"

"As well as I may." Junko shrugged. "I hunt and fish for the folk here, and mend their poor flimsy dams and weirs, as I was raised to do. And they in turn shelter me, and call me *Wayfarer,* and ask no questions. I am where I belong."

To this Yukiyasa knew not what to say, and they two were silent again, until Junko asked finally, "Akira Yamagata, the horsemaster—he is well?"

"Gone these two years and more," the priest replied gently, for he knew of the friendship. Junko inquired after a few other members of Lord Kuroda's household, but not once about the *daimyo* himself, or about Lady Hara. Wondering on this, and thinking to provoke Junko beyond prudence, Yukiyasa began to speak of the successes of Masanori Morioka. "Since you...since you left, the ascent in his fortunes has been astonishing. He is very nearly a Council of Ministers in himself now—and the lord being old, and without children..." He shrugged, leaving the sentence deliberately unfinished.

"Well, well," Junko said mildly, almost to himself. "Well, well." He smiled then, for the first time at the puzzled priest, and it was a smile of such piercing amusement as even Yukiyasa had never seen in all his long life. "I am pleased for him, and wish him all success. Let him know of it."

"This after you sent an *ushi-oni* to destroy him?" It was not Yukiyasa's custom ever to raise his voice, but perplexity was bringing him close to it. "You said yourself that you wished Minister Morioka dead and out of your way. Sayuri died of that envy." Startled and frightened by the anger in his words, he repeated them nevertheless, realizing that he had loved the woman who was no woman. "She died because you were insanely, cruelly jealous of that man you praise now."

Junko's smile vanished, replaced, not by anger of his own, but by the same weary knowledge that had aged his face. "Not so, though I wish it were. You have no idea how I wish that were true." He was silent for a time, looking away as he began to gather the seven salmon into a rush-lined basket. Then he said, still not meeting the priest's eyes, "No. My wife died because she understood me."

"What nonsense is this?" Yukiyasa cried out. He was deeply ashamed of his loss of control, yet for once refused to restrain himself. "I warned you, I *warned* you, in so many words, never again to coax her to change form—never to let her do it, for your sake and her own—and see what came of your disregard! She yielded once more to your desire, set forth to murder Minister Morioka, as she had slain others, and thereby redis-covered the terrible truth she had forgotten for love of you. For love of you!" The old priest was on his feet now, trembling and sweating, jab-bing his finger at Junko's expressionless face. "Understand you? How could she understand such a man? She only loved, and she died of it, and it need not have happened so. It need not have happened!"

The sky was going around in great, slow circles, and Yukiyasa thought that it would be sensible to sit down, but he could not find his feet. Someone was saying somewhere, a long way off, "She loved me when she was an otter." Then Junko had him by the shoulders, and was guiding him carefully through the long journey back to the grass and the ground. In time the sky stopped spinning, and Yukiyasa drank cold brook water from Junko's cupped hands and said, "Thank you. I am sorry."

"No need," Junko replied. "You have the right of it as much as any-one ever will. But Sayuri knew something that no one else knew, not even I myself." He paused, waiting until the priest's color had returned and his heartbeat had ceased to shake his body so violently. Then he said, "Sayuri knew that in my soul, in the darkest corner of my soul, I wished her to go exactly where she did go. And it was not to Minister Morioka's quarters."

It took the priest Yuriyasa no time at all, dazed as he still was, to comprehend what he had been told, but a very long while indeed to find a response. At last he said, almost whispering, "The Lord Kuroda loved you. Like a son."

Junko nodded without answering. Yukiyasa asked him hesitantly, "Did you imagine that if Sayuri...if Lord Kuroda were gone, you might somehow become *daimyo* yourself?"

"'Like a son' is not like being a son," Junko replied. "No, I had no such expectations. My master, in his generosity, had raised me higher than I could possibly have conceived or deserved, being who I am— *what* I am. In a hundred lifetimes, how should I ever hold any grievance against the Lord Kuroda?"

Twilight had arrived as they spoke together, and fires were being lighted in the nearest huts. Junko stood up, slinging the fish basket over his shoulder. Looking down at Yukiyasa, his face appearing younger with the eyes in shadow, he said, "But Sayuri knew the *ushi-oni* in me, the thing that hated having been shown all that I could not have or be, and that wished, in the midst of luxury, to have been left where I belonged—in a place just like this one, where not one person knows how to write the words *daimyo* or *shogun,* and *samurai* is a word that comes raiding and killing, trampling our crops, burning our homes. Do you hear what I am telling you, priest of the *kami*? Do you hear?"

He pulled Yukiyasa to his feet, briefly holding the old man close as a lover, though he did not seem to notice it. He said, very quietly, "I loved Lord Kuroda for the man he was. But from the day I entered his castle—a ragged, ignorant boy from a ragged village of which *he* was ignorant—I hated him for *what* he was. I spent days and years forgetting that I hated him and all his kind, every moment denying it in my heart, in my mind, in my bones." For a moment he put his hand hard over his mouth, as though to stop the words from coming out, but they came anyway. "Sayuri...Sayuri knew my soul."

A child's voice called from the village, the sound sweetly shrill on the evening air. Junko smiled. "I promised her family fish tonight. We must go."

He took Yukiyasa's elbow respectfully, and they walked slowly away from the river in the fading light. Junko asked, "You will rest here for a few days? It is a long road home. I know."

The priest nodded agreement. "You will not return with me." It was not a question, but he added, "Lord Kuroda has not long, and he has missed you."

"And I him. Tell him I will forget my own name before I forget his kindness." A sudden whisper of a laugh. "Though I am Toru now, and no one will ever call me Junko again, I think."

"Junko-*san*," Yukiyasa corrected him. "Even now, he always asks after Junko-*san*."

Neither spoke again until they had entered the village, and muddy children were clinging to Junko's legs, dragging him toward a hut further on. Then the priest said quietly, "She really believed she was human. She might never have known." Junko bowed his head. "Did you believe it yourself, truly? I have wondered."

The answer was almost drowned out by the children's yelps of happiness and hunger. "As much as I ever believed I was Junko-*san*."

The Rock in the Park

Van Cortlandt Park begins a few blocks up Gunhill Road: past the then-vacant lot where us neighborhood kids fought pitched battles over the boundaries of our parents' Victory Gardens; past Montefiore Hospital, which dominates the entire local skyline now; past Jerome Avenue, where the IRT trains still rattle overhead, and wicked-looking old ladies used to sit out in front of the kosher butcher shops, savagely plucking chickens. It's the fourth-largest park in New York City, and on its fringes there are things like golf courses, tennis courts, baseball diamonds, bike and horse trails, a cross-country track and an ice-skating rink—even a cricket pitch. That's since my time, the cricket pitch.

But the heart of Van Cortlandt Park is a deep old oak forest. Inside it you can't hear the traffic from any direction—the great trees simply swallow the sound—and the place doesn't seem to be in anybody's flight path to JFK or LaGuardia. There are all sorts of animals there, especially black squirrels, which I've never seen anywhere else; and possums and rabbits and raccoons. I saw a coyote once, too. Jake can call it a dog all he likes. I know better.

It's most beautiful in fall, that forest, which I admit only grudgingly now. Mists and mellow fruitfulness aren't all that comforting when bloody school's starting again, and no one's ever going to compare the leaf-changing season in the Bronx to the shamelessly flamboyant dazzle of October New Hampshire or Vermont, where the trees seem to turn overnight to glass, refracting the sunlight in colors that actually hurt your eyes and confound your mind. Yet the oak forest of Van Cortlandt Park invariably, reliably caught fire every year with the sudden *whoosh* of a building going up, and it's still what I remember when someone says the word *autumn*, or quotes Keats.

It was all of Sherwood to me and my friends, that forest.

Phil and I had a rock in Van Cortlandt that belonged to us; we'd claimed it as soon as we were big enough to climb it easily, which was around fourth grade. It was just about the size and color of an African elephant, and it had a narrow channel in its top that fit a skinny young body perfectly. Whichever one of us got up there first had dibs: the loser had to sit beside. It was part of our private mythology that we had worn that groove into the rock ourselves over the years, but of course that wasn't true. It was just another way of saying *get your own rock, this is ours*. There are whole countries that aren't as territorial as adolescent boys.

We'd go to our Rock after school, or on weekends—always in the afternoons, by which time the sun would have warmed the stone surface to a comfortable temperature—and we'd lie on our backs and look up through the leaves and talk about painters Phil had just discovered, writers I was in love with that week, and girls neither of us quite knew how to approach. We never fixated on the same neighborhood vamp, which was a good thing, because Phil was much more aggressive and experienced than I. Both of us were highly romantic by nature, but I was already a *princesse lointaine* fantasist, while Phil had come early to the understanding that girls were human beings like us. I couldn't see how that could possibly be true, and we argued about it a good deal.

One thing we never spoke of, though, was our shared awareness that the oak forest was magic. Not that we ever expected to see fairies dancing in a ring there, or to spy from our warm, safe perch anything like a unicorn, a wizard or a leprechaun. We knew better than *that*: as a couple of New Yorkers, born and bred, cynicism was part of our bone marrow. Yet even so, in our private hearts we always expected something wild and extraordinary from our Rock and our forest. And one hot afternoon in late September, when we were thirteen, they delivered.

That afternoon, I had been complaining about the criminal unfairness of scheduling a subway World Series, between the Yankees and the Dodgers, during school hours, except for the weekend, when there would be no chance of squeezing into little Ebbets Field. Phil, no baseball fan, dozed in the sun, grunting a response when absolutely required ("Love to do a portrait of Casey Stengel; *there's* a face!"). I was spitballing ways to sneak a portable radio and earpiece into class, so I could follow the first game, when we heard the hoofbeats. In itself, that wasn't unusual—there was a riding stable on the western edge of the Park—but there was a curious hesitancy and wariness about the sound that had us both sitting up on our Rock, and me saying excitedly, "Deer!"

These days, white-tail deer dropping by to raid your vegetable garden are as common in the North Bronx as rabbits and squirrels. Back then, back when I knew Felix Salten's *Bambi* books by heart, they were still an event. But Phil shook his head firmly. "Horse. You don't hear deer."

True enough: like cats, deer are just *there,* where they weren't a moment before. And now that it was closer it didn't sound like a deer to my city ears—nor quite like a horse, either. We waited, staring toward a grove of smaller trees, young sycamores, where something neither of us could quite make out was moving slowly down the slope. Phil repeated, "Horse—look at the legs," and lay back again. I was just about to do the same when the creature's head came into view.

It didn't register at first; it couldn't have done. In that first moment what I saw—what I allowed myself to see—was a small boy riding a dark-bay horse not much bigger than a colt. Then, somewhere around the time that I heard myself whisper "Jesus *Christ,"* I realized that neither the boy nor the horse was *that* small, and that the boy wasn't actually riding. The two of them were *joined*, at the horse's shoulders and just below the boy's waist. In the Bronx, in Van Cortlandt Park, in the twentieth century—in our little lives—a centaur.

They must operate largely on sight, as we do, because the boy only became aware of us just after we spotted him. He halted instantly, his expression a mix of open-mouthed curiosity and real terror—then whirled and was gone, out of sight between the great trees. His hoof-beats were still fading on the dead leaves while we stared at each other.

Phil said flatly, "Just leave me out of your hallucinations, okay? You got weird hallucinations."

"This from a person who still thinks Linda Darnell's hot stuff? You know what we saw."

"I never. I wasn't even here."

"Okay. Me neither. I got to get home." I slid down off the Rock, picking up my new schoolbook bag left at its base. Less than a month, and already my looseleaf notebook looked as though I'd been teething on it.

Phil followed. "Hell, no, it was your figment, you can't just leave it on a doorstep and trust to the kindness of strangers." We'd seen the Marlon Brando *Streetcar Named Desire* a year earlier, and were still bellowing "STELLA!!!" at odd moments in the echoing halls of Junior High School 80. "You saw it, you saw it, I'm gonna tell—Petey saw a centaur—*nyaahh, nyaahh*, Petey saw a centaur!" I swung the book bag at him and chased him all the way out of the Park.

On the phone that evening—we were theoretically doing our Biology homework together—he asked, "So what do the Greek myths tell you about centaurs?"

"Main thing, they can't hold their liquor, and they're mean drunks. You don't ever want to give a centaur that first beer."

"I'll remember. What else?"

"Well, the Greeks have two different stories about where they came from, but I can't keep them straight, so forget it. In the legends they're aggressive, always starting fights—there was a big battle with the Lapiths, who were some way their cousins, except human, don't ask, and I think most of the centaurs were killed, I'm not sure. But some of them were really good, really noble, like Cheiron. Cheiron was the best of the lot, he was a healer and an astrologer and a teacher—he was the tutor of people like Odysseus, Achilles, Hercules, Jason, Theseus, all those guys." I paused, still thumbing through the worn Modern Library Bulfinch my father had given me for my tenth birthday. "That's all I know."

"Mmmff. Book say anything about centaurs turning up in the Bronx? I'll settle for the Western Hemisphere."

"No. But there was a shark in the East River, a couple of years back, you remember? Cops went out in a boat and shot at it."

"Not the same thing." Phil sighed. "I still think it's your fault, somehow. What really pisses me off, I didn't have so much as a box of Crayolas to draw the thing with. Probably never get another chance."

But he did: not the next day, when, of course, we cut P.E. and hurried back to the Park, but the day after that, which was depressingly chilly, past pretending that it was still Indian Summer. We didn't talk much: I was busy scanning for centaurs (I'd brought my Baby Brownie Special camera and a pair of binoculars), and Phil, mumbling inaudibly to himself, kept rummaging through his sketch pads and colored pencils, pastels, gouaches, charcoals and crayons. I made small jokes about his equipment almost crowding me off the Rock, and he glared at me in a way that made me uneasy about that "almost."

I don't remember how long we waited, but it must have been close to two hours. The sun was slanting down, the Rock's surface temperature was actually turning out-and-out cold, and Phil and I were well past conversation when the centaurs came. There were three of them: the young one we had first seen, and the two who were clearly his parents, to judge by the way they stood together on the slope below the sycamore grove. They made no attempt to conceal themselves, but looked directly at us, as we stared back at them. After a long moment, they started down the slope together.

Phil was shaking with excitement, but even so he was already sketching as they came toward us. I was afraid to raise my camera, for fear of frightening the centaurs away. They had a melancholy dignity about them, even the child, that I didn't have words for then: I recall it now as an air of royal exile, of knowing where they belonged, and knowing, equally, that they could never return there. The male—no, the *man*—had a short, thick black beard, a dark, strong-boned face, and eyes of a strange color, like honey. The woman...

Remember, all three of them were naked to the waist, and Phil and I were thirteen years old. For myself, I'd seen nude models in my uncles' studios since childhood, but this woman, this *centauride* (I looked the word up when I got home that night), was more beautiful than anyone I knew. It wasn't just a matter of round bare breasts: it was the heartbreaking grace of her neck, the joyous purity of the line of her shoulders, the delicacy of her collarbones. Phil had stopped sketching, which tells you more than I can about what we saw.

The boy had freckles. Not big ones, just a light golden dusting. His hair was the same color, with a kind of reddish undercoloring, like his mother's hair. He looked about ten or eleven.

The man said, "Strangers, of your kindness, might either of you be Jersey Turnpike?"

He had a deep, calm voice, with absolutely no horsiness in it—nothing of a neigh or a whinny, or anything like that. Maybe a slight sort of funny gurgle in the back of the throat, but hardly noticeable—you'd really have to be listening for it. When Phil and I just gaped, the woman said, "We have never come this way south before. We are lost."

Her voice was low, too, but it had a singing cadence to it, a warm offbeat lilt that entranced and seduced both of us even beyond her innocent nudity. I managed to say, "South....you want to go south...um, you mean south like down south? Like *south* south?"

"Like Florida?" Phil asked. "Mexico?"

The man lifted his head sharply. "Mexico, yes, that was the name, I always forget. It is where we go, all of us, every year, when the birds go. *Mexico.*"

"But we set out too late," the woman explained in her soft, singing voice. "Our son was ill, and we traveled eastward to seek out a healer, and by the time we were ready to start, all the others were gone—"

"And Father took the wrong road," the boy broke in, his tone less accusatory than excited. "We have had such adventures—"

His mother quelled him with a glance. Embarrassment didn't sit easily on the man's powerful face, but he flushed and nodded. "More than one. I do not know this country, and we are used to traveling in company. Now I am afraid that we are completely lost, except for that one name someone gave me—Jersey Turnpike. Can Jersey Turnpike lead us to Mexico?"

We looked at each other. Phil said, "Jersey Turnpike isn't a person, it's a road, a highway. You can go south that way, but not to Mexico—you're way off course for Mexico. I'm sorry."

The boy mumbled, "I *knew* it," but not in a triumphant, wise-ass sort of way; if anything, he appeared suddenly very weary of adventures. The man looked utterly stricken. He bowed his head, and the color seemed to fade visibly from his bright chestnut coat. The woman's manner, on the other hand, hardly altered with Phil's news, except that she moved closer to her husband and pressed her light-gray flank against his, in a gesture of silent trust and confidence.

"You're too far east," I said. "You have to cut down through Texas." They stared uncomprehendingly. I said, "Texas—I *think* you'd go by way of Pennsylvania, Tennessee, maybe Georgia..." I stopped, because I couldn't bear the growing fatigue and bewilderment in their three faces, nor in the way their shining bodies sagged a little more with each state name. I told them, "What you need is a map. We could bring you one tomorrow, easy."

But their expressions did not change. The man said, "We cannot read."

"Not now," the woman said wistfully. "There was a time when our folk were taught the Greek in colthood, every one, and some learned the Roman as well, when it became necessary. But that was in another world that is no more...and learning unused fades with long years. Now only a few of our elders know letters enough to read such things as maps in your tongue—the rest of us journey by old memory and starlight. Like the birds."

Her own eyes were different from her husband's honey-colored eyes: more like dark water, with deep-green wonder turning and glinting far down. Phil never could get them right, and he tried for a long time.

He said quietly now, "I could draw you a picture."

I can't say exactly how the centaurs reacted, or how they looked at him. I was too busy gawking at him myself. Phil said, "Of your route, your road. I could draw you something that'll get you to Mexico."

The man started to speak, but Phil anticipated him. "Not a map. I said a *picture*. No words." I remember that he was sitting crosslegged on the Rock, like our idea of a swami or a yogi; and I remember him leaning intensely forward, toward the centaurs, so that he seemed almost to be joined to the Rock, growing out of it, as they were joined to their horse bodies. He was already drawing invisible pictures with his right forefinger on the palm of his left hand, but I don't think he knew it.

I opened *my* mouth then, but he cut me off too. "It'll take me all day tomorrow, and most likely all night too. You'll be okay till the day after tomorrow?"

The woman said to Phil, "You can do this?"

He grinned at her with what seemed to me outrageous confidence. "I'm an artist. Artists are always drawing people's journeys."

I said, "You could wait right here, if you like. We hardly ever see anybody but us in this part of the park. I mean, if it would suit you," for it occurred to me that I had no idea what they ate, or indeed how they survived in the twentieth century. "I guess we could bring you food."

The man's teeth showed white and large in his black beard. "The forage here is most excellent, even this late in the year."

"There are lots of acorns," the boy said eagerly. "I love acorns."

His mother turned her dark gaze to me. "Can you also make such pictures?"

"Never," I said. "But I could maybe write you a poem." I wrote a lot of poems for girls when I was thirteen. She seemed pleased.

Phil was gathering his equipment and scrambling off the Rock, imperiously beckoning me to follow. "Quit fooling around, Beagle. We got work to do." Standing among them, the size and sheer presence of all three centaurs was, if not intimidating, definitely daunting. Even the boy looked down at us, and we barely came up to the shoulders of his parents' horse-bodies. I've always enjoyed the smell of horses—in those days, they were among the very few animals I wasn't allergic to—but centaurs in groups smell like thunder, like an approaching storm, and it left me dizzy and a bit disoriented. Phil repeated briskly, "Day after tomorrow, right here."

We were halfway up the slope when he snapped his fingers, said, "Ah, *shit!*", dropped his equipment and went running back toward the centaurs. I waited, watching as he moved swiftly between the three of them; but I couldn't, for the life of me, make out what he was doing. He came back almost as quickly, and I noticed then that he was tucking something into his shirt pocket. When I asked what it was, he told me it was nothing I needed to trouble my pretty little head about. You couldn't do anything with him in those tempers, so I left it alone.

He didn't say much else on the walk home, and I managed to keep my curiosity in check until we were parting at my apartment building. Then I burst out with it: "Okay, you're going to draw them a picture that's going to get a family of migrating centaurs all the way to Mexico. This, excuse me, I want to hear." His being on the hook meant, as always, *us* being on the hook, so I felt entitled to my snottiness.

"I can do it. It's been done." His jaw was tight, and his face had the ferocious pallor that I associated entirely with street fights, usually with fat Stewie Hauser and Miltie Mellinger, who never tired of baiting him. "Back in the Middle Ages, I read about it—Roger Bacon did it, somebody like that. But you have to get me some maps, as many as you can. A *ton* of maps, a *shitload* of maps, covering every piece of ground between here—right here, your house—and the Texas border. You got that? *Maps*. Also, you should stop by Bernardo's and see can you borrow that candle of his mother's. He says she got it from a *bruja*, back in San Juan, what could it hurt?"

"But if they can't read maps—"

"Beagle, I have been extraordinarily lenient about that two bucks—"

"Maps. Right. Maps. You think they came down from Canada? Summer up north, winter in Mexico? I bet that's what they do."

"*Maps*, Beagle."

The next day was Saturday, and he actually called me around seven in the morning, demanding that I get my lazy ass on the road and start finding some maps for him. I said certain useful things that I had picked up from Angel Salazar, my Berlitz in such affairs, and was at the gas station up the block by seven-thirty. By ten, I'd hit every other station I could reach on my bike, copped my parents' big Rand McNally road atlas, and triumphantly dumped them all—Bernardo's mother's witch-candle included—on Phil's bed, demanding, "*Now* what, fearless leader?"

"Now you take Dusty for her morning walk." He had his favorite easel set up, and was rummaging through his paper supplies. "Then you go away and write your poem, and you come back when it's time to take Dusty for her evening walk. Then you go away again. All well within your capacities."

Dusty was his aged cocker spaniel, and the nearest thing I had to the longed-for dog of my own. I went home after tending to her, and sat down at the desk in my bedroom to write the poem I'd promised to the centaur mother. I still remember the first lines:

> *If I were a hawk,*
> *I would write you letters—*
> *featherheaded jokes,*
> *scribbled on the air.*
> *If I were a dog*
> *I would do your shopping.*
> *If I were a cat*
> *I would brush your hair.*
> *If I were a bear,*
> *I would build your fires,*
> *bringing in the wood,*
> *breaking logs in two.*
> *If I were a camel*
> *I'd take out the garbage.*

> *If I were a fox*
> *I would talk to you...*

There was more and sillier, but never mind. I was very romantic at thirteen, on very short notice, and I had never seen beauty like hers.

Okay, a little bit extra, because I do like the way it ended:

> *If I were a tiger,*
> *I would dance for you.*
> *If I were a mouse,*
> *I would dance for you.*
> *If I were a whale,*
> *I would dance for you...*

When I came back in the evening to walk Dusty again, Phil was working in his bedroom with the door closed, and an unattended dinner plate cooling on the sill. His parents were more or less inured to his habits by now, but it fretted at them constantly, just as my unsociability worried my mother, who would literally bribe Phil and Jake to get me out of the house. I reassured them, as I always did, that he was working on a really demanding, really challenging project, then grabbed up dog and leash and was gone. It was dark when I brought her back, but Phil's door was still shut.

As it was the next morning, and remained until mid-afternoon, when he called me to say, "Done. Get over here."

He sounded awful.

He looked worse. His eyes were smudgy red pits in a face so white that his own small freckles stood out, and he moved like an old man, as though no part of his body could be trusted not to hurt. He said, "Let's go."

"You're kidding. You wouldn't make it to Lapin's." That was the candy-and-newspaper store across the street. "Take a nap, for God's sake, we'll go when you wake up."

"*Now.*" When he cleared his throat, it sounded exactly like my father's car trying to start on a cold morning.

He was holding a metal tube that I recognized as a tennis-ball can. I reached for it, but he snatched it away. "You'll see it when *they* see it." Just then, he didn't look like anyone I'd ever known.

So we trudged to Van Cortlandt Park, which seemed to take the rest of the afternoon, as slowly as Phil was walking. He had clearly been sitting in more or less the same position for hours and hours on end, and the cramps weren't turning loose without a fight. Now and then he paused to shake his arms and legs violently, and by the time we reached the Park, he was moving a little less stiffly. But he still hardly spoke, and he clung to that tennis-ball can as though it were a cherished trophy, or a life raft.

The centaurs were waiting at the Rock. The boy, a little way up the forest slope from his parents, saw us first, and called out, "They're here!" as he galloped to meet us. But he turned shy midway, as children will, and ran back to the others as we approached. I remember that the man had his arms folded across his chest, and that there were a couple of dew-damp patches on the *centauride*'s coat, the weather having turned cloudy. They said nothing.

Phil said, "I brought it. What I promised. Here, I'll show you."

They moved close, plainly careful not to crowd him with their bodies, as he opened the air-tight can and took out a roll of light, flexible drawing paper. He handed the free end to the man, saying, "See? There you are, all three of you. And there's your road to Mexico."

Craning my neck, I could see a perfectly rendered watercolor of the oak forest, so detailed that I saw not only our Rock with its long groove along the top surface, but also such things as the bird's nest in the upper branches of the tallest sycamore and its family of occupants. I couldn't tell what sort of birds they were, but I knew past doubt that Phil knew. The centaurs in the painting, on the other hand, were not done in any detail beyond the generic, except for relative size, the boy being obviously smaller than the other two. They might have been pieces in a board game.

The man said slowly, not trying to conceal his puzzlement, "This is very pretty, I can see that it is pretty. But it is not our road."

"No, you don't understand," Phil answered him. "Look, take both ends, so." He handed the whole roll to the centaur. "Now…hold it up so you can watch it, and walk straight ahead. Just walk."

The man moved slowly forward, his eyes fixed on the image of the very place where he stood. He had not gone more than a few paces when he cried out, "But it moves! It moves!"

His wife and son—and I—pressed close now, and never mind who stepped on whose feet. The watercolor had changed, though not by much; only a few paces' worth. Now it showed a distinctly marked path in front of the centaur's feet: the path we ourselves took, coming and going in the oak forest. He said again, this time in a near-whisper, "*It moves…*"

"And we too," the woman said. "The little figures—as we move, so do they."

"Not always." Phil's voice was sounding distinctly fuller and stronger. "Go left now, walk off the path—see what happens."

The man did as directed—but the figures remained motionless in the watercolor, reproving him with their stillness. When he returned to the path and stepped along it, they moved with him again, sliding like the magnet-based toys we had then. I noticed for the first time that each one's painted tail had a long, coarse hair embedded in the pigment: chestnut, gray, dark-bay.

Almost speechless, the man turned to Phil, holding up the roll to stare at it. "And all our journey is in this picture, truly? And all we need do is follow these...poppets of ourselves?"

Phil nodded. "Just pay attention, and they won't let you go wrong. I fixed it so they'll guide you all the way to Nogales, Texas—that's right on the Mexican border. You'll know the way from there." He looked up with weary seriousness at the proud, bearded face above him. "It's a very long way—almost two thousand miles. I'm sorry."

"We have made longer journeys, and with no such guide." The man was still moving forward and back, watching in fascination as the little images mimicked his pacing. "Nothing to compare," he murmured, "not in all my life..." He halted and faced Phil again. "One with the wisdom to create this for us is also wise enough to know that there is no point in even trying to show our gratitude properly. Thank you."

Phil reached up to take the proffered hand. "Just go carefully, that's all. Stay off the main roads—the way I drew it, you shouldn't ever have to set foot on a highway. And don't ever let that picture out of your sight. Definitely a one-shot deal."

He climbed up onto the Rock and instantly fell asleep. The man seemed to doze on his feet, as horses do, while the boy embarked on one last roundup of every last acorn in the area. For myself, I spent the time saying my poem over and over to the *centauride,* until she had it perfectly memorized, and could repeat it back to me, line for line. "Now I will never forget it," she told me. "The last time anyone wrote a poem for me, it was in the Greek, the oldest Greek that none speak today." She recited it to me, and while I understood not one word, I would know it if I heard it again.

Phil was still asleep when the centaurs left at twilight. I did try to wake him to bid them farewell, but he only blinked and mumbled, and was gone again. I watched them out of sight among the oaks: the man in the lead, intently following the little moving images on Phil's painting; the boy trotting close behind, exuberant with adventure, for good or ill. The woman turned once to look back at us, and then went on.

I don't remember how I finally got Phil on his feet and home; only that it was late, and that both sets of parents were mad at us. The next day was school, and after that I had a doctor's appointment, and Phil had flute lessons, and what with one family thing or another, we had almost no time together until close to the end of the week. We didn't go to the Rock—the weather had turned too grim even for us—rather we sat shivering on the front stoop of my apartment building, like winter birds on a telephone line, and didn't say much of anything. I asked if Phil thought they'd make it all the way to Mexico, and he shrugged and answered, "We'll never know." After a moment, he added, "All *I* know, I got a roomful of stupid maps, and my whole body hurts. Never again, boy. You and your damn hallucinations."

I said, "I didn't know you could do stuff like that. Like what you made for them."

He turned to stare intently into my face. "You saw those hairs in those little figures? I saw you seeing them." I nodded. "Well, each was from one of their tails—Mom, Pop or the Kid. And I plucked a few more hairs, wove those into my brushes. That was the magic part: centaurs may have a lousy sense of direction, but they're still magic. Wouldn't have worked for a minute without that." I stared, and he sighed. "I keep telling you, the artist isn't the magic. The artist is the *sight,* the artist is someone who knows magic when he sees it. The magic doesn't care whether it's seen or not—that's the artist's business. My business."

I tried earnestly, stumblingly, to absorb what he was telling me. "So all that—I mean, the painting moving and guiding them, and all…"

Phil gave me that crooked, deceptively candid grin he's had since we were five years old. "I'm a good artist. I'm really good. But I ain't *that* good."

We sat in silence for a while, while the leaves blew and tumbled past us, and a few sharp, tiny raindrops stung our faces. By and by Phil spoke again, quietly enough that I had to lean closer to hear him. "But we were magic too, in our way. You rounding up every single map between here and Yonkers, and me…" He hunched over, arms folded on his knees, the way he still does without realizing it. "Me at that damn easel, brush in one hand, gas-station map in the other, trying to make art out of the New Jersey Turnpike. Trying to make all those highways and freeways and Interstates and Tennessee and Georgia come alive for a family of mythological, nonexistent…hour after goddam miserable, backbreaking, cockamamie hour, and that San Juan candle dropping wax everywhere…"

His voice trailed off into the familiar disgusted mumble. "I don't *know* how I did it, Beagle. Don't ask me. All I knew for sure was, you can't let centaurs wander around lost in the Bronx—you can't, it's all wrong—and there I was."

"It'll get them to Mexico," I said. "I know it will."

"Yeah, well." The grin became a slow, rueful smile, less usual. "The weird thing, it's made me...I don't know *better*, but just *different,* some way. I'm never going to have to do anything like that again, thank God—and I bet I couldn't. But there's other stuff, things I never thought about trying before, and now it's all I'm doing in my head, right now—my head's full of stuff I have to do, even if I can't ever get it right. Even *though*." The smile faded, and he shrugged and looked away. "That's them. They did that."

I turned my coat collar up around my face. I said, "I read a story about a boy who draws cats so well that they come to life and fight off demons for him."

"Japanese," Phil said. "Good story. Listen, don't tell anybody, not even Jake and Marty. It gets out, they'll want me to do all kinds of stuff, all the time. And magic's not an all-the-time thing, you're not ever *entitled* to magic—not ever, no matter how good you are. Best you can do—all you can do—is make sure you're ready when it happens. If."

His voice had grown somber again, his eyes distant, focusing on nothing that I could recognize. Then he brightened abruptly, saying, "Still got the brushes, anyway. There's that. Whatever comes next, there's the brushes."

We Never Talk About My Brother

Therefore, since the world has still
Much good, but much less good than ill,
And while the sun and moon endure
Luck's a chance, but trouble's sure,
I'd face it as a wise man would,
And train for ill and not for good.

—A. E. Housman

Nobody does anymore, haven't for years—well, that's why you're here, ain't it, one of those "Where Are They Now" pieces of yours?—but it's funny, when you think about it. I mean, even after what happened, and all this time, you'd think Willa and I—Willa's my sister—you'd think we'd say at least Word One about him now and then. To each other, maybe not to anyone else. But we don't, not ever, even now. Hell, my wife won't talk about Esau, and she'd have more reason than most. Lucky you found me first—she'd have run you right on out of the house, and she could do it, too. Tell the truth, shame the devil, the only reason I'm sitting here talking to you at all is you having the mother wit to bring along that bottle of Blanton's Single Barrel. Lord, I swear I can *not* remember the last time I had any of that in the house.

Mind if you record me? No, no, you go ahead on, get your little tape thing going, okay by me. Doesn't make a bit of difference. You're like to think I'm pretty crazy before we're through, one way or another, but that don't make any difference either.

Well, okay then. Let's get started.

Last of the great TV anchormen, my brother, just as big as newsmen ever used to get. Not like today—too many of them in the game, too much competition, all sort of, I don't know, interchangeable. More and more folks getting the news on their computers, those little earphone gadgets, I don't know what-all. It's just different than it was. Way different. Confess I kind of like it.

But back then, back then, Esau was just a little way south of a movie star. Couldn't walk down the street, go out grocery-shopping, he'd get jumped by a whole mob of his fans, his groupies. Couldn't turn on the TV and not see him on half a dozen channels, broadcasting, or being interviewed, or being a special guest on some show or other. I mean everything from big political stuff to cooking shows, for heaven's sake. My friend Buddy Andreason, we go fishing weekends, us and Kirby Rich, Buddy used to always tease me about it. Point to those little girls on the news, screaming and running after Esau for autographs, and he'd say, "Man, you could get yourself some of that so easy! Just tell them you're his brother, you'll introduce them—man, they'd be all over you! All *over* you!"

No, it's not a nickname, that was real. Esau Robbins. Right out of the Bible, the Old Testament, the guy who sold his birthright to his brother for a mess of pottage. Pottage is like soup or stew, something like that. Our Papa was a big Bible reader, and there was...I don't know, there was stuff that was funny to him that wasn't real funny to anyone else. Like naming me and Esau like he did.

A lot easier to live with Jacob than a funny name like Esau, I guess— you know, when you're a kid. But I wasn't all that crazy about my name either, tell you the truth, which is why I went with Jake first time any-body ever called me that in school, never looked back. I mean, you think about it now. The Bible Esau's the hunter, the fisherman, the out-door guy—okay, maybe not the brightest fellow, not the most mannerly, maybe he cusses too much and spits his tobacco where he shouldn't, but still. And Jacob's the sneaky one, you know? Esau's come home beat and hungry and thirsty, and Jacob tricks him—face it, Jacob *tricks* him right out of his inheritance, his whole future, and their mama helps him do it, and God thinks that's righteous, a righteous act. Makes you wonder about some things, don't it?

Did he have a bad time of it growing up, account of his name? 'Bout like you'd expect. I had to fight his battles time to time, if some big fel-low was bullyragging him, and my sister Willa did the same, because we were the older ones, and that's just what you do, right? But we didn't *see* him, you know what I mean? Didn't have any idea who he *was*, except a nuisance we had to take care of, watch after, keep out of traffic. He's seven years younger than Willa, five years younger than me. Doesn't sound like much now, but when you're a kid it's a lot. He might have been growing up in China, for all we knew about him.

I'm embarrassed to say it flat out, but there's not a lot I really recall about him as a kid, before the whole thing with Donnie Schmidt. I remember Esau loved tomatoes ripe off the vine—got into trouble every summer, stealing them out of the neighbors' yards—and he was scared of squirrels, can you believe that? Squirrels, for God's sake. Said they chased him. Oh, and he used to hurt himself a lot, jumping down from higher and higher places—ladders, trees, sheds and all such. Practicing landing, that was the idea. Practicing landing.

But I surely remember the first time I ever really looked at Esau and thought, wow, what's going on here? Not at school—in the old Pott Street playground, it was. Donnie Schmidt—mean kid with red hair and a squinty eye—Donnie had Esau down on his back, and was just beating him like a rug. Bloody nose, big purple shiner already coming up...I came running all the way across the playground, Willa too, and I got Donnie by the neck and hauled him right off my brother. Whopped him a couple of times too, I don't mind telling you. He was a nasty one, Donnie Schmidt.

Esau had quit fighting, but he didn't bounce up right away, and I wouldn't have neither, the whupping he'd taken. He was just staring at Donnie, and his eyes had gone really pale, both of them, and he pointed straight at Donnie—looked funny, I'm bound to say, with him still lying flat down in that red-clay mud—and he kind of whispered, "*You* got run over." Hadn't been as close as I was, I'd never have heard him.

"You got run over." Like that—like it had already happened, you see? Exactly—like he was reading the news. You got it.

Okay. Now. This is what's important. This is where you're going to start wondering whether you should have maybe sat just a little closer to the door. See, what happened to Donnie, didn't happen then—it had already happened a week before. Seriously. Donnie, he didn't disappear, blink out of sight, right when Esau said those words. He just shrugged and walked away, and Willa took Esau home to clean him up, and I got into a one-a-cat game—what you probably call "horse" or "catcher-flies-up"—with a couple of my pals until dinnertime. And Ma yelled some at Esau for getting into a fight, but nobody else thought anything more about it, then or ever. Nobody except me.

Because when I woke up next morning, everybody in town knew Donnie Schmidt had been dead for a week. Hell, we'd all been to the funeral.

I didn't see it happen, but Willa did—or that's what she thought, anyway. Donnie'd been walking to school, and old Mack Moffett's car went out of control somehow, crossed three lanes in two, three seconds, and pinned him against the wall of a house. Poor kid never knew what hit him, and neither did anyone who ever went over the car or gave poor

Mack a sobriety test. The old man died a couple of months later, by the way. Call it shock, call it a broken heart, if you like—I don't know.

But the point is. The point is that Donnie Schmidt was alive as could be the day before, beating up on Esau on the playground. I remembered that. But I'd also swear on a stack of Bibles that he'd been killed in an accident the week before, and Willa would swear on the Day of Judgment that she was there. And we'd both pass any and every lie-detector test you want to put us through. Because we *know*, we know we're telling the truth, so it's not a lie. Right?

It's just not true.

Told you. Told you you'd be looking at me like that about now...no, don't say nothing, just *listen*, okay? There's more.

Now I got no idea if that was the first time he did it—made something happen by saying it already had. No idea. Like I said before, it was just the first time I ever really saw my brother.

Nor it didn't change a lot between us, him and Willa and me. Willa was all books and choir rehearsals, and I was all cars and trucks and hunting with my Uncle Rick, and Esau pretty much got along on his own, same as he'd always done. He was just Esau, bony as a clothes rack, all elbows and knees—Papa used to say that he was so thin you could shave with him—but if you looked closely, I guess you could have seen how he might yet turn out good-looking. Only we weren't looking closely, none of us were, not even me. Not even after Donnie. One of anything is still just one of anything, even if it's strange. You can put it out of your mind. So across the dinner table was about it for Willa and me. If we were home.

But while I wasn't really looking, I can't say I didn't pay a little more attention in the looking I did, if you know what I mean.

One time I do recall, when Esau was maybe twelve, maybe thirteen, in there somewhere. Must have been thirteen, because I was already out of high school and working five days a week to help with the rent. Anyway I'm up on the roof of the house on a Saturday, replacing a few shingles got blown off in the last windstorm. Hammering and humming, not thinking about much of anything, and suddenly I turn my head and there's Esau, a few feet away, squatting on his heels and watching me. Never heard him climbing up, no idea how long he's been there, but I know I don't like that look—sets me to thinking about the one he gave Donnie. What if he says to me, "*You* fell off the roof," and it turns out I'm dead, and been dead some while? So I say "Hey, you want to hand me those nails over there?" friendly and peaceable as you like. Probably the most I've said to him in a week, more.

So he hands me the nails, and I say thanks, and I go back to work, and Esau sits watching me a few minutes more, and then he asks, right out of nowhere, "Jake, you believe in God?"

Like that. I didn't even look up, just grunted, "Guess I do."

"You think God's nice?"

His voice was still breaking, I recall—went up and down like a seesaw, made me laugh. I said, "Minister says so."

He wouldn't quit on it, wouldn't let up. "But do *you* think God's nice?"

I dropped a couple of shingles, and made him go down and bring them back up to the roof for me. When he'd done that, I said, "You look around at this world, you think God's nice?"

He didn't answer for a while, just sat there watching me work. By and by he said, "If I was God, I'd be nice."

I set my eye on him then, and I don't know what made me do it, but I said, "You would, huh? Tell it to Donnie Schmidt."

I'd never said anything like that to him before. I'd never mentioned Donnie Schmidt since the funeral, because I knew in my mind—like Willa, like everyone else—that Donnie was dead and buried a week before him and Esau had that fight. Anyway, Esau's eyes filled up, which hardly ever happened, he wasn't ever a crier, and his face got all red, and he stood up, and for a minute I thought he actually was about to come at me. But he didn't—he just screamed, with that funny breaking voice, "I *would* be a nice God! I *would!*"

And he was off and gone, I guess down the ladder, though maybe he jumped, the way he was doing then, because he was limping a bit at dinnertime. Anyway, we never talked about God no more, nor about Donnie Schmidt neither, at least while Esau still lived here.

I never talked about any of this with Papa. He was pretty much taken up with his Bible and his notions and his work at the tannery, before he passed. But Ma saw more than she let on. One time...there was this one time she was still up when I come home from little Sadie Morrison's place, she as later married that Canuck fellow, Rene Arceneaux, and she said—that's Ma, not Sadie—she said to me, "Jacob, Esau's bad."

I said, "Ma, goodness' sake, don't say that. There's nothing wrong with the kid except he's kind of a pain in the ass. Otherwise I got no quarrel with him." Which was true enough then, and maybe still is, depending how you measure.

Ma shook her head. I remember, she was sitting right where you are, by the fireplace—this was their house, you know—just rocking and shelling peas—and she said, "Jacob, I ain't nearly as silly as everybody always thinks I am. I know when somebody's bad. Esau, he makes people into ghosts."

I looked at her. I said, "Ma. Ma, don't you never go round saying stuff like that, they'll put you away for sure. You're saying Esau kills people, and he never killed nobody!" And I believed it, you see, absolutely, even though I also knew better.

And Ma...Ma, whatever she knew, maybe she knew it because she was just as silly as folks thought she was. Hard to say about Ma. She said, "That girl last year, the one he was so gone on, who wanted to go off to New York to be an actress. You remember her?"

"Susie Harkin," I said. "Sure I remember. Plane crashed, killed everybody on board. It was real sad."

Ma didn't say nothing for a long time. Rocked and shelled, rocked and shelled. I stood and watched her, snatching myself a pea now and then, and thinking on how wearied she was getting to look. Then she said, almost mumbling-like, "I don't think so, Jacob. I'm *persuaded* she got killed in that crash, but I don't *think* so."

That's exactly how she put it—exactly. I didn't say anything myself, because what could I say—Ma, you're right, I remember it both ways too? I remember you telling me she gave him the mitten—that's the way Ma talks; she meant the girl broke up with him—and left, and I remember Susie doing just fine up there in the city, she even sent me a letter... but I also remember her and Esau talking about getting married someday, only then she stepped on that flight and never got to New York at all...I'm going to tell Ma that, and get her going, when the city health people already thought she ought to be off in some *facility* somewhere? Not hardly.

Things wandered along, way they do, just happening and not happening. Willa went all the way on to state college and become a teacher, and then she got married and moved all that way to Florida, Jacksonville Beach. Got two nice kids, my niece Carol-Ann and my nephew Ben. Ma finally did have to go away, and soon enough she passed too. Me, I kept on at the same hardware store where you found me, only after a while I came to own it—me and the bank. Married Middy Jo Staines, but she died. No children.

And Esau....well, he graduated the town high school like me and Willa—unless maybe we just think he did—and then the University of Colorado gave him a scholarship, unless they just think so, and he was gone out of here quicker than scat. Never really came home after that, except the once, which I'll get to in a bit. Got through college, got the job with that station in Baltimore, and the next time we saw him he was on the air, feeding stories to the network, the way they do—like, "And here's Esau Robbins, our Baltimore correspondent to tell you more about today's tragic explosion," or whatever. And pretty soon it was D.C. and the national news, every night, and you look up and your baby brother's famous. Couldn't have been over thirty.

And looking good, too, no question about it. Grew up taller than me, taller than Papa, with Ma's dark hair and dark blue eyes, and that look—like he belonged right where he was, telling you things he knows that you don't, and telling them in that deep, warm, friendly voice he had. Lord, I don't know where he rented that voice—he sure didn't have it when he lived in this town. Voice like that, he could have been reciting Mother Goose or something, wouldn't have mattered. When you heard it you just wanted to listen.

I used to watch him on the TV, my brother Esau, telling us what's really doing in Afghanistan, in Somalia, in France, in D.C., and I'd look at his eyes, and I'd wonder if he ever even thought about poor, nasty Donnie Schmidt. And I'd wonder how he found out he could do it, how'd he discover his talent, his knack, whatever you want to call it. I mean, how does a little boy, schoolyard-age boy—how does he deal with a thing like that? How does he even practice it, predicting something he wants to happen—and then, like that, it's true, and it's always been true, it's just a plain fact, like gravity or something, with nobody knowing any better for sure but me? Town like this, there's not a lot of people you can talk to about that kind of thing. Must of made him feel even more alone, you know?

The visit. Whoo. Yeah, well—all right. All right.

It wasn't hardly a real visit, first off. See, he'd already been the anchorman on that big news program for at least ten, twelve years when they got the notion to do a show on his return to the old home town. So they sent a whole crowd along with him—a camera crew, and a couple of producers, the way they do, and there was a writer, and some publicity people, and some other folks I can't recall. Anyway, I'll tell you, it was for sure the biggest thing to hit this place since Ruth and Gehrig barnstormed through here back in the Twenties. They were here a whole week, that gang, and they spent a lot of money, and made all the businesses happy. Can't beat that with a stick, can you?

And Esau walked through it all like a king—just like a king, no other word for it. They filmed him greeting old friends, talking with his old teachers, stopping in at all his old hangouts, even reading to kids at the library. Mind you, I don't remember him ever having any hangouts, and the teachers didn't seem to remember him much at all. As for the old friends...look, if Esau had any friends when we were all kids, I swear I don't recall them. I mean, there they were in this documentary thing, shaking his hand, slapping his back, having a beer with him in Henry's—been there fifty, sixty years, that place—but I'd never seen any of them with him as a kid, 'ceptin maybe a few of them were pounding on him, back before Donnie. Thing is, I don't imagine Esau was trying very hard to get the details right. Wouldn't have hardly thought we was worth the trouble. Willa thought she recognized one or two, and remembered this and that, but even she wasn't sure.

Oh, yeah, her and me, we were both in it. They paid for Willa to come from Florida—flew little Ben and Carol-Ann, too, but not her husband Jerry, cause they just wanted to show Esau being an uncle. They'd have put her and the kids up at the Laurel Inn with the crew, but she wanted to stay here at the old house, which was fine with me. Don't get to be around children much.

We didn't see much of Esau even after Willa got here, but a day or two before they wrapped up the film, he dropped over to the house for dinner, which meant that the whole crew dropped over too. We were the only ones eating, and it was the strangest meal I've ever had in my life, what with all those electricians setting up lights, and the sound people running cables every which way, and a director, for God's sake, a director telling us when to start eating—they sent out to Horshach's for prime rib—and where to look when the camera was on us, and what Willa should say to the kids when they asked for seconds. Carol-Ann got so nervous, she actually threw up her creamed corn. And Willa got so mad at the lighting guy, because Ben's got eye trouble, and the lights were so bright and hot...well, it was a real mess, that's all. Just a real mess.

But Esau, he just sat through it all like it was just another broadcast, which I guess to him it was. Never got upset about all the retakes—lord, that dinner must have taken three hours, one thing another—never looked sweaty or tired, always found something new and funny to say to the camera when it started rolling again. But that's who he was talking to, all through that show—not us, for sure. He never once looked straight at any of us, Willa or the kids or me, if the camera wasn't on him.

He was a stranger in this house, the house where we'd all grown up—more of a stranger than all those cameramen, those producers. He could just as well have been from another country, where everybody's great-looking, but they don't speak any language you ever heard of. With all the craziness and confusion, the lights and the reflectors, and the microphones swinging around on pole-things, I probably studied on my brother longer and harder than I'd ever done in my life before. There at that table, having that fake dinner, I studied on him, and I thought a few new things.

See, I couldn't believe it was just Esau. What I *could* believe is there's no such thing as history, not the way they teach it to you in school. Wars, revolutions, all those big inventions, all those big discoveries...if there's been a bunch of people like Esau right through time—or even a few, a handful—then the history books don't signify, you understand what I'm saying? Then it's all just been what any one of them wanted, decided on, right at this moment or that, and no great, you know, patterns to the way things happen. Just Esau, and whatever Others, and *you got run over.* Like that. That's what I came to think.

And I know I'm right. Because Susie Harkin was in that film.

Yeah, yeah, I know what I told you about the plane crash, the rest of it, I'm telling you this now. She walked in by herself, bright as you please, just before they finally got around to putting real food on the table, and sat right down across from Esau, between me and little Ben. The TV people looked at the director for orders, and I guess he figured she was family, no point fussing about it, and let her stay. He was too busy yelling at the crew about the lights, anyway.

Esau was good. I am here to tell you, Esau was *good.* There was just that one moment when he saw her...and even then, you might have had to be me or Willa, and watching close, before you noticed the twist of blank panic in his eyes. After that he never looked straight at her, and he sure never said her name, but you couldn't have told one thing from his expression. Susie didn't waste no time on him, neither; she was busy helping little Ben with his food, cutting his meat up small for him, and making faces to make him laugh. Ma had said "Esau makes people into ghosts," but I don't guess you'd find a ghost cutting up a boy's prime rib for him, do you? Not any kind of ghost I ever heard about.

When she'd finished helping Ben, she looked right up at me, and she winked.

As long as she'd been gone, Susie Harkin didn't look a day different. I don't suppose you'd ever have called her a beauty, best day she ever saw. Face too thin, forehead a shade low, nose maybe a bit beaky—but she had real nice brown eyes, and when she smiled you didn't see a thing but that smile. I'd liked her a good bit when she was going out with Esau, and I was real sorry when she died in that plane crash. So was Willa. And now here Susie was again, sitting at our old dinner table with all these people around, winking at me like the two of us had a secret together. And we did, because I knew she'd been dead, and now she wasn't, and *she* knew I knew, and she knew *why* I knew besides. So, yeah, you could say we had our secret.

Esau didn't do much more looking at me during the dinner than he did at Susie, but that was the one time he did. I saw him when I turned to say something to Willa. It wasn't any special kind of a look he gave me, not in particular; it was maybe more like the first time I really looked at him, when he did what he did to Donnie Schmidt. As though he hadn't ever seen me either, until that glance, that wink, passed between Susie Harkin and me.

Anyway, by and by the little ones fell asleep, and Willa took them off to bed, and the crew packed up and went back to the Laurel Inn, and Susie right away vanished into the kitchen with all the dirty dishes— "No, I insist, you boys just stay and talk." You don't hear women say that much anymore.

So there we were, me and Esau, everything gotten quiet now— always more quiet after a lot of noise, you notice?—and him still not really looking at me, and me too tired and fussed and befuddled not to come straight at him. But the first thing I asked was about as dumb as it could be. "Squirrels still chasing you?"

Whatever he was or wasn't expecting from me, that sure as hell wasn't it. He practically laughed, or maybe it was more like he grunted in a laugh sort of way, and he said, "Not so much these days." Close to, he looked exactly like he looked on the TV—exactly, right down to the one curl off to the left on his forehead, and the inlaid belt buckle, and that steepling thing he did with his fingers. Really was like talking to the screen.

"Susie's looking fine, don't you think?" I asked him. "I mean, for having been dead and all."

Oh, that reached him. That got his attention. He looked at me then, all right, and he answered, real slow and cold and careful, "I don't know what you're talking about. What *are* you talking about?"

"Come on, Esau," I said. "Tomorrow I might wake up remembering mostly whatever you want me to remember, the way you do people, but right now, tonight, I'm afraid you're just going to have to sit here and talk to me—"

"Or *what?*" Those two words cracked out of him just like a whip does—there's the forward throw, almost gentle, like you're fly-fishing, and then the way you bring it back, that's what makes that sound. He didn't say anything more, but the color had drained right out of his eyes, same way it happened with Donnie Schmidt. Didn't look much like the TV now.

I asked him, "You planning to make me a ghost too? Kill me off in a plane crash a few weeks ago? I ought to tell you, I hate flying, and everybody knows it, so you might want to try something different. Me, I always wanted to get shot by a jealous husband at ninety-five or so, but it's your business, I wouldn't presume." I don't know, something just took me over and I didn't care what I said right then.

He didn't answer. We could hear Susie rattling things in the kitchen, and Willa singing softly to her kids upstairs. Got a pretty voice, Willa does. Wanted to do something with it, but what with school, and then there was Jerry, and then there was the trouble starting with Ma...well, nothing ever came of it somehow. But I could see Esau listening, and just for a minute or so he looked like somebody who really might have had a sister, and maybe a brother too, and was just visiting with them for the evening, like always. I took the moment to say, "Papa was funny, wasn't he, Esau? Getting us backwards like that, with the naming?"

He stared at me. I shrugged a little bit. I said, "Well, you think about it some. Here's Jacob, which I'm named for, cheating Esau out of his inheritance, tricks him into swapping everything due him for a mess of chicken soup or some such. But with us...with us, it kind of worked out t'other way round, wouldn't you say? I mean, when you think about it."

"I don't know what you're talking about." He said it in the TV voice, but his eyes still weren't his TV eyes, reassuring everyone that the world hadn't ended just yet. "Papa was as crazy as Ma, only different, and our names don't signify a thing except he was likely drunk at the time." He slammed his hand on the table, setting all the dishes Susie hadn't cleared off yet to rattling. Esau lowered his voice some. "I never stole *anything* from you, Jake Robbins. I wouldn't have lowered myself to it, any more than I'd have lowered myself to take along a lump of sand-covered cat-shit from this litterbox of a town, the day I finally got out of here. The one thing I ever took away was *me,* do you understand that, brother? Nothing more. Not one damn thing more."

His face was so cramped up with anger and plain contempt that I couldn't help putting a finger out toward him, like I was aiming to smooth away a bunch of rumples. "You want to watch out," I said. "Crack your makeup." Esau came to his feet then, and I really thought he was bound to clock me a good one. I said, "Sit down. There's ladies in the house."

He went on glaring in my face, but by and by he kind of stood down—didn't quite sit, you understand, but more leaned on the table, staring at me. He'd cracked his makeup, all right, and I don't mean the stuff they'd put on his skin for the filming. You wouldn't want that face telling you any kind of news right then.

"I bet Papa knew," I said. "Ma just had like a glimmer of the truth, but Papa...likely it's how come he drank so much, and read the Bible so crazy. It's his side of the family, after all."

Esau said it again. "I don't know what you're talking about," but there wasn't much what you might call conviction in the words. It's an odd thing, but he was always a real bad liar—embarrassing bad. I'd guess it's because he's never had to lie in his life: he could always make the lie be true, if he cared to. Handy.

I said, "I'm talking about genetics. Now there's a word I hadn't had much use for until recently—knew what it meant, more or less, and let it go at that. But there's a deal *to* genetics when you look close, you know?" No answer; nothing but that bad-guy stare, with something under it that maybe might be fear, and maybe not. I kept going. "Papa and his Bible. There's a lot in the Bible makes a lot more sense that way, genetics. What if...let's say all those miracles didn't have a thing to do with God, nor Moses, nor Jesus, nor Adam's left ball, whatever. What if it was all people like you? Two, three, four, five thousand years of people like you? The Bible zigs and zags and contradicts itself, tells the same story forty ways from Sunday, and don't connect up to nothing half the time, even to a preacher. But now you back off and suppose for one moment that the Bible's actually trying to record a world that keeps shifting this way and that, because people keep messing with it. What would you say about that, Esau?"

Nothing. Not a word, not a flicker of an eyelid, nothing for the longest time—and then, of all things, my brother began to smile. "Declare to goodness," he said, and it wasn't the smooth TV voice at all, but more like the way his mouth was born, as we say around here. "Even a blind hog finds an acorn once in a while. Continue, please. You have all my attention."

"No, I don't yet," I said back to him, "but I will. Because with genetics, it's a family thing. Somebody in a family has a gift, a talent, there's likely to be somebody else who has it too. Oh, maybe not the same size or shape of a gift, but close enough. Close enough."

I surely had his attention now, let me tell you. His hands were opening and closing like leaves starting to stir when a storm's coming. "Willa doesn't have that thing you have," I said, "none of it, not at all. She's the lucky one. But *I* do. Wouldn't have guessed it before, not even seeing what you'd done, but now I know better. That same power to mess with things, only I guess I never needed to. Not like you."

Esau started to say something, but then he didn't. I said, "I turned out pretty lucky myself. I had Middy Jo—for a while, anyway. I got a job suited me down to the ground. Didn't have nearly so many people to get even with as you had, and the ones I did I have I mostly forgot over time. I was always forgetful that way. Forget my head, it wasn't screwed on." Papa always used to say that about me, the same way he used to say Willa'd make some woman a great husband, because she could get the car started when he couldn't. Never yet heard old Jerry Flores complain.

"What you did to Donnie Schmidt," I said. "What you did to Susie. What I know you did to a few other folks, even though you made sure the rest of everybody didn't remember. It all scared me so bad, I would never gone anywhere *near* power like that, if I'd known I had it."

Esau's voice was sort of thickish now, like he was trying not to cry, which surely wasn't the case. He said, "You can't do what I do."

"You know better than that, Esau. Same way I know you've never bent reality towards even one good thing. I watch you on the TV, every night, just about, and everything you report on—it's death, it's all death, nothing but death, one way or another. A million baby girls left out on the street in China, a raft full of people capsizes off Haiti, some kid wipes out a whole schoolyard in Iowa, there's more people starving in Africa, getting massacred, there's suicide bombers and serial killers all over the place—it's you, it's your half of the genetics. It's what you are, Esau, and I'm sorry for you."

"Don't be." It was only a whisper, but it came at me like a little sideways swipe from one of those oldtime straight razors, the kind Papa had. Esau said, "You're the good one." It wasn't a question. "Well, who'd have thought it? My loud-mouthed, clumsy, stupid big brother turns out to be the superhero in the closet, the champion with a secret identity. Amazing. Just shows you something or other. Truly amazing."

"No," I said. "No, I don't care about that. I just wanted you to know I know. About the genetics and so forth." And then I said it—because he's right, I am stupid. I said, "You're trying to be the Angel of Death, Esau, and I'm just so sorry for you, that's all."

He'd been looking toward the kitchen, like he expected something—or maybe didn't expect it—but now he turned around on me, and I'm not ever about to forget what I saw then. It was like we were kids again, and he was screaming at me, "I *would* be a nice God! I *would!*" Except now the scream was all in his eyes: they were stretched wide as wide, like howling jaws, and the whites had gone too white, so they made the pupils look, not black, but a kind of musty, crumbly gray, like his eyes were rotting, nothing left in there but gray anger, gray pain, gray brick-lined schoolyards, where my brother Esau learned what he was. I'd been halfway joking when I'd said that about the Angel of Death. Not any more.

"Sorry for me, Jake?" It wasn't the razor-whisper, but it wasn't any voice you'd have recognized, either. Esau said, "*Sorry* for me? I'm on television, asshole. I'm a *star.* Have you the slightest notion of what that means? It means millions—*millions*—of people inviting me into their homes, listening to me, believing in me, *trusting* me. Hell, I'm a family member—a wise old uncle, a mysteriously well-traveled cousin, dropping by to tell them tales of the monsters and fools who run their lives, of the innocents who died horribly today, the people murdered to please somebody's god, the soldiers being sent to die in some place they never heard of, the catastrophes waiting to happen tomorrow, unless somebody does something right away. Which they won't, but that isn't *my* work. I can't claim credit there."

He smiled at me then, and it was a real smile, young and joyous as you like. He said, "Don't you understand? They *love* death, all those people, they love what I do—they *need* it, no matter how awful they say it is. It's built into the whole species, from the beginning, and you know it as well as I do. You may be the Good Angel, but I'm the one they hang out with in the kitchen and the living room, I'm the one they have their coffee with, or a beer, while I smile and lay on some more horror for them. Meaning no offense, but who wants what *you're* selling?"

"Those people who watch you don't know what they're buying," I said back. "Your stories aren't just stories, you aren't just reporting. You're making real things happen in the real world. I see you on the TV and I can feel all those things you talk about, and explain about, and tell folks to be afraid of, I can feel them coming true, every night. It's like Ma said, your stories kill people." He didn't turn a hair, or look away, and I didn't expect him to. I said, "And I keep wondering, how many like us might be doing the same right now, all over everywhere. Messing with people, messing with the world so nothing makes no sense, one day to the next, so most everybody gets run over in the end, like Donnie Schmidt. You suppose that's all we can do? That's all it's for, this gift we've got? This heritage?"

Esau shrugged. "No idea. It suits me." He gave me that smile again, made him look like a happier little kid than he ever was. "But why should it concern you, Jake? Are you planning to devote the rest of your life to writing letters to my sponsors, telling them I'm the source of all the pain and misery in the world? I'll be very interested in watching your efforts. Fascinated, you could say."

"No," I told him. "I've got a store to run, and I meet Earl Howser and Buddy Andreason for breakfast at Buttercup on Tuesdays, and it's not my place to chase around after you, fixing stuff. What I know's what I know, and it don't include putting the world back the way it ought to be. It's too late for that. Way too late for heroes, champions, miracles. Don't matter what our heritage was maybe meant for—your side got hold of it first, and you won long ago. No undoing that, Esau, I ain't fool enough to think otherwise. I'm still sorry for you, but I know your side's won, this side the grave."

He wasn't listening to me, not really. Just about all his attention was focusing on the kitchen right then, because Susie'd begun whistling while she was clattering pots in the sink. She could always whistle like a man, Susie could. Esau took a step toward the sound.

"I wouldn't," I advised him. "Best leave her be for a bit. What with one thing another, she's not real partial to you just now. You know how it is."

He stopped where he was, but he didn't answer. Halfway crouched, halfway plain puzzled—I've seen dogs look like that, when they couldn't figure what to do about that big new dog on the block. He said, real low, "I didn't bring her back."

"No," I said. "You couldn't have."

He didn't hear that right off; then he did, and he was just starting to turn when Susie came out of the kitchen, drying her hands on a dishtowel and asking, "Jake, would you like me to wash that old black roasting pan while I'm at it?" Then she saw Esau standing there, and she stood real still, and he did too. Lord, if I closed my eyes, I'd see them like that right now.

I stood up from the table, so that made three of us on our feet, saying nothing. Esau was breathing hard, and I couldn't hardly tell if Susie was breathing at all. That made me anxious—you know, considering—so I said, "Esau was just leaving. Wanted to say goodbye."

Neither of them paid the least bit of attention to me. Susie finally managed to say, "You're looking well, Esau. That's a really nice tie."

Esau's voice sounded like a cold wind in an empty place. He said, "You're rotting in the ground. You're bones."

"No." Susie's own voice was shaky, but stronger than his, some way. "No, Esau, I'm not. I refuse."

She sort of peeked past him at me as she said that, and Esau caught it. He turned.

"Susie stays," I said. I was madder than I ever remembered being, and I was wound up, ready to go at whoever, let's do it, just pick your weapons. And I was heavily spooked, too, because pretty much the only mixups I've been in my whole life, they were always about hauling some guy off my baby brother one more time. Heritage or not, I'm no fighter, never wanted to be one. It's just I always liked Susie.

As for the way Esau stared at me, it did clear up a few things, and that's about all I'm going to tell you. I looked back into those TV eyes, and I saw what lived in there, and I thought, well, anyway, I've still got a sister. If you can get through the rest of your life without ever having that feeling, I'd recommend it.

Esau said, "She goes back where she belongs. Now."

"She didn't belong there in the first place," I said to him. "Leave her be, Esau. She's got no business being dead."

"You don't know what you're doing," he said. His lips were twitching like they didn't belong to his face. "Stay out of it, Jake."

"Not a chance," I said. "I can't fix up all the things you do, what you've already done. Might be Superman, Spider-Man, Batman could, but it's not in me, I'm no hero. I'm just a stubborn man who runs a hardware store. But I always liked Susie. Nice girl. Terrific whistler. Susie's not going back nowhere."

Even a little bit younger, I'm sure I'd have been showing off for her, backed away against the wall as she was, looking like a lady tied up for the dragon. But I wasn't showing off for anybody right then, being almost as scared as I was angry. Esau sighed—very dramatic, very heavy. He said, "I did warn you. Nobody can say I didn't warn you. You're my brother, after all."

I started to answer him, but I can't remember what I meant to say, because that was when Esau hit me. Not with his fists, but with such a blast of—I still don't know what to call it...hatred? Contempt? Plain meanness?—that it knocked me off my feet and right over my chair. For a moment I swear I thought I'd caught on fire. My head wouldn't work; *nothing* worked; it was like every single string in my body had been cut—I couldn't even flop around on the floor. I didn't know who I was. I didn't know *what* I was.

Susie screamed, and Esau hit me again. That time I did flop around, after I slid across the floor and fetched up against the wall. To this day I can't honestly explain how it felt—been trying to describe it to myself for years. Best I can do is that it wasn't like an electric shock, and it wasn't really like being burned, or beaten up either, although I was all over bruises next day. It was more...it was more like he was *unmaking* me, like he was starting to take me apart, atom by atom, molecule by molecule, so I wouldn't exist anymore—I wouldn't ever *have* existed, he'd never have *had* a brother. I could feel it happening, and I tell you, I'll never be scared of anything again.

But I didn't die. I mean, I didn't get *lost,* the way he wanted me to. Susie ran to me, but I managed to wave her off, because I didn't want her getting caught between us. Esau went on hammering me with whatever it was he had that let him smash planes out of the sky, trains off the tracks, set mudslides boiling down on little mud villages. But it wasn't hurting me any more, not like it had been. I was still me. He hadn't been able to make me not *be,* you understand?

I got my back against the wall and pushed myself up till I was on my feet. Took more time than you might think—I work, I don't work *out*—and anyway Esau just kept at me, like point-blank, coming close up to me now and knocking me this way and that, one belt of crazy rage after another. I couldn't do much about it yet, but he couldn't quite put me down again, either.

I did tell him to stop it. Same way he warned me, I told him to stop. But he wouldn't.

So I stopped him. Or the thing stopped him, the thing that had been rousing up in me all this time, while he was whupping the daylights out of me. It burst out of me like from a flamethrower, searing me—mouth, throat, chest, guts—way worse than anything Esau'd done to me, and slamming me back against the wall harder than he had. I couldn't see, and I couldn't hear a thing, and right that moment, that's when I did think I was going to die. Looked forward to it, too, just then.

When my eyes cleared some—ears took a lot longer—I saw Esau lying on the floor. He wasn't moving.

If it was just me, the way I was feeling, I'd likely have left him lying there till the neighbors started complaining. But...see, I already told you how Willa and me, we were always supposed to watch over our baby brother—protect him in those schoolyard fights, make sure he did his homework, all that—and I guess old habits die hard. I said, "Esau? Esau?" and when he didn't answer, I tried to get to him, but he seemed an awful long way off. Susie helped me. She'd been crying, but she stopped, and she got me to Esau.

He was trying to sit up by the time we reached him, and we helped him onto his feet in a while. He looked like pounded shit, excuse my French, what with his nice shirt in rags, and that tie Susie liked gone, and an arm of his suit jacket dangling by a few threads. I'd seen him wear that same jacket on the TV, I don't know how many times. His face was gray. I don't mean pale, or white—it was gray like old cement, old grout, and it was like the gray went all the way through. Susie and me, we might be the only people in the world ever saw him like that.

He actually tried to smile. He said, "I should have made you check your guns at the door. Where on earth did you pick up *that* trick?"

"Just got pissed off," I said. "And I'll do worse if you're not out of here in two minutes by Papa's watch. Susie stays."

Esau shrugged, or he tried to. "Got to catch a plane tomorrow, anyway. Back to the old grindstone." He looked at Susie. She kind of edged behind my shoulder some, and Esau's smile widened. He said, "Don't worry, my dear. You really should have stayed dead, you know, but it's not your fault." He turned back toward me. "Your doing, of course."

"Watching those folks pile in," I told him. My head was still ringing. "That whole crew, all those people come to paint up your homecoming for the world to see. Couldn't help thinking there ought to be someone like Susie there too. Like Donnie Schmidt. I swear, I was just thinking on it."

"Glad it wasn't Donnie who showed up," Esau murmured. He tugged on the loose arm of his ruined jacket; it came free, and he dropped it on the floor. "Sneaky old Brother Jake," he said. "You've likely got more of the family inheritance than I do. Just like in Papa's Bible, after all."

I was still feeling hollowed-out, burned-out, not by anything he'd done, but by whatever it was I'd had to do. I said, "I can't let you go on, Esau."

He smiled. "You can't kill me, Jake. We both know you better than that."

"You might not know me well enough," I said. "Gone as long as you've been. There's worse things than killing you. Maybe way worse."

And he saw. He looked into my eyes, for a change, and he saw what I had it in mind to do. "You wouldn't dare," he said in a whisper. "You wouldn't dare."

"I wouldn't dare *not* do it," I answered him straight. "You're a time bomb, Esau, you're a loaded gun. Didn't matter before, when I could pretend I didn't really know—but now, if I don't take the bullets out of you, I'm as bad you are. Can't see that I've got a choice."

He's Esau. He didn't beg, and he didn't bother with threatening. All he said was, "It won't be easy for you. It's my life you're talking about. I'll fight you for it."

"I know you will," I said. "And you'll have a better chance than Donnie Schmidt."

"Or me," Susie said, standing right next to me. "Goodbye, Esau."

He gave her a different kind of smile than he'd given me—practically kind, practically real. It looked nice on him. He said, "Goodbye, Susie. See you on the six o'clock." And he was away, that fast, vanished into the dark. I looked after him for some while, then said what I had to say, and closed the door.

Susie had heard me, of course. "He always meant to be a good God," I told her. "A good God, a good angel, whatever. Don't know how he got to be...what he was."

Susie picked up Esau's torn-off sleeve and turned it around and around in her hands, not looking at it, not looking at anything much. She said finally, "I read once, in India they've got gods that are also demons. Depends on their mood, I guess, or the time of year. Or maybe just their lunch."

"Well, I wasn't planning to go into the god business myself," I told her. "Really wasn't looking to set up in competition with any Angel of Death. Piss-poor job, you ask me. No benefits, no paid vacations. And damn sure no union."

Susie shook her head and laughed a little bit, but after that she got quiet again, and sort of broody. By and by, she said, "There's a union. There's always been others like you, Jake. The ones who mend the world."

"The world's no torn shirt," I said. My insides felt like they'd been scooped out, dragged over gravel and put back. "I got a store to run." Susie looked at me, didn't say anything. I said, "There's others like him out there, I don't know how many. Can't stop them all." I put my hand on Susie's shoulder to steady myself.

Willa came in behind us in her bathrobe, looked around at the dining room, and demanded, "What was all that tarryhooting around in here after we went to bed? Did you and Esau get to wrestling or something?"

"Kind of," I mumbled. "Boys with beers. I'll clean up, I promise."

Willa shrugged. "Your house. I was just afraid you'd wake up the kids. Esau already gone?" I nodded, and she peered at me in that older-sister way of hers. "You sure nothing happened between you two?" She wasn't expecting an answer, so I didn't have to fix one up. She studied Susie a lot more closely and carefully than she'd done during dinner, and there wasn't any question what she was thinking. But what Willa thinks and what Willa says never did spend a lot of time together. This time she just said, "Good of you to take the time with Ben, Susie. I was just frazzled out, dealing with those crazy TV people and Carol-Ann."

"It's been some time since I've been around children," Susie said. "I like yours."

Willa said, "Stay the night, why don't you? It's late, and there's a spare bedroom downstairs." As she left, she said over her shoulder, "And I make great Mexican eggs. My husband loves them, and *he's* Mexican."

Susie looked at me. I said, "If you aren't worried about compromising your reputation, that is, staying over in the house of a widower man. There's still folks in this town would raise their eyebrows."

Susie laughed full-out then, for the first time. That was nice. She said, "I'm older than I look."

Well.

What else? The network never ran that show, of course, what with one thing another. Didn't get the chance. Seems like it all started turning bad for Esau, just about then, slow but steady. That stock-option business. Those people who sued the whole network about his fouled-up dirty-bomb story. The sexual harassment charges. *Those* got settled out of court, like a bunch of other stuff, but there was a mountain landing on his head and he couldn't duck it all. Still, he hung on like a bullrider. He's almost as stubborn as I am. Almost.

Tell the truth, he might have ridden that bull all the way home, if he'd still been selling the same kind of stories. But the things that had made him who he was, the big disasters and the common-man nightmares, somehow there just weren't as many of them as there had been. The news got smaller, and so did he.

Did I feel bad? Interesting, you asking me that. Yeah, I did feel bad for him, I couldn't help it. I still wonder how he felt when he woke up—the morning *after* the night he told the country all about those Kansas cult-murders, with the ritual mutilating and all—only it turned out they hadn't ever happened, even though he'd made them up just as pretty and scary as all the other lies he'd always made real. How's the Angel of Death supposed to do his job with clipped wings?

I got a call in the store that day. Picked up on the second ring, but when I said hello there wasn't anybody on the line.

The guns were the last straw. The automatics and the Uzis and whatever in his office, in the dressing-room, those were bad enough, the tabloids had a field day with those. But trying to go through Los Angeles airport security with a pistol butt just sticking out of his coat pocket... lord, that did him in. Network hustled him out of there so fast, his desk was smoking behind him. That wasn't me, by the way, all those guns. That was just the state he was in by then. Poor Esau. All those years jumping off things, he still never did learn how to land.

Or maybe I should have chosen my words better as he walked away that night. Probably would have, if I'd had more time. All I knew then was I had to speak up before he did. Jam my foot in the door.

"My brother thinks he's an angel," I'd said. "He thinks he can change anything in the world just by saying so. But that's crazy. *He can't do that.*"

Didn't know what else to say. Might have had a little too much what we used to call *English* on it, but I done what I could.

Lord, don't I wish I had a movie of you for the last half-hour or so, the way you've been looking at me. You'd get to keep *that*, anyway, even though there won't be nothing on your tape tomorrow, nor nothing in your memory. Couple of hours, you couldn't even find this house again, same as your editor won't ever remember giving out this assignment. Because nobody talks about my brother anymore. Nobody's talked about him in years. And it's a sad thing, some ways, because being Esau Robbins every night, everywhere, six o'clock...that *mattered* to him. Being the Angel of Death, that *mattered* to him. They were the only things that ever filled him, you understand me? That's all he ever could do in his life, my poor damn brother—get even with us, with people, for being alive. And I took all that away. Stole his birthright and shut down the life he built with it. That don't balance the scales, nor make up for all he did, but it's going to have to do.

Esau Robbins no longer exists. He's not dead. He's just...gone. Maybe someday I'll go and look for him, like an older brother should, but right now gone is how it stays. Price of the pottage.

Thanks for the Blanton's, young man. Puts a smile on my face, and even though it isn't her drink Susie will certainly applaud your thoughtfulness.

You'll likely be finding a bonus in your next paycheck. Nobody in accounting will be able to explain why—and you sure as hell won't, either—but just you roll with it.

The Rabbi's Hobby

It took me a while to get to like Rabbi Tuvim. He was a big, slow-moving man with a heavy-boned face framed by a thick brown beard; and although he had spent much of his life in the Bronx, he had never quite lost the accent, nor the syntax, of his native Czechoslovakia. He seemed stony and forbidding to me at first, even though he had a warm, surprising laugh. He just didn't look like someone who would laugh a lot.

What gradually won me over was that Rabbi Tuvim collected odd, unlikely things. He was the only person I knew who collected, not baseball cards, the way all my friends and I did, but *boxers*. There was one gum company who put those out, complete with the fighters' records and a few lines about their lives, and the rabbi had all the heavyweights, going back to John L. Sullivan, and most of the lighter champions too. I learned everything I know about Stanley Ketchel, Jimmy McLarnin, Benny Leonard, Philadelphia Jack O'Brien, Tommy Loughran, Henry Armstrong and Tony Canzoneri—to name just those few—from Rabbi Tuvim's cards.

He kept boxes of paper matchbooks too, and those little bags of sugar that you get when you order coffee in restaurants. My favorites were a set from Europe that had tiny copies of paintings on them.

And then there were the keys. The Rabbi had an old tin box, like my school lunch box, but bigger, and it was filled with dozens and dozens of keys of every shape and size you could imagine that a key might be. Some of them were *tiny*, smaller even than our mailbox key, but some were huge and heavy and rusty; they looked like the keys jailers or housekeepers always carried at their belts in movies about the Middle Ages. Rabbi Tuvim had no idea what locks they might have been for—he never locked up anything, anyway, no matter how people warned him— he just picked them up wherever he found them lying loose and plopped them into his key box. To which, by the way, he'd lost the key long ago.

When I finally got up the nerve to ask him why he collected something as completely useless as keys without locks, the rabbi didn't answer right away, but leaned on his elbow and thought about his answer. That was something else I liked about him, that he seemed to take everybody's questions seriously, even ones that were really, *really* stupid. He finally said, "Well, you know, Joseph, those keys aren't useless just because I don't have the locks they fit. Whenever I find a lock that's lost its key, I try a few of mine on it, on the chance that one of them might be the right one. God is like that for me—a lock none of my keys fit, and probably never will. But I keep at it, I keep picking up different keys and trying them out, because you never know. *Could* happen."

I asked, "Do you think God wants you to find the key?"

Rabbi Tuvim ruffled my hair. "*Leben uff der keppele.* Leave it to the children to ask the big ones. I would like to think he does, Yossele, but I don't know that either. That's what being Jewish is, going ahead without answers. Get out of here, already."

The rabbi had bookshelves stacked with old crumbly magazines, too, all kinds of them. Magazines I knew, like *Life, Look* and *Colliers* and *The Saturday Evening Post*; magazines I'd never heard of—like *Scribners, The Delineator, The Illustrated London News,* and even one called *Pearson's Magazine,* from 1911, with Christy Mathewson on the cover. Mrs. Eisen, who cleaned for him every other week, wouldn't ever go into the room where he kept them, because she said those old dusty, flappy things aggravated her asthma. My father said that some of them were collector's items, and that people who liked that sort of stuff would pay a lot of money for them. But Rabbi Tuvim just liked having them, liked sitting and turning their yellow pages late at night, thinking about what people were thinking so long ago. "It's very peaceful," he told me. "So much worry about so much—so much certainty about how things were going to turn out—and here we are now, and it *didn't* turn out like that, after all. Don't ever be too sure of anything, Joseph."

I was at his house regularly that spring, because we were studying for my Bar Mitzvah. The negotiations had been extensive and complicated: I was willing to go along with local custom, tradition and my parents' social concerns, but I balked at going straight from my regular classes to the neighborhood Hebrew school. I called my unobservant family hypocrites, which they were; they called me lazy and ungrateful, which was also true. But both sides knew that I'd need extensive private tutoring to cope with the *haftarah* reading alone, never mind the inevitable speech. I'd picked up Yiddish early and easily, as had all my cousins, since our families spoke it when they didn't want the *kindelech* to understand what they were talking about. But Hebrew was another matter entirely. I knew this or that word, this or that phrase—even a few songs for Chanukah and Pesach—but the language itself sat like a stone on my tongue, guttural and harsh, and completely alien. I not only couldn't learn Hebrew, I truly didn't *like* Hebrew. And if a proper Jew was supposed to go on studying it even after the liberating Bar Mitzvah, I might just as well give up and turn Catholic, spending my Sunday mornings at Mass with the Geohegans down the block. Either way, I was clearly doomed.

Rabbi Tuvim took me on either as a challenge or as a penance, I was never quite sure which. He was inhumanly patient and inventive, constantly coming up with word games, sports references and any number of catchy mnemonics to help me remember this foreign, senseless, elusive, *boring* system of communication. But when even he wiped his forehead and said sadly, *"Ai, gornisht helfen"* which means *nothing will help you,* I finally felt able to ask him whether he thought I would ever be a good Jew; and, if not, whether we should just cancel the Bar Mitzvah. I thought hopefully of the expense this would save my father, and felt positively virtuous for once.

The rabbi, looking at me, managed to sigh and half-smile at the same time, taking off his glasses and blinking at them. "Nobody in this entire congregation has the least notion of what Bar Mitzvah *is*," he said wearily. "It's not a graduation from anything, it is just an acknowledgment that at thirteen you're old enough to be called up in temple to read from the Torah. Which God help you if you actually are, but never mind. The point is that you are still Bar Mitzvah even if you never go through the preparation, the ritual." He smiled at me and put his glasses back on. "No way out of it, Joseph. If you never manage to memorize another word of Hebrew, you're still as good a Jew as anybody. Whatever the Orthodox think."

One Thursday afternoon I found the rabbi so engrossed in one of his old magazines that he didn't notice when I walked in, or even when I peered over his shoulder. It was an issue of a magazine called *Evening,* from 1921, which made it close to thirty years old. There were girls on the cover, posing on a beach, but they were a long way from the bathing beauties—we still called them that then—that I was accustomed to seeing in magazines and on calendars. These could have walked into my mother's PTA or Hadassah meetings: they showed no skin above the shin, wore bathing caps and little wraps over their shoulders, and in general appeared about as seductive as any of my mother's friends, only younger. Paradoxically, the severe costumes made them look much more youthful than they probably were, innocently graceful.

Rabbi Tuvim, suddenly aware of me, looked up, startled but not embarrassed. "This is what your mother would have been wearing to the beach back then," he said. "Mine, too. It looks so strange, doesn't it? Compared to Betty Grable, I mean."

He was teasing me, as though I were still going through my Betty Grable/Alice Faye phase. As though I weren't twelve now, and on the edge of manhood; if not, why were we laboring over the utterly bewildering *haftarah* twice a week? As though Lauren Bacall, Lena Horne and Lizabeth Scott hadn't lately written their names all over my imagination, introducing me to the sorrows of adults? I drew myself up in visible—I hoped—indignation, but the rabbi said only, "Sit down, Joseph, look at this girl. The one in the left corner."

She was bareheaded, so that her whole face was visible.

Even I could tell that she couldn't possibly be over eighteen. She wasn't beautiful—the others were beautiful, and so what?—but there was a playfulness about her expression, a humor not far removed from wisdom. Looking at her, I felt that I could tell that face everything I was ashamed of, and that she would not only reassure me that I wasn't the vile mess I firmly believed I was, but that I might even be attractive one day to someone besides my family. Someone like her.

I looked sideways at Rabbi Tuvim, and saw him smiling. "Yes," he said. "She does have that effect, doesn't she?"

"Who is she?" I blurted out. "Is she a movie star or something?" Someone I should be expected to know, in other words. But I didn't think so, and I was right. Rabbi Tuvim shook his head.

"I have no idea. I just bought this magazine yesterday, at a collectors' shop downtown where I go sometimes, and I feel as though I have been staring at her ever since. I don't think she's anybody famous—probably just a model who happened to be around when they were shooting that cover. But I can't take my eyes off her, for some reason. It's a little embarrassing."

The rabbi's unmarried state was of particular concern in the neighborhood. Rabbis aren't priests: it's not only that they're allowed to marry, it's very nearly demanded of them by their congregations. Rabbi Tuvim wasn't a handsome man, but he had a strong face, and his eyes were kind. I said, "Maybe you could look her up, some way."

The rabbi blinked at me. "Joseph, I am curious. That's all."

"Sure," I said. "Me too."

"I would just like to know a little about her," the rabbi said.

"Me too," I said again. I was all for keeping the conversation going, to stall off my lesson as long as possible, but no luck. The rabbi just said,

"There is something about her," and we plunged once more into the cold mysteries of Mishnaic Hebrew. Rabbi Tuvim didn't look at the *Evening* cover again, but I kept stealing side glances at that girl until he finally got up and put the magazine back on the bookshelf, without saying a word. I think I was an even worse student than usual that afternoon, to judge by his sigh when we finished.

Every Monday and Thursday, when I came for my lessons, the magazine would always be somewhere in sight—on a chair, perhaps, or down at the end of the table where we studied. We never exactly agreed, not in so many words, that the girl on the cover haunted us both, but we talked about her a lot. For me the attraction lay in the simple and absolute aliveness of her face, as present to me as that of any of my schoolmates, while the other figures in the photograph felt as antique as any of the Greek and Roman statues we were always being taken to see at museums. For Rabbi Tuvim…for the rabbi, perhaps, what fascinated him was the fact that he *was* fascinated: that a thirty-year-old image out of another time somehow had the power to distract him from his studies, his students, and his rabbinical duties. No other woman had ever done that to him. Twelve years old or not, I was sure of that.

The rabbi made inquiries. He told me about them—I don't think there was anyone else he *could* have told about such a strange obsession. *Evening* was long out of business by then, but his copy had credited the cover photograph only to "Winsor & Co., Ltd., Newark, New Jersey." Rabbi Tuvim—obviously figuring that if he could teach me even a few scraps of Hebrew he ought to be able to track down a fashion photographer's byline—found address and phone number, called, was told sourly that he was welcome to go through their files himself, but that employees had better things to do. Whereupon, he promptly took a day off and made a pilgrimage to Winsor & Co., Ltd., which was still in business, but plainly subsisting on industrial photography and the odd bowling team picture. A clerk led him to the company archive, which was a room like a walk-in closet, walled around with oaken filing cabinets; he said it smelled of fixatives and moldering newsprint, and of cigars smoked very long ago. But he sat down and went to work, and in only three hours, or at most four, he had his man.

"His name is Abel Bagaybagayan," he told me when I came the next day. I giggled, and the rabbi cuffed the side of my head lightly. "Don't laugh at people's names, Joseph. How is that any stranger than Rosenwasser? Or Turteltaub, or Kockenfuss, or Tuvim, or your own name? It took me a long time to find that name, and I'm very proud that I did find it, and you can either stop laughing right now, or go home." He was really angry with me. I'd never before seen him angry. I stopped laughing.

"Abel Bagaybagayan," Rabbi Tuvim said again. "He was what's called a free-lance—that means he wasn't on anyone's staff—but he did a lot of work for Winsor through the 1920s. Portraits, fashion spreads, architectural layouts, you name it. Then, after 1935 or so…nothing. Nothing at all. Most likely he died, but I couldn't find any information, one way or the other." The rabbi spread his hands and lifted his eyebrows. "I only met a couple of people who even remembered him vaguely, and nobody has anything like an address, a phone number—not so much as a cousin in Bensonhurst. Nothing. A dead end."

"So what are you going to do?" I asked. The old magazine lay between us, and I marveled once again at the way the mystery-girl's bright face made everyone else on the cover look like depthless paper-doll cutouts, with little square tabs holding their flat clothes on their flat bodies. The rabbi waggled a warning finger at me, and my heart sank. Without another word, I opened my Hebrew text.

When we were at last done for the day—approximately a hundred and twenty years later—Rabbi Tuvim went on as though I had just asked the question. "My father used to tell me that back in Lvov, his family had a saying: *A Tuvim never surrenders; he just says he does.* I'm going to find Abel Bagaybagayan's family."

"Maybe he married that girl on the cover," I said hopefully. "Maybe they had a family together."

"Very romantic," the rabbi said. "I like it. But then he'd probably have had mouths to feed, so if he didn't die, why did he quit working as a photographer? If he did quit, mind you—I don't know anything for sure."

"Well, maybe she was very rich. Then he wouldn't *have* to work." I didn't really think that was at all likely, but lately I'd come to enjoy teasing the rabbi the way he sometimes teased me. I said, "Maybe they moved to California, and she got into the movies. That could have happened."

"You know, that actually could," Rabbi Tuvim said slowly. "California, anyway, everybody's going to California. And Bagaybagayan's an Armenian name—much easier to look for. I have an Armenian friend in Fresno, and Armenians always know where there are other Armenians… thank you, Detective Yossele. I'll see you on Monday."

As I left, feeling absurdly pleased with myself, he was already reaching for the old *Evening,* sliding it toward him on the table.

In the following weeks, the rabbi grew steadily more involved with that face from 1921, and with the cold trail of Abel Bagaybagayan, who wasn't from Fresno. But there were plenty of people there with that name; and while none of them knew the man we were looking for, they had cousins in Visalia and Delano and Firebaugh who might. To my disappointment, Rabbi Tuvim remained very conscientious about keeping his obsession from getting in the way of his teaching; at that point, the Fresno phone book would have held more interest for me than *halakha* or the Babylonian Talmud. On the other hand, he had no hesitation about involving me in his dogged search for either photographer or model, or both of them. I was a great Sherlock Holmes fan back then, and I felt just like Doctor Watson, only smarter.

This was all before the Internet, mind you; all before personal computers, area codes, digital dialing...that time when places were further from each other, when phone calls went through operators, and a long-distance call was as much of an event as a telegram. Even so, it was I, assigned to the prairie states, who found Sheila Bagaybagayan, only child of Abel, in Grand Forks, North Dakota, where she was teaching library science at the university. I handed the phone to Rabbi Tuvim and went off into a corner to hug myself and jump up and down just a bit. I might not know the *Midrash Hashkern* from *"Mairzy Doats"* but, by God, I *was* Detective Yossele.

Watching the rabbi's face as he spoke to Sheila Bagaybagayan on the phone was more fun than a Saturday matinee at Loew's Tuxedo, with a double feature, a newsreel, eighteen cartoons, Coming Attractions and a Nyoka the Jungle Girl serial. He smiled—he laughed outright—he frowned in puzzlement—he spoke rapidly, raising a finger, as though making a point in a sermon—he scratched his beard—he looked suddenly sad enough to weep—he said "Yes...yes...yes..." several times, and then "Of course—and *thank* you," and hung up. He stood motionless by the phone for a few minutes, absently rubbing his lower lip, until the phone started to buzz because he hadn't got it properly back on the hook. Then he turned to me and grinned, and said, "Well. That was our Sheila."

"Was she really the right one? Mr. Baba...uh, Abel's daughter?" The passing of weeks hadn't made me any more comfortable around the photographer's name.

Rabbi Tuvim nodded. "Yes, but her married name is Olsen. Her mother died when she was practically a baby, and Abel never remarried, but raised her alone. She says he stopped working as a photographer during the Depression, when she was in her teens, because he just couldn't make a living at it anymore. So he became a salesman for a camera-equipment company, and then he worked for Western Union, and he died just after the war." He smacked his fist into his palm. *"Rats!"*— which was his strongest expletive, at least around me. "We could have met him, we could have asked him...*Ach, rats!*" I used to giggle in *shul* sometimes, suddenly imagining him saying that at the fall of Solomon's Temple, or at the news that Sabbatai Zevi, the false Messiah, had turned Muslim.

"The girl," I asked. "Did she remember that girl?"

The rabbi shook his head. "Her father worked with so many models over the years. She's going to look through his records and call me back. One thing she did say, he preferred using amateurs when he could, and she knows that he sneaked a lot of them into the *Evening* assignments, even though they ordered him not to. She thinks he was likely to have kept closer track of the amateurs than the professionals, in case he got a chance to use them again, so who knows?" He shrugged slightly. "As the Arabs say, *inshallah*—if God wills it. Fair enough, I guess."

For quite some time I cherished a persistent hopeful vision of our cover girl turning out to be Sheila Olsen's long-gone mother. But Abel Bagaybagayan had never employed his wife professionally, Sheila told us; there were plenty of photographs around the Grand Forks house, but none of the young woman Rabbi Tuvim described. And no magazine covers. Abel Bagaybagayan never saved the covers.

All the same, Sheila Olsen plainly got drawn into the rabbi's fixation—or, as he always called it—his hobby. They spoke on the phone frequently, considering every possibility of identifying the *Evening* girl; and my romantic imagination started marrying them off, exactly like the movies. I knew that she had been divorced—which was not only rare in our neighborhood then, but somehow exotic—and I figured that she had to be Rabbi Tuvim's age, or even younger, so there we were. Their conversations, from my end, sounded less formal as time went on; and a twelve-year-old romantic who can't convert "less formal" into "affectionate" at short notice just isn't trying.

No, of course it never happened, not like that. She wasn't Jewish, for one thing, and she really *liked* living in North Dakota. But her curiosity, growing to enthusiasm, at last gave the rabbi someone besides me to discuss his hobby with, and fired up his intensity all over again. I wasn't jealous; on the contrary, I felt as though we were a secret alliance of superheroes, like the Justice Society of America, on the trail of Nazi spies, or some international warlord or other. The addition of Sheila Olsen, our Grand Forks operative, made it all that much more exciting.

I spoke to her a couple of times. The first occasion was when a call from old Mrs. Shimkus interrupted my Monday Hebrew lesson. I was always grateful when that happened, but especially so in this case, since we were doing vowels, and had gotten to *shva*. That is all you're going to hear from me about *shva*. Mrs. Shimkus was always calling, always dying, and always contributing large sums for the maintenance of the temple and scholarships for deserving high-school students. This entitled her, as the rabbi said with a touch of grimness, to her personal celestial attorney, on call at all times to file suit against the Angel of Death. "Answer the phone, if it rings. Go back to page twenty-nine, and start over from there. I'll be back sooner than you hope, so get to it."

I did try. *Shva* and all. But I also grabbed up the telephone on the first ring, saying importantly, "Rabbi Tuvim's residence, to whom am I speaking?"

The connection was stuttery and staticky, but I heard a woman's warm laughter clearly. "Oh, this has simply got to be Joseph. The rabbi's told me all about you. *Is* this Joseph?"

"All about me?" I was seriously alarmed at first; and then I asked, "Sheila? Olsen? Is this you?"

She laughed again. "Yes, I'm sure it is. Is Rabbi Tuvim available?"

"He's visiting Mrs. Shimkus right now," I said. "She's dying again. But he ought to be back pretty soon."

"Very efficient," Sheila Olsen said. "Well, just tell him I called back, so now it's his turn." She paused for a moment. "And Joseph?" I waited. "Tell him I've looked all through my father's files, all of them, and come up empty every time. I'm not giving up—there are a couple of other possibilities—but just tell him it doesn't look too good right now. Can you please do that?"

"As soon as he gets back," I said. "Of course I'll tell him." I hesitated myself, and then blurted, "And don't worry—I'm sure you'll find out about her. He just needs to find the lock she fits." I explained about the rabbi's key collection, and expected her to laugh for a third time, whether in amusement or disbelief. But instead she was silent long enough that I thought she might have hung up. Then she said quietly, "My dad would have liked your rabbi, I think."

Rabbi Tuvim, as he had predicted, returned sooner than I could have wished—Mrs. Shimkus having only wanted tea and sympathy—and I relayed Sheila Olsen's message promptly. I hoped he'd call her right away, but his sense of duty took us straight back to study; and at the end of our session we were both as pale, disheveled and sweating as Hebrew vowels always left us. Before I went home, he said to me, "You know, it's a funny thing, Joseph. Somehow I have connected that *Evening* model with you, in my head. I keep thinking that if I can actually teach you

Hebrew, I will be allowed to find out who that girl was. Or maybe it's the other way around, I'm not sure. But I know there's a connection, one way or the other. There *is* a connection."

A week later the rabbi actually called me at home to tell me that Sheila Olsen had come across a second *Evening* with what—she was almost certain—must be the same model on the cover. "She's already sent it, airmail special delivery, so it ought to be here day after tomorrow." The rabbi was so excited that he was practically chattering like someone my age. "I'm sure it's her—I took a photo of my copy and sent it to her, and she clearly thinks it's the same girl." He slowed down, laughing in some embarrassment at his own enthusiasm. "Listen, when you come tomorrow, if you spot me hanging around the mailbox like Valentine's Day, just collar me and drag me inside. A rabbi should never be caught hanging around the mailbox."

The magazine did arrive two days later. I used my lucky nickel to call Rabbi Tuvim from school for the news. Then I ran all the way to his house, not even bothering to drop my books off at home. The rabbi was in his little kitchen, snatching an absent-minded meal of hot dogs and baked beans, which was his idea of a dish suitable for any occasion.

The *Evening* was on a chair, across from him. I grabbed it up and stared at the cover, which was an outdoor scene, showing well-dressed people dining under a striped awning on a summer evening. It was a particularly busy photograph—a lot of tables, a lot of diners, a lot of natty waiters coming and going—and you had to look closely and attentively to find the one person we were looking for. She was off to the right, near the edge of the awning, her bright face looking straight into the camera, her eyes somehow catching and holding the twilight, even as it faded. There were others seated at her table; but, just as with the first cover photo, her presence dimmed them, as though the shot had always been a single portrait of her, with everyone else added in afterward.

But it was just this that was, in a vague, indeterminate way, perturbing the rabbi, making him look far less triumphant and vindicated than I had expected. I was the one who kept saying, "That's her, that's her! We were right—we found her!"

"Right about what, Joseph?" Rabbi Tuvim said softly. "And what have we found?"

I stared at him. He said, "There's something very strange about all this. Think—Abel Bagaybagayan kept very precise records of every model he used, no matter if he only photographed him or her once. Sheila's told me. For each one, name, address, telephone number, and his own special filing system, listing the date, the magazine, the occasion, and a snapshot of that person, always. But not *this* one." He put his finger on the face we had sought for so long. "Not this one girl, out of all those photographs. Two magazine covers, but no record, no picture—*nothing.* Why is that, Detective Yossele? Why on earth would that be?"

His tone was as playful as when he asked me some Talmudic riddle, or invited me to work a noun suffix out for myself, but his face was serious, and his blue eyes looked heavy and sad. I really wanted to help him. I said, "She was special to him, some way. You can see that in the photos." Rabbi Tuvim nodded, though neither he nor I could ever have explained what we meant by *seeing.* "So maybe he wanted to keep her separate, you know? Sort of to keep her for himself, that could be it. I mean, he'd always know where she was, and what she looked like—he'd never have to go look her up in his files, right? That could be it, couldn't it?" I tried to read his face for a reaction to my reasoning. I said, "Kind of makes sense to me, anyway."

"Yes," the rabbi said slowly. "Yes, of course it makes sense, it's very good thinking, Joseph. But it is *human* thinking, it is *human* sense, and I'm just not sure..." His voice trailed away into a mumble as he leaned his chin into his fist. I reached to move the plate of baked beans out of range, but I was a little late.

"What?" I asked. "You mean she could be some kind of Martian, an alien in disguise?" I was joking, but these were the last days of the pulp science-fiction magazines (*and* the pulp Westerns, *and* romances, *and* detective stories), and I read them all, as the rabbi knew. He laughed then, which made me feel better.

"No, I didn't mean that." He sighed. "I don't know what I meant, forget it. Let's go into the living room and work on your speech."

"I came to see the magazine," I protested. "I wasn't coming for a lesson."

"Well, how lucky for you that I'm free just now," the rabbi said. "Get in there." And, trapped and outraged, I went.

So now we had two photographs featuring our mystery model, and were no closer than we'd ever been to identifying her. Sheila Olsen, as completely caught up in the quest as we two by now, contacted every one of her father's colleagues, employers, and old studio buddies that she could reach, and set them all to rummaging through their own files, on the off-chance that one or another of them might have worked with Abel Bagaybagayan's girl twenty or thirty years before. (We were all three calling her that by now, though more in our minds than aloud, I think: "Abel's girl.") Rabbi Tuvim didn't hold much hope for that course, though. "She didn't work with anyone else," he said. "Just him. I know this." And for all anyone could prove otherwise, she never had.

My birthday and my Bar Mitzvah were coming on together like a freight train in the old movies, where you see the smoke first, rising away around the bend, and then you hear the wheels and the whistle, and finally you see the train barreling along. Rabbi Tuvim and I were both tied to the track, and I don't know whether he had nightmares about it all, but I surely did. There was no rescue in sight, either, no cowboy hero racing the train on the great horse Silver or Trigger or Champion, leaping from the saddle to cut us free at the last split-second. My parents had shot the works on the hall, the catering, the invitations, the newspaper notice, and the party afterward (the music to be provided by Herbie Kaufman and his Bel-Air Combo). We'd already had the rehearsal—a complete disaster, but at least the photographs got taken—and there was no more chance even of postponing than there would have been of that train stopping on a dime. Remembering it now, my nightmares were always much more about the rabbi's embarrassment than my own. He had tried so hard to reconcile Hebrew and me to one another; it wasn't his fault that we loathed each other on sight. I felt terrible for him.

A week before the Bar Mitzvah, Sheila Olsen called. We were in full panic mode by now, with me coming to the rabbi's house every day after school, and he himself dropping most of his normal duties to concentrate, less on teaching me the passage of Torah that I would read and comment on, but on keeping me from running away to sea and calling home from Pago Pago, where nobody gets Bar Mitzvahed. When the phone rang, Rabbi Tuvim picked it up, signed to me to keep working from the text, and walked away with it to the end of the cord. Entirely pointless, since the cord only went a few feet, it was still a request for privacy, and I tried to respect it. I did try.

"What?" the rabbi said loudly. "You found *what?* Slow down, Sheila, I'm having trouble...When? You're coming...Sheila, slow *down!*...So how come you can't just tell me on the phone? Wait a minute, I'm not understanding—you're *sure?*" And after that he was silent for a long time, just listening. When he saw that that was all I was doing too, he waved me sternly back to my studies. I bent my head earnestly over the book, pretending to be working, while he tried to squeeze a few more inches out of that phone cord. Both of us failed.

Finally the rabbi said wearily, "I do not have a car, I can't pick you up. You'll have to...oh, okay, if you don't mind taking a cab. Okay, then, I will see you tomorrow...What? Yes, yes, Joseph will be here....yes— goodbye, Sheila. Goodbye."

He hung up, looked at me, and said *"Oy."*

It was a profound *oy,* an *oy* of stature and dignity, an *oy* from the heart. I waited. Rabbi Tuvim said, "She's coming here tomorrow. Sheila Olsen."

"Wow," I said. *"Wow."* Then I said, "Why?"

"She's found another picture. Abel's girl. Only this one she says she can't send us—she can't even tell me about it. She just has to get on a plane and come straight here to show us." The rabbi sat down and sighed. "It's not exactly the best time."

I said, "Wow," for a third time. "That's *wonderful.*" Then I remembered I was Detective Yossele, and tried to act the part. I asked, "How did she sound?"

"It's hard to say. She was talking so fast." The rabbi thought for a while. "As though she *wanted* to tell me what she had discovered, really wanted to—maybe to share it, maybe just to get rid of it, *I* don't know. But she couldn't do it. Every time she tried, the words seemed to stick in her throat, like Macbeth's *amen."* He read my blank expression and sighed again. "Maybe they'll have you reading Shakespeare next year. You'll like Shakespeare."

In spite of that freight train of a Bar Mitzvah bearing down on us, neither the rabbi nor I were worth much for the rest of the day. We never exactly quit on the Torah, but we kept drifting to a halt in the middle of work, speculating more or less silently on what could possibly set a woman we'd never met flying from Grand Forks, North Dakota, to tell us in person what she had learned about her father and his mysterious model. Rabbi Tuvim finally said, "Well, I don't know about you, but I'm going to have to drink a gallon of chamomile tea if I'm to get any sleep tonight. What do you do when you can't sleep, Joseph?"

He always asked me questions as though we were the same age. I said, "I guess I listen to the radio. Baseball games."

"Too exciting for me," the rabbi said. "I'll stick with the tea. Go home. She won't be here until your school lets out." I was at the door when he called after me, "And bring both of your notebooks, I made up a test for you." He never gave up, that man. Not on Abel Bagaybagayan, not on me.

Sheila Olsen and I arrived at Rabbi Tuvim's house almost together. I had just rung the doorbell when her cab pulled around the corner, and the rabbi opened the door as she was getting out. She was a pleasant-faced blonde woman, a little plump, running more to the Alice Faye side than Lauren Bacall, and I sighed inwardly to think that only a year before she would have been my ideal. The rabbi—dressed, I noticed, in his second-best suit, the one he wore for all other occasions than the High Holidays—opened the door and said, "Sheila Olsen, I presume?"

"Rabbi Sidney Tuvim," she answered as they shook hands. To me, standing awkwardly one step above her, she said, "And you could only be Joseph Makovsky." The rabbi stepped back to usher us in ahead of him.

Sheila—somehow, after our phone conversations, it was impossible to think of her as Mrs. Olsen—was carrying a large purse and a small overnight bag, which she set down near the kitchen door. "Don't panic, I'm not moving in. I've got a hotel reservation right at the airport, and I'll fly home day after tomorrow. But at the moment I require—no, I request—a glass of wine. Jews are like Armenians, bless them, they've always got wine in the house." She wrinkled her nose and added, "Unlike Lutherans."

The rabbi smiled. "You wouldn't like our wine. We just drink it on Shabbos. Once a week, believe me, that's enough. I can do better."

He went into the kitchen and I stared after him, vaguely jealous, never having seen him quite like this. Not flirtatious, I don't mean that; he wouldn't have known how to be flirtatious on purpose. But he wasn't my age now. Suddenly he was an adult, a grownup, with that elusive but familiar tone in his voice that marked grownups talking to other grownups in the presence of children. Sheila Olsen regarded me with a certain shrewd friendliness in her small, wide-set brown eyes.

"You're going to be thirteen in a week," she said. "The rabbi told me." I nodded stiffly. "You'll hate it, everybody does. Boy or girl, it doesn't make any difference—everybody hates thirteen. I remember."

"It's supposed to be like a borderline for us," I said. "Between being a kid and being a man. Or a woman, I guess."

"But that's just the time when you don't know *what* the hell you are, excuse my French," Sheila Olsen said harshly. "Or *who* you are, or even *if* you are. You couldn't pay me to be thirteen again, I'll tell you. You could not pay me."

She laughed then, and patted my hand. "I'm sorry, Joseph, don't listen to me. I just have…associations with thirteen." Rabbi Tuvim was coming back into the room, holding a small tray bearing three drinks in cocktail glasses I didn't know he had. Sheila Olsen raised her voice slightly. "I was just telling Joseph not to worry—once he makes it through thirteen, it's all downhill from there. Wasn't it that way for you?"

The rabbi raised his eyebrows. "I don't know. Sometimes I feel as though I never did get through thirteen myself." He handed her her drink, and gave me a glass of cocoa cream, which is a soft drink you can't get anymore. I was crazy about cocoa cream that year. I liked to mix it with milk.

The third glass, by its color, unmistakably contained Concord grape wine, and Sheila Olsen's eyebrows went up further than his. "I thought you couldn't stand Jewish wine."

"I can't," the rabbi answered gravely. "*L'chaim.*"

Sheila Olsen lifted her glass and said something that must have been the Armenian counterpart of "*To life.*" They both looked at me, and I blurted out the first toast that came into my head. "*Past the teeth, over the gums / Look out, gizzard—here she comes!*" My father always said that, late in the evening, with friends over.

We drank. Sheila Olsen said to the rabbi, clearly in some surprise, "You make a mean G-and-T."

"And you are stalling," Rabbi Tuvim said. "You come all this way from Grand Forks because you have found something connecting your father and that covergirl we're all obsessed with—and now you're here, you'll talk about anything but her." He smiled at her again, but this time it was like the way he smiled at me when I'd try in every way I knew to divert him from *haftarah* and get him talking about the Dodgers' chances of overtaking the St. Louis Cardinals. For just that moment, then, we were all the same age, motionless in time.

I wasn't any more perceptive than any average twelve-year-old, but I saw a kind of grudging sadness in Sheila Olsen's eyes that had nothing in common with the dryly cheerful voice on the phone from North Dakota. Sheila Olsen said, "You're perfectly right. Of course I'm stalling." She reached into her purse and took out a large manila envelope. It had a red string on the flap that you wound around a dime-sized red anchor to hold it closed. "Okay," she said. "Look what I found in my father's safety-deposit box yesterday."

It was a black-and-white photograph, clipped to a large rectangle of cardboard, like the kind that comes back from the laundry with your folded shirt. The photo had the sepia tint and scalloped edges that I knew meant that it was likely to be older than I was. And it was a picture of a dead baby.

I didn't know it was dead at first. I hadn't seen death then, ever, and I thought the baby was sleeping, dressed in a kind of nightgown with feet, like Swee'Pea, and tucked into a little bed that could almost have fitted into a dollhouse. I don't know how or when I realized the truth. Sheila Olsen said, "My sister."

Rabbi Tuvim had no more to say than I did. We just stared at her. Sheila Olsen went on, "I never knew about her until yesterday. She was stillborn."

I was the one who mumbled, "I'm sorry." The rabbi didn't bother with words, but came over to Sheila Olsen and put his arm around her.

She didn't cry; if there is one sound I know to this day, it's the sound people make who are not going to cry, *not going to cry*. She put her head on the rabbi's shoulder and closed her eyes, but she didn't cry. I'm her witness.

When she could talk, she said in a different voice, "Turn it over."

There was a card clipped to the back of the mounting board, and there was very neat, dark handwriting on it that looked almost like printing. Rabbi Tuvim read it aloud.

> *"Eleanor Araxia Bagaybagayan.*
> *Born: 24 February 1907*
> *Died: 24 February 1907.*
> *Length: 13½ inches.*
> *Weight: 5 lbs, 9 oz.*
> *We planned to call her Anoush."*

Below that, there was a space, and then the precise writing gave way to a strange scrawl: clearly the same hand, but looking somehow shrunken and warped, as though the words had been left out in the rain. The rabbi squinted at it over his glasses, and went on reading:

> *"She has been dead for years—she never lived—how can she be invading my pictures? I take a shot of men coming to work at a factory—when I develop it, there she is, a little girl eating an apple, watching the men go by. I photograph a train—she has her nose against a window in the sleeping car. It is her, I know her, how could I not know her? When I take pictures of young women at outdoor dinner parties—"*

"That's your magazine cover!" I interrupted. My voice sounded so loud in the hushed room that I was suddenly embarrassed, and shrank back into the couch where I was sitting with Sheila Olsen. She patted my arm, and the rabbi said patiently, "Yes, Joseph." He continued:

> *"—I see her sitting among them, grown now, as she was never given the chance to be. Child or adult, she always knows me, and she knows that I know her. She is never the focal point of the shot; she prefers to place herself at the edge, in the background, to watch me at my work, to be some small part of it, nothing more. She will*

*not speak to me, nor can I ever get close to her; she fades
when I try. I would think of her as a hallucination, but
since when can you photograph a hallucination?"*

The rabbi stopped reading again, and he and Sheila Olsen looked
at each other without speaking. Then he looked at me and said, somewhat hesitantly, "This next part is a little terrible, Joseph. I don't know
whether your parents would want you to hear it."

"If I'm old enough to be Bar Mitzvah," I said, "I'm old enough to hear
about a baby who died. I'm staying."

Sheila Olsen chuckled hoarsely. "One for the kid, Rabbi." She gestured
with her open hand. "Go on."

Rabbi Tuvim nodded. He took a deep breath.

*"She was born with her eyes open. Such blue eyes,
almost lavender. I closed them before my wife had a
chance to see. But I saw her eyes. I would know her eyes
anywhere...is it her ghost haunting my photographs? Can
one be a ghost if one never drew breath in this world? I
do not know—but it is her, it is her. Somehow, it is our
Anoush."*

Nobody said anything for a long time after he had finished reading. The rabbi blew his nose and polished his glasses, and Sheila Olsen
opened her mouth and then closed it again. I had all kinds of things I
wanted to say, but they all sounded so stupid in my head that I just let
them go and stared at the photo of Sheila Olsen's stillborn baby sister.
I thought about the word *still*...quiet, motionless, silent, tranquil, at rest.
I hadn't known it meant *dead*.

Sheila Olsen asked at length, "What do Jews believe about ghosts?
Do you even *have* ghosts?"

Rabbi Tuvim scratched his head. "Well, the Torah doesn't really
talk about supernatural beings at all. The Talmud, yes—the Talmud
is up to here in demons, but ghosts, as we would think of them...no,
not so much." He leaned forward, resting his elbows on his knees and
tenting his fingers, the way he did when he was coaxing me to think
beyond my schooling. "We call them *spirits,* when we call them anything, and we imagine some of them to be malevolent, dangerous—
demonic, if you like. But there are benign ones as well, and those are
usually here for a specific reason. To help someone, to bring a message.
To comfort."

"Comfort," Sheila Olsen said softly. Her face had gone very pale; but as she spoke color began to come back to it, too much color. "My dad needed that, for sure, and from Day One I couldn't give it to him. He never stopped missing my mother—this person I never even knew, and couldn't be—and now I find out that he missed someone else, too. My perfect, magical, *lost* baby sister, who didn't have to bother to get herself born to become legendary. Oh, Christ, it explains so much!" She had gone pale again. "And you're telling me she came back to comfort him? That's the message?"

"Well, I don't know that," the rabbi said reasonably. "But it would be nice, wouldn't it, if that turned out to be true? If there really were two worlds, and certain creatures—call them spirits, call them demons, angels, anything you like—could come and go between those worlds, and offer advice, and tell the rest of us not to be so scared of it all. I'd like that, wouldn't you?"

"But do you believe it? Do you believe my stillborn sister came back to tell my father that it wasn't his fault? Sneaking into his photographs just to wave to him, so he could see she was really okay somewhere? Because it sure didn't comfort him much, I'll tell you that."

"Didn't it?" the rabbi asked gently. "Are you sure?"

Sheila Olsen was fighting for control, doggedly refusing to let her voice escape into the place where it just as determinedly wanted to go. The effort made her sound as though she had something caught in her throat that she could neither swallow nor spit up. She said, "The earliest memory I have is of my father crying in the night. I don't know how old I was—three, three and a half. Not four. It's like a dream now—I get out of my bed, and I go to him, and I pat him, pat his back, the way some-one…someone used to do for me when I had a nightmare. He doesn't reject me, but he doesn't turn around to me, either. He just lies there and cries and cries." The voice almost got away from her there, but she caught it, and half-laughed. "Well, I guess that *is* rejection, actually."

"Excuse me, but that's nonsense," Rabbi Tuvim said sharply. "You were a baby, trying to ease an adult's pain. That only happens in movies. Give me your glass."

He went back into the kitchen, while Sheila Olsen and I sat staring at each other. She cleared her throat and finally said, "I guess you didn't exactly bargain for such a big dramatic scene, huh, Joseph?"

"It beats writing a speech in Hebrew," I answered from the heart. Sheila Olsen did laugh then, which emboldened me enough to say, "Do you think your father ever saw her again, your sister, after he stopped being a photographer?"

"Oh, he never stopped taking pictures," Sheila Olsen said. "He just quit trying to make a living at it." She was trying to fix her makeup, but her hands were shaking too much. She said, "He couldn't go through a day without taking a dozen shots of everything around him, and then he'd spend the evening in his closet darkroom, developing them all. But if he had any more photos of...*her*, I never saw them. There weren't any others in the safe-deposit box." She paused, and then added, more to herself than to me, "He was always taking pictures of me, I used to get annoyed sometimes. Had them up all over the place."

Rabbi Tuvim came back with a fresh drink for her. I was hoping for more cocoa cream soda, but I didn't get it. Sheila Olsen practically grabbed the gin-and-tonic, then looked embarrassed. "I'm not a drunk, really—I'm just a little shaky right now. So you honestly think that's her, my sister...my sister Anoush in those old photographs?"

"Don't you?" the rabbi asked quietly. "I'd say that's what matters most."

Sheila Olsen took half her drink in one swallow and looked him boldly in the face. "Oh, I do, but I haven't trusted my own opinion on anything for...oh, for years, since my husband walked out. And I'm very tired, and I know I'm halfway nutsy when it comes to anything to do with my father. He was kind and good, and he was a terrific photographer, and he lost his baby and his wife, one right after the other, so I'm not blaming him that there wasn't much left for me. I'm *not!*"—loudly and defiantly, though the rabbi had said nothing. "But I just wish...I just wish..."

And now, finally, she did begin to cry.

I didn't know what to do. I hadn't seen many adults crying in my life. I knew aunts and uncles undoubtedly *did* cry—my cousins told me so—but not ever in front of us children, except for Aunt Frieda, who smelled funny, and always cried late in the evening, whatever the occasion. My mother went into the bathroom to cry, my father into his basement office. I can't be sure he actually cried, but he did put his head down on his desk. He never made a sound, and neither did Sheila Olsen. She just sat there on the couch with the tears sliding down her face, and she kept on trying to talk, as though nothing were happening. But nothing came out—not words, not sobs; nothing but hoarse breathing that sounded terribly painful. I wanted to run away.

I didn't, but only because Rabbi Tuvim did know what to do. First he handed Sheila Olsen a box of tissues to wipe her eyes with, which she did, although the tears kept coming. Next, he went to his desk by the window and took from the lowest drawer the battered tin box which I knew contained his collection of lost keys. Then he went back to Sheila

Olsen and crouched down in front of her, holding the tin box out. When she didn't respond, he opened the box and put it on her lap. He said, "Pick one."

Sheila Olsen sniffled, "What? Pick *what?*"

"A key," Rabbi Tuvim said. "Pick two, three, if you like. Just take your time, and be careful."

Sheila Olsen stared down into the box, so crowded with keys that by now Rabbi Tuvim couldn't close it so it clicked. Then she looked back at the rabbi, and she said, "You really *are* crazy. I was worried about that."

"Indulge me," the rabbi said. "Crazy people have to be indulged."

Sheila Olsen brushed her hand warily across the keys. "You mean, you want me to just *take* a couple? For keeps?" She sounded like a little girl.

"For keeps." The rabbi smiled at her. "Just remember, each of those keys represents a lock you can't find, a problem you can't solve. As you can see…" He gestured grandly toward the tin box without finishing the sentence.

I thought Sheila Olsen would grab any old key off the top layer, to humor him; but in fact she did take her time, sifting through a dozen or more, before she finally settled on a very small, silvery one, mailbox-key size. Then she looked straight at Rabbi Tuvim and said, "That's to represent *my* trouble. I know it's a little bitty sort of trouble, not worth talking about after a war where millions and millions of people died. Not even worth thinking about by myself—nothing but a middle-aged woman wishing her father could have loved her…could have *seen* her, the way he saw that strange girl who turned out to be my sister, for God's sake." Her voice came slowly and heavily now, and I realized how tired she must be. She said, "You know, Rabbi, sometimes when I was a child, I used to wish *I* were dead, just so my father would miss me, the way I knew he missed my mother. I did—I really used to wish that."

The rabbi called a taxi to take her to her airport hotel. He walked her to the cab—I noticed that she put the little key carefully into her bag—and I saw them talking earnestly until the driver started looking impatient, and she got in. Then he came back into the house, and, to my horrified amazement, promptly gave me the Torah test he'd written up for me. Nor could I divert him by getting him to talk about Sheila Olsen's photographs, and her father's notes, and the other things she had told us. To all of my efforts in that direction, he replied only by pointing to the test paper and leaning back in his chair with his eyes closed. I mumbled a theatrically evil Yiddish curse that I'd learned from my Uncle

Shmul, who was both an authority and a specialist, and bent bitterly to my work. I did not do well.

I didn't imagine that I would ever see Sheila Olsen again. She had a job, a home and a life waiting for her, back in Grand Forks, North Dakota. But in fact I saw her that Saturday afternoon, in the audience gathered at the Reform synagogue to witness my Bar Mitzvah. Rabbi Tuvim's other students had all scheduled their individual ceremonies a year or more in advance, and I didn't know whether to be terrified at the notion of being the entire center of attention, or grateful that at least I wouldn't be shown up for the pathetic *schlemiel* I was by contrast with those three. We had a nearly full house in the main gathering room of the synagogue, my schoolmates drawn by the lure of the after-party, the adults either by family loyalty or my mother's blackmail, or some combination of both. My mother was the Seurat of blackmail: a dot here, a dot there…

The rabbi—coaching me under his breath to the very last minute— was helping me tie the *tefillin* around my head and my left arm when I messed up the whole process by pulling away to point out Sheila Olsen. He yanked me back, saying, "Yes, I know she's here. Stand still."

"I thought she went home," I said. "She said goodbye to me."

"Hold your head up," Rabbi Tuvim ordered. "She decided she wanted to stay for your Bar Mitzvah—said she'd never seen one. Now, remember, you stand there after your speech, while I sing. With, please God, your grandfather's *tallis* around your shoulders, *if* your mother remembers to bring it. If not, I guess you must use mine."

I had never seen him nervous before. I said, "When this is over, can I still come and look at your old magazines?"

The rabbi stopped fussing with the *tefillin* and looked at me for a long moment. Then he said very seriously, "Thank you, Detective Yossele. Thank you for putting things back into proportion for me. You have something of a gift that way. Yes, of course you can look at the magazines, you can visit for any reason you like, or for no reason at all. And don't worry—we will get through this thing today just fine." He gave the little leather phylactery a last tweak, and added, "Or we will leave town on the same cattle boat for Argentina. Oh, thank God, there's your mother. Stay right where you are."

He hurried off—I had never seen him hurry before, either—and I stayed where I was, turning in little circles to look at the guests, and at the hard candies ranged in bowls all around the room. These were there specifically for my friends and family to hurl at me by way of congratu-lations, the instant the ceremony was over. I don't know whether any other Jewish community in the world does this. I don't think so.

Sheila Olsen came up to me, almost shyly, once Rabbi Tuvim was gone. She gave me a quick hug, and then stepped back, asking anxiously, "Is that all right? I mean, are you not supposed to be touched or anything until it's over? I should have asked first, I'm sorry."

"It's all right," I said. "Really. I'm so scared right now…" and I stopped there, ashamed to admit my growing panic to a stranger. But Sheila Olsen seemed to understand, for she hugged me a second time, and it was notably comforting.

"Your rabbi will take care of you," she said. "He'll get you through it, I know he will. He's a good man." She hesitated then, looking away. "I'm a little embarrassed around both of you now, after yesterday. I didn't mean to carry on like that." I had no idea what to say. I just smiled stupidly. Sheila Olsen said, "I'll have to leave for the airport right after this is over, so I wanted to say goodbye now. I guess it was all foolishness, but I'm glad I came. I'm glad I met you, Joseph."

"Me, too," I said. We saw Rabbi Tuvim returning, waving to us over the heads of the milling guests. Sheila Olsen, shy again, patted my shoulder, whispered "*Courage,*" and began to slip away. The rabbi intercepted her deftly, however, and they talked for a few minutes, at the end of which Sheila Olsen nodded firmly, pointed to her big purse, and went to find a seat. Rabbi Tuvim joined me and went quietly over my Torah portion with me again. He seemed distinctly calmer, or possibly I mean resigned.

"All right, Joseph," the rabbi said at last. "All right, time to get this show on the road. Here we go."

I'm not going to talk about the Bar Mitzvah, not *as* a Bar Mitzvah, except to say that it wasn't nearly the catastrophe I'd been envisioning for months. It couldn't have been. I stumbled on the prayers, lord knows how many times, but Rabbi Tuvim had his back to the onlookers, and he fed me the lines I'd forgotten, and we got through. Oddly enough, the speech itself—I had chosen to discuss a passage in Numbers 1-9, showing how the Israelites first consolidated themselves as a community at Sinai—flowed much more smoothly, and I found myself practically enjoying the taste of Hebrew in my mouth. If the rabbi could teach me nothing else, somehow I'd come to understand the sound. Not the words, not the grammar, and certainly not the true meaning…just the *sound*. Nearing the grand finale, I wasn't thinking at all about the gift table in the farthest corner of the room. I was already beginning to regret that the speech wasn't longer.

That was when I saw her.

Anoush.

Small and dark, olive-skinned, she was no magazine covergirl now, but a woman of Sheila Olsen's age. She stood near the back of the room, away on the margins, as always. Sheila Olsen didn't see her, but I did, and she saw that I did, and I believe she saw also that I knew who and *how* she was. She didn't react, except to move further into shadow—she cast none of her own—but I could still see her eyes. No one else seemed to notice her at all; yet now and then someone would bump into her, or step on her foot, and immediately say, "Oh, sorry, excuse me," just as though she were living flesh. I tried to catch Sheila Olsen's eye, and then Rabbi Tuvim's, to indicate with my chin and my own eyes where they should look, but they never once turned their heads. It was very nearly as frustrating as learning Hebrew.

I finished the speech any old how, and when I was done, my mother came out and put her father's *tallis* on my shoulders, and everybody cheered except me. All I wanted to do was to draw Sheila Olsen's attention to the shy, ghostly presence of her sister, but I lost track of both of them when the hard round candies began showering down on me. It was going to make for an uncertain dance floor—Herbie Kaufman's Bel-Air Combo were busily setting up—but a number of my schoolmates were crowding onto it, followed by a few wary older couples. I was down from the little stage and weaving through the crush, *tallis* and all, pushing past congratulatory shoulder-punches and butt-slaps, not to mention the flash cameras—forbidden during the ceremony itself— going off in my face as I hunted for Sheila Olsen, frantic that she might already have left. She had a plane to catch, after all, and things to decide to remember or forget.

I was slowing down, beginning to give up, when I spotted her heading for the door, but slowed down by the press of bodies, so that she heard when I called her name. She turned, and I waved wildly, not at her, but toward the shadowless figure motionlessly watching her leave. And for the first time, Sheila Olsen and Eleanor Araxia Bagaybagayan saw each other.

Neither moved at first. Neither spoke—Sheila Olsen plainly didn't dare, and I don't think Anoush could. Then, very slowly, as though she were trying to slip up on some wild thing, Sheila Olsen began to ease toward her sister, holding out her open hands. She was facing me, and I saw her lips moving, but I couldn't hear the words.

But for every step Sheila Olsen took, Anoush took one step back from her, remaining as unreachable—*there, not there*—as her father Abel had found her, so many years before. Strangely, for me, since I had never seen her as beautiful on the magazine covers—only hypnotically *alive*—now, as a middle-aged woman, she almost stopped my newly-manly heart. There was gray in her hair, a heaviness to her face and midsection, and in the way she moved...but my heart wanted to stop, all the same.

I was afraid that Sheila Olsen might snap, out of too much wishing, and make some kind of dive or grab for Anoush, but she did something else. She stopped moving forward, and just stood very still for a moment, and then she reached into her purse and brought out the lacy little key that she had taken from Rabbi Tuvim's collection. She stared at it for a moment, and then she kissed it, very quickly, and she tossed it underhand toward Anoush. It spun so slowly, turning in the light like a butterfly, that I wouldn't have been surprised if it never came down.

Anoush caught it. Ghost or no ghost, ethereal or not, she picked Sheila Olsen's key out of the air as daintily as though she were selecting exactly the right apple on a tree, the perfect note on a musical instrument. She looked back at Sheila Olsen, and she smiled a little—I *know* she smiled, I *saw* her—and she touched the key to her lips...

...and I don't know what she did with it, or where she put it—maybe she *ate* it, for all I could ever tell. All I can say for certain is that Sheila Olsen's eyes got very big, and she touched her own mouth again, and then she turned and hurried out of the synagogue, never looking back, I was going to follow her, but Rabbi Tuvim came up and put his hand gently on my shoulder. He said, "She has a plane to catch. You have a special party. Each to his own."

"You saw," I said. "Did you see her?"

"It is more important that you saw her," the rabbi answered. "And that you made Sheila Olsen see her, you brought them together. That was the *mitzvah*—the rest is unimportant, a handful of candy." He patted my shoulder. "You did well."

Anoush was gone, of course, when we looked for her. So was the rabbi's key, though I actually got down on my knees to feel around where she had stood, half-afraid that it had simply fallen through her shade to the floor. But there was no sign of it; and the rabbi, watching, said quietly, "One lock opened. So many more." We went back to the party then.

Film took longer to develop in those days, unless you did it yourself. As I remember, it was more than a week before friends and family started bringing us shots taken at my Bar Mitzvah party. I hated almost all of them—somehow I always seemed to get caught with my mouth open and a goofy startled look on my face—but my mother cherished them all, and pored over them at the kitchen table for hours at a time.

"There you are again, dancing with your cousin Marilyn, what was Sarah ever *thinking,* letting her wear that to a Bar Mitzvah?" "There you are in your grandpa's *tallis,* looking so grownup, except I was so afraid your *yarmulke* was going to fall off." "Oh, there's that one I love, with you and your father, I *told* him not to wear that tie, and your friend what's-his-name, he should lose some weight. And there's Rabbi Tuvim, what's that in his beard, dandruff?" Actually, it was cream cheese. The rabbi loved cream cheese.

Then she turned over a photo she'd missed before, and said in a different tone, "Who's that woman? Joseph, do you know that woman?"

It was Anoush, off to one side beyond the dancers I'd been shoving my way through to reach Sheila Olsen. She had her arms folded across her breast, and she looked immensely alone as she watched the party; but she didn't look lonely at all, or even wistful—just alone. As long as it's been, I remember a certain mischievousness around her mouth and eyes, as though she had deliberately slipped into this photograph of my celebration, just as she had slipped comfortingly into her father's work—yes, to wave to him, as Sheila Olsen had said mockingly then. To wave to her sister now...and maybe, a little, to me.

I practically snatched the picture our of my mother's hand—making up some cockamamie story about an old friend of Rabbi Tuvim's—and brought it to him immediately. We both looked at it in silence for a long while. Then the rabbi put it carefully into a sturdy envelope, and addressed it to Sheila Olsen in Grand Forks, North Dakota. I took it to the post office myself, and paid importantly, out of my allowance, to send it Airmail Special Delivery. The rabbi promised to tell me as soon as Sheila Olsen wrote back.

It took longer than I expected: a good two weeks, probably more. After the first week, I was badgering the rabbi almost every day; sometimes twice, because they still had two postal deliveries back then. How he kept from strangling me, or anyway hanging up in my ear, I have no idea—perhaps he sympathized with my impatience because he was anxious himself. At all events, when Sheila Olsen's letter did arrive, he called me immediately. He offered to read it to me over the phone, but I wanted to see it, so I ran over. Rabbi Tuvim gave me a glass of cocoa cream soda, insisted maddeningly on waiting until I could breathe and speak normally, and then showed me the letter.

It was short, and there was no salutation; it simply began:

> *"She sits on my bedside table, in a little silver frame.*
> *I say goodnight and good morning to her every day. I*

have tried several times to make copies for you, but they never come out. I'm sorry.
   Thank you for the key, Rabbi.
   And Joseph, Joseph—thank you."

I still have the letter. The rabbi gave it to me. It sits in its own wooden frame, and people ask me about it, because it's smudged and grubby from many readings, and frayed along the folding, and it looks as though a three-year-old has been at it, which did happen, many years later. But I keep it close, because before that letter I had no understanding of beauty, and no idea of what love is, or what can be born out of love. And after it I knew enough at least to recognize these things when they came to me.